The crowd bunc[...]
halted. Bellies an[...]
his breath. His ri[...]
Someone's pompo[...] across Arto's face in a
floppy woollen cuddle; he shook his head from
side to side. Cries, pandemonium.

'Scatter, scatter —!'

'Stop the devil wagon —!'

A lurch, and Arto's arms were free. He gasped.
His fingers clawed upward. Bodies collided again.
Corklike, Arto rose. A couple of buttons popped
from his stressed waistcoat. The black vehicle
blared again: *Aaaaannnggg*. Its eyes glared.
Those great hard rubber wheels crunched pebbles.
Foul smoke gouted from its rump. Two slanted
windows wrapping around the front of the
machine were black and glossy as obsidian in the
furnace light. No one, nothing, was evident
behind the windows. The metal beast was raging
of its own volition.

The Fallen Moon

THE SECOND BOOK OF
MANA

IAN WATSON

VGSF

First published in Great Britain 1994
by Victor Gollancz

First VGSF edition published 1995
by Victor Gollancz
An imprint of the Cassell Group
Wellington House, 125 Strand, London WC2R 0BB

© Ian Watson 1994

The right of Ian Watson to be identified as author of
this work has been asserted by him in accordance with
the Copyright, Designs and Patents Act, 1988.

A catalogue record for this book is
available from the British Library.

ISBN 0 575 06098 0

Printed and bound in Great Britain
by Cox & Wyman Ltd, Reading, Berks

CHARACTER GUIDE
to most Persons in the two books of MANA

(omitting several lumberjacks, hairdressers, sauna patrons and such, as well as all nakki personages engendered by the Ukko-child; and according to the most regular usage of a person's first or second name)

ALEKSONIS, VIKTOR: Lucky's General
ALVAR VAN MAANEN: chronicler, father of Osmo
AMBERMAN: Goldi's lover at Kip'an'keep
AMELIE: cockeyed maid at Maananfors keep
ANDERSEN: bailiff of the aitch-house
ANNA: echo of Gunther Beck's dead wife
ANNETTA: informant of Johanna van Maanen who becomes under-housekeeper at Maananfors keep
ANNI: sex-slave of the Brazen Isi, nurse to Jack, lover of Jatta
ARNI: mutant at Outo who only hears voices
ARTO NURMI: glovemaker, tango conductor, father of Juke
ARVID BLOMBERG: apprentice to shaman Sven Hartzell

BECK, GUNTHER: longlife dream lord of Castlebeck
BEKKER: Captain of Lucky's wooden soldiers
BEN PRUT: aide to General Aleksonis
BEN: diabetic guard in Lucky's service
BERGMAN: baker of the aitch-house
BERTEL OKKONEN: Lucky's longlife consort
BERTHA: Gunther's cook at Castlebeck
BOSCO: Pootaran consul at Landfall
BRILLE-ESTIVAN: Brazen Isi mage responsible for Jack's nurture
BURGDORF, MAXI: Lord of Yulistalax, patron of Gala
BURGDORF, MITZI: Maxi's wife

CAMMON, TYCHO: former tyrant whom Osmo turned to stone
CARTER: Earth's cartographic satellite
CONWAY, PENELOPE: Earth's Resident at Landfall
CULLY: Gunther's 'nephew', son of Cal and Marietta

EDITH KIPPAN: wife of Tapper the forest lord of Kip'an'keep

7

ELIAS: a guard of Lucky's
ELMER LOXMITH: instinctive engineer of the aitch-house who weds Eva
ESTER NURMI: mother of Eyeno and Juke
ESTER SARIOLA: pestery junior daughter of Lucky's
EVA SARIOLA: Jatta's sumptuous, bumptious younger sister who weds Elmer
EYENO NURMI: one-eyed mutant poetess from Outo

GERDA: an echo lass
GOLDI: Juttahat Girlem seductress bred by the Brazen Isi
GRANNY: concierge of Lucky's portrait gallery
GRETEL: an echo lass
GRÜNWALD, MA: wisewoman at the aitch-house
GUNTHER BECK: the dream lord
GURRUKAL, MATHAVAN: pilot and medic on tour of duty from Earth

HAAVIO, JUUSI: mana-priest of Forssa, obsessed with cuckoos
HAAVIO, LEENA: Juusi's wife, obsessive cook
HAKULINEN, SEPPO: the van Maanens' inept mana-priest
HANNES: groom at Maananfors keep
HARTZELL, SVEN: shaman of Niemi
HAXELL, ROLF: Captain of Defence Volunteers of the aitch-house
HAXTHAUSEN, JULIUS: Lucky's palace tailor
HEAD (and SHOULDERS): mutants at Outo
HELENIUS, JOHANN: Lord of Saari, Master of Mint, Kyli's father
HENZEL LOXMITH: Elmer's paralysed father
HERMI: shaman, intermediary with the Velvet Isi
HILDA, GOODY: bent mutant wisewoman from Halvek
HOLMBERG, MRS: housekeeper of Maananfors keep
HUBERTUS JAEGER: longlife Lord of Luolalla, Kay Sariola's husband, son
    of Bella
HUKKINEN: mana-priest of Niemi

INGA: echo lass attracted to Eyeno
INGA KENNAN: Dame of Niemi, Minkie's mother
IMBRICATE: Brazen Isi mage imprisoned in Pohjola Palace then in Velvet
    Isi nest, somaseer and body-adept, responsible for the Jarl project

JACK PAKKEN: son of Jatta and, conceptually, of Jarl; the demon fastboy,
    the mana-kid
JARL PAKKEN: Jatta's Juttahat seducer, bred by the Brazen Isi
JATTA SARIOLA: defiant princess seduced by Jarl, mother of Jack
JOHANN: brother of jump-biker Jurgen
JOHANNA VAN MAANEN: mother of Osmo
JOHANNES KENNAN: a baby, also known as Piglet
JUKE NURMI: mutant proclaimer from Outo, Eyeno's brother
JUMALA: mana-bishop in Tumio
JUNE: pathogenic mutant lass who weds Jack, mother of Maids of Horror

JURGEN: jump-biker, Captain of Osmo's garrison of the aitch-house
JUTTAHATS: servants of the Isi, including Tulkis who can interpret, and Pelkis who assist at games; Jarl and Goldi being the only two 'free' Juttahats without a voice in their heads

KARL KENNAN: younger brother of Minkie
KARLO: Juke's jump-bike companion
KAY SARIOLA: wife of Hubertus Jaeger
KIPPAN, TAPPER: longlife forest lord of Kip'an'keep, husband of Edith Sariola, father of Tilly
KOSTI: younger brother of Minkie
KNOTTY: mutant from Outo, plays the fiddle
KURO: mutant at Outo who is deaf to voices
KYLI KENNAN: née Helenius, wife of Minkie

LAMMAS: werewool mutant and tango singer
LINQVIST: Lucky's chamberlain
LOKKA LOXMITH: Elmer's mother
LUCKY: Queen of Kaleva. Those of her daughters who are featured (in descending age, but excluding echoes) are: Edith, Helena, Kay, Jatta, Eva, Minnow, Ester, Sal, Kaisa, Martha, Mary, and Hanna the lastborn
LUTAINEN: Maxi Burgdorf's laureate
LUNDAHL, MRS: a Christian at Maananfors
LYLE MELATOR: Elmer's assistant

MAGNUS: clerk at the aitch-house
MAIDS OF HORROR: the daughters of June and Juke, being Minx, Minxie, Jinx, and Jinxie
MARIA: an echo lass
MARIETTA: mother of Cully, sometime bedmate of Gunther
MARKO: Osmo's watchman
MARTI: a guard to Jatta
MARTIN (AND YOUNG MARTIN): retainers of Gunther
MELATOR, LYLE: Elmer's assistant
MAX: elderly guard of Minnow
MIKAL: Lucky's court painter
MINKIE KENNAN: rapscallion and seducer, son of Ragnar and Inga
MINNOW SARIOLA: pert princess whom Osmo weds
MIRIAM: manageress of the Pootaran emporium in Landfall
MOLLER: mana-priest of the aitch-house
MUSKULAR: Velvet Isi mage

NIKKI LOXMITH: Elmer's sister
NILS CARLSON: Lucky's young proclaimer

OLGA: peasant girl, namesake of Cully's sister
OLLI: a guard to Jatta

9

OSMO VAN MAANEN: prime proclaimer, Lord of Maananfors
OTTO: a guard of Lucky's
OUT: a talking dog

PAAVO SERLACHIUS: Lucky's mana-priest
PASQUIL: retainer to Gunther
PAULA: Lucky's doppelgänger
PEKULAR: Velvet Isi strategist
PELLER, SAM: Osmo's paranoid, prematurely aged security chief, son of
    Felix
PENELOPE (PEN) CONWAY: Earth's Resident at Landfall
PIEMAN: whistling mutant of Outo
PIERRE, MISSIEUR: jeweller of Threelakes
PRUT, BEN: aide to General Aleksonis

RINTALA, VICTOR: father of Vivi, Osmo's former mistress
ROGER 'WETHEAD' WEX: Earth's special agent with wetwear in his skull
RUOKOKOSKI: glassmaker at Niemi, his daughter being Ellen

SAL: farmer's daughter seduced by Minkie
SAM PELLER: Osmo's security chief, son of Felix
SEPTIMUS: Osmo's bailiff
SERLACHIUS, PAAVO: Lucky's mana-priest
SIMBURG, MRS: governess in Lucky's palace
SNOWY: Minkie's crony
STUMPY THE ECSTATIC: charismatic village boss of Kaukainkyla

TAIKU SETALA: deceased shaman acquainted with Gunther
TAPPER KIPPAN: forest lord of Kip'an'keep
TILLY KIPPAN: Tapper's daughter
TOMI: a gay lumberjack
TOMMI: Nikki Loxmith's talking cat
TYCHO CAMMON: ex-tyrant, turned to stone

VAARA, PETER: dramatist and actor manager, whose troupe consists of
    Natalya, Sophie, Stanislav, and Tancred
VANNI, NANNY: nanny in Pohjola Palace
VENNI: odorous cook in Maananfors keep
VILLANEN, PER: Victor Rintala's son-in-law
VIPER: monstrous mutant Brindled mage
VIVI RINTALA: Osmo's erstwhile mistress

WERNER, HANS: fisherman of Maananfors whose hand Osmo petrifies
WETWEAR: protoplasmic computer sharing Roger Wex's skull
WEX, ROGER: alias Wethead, Earth's special agent

YŪ: aide to Penelope Conway

CONTENTS

11

Part Three: MOONRISE

Prologue · FROM *THE CHRONICLES OF KALEVA* OF ALVAR VAN MAANEN*

This is a cuckoo's summary, recited by one of our gossipy Kalevan birds eager for a dollop of lamb offal . . .

During the celebration for the 402nd anniversary of Lucky Paula Sariola entering the Ukko entity adrift in Earth's asteroid belt, Lucky's daughter Jatta came to Osmo van Maanen's keep at Maananfors as a vagabond along with her demon child Jack, the fastboy.

In actuality Jatta had been seduced by an alien Juttahat cunningly bred in the guise of a human being – who assumed the name of Jarl Pakken. This servant of the Isi serpents perhaps hoped to steal the secret of longlife with which all Sariola princesses could endow the man who first bedded them. Lucky's daughters themselves all lived a normal lifespan unlike their ever-youthful mother, the Queen in the North, whom the Ukko had altered before it began transporting human immigrants to this new world of Kaleva.

Lord Osmo (my son, incidentally – no not the cuckoo's son but mine, Alvar's) presumed that Jatta had slept with one of the mutant mocky-men whom he abhorred. Using his power as a proclaimer, he who had changed the tyrant Tycho Cammon into stone bespoke Jatta to seek refuge in some mutant hovel far away in Saari (much to my chagrin, since I'd hoped to question Jatta!).

Juke Nurmi, son of mutants – but not himself visibly marked – had nursed a mania to trounce Lord Osmo. Following that Lucky's Day feast Juke freed Cammon from his stone stasis so that the ex-tyrant might take revenge. Cammon murdered Osmo's sometime bed-partner Vivi before being destroyed (and his bones burned to ash).

Decamping, the mutie proclaimer imposed himself upon Jatta and Jack as their escort – as far as Speakers' Valley above Yulistalax. There, amidst a mana-blizzard and a stampede of sheep set on fire by young Demon Jack, a sky-boatful of armed Juttahats brawled with a boatful of the Queen's guards. The Jutties kidnapped Jack (but Jarl Pakken proved to have become a zombie). Abandoning the little boy to his fate, Lucky snatched the Brazen Isi mage, Imbricate, and retrieved Jatta (who was desolate) along with her escort.

In that same valley two months later, at the autumn gala, Lucky's consort

---

* All of his pesky abbreviations have been expanded.

13

Prince Bertel introduced their marriageable daughter Eva to our champion proclaimer Osmo – and to Osmo's friend from over the turquoise lake, Elmer Loxmith the instinctive engineer. Bertel had fathered a hundredsome daughters and was privately bone-sick of longlife and of his wife's caprices.

Queen Lucky was sure that part of her soul and sanity had been kept by the Ukko entity and that this echo of herself might now dwell in an offspring of the original Ukko somewhere upon Kaleva itself. Lucky had stolen an everything machine (an all-purpose nanotek, no, nanotechno – Penelope Conway in the Earthkeep at Landfall must know the right name!). Well, Lucky's General Aleksonis had looted this from a crashed Isi shuttle-ship. The Queen hoped the machine would build a device with which she could locate this Ukko offspring and consequently her lost self. The everything machine was kept under guard by Lucky's wooden soldiers inside the Fortress in the Fjord at Sariolinna. It remained stubbornly inactive.

Could Osmo bespeak it to work in exchange for daughter Eva's hand? Or could Elmer tinker it to work? Could Roger Wex, the Earth agent with wetwear in his head, compel the captive mage Imbricate to reveal how the everything machine functioned?

At the gala Osmo was beset with an erotic frenzy for Eyeno Nurmi, the one-eyed mutie poetess who was Juke's sister and for whom Juke guiltily nursed incestuous feelings. Eyeno wore a convincing false eye obtained from the Velvet Isi, and she resented Osmo's advances. When the mutie proclaimer's challenge against Osmo failed, to save his skin Juke bartered his sister to the victor. To Osmo's horror, Eyeno plucked out her eye. Enraged, Osmo bespoke Eyeno to drown herself in a lake far away.

Hear the story, hark to the tale. Thinking to kill herself in Loom Lake, Eyeno was instead sucked in to the junior Ukko concealed beneath those waters. (Though we did not learn about this till later!) Therein, she met Paula Sariola's echo and the echoes of dead Sariola daughters whom Eyeno previously used to glimpse with her inward eye. The only other living person to have entered this inner domain, this wishworld within the junior Ukko, had been the father of a certain rapscallion, name of Minkie Kennan.

Osmo's venom at Eyeno had arced through mana-space, killing his mother in Maananfors (my wife Johanna, who never cared a hoot about my Chronicles). Johanna's death caused Osmo such grief that he was disinclined to proclaim for many months. Elmer Loxmith, for his part, had been commissioned to build a sleep-monitor for the longlife Gunther Beck, who planned to hibernate by drinking serpent hormone. Through deep dreams Lord Beck hoped to find the echo of his beloved wife Anna Sariola who died two centuries previously.

Hark to the story! During the winter Wethead Wex's status at the Queen's court diminished, but he conceived an affection for Minnow Sariola, Jatta's elfin younger sister who chattered to herself. In the spring Demon Jack landed at the palace in a stolen sky-boat. In the space of a mere nine months in Isi hands, Jatta's

fastboy had grown speedily to adolescence, and now had escaped from the alien serpents. Once the winter ice thawed, Lucky summoned Osmo and Elmer to Pohjola
Palace to compete at activating the everything machine. Elmer succeeded, winning
Eva as his bride. To pique Osmo, the Queen invited mutants from Juke Nurmi's
village as wedding guests. (The mutie proclaimer himself had disappeared after the
gala.) Enraged, Osmo departed in his sky-boat only to find that Vivi's father – one
of Osmo's small entourage – had abducted Minnow for him as a consolation prize.
En route, Juke lay in ambush with missiles given him by the Velvet Isi (who had
formerly given his sister her artificial eye). Damaged, Osmo's sky-boat strayed way
off course before crashing. Only he (ah my son!) and Minnow survived.

As well as mutants, Bertel brought Minkie Kennan to the wedding at Pohjola
Palace. Alas, Elmer proved unable to consummate his nuptials. Back in Loxmithlinna, Elmer began to whip his new bride nightly. Gunther Beck's missing nephew
Cully arrived at the Loxmiths' keep in a seriously confused state of mind. This
young man's plight intrigued Eva almightily.

Hark and hear: the Queen's everything machine began to produce exotic
weapons, amongst which was an armed jump-bike. Bertel goaded Minkie into a
rage. Young Kennan seized this jump-bike, gunned the prince down, and escaped
together with the Isi mage (of whom he quickly rid himself). Chasing after the
murderer by sky-boat, fastboy Jack came across Juke instead. He brought the mutie
proclaimer back to the palace where the widowed Queen raged and grieved.

Osmo (oh my son!) discovered sterling qualities in Minnow when the two
castaways made their way through a deathmaze in the western forests to the den
of the giant Isi mana-mage known as Viper. Minnow saved Osmo's spirit from
being raped by the mage. Now the two would wed as equals on their return to
Maananfors – where Osmo's paranoid bondsman Sam Peller was stockpiling new
weapons. These were unexpectedly being supplied by Isi of the Brindled faction.
News of Juke's welcome at the royal palace inflamed Osmo. Word of the survival
of Minnow's kidnapper fevered Lucky.

Bertel's assassin had vanished. Minkie was in seventh heaven in the Ukko under
Loom Lake, seducing maidens – until Eyeno began to rouse the exotic inhabitants
to war against him. (Which we only discovered subsequently!) Wex was pursuing
a quest to rescue Minnow. Broken-legged, Wex stumbled upon a conclave of our
enigmatic gossip-birds, where all the cackle was about looming war. By now Osmo
was eyeing nearby Loxmithlinna as of strategic importance; surely Lucky would
reason likewise. At Loxmithlinna itself, Eva's probings finally maddened Cully.
The Isi had filled this young man's mind with false memories so that he would
murder the dreamlord out of hatred – and Lord Beck's nephew had been bemusedly
resisting their sway. In anguish Cully put out one of Eva's prying eyes with his
dinner knife, and fled during the confusion.

'Bloodshed and war,' cackled a cuckoo ...

One day Moon will plunge
Into warm world
Shattering herself
In a rupturous and
Forced embrace.

– Eyeno Nurmi

PART ONE

MATINGS
AND
MAJESTY

1 · TANGO INTERRUPTED

On a blithe evening early in June the timbered village hall of
Onnekyla was decked with freshly cut foliage. Amid the bristly
verdant sprays hung many bunches of herbs, splendid for warding off gadflies and such. The scent of evergreen sap and tart
midgebane mingled in a duet of odours, puckish to people but
pukey to insects.

The women wore bright woollen robes of all hues of blue,
banded and striped in yellow and crimson. The men: purple
tunics embroidered with gilt braid. Unruly pompons spilled from
the men's caps, wild mop-heads of red wool. Maybe a sixth of
the assembly were dancing to the wistful tango melody, couples
slow-stepping sideways by the mellow light of oil-lamps. Double
doors stood open upon a dusky tree-fringed forecourt. Occasional
exuberant *yoiks* resounded from a cluster of drinkers at a can-
opied booth. The buffet table inside the hall was nearly denuded
of pasties and pies. A lone dedicated glutton browsed upon some
remnants. Most villagers in the hall simply harkened to the
plangent tones of the singer. The bulk of Lammas's audience
lolled in all available chairs; they leaned against the plank walls;
they stood swaying to his song, eyes moist with sentiment. Surely
this must be the woolly mutant's final encore of the evening.
Penultimate, anyway.

> 'To you I may look like a beast,
> 'To your eyes I may seem nature's jest.
> 'One pitying glance from you, Rita, the least
> 'Little nod, and love beats a drum in my breast.
>
> 'You're such a fine hen, charming chick,
> 'Dainty bird – any man will avow.
> 'How it wounds me to the quick
> 'When a *beast* can't woo a *bird*, thou . . .'

Lammas warbled so soulfully. Except upon his endearingly
winsome face and upon the palms of his hands, tufty grey curls
entirely covered the mutant. He only wore a token pair of brown

19

cotton shorts (and sandals). More clothes, and he would sweat uncomfortably. His fellow mutie, Knotty, accompanied Lammas on the fiddle. Knotty wore a hessian tunic to complement his own ridgy ropy skin, which seemed woven of tangled string. The third musician, Pieman, whistled melodiously while chiming a couple of cymbals together – the soul of shining silver transformed into sound. His face and his fists (and his other tunic-clad parts) were as crusty as well-baked bread.

Arto Nurmi conducted the combo. Arto was short and bowlegged. He sported a natty (if frayed) waistcoat of gold and blue stripes over a baggy embroidered white shirt, the sleeves being rolled up to the elbows. Cross-gartered moccasins tethered the lower reaches of his roomy black breeches. On his hands: white kid gloves, of his own crafty cutting and nimble sewing. In the right glove (with six fingers – or rather, five fingers and a thumb) Arto waved an open red fan as baton while conducting, signalling that the current choice of dancing partners was at the women's behest. In the other glove (likewise with six fingers) Arto clutched a closed blue fan. His ears, long and pointy as a goat's, were alert to every nuance of Knotty's fiddle and of Pieman's fluting whistle. Also to Lammas, of course, the star of the occasion.

> 'Dear duckling, you'll forever be my only.
> 'Yet ne'er I'll tiptoe to your downy nest.
> 'Forever must my aching heart be lonely,
> 'Never shall my love for you be blessed . . .'

The Queen's two guards were as deeply affected as the villagers of Onnekyla. Maybe more so. For the past three weeks blond Elias and sandy Otto had been guiding the mutie combo on their tango tour through the Northland, and they had heard the werewool perform every evening. In their camouflage leathers, lightpistols at their waists, that tough duo were misty-eyed.

Yet now the crook-legged conductor missed a beat. His sensitive ears twitched. He frowned.

A grumbling.

A rumbling.

A muted blare. *Aaaaannnggg*. As of an ill-tempered hervy blundering through woodland in rut.

The Northland wasn't home to any of those horn-crowned beasts. No hervies dwelled north of the Great Fjord – not so far as Arto knew! Admittedly the bow-legged glovemaker had never strayed far from his hovel in southernmost Saari until quite recently when the crazy Queen required a gaggle of mocky-men to be guests at a certain wedding. Arto in particular. Him being the dad of the lad who'd helped out Queen Lucky's unlucky daughter Jatta and her miracle boy, the lad who was Lord van Maanen's bane.

The lad who had betrayed his own sister.

Who sold out precious Eyeno.

Arto didn't wish to think too much about that business. Likely he'd never see Juke again, no more than he'd see the lad's sister. Juke might be roaming incognito anywhere between Tumio and Kip'an'keep. Anyplace between Landfall and the Velvet Serpent nest beyond Saari city. Lying low, or trying to get himself killed by hobnobbing with alien snakes or bumping into tetchy hervies.

The sounds which Arto's preternaturally keen lugs were picking up couldn't possibly be those of a hervy . . .

Damn Juke for looking so normal! For being that freak among freaks, that mockery among mocky-men: a child without visible flaw or blemish or abnormality. The lad's birth had been a curse – as Eyeno might have rhymed it.

Might have, indeed. Before she was sent to her death.

Insufferable sadness possessed the glovemaker. Loss. Grief. Poignant pangs. Soulfully he wagged the red fan. His thoughts homed upon his creaky cott in humble Outo. Each groan of its ramshackled fabric was dear to him, engraved in memory. Ester must be fretting somethink chronic about her hubby's prolonged absence. Dear plump, hairy, goat-eyed Ester, left alone these four long weeks ever since the prince descended upon the mutants' village in the royal sky-boat.

The *murdered* prince . . . killed, now, by that raffish fellow-me-lad Minkie Kennan. Bertel, the dad of all Lucky's harvest of daughters, assassinated!

A cuckoo had cackled this shocking news a fortnight previously while the mutie combo were on tour. How might the murder twist the Queen's fickle mind? Would it sour the guarantee to the mocky-men to return them safely home once their tango trip was over? Would the grief-stricken Queen honour her dead husband's promises? Onnekyla was just thirty keys from Sariolinna and Pohjola Palace. The lap of honour around assorted towns and hamlets of the Northland was almost complete. An honour, indeed. Quite a novel experience for mocky-men! Ester would be amazed. So would Juke have been, damn the boy.

Poor precious tumbledown cott in Outo, so far away! Home was as distant as any lovesick lad from his forbidden sweetheart in one of Lammas's heart-wrenching songs. Poor cherished comfy missus, waiting and wondering all this while. Small comfort their two fine children had proved to be.

On the journey by air from Niemi to Sariolinna that rascal Kennan had acted standoffish enough towards *muties*. Snooty was the word. Even so, once or twice Kennan had been on the verge of glad-eyeing young June. Just as well for the scoundrel that he didn't! That particular dish of peaches and cream could give a fellow a disease if old Goody Hilda, the shrivelled chaperon, were to look the other way. Actually the wisewoman almost always *did* look the other way, her being so stooped over that she could only squint sidelong at you. Goody Hilda kept the lass under control; that was the point. June was the mocky-men's security, so to speak, their safe conduct.

Not on this present tour of the hinterland, mind you. The Queen had *interested* herself in June: buxom young June of the double bosoms – four bubs plumping forth beneath the mocky-girl's roomy blouse, twin titties above twin titties. Lucky had kept June and Hilda behind at the palace.

Unlucky Queen. Her consort of the last four centuries had been snuffed by that rapscallion. How crazy would Lucky be by the time the combo returned to Pohjola Palace?

Aaaaannnggg ...

A shrill threadlike scream came from the far end of the hamlet. A blade sliced through softness which was suddenly brittle ...

An abrupt *whump*. Treetops lit up ruddily. '*How far from here to happiness* ... ?' – the werewool faltered in his song. 'Fire!' bellowed a boozer out in the forecourt.

Bones of a house were ablaze. Disjointed timbers flared in silhouette against an ashen skyline: a furnace cage. A constellation of wild sparks flew upward. Another home erupted with a clap of thunder, spouting an inferno. Somewhere children were screaming.

Hubbub, as the crowd poured along the dark pebbled street in their finery. Propelled like flotsam in a flood, Arto gimped valiantly to avoid being overwhelmed.

'Bucket brigade—!'

'The well, the pond—!'

'The kids, our babes—!'

Brilliant saucer eyes glared. Bright rays lanced from a black shape with broad high wheels, the bulk of a laden wagon. The unknown vehicle trundled forward. Those eyebeams raked aside to spotlight a dwelling. Fat phosphorbugs streaked from the wagon as swiftly as firebullets from a crossbow, etching after-images, bursting against the vertical boards of the house, against the gutter eaves above, swarming through shattering windows, kindling curtains, illuminating rooms from within, clinging, igniting a radiant bonfire. With a vast exhalation of hot breath the wooden building became another furnace cage, enclosing little shrieks of terror and agony which soon were smothered.

'Devil cart—!'

'All the fire-nakkis together in a coach—!'

'Of black metal, look . . .'

'Serpent war-wagon—'

'No!'

'Yes!'

'Burning our homes—'

'Slaughtering our bairns in bed. The bairns—'

The crowd bunched tight as their onward rush halted. Bellies and bums crushed Arto, expelling his breath. His ribs were in danger of cracking. Someone's pompon cap fell across Arto's face in a floppy woollen cuddle; he shook his head from side to side. Cries, pandemonium.

'Scatter, scatter—!'

'Stop the devil wagon—!'

A lurch, and Arto's arms were free. He gasped. His fingers clawed upward. Bodies collided again. Corklike, Arto rose. A couple of buttons popped from his stressed waistcoat. The black vehicle blared again: *Aaaaannnggg*. Its eyes glared. Those great hard rubber wheels crunched pebbles. Foul smoke gouted from its rump. Two slanted windows wrapping around the front of the machine were black and glossy as obsidian in the furnace light. No one, nothing, was evident behind those windows. The metal beast was raging of its own volition.

'Mr Nurmi!' Elias was taking his escort duty seriously. Trying to shoulder through the throng, the blond guard waved his lightpistol – and the crowd parted, opening a channel to the front for him, and then for Otto too.

Voices appealed: 'Shoot its eyes! Blind it!'

23

Almost all knives had been left at home on account of, and out of respect for, the tango concert. Only a couple of villagers were brandishing blades. What use would even the sharpest knives be against the juggernaut? Lightpistols, ah! Maybe. Possibly. Hopefully.

'Blind its eyes, Queen's-men!'

'Come on, Lucky's leatherboys!'

'*What is it?*' Cuckoo cackle hadn't forewarned the villagers of this menace.

'Before it torches another house!'

'Get out of my way, you fool. *Run for it.*'

'Babes in their beds—'

'Leatherboys, leatherboys!'

Illuminated by the blazing house, the destroyer had paused less than two hundred metres from the front of the crowd. Willy-nilly the glovemaker felt himself being levered to the fore.

'Let the conductor through! That thing needs *charming*.'

Maybe that many-bodied beast, the crowd, judged with insensate instinct that in the present extremity a mutie might serve as a suitable scapegoat to appease the metal beast. Notwithstanding their sentimental tears shed so recently. All because Arto came from a *goaty* region, and sported goaty ears. His baggy sleeve snagged on a belt buckle and promptly tore loose. Nothing would halt his forward progress.

Just as Otto and Elias were levelling their pistols with wary determination, the mob squeezed Arto out like pus from a boil behind the duo. The glovemaker collapsed. He struggled to his feet. Here he was, out in front of the cordon, breathless and bandy-legged.

The great black vehicle basked in the heat and glare. *Aaaaannnggg*, it brayed.

A drumming . . .

. . . of hooves.

'*In the Queen's name let us through!*'

At this cry Lucky's guards delayed firing their guns. A pair of ponies, stocky and shaggy, came forging through the crowd. One mount bore the fastboy from the Queen's court: Jatta Sariola's miracle lad who had escaped from the Isi after growing up as fast as a mushroom. His skin was the cinnamon hue of a penny-bun fungus, too. A wiry lad, with cropped jet hair just like his mum's. As usual he was wearing that coppery Juttahat livery — which the light from the blazing house bronzed and burnished.

24

A black wriggle-glyph decorated Demon Jack's right shoulder. An inky vesperbird seemed to cling claw-hooked, as if flattened against a branch.

Not for a moment did Arto mistake the fastboy for an actual servant of the serpent. Some villagers did, though. Some did.

'It's a Juttie—!'

'A Juttie from the south—!'

'Told you yon war-wagon was Isi, didn't I—?'

'Wagon'll know its proper master—'

Jack reined in and leapt from the saddle. He was unarmed. As was his riding companion, apart from a sheathed knife at the belt.

That companion dismounted swiftly, abandoning his drooling pony to its own devices. Fawn hair swept back from his brow. Icy blue eyes were intent on their target: the berserk war-wagon, the mad hervy-machine. That muscle-corded neck, that vigorous build – so unlike Arto's own physiology. Smart new grey travelling cloak . . .

He was Juke. He was none other than the glovemaker's own flesh and blood. Arto reeled in astonishment.

Neither Arto's son nor the fastboy paid any heed to the old man. Not right now. Oh no.

'Don't you fire those guns,' Demon Jack cried at the guards. 'You'll only provoke it.'

Side by side, the fastboy and Juke advanced cautiously towards the war-wagon. The juggernaut glared balefully at them, flood-lighting the pair.

Juke stretched out his hands as if to wrestle with the manic fighting vehicle. 'I bespeak you, spawn of the everything machine!' he bellowed. 'Cease and desist! Be tame! This is spoken, spoken.'

'—he's a proclaimer—'

'—he'd better be a paragon at it—'

'Your origin was Isi and Juttie, Steel Hervy!' Juke certainly perceived the analogy with that irascible beast. The fastboy flashed the proclaimer a grin of complicity as if both shared a secret or a special memory. 'You were made for the human Queen, Steel Hervy – to serve Lucky Sariola. Elmer Loxmith aroused the everything machine, and it built you out of atoms from the patterns stored inside itself. You'll submit to us, Hervy. This is spoken and bespoken.'

Aaaaannnggg.

Phosphorbugs gushed from a nozzle atop the vehicle. Not at the two challengers nor the crowd behind them – who squealed nonetheless. Not at Juke and Jack nor at Arto – nor at the houses of white boards and steep shingled roofs. Those firebullets winged overhead towards far woodland beyond street and hamlet. And the crowd sighed.

Huge wheels ground a few paces forward, backward, grooving the pebble road. *Aaaaannnggg*. Suddenly the bright eyes of the war-wagon extinguished themselves.

Only momentarily – as if the machine had blinked. Spotlight beams sprang forth again. The nozzle dipped to point at people. Arto quaked. Dozens were about to die, torn by firebullets, their fine garments ignited. Himself in the forefront; and Juke too. Juke and Jack.

The demon boy stiffened. He rose on tiptoe. He *shone*. He was as lustrous as brass. As sunlight at noon.

Mana-magic. The furnace-house was a grey ghost. The eyes of the hervy-wagon were pale and feeble; barely visible at all. Almost all the light in the vicinity clad Jack. The bulk of the war-machine became a black silhouette, as anchored as a boulder on a ridge at sunset.

Cold gusted over Arto. This sudden chill burned as much as it froze. His long ears crisped to crêpe. His eyes smarted, tears freezing.

Juke cried, 'Yield to us, Hervy! This is spoken.' Sounded as if Juke's teeth were chattering. Hoarfrost stood in stiff white hairs along the black outline of the war-vehicle. Such a numbing freeze in June, with a glowing sun-child presiding. *Mana-magic*. Gradually light and darkness combined once more; cold and heat mingled together. The house burned more brightly. In its glow the war-machine sat inertly, its headlamps modest, flanks and windows and canopy slicked with moisture from melting rime.

Jack wobbled. He was no longer radiant. 'I'm hungryungry,' Arto heard the lad babble at Juke.

Juke beckoned Elias and Otto. The three men trotted towards the calmed juggernaut. They scaled rungs on its flank. A hatch opened. For a while Juke and the two guards conferred, then Elias entered the cabin. The demon boy was plodding around in a circle, drained. He might have been asleep on his feet, or walking to keep himself awake.

Juke stood tall atop the war-wagon, his hair swept back. To

the crowd he shouted, 'It'll take us a while to learn the workings of this monster, but I swear it's safe now—'

Only then did he spy his father.

'Lad . . .'

'Dad . . .'

This reunion was an embarrassment both for the glovemaker and for the hero of the hour. (Co-hero, more exactly; the other star being Demon Jack. The fastboy hadn't scaled the war-wagon to pose there briefly like a hunter with his trophy.)

'Likely you saved me life, lad—'

'The Queen has honoured us, Dad. You and me, and—'

And Lammas and Knotty likewise – who hurried, just then, from the mêlée of villagers. Folks were scurrying hither and thither, trying to organize a bucket brigade and beaters to stop the fire from spreading. Men and women dashed warily past the dormant juggernaut. A few people wailed. Others wept with relief, and some with sorrow – a bitter appendix to the indulgent melancholy Lammas had conjured in the dance hall. A number raged. A fair few stood enthralled. Kids were sneaking from houses which had been spared. Lammas slapped at sparks which had swirled into his wool, singeing a tuft here and there. With stringy hands Knotty clapped Juke upon both shoulders and clasped him tightly. The embrace was rigid. Knotty was holding Juke away from him quite as much as he was clutching him in acclaim. By interposing himself thus between father and son Knotty certainly forestalled a parental hug, or filial hug, which might have proved similarly stiff. Or which might not even have occurred. Knotty had filled an awkward vacuum.

'Queen Lucky has honoured us mocky-men, Knotty,' said Juke.

Arto shuffled his feet indecisively. By now Pieman had turned up to scrutinize the saviour (or co-saviour) of the village.

'Quite a show, Master Juke!' Pieman's tone verged on the derisive. 'Pity your sister can't be here to applaud.'

There: Pieman had said the needful for Arto.

'Shut up,' muttered Lammas. '*Hwisht!*'

Pieman shrugged. 'Can't help being a bit crusty, can I? Can't change facts.'

Juke's face flushed in the firelight. 'What do you know, Pieman? Do you know *anguish*?'

'Oh you can *try* to proclaim it otherwise, Master Juke—'

27

The werewool grabbed Pieman by his collar. 'Don't be such a know-all, eh?'

For ten, for twenty seconds Lammas and Pieman and Knotty and Juke might each have been part of a tableau. None of the participants dared move, or were able to. A frown creased Juke's brow. Hesitantly he reached out his own hand toward his critic's crusty neck.

'It was in the woods outside Threelakes,' Juke muttered. 'When we were selling gold for the Halvek folk . . . Do you remember? After my . . . *sister* got that false eye from Missieur Pierre the jeweller . . . A few years ago now, isn't it? We four met up in the woods. You, Pieman, were all for spoiling her joy at her new eye with your wisdom about aquamarines. I grabbed you by the scruff, didn't I?'

'*Five* of us met up in the woods,' Pieman corrected Juke. 'There were five of us. The fifth person was—'

'I know. My own dear sister.' Juke refrained from saying her name.

'You've gone on to such grand deeds since then—'

'And now,' warned Lammas, 'we're in danger of ruining another reunion unless we're careful.'

'That's true enough,' agreed Arto. He didn't exactly look at his son. 'I suppose one child's better than none.'

'I was compelled,' whispered Juke. 'Compelled . . . But I paid van Maanen back and no mistake.'

'How do you mean, son?'

'Why, I shot Lord Osmo down on his way home from Sariolinna in his sky-boat – with a missile. Smoke and fire poured from the tail.'

'You shot *him* down? Just *him*?'

'I used an Isi missile, Dad. Given me by the same Velvet Isi who gave . . . who gave . . . my sister her . . .' Words swallowed themselves. Again, the evasion of her name.

One of the ponies was cantering to and fro, snickering, a mad look in its eye. The fastboy was leaning against the other beast, mumbling to it sleepily while it supported him.

Arto said carefully, 'I'm thinking that yon Lord was on his way home with a certain *Miss* Sariola – the kidnapped Princess Minnow.'

Juke was silent.

'You must have killed Minow an' all, son. Did the Queen smile at this news? Is she completely crazy now that her hubby's dead?'

'Dad, Lucky needs an overseer for this everything machine of hers and for some of its products, as the good folks here can attest. Then there's the matter of revenge upon Minkie Kennan some day . . .'

'I'm thinking, by all accounts you were more deeply compelled than just by yon lord you shot down. Self-compelled in the matter of your sister.'

Pieman was nodding aye to this. Lammas shook his woolly head warily.

'I'd give almost anything,' Juke whispered, 'to call her back.'

'Her, being Princess Minnow?'

'Eyeno, Dad. Eyeno.' Juke could hardly pronounce her name; he almost choked.

Arto dithered. 'Well then, there's a wish. 'Course, the swan of death doesn't heed any such wishes. I suppose you're still my flesh and blood, Juke, when all's said and done. I don't expect you'll be coming home with me to see your mum? 'Course you won't, lad. Not yet-a-while. I'll tell her that you're sorry your sister died. I'll tell her truthfully. Meanwhile you'll hunt Minkie Kennan for the Queen.'

A discreet cough from Lammas. 'Kennan's from Niemi. That ain't exactly far from our own home cotts, you might recall, Master Juke. Minkie's mum the Dame is a tough bird. Couple of younger sons too. Revenge breeds revenge, mm? We wouldn't wish our cotts to be burned down in retaliation.'

'That shouldn't happen! Oh no, never; this is spoken, Lammas.' Did Juke mean that such a calamity *wouldn't* ever happen – or that it *oughtn't* to? 'Tell you what,' Juke promised grandly, 'tomorrow morning we'll ride back together to the palace in the battle-hervy. On top of it too,' he qualified. The cabin itself could obviously only accommodate three passengers. 'I'll ride up top so that people en route won't feel alarmed. We'll travel in style, my fellow mocky-men.'

And so they did, the following day: the tango combo, the guards, and the Queen's two mana-men (one of them little more than a lad).

The notion of tethering ponies behind the vehicle on long leads had swiftly been rejected. The *aaaaannnggg* of that engine and the gust of exhaust gases would panic and choke the animals. Those sturdy mounts stayed in Onnekyla as partial recompense for three burned houses and several dead children. Elias sat inside the war-machine with Jack. Elias steered and Jack cajoled

29

the vehicle. Arto also rode within, resting his bow legs. On top, in a recessed bay ringed by a rail, lounged Elias and Pieman and the werewool and Juke.

The bulky vehicle swayed as its four great wheels grooved the dirt road which summer had softened. Sunlight dappled warmly through the viridian-needled veras and jade-scaled larixes and hoary sylvesters. Gnats floated by like puffs of fumes. Now and then the sprawling boughs of chartreuse curver trees and those of fleecy-fronded horzmas (both at the northern extreme of their habitat) swept across the top of the hervy-vehicle. The passengers were obliged to crouch low or even prostrate themselves.

'What *use* is this thing, anyway?' Pieman demanded after one such close brush. 'Bit on the burly side for forests, isn't it?'

'You might say the same of the flesh-and-blood hervy,' Juke retorted. 'Doesn't it get foliage tangled in its rack of horns? This beast will make a fine big watchdog for the palace. Eyes gleaming, spitting fire.'

Pieman clawed a frond loose from his crusty neck. 'Let's hope Lucky likes her new pet. Maybe us mocky-men can go home to our mocky-cotts.'

'Aye to that,' agreed Lammas as the war-machine rolled onward.

2 · COITUS CONTEMPLATED . . .

Goody Hilda, the wisewoman from Halvek, saw the world obliquely and aslant. The curvature of her spine was so extreme that she must crane her head sideways to carry on a conversation. Even for a mocky-woman, Hilda's perspective upon affairs was out of kilter. Thus she perceived the Queen's perverse *drift* as regards June and young Demon Jack Pakken rather earlier than anyone else in Pohjola Palace.

That included Jack's mother Jatta, whom Queen Lucky had tormented twice already. On the first occasion, by marooning her errant daughter in wild woodland over winter, pregnant with Jack. On the second occasion, by rescuing the disgraced princess from that affray at Speakers' Valley yet letting Jatta's child be snatched away by alien Juttahats.

It also included the peasant girl Anni, whom Jutties had abducted from her parents' farm to become a sex-slave for Jarl Pakken in his rehearsals for the ravishing of Jatta; then to act as nurse to Jatta's own son who grew so rapidly. Of course, Jack had rescued Anni from the serpents' nest, and she now shared Jatta's chamber in the palace. Anni was Jatta's confidante now that sisters Eva and Minnow had departed from the palace, the one to the Loxmiths' aitch-house far south beyond the Great Fjord, the other abducted to her death.

The mutie girl June, of the double bosoms, was Goody Hilda's responsibility. Buxom and bonny with blonde bushy pigtails, June's rosy features nevertheless often showed a petulant cast. Sometimes her air was saucy. Frequently the girl was sulky and moody. As well she might be. Were she to touch a fellow, or a fellow touch her, he would be afflicted with thirst or itch or shivers or shits – unless Hilda were holding June's hand so as to disarm this lamentable diseased faculty. Cause enough for much pouting and heartache on June's part.

As for Jack himself . . . to outward appearances he was an energetic adolescent (given to sudden torpor or ravenous hunger if he strained himself). As regards experience of life, Jatta's miracle lad was a mere thirteen months old. A year and a month. Yet Jack had begun speaking almost as soon as he was born. Within a handful-and-a-half of weeks he had grown as big as a two-year-old and was scampering around, very much of a handful for his refugee mother. Jack's subsequent experience included training in the mystery of wind and light and cold by an Isi mana-mage. Would he continue to mature at the same hectic pace, so that within a decade or even half that span he might become a sage, or an old codger? Such was Jatta's fear.

The demon boy's first birthday had fallen on the day following the marriage of Princess Eva to Elmer Loxmith; the same date on which the newly-weds departed for Loxmithlinna by sky-boat – which was a week prior to Prince Bertel's murder by Minkie Kennan. When Jack looked to be sixteen or seventeen if he was a day could you properly speak about a *first* anniversary?

In the month since that 'birthday' Jack had sprouted a meagre moustache. Just a touch of 'tache, mind you. The darkness of the hair made that male plumage rather more noticeable. As yet Jack showed no sign of a beard. Ought he to? Ought he not to? Jack's sire, Jarl Pakken, had possessed curly red hair, at least before he became a zombie. Yet Jarl Pakken had really been a

Juttahat – and Jutties did not normally sprout whiskers. Jatta's hair was jet-black, as were all Sariola daughters' tresses, and Queen Lucky's too. Jack might be regarded as a lad self-born from his mum, fermented and catalyzed in her by her seducer rather than being a blend of herself and that sham-man, that impostor. Not a duplicate, in male form, of his mother: Jack certainly wasn't that. Neither was he an amalgam of two parents. Say, rather, that he was the synthesis of his mother and of mana itself. He was Jatta's mana-kid.

Ought Jack ever to sprout a beard? Maybe not. But anyhow, some hair now decorated his upper lip, sign of a jejune manliness – and of certain stirrings. No matter if he was properly eighteen years old, or only thirteen, or one-and-a-bit. No matter if he was callow, or contrariwise precocious.

Emotionally, just who *was* Jack? He had escaped with Anni from the alien serpents' nest to Sariolinna to rejoin his mother and to meet his grandmother the Queen so as to confirm his own true identity. Now that his selfhood was more secure, in what direction might he extend himself?

June . . .

June seemed to be of an age for Jack.

Would any normal lass harbour feelings for a fastboy who was the offspring, if only conceptually, of an alien? Maybe a lass might! With his cinnamon skin and his dark cropped hair, with his ambery eyes and neat features and lithe figure, Jack was handsome enough, if a mite on the short side. He could shine with power. He could compel with his body – with the lingo of his legs and arms and torso. Yet would any young hen truly take a shine to him?

The mana-kid doubted this. This much Goody Hilda had observed, askew. Jack was unsure of himself. Stirrings (and a modest 'tache) had come upon the lad so suddenly. He wouldn't be a devil with the chicks the way Minkie Kennan reputedly had been. In this regard Jack was shy, awkward. When the lad eyed curvaceous June the mocky-girl seemed . . . so out of reach. Hygienically so!

The taboo girl wasn't exactly *oblivious* to this furtive attention on the fastboy's part. It made her sulk in frustration . . .

The Queen also took heed.

Even in her widow's weeds, Lucky noted the kindling of her grandson's itch for June. An itch which June could hardly

32

scratch! Lucky spied this through her black lace veil of mourning, and slyly she began to encourage this delicate relationship.

Only Hilda was fully aware of this, at first. And she was wary. If need be, she'd challenge Queen Lucky even in the throes of mourning. What did a twisted antique such as Hilda with only a scant few years (or months) left in her have to worry about from a Queen?

Lucky's mutie guests could hardly mean more to the Queen than playthings. Cute, grotesque *toys*. Honouring them at court had been a way of smacking Lord Osmo van Maanen in the gob. The celebrated tango tour of the northern hinterland, likewise. When word had come of Lord Osmo's death-crash – caused by Juke, the bearer of these tidings – the news had been a source of considerable ambivalence. Lucky had lost her enemy and kidnapper of Princess Minnow. She was avenged – yet she was cheated of her revenge. Minnow was dead (but Lucky had borne a hundred and more daughters). Juke had been Osmo's bane; now he was that cocky lord's executioner. Juke was the Queen's champion, give or take a dead daughter.

Surely the girl with the double bosoms and her crook-backed duenna were merely toys for a Queen. Why, then, would Lucky risk the well-being of her grandson by encouraging him to consort with June? And June, with Jack?

Irrespective of van Maanen's demise, a major preoccupation of Lucky seemed to be *weapons* from her everything machine . . . Hilda felt suspicious in her very waters, thin and gruelly though those were these days.

When Goody Hilda grew suspicious, she betook herself to the picture gallery, Lucky's Pinacotek. This was up a spiral stone stairway along from the fur factory where twenty or so women steamed and beat and combed and cut and sewed the coats of arctic goats and tarandras from the tundra. It was some way beyond the counting house court, a plaza domed with glass in the chambers around which clerks kept tally of the Queen's treasury. Woe betide those fellows if they filched a golden or, or a silver mark. In a nearby refectory, hands (and a mouth, and a nose) protruded from the plastered wall where a thieving clerk had been entombed some decades previously by a proclaimer on Lucky's orders. The mostly invisible wretch was virtually part of the décor, his palms a receptacle for coins, his mouth a hole for scraps.

33

What a heave it was for Hilda up that spiral stairway, even with the aid of a hairy white rope looped through rungs. Stooped over so chronically, the wisewoman's head inclined in one direction while the stone steps screwed the other way. On this occasion June wasn't on hand to haul and push the bent beldame upward, in the way the girl had helped out during previous explorations of the palace.

Expeditions, indeed. Tours and excursions. Hilda must have hobbled around most of Pohjola Palace arm in arm, or hand in hand, with the querulous if inquisitive lass. They had trod through pillared arcades and long halls akin to covered streets, through little piazzas under cupolas, by way of busy work-shops, apartments, refectories, armoury, storerooms, parlours. They had rested on sofas embroidered with faces in the Dome of Favours watching Mikal the painter crouched on his plat-form adding midget figures to the frieze of heroes. In the ballroom, with its *trompe-l'oeil* of waltzing beaux and belles, June had danced wistfully with herself, following the footstep pattern on the floor. One particular area of orange and blue parquet blocks showed signs of a vigorous scrubbing. That was where Minkie Kennan had gunned Prince Bertel down before leaping away on the jump-bike. In Perfume Passage, where civet and musk were treated, June had inhaled in tantalized pique . . .

One chamber in the palace known as the Replica Room housed a scale model, made of thin lacquered wood and leaves of trans-lucent mica, of the entire complex – though excluding the net-work of cellars and crypts beneath – with cut-away roofs and domes and walls. This was the long-dead architect's original scheme, to which later accretions had been, and were still, faith-fully added by the Queen's current surveyor. Naturally, the miniature of the Replica Room within the model itself contained a tiny replica of the whole model. This was executed in highly detailed pottery. No one could see inside the wee pottery palace. Gossip had it that the Queen's ruby ring had included an even tinier pattern of Pohjola, inscribed on the backside of the large gem a couple of centuries earlier by a lapidary-proclaimer peer-ing through a lens. Lucky had carried the palace around with her upon her finger. Whether this was true or not, the Queen's ruby ring had been immured in her dead consort's coffin along with her diamond tiara to rest in a crypt which certainly wasn't part of the replica.

Huff, puff: Hilda reached the top of the stairway and swung towards the picture gallery. Really, she *must* take up using a walking stick instead of whispering cantrips to uphold herself.

All the portraits along the gallery were of Lucky in a medley of moods: radiant, glowering, serene, frenetic. Which one would be Mikal's painting of her? Impossible to say, when none was signed with a name – which few visitors would know how to read, even if so. Several bore emblems down in their bottom right corners, at squinting height for Hilda: a tiny palette, a dripping brush, an eye with a finger shading it. Lucky past and Lucky present; Lucky a century since or three centuries prior: no telling one from t'other. Hilda's bones ached from the climb.

The sunshine of mid-June bedazzled the sloping skylights. No direct rays reached the paintings to fade their oils, but random reflections dappled many of the variously carved frames, and their somewhat repetitive contents, and the yellower panelling. Motes speckled the air. At the far end of the gallery the fat old concierge known only as Granny snoozed in a stout easy chair, its green leather back deeply buttoned. Across her lap lay a white goose-feather duster. A tin spittoon drawer jutted open by several fingers' width from under the front of the seat. Granny's long baggy grey woollen gown was rucked up at the rear, exposing muscle-knotted white shanks. The tray pressed against the back of her legs.

Hilda knew by now to press a penny into Granny's palm. Batting an eye, the tubby old woman squinted at the bronze coin: anchor on the front of it for security. (And on the reverse an eye for prudence.) For safe-keeping Granny tinkled the coin down into the tin drawer. The shallow spittoon must be empty except of other such gratuities, and dry. Maybe a former concierge of the art collection had required the flat cuspidor under her seat, for phlegm. Granny had other uses for the receptacle. It was her money-box.

And it was something else besides.

Granny rubbed her muscular shanks to and fro against the tin. 'That's better now . . .' She wagged the duster. 'You're peering at me summat meddlesome.'

'I can't straighten up, that's why. I'm Hilda from Halvek, if you recall.'

Granny ummed, digesting this information. 'It's me sciatica, if you must know. The tin takes the pang away.'

'Ah . . . we're two of a kind, old cousin.' Dangling her hand,

Goody Hilda patted Granny's left leg and murmured a soothing mana-charm.

The concierge sighed. 'That's kind of you . . . So where's Halvek when it's at home?'

'Far away. Are all the Queen's moods on show here?'

Granny chuckled. Then, in the irritating fashion of those who possess a little much-prized knowledge, she added: 'I know what I know, Hilda from Halvek.'

'Undoubtedly. Never a truer word.'

Opposite the concierge hung a framed foggy mana-mirror, the only item on display without any coherent visual content. Cottony mist eddied in the glass.

'Granny's supposed to keep watch on that for when Her Majesty's future face shows. That'll be her elderly face, when Lucky grows old like you and me . . .'

'So I've heard.'

'Has to happen some day. Maybe it'll be the next Granny as sees it.'

Hilda nodded, sidelong. 'The glass can show people's fortunes too?'

'Happens now and then.'

'With so many of the Queen's moods on show here, maybe the mirror can reflect her intentions?'

'What Granny sees, Granny will tell Her Majesty.'

The wisewoman peered into the rutted prune face. 'Maybe the Queen confides in you? Do tell.'

'Tell? I could tell. Granny knows a thing or two.' The old woman's breath smelled of musty cobwebs and mild vinegar.

'Unknot yourself, old aches; and unknot yourself as well, old tongue. What would such a *thing* be?'

Granny cackled gleefully. 'Prince Bertie and her were talking, right here as plain as you and me. She wants to find where her real self is. That's everything to Her Majesty. She thinks as her real self's held prisoner in an Ukko-child – and the Jutties made Princess Jatta bake a bun in her oven, by name of Jack, as a way of finding Lucky's lost self before Her Majesty does—'

Before long, if the Queen had her way, Jack might bake some buns in June's hot unique oven . . .

Hilda shuffled to stand beside the swirly glass, peering up sidelong at it.

'Mana-mirror on the wall,' she asked.

'What'll befall?'

All remained as misty as ever. From her easy chair Granny began reminiscing.

'Well, I was as sleek and soft as water once. As slippery and as moist and as bendy. As supple and sweet. A real water-girl's what I was before I settled into lard. Can hardly credit it now! Why, the sheen of my skin was sheer silk. So sweet on the tongue, would you believe? I kissed and licked myself whenever t'other lads and lasses were looking the other way. I was the fresh morning dew all condensed into a body, a nakki-girl, a changeling. As soft and sleek and shiny and sweet as the dew. Oh I'd never dry up. Aye, I was a lustrous nakki-girl walking upon the land. I was as moist and as bendy once—'

Granny rocked about in her easy chair. She was under a mild sway, the compulsion of memory making her repeat herself. *Water, silk . . . Sheen, sweet . . .*

Goody Hilda wasn't a proclaimer who could compel serious events to occur, yet she was sensitive to the inner waters of a body. She could expand health and restrain sickness. She could discern some of the tides of mana. Granny was caught in an eddy of reverie. Mana was waxing. Past circumstances were repeating themselves obsessively as if what had once occurred might now recur in some new guise.

As clearly as though it were yesterday Hilda remembered stooping over the newly-born Eyeno Nurmi, who would become a poetess. A lovely baby with one eye lacking; the other eye hidden inside her head, an inner eye – so Hilda had detected. Back then, the wisewoman had been somewhat less bent. When Hilda was a girl, she had stood almost straight. In due course she began to bend like the sky-sickle, the debris of the shattered ancient moon which had strayed too close to Kaleva long ago before people were even fish on a world far away – as the dead poetess had proclaimed in verses. (Poetry was a different sort of proclaiming.)

That bulgy-eyed mocky-man Arni, who could read and who taught Eyeno to read, had discovered those verses after a cuckoo had brought news of Eyeno's condemnation to death by Osmo van Maanen at the gala – abetted by Juke's cowardice. Arni had read the verses to grieving mocky-men, as a memorial. Hilda had been visiting Outo village at the time.

Shattered moon, shattered life . . .

Were other lives soon to be shattered? June's, and Jack's? In a rupturous embrace!

Bright specks of dust lazed in the pool of illumination below the skylights. Fog billowed in the mana-mirror.

'Shattered moon,' begged Hilda.

'Shed light on June.'

Squinting up at the glass, Hilda saw two faces together cheek by cheek. One was June's rosy countenance. The other was Jack's. Those four cheeks of theirs were in motion. Were the pair chewing lustily in addition to grinning broadly? Hectic colours painted their mobile flesh: slashes of feverish red and bilious green and suffocated blue.

Each cheek was a tiny mannekin girl wearing a wide hooped skirt belling out from the slenderest of waists. Four little maids, royally dressed. A swirling nausea gripped Hilda. She flushed, she shivered. A constipated cramp panged her bowels. Her noddle ached. Nevertheless June looked so buoyant, and Jack so blithe.

Might those four girls conceivably be June's future brood? Her clutch of chicks by Jack? Four breasts, four sucklings . . . Who had dressed the little misses up so richly and fancifully? Queen Lucky? Each pretty child seemed to be the epitome of a malady, the essence in miniature of a foul malaise: delirium, poisoned bile, asphyxiation. Yet they appeared perky enough in themselves; whilst June and Jack looked perfectly fine.

Could June rid herself of her curse by giving birth to *embodiments* of that jinx? Little girls who could spread sicknesses if they chose to? Supposing they were sufficiently peeved – or prevailed upon! Bribed with beautiful dresses! What would the quadruplets' names be? Jinx? And Minx? And Minxie and Jinxie?

How could the fastboy survive courting June with his health intact? Evidently he would not only survive, but thrive, if the image in the mana-mirror was accurate! Two young folk cheek to cheek, aglow with health and high spirits.

Yet what of those four little daughters? What would *their* future be, if manipulated by the Queen? Not to mention the future of all those with whom they came into contact? Plague Girls . . . (Hilda felt it in her waters, which were churning, and curdling.) Lasses of Menace. Maids of Horror . . .

Already the image in the mana-mirror was evaporating into swirls of mist.

Had Granny noticed the fortune? If so, what did she make of it? This was certainly a matter to cackle about into the Queen's ear, whether or not Lucky had already glimpsed such a presage in this mirror or another. Yet Granny seemed so bound up in her own inner vision, her reverie of having once been as lovely and seductive as a water-sprite. The mirror was once again a square of milky cloud. Hilda hobbled back towards the easy chair. *Really, she must avail herself of a short walking stick.* That nauseous queasiness in her guts was abating. Spasms were fewer.

The fat old woman swayed as she wagged her duster to and fro. 'And did you see me, all sleek as silk? All shiny and sweet as dew?'

'Wake up, Granny.' Once, Hilda might have snapped her fingers. Not for many a long year now. 'Wake up.'

The concierge blinked. 'Hmm, so did I doze off? Oh I dreamt such a lovely dream but now it's gone away. Why did you spoil my dream? Everything gets spoiled sooner or later, turned into lard.' She stared perplexedly at her puffy white hand. 'A good dusting's what these here pictures need. Of course, dust just settles somewhere else instead. Good thing too, else what would Granny have to do with herself all day? Dust and lard: that's life in a word. The greasy side and the dry side. Dross clogs together, crumbs fall apart.'

'Granny knows a thing or two,' Hilda coaxed. 'More than lard and dust.' She scrutinized the old woman lopsidedly.

Granny fixed Hilda with a canny eye. 'I knows what I know,' was the reply.

The wisewoman prised a second penny from the pocket of her gown, and presented it. An eye and an anchor. The coin rattled speedily into the spittoon tray underneath the easy chair.

The climb back down the spiral stairway proved even more bothersome for Goody Hilda than the ascent had been. Nevertheless her visit to the picture gallery had been well worthwhile, if perhaps ambivalent.

A few afternoons later, Hilda was perched crookedly in one of the three lobes of a circular six-seater sofa embroidered with hearts large and small. Beside her: pigtailed June, in a loose creamy satin gown which the Queen had given her, smart new peaked bootees of matching suède on her feet. Pert sulky peaches, dressed in soft cream. The wisewoman held June's hand.

The only window looked out upon an inner courtyard cloistered along two sides. Beds of dill alternated with parsley. A fountain sprang from the mouth of a bronze leaperfish balancing upon its tail. Tapestries decked the rest of the chamber. Auroras danced upon a white landscape: green and blue and scarlet skirts, wild fiery hair a-swirl, veils and gossamer shawls. The weave suggested that women were dancing rather than clearly picturing women as such. In between the effervescent figures, sparkling stars picked out constellations. There was the Archer, there was the Cow – and the Cuckoo, and the Harp.

The big round sofa had been a gift to Lucky a century previously from a suitor name of Valentin who was intent on winning a Sariola daughter and longlife. The hundreds of faded hearts – some as large as a head, others as small as a thumbnail – were all pastel in hue by now: rose and pink and coral.

In the adjoining division of the sofa, separated from June by an upholstered arm of hearts, sat Jack in his long-wearing coppery livery. He might have been a proud, if diffident, junior lieutenant in some regiment newly raised by Lucky – except that his uniform was that of the servants of the alien Brazen Isi serpents.

Jack was telling Hilda (and thus June too, of course) about the snakes' nest he had been reared in; about the frequent twangs and chimes, the fruity air, the speed with which Juttie kids, in their elastic suits, grew to maturity. Jack harped on about how swiftly Juttie brats grew ...

On a little ivorywood table stood a plate bearing scraps of apple skin, three used forks, and one remaining intact baked apple. This, and its now consumed companions, had been cored and filled with syrup sprinkled with cinnamon then dressed with cloves before cooking. Useful for warding off epidemics, so Hilda believed – not that many apples had ever arrived in the far south of Saari where the mocky-men had their homes and herded their goats. Nor cinnamon nor cloves. Those were the produce of the island of Pootara much further south across the many-islanded sea, grown by the black rationalists who knew little of mana. Here in Pohjola Palace one could just ask for such things.

A lovely melting treat for herself and June and Jack; though serving a prophylactic purpose as well. The lingering spicy aroma masked a certain acrid hint to June's yeasty perspiration.

The chaperon's face bent (inevitably) towards the fastboy as he reminisced. She squeezed June's hand softly as a lover might have done, as proxy for Jack who shouldn't touch her ... quite yet. All the embroidered pastel hearts suggested to Hilda not merely amorousness, which must have been the Queen's idea in encouraging Jack and June to make use of this particular chamber – with duenna in tow – but also medical conditions (which may have been Lucky's notion too). Heartbeats, blood pumping, ruddy health – and morbidity. Diseases of the blood. Purpura, when a scratch could bleed a person to death. White-blood. Vein-pain.

'Will you have the last apple?' Jack offered Hilda gallantly. His question was really addressed to June; so Hilda kept quiet.

The girl eyed the delicacy. Four breasts and chubby cheeks needed feeding, didn't they? Hilda, who was wise in many respects and possessed a sense of etiquette, had instilled a modicum of this into the girl – not that the fastboy himself was particularly polished in his manners.

'*You* have it, Jack. You're usually *ravenous.*' Especially after exerting himself . . . It was over a week now since Jack (and Juke) had returned in triumph with the war-machine.

'But I don't need another apple,' Jack protested.

If he devoured the syrup-soaked fruit, would his body promptly burn this fuel and become another day older?

Would sexual congress with him be just as precipitate? Would he come very quickly indeed like some randy billygoat? So swiftly that he actually escaped becoming diseased?

The fruit remained untouched. June's eyes were limpid. They were still pools, waiting to reflect a lover and to be filled with him – just as her body waited, in vain, to be filled.

'Tell me again how you tamed the hervy!' June was alluding to the battle-wagon. What did her sudden glance of challenge signify? An allurement, to risk his health? A disregard of his interests for the sake of her own satisfactions?

'The hervy, Jack. It's something to tame a hervy. Maybe you can tame anything—' Even including her curse?

'When I was very young I tamed a real wild hervy.' Jack's words fairly spilled out. 'Mum and me and Juke were on the way to a town with rapids. We were hurrying away from Lord Osmo's keep because he'd bespoken Mum to flee even though she was tired and desperate. I hated Osmo! Well, and now he's dead, thanks to Juke. A hervy appeared on the path by a rushing river. A living breathing hervy. Mum needed a ride. I tamed that beast, so we rode it. At the town the people chopped our hervy's head off and hung its heart on its horns for cuckoos to feed on. The mana-priest asked us to dinner.' (Breathlessly.) 'I climbed up on his cuckoo perch to get some more meat. Leg of lamb, it was.'

'Be careful, child,' croaked Hilda.

June giggled as Jack raced onward. 'The perch snapped and I fell on the shore. The priest was furious. Yet his people had hacked my hervy's head off, hadn't they? On the way to that town, riding my hervy, we met a gang of woodmen. One of them called us *the holy family*. Daddy, Lady, and Holy Echo, that's what. Juke wasn't my Daddy. I had to tell the woodmen a story before they would let us pass by—'

'Careful,' repeated Hilda.

'I told them what Mum told me before I was born, how Queen-Louhi-wanted-a-magic-mill-to-make-all-sorts-of-things, how-Vai-could-have-her-daughter-if-he-could-make-the-mill.' Breathlessly Jack rushed on. His story doubled back into a tale from the *Book of the Land of Heroes*, a tale such as Lucky had told to the Ukko in exchange for transport to this world of Kaleva. A tale such as Jatta had told to her demon child while he was growing in her womb. A captivating tale, a compelling tale. One which could enthral and impel a person to act it out in some way or other. Jack hadn't even touched on the matter of the battle-hervy yet.

''Ware,' said Hilda, 'this is a trap-story, yours.'

Jack lurched onwards. Now each sentence was a single word. 'Queen-Louhi-said-the-next-hero-had-to-catch-a-terrible-wild-hervy.' Jack gulped. 'He-HAD-to-BRIDLE-the-FIRESTEED. He-SUCCEEDED. He'd-HAVE-to-SHOOT-the-SWAN-of-DEATH.' The tale was thumping along, though it wasn't Jack's tale at all any more.

'A trap-story!' Hilda cried. Her goat-hide boot kicked out. The ivorywood table flew over. Tumbling, the plate cracked into three. That final apple rolled squashily across the waxed boards for a short distance. Snow whirled briefly in the air, a flurry of white flakes quite like petals of icing sugar. Jack's neat jaw hung open.

June asked excitedly: 'What's a trap-story?'

'Next it would be a nest within a nest!' exclaimed the wise-woman. The turbulent flakes disconcerted her.

Instead of snow or sugar, small white feathers gyrated down to the floor. The fastboy bounded from the sofa. June gaped at Jack as, down on his knees, he seized the cooked fruit and crammed it into his mouth; which put a stopper to his story.

'*Are we squabbling about a baked apple?*'

The Queen had slipped quietly into the courtship chamber, into

42

the salon of pastel hearts where veiled aurora maidens danced effervescently. As usual since her husband's death Lucky was dressed in crinkled black crêpe de chine over glossy black satin. The black lace veil hid her expression. She seemed at once abstracted from reality, an inky silhouette figure, yet her presence was so solid and dense. Securing the veil on the unkempt crown of her head: a chaplet of amber beads from the shores of the Great Fjord. This was her first concession to adornment since the funeral.

'Jack was getting himself tangled in a trap-story,' explained the wisewoman. 'Or even in a story-trap.'

'Was he indeed?' How whimsically ebullient Lucky sounded at the prospect of her grandson ensnared.

('What's a trap-story?') whispered June.

('Later.')

('No, *now!*') That pout of June's . . . *Now, or I shan't heed you any longer.*

Sticky-lipped, Jack grinned at his grandmother. June's moods were provocative to him. Jack could be so transparent, so gauche. What else might one expect from someone who was only a year and a bit old, or fourteen years or whatever? The feathers on the floorboards had all but disappeared, shrivelled to mere threads.

Said Hilda, 'A trap-story snares you into running on and on compulsively. Soon you'll be trying to act out the tale yourself as if you're the hero of it, or the heroine. A story-trap, on the other hand – that's what I meant by a nest within a nest – is when part of a story causes a new story to start within itself. Then that story opens up another story till you can never find your way back to the beginning. In my time I've treated a patient or two who fell into that kind of sway.'

'Oh *I'll* find my way back to the beginning—' Lucky was staring towards the window, beyond which the dill and parsley grew. She might have been addressing her faint reflection in the glass. 'I'll find the way even without my Prince; and maybe more easily without him. You see, now there'll be no more daughters in the line, no more seed springing within me; I don't suppose. I escape from the trap of generation, generations . . .'

Seed, and generation . . . A flush suffused June's already rosy cheeks. Jack found an itch on his arm which needed scratching imperatively. He ducked back to his seat next to June though separated from her by the padded arm of the sofa.

43

Hilda thought she understood the Queen's drift. Granny in the gallery had supplied the key: Queen Lucky was seeking for a lost soul, namely her very own, which the Ukko had kept when it made Lucky immortal, and which it had stored within its supposed offspring.

The union of her grandson and June – supposing that this could take place without Jack becoming seriously, fatally, ill – would cause those maids of horror to be born. Those lasses of menace, whom Hilda had spied in the mana-mirror. Four little daughters who could spread sickness and death.

Did Lucky have any inkling that this would be the result of Jack's and June's mutual desire? Had she already stared into a mana-mirror and beheld this? Had she tossed liquid tin into a bowl of water and seen such shapes congeal?

Murmuring to herself, the widowed Queen roamed the room, and came to rest on the vacant lobe of the heart sofa, with her back to its other occupants. They might no longer have existed for her: these, her human dolls. Mere dayflies, born at dawn and dead at eve. Even Hilda, with her few scores of years, was a dayfly by comparison with Lucky, four centuries old. As for Jack, he might be the person most like a dayfly ever, fated to age and succumb to old age within four years, five, or six – unless June's touch put paid to him first. Perhaps that was an essential part of the shy attraction Jack felt for June. June was a death-bringing girl. Suitors would fall sick because of her. Yet a lad who lived so fast was already in a sense a *dying* boy. So the two qualities, both the fruit of mana-energy acting upon the flesh, might cancel one another out, and discharge themselves – resulting in the birth, instead, of those little menace lasses, Minx and Jinx and Minxie and Jinxie . . .

Lucky's daughters conferred longlife on their first lover, their husband. If the offspring of Lucky's grandson and June bestowed mortality – *rapid* mortality – upon those whom they touched with deadly intention, the line of Lucky would be tied in a knot, terminated. Or at least one string of that line would be tied; and maybe one was enough. Lucky would be liberated. Free to find herself. Was this in the Queen's mind?

Minx and Minxie, Jinx and Jinxie: those were merely names which Hilda had imagined. The children did not exist as yet, to bring death to people. Surely there could be a way for Jack and June to become lovers – curing June, and stabilizing Jack – without any virulent children actually being conceived . . .

44

'Pull an egg into a knot,' mumbled the wisewoman, 'so that the knot doesn't show ...' That was one of the tasks which a maiden had set for the old hero Vai who wanted to wed her. *Pull an egg into a knot*. Prevent the egg from hatching. Prevent the egg from fertilizing. A contraceptive charm.

Now was surely high time for such a charm.

'Children,' said Hilda to June, then to Jack, 'let's play a knot game, shall we? A game with string. With cord. If you can't quite touch each other yet,' and she squeezed June's hand reassuringly, 'at least you can do so with cord. Maybe after you've used cord, touching with fingers will become easier and safer, hmm?'

Let them believe that she was assisting their courtship. Why, indeed she was! Yet at the same time, let a knot be tied in an egg. Without the knot showing, of course.

'I'll run and fetch some cord.' Whilst licking his sticky palm and rubbing it on his liveried thigh, Jack darted for the door. Ach, you oughtn't to dash at the same time as you were rubbing your leg. Jack seemed to be gimping in a mockery of Hilda's affliction. 'With your permission, Grandmother,' the fastboy called back; and he was gone.

Lucky spoke distractedly: 'The ropes of love ... they bind a cock and a hen in wedlock. Tie your bride to the bedstead then whip her lightly with switches cut from a curver tree. Whip her buttocks and tickle her loins. Tie your fresh-plucked goose to the bed. Speak the word of unlocking of her girdle. Don't you forget the word of unlocking! You can't forget, can you? Knots are for memory. Tie your hen upon the mattress and utter the word and tickle her buttocks—'

What *recipe* was this? What instructions were these, which Lucky must have uttered many times before? Uttered in what circumstances? Why, as advice to bridegrooms! To grooms who were about to wed one of her many daughters and win longlife from their virgin bride.

'Though June wears no girdle except for the girdle of disease—'

All Sariola daughters must have been compelled to wear chastity girdles, which a secret word would unlock ...

As Hilda grappled with this revelation, she understood that Lucky perceived a similarity between the mocky-girl June and her own princess daughters – whom Lucky could never have treated with too much tenderness except when sentimentality overtook her. With regard to the forbidding girdle, June was akin to a daughter.

45

Advice to eager bridegrooms? No, not advice – but orders from their mother-in-law.

The Queen roused herself. 'Wisewoman—' Hilda craned her neck further so as to gaze backwards. Lucky had swung around, hoisting a crêpe-and-satin-clad leg and black pointy-toed boot on to the upholstery of hearts. The Queen stared at Hilda over the padded divide.

'Jack was weaned so quickly, wasn't he? A baby one moment; and then no longer a baby. Maybe that's why he's attracted by an abundance of breasts. A bounty of bosom.'

June sniggered, and Hilda squeezed her hand sharply.

'I'm sure there's more to this than meets the eye,' the wisewoman said warily.

'Will this string game of yours protect Jack, Goody Hilda?'

'If he needs protecting, Your Majesty.'

'Do you feel *in your waters* that he mightn't?'

Cautiously: 'That's as maybe.' (*I knows what I knows*. She mustn't echo Granny.)

'And maybe my mana-priest and my shaman could join in your next string game . . .' To reinforce protection for Jack; to bind him more closely to June, until Jack netted June, and June netted Jack.

Hilda neither asked why, nor disagreed. Behind her veil the Queen chuckled. She and the wisewoman were by way of becoming conspirators in the matter of the fastboy and the mocky-girl.

Jack returned eagerly with loops and loops of worming white cord, which he threw upon the rug by the window. He sat down there expectantly. Prompted by Hilda, June abandoned the sofa of hearts.

The two young people faced each other cross-legged upon the rug. They eyed one another, smiling bashfully. Laboriously Hilda settled by June. Bowed over and neck crooked, she no longer held the girl's hand.

The Queen joined in, squatting down in her mourning garb as if grief had distracted her so much that now she would romp upon a floor. Yes, Lucky completed the circle.

Heeding Hilda's instructions, June began paying out cord into Jack's hands without actually touching him, and onward into Lucky's hands until each of the three participants commanded many loose metres of cord. June held out a length. Jack looped doubled cord over. Lucky thrust folded cord through . . . Soon the threesome were connected by an ever more elaborate open knot or network.

Loop over, loop through, all the while pulling more cord into play. When the two ends of the cord were finally reached, those who held the ends would haul them tight. What knotty shape, or shapes, would quiver in mid-air between them?

Over, under, through . . .

('Tie a knot in an egg,') whispered Hilda. ('Tie the egg into a knot.')

'What are you mumbling?' demanded Lucky.

'Knit-knot, knitty-knotty,' Hilda said aloud. And under her breath, ('Tie the egg into a knot so the knot doesn't show.')

Whether or not Lucky heard that whisper, she began to chant softly, 'Tie the ropes of love twice! But first say the word of unlocking. Unblocking, uncorking, unknotting—'

('Tie the egg—')

'Untie, unlace, unbind—' Aye: a girl from her girdle. For June wore an intangible corset of disease.

('Knot the egg—') June shouldn't conceive those bothersome babes.

'Unknot—'

Not that Jack and June were likely to dash off together to the fastboy's bedchamber immediately that the game of string was over! This game was only a prelude. But even so!

Over and under and through. Not much spare cord remained. The two youngsters and the veiled Queen were shuffling closer together.

('Tie—')

'Untie and unite. Unite and untie—' purred Lucky. At last she let go of her stretch of cord. The youngsters' hands were almost touching. Over and through again – and the ends of the cords were in Jack's fists, and in June's.

'Now *pull*!'

Shuffling back from one another, Jack and June hauled cord through their hands, tightening the labyrinthine knot . . .

'And heave!' Lucky was a mistress of this game.

Between Jack and June four distorted knotty figures cavorted. A quartet of dollies danced. Side by side, joined to one another: four adjacent knot figures.

Tie a knot in a fertile egg: to split the egg, and split it again . . . Hilda stared crookedly at the outcome of her whispered charm and of the Queen's chant.

47

Jack grinned at June. The mana-kid tugged the thick string and she tugged too. To and fro. How the cord dollies jigged.

3 · HEARTBELLS

What exactly did Jack feel with regard to June? Adolescent passion? Curiosity? *Love?*

This was a knotty question. The fastboy's mother and Anni had tussled with various answers once they finally realized the drift of events.

Jatta's chamber overlooked, from a stubby tower, that same cloistered courtyard where the dill and parsley grew and the bronze leaperfish spouted. Soft woolly cumulus clouds drifted above, like foamy billows on an upside-down blue sea. She once used to imagine that a summer storm might present itself thus in the balmy climate around Pootara island away in the south. Shaggy white horses prancing upon the hot azure, performing capers.

Warm here, too. Soon be noon. Cumulus had formed too late in the morning to be a harbinger of rain. The afternoon would be fine; perhaps with a cooling breeze.

Jatta's – and Anni's – cream-plastered walls were painted with curlicues of flower chains. Pink heartbells twined with apricot bellflowers and with those violet starflowers which sister Eva – now wedded to engineer Elmer – wore as petite teasing tattoos upon her cheek and neck and wrist.

Jatta had shared this chamber with Anni ever since Jack freed Anni and himself from the Brazen Isi nest three months previously, in March. Two smaller beds, carved with leafy trefoils, had replaced a larger one in the modestly sized apartment. A black-varnished wardrobe loomed. In front of the only window stood a triple-mirrored bureau dressing table and two balloon-back chairs, frequently occupied by Jatta and Anni.

Maybe the chamber was somewhat congested. Yet Anni and Jatta had both known pressure, as well as isolation. Anni had been isolated from human company in the Isi nest until Jack's arrival, prior to which she was subject to compelling erotic pressure from that sham man, Jarl Pakken. Jarl had ravished Jatta irresistibly; then she had known solitude during a whole winter spent in a hut, pregnant with Jack.

If Anni and Jatta crowded one another now, it was a welcome crowding; an intimacy more gratifying than Jatta had experienced with her departed sisters Eva or Minnow. The one, suave; the other, intrusive. Both full of themselves. Ester, Minnow's immediate junior, at fourteen years of age was hardly Jatta's peer.

Whereas Anni . . . !

When Jatta first set eyes on the erstwhile peasant girl in alien harness at Speakers' Valley, Anni had seemed to be a distorted reflection of her own self: with the pear-shaped face, the jet-black hair, and large dusky eyes. Jatta's dark eyes were narrower, without much fold to the lids at all. Anni's tresses had been greasy and unkempt; now they were glossy. Jatta's hair had been hacked short; she still wore it thus, though less spikily, less like a broom-head. Of late, Anni had adopted Jatta's own preferred clothing. Her room-mate had exchanged a blue woollen gown for a suède tunic of lavender hue (Jatta's was purple) sewn with strips of green and orange and crimson felt. A similar frilled chemise; similar fawn calfskin trousers.

The two women had grown closer – the ex-peasant and the ex-princess converging. (Being unwedded, presumably Jatta still *was* a princess despite her seduction and her year of exile and the demon child to whom she had given birth.) Anni could never go back to her family. Her life was in the northland now, with Jatta. Jatta had found a sister unlike any other Sariola sister, affiliated to her by suffering, by a shared seducer, and by their past care for Jack – who was now causing renewed concern.

The two women sat alongside one another in front of their reflections rather than looking directly at either's face. Jatta eyed Anni's image in the central mirror of the triptych, and Anni watched Jatta's. Essentially the same face was there for each, in the silvered glass, save for the style of hair, more fullness to Anni's eyes, and her lighter skin. Likely there was some Sariola blood in Anni from a century back or longer – wild oats sown by a scion of some family mothered by a bygone princess, fathered by a longlife. During Jatta's wandertime her features had become sunbrowned. She still retained her tan. The peasant girl had paled during some years of captivity in the Isi nest. Yet oh, they were similar.

Anni's left hand rested on her calfskin-clad knee. Jatta's right hand rested upon her room-mate's. On the dressing table were a comb of horn, a silver-backed brush, a cut-glass bowl of little gingerbread men (or were those gingerbread women?), tiny bottles of fragrances, a few brass bangles.

'Does he feel love?' Jatta asked. 'Should his two mothers ask him about his feelings?'

'Oh I'm not,' demurred Anni, 'not his true mum.'

'You shared his care. Now we share: a brush and comb and a looking glass. Does he feel love for you and me?'

'Do *we*?' mumbled Anni.

Jatta squeezed Anni's hand softly. 'Having you with me is . . . a delight, don't you think?' She spoke as though each person were an aspect of the other.

Anni shivered. 'I don't *think* about it, Jatta — it ain't to be thought about.'

'Because it's wayward?' Jatta chuckled. 'I've always been that.'

'Because it ain't a thinking thing at all. It ain't something we decide about.'

'Is this a sway that we're coming under, you and me?'

'If so, then it's a tender sway—'

'We were both victims of Jarl's sway, weren't we?'

Questions echoed. This exchange might well continue for an hour as a prolonged exploration of each other, a communion. Increasingly it was this way between them. Maybe they needed to sit thus side by side, not directly watching one another, so as to preserve a sense of identity. But identity also meant oneness. Anni's countenance in the mirror smiled; and hers was Jatta's full-cheeked smile.

'My mother still has the skin-suit,' remarked Jatta.

That body-glove made of sloughed serpent skin, bespoken by an Isi mage, had been used by Jarl to control Anni during his erotic manipulations of her . . .

A flutter of apprehension: 'Oh we don't need that, do we?'

'No, no, of course not. *We* don't. Don't be such a silly. I'm wondering whether my mother might take it into her head that June could use the skin as a way of controlling her bestowing of diseases. It's the sort of trick my mother would think of. Affection, without infection, do you see?'

'Affection?' queried Anni. 'Or *love*?'

That was the question which rebounded between Jatta and Anni, as their mutual glances reflected in the glass. If they had

50

not been so concerned to solve this conundrum in their own regard, they might have been more inclined to intervene and offer parental counsel to the fastboy.

Did Jack really love Jatta – or Anni – sufficiently to heed advice? The sheer speed of Jack's seeming maturity deeply disconcerted his mother.

'I might seem to be condemning him to childishness, mightn't I? I might seem to be saying that he's a lad who shouldn't ever grow up. That would be true! Though what if love makes him sick – sick to death?'

'He ought to know love, do you mean? With June? Even though she's—'

'A mutie? Isn't Jack just as unusual?'

'Are you hinting that you ought – that *we* ought to make a suggestion about June using the skin-suit? We'd be just like Jarl and the Jutties.'

'Even if it's for Jack's protection?' Jatta frowned. 'I know, I know! Why should the suit safeguard him? I was about to say – as if I believed it! – that I won't let my mother manipulate him and put his health at risk—'

'He volunteered to serve Lucky, didn't he?'

'I don't *know* my own son. Not in the way that I know you, dear Anni. Do we know what to do? Do we?'

Questions only reflected questions.

Two chairs, two beds, and a triple mirror.

'Is it love?' asked Jatta.

About whom was the question asked?

'Remember the song? One of Lammas's songs.' Anni began to sing in a wavering voice:

> 'We're so different, yet the same
> 'At heart: a mocky-girl, and prince.
> 'Why ever should I be to blame
> 'For yielding to your hints?'

Theirs was a kind of happy mesmerism. The mirror, the two faces, the talk. The continuing revelation of Jatta's ecstatic bemusement by Jarl. The disclosure of Anni's enforced submission to that seducer which had reverberated in her very nerves, in the most sensitive nubs of Anni, paradoxically awakening sensitivities which up until then had been quite callow; awakening those maddeningly, only for those to be played upon, and resisted, often unavailingly.

Now that Anni was liberated in company with the target of Jarl's usage, how should the two women best raise solace to a pitch of delight, as they surely deserved? How best recapture and recuperate Jatta's lost rapture along with Anni's intimate knowledge of this rapture – which no one else in the world could surely understand, except for the two of them? Thus joyfully, too, redeem Anni's time of slavery . . .

To regain, freely together, the sensations of bliss without the hoaxery and pressure, in the blessed absence of that false man who had imposed himself on them, and of any man whatever . . .

No one else should intrude ever again between the image and its reflection, between the like and the likeness.

Even Jatta's fastboy – Anni's fastboy, too! – was a poignant link yet also, in a way, a distraction.

Jatta imagined herself trying to shout sense into Lucky as she had done in the immediate aftermath of Bertel's murder; railing at her mother. True enough, Jatta had formerly thwarted her mother in the matter of welcoming suitors for her hand, her flesh, and longlife. Lucky had paid Jatta back. Then of course there had been an equivocal reunion between mother and daughter. Jatta could stand up to Lucky to the extent that this made much difference. At least she wasn't a *silly* daughter! In this business of Jack's crush on bounteous-breasted June, Jatta *could* be strong. To her son's detriment, or to save him, which?

To try to intervene seemed curiously irrelevant compared to her deepening relationship with Anni, to the duet of self-discovery. Jack the child had been a token of Jarl, a bedevilling souvenir. On Jack's return to the palace the sway which Jarl had cast over Jatta had finally vanished – in the presence of her grown-up boy, her dusky amber-eyed son with such mana in him. Jatta was cleansed. She could begin to reconstruct herself; though not, as she discovered by and by, with her son's assistance, even if Jack had come to Pohjola Palace to find his mother, and so confirm his own identity.

Jatta sang softly in reply:

> 'A princess and a mocky-man;
> 'He came to her palace door.
> 'Her brother had ravished his sister
> 'Whom he had claimed to adore . . .'

In the song the pregnant mocky-girl had hanged herself from a curver tree, an odd choice in the circumstances since a curver bough might bend considerably under her weight.

'Why don't we invent our own words for the song?' suggested Jatta. 'About a princess who falls from grace and a peasant girl who lives in a palace? How they sit in a garden, perfectly balanced upon a see-saw, unless one or other of them makes a sudden motion – or leaps off in alarm! One says "love?" And the other says "move?" Slowly they inch together.'

Perhaps there was a subtle, sly sway at work, a residue of Jarl's original enchantment which Jack's return had seemed conclusively to oust; a remnant now growing anew though in a different direction, involving Jatta compellingly with Anni, whom Jarl had also swayed so dominatingly. Thus the sway was shared.

With her left hand, Jatta reached to open her drawer in the dressing table. From under a kerchief she removed an egg. Keeping her gaze on the mirror, she passed the egg to her companion, who took the offering in her right hand. Still Jatta's other hand rested upon Anni's.

'It's *heavy*—' Not the pressure of the hand, oh no. The egg.

'Too heavy, dear? It's full of sweet chocolate. A mignon egg; a darling egg. Shall we crack it, and both of us lick it and bite it at once?' Until their lips might meet.

Single-handedly Anni rotated the egg till she spied the plug where molten sweetness had been poured into the snowy white receptacle. She tightened her grip. Cracks crazed the shell yet no fragments fell off. Should she peel the hard wrapping from the chocolate with her teeth?

'We *do* have teeth,' said Jatta. 'If we're obliged to we can bite and scratch and fight.'

'To rescue Jack from June . . .'

'From my mother, really.'

Yet Jack had volunteered to play the Queen's games. This predicament regarding the mutant girl still seemed lacking in urgency, a distraction compared with what was transpiring between Jatta and her soulmate.

Once, the pressure of Jarl Pakken had almost swamped Anni's identity. And once too, beside a secluded little lough near Lokka village that same force had immersed and glutted Jatta until Jarl seemed indispensable, as crucial as an organ of her own body. As vital to her.

Now Jatta and Anni were beginning – so it seemed – to dissolve in personality, into one another. This dulcet melting affirmed each of them in the kernel of her being. Each had been submerged: Jatta by Jarl, and Jatta's *other* self, Anni, also by Jarl. Thus these two women came together to make one whole shared soul, entire: one *twin* person, a duo.

This was, Jatta realized, the second miracle in her life. First there had been her miracle child. (Was he now in peril? His jeopardy seemed remote. Had Jarl also been a miracle? Say rather: a prodigy, who had left a compelling afterglow.) The second miracle was the miracle of Anni. Miracles had a way of eclipsing other events in their vicinity . . .

Had Jatta suspected, when first she invited Anni to share her room, that this convergence would occur? No. Her invitation had been partly prompted by penitence for abandoning Anni in Speakers' Valley, clad in her snakeskin body-stocking, in the thrall of zombie Jarl. Partly it had been payment for Jack's subsequent upbringing. And also, so as to assert herself in her mother's presence, in the euphoria of her son's return. Anni had been anxious that Jatta might be jealous of her. Oh but now they were both jealous, each of them, of one another!

Just three months previously in the Dome of Favours, Jatta had announced – presciently – that she and Anni were, or should be or would be, *closer than sisters* . . . Well, this had been no brash claim. Lucky's harvest of rival daughters did not generally feel too deeply endeared to one another, whatever affectionate pretences they might indulge in.

Anni made a claw of her middle finger to prise some cracked shell loose, exposing chocolate.

Jatta wrinkled her nose. For what assailed her nostrils fleetingly was an odour of baked bread and weed from sea pools. Of yeast and foreshore – a memory of her mother's odour, when Lucky Paula Sariola had burst into a young girl's bedroom one day high up a different tower overlooking the town and the fjord and had crushed close to the girl, squeezing her tightly, overwhelming, tormenting her with questions, presenting a nougat mignon egg to her as a reward or a tease, till the girl exclaimed to appease her, '*I shan't ever get married.*'

Fluffy clouds coasted by as quickly as a pony could gallop, though seeming to be more sedate.

'Let's keep the mignon for dessert,' proposed Jatta. 'We'll collect a couple of pasties from the kitchens, and pots of roe and a bottle. We'll ride out for a picnic in the woods, shall we? I've remembered a lovely place.'

A perfect spot, where a secluded little lake – a modest pool, really – nestled among henna-scaled larix trees and viridian-needled veras and hoary sylvesters, and the occasional hardy horzma dripping fronds . . . About ten keys north-west of Sario-linna town. It was several years since Jatta had been there. She hadn't revisited the spot. Yet now the scene came vividly into her mind's eye. Even as she visualized the place, the image diverged and altered somewhat. The pool *did* bear quite a resemblance in miniature to that lough in the woodland beyond Lokka, didn't it; to that dell where Jarl had sung for her and sported with her?

Might somebody recently have built a chalet by the pond? Perhaps not. Her guard at the time had muttered that the wee navel of water seemed like a nakki-pool. A water-sprite probably haunted it.

'Ideal place for a picnic on a day like this, Anni. We'll ride out there inside, oh, half an hour.'

Providing that Jatta could find that pond again, not far from where a certain forest track bent around a pile of pink granite boulders. The route was coming clearer to her.

'Truth to tell, I don't *like* ponies too much,' admitted Anni.

'A farm girl not liking ponies?'

'I'm not much use at riding them.'

'Tell you what. We'll borrow a Percheron. How about that? We'll both ride on its back together. I've seen a double saddle hanging in the stables. No risk of falling off a Perch'. Might take us a while longer to amble there, that's all.'

Anni's eyes twinkled. 'We could hardly ask our fastboy to fly us there in the sky-boat he stole, could we now?'

'Apart from there being nowhere suitable for us to land . . .'

Apart from Jack being otherwise engaged. Not to mention the fact that any fellow-me-lad whatever was surplus to requirement on this particular outing.

Complicity knitted Jatta to Anni. 'We don't need a guard,' Jatta murmured. Hardly any need to say so. No soldiers nor any other men. Besides which, this princess had given her gift away; Jarl had taken it. 'We'll have knives with us.'

Anni turned and touched Jatta's cheek where the faintest of scars still showed across the skin, souvenir of a clumsy and unsuccessful assault while en route to Maananfors with her child.

Jatta's friend beamed. 'Don't forget spoons for the roe!'

Indeed Jatta's soul had grown firmly into Anni's, like a graft. Anni's, into Jatta's. What fruit might burgeon from this mutual graft? Only flowers, lovely blossoms. Heartbells.

Juke Nurmi was chin-wagging in the corridor with the young proclaimer, Nils Carlson.

Nils was fresh-faced with unruly flaxen hair and eyes of a watery blue. Juke overtopped him by a hand's breadth and possessed the edge in muscle too. But Nils was a determined young man. He'd had tattoos of bespeaker's lips pricked upon his own lips in mauve dye to reinforce his words. His livid mouth looked bruised by a blow. Juke's own twin tattoos, of red lips around his nipples, were flamboyant – as Jatta knew – yet those were hidden by his clothing. Nils had chosen a more conspicuous mark of his mana-talent. The tattooing must have hurt. It professed a defiance of pain. Would a lass wish to kiss such lips? No doubt if Nils Carlson *said* she should!

'*I've* never had a partner,' Nils was saying – and Jatta drew Anni into a dark archway close by. Juke's back was turned; he hadn't noticed the two women approach. The young proclaimer was preoccupied. 'So what's it like having one?' he quizzed Juke. He sounded truculent, though a mite awed. Was he asking Juke what he seemed to be asking? Was the mauve-lipped young man confessing to virginity? Jatta pressed close against Anni, hand in hand, eavesdropping.

Was Nils intent on provoking Juke? On sparking a feud the like of Juke's with dead Lord Osmo? The jealousy of one novice proclaimer for a rather more powerful one! Jatta had no particular desire to waste time, yet she lingered. Anyway, the quickest route to the stables was past that pair of proclaimers.

Hadn't Tattoo-Lips heard, from cuckoo cackle or palace gossip, that Juke quite likely had never known a woman sexually? Juke had been too infatuated with his unfortunate sister. Juke said something which Jatta failed to make out – speaking softly, with menace? Squeezing Anni's hand cautioningly, Jatta squinted from shadow.

Noonlight spilled through long squat windows of thick glass high up. Sconces held dead candles. The corridor was floored with orange and green majolica tiles, faded and worn by the tread of a million boots and shoes coming and going down the years. Near the two men hung a gilded picture frame intricately carved with corpses of birds interwoven bill to tail, beak to tail: harnies and soarfowl and gyrebirds, and more. At first glance the frieze appeared to be a carving of copious foliage rather than masses of plumage, a hunter's delirium.

The varnished painting itself depicted seven raven-haired girls of assorted ages all dressed in tunics gaudy with felt and calfskin trousers. Panicked and amazed, the girls had variously taken, and still were frantically taking, refuge on top of a huge solitary boulder set in a tree-girt glade. Shaggy horned beasts of indeterminate species rushed towards that crag amidst the herbage, heads lowered. These were shadow creatures, really; nightmares, nightbulls. Three of the smaller sisters were only halfway up the rock, their scramble unassisted by the others. The stony platform was about wide enough for seven sisters crowding together. If one of those maddened beasts reared up and planted its forelegs against the flank of the boulder, its jabbing horns might just reach a girl's boots. The sisters would be forced to shuffle their positions. One of the girls might fall off; or be pushed.

Juke leaned a palm against the plastered wall, boxing the young proclaimer in. Nils' square chin jutted pugnaciously. A bruiser with words. Nils wagged his chin, as if a fly had settled on it. His washed-out gaze challenged Juke. Some scurf speckled the shoulders of his brown leather jerkin. Pinned to a lapel, the clawfoot of some bird. Dangling from each large ear lobe, a little silver sickle such as spanned the southern sky. So here was a fellow in the ascendancy – who had heeded the Queen's call for proclaimers in the wake of Lord Osmo's kidnap of Minnow. The Queen's revenge was pre-empted, though. Juke had destroyed Lord Osmo, not with words but with an Isi missile.

Juke was wearing bottle-green breeches and an embroidered linen shirt; no sign of a knife at his belt.

'—he isn't exactly a *partner*.'

'A good proclaimer could have tamed the steel hervy all on his own?'

They were talking about her miracle boy. About the exploit in which Nils had *not* been involved. The young proclaimer's tone hinted that Juke had needed help.

'I did sink up to my nose in muck once,' Juke conceded crossly, 'as most people know, especially including the Queen. But I almost took van Maanen – and he took Tycho Cammon, don't forget.' Juke sounded as though he was trying to be reasonable. Oh but he *could* seem reasonable.

57

'What's your main goal, if you don't mind my asking?' Nils enquired in that same tone of abrasive respect. 'Now that Lord Osmo's out of the way?' He chuckled. 'Distinguished, then extinguished, eh? Do we punish Minkie Kennan? Will you go to another gala? What does Queen Lucky want?'

'Right now she wants us in the Courtship Chamber to play a cord game.'

Jatta listened intently; as did Anni.

'Jack and the busty girl, hmm? *Busty-lusty*.'

Juke sniffed disapprovingly. 'I'll remind you that June's from my own part of the world.'

'One doesn't need to be priggish . . .'

But Juke *could* be priggish in the matter of females from the mocky-villages. He could be a seething prude – who had loved his sister too devotedly, and then betrayed her and himself. Something in Juke's expression must have alarmed Nils, for he promptly apologized.

'Ach, I spit in my mouth, Juke. Do you think this curious courtship is a way whereby the Queen hopes to, well . . . ?'

'Well what?'

'So to speak, renew her own circumstances vicariously by proxy.'

'*Circumstances?*'

'Husband being dead; no more princesses ever again. Unless . . .'

'Unless some enchantment stirs close to her? Damned if *I'd* be the Queen's gallant!' Had Juke contemplated such a notion? 'Her still in mourning . . .' Juke himself ought to be in furtive, agonized mourning, in some dark chamber of his heart – for his sister.

'Queen's interested enough in new weapons, without any Osmo to use them against, either.'

'Maybe they distract her from brooding. Wherever Minkie Kennan fled to on that jump-bike, he's no more than a squib of a fellow – with a talent for ingratiating himself. I've sprinkled salt on his tail in the past. Personally I think the Queen's planning to take on the Brazen Isi – for arranging the ravishing of Jatta. Teach the Isi a lesson.'

'Learn one too, maybe? Do you know what she was hoping to find out from that Isi mage she kept in her dungeon till Kennan sprung it free?'

Was Nils trying to find out how cosy Juke was with the Queen these days? Whether he might indeed harbour some ambition in that risky direction? When Juke had come north, desolate but avenged, he was putting his fate in Lucky's hands. Lucky had reprieved him. Juke still remained bony-guilty of treachery to his sister. He resented lords and princesses, didn't he? Could he contemplate serving his Queen in the loving way? As a Bertel substitute? Should Lucky's desires flare up . . .

Very likely, guilty virgin that he was, he'd fail to satisfy her. Nobody could bespeak Lucky. No one could fool her in that fashion. Juke had tried to, once, when he and Jatta were aboard the royal sky-boat escaping from Speakers' Valley. Lucky had cottoned on in a trice.

'Presumably she was trying to discover how to operate the everything machine,' said Juke.

'To produce weapons? Then to attack the Isi with them?'

This seemed to be a spuriously circular reason. Juke surely knew what Lucky most desired, namely to find her own lost self, the real Paula Sariola who had remained in the Ukko while her dark echo had returned to the real world; or so she imagined! When Juke bespoke Jatta during their trek together to spill out her story from childhood onwards – ravishing her memory though never her body – Jatta had told Juke this, hadn't she? Perhaps Juke had dismissed that part of her tale as childish fantasy or misunderstanding. Maybe he failed to connect the Queen's crazy hope with the everything machine. Surely the two *were* connected . . .

Juke yanked his hand from the wall, releasing Nils.

'We'd best not keep Her Majesty waiting.' And they headed off together.

But Juke swung round unexpectedly. Had he felt a prickle between his shoulder blades? Seeing Jatta haul Anni from the nook, he flinched and raised a hand in a doubtful greeting. Or was his gesture one of warding off? Then he was striding onward.

'Wait, Jatta, please!' A girl's voice, from back along the corridor. It was Jatta's turn to swing round.

Younger sister Ester was hurrying to catch up. Her of the wandering eye. She wore a slack pink satin gown, and a white lace shawl around otherwise bare shoulders. Soft, quiet moccasins on her feet. The girl's ebon hair was pinned up high with glittery combs to heighten her, exposing a long swoop of neck. The fourteen-year-old looked as if she had dressed up for a ball, or for her idea of a ball. Which clothes basket, whose wardrobe, had she ransacked in an attempt to ape maturity? Failing to find shoes to match . . . unless moccasined stealth was a greater priority.

'Isn't it exciting? Are you going to help Juke and Mother?' Ester's glance meandered wistfully past her sister in the direction of the departing men.

'You look . . .' *Ridiculous?* Like a junior Eva, with all those combs in her hair. But hardly as lushly endowed. Ester's shoulders were scrawny, with several pimples on them . . . 'dressed for a party.'

'Well, it's a *kind* of party, isn't it? A courtship party.'

'Don't be,' (yes, say it), 'absurd.'

'Pooh, a big sister *would* say that.' Undeterred, Ester gaped along towards the now vacant further reach of corridor. 'Are you going to give Jack and June your blessing?' The girl's squint wasn't unattractive. It lent her an appearance of quirky intensity. 'Juke'll bespeak them, won't he?' she added dotingly.

Juke's gesture – when he'd spied Jatta and Anni, and *beyond them* Ester – assumed a new significance. A wave of greeting yet discouragement. Not a strong rebuff. More like: leave me alone just now, Ester the Pester. Leave me alone for a year or two or three.

'He'll talk the evil touch away from her—'

The silly girl had a crush on Juke. At the moment Jatta was a channel whereby she could learn more about that moody proclaimer. Ester also wanted to reassure herself that Jatta had no abiding interest in the man who had formerly protected her.

Evidently Juke was aware of Ester's infatuation. A Sariola daughter gauchely setting her sights on him, fixing him with her intriguing squint. Not yet marriageable, nor fleshed out. A kid, nearly on the borderline of nubile. Wait two or three years more? Be rewarded with longlife, if he performed some great deeds for Lucky? *Was that it?* No funny business, mind you. No premature attempt to bespeak the girdle off the girl. Nor botched abductions; not after he had shot down Princess Minnow by accident. Avoid the rage of Lucky; let Ester mature yet a while.

If a mocky-maid from Juke's own home pastures – that harsh terrain of boulders and goats – could be wooed by the Queen's own bizarre grandson, why shouldn't a mutant fellow who looked perfectly normal, and who was a powerful proclaimer besides, entertain the idea of one day wedding a squinty princess? The previous year Juke had denied any such possibility. Hadn't he firmly told Jatta *no* – since he carried mutie seed within him? He might become a zombie.

The year before, any such possibility *had* been remote. Now Juke was here in Pohjola Palace, and no longer nearly so distant from such temptation!

Was that it?

'Juke's Demon Jack's friend, after all,' Ester pointed out. 'Otherwise they wouldn't have faced the war-wagon together – and tamed it! *You're* both off together to the Courtship Chamber.'

'Actually we're planning a picnic—'

'On our ownsome,' added Anni.

'If we can ever get near the kitchens, let alone the stables.'

Ester's glare was accusatory. 'I don't believe you! I'm nearly grown up!' Her gaze skittered to the painting where a younger sister might quite soon be pushed off that boulder to tumble under the hooves of those horny black beasts.

'If you'd like a word of advice, little sister—' Which was patronizing, in what must seem all too typical Sariola sister fashion.

Ester shut one eye, so that she regarded Jatta unswervingly. In that dark pupil within a brown iris, within a silky cream setting (really, the girl *could* be classed as quite pretty) Jatta saw her own chubby-cheek face captured in miniature. Her *I*, within the eye of another. She suffered momentary guilt. Such intimacy was reserved for the sister of her soul. Fury stirred briefly – at how she was being drawn into *politics* of the heart.

'Advice about what?' asked the girl.

What did Jatta care about Juke's future prospects? He had escorted her in his own interests. The two of them may have become friendly after a fashion – and quarrelled, then come to a rapport. She'd been a sort of surrogate sister to him! Juke was responsible for his own sister's death and for Minnow's death too. Now he was helping their mother to meddle with the mystery of Jack's future. (*Please don't let Jack die too soon.*)

'About what?' pestered Ester.

'About Juke Nurmi . . . Women die because of him.' A weak explanation, unsatisfying and incomprehensible to Ester.

'He's helping to stop Jack *dying* because of *June*' – a barbed hint – 'then he'll be quits for Minnow's accident, won't he?'

Ester didn't especially grieve for Minnow. Minnow had looked to be of an age with Ester, although in reality she was three years her senior. Naturally Minnow had dissociated herself from

Ester lest Minnow seem to be just a kid too. With Minnow out of the way, Ester was the next in line to wed, by and by. Important Ester! Jatta appraised the girl's filched décolleté gown wryly.

. . . And here came Mrs Simberg, accompanied by Nanni Vanni. The stout old nurse toddled, shortened by her years into a little barrel of black-clad body. The governess stalked forward like a tall grey hikerbird. Censorious spectacles were perched upon her nose. A silver pomander of herbs hung around her scraggy neck. Mrs Simberg was carrying Nakkinook, the much-used boy bisque doll in its latest sartorial incarnation of red-striped jacket, green breeches, and mustardy waistcoat. The flirt doll, the fetish doll, owned by all Sariola daughters in turn for several years on end during which he would ogle them and they would confide in him. Seemingly the doll had been confiscated from six-year-old sister Martha, to be conveyed in the direction of the Courtship Chamber.

Was Lucky recruiting everybody in this enterprise? Even including a doll! (Though excluding Jack's own mother, who might be *prejudiced* . . .) Or was a powerful intimation – a mana-current generated by Jack's burgeoning apprentice desires – wafting governess and nanny and Ester and whoever else towards that antechamber, prelude to a bed of love?

Should Jatta quiz her erstwhile governess? The vinegary woman had miscarried of *her* only child years and years ago when her husband deserted her . . .

Right now Jatta had more important business.

'A pot of luckyfish roe,' she promised Anni, 'and one of sweetfin, and a jar of sour cream.'

4 · In the Sway of Desire

Jack and June sat cross-legged upon the rug in the Courtship Chamber, but now side by side. Both wore gloves. His were of tan kidskin, with flared cuffs. Hers were cream.

At Lucky's request Arto Nurmi had sewn the two pairs of covers for the young folks' hands. The seams were noticeably raised, executed in exaggerated glover's stitch. Arto had demurred at this specification, concerned that palace denizens who observed these sole examples of his craftsmanship might suppose that he was incompetent. Such, however, was the manner in which wounds were sewn up so as to ensure healing. Surgeon's stitch, as well as glover's! These were prophylactic gauntlets. They reeked of cinnamon and crushed cloves.

Goody Hilda crouched awkwardly alongside June, the girl's left hand in hers. In June's lap reposed the quartet of cord dollies, severed several days since by the Queen's shaman from the midst of their long white looping umbilicus. A fresh pile of cord lay beside Jack.

The shaman tapped a rattle upon his broad shallow drum. Garbed in harnie wings and pelts, he was. Dozens of tin discs jingled as he shuffled. A rooster mask, coated with orange feathers, hid his head. The masked man peered through yellow glass eyes. Scarlet comb and wattle were of leather; the beak of sharp tin. A couple of clawfoot legs with spurs served as earrings.

Mana-priest Paavo Serlachius stood portly in his grey serge suit and stiff white wing collar. The priest's face was almost as ruddy as the rooster's wattle. Juke and Nils had ranked themselves on either side of him. Only the Queen occupied the sofa of hearts, in her black weeds, her veiled head crowned with amber beads.

Tump, tump. The shaman's percussion was a constant heartbeat.

Lucky rhapsodized in a low choked voice about her dead husband and the wellspring of their love. Her audience were attentive not only because she was a queen of quirks who could easily veer from sentiment to vexation. These were precious revelations, to the extent that what she said did genuinely reveal the feelings of the mother of a world, Kaleva's patron saint and delinquent. Lucky harped on about the source of love, of mutual intoxication, setting a theme for Jack and June.

'My Bertie's field was flowers. Botany, did I say? Blossoms and herbage and trees. Bouquets and posies: all for me, his bonny blossom.'

'Bliss in bowers,' Serlachius warbled sympathetically. 'Honeyed hours.'

'Quite! Of course we'd be bound to live here in the Northland, where else, in the palace of our desires . . . We met at Landfall, did I say? This was before Sariolinna was founded or Threelakes or Kip'an'keep and long before the Isi came. Thus Kaleva was all our world, virgin as was I. When my prince-to-be arrived as an immigrant in the fourth year after the Ukko had altered my hair from blonde to black as night, it was as if I'd been awaiting *him* and none other. As soon as he set eyes on me, he discovered his destiny too. I was nineteen when I bedded my love, and ceased to age. *Bedded my love and ceased to age*, do you hear?

'*Ceased to age*, Jack. As did *he* – apart from acquiring a plumper pot of a tummy. Oh but I acquired the very same tum from his seed every three years or so. Childbirth never harmed or hurt me the least little bit, do you heed, June? Baby daughters slip out as smoothly as turds from a bum.'

June began to snigger, and Hilda squeezed the girl's gloved hand sharply. Lucky drew her feet up on to the sofa, the heels of her black boots digging into hearts, and held herself thus with laced fingers.

'His *scent* – the scent of his skin – always appealed to me, though I'm sure only I ever noticed. It was . . . waxen. The smell of waxy cream petals in a nowhere-meadow. I miss it so! My other self still sniffs that scent: attar of Ukko.'

Juke's eyes narrowed and his brow knit in a frown.

'Such a delicate fragrance could lead me by the nose to the end of the world if I could catch a hint of it. Still, with *him* by me' – yet she refrained from uttering Bertel's name – 'my senses were satisfied . . .'

Dissatisfied, now? All be it teased at the prospect of dusky Jack and chubby June so close together?

Out in the herb garden a cuckoo had alighted on the nearer lip of the basin where the bronze leaperfish balanced upon its tail fins. The fish blew a glassy rod of water which fractured into splinters; a sleek stem forever shedding tiny petals. A wrought-iron cuckoo perch beyond the fountain held a dead chick spitted on a spike, but the gossip-bird disregarded the offering. Fluffing out its shingled verdigris plumes, the cuckoo stared unblinkingly at their window from its big yellow eyes. Its feline ears cupped toward the room. Out there, the leaperfish must be burbling audibly. Could that stare read lips so as to assist the bird's keen hearing?

Lucky hugged herself. 'I was nineteen, did I say?' She was reiterating herself, as if once every three or four years she had been abruptly restored to what she had previously been; wedding Bertel afresh, to spawn another daughter. *If she failed to conceive another daughter now that her prince was dead, might she resume a normal rate of aging?*

The rooster shaman drummed heartbeats. Jack swayed from side to side, almost bumping June. Jack was aging. Not to the casual eye. Nor even if you observed him for several days on end. Yet nevertheless!

'I was intoxicated with him. He, with me.' Lucky's voice caressed her listeners. 'We both possessed such a flair for one another, such a talent for *loving* one another. What a peerless, precious faculty – transcending time, outstripping the hours and years. A talent, I tell you.' The Queen threw up her veil, baring for the first time in a month her face: that full oval countenance with the spiced bun cheeks, those narrow smoky eyes. Addressing herself to Juke and Nils and the mana-priest: 'Proclaimers, say as I say: a talent to cheat time. Bestow it on that boy. Bless my grandson and,' she wavered mischievously, 'his bosom playmate. Banish harm or hurt. Let hurt and harm find an outlet other than in Jack. Let harm and hurt tie knots in themselves, such as lie in June's lap.' *The cord dollies.* 'Let ill be expelled from her.'

Juke breathed in deeply and began to proclaim as requested. Nils joined in. Serlachius added his voice. Jack rocked, crooning to himself. The shaman bumped the rattle against his drum. June blushed, though there was eager hope in her eyes.

('Tie an egg into a knot,') Hilda whispered without much conviction. Hadn't she originally claimed that her purpose in bringing June to the palace was to relieve the mocky-girl of her curse? An egg would indeed be tied into a knot; into a quartet of knots, a quadruplet of warm baby flesh and throbbing blood and bendy bone instead of cord, one bairn to hang from each of June's teats, piglets nuzzling at her paps . . .

The aurora dancers around the walls were aglow, aswirl. Out in the garden a sudden excess of white water jetted high and foamy from the bronze lips of the fish, cascading back upon the basin to drench the peering cuckoo – which promptly took flight, a fluster of scaly plumes. Flooded, the basin overflowed.

'That's enough!' The Queen's voice shrilled as if prudery had suddenly afflicted her. 'That'll do! Let's see if Jack breaks out in pimples. And pus. And *pestilence*.' She laughed giddily. 'Take the gloves off, you two.'

Jack quickly tossed Arto's work aside. June (once Hilda had released the girl's hand) teased each finger slowly free in turn, a flirtatious striptease of the digits. Soon enough the fastboy slid

65

his hand into hers. When June uncrossed her legs, the linked dollies slid down her satin lap.

Perched upon embroidered hearts, Lucky hugged her ankles jubilantly. 'Play the rope game again! With proclaimers present, this time!' She chortled, she shed some tears.

In the Courtship Chamber the gloves were off . . . but no other garments. Nor would *intimacies* occur for several days yet, and then in circumstances of rather more privacy.

In another chamber hundreds of paces away, the breeches weren't yet on, and a visitor of some consequence was due to call on General Viktor Aleksonis. Thick curtains of green and gold brocade cloaked the windows, though by the ormolu twenty-four-hour clock on the mantelshelf noon, not midnight, was nigh. Requirements of privacy! Several brass oil-lamps illuminated the General's office.

'Can't you hurry up?' Lucky's commander growled in exasperation at the finicky little tailor, Julius Haxthausen. 'Do a few creases matter, man?' The General appealed to his lanky aide, Ben Prut: *'Can't you help?'*

Tapestries of battles-such-as-never-were decorated two of the walls. Amidst sparse boulder-strewn woodland near a lake scummed with gold – and again in a bleak snow-dusted mountain valley – gaudily uniformed cavalry skirmished with robotic formations of black-liveried Juttahats. The human cavalry, on their stocky ponies, brandished swords. The Juttie infantry bore lances resembling long blue needles. Some threw these as javelins. Transfixed, a cavalryman was cartwheeling off his mount. Numbers of Juttahats lay like broken insects, leaking orange blood. Each Juttie wore on its back a long upright sheath containing at least one spare lance. Those aliens could hardly rush about too rapidly. Each tight formation was a-bristle with seeming antennae which might be controlling those alien troopers, marshalling and marching them. Jagged, crimson-edged clouds jig-sawed through the skies.

Hand-inked illustrated maps littered a campaign table. Weighing these down were a lightpistol in a leather holster, various geometrical instruments, pens and inkwell, and a marble ashtray housing a tobacco pipe of purple tammywood. The General's apartment smelled of sweet nutty fumes. Charts protruded from cubby-holes in a roll-top bureau. A communicator occupied a pedestal table, quietly hissing static.

Aleksonis, in his underpants, leaned back along a chaise-longue. He supported himself on his elbows whilst raising his buttocks as the tailor struggled to haul white buckskin breeches up over his hips. Those breeches were tight. They were wet to facilitate pulling them on. A mighty struggle, even so. The tailor had divested himself of his silk and leather waistcoat and had rolled up his sleeves. Still he puffed. Hair slicked across his sweating forehead. He was a stickler that there should be no wrinkles.

Haxthausen panted. 'Your underlinen keeps rumpling up, sir. Next time it would be better if you wear nothing underneath.'

'How undignified! My visitor's due in—' Aleksonis strained to see the clock, but couldn't quite.

'I'll build a framwork to hold the breeches so that you can step down into them from off a chair—'

'Leap into 'em, and snap a toe?'

The rest of the General's new dress uniform hung on a faceless dummy: a white tunic with silver collar and chevrons, and over this a scarlet supervest emblazoned with the newly conceived Order of the Ukko. First recipient: Viktor Aleksonis, who had retrieved the everything machine for his Queen. A dozen stars surrounded what appeared at first glance to be a potato-shaped womb, of silver, embossed with the curly foetus of some creature which was evidently destined to have a long tail. This was really the outline of an inner ear: the cochlea, labyrinths, and canals. The blank head of the dummy wore a silver helmet bearing the emblem of a winged eye. From the peak rose a high green plume. Tall leather jackboots stood waiting by the dummy. A long sword with damascened full-bowl guard hung, scabbarded.

'New weapons call for a fine new costume, my General,' Lucky had informed Aleksonis recently.

Ben Prut stooped over his superior to lend a hand heaving. Silver chevrons were newly appended to Prut's camouflage leathers, and he wore a splendid matching shoulder belt. His new regalia was less complicated than the General's. The Queen preferred her palace guards to look functional. But their commanding officer must seem imposing.

Tall Ben Prut, a distant younger relative of Mrs Simberg, shared with that sad governess a lean and bony frame, thin features, and an unfortunate degree of short-sightedness. His vision was excellent for inking tiny pictures and emblems on maps. In a brass case in a pocket of his leathers he carried spectacles. Prut preferred not to wear these in the palace, though he must don the specs for target practice which it fell to him to organize. As a Queen's guard, he was less élite than the eerie dollied-up soldiers at the Fortress in the Fjord of whom Aleksonis was also in nominal overall command.

'Ach, *hurry*! Can't hold my crupper up for ever.'

Ben's fingers, and the tailor's, plucked and yanked at the damp recalcitrant waistband. Four crustaceans feeding on the white belly of a corpse. The General kept himself in reasonable trim. His limbs were sinewy and his torso firm, thinly marked by several olden scars, souvenirs of knife fights in his youth. On his right shoulder: a blue tattoo of a horse for strength and stamina. The present posture was not one of his regular exercises.

'I'll get aches in my joints from wearing damp breeches!'

'Your body heat'll soon dry them out, sir. Her Majesty insisted on tight buckskins, so they need to be wetted.'

'*Too* tight, imbecile.'

'Your underpants are the real problem.' Julius Haxthausen was not going to be criticized in matters of togs and measurement. 'Ah! *Aha!*' With a final hoist at last the breeches fitted snugly. Aleksonis relapsed upon the chaise-longue, but only briefly. Quickly he lurched to his feet and stamped towards the jackboots, to plunge one leg deep, then the other. Already Ben Prut had separated the supervest from the tunic. He held the latter wide open. *Cling*, chimed the clock on the mantelshelf. The General finished buttoning himself just as the twelfth note struck and a fist thumped punctually on the door.

Ben Prut admitted Bekker, Captain of the Fortress; and shooed the tailor on his way.

A dark blue uniform trimmed with gold and crimson lace . . . Tall shako hat with tufted crimson pompon set upon a hairless head. The Captain's dark hard ruddy face was distinctly grained in texture. Side-arm holstered on his belt; scabbarded sabre dangling. Brown gloves . . .

Captain Bekker gazed at the faceless dummy which still wore the plumed helmet. For a moment Bekker seemed inclined to salute it rather than the flesh-and-blood General. Then expressionlessly he faced Aleksonis. A gloved hand snapped to his brow.

'Will you take some wine?' the General invited. 'Or berry liqueur?'

Notwithstanding that wooden grain, how smoothly polished was the Captain's face, the curved planes of his cheeks and chin and brow. Bekker's deep-set eyes, of kastanut hue, regarded Aleksonis from unpuckered cups. The General's orbital flesh was rucked and tucked and grooved.

'Some mustaberry, Captain?'

'A little, thank you.'

Prut poured two and a half glasses of the liqueur. In the squat decanter the drink was virtually black. In a slimmer glass it took on the magenta hue of a resin or varnish. Bekker moistened his flexible ligneous lips.

How clammily the General's breeches clung to him. The Captain – wooden but abundantly alive – seemed more comfortable than Aleksonis felt. Did Bekker heed discomfort? Did he even notice? Did he experience much pleasure except in those blissful dreams which he dreamt when he was in a rigid trance, immobile and inflexible? Ever since the everything machine began to produce weapons in the ruins of the donjon on that isle in the Fjord, Bekker and his fifty wooden sentries had been alive and alert, dutifully occupied with inspecting and testing and sorting the new weaponry fabricated from the quarried atoms of the island. Duty was their delight. Their other appetites were modest. If those sentries remained active for a protracted period might they begin to yearn for their previous state of blissful wooden torpor? They might catnap at night now, drowse and doze and even slumber, but they wouldn't be profoundly inert.

Supposing that a campaign was called for, how might they cope with leaving their familiar fort in the fjord? A stockpile of weaponry such as they were amassing implied an offensive rather than merely the passive defence of a fortress. An assault upon the Isi, surely.

'Why am I here, away from my command?' the Captain asked calmly.

The very question.

'The machine hasn't produced any kind of . . . homing device? Nothing recognizable as an instrument for . . . seeking something out? A detector of distant objects? A sort of compass?' Aleksonis was being deliberately vague, since the Queen was likewise evasive in this regard.

'There are three more jump-bikes. We can use them to reach a target. In one jump, or more, depending on the distance.'

69

'Could you reach an unknown destination far away, Captain Bekker? Can a bike carry you somewhere of its own accord if you wish?'

'I find that hard to imagine. The world of dreams is not the world of war.'

'Quite.' Setting down his glass, Aleksonis stalked – magnificent in his scarlet supervest and silver-collared tunic – to the map table. He pressed his pipe into a pouch of Pootaran tobacco. He tamped with his thumb. A match flared. He sucked flame into weed. Smoke billowed, sweet and nutty.

Bekker's nostrils twitched. But fire would not disconcert this wooden soldier – neither the hostile variety, nor a bonfire. He was as impervious as the lathe-turned tammywood of Viktor's pipe.

(Puff.) 'How far have any of you actually jumped a bike?'

'To the shore. Up the shore. Along the shore.' As if those jaunts added up to a significant journey.

'Always within sight of the fortress?'

'It's our duty to guard our fortress and the everything machine.'

'What were your feelings on coming here, Captain?'

'I was summoned.'

'How do you feel at not being able to see your fortress any longer?'

Bekker gestured at the radio communicator.

'What if some of your sentries are seconded here to the palace?'

'Here they will serve. Does the Queen require this?' (Was the Captain subtly questioning the General's authority?) Bekker sipped a few drops of his liqueur.

Pausing by the communicator, Aleksonis switched off the machine. A green light vanished. Keep the Captain here, watch him, see if he becomes at all anxious. How does wood express disquiet?

Wood abides. Wood stands its ground.

'I need you to remain here for several days, Captain.'

'In this room?' Bekker looked around. 'May I examine your maps?'

'. . . of far-away places, indeed. I may need to send you on a mission. You and your men. Leaving the fortress undefended.'

'A soldier glories in an expedition.'

'Does a sentry rejoice?'

'We wish to be heroes.'

70

How agreeably warm the pipe bowl was. The breeches did seem less damp. Unfortunately an itch began to tease Viktor's shank down inside the jackboot out of reach.

'You can stay in the regular guards' quarters.' Those of the workaday flesh-and-blood guards. That itch was fast becoming worse, as soon as noticed, as unappeasable provocations had a habit of doing.

'Have I been there before?' Had the woodman forgotten his own past? How long ago, thirty-odd years? When Bekker had been a bit of a proclaimer, as Aleksonis recalled from his youth. A minor proclaimer, who volunteered to take advantage of Tapper Kippan's courtship gift to Lucky when the forest lord came wooing – some daughter, the name had gone. By a transfusion of sap from a certain tree which only grew in the southern forests, Bekker had become remarkable, and would live long, though not in the way that the husbands of Lucky's daughters lived long.

Tapper Kippan must have many such stalwart woodmen protecting his forest domain. Sentinels, never venturing far, no more than the wood lord himself strayed far from home by all accounts.

'Prut will show you the way. Each guard has his own room. Married guards have a couple. Those with sprats, three. We don't stint.' Oh to pull off the boot and attack that pesky itch.

Bekker put down his glass. He seemed disappointed. 'I thought I was to study maps. Charting where, and how, to be a hero.'

'Yes, tomorrow. First I have some work I must do.' With scritchy-scratchy fingernails. 'Capital notion of yours, to scan the maps. Take some with you. I want you to imagine yourself travelling far, a long way from the fortress, and for a long time.' Aleksonis experimented with stiffening his leg, clenching the sinews, though he risked a cramp. These damned breeches. His shank had become a mass of bedevilling formicks. The insects wouldn't administer a decisive bite. Only his own hand could oblige.

'Do you *dream* about being a hero?' Prut asked the Captain. Bekker reacted not one whit. Wooden man, indeed. Oblivious of the General's distress, Prut pursued the enquiry: 'Do tell me, Captain, are your dreams heroic?' As if Aleksonis wished to hear of this, right now!

Well, he *did*. This was certainly germane to the matter of whether Bekker and his wooden sentries were imprinted upon their fort in the fjord, or whether they could range far and wide with ease. Presumably they could be bespoken to do so. Yet if

71

there was any sort of reluctance one didn't wish to appeal to Juke Nurmi or to young Demon Jack. Plain orders ought to suffice. Aleksonis had never hitherto commanded wooden soldiers in action . . .

Ach, heroism. He'd certainly acted the hero when he captured the everything machine from a squad of suicidal Jutties who fought to the last alien! Resisting an imperative to tear at his flesh was also a mite heroic. How much worse must be an itch of the mind! What fingernails could scratch such an itch to distract it? Compulsions must be obeyed.

Orders too; unless in conflict with some compulsion.

'Ben, will you *kindly* show Captain Bekker to his billet!' Aleksonis seized a bundle of maps and thrust them at his aide.

Here was the pool, and almost as Jatta had remembered, give or take that bend in the mossy bank, quite so many sheaves of reeds, and the redoubtable span of that stout horzma tree dangling its skirt of fleecy emerald fronds almost to the water. Actually, there was only a single horzma, not several smaller ones as in her memory. And likewise only one sylvester tree with its chalky bark and blue bristles. Larixes and veras screened the dell with a stitchery of scales and needles, gingery red and vivid green.

In the past several weeks she and Anni had quite often strolled the streets of Sariolinna, with a guard lagging watchfully behind. Guards needed to be kept occupied. Such a fellow was useful for glaring at overly inquisitive townsfolk. The two young women would leave by way of the Zig-Zag Gate then head down Sariola Boulevard to the harbour to admire the boats and the fish market. Or else they might promenade along Katarina Avenue as far as Lucky Square with its jetting fountain.

But no guard now.

As well as a picnic for themselves, Jatta had brought a nosebag of oats for the Perch'. The double saddle and a couple of riders had been no more bother for so burly an animal than for a pony to carry a child. The real question might have been whether such a heavy beast could propel itself on a trip of any significant length rather than simply remain standing massively still. Yet their grey mare (blotched moderately with white) had clomped along on its hard blue feet, its great muscles in leisurely motion upon flat flinty bones. So broad was its back and rump that there could be no fear of falling. The Perch' was a kind of giant sofa, smelling of hot horsehair. Now it nuzzled its oats contentedly beyond a lattice of henna and green, reined to a branch.

Jatta had set out on a linen kerchief crisp pasties filled with mashed potatoes, a jar of orange luckyfish roe, a jar of gingery sweetfin roe, a pot of sour cream, rusks, a saucer of chopped onion, a bottle of black mustaberry wine. Also, the cracked mignon egg. Transported in a saddlebag stuffed with melting ice and damp towels, wine and roe and cream still retained the chill of the palace ice-house below the kitchens. This was almost the self-same picnic with which Jarl had wooed her in a kindred dell beside a larger pool.

The two women drank. In passing the bottle the lingering brush of hand against hand was tentative, enchanted. They fed each other roe on rusk, dabbed with cream, sprinkled with onion. Jatta inhaled the fishy tang. No ghost of cinnamon and mushroom gills and roasted kasta nuts arose to trouble her. Jarl's fragrance was far away, long ago.

Anni shifted. She shook her glossy tresses. 'I need a pee—'

Sun, of boiling butter. The dell, a sultry bowl. Barely a wisp of breeze intruded. Gnats eddied at the far side of the pool, a vague vibrating funnel.

Jarl had lured Jatta to bathe with him.

'Me too,' she answered Anni. 'Why don't we both make water in the pool?'

Trousers *were* a bit hot for such an afternoon in a dell. Suède tunics too, for that matter. Soon it was only chemises and skin as they crouched in the pool, Jatta's arms and shoulders as golden as Jarl's had been, beside Anni's ivorywood flesh.

'So we purify ourselves of that sham man,' Jatta murmured.

'Ain't it so.'

'We mingle. We perfect ourselves.'

'Ain't it true.'

'Rapture, not capture.' Jatta chuckled. 'I can't exactly carry you ashore, can I?'

'Don't know as a pond has a *shore*, really.' Anni rose, half dry, half soaked. She led her friend by the hand. Two pairs of muddy feet. Bare to the midriff, they lay together beside the picnic.

'When *it* happened,' breathed Jatta, 'I glimpsed you naked in the snake-suit. It seemed a web of strings. You squirmed, you wiggled.'

'Didn't I just.'

'You smiled, yet your eyes were confounded.'

'The very word.'

'We first met then, though we didn't know it.' A frenzy of the spirit coursed through Jatta. She trembled with an inner turbulence. 'We're seized by freedom now, Anni.'

'Ain't we.'

They pressed close. Palms, fingers wandered in caress. Noses nuzzled, breathing in the other's roe-scented exhalations. Tongues touched. Each body was a beloved voice in a duet of fondling. They breathed each other in, and out, in exaltation. Each: a fluttering, volatile wing of the same heart-throbbing bird, which ascended above their two bodies bedded there upon the soft moss . . .

The Perch' snickered. Anni uttered a small cry of surprise. 'Look, look—'

Across the pool where the funnel of midges had swayed, now there were many more – a thousand more – in the faint shape of a person. A woman, yes. Tall, slender, hazy, composed of gnats and yet more gnats and midges. Tiny insects were still massing, gathered by mana, swept up into that figure, that cloudy column.

'A nakki,' squeaked Anni, more in astonishment than alarm.

Did the sprite wear a gown? Were her limbs merely indefinite and fused? Sleek hair cascaded about the spectral woman's shoulders. Her left eye gleamed. A pair of glitterbugs hovered there, joined in aerial copulation. Poised upon the water, did the presence watch Jatta and Anni with that glinting eye? Would she speak? Would wee wings of innumerable gnats vibrate in unison to conjure a voice from the air?

Was this truly a nakki, native to a charmed pond? Or was this perhaps the visible, volatile form of the union of Jatta's soul with Anni's?

'Ourselves as one,' Jatta whispered. Why, it was their own passion which had enchanted this pond. Yet the woman who stood on the water was unlike them in almost every respect. Taller, more slender. Her hair so light; wings reflecting sunshine. Why did one of her eyes gleam so, when the other did not? She couldn't possibly be jinxing Jatta and Anni's intimacy – no, no – but surely was blessing their love.

Anni called, 'Did you once drown yourself in this pool, bright maid?'

This pond was hardly deep enough for other than the most vehement and desperate suicide. Nor was this hot joyous dell at all forlorn.

'Were you drowned by a false lover?'

The question transfixed the apparition. Her whole body quivered. Her left eye shone. Midges flowed to form a luminous rod, clasped in her blended fingers. The outline of a lightrifle, perhaps . . . What nakki would clutch a lightrifle?

Jatta knew who the woman was.

Desolately, almost disinterestedly, Jatta had seen her when the royal sky-boat landed briefly at the mocky-village after her fastboy had been lost to the Brazen Jutties, there to disgorge Juke – as well as her mother for a flamboyant half-minute.

She was Eyeno. She was Juke's dead sister. Betrayed by him, then bespoken by lusty Lord Osmo to drown herself after she tore out her false eye. While Jatta watched numbly from a porthole of the sky-boat, Eyeno had run from a hovel to greet her brother. Eyeno Nurmi was dead; must be dead.

'Eyeno!' cried Jatta, nonetheless. The apparition must be Eyeno's echo. She couldn't conceivably have drowned herself *here*. Not in the Northland, in a pond.

As the figure took a step forward over the water, the component gnats and midges dragged apart in disorder. How quickly the cloud dispersed.

'She's gone—'

'*Eyeno's* gone, Anni. That's who it was. I recognized her.'

'Juke's sister. Why should she—?'

'—preside over our union? I think . . . to remind us to be true! Unlike the Jukes of this world, unlike all those. This has to be our secret, dear.'

'Ain't it so.'

'We shan't be tempted to tell.'

'Who could tempt us? We'd be fools.'

'You and I, we're a power together in ways we don't yet know.'

'We'll find out, won't we?'

'We conjured up her echo out of magic rapture, Anni.'

Ukko-ukkoo: distant cackle. And the Percheron uttered a muffled neigh of rebuff.

'Cuckoo, coming to spy on us?' The gossip-bird's journey from somewhere to somewhere had been deflected by the sway of desire. It sensed the mana, it sighted the horse . . .

'Maybe it already spied on us.'

'We'd have seen it.'

'Would we, Anni?' What, while they themselves, Jarl's

ravishees, were taking wing on such a maiden voyage? A fleeting sadness pierced Jatta – a poignancy – a sharp sparkling seam in the smooth marble of their love. This, too, belonged. Without it, they would be fools.

5 · ... AND CONSUMMATED

How right Jatta was regarding the skin-suit!

'Now promise me you'll wear this,' the Queen insisted fondly. Lucky was wearing her veil again. June found this less disconcerting when such intimate matters were being aired.

A double window stood open to admit a gentle breeze. Its waft stirred several layers of finest white netting hanging like great delicate cobwebs spun by a host of hammockis on a pasture overnight. The view of Sariolinna's sun-kissed rooftops, neighbouring forest, fjord beyond and the harsh mountains over the water, was nebulous indeed, merely a patterned mist, even if the forenoon itself was far from hazy.

Forenoon of June's wedding day ... in a sense.

The royal marriage bed was also being aired. Its embroidered counterpane was turned down to expose silken sheets on which were scattered sachets of sweet herbs. The silk was iridescent: violet, mauve, shot with sapphire like the skirts of aurora dancers. When candles in the sconces were alight and dancing too how those sheets would shimmer. But the summer night wouldn't call for candles. Ruched pink satin hung from the bed canopy and alongside the window. The filmy body-stocking was laid out upon the sheet like some peculiarly tight nightdress or article of lingerie. Lucky had insisted on loaning this room where almost all Sariola daughters had been conceived. You could hardly refuse such an offer. Would the Queen's nocturnal presence in her own adjoining chamber prove intimidating? Not one but two stout doors – with a generous gap in between – separated Lucky's private apartment from the nuptial bower. A second pair of doors, flanked by a stove, gave entry to the suite which Bertel had occupied until his death. No longer, no longer.

'I've advised *many* daughters before,' Lucky hinted as they eyed the snakeskin. 'Lasses made in this bed, born in this bed. A *hundred* girls, and more.' This bed was bountiful.

June clutched the quartet of cord dollies. That a mocky-girl should sleep with her lover for the first time in the Queen of Kaleva's own sheets, at her invitation: a marvel! To lie with her eager lover, grandson of a Queen, full of mana-magic, in this silken royal bed! A mocky-girl from humble Halvek . . .

Which reminded her: 'Your Majesty, Lammas asked me – he's wondering when Knotty and Pieman and him can be going home to their cotts.'

Lightly Lucky cuffed one of June's blonde pigtails. 'Soon,' she cooed, 'soon.'

'Can my Jack fly them home, do you think?'

Lucky gripped the pigtail tightly. 'Where do you think you'll be giving birth to your brats? Who'll be your midwife?'

'Here, of course. Here, Your Majesty. With Hilda.'

'Good girl. Jack's such a fine boy . . . Some day he'll catch Minkie Kennan for me, him and Juke. *Where has Kennan gone to ground? Damn and damn him.* My chamberlain once surprised him loitering in the corridor—' Her hand jerked.

June yelped at the pull on her hair. Lucky gazed at the closed door of Bertel's former suite.

'In that corridor outside. Linqvist told me much later, after—' After what occurrence, she did not specify. Little need to do so. 'I wonder whether Kennan had sneaked into the other parlour . . . and through into here?'

This chamber, where Lucky and her consort had come together when the passion arose in her, could only be entered from her suite, or from the other, closed suite.

Slowly the pressure on the pigtail eased. 'We have bridal details to think about, June—'

Her 'brats', indeed. Not babes or bairns or wee mites . . .

'—especially about sheathing yourself in the serpent-skin.'

The Queen was distracting herself from painful thoughts of a murdered prince. That was why she was loaning the bed: to divest it of memories. Centuries of memories. To expel those. Maybe she imagined the snake-skin as her own skin, sloughed off, and stretched over June. It wouldn't merely tease and provoke Jack coquettishly and guard him from any sickness caused by her touch. It might also control June's limbs and feelings.

When Lucky's hand brushed the cord dollies, June clasped those possessively to her bosoms.

'Four knots of love,' Lucky whispered into the mocky-girl's ear, 'means two braces of brats.'

It was a long day and a late-light evening before June returned to Lucky's parlour. Chattering and chuckling, the Queen led her and Jack from the Courtship Chamber where the lovers-to-be had dined in company with Goody Hilda on pungent tarandra heart stew with puffballs, followed by squeaky cheesebread. Each bite of the cheesebread which Jack and June took had made a little noise like a stiff key turning in a lock. The mutie combo had serenaded their supper from outside in the herb garden. By and by the wisewoman had dozed off crookedly upon the embroidered hearts.

On arrival at the antechamber to the bridal suite, who should June and Jack find waiting in Lucky's parlour to wish them well than the two proclaimers, the mana-priest, and even chamberlain Linqvist in his frock-coat, cummerbund, and powdered white wig? Maybe there was to be an intimate wedding ceremony after all.

But no: Linqvist was there to serve drinks, set out upon a drum table. This table, with drawers set around its circumference, and a couple of soft settees and a cabinet, were multiplied many-fold in long gilt-framed mirrors hugging the walls. Here was the salon where Lucky entertained her reflections.

The drinks were sweet pink tonics, of the juice from nipple-hued bubberries. Tilting his glass at the fastboy in his golden livery, Juke proposed a toast.

'You're the wind and the light, lad. You're tempest and sunbright. You're hurry and scurry. But tonight you'll slow down.'

Jack raked a hand through his tight black hair.

'Grow old at a normal rate, Demon Jack. A bird in mid-air doesn't come to a sudden stop or it'll fall like a brick.'

Nils flicked the bird's claw fetish pinned on his lapel. 'Long life to you, mana-kid.'

'*Longlife?*' cried Lucky. 'Did you say *longlife?*' Spying her own expression in the silvered glass, she sweetened her countenance. She positively simpered even as Nils was rubbing his tattooed lips together to erase ill-chosen words. Mirrors were crowded with multiple eclipsing images of those present, queues of Queen and priest and chamberlain, proclaimers and fastboy and his girl. Naturally, half of the figures had their backs turned, and the most distant were foggy.

'Somewhere out there, *Pappi* Paavo,' Lucky remarked to Serlachius, 'she has blonde hair, not black. But I never see far enough. The question is: does she see me?'

The mana-priest ahem-ed. 'These are ordinary mirrors, Majesty.'

'Aren't my *daughters* also mirrors of myself? I've come to the end of the series. Baby Hanna's the last princess.'

'You also have a remarkable grandson,' Serlachius reminded her.

'Ah yes, Jack paralysed you, didn't he? You were totally numbed and stupefied.'

Serlachius's face was already too florid to betray much embarrassment. The fastboy looked bashfully rueful, though only briefly. Excitement was mounting in him, mingled with apprehension. When June brushed against him skittishly, he quivered. A lace shawl hid her plump shoulders, otherwise the skin-suit she wore under her gown would have shown. She hugged her bouquet of cord dollies.

When Lucky threw open the doors to the nuptial chamber, heady scent surged – from a bed heaped with great white flowers like so many dwarf white swans a-sail upon sheets and counterpane. Swans there weren't on Kaleva, except in images and carvings.

Serlachius peered past, and shuddered. '*Soulflowers*, Majesty?'

The floral likeness of the swan of death . . . Soulflowers were the epitome of that absent bird – bigger than the harny, and snowy – which bore the spirit away to the far shore. If you could find or afford such blooms, they belonged on coffins. None had graced Bertel's casket after his unseasonable death. Now a profusion of soulflowers littered the bed where he and Lucky had given the spark of life to so many daughters.

Lucky chuckled. 'I had those shipped from the south packed in ice. Souls will gather here. Souls waiting to be conceived.'

'More like spirits of death,' Serlachius muttered.

'Oh *quite*,' agreed Lucky. 'Do you like your big bridal bouquet, June?'

The mocky-girl gazed wide-eyed. 'Never saw a soulflower before.'

Jack skipped to the bedside. He buried his face in a flower. He inhaled. He rummaged among great white petals. 'Death drives death away, doesn't it, Grandmother?'

'Exactly!'

A tripod table inlaid with marquetry bore a carafe of more pink cordial, two fluted glasses, and a plate heaped with gingerbread persons.

'Do eat at least four during the night,' Lucky advised.

'Four! I'll remember. Oh but this one here,' and June poked, 'has had its head nibbled off.' She held the biscuit up. 'Ooh, by tiny little teeth. I'm thinking a *mus* 'as bin in the room, Yer Majesty. Oh here's a *dropping*, just under the rim of the plate!'

Lucky hastened to see. Smearing her fingertip across the morsel of excrement, she removed the dirt from the marquetry. 'Must have scrambled in through the window.'

Displeased, Linqvist headed towards the veils of netting. Dithering, he changed direction. From behind a firescreen he plucked a poker, and resumed his stalk towards the concealed casement. Juke was scrutinizing the tufty rugs on the floor as if the tiny animal might be crouching tremblesome, pointy head bowed in camouflage, front paws prayerfully clasped together like foetal hands.

Lucky shoved her stained finger at June's nose; and the girl jerked back. 'It's the smell of madness, that, Your Majesty. Don't you know what they say about a *mus in the mind*?'

'Sniff, and you'll be safe.'

'My babes,' protested the girl.

'They'll be such maddeningly provocative little maids!'

June wrung the dollies in her hands. 'I dunno—'

'Come now, your offspring will rid you of your curse. Don't forget to eat four biscuits.'

'I shan't—' As Lucky's expression darkened: 'I shan't forget, honest.'

'Now smell the mus dropping, June.'

'Can't smell nothing 'cept for all the lovely flowers.'

Lucky licked her own soiled fingertip. Promptly she kissed June full on the lips. Just then, from among the blooms Jack had plucked one which was smaller and creamier in hue.

'What's this? A bud?' Long-stemmed, waxen, spoon-shaped petals cupped like ears . . .

Lucky rushed upon him. She seized the flower. She breathed deep. She moaned: 'Oh faithful scent, oh home of memory . . . !' She shed a tear into the flower. *'How can it be?* Can Bertie have sent me this to breathe? To sniff his dear skin again! Oh Ukko-flower, are you thirsty?' Circuiting the bed, she slid the stem into the carafe of cordial.

'*Ukko-flower*, Majesty?' queried Serlachius.

'A mana-bloom from the Ukko meadow that only I ever saw!' Gently she cradled the creamy petals in both hands. 'Are you from him? Hasn't he flown to the shore of death after all? Is Bertie in an Ukko meadow?' Panic ignited an echo in her speech. 'Only I ever saw such a bloom, only me and my twin, my twin and me, my other. Is Bertie with my good twin, mana-flower? Is Bertie in bliss with my blonde sister? Is that it, is that it? How dare he dally with *her*? Yet she's me, my true self. Are you from *her*, Ukko-flower? Will my twin show herself in mirrors now?'

Serlachius ogled the bloom. 'A manifestation of the mysterium!'

'Don't anyone touch that flower!' Deserting the waxen bloom, Lucky dashed to her parlour.

A mad-making mus had chewed the head off a gingerbread intended for the lovers to snack on, and now a flower from inside a star-entity was sipping their bubberry cordial. June called weakly over the sheets to her fastboy, 'Won't she let us use the bedroom any more?'

'Mysterium of mysteria,' marvelled Serlachius.

Lucky returned disconsolate. 'I'm not there . . .'

Nils had a suggestion. 'A flower with petals shaped like ears – maybe you'll hear a voice in it if your grandson calls up a wind. Maybe you'll hear your Bertie's voice, if the flower's a message from him.'

'Don't you call him that!'

Nils was bewildered.

'Bertie's a bed-name, my young proclaimer. Only I called him Bertie – at times! Wait, *was* it only me? Years and years ago, before you were the seed of a seed, don't I recall . . . ? Why, it would be that lovestruck longlife, his crony the dreamlord. How terrible to love so unremittingly.' She addressed the flower: 'Did Bertie really send you to me, mana-bloom? How else could you have come to be amongst these soulflowers? You weren't there when Linqvist and I dressed the bed.' She stooped to inhale deeply. 'The smell of his skin, this dear waxy balm.' Her fingers fluttered. Those petals might have been peeled from her consort's body, flowers of flesh.

Juke spoke haltingly. 'But I've seen that kind of bloom before—' (And Jack nodded momentarily, but restrained himself.)

Emerging from behind the netting: the chamberlain. With that poker in his white-gloved hand, he seemed an intruder in spite of his courtly wig and frock-coat. His other hand displayed a streak of dowdy green.

'I found a cuckoo's plume, Majesty—' A scaly mottly verdigris plume.

'A cuckoo brought the flower in its beak to lay on my bed?' From Linqvist to Juke, and from Juke to Linqvist she turned, overwhelmed: 'Where did you see such a flower?'

The chamberlain held out the plume in perplexity.

'I saw one like it in the Velvet Isi nest,' said Juke, 'when I went there with—' The muscles in the proclaimer's neck stiffened.

'With your sister: is that who you mean?'

Juke shuddered. 'An Isi mana-mage was making use of a flower like that and a glass model of an Ukko. The flower was responding to the model. But I was sent away.'

'She stayed with the mage, and told you afterwards?'

Juke nodded resentfully.

In that full oval face of Lucky's, narrow eyes smouldered. 'We shan't use her name. Not even the word *she*. We'll refer to . . . the *eye*. The eye that saw the flower and the model. Give me that feather, Linqvist. Have guards climb on the roofs to look for the cuckoo that shed it and for anything else it dropped.'

Linqvist expressed reservations. The light was failing. Rooftops would be dim and dodgy.

In that case let all the seeing-eye dogs be loosed from the kennels too! All the cock-eared, pointy-muzzled Spitzes whose trainers could look in a mana-mirror to see whatever the watchdog saw . . .

Guards scrambling about on rooftops in the vicinity of the nuptial chamber? Dogs yapping. Where was the decorum?

'Just close the window, Linqvist. Put that poker back in the fireplace. And take our young proclaimer away with you.'

'I can wait next door while Juke's being questioned—' Nils had thought he was essential to the proceedings.

'Get him out of here! Find that bird.'

Serlachius seized Nils by the arm and propelled him out of the Queen's presence, murmuring, 'Discretion, my son.'

Linqvist lingered. 'There's almost bound to be *some* cuckoo or other around . . .'

'Do we want a gossip-bird roosting on the windowsill outside this room tonight?' Lucky smirked sympathetically at Jack and June. 'No, Linqvist. Station a Spitz on the roof below as a deterrent. Winch another one up to the ridge above.'

Was she intent on seeking a bird or on scaring birds away?

'A dog might howl, at the height.'

'I might have its trainer whipped if my young guests are disturbed. My spy-dogs don't mind offending cuckoos,' she confided to Juke. 'Maybe they feel a sense of rivalry. Or else of inferiority, since dogs can't usually speak. *Genius* could. That was years ago. The mutie bitch is dead.'

Juke winced. Lucky's words – whether heedless or mischievously intentional – rasped the scab in his soul. The mutie bitch was dead indeed. His sister.

'If they see a cuckoo fluttering lamely, track it to hear what it cackles about. Do you hear?'

The chamberlain departed, confused as to his mission.

'I wonder,' Lucky mused, 'whether the flower-bringer might have pulled out its plume deliberately to leave as a memento? So what,' she asked Juke, 'did the *eye* observe in the Isi nest?'

The eye. How wickedly apt. His sister had gone with him to the Velvet Isi to ask for a fine false eye in place of the dull paste aquamarine she had bought from Missieur Pierre the jeweller in Threelakes.

'What do you know about mana-blooms and a model of an Ukko?'

The fastboy was begging Juke with those soft ambery eyes to say something suitable but succinct, and June was twisting her dollies. Let Lucky not fly into a frustrated rage on their evening of joy and love.

'These flowers grow among the echoes of the dead. The mage's mouthpiece said that the Isi call it the ear-flower . . .'

'Do you hear me, flower?' Lucky asked the waxen petals. 'Is the Ukko-child reaching out to me with a clue? Does my twin yearn for me as I for her?' She listened – to silence. 'Does this have nothing to do with my consort? His spirit isn't reproaching me that this was *our* bed of love?'

Anguish gripped Juke. 'The eye saw the flower – but the flower also saw the eye!'

'How do you mean?'

'After I'd been sent away, a Juttie took hold of the flower. The flower tightened into a bud and the bud entered the empty socket where her false eye had been. The bud opened up again to map the space so that the Jutties could make a better and more convincing eye—'

'For her, whom we shan't name. So a Velvet Isi mage possesses skills with such a flower? Colonists coming here on my Ukko haven't seen these flowers, or gathered any. Roger Wex would have told me so to curry favour. The Velvet Jutties have plucked at least one, and can use it as a way to probe an Ukko. And to probe *for* an Ukko, no doubt! Ear-flower, eye-flower . . . eye and ear of an Ukko.' She peered intently at Juke. 'Yet you know how to approach that Isi nest, and how to enter it.'

'It's protected by mana-mists and a maze of a road, and by roving Jutties and gun-domes at the tunnel mouth. I was shown the way by two Jutties—' He gestured: too many circumstances to explain.

'You never told me because the *eye* was there as well as you, and the memory hurts. Do you think I don't understand hurt? You know that nest and the way there more than you're admitting. Our Jack was bred in a snakes' nest too. Maybe, my Juke, we need to attack that Velvet Isi nest beyond Saari. We can battle for the mage's bloom. Or at least deny them the use of it before they come any closer to the Ukko-child where my real self hides away . . . Bless that bird for bringing me this bloom. Or I might never have known that Velvets possess this guide.'

Lucky lifted the flower from the carafe of cordial and rotated it to and fro: a key which might unlock an invisible door.

'How long since you were in the Velvets' nest?'

'Long enough to forget.' This was a lie.

'So they haven't found out yet how to use this guide fully.'

'*I* wouldn't be much of a guide, unlike—'

'Unlike *whom*, Juke?'

'Somebody who knew the ways through those misty woods.'

'*Who is it?*'

'Kennan . . .' The proclaimer's gaze was abstracted, and afar. 'Met him when I was returning. He'd been raiding. He tried to assault . . .'

'To assault the *wearer of the eye*?'

Juke squirmed.

'Kennan.' Now the bloom was a blade, stabbing empty air. '*He* can hardly have taken refuge with the Velvet Isi – not when ambushing their Jutties was his hobby! This flower can't possibly be that family secret of his. When you and Jack catch him for me, we mustn't kill him right away. Compel him to lead you through those woods. And lead my woodmen too. You can barter him to the Velvets to gain entry to their nest. Then seize their mana-flower for me.'

Bitterly: 'So your prince's murderer is going to prove useful . . .'

'My Juke, you're distressed at your own act of betrayal. I understand that. Didn't Bertel betray me too by dying?' Lucky inhaled the waxy odour of the flower which had trespassed on to the bed of love. 'His very scent, his very skin . . . No, he didn't send this bloom to me. The cuckoos serve the Ukko. If this flower's a sensitive organ of the Ukko is it sustained by the flow of mana? Can it drink bubberry cordial?'

A thorn of memory pricked Juke. 'They kept the flower in a flask of fluid. I don't know what the fluid was.' If Minkie Kennan could be found, would Jack and himself really have to invade the Velvets' nest?

'So it does need special sustenance, but we've no idea what.'

Again, was Jack for just a moment on the point of adding his penn'orth?

Juke hesitated. 'Might this flower have been carried here to provoke you into attacking the Velvets? To cause mayhem?'

'On account of what you just told me about the flower in their nest? Who else knew you knew this?'

'The *eye* knew,' he whispered, 'but she's dead.'

Lucky surveyed the scatter of soulflowers. 'This bed's for Jack and June, and high time too.'

At last the young couple were left alone – though how alone? Weren't Juke and the mana-priest chanting quietly in the adjacent room at the Queen's behest? Were guards clambering below, and was a dog already balancing on the roof ridge, its ears cocked?

Though the window was shut, a breeze sprang up whenever Jack moved. The fast-failing light gathered around him, brightening. He was his own candle, illuminating the heart of the room, while the walls were inky black. Cloying perfume ached from the soulflowers as the fastboy swept them all to the floor; and now the sheets shimmered, rendered phosphorescent by his touch. Quickly he unpeeled his coppery livery, exposing glossy cinnamon skin. How trim he seemed, how tight-buttocked. A person of such a hue didn't seem conspicuously nude, until he turned to face June. His pecker had risen.

85

She shucked off her shawl, exposing her chubby shoulders faintly webbed with supple snake-skin. Fumbling, she unhooked her gown. His presence illuminated her. As creamy satin fell about her feet Jack gaped at the four pink-nippled fruits of her bosoms. Those pale peeled plump pears rested upon one another within a cuddling gauzy net. The same tracery hugged all her fullness from neck to ankles, and down to her wrists. The web conducted the orchestra of her curves, at once hushing and emphasizing, except at her loins where blonde quiffs frizzed free.

A moan escaped from him. His cock quivered, so urgently lonesome in mid-air that he clutched at it. Such seizure by desire astonished him. It was as though that swollen growth, which all of his nerves and his blood now nurtured, were the robberbird which he had once lifted and hurled, forcing it to fly . . . towards that downy hen's nest which he beheld. His trembling lips craved those bosoms which were lightly yet firmly sheathed in . . . *revelation*; those four bubs which were both gossamer-swathed yet plumply exposed. His tongue thirsted for her pink mouths: the one above, which smiled with anxious coquetry, the other hiding within her nest. His nostrils twitched to capture a hint of piquant oils. His cock fretted and seethed, agog to burrow, frantic to delve.

'Jack—' She held out her arms.

And he sneezed thunderously. He tishooed explosively.

Again, and yet again.

How could this be? When he was the wind, when he was the storm. How should storm and wind possess him, rather than he, them?

He sneezed rain, he sneezed snow. Bright flakes flurried in the bedchamber. Auroras frisked upon the bed. Jack clasped his nose. It leaked gluey rheum, it wept sticky lymph. Every few seconds: another detonation – a host of ejaculations from his nostrils, forever refilling with fluids, fat raindrops and fluffy snow.

June uttered the bleat of a lamb, then the squeal of a blush-rosy piglet.

In frustration the fastboy hurtled around the room, distributing outbursts of weather and explosions of bright popping light.

Wrenching open the doors to Bertel's suite he careered through into a suite of shrouds; and his light went with him. Starched white dustsheets cloaked every item of furniture as if snow had banked high and deep, forming vague blanched statuary.

Amongst which he dashed. He needed all that extra space in which to outrun himself, to outstrip himself: a beige-skinned naked youth squeezing his snozzle, in vain – snowflakes swirled and settled on the dustcovers.

Jack grabbed a shroud to wrap around himself to quell the storm as a blanket might douse a fire. An armchair upholstered in green leather stood exposed; spring-thaw had come suddenly to that portion of the prince's parlour.

The mana-kid's sneezes ceased as suddenly as they had begun. Cloaked in linen, Jack scampered back to the love chamber where June stood flabbergasted. He dashed past her – 'I'll be back, I'll be back!'

Yanking open the other door and leaping into the in-between – no, he did not collide with a lurking Queen. Banging the door shut behind him, he trapped the tail of his sheet. Linen tore as Jack tossed the twin door wide and erupted into the parlour. Lucky was clasping her flower and the cuckoo's plume with dreamy concern.

'Juke, help me!'

Oh, Juke helped.

He hurried Jack barefoot in his sheet along a corridor, down two flights of stairs, then along another passage till they came to the nearest men's sauna. The proclaimer shed his clothes, and appropriated a small tureen of sausages.

The hot-room was crowded. Juke soon emptied it of all bare flesh but their own. He begged and bespoke the occupants to quit the tiers of slatted yellover benches. Be off, be off.

'Queen's business, fellows! There'll be mana-steam in here shortly. You'll have heard the tale of the mutton on fire in Speakers' Valley?'

Well, people had no wish to be *scalded*. Flushed bodies decamped with a tittle of grumbling and a rib of banter. Juke ladled a snake of water across the brazier coals. Steam hissed forth. He hooked out a sausage.

'Get that inside you, lad. It'll stiffen you.'

He tossed a second sausage upon the coals, where it soon burst, releasing a penetrating porky aroma.

'Gobble up, Jack. Pack some meat into you.'

Hot juice ran down the fastboy's chin, and perspiration down the rest of him.

'I just couldn't stop sneezing—'

87

'Too many flowers, and too much perfume, eh? You got pollen up your beak. Sweat it all out of you.'

'*You've* (gulp) been to bed with a woman . . . (gobble) with girls—'

Juke looked away. The tattooed lips around his nipples heaved. 'You've encountered a surfeit of desire, fastboy. Too much eagerness, too much perfume. Pack a humble sausage in!'

'I already ate tarandra heart and puffballs.'

'Heart and balls; so therefore you're ready to rut, eh? Far too ready in my opinion, too keen by far. You need rough ballast.'

'Are you sure?'

'There's lust, lad, and there's love,' was Juke's disjointed reply. 'When the two are hopelessly mixed up . . . frenzy and friendship can't tango together without some kind of calamity.'

Jack's amber eyes were wide. Sweat leaked from his brow. He rubbed his peepers roughly with the back of his hand. 'Am I really in love?' he asked.

'You have an appetite, sonny, and it's a potent one. Don't let your imagination torment you or you'll explode in sneezes or worse.'

'I don't *understand*!'

'You're too keyed up.' So saying, Juke hauled the fastboy from the steam-room through into the tiled annex.

A marble pool of cold water awaited. Juke propelled Jack into the pool, then hauled him out, spluttering and gasping. A convulsion seized the fastboy. As Juke held him from behind, he vomited a brown mess upon the tiles. Juke lowered him. 'Now rinse your mouth out in the water.'

While a shocked Jack was complying, Juke fetched a towel and the lad's sheet and one more sausage.

'Eat this now. You'll need it. Can't keep your ladylove waiting *too* long.' He wiped the lad down and patted him dry; then himself. 'I'll be with you in spirit tonight, Demon Jack.'

Jack swayed, then stood firm. 'I was too eager. I'll still be eager.'

'Controllably, lad. You've had something else to think about.'

When the two of them returned to the parlour Serlachius was snoozing on the sofa. Through in the nuptial chamber, where a couple of candles now burned, Lucky perched in her black weeds upon the bed, consoling and cheering June. Waxy mana-flower in one hand, the Queen was stroking June's snakeskin-clad knee, a seeming seductress.

'—a bit of a confession, my dear,' they heard. 'Even my prince sometimes – helplessly besotted with me though he was! Well, he drank too much . . . And here they come already! Wasn't long, was it?'

Across June's lap lay Jack's loose livery. Upon that coppery fabric: the four cord dollies as well as a scatter of crumbs from the gingerbreads into which she had made considerable inroads.

With a shy indignation June addressed Juke. 'What did you *do* with him?' She didn't trouble to cover her visible, if skin-suited, bosoms. Why, Juke was a fellow mutant – even if he did look normal.

'Quick sauna.' Juke began gathering up trampled soulflowers. 'Too much pollen, hmm?' He refrained from any mention of sausages.

'Dog fell off the roof,' June told her sheet-wrapped beau. 'Ooh it yowled. Must 'ave broke its back. That's a bit unlucky.'

'Not at all,' the Queen assured her. 'Death feasted on a doggy soul. Death's been duped and led astray, do you see? All harm's gone from here, and Jack's cured of his sneezes by the steam.' Bestowing a final pat, Lucky arose. 'Juke: you'll stay with my priest, in case . . .' Of another outburst of sneezing? She wagged the mana-flower. 'I'm for a sauna too, Juke. This bloom'll wilt without the right care.'

To carry the flower into a steamy semblance of a furnace? Surely an extreme expedient.

So once again the young couple were alone together, and now in one another's arms, June's skin-suit sleek against the silk sheets.

In the candlelight Jack glowed softly. No wild spasms of illumination pulsed, nor did sudden gusts drag at the flames. No snow flurried; he was contained within himself. He wouldn't release his power prematurely into the room but into June herself.

She gazed enchanted at his darkly darling eyelashes, registering them fully for the first time. She touched them ever so lightly with a fingertip. His lids fluttered trustfully: the hair of the eye, the delicate sleeves of flesh guarding tender moisture – as, much lower down, her curly fleece girt her moist declivity.

He was freckled across the bridge of his slim nose. You hardly noticed on account of that wholesale freckle-hue to his skin.

Their kisses were savoury, greedy, and sticky. They fed one

another with tongues as urgently as a bird regurgitating food into a chick and the chick gulping.

And now he could wait no more. Vibrancy met the voluptuous. He was young and timeless. She had watched billies humping the girl goats, billies who first sprayed their own heads and chests with piss and spunk. She had watched drakes treading ducks. Oh he was a force of nature, this fastboy. He exploded within her. She could swear she felt the spatter of his seed.

'*Four* times,' she insisted, hugging him with arms and legs.

Her own nerves were becoming alert and impatient, then impetuous. She clasped his buttocks. Her fingernails pricked him and pried at the solidity between the root of his scrotum and shaft – in that place where she herself was cleft. She explored the pucker of his bum. Yes, and yes. White hen clutching hard brown egg within her parted feathers, clucking broodily deep in her throat, her four breasts cushioning him . . .

They continued.

After a while he broke off to gobble gingerbreads.

Lucky chased all the users out of the sauna, too. A women's sauna. Word spread: '*The Queen's taking the steam—!*' Not within living memory had Lucky Sariola done so, nor had any of her many daughters, no never.

Inside the emptied steam-room Lucky shed her black weeds, swiftly as could be. Even after she stripped, the hot air stifled her. Dizzily she hunched upon the yellover bench close by the brazier box. She inhaled from the mana-bloom to refresh herself.

'Can't risk you fading, flower—'

She dunked the Ukko-bloom into the wooden water bucket. Then she laid the dripping stem and head of petals upon the charcoals. Such a sizzling and spitting! A wraith of smoke and sweet sickly fragrance sucked into her lungs. The flower writhed. She tried to hear words, but in vain.

Above the grilling twisting bloom a figure was taking hazy shape as if the flower's spirit stood erect to escape. A doll of smoke. A young woman with ash-white hair . . . Her twin! Her blonde sister! She was armed with a sword – or was it a rifle? Come to me, Find me, Fight for me. Robes of fumes. One of her eyes was a wee hovering bright spark.

The twin had altered since Lucky last saw her in a mirror in her tiny cabin aboard that steel eggshell of a spaceship, *Katarina*. In the gentler gravity of an Ukko she had become taller, more willowy and lissom. Yet this could only be her very own lost self hovering in miniature above the charcoals: Queen of an Ukko.

Exultation fevered Lucky. In sheer yearning she sang out, 'Paula, my Paula!' Beguiled by the sight and scent and touch of her, her prince had cried similarly – almost involuntarily – in that bedchamber where Jack and June now lay entwined.

Such a glimpse was well worth the physical loss of the flower. A message from her self to herself. A militant message, too. Fight to regain her self and soul and her sanity! Her twin was aware of her and craved for her quite as much as she herself craved – even though her twin was no longer a perfect reflection at all, indeed almost wore the semblance of a stranger. But then, Lucky was a stranger to herself; and had been so for centuries. Thus this vision could only flood her with hope.

Lucky stared, transfixed. As the last trace of the ear-flower disintegrated to hot dust the figure faded.

Knotty passed the second vodka bottle of the night onward to Pieman. The recipient's palms were less crusty than his knuckles. After swigging, he rubbed his lips with the bowl of his hand rather than the backside before thrusting the spirit at Lammas, who was usually so temperate. 'Oodles of royal vodka's all very nice,' he groused. 'We can pickle ourselves, an' we never need leave.'

Lammas wetted his whistle. 'Ah, but we do need *leave* – from Herself. We need leave to leave.'

The woolly crooner perched on the edge of one of the double beds. Three fellow mocky-men crowded the other bed for mutual support. The final inmate of the chamber lolled in an arm-chair. Arto was fairly sozzled. His stockinged feet failed to reach the floor. His striped waistcoat was unbuttoned, though the two buttons torn off at Onnekyla had been replaced. One white glove on, and one off. He waved limply, conducting the discussion.

Brocade drapes were closed, but an open window admitted breeze. An oil-lamp burned. A tapestry on the wall showed heroes with long white windblown hair in an open boat upon surging choppy jade-green waves, with an orange-hued storm rolling by.

'Are we *tied up* here, then?' Knotty's hessian tunic had rucked up; he scratched a ropy brown knee. 'I say we slip loose without any by-your-leave at all. Tomorrow's as good a day as any. Asking invites refusal.'

Arto belched. 'Me old cott'll be squeaking and groaning for me. And as for the missus . . . Ach my boy's no use to me. I wouldn't beg his help.'

'Do we *walk* all the way home?' asked Lammas.

Pieman leered at the crooner. 'You'll sing for our suppers on the way, right? I don't see us being brought back forcibly to the palace. We'll be leaving June and Hilda here.'

'Well, that's plain as pie.'

'What do you mean by that, Knotty?'

'Oh, *nothing*. But listen: we mustn't steal anything, not ponies nor a boat. Arto: are you really up to tramping all those hundreds of keys?'

'I'll squeak along, never you fret.'

'Couldn't we at least fork out for a boat trip to the end of the fjord to get us started?' asked Lammas.

'Waste of money,' was Arto's opinion.

'Pride's all very well.'

'Don't flaunt our assets. Gives people bad ideas. Might invite robbery. Our cotts back home could be pillaged.'

'Do we have to be so mean?'

'What with all the applause, you've been picking up airs and graces, Lammy. We're *mocky-men*. Don't be precious.'

Pieman agreed. 'Discreet's the word.'

Chinwag continued tipsily. They would trek eastward till the Great Fjord narrowed to a trickle. Maybe the fjord petered out into bogs. Next, head south-east towards the domain of Saari. Take care to avoid yon serpents' nest up to the north-east of Threelakes. Why, they'd be back home in Outo in a month or so, unforeseen circumstances permitting.

'Here's to absconding,' proposed Knotty, who had the bottle again.

6 · CURSE OF THE CUCKOO

Minnow van Maanen, née Sariola, swanked into the banqueting hall hand in hand with Osmo. Her brand-new gown of magenta satin cut a dignified dash. So did her new husband in a green and gold waistcoat, creamy silk shirt, matching breeches with golden ribbon rosettes on the knees, and brass-buckled shoes. Purse and keys, sheathknife and lightpistol adorned Osmo's favourite belt which had been freshly oiled and polished. (The clasp was that bulgy-eyed brass fish swallowing its own tail.) High-heeled and high-soled black boots, on which a cobbler in town had worked overtime, elevated Minnow shoulder-high to Osmo. She had plunged several spangled combs into her frizz of black hair in emulation of sister Eva. Minnow also wore Osmo's cygnet ring with the swan of death engraved in minuscule.

He needn't wear such a ring any longer; not after the previous night when she had at last bestowed her gift on him, of her maidenhead, and longlife.

Nodding to left and right, Minnow acknowledged those who were waiting in the hall that morning. *Late* that morning. She and Osmo had both slept in. He had spent well over an hour bathing and shaving, trimming his moustache, combing his wavy chestnut hair to perfection, considering his outfit for the day, and admiring himself in the mirror.

Maybe he'd been looking for subtle hints of longlife several years before he could possibly notice any; or rather, *fail* to observe – any further sign of ageing. Unless, of course, he'd been inspecting himself for early symptoms of the alternative to long-life . . . That would have been rather rude of him in the circumstances! Truth to tell, he'd seemed perfectly purry – cat with its cream – humming to himself.

('And there's Mrs Holmberg,') Minnow reminded herself. The dumpy frumpy owl of a housekeeper stood close to Annetta, the under-housekeeper. Apparently Mrs Holmberg didn't see eye to eye with that lass. Annetta's girlish pigtails and big brown eyes conveyed an impression of guilelessness which was quite bogus since Annetta made it her business to know what was worth knowing. Osmo's dad seemed to prefer her to the older servant.

Dear old chap, Alvar! He could have worn something less casual for this levee than an old mulberry dressing gown. A black notebook poked from its pocket, his fingers were stained with ink, and smoke puffed from his droop-bowl tammywood pipe. Mrs Holmberg was wrinkling her nose at the drifting odour of weed soaked in nutmeg and rum. Such a sourpuss. Still, it was she who was in charge of the household; so would she repay cultivating in preference to Annetta?

And did Lady Minnow van Maanen really need to bother herself about the moods of Annettas and Holmbergs? Maybe yes!

Looking so young and little, despite her high boots, Minnow ought to impress.

How would Eva be faring as chatelaine of the aitch-house at the other side of the turquoise lake? Minnow's elder sister always had more presence. More body. More flesh and more of a coiffure.

However, Osmo was taking his Minnow very seriously; as well he should, seeing as she'd saved his bacon – and his spirit, from invasion by the monstrous Isi mana-mage. She'd become a bit of a shamaness in the process. For the first time ever someone had glimpsed an alien world and a serpent's mind.

('There's Septimus the Bailiff . . .') Plump and roguish and a bit of a toper judging by the amount he'd put away during the celebrations the previous evening. It was still necessary to remind herself who everybody was. Yet what a relief to be away from Pohjola Palace and her mad mother, even if Osmo's keep wasn't half as grand.

The previous night *Minnow* had taken Osmo. She had ridden bare-belly upon him, deflowering herself upon his pommel, working herself into a lather – and him climactically into a froth, chattering to herself the while: *'The arrow's in her quiver, the fist's in the glove, deep in the velvet, eh?'* First time ever, even if her actual girdle had been lost in Viper's den three whole weeks beforehand.

Wasn't bad, wasn't bad at all. Could get quite attached to it. So long as she was the rider. Also, his froth ran out of her promptish, gluing up his curlies and not hers. He wouldn't beget a bun in her oven before she was ready for a bairn. That was her theory, at least. It seemed eminently plausible.

Otherwise, might she have been fertile the night before?

In Viper's den she'd still been having the last seep of her bleeding. When Viper swayed her and Osmo to imagine they were in a bridal bed, her scrap of rag had come loose along with her borrowed baggy breeches. Osmo hadn't exactly noticed the rag at the time, nor had he enquired subsequently. He hadn't much appreciated her earlier account of *bungs*, made from tundra spongemoss.

Down south here, so it seemed (*thanks, Annetta*), women used cotton wadding instead.

Three weeks had passed since that business in the mage's cave. Hence her wedding night probably hadn't been baby-time. Nevertheless she had insisted on riding her hubby-horse as opposed to being ridden, and she intended to continue to do so.

First time ever; not bad at all. Thanks to her equestrian activity in bed Osmo was longlife. And she was the Lady of Maananfors. Maananfors seemed a pleasant town. She was dying to talk to Eva; hence all the combs in her hair. In hindsight her abduction seemed almost romantic. Almost!

All these strangers to get to know.

('There's Sam Peller.')

Osmo's silver-haired bondsman with the trim white beard and whey face and paranoiac alertness . . .

It had been a busy five days since Osmo and Minnow arrived in Maananfors after tramping past ten million trees and circling a hundred lakes before finally catching a boat ride. A prime item on the agenda – aside from the wedding – had been the armoury, brimful with weapons recently sold by Juttahats of the Brindled Isi nest at a very cheap price in golden ors. Neither the serpents nor their servants were known to have much use for coins even as trinkets.

What was their precise motive? Alien motives weren't precise. The Brazen Isi had recently sent a few raiders into the van Maanen domain. Were the Brindleds hoping to spur Maananfors to mount a punitive attack against the Brazens? Were they hoping to forestall an invasion by the Brazens, launched while Osmo was missing, presumed dead?

Sam's surmises were irrelevant now that Osmo had come home, infuriated at Minnow's mother.

'My dear gosling,' Osmo murmured to her who had perched on him the previous night, and that morning too when he woke aroused. 'My duckling, my chick, my wife, my *life*.' He squared his shoulders and stuck out his chest, displaying to all in the hall his wholehearted approval of his bride, his perfect satisfaction with her. 'We'll fix your mother's tricks.' He hadn't yet indicated how. Osmo was as firmly set on this venture as he was intoxicated with the same Queen's daughter.

Minnow teetered as Osmo handed her up on to the dais, to sit at the high table. She tottered. Maybe the boots were a bit excessive. She'd wished to stand tall, and walk tall.

But she couldn't sit tall. Not until the housekeeper, in her dowdy gingham frock of dark blue and brown check, hastened to the dais bearing a tapestry cushion which she must have been hiding behind her back for this express purpose. Why couldn't there have been a cushion on the chair already, as yesterday? Had Mrs Holmberg removed it deliberately? Was the cushion a snub, a put-down as well as a lift-up?

A maid bore a tray of coffee and spiced buns. The housekeeper favoured Minnow with a sweet smile as she eased the cushion into position. Around her eyes were birds' feet of disappointment, bravely borne.

'That wasn't quite necessary, Mrs Holmberg,' Minnow said brightly, mingling bonhomie with rebuke.

The housekeeper turned her attention to Minnow's husband. 'I thought you weren't coming back, Lord Osmo! I thought you were dead like poor Vivi.' Oh, this was impertinent, almost verging on outrageous. To mention Osmo's former amusement on the morning after the wedding night! 'Annetta isn't a *patch* on Vivi. Whereas Amelie—'

'Whereas Amelie is your niece,' growled Osmo.

'It was your father who persuaded your mother, bless her memory, to appoint Annetta just because Amelie has this wee bias against paintings hanging straight in case bad luck sits upon them.' (Surely not in the same manner as Minnow sat upon the cushion!) 'Annetta used to report all about you to Lady Johanna, bless her bones, so I suppose that was why your mother favoured her. Dear me, I hadn't wanted to mention this now that your mother's dearest wish has come true,' nodding at Minnow, 'bless her heart.'

So that was why Mrs Holmberg had sequestered the cushion: to bend Osmo's ear while he was in the mood for making grand decisions. The housekeeper must have been bottling grudges up inside her till their buzzing had befuddled her. Though Annetta couldn't hear the exchange, she was looking smug.

'My husband's rather busy this morning,' piped Minnow. 'Maybe I can arbitrate in a few weeks' time when I'm more familiar with everyone.'

'Definitely you must decide about such things, my duckling,' agreed Osmo, and he waved the housekeeper away. 'Scoot, Mrs Holmberg; be off with you.'

The aproned maid poured steamy coffee. In the rest of the hall scullyboys were offering trays of cordials. Tapestries of trees draped the speckly pink granite walls. Tubby black stoves wore flue hats all the way up to the heavily timbered roof. Tall windows stood ajar. Chandeliers were wide glass nests where birds of crystal might roost, tinkling. Really rather grand, if not quite a palace. Out in the courtyard, held back by guards with lightrifles, knots of townsfolk were waiting to spill into the hall for the levee.

Levy, too; those new guns would need hands to wield them.

'I'll be deciding about other things as well,' Minnow reminded Osmo. 'More than mere housework.'

'*That*,' and he grinned, 'goes without saying.'

When Osmo had returned to his keep with Minnow just short of the mid-cusp of July, preparations for the usual Lucky's Day feast had been in train, though without much enthusiasm. It was well over a month since a cuckoo had cackled in Maananfors town square that Juke Nurmi had shot Lord Osmo's sky-boat down in flames, and that the Queen had welcomed Osmo's assassin at court; welcomed him even though a Sariola daughter had been aboard the sky-boat, seized by their lord after Lucky insulted him! (By now it seemed more as if the princess in question had *eloped* – even if she hadn't actually done so to begin with.)

In the wake of the awful news old Alvar had resumed the reins of lordship which he'd forsaken in his son's favour to concentrate on his *Chronicles*. Alvar's grief was peppered with resentment (Sam had hinted) and even outrage. Would Alvar be forced to take on the nuisance of a young new wife so as to beget another heir? Alvar had greeted Minnow's advent with open arms. She was his deliverance as well as his son's salvation.

Out of respect for tradition, the chronicler hadn't quite been able to bring himself to cancel the impending feast. This had easily metamorphosed into a celebration of Lucky's elfin daughter, of her wedding to Osmo, and of his salvation from sky-boat crash, marooning, and Isi enchantment.

For the wedding ceremony Minnow's father-in-law (to-be) had dressed sprucely in black and gold striped jacket and scarlet cummerbund – whereas the dressing gown he wore today declared: farewell to humdrum cares. How Alvar had grinned last night (and scribbled in his notebook at high table) while Osmo narrated Minnow's merits and his adventures with her in a woodland mana-maze. No one could have been unimpressed, despite her girlish looks and diminutive stature.

The mana-priest had bumbled his way earnestly through the ceremony. Baldy Seppo Hakulinen was such a twit compared with Serlachius back in Sariolinna. Afterwards, a tattooist had pricked a petite black picture of a leaping sprat just below the image of speaker's lips on Osmo's right arm. Black, for her coaly Sariola hair.

This morning Osmo had additional revelations to impart about the *delirium* of the Queen which could prove very dangerous for everybody on Kaleva. Hubbub was brewing out in the courtyard. People were becoming impatient.

'Admit everybody,' Osmo bid Sam Peller. Sam signalled accordingly to the guards; and in flooded blue-clad fellows of the town watch and farmers and fishermen and tradesmen and burgesses, and the skipper of the paddle-steamer and the priest from the kirk; and also—

The cause of commotion had been a prim-faced fellow with curly black hair. A gaberdine cloak was slung around him. His left leg was swathed in a puttee of dirty bandage. His crudely fashioned crutch of tammywood stomped the waxed yellover floorboards. And on his right shoulder there perched a cuckoo.

The bird's claws clung tight to him. Accumulated droppings whitened the top of his cloak. Never had anyone seen a cuckoo seated upon a person's shoulder – like a second head of scaly green plumes with big feline eyes and ears! The stranger gimped to a halt. Surely he was a most remarkable shaman, but also a singularly scruffy one.

Minnow burst out laughing. 'Wethead, Wethead,' she gasped. 'Whatever are you doing here?'

For the moment her husband failed to understand her merry astonishment. 'Who *is* this freak? What's the meaning of this?'

The bird cackled. Seizing a clump of the oddity's hair in its beak, it launched itself. All of the fellow's locks tore loose at once. He cried out, suddenly bald as a stone. He dropped the crutch to clutch at his denuded skull as the cuckoo beat its way up to one of the timbers of the tie-beam roof. There it settled, a wig hanging from its mouth. Indeed, a wig.

Spectators couldn't decide whether to chortle or marvel. Set in the right side of the man's denuded cranium were two steel discs the size of pennies.

And Osmo realized: *it was the Earthman, Roger Wex.* An artificial mind shared Wex's brain with him, poured into him through those plugged holes in his head. Wex had been advising the

Queen in a buffoonish fashion. He had prattled about mana-energy while Osmo was bespeaking the everything machine to activate itself.

He'd succeeded, too! Virtually. Almost. He'd brought that machine to the very brink of obeying – only for Elmer to barge in and reap the reward, Princess Eva.

Ah but had the pernicious Queen not cheated him, precious Minnow would never have been at his side right now; his wife, his life, his darling duckling . . .

Minnow's glee trickled into giggles.

'We took my mother's statue apart together, him and me,' she told Osmo. 'That was splendid,' she told herself. 'Greetings, Roger!' she called to the discomfited figure.

Osmo did recall Eva mentioning some such prank, when they tangoed in the palace ballroom. In evident perplexity Wex eyed Minnow seated at high table daintily gorgeous in her satin.

'Am I too late?' he exclaimed.

Up on the roof beam the cuckoo was wagging his wig to and fro. Was the bird contemplating tearing his hairpiece apart though it failed to sniff any meat attached? Wex raised his hand. He might have been about to reach out to Minnow. Second thoughts converted this motion into a plea to the cuckoo. Control exerted itself. He practically stood to attention. 'May I congratulate you?'

'You may congratulate us both,' Osmo said acidly.

Gripped by a further spasm of hilarity, Minnow beckoned the Earthman closer.

{*She's convulsed with gaiety, my Roger.*} Thus his other half diagnosed.

'It's the hilarity of relief,' he retorted; 'relief at a chance of escape—' From her abductor and ravisher.

{*No! Minnow's in genuine good humour.*}

Up until this moment Wex had been envisaging sanctuary for Minnow at the Earthkeep in Landfall, and never mind any qualms on Pen Conway's part. The black woman with her womb ripped out might well be Earth's official Resident on Kaleva – {*Penelope Conway's hysterectomy was a voluntary political decision on her part to minimize mana-mania and false consciousness.*} – but Wex was Earth's roving agent, with liberty to make unusual decisions provided that these were upheld by his wetwear.

'She can't be happy,' he argued.

*

99

'Does he normally talk to himself?' Osmo enquired of his wife.

'Not to himself exactly. To his *other* self.'

'Ah . . .' Gently: 'Do I take it that you nursed a certain fellow-feeling for him, my gosling? A certain mischievous sympathy?'

'Oh yes,' she agreed cheerfully. 'I would, wouldn't I?' she asked herself. 'Mum-mum-mumble, eh?'

'Now you have me to mumble to.'

'Oh dear. Well, I *was* abducted, wasn't I? Roger must have supposed. Roger must have presumed. He travelled all this way. How perfectly daftly romantic. What *are* you doing here, Wethead? Roger?' Leaning towards the Earthman, she mouthed: 'We're blissfully married, Osmo and I!'

{*She doesn't appear to be under a sway, my Roger. Not remotely so.*}

'So what *happened*?' Wex stood slack-jawed till his features reset themselves, and he announced: 'Lord Osmo, I have some news for you—'

'And I, for you,' Osmo replied. 'If I read the situation accurately – please correct me if I'm wrong – you seem to have marched into my hall labouring under a considerable illusion about myself and my bride.' (Minnow was nodding emphatically.) 'Though at least the bird doffed your cap for you!'

Bailiff Septimus jerked his thumb upward smartly in the direction of the roof beam, prompting guffaws. However, with security ever in mind, Sam Peller was keeping a tight eye on the cloaked intruder, and his hand was on his lightpistol.

'If you want my opinion, Lord Osmo—' began Sam.

Wex said, 'That cuckoo's been bothering me for weeks. I stumbled upon a whole conclave of cuckoos in a cave—'

'You stumbled,' asked Minnow, 'and broke your leg?'

'No, that happened earlier. My other self told me to *break a leg* for luck—'

'Few fellows,' said Osmo in good humour, 'would limp into my hall and blab so blatantly about rescuing a maiden.'

'I spoke out of turn, Lord Osmo. The bird confused me by snatching my hair.'

Sam had eased his pistol out, and was moving alongside Wex. He signed to a guard to cover the Earthman with his lightrifle.

'I notice,' said Sam, 'you're standing up straight enough without your crutch. That crutch was a hoax. *Eh?*' With the muzzle Sam tapped one of the steel pennies implanted in Wex's scalp. At once Wex stiffened. His arms flexed. His hands became hard blades. Sam had skipped away, and held his gun level. 'Don't you move. He could easily be acting for the Queen, my Lord.'

'I *did* break my leg!'

'He could be here to avenge the felicitous elopement.'

'I'm not involved with the Queen. I'm not interested in vengeance. I needed a crutch but maybe it's time to get rid of it.'

Osmo took a deep breath.

'Roger Wex: you'll not attempt any harm against my person, or any of my personnel. *This is spoken.* You'll tell me if harm was your intention. You'll tell me if the Queen sent you. *I bespeak you.*'

The Earthman shuddered. His eyelids fluttered, interrupting his view of Osmo, freezing what he saw into separate segments. His facial and throat muscles became supple fingers manipulating his organ of speech, and a rolling fruity voice issued from his lips.

'*We are immune to mana-effects, Lord Osmo. I am the wetwear that guards his mind. I can prevent my host from being coerced and impelled.*'

'Roger, poor you!' squealed Minnow.

The Wex-body regarded her with a mixture of exasperation and affection. '*Except perhaps by yourself, Princess. I have been trying to cope with this distracting flux of feeling, which I must admit to appreciating even if I cannot approve it. Earth's security is paramount. Your happiness is noted by us. My Roger will not upset that happiness, Lord Osmo,*' the voice assured her husband.

('What can a Minnow say to *that*?') she asked herself.

'You appear to be cherished,' Osmo murmured. 'Quite rightly so.'

Minnow laughed, she shed a tear, she clasped her husband's hand. 'He's harmless – but how sad for him.'

'*I am somewhat in flux,*' confessed the wetwear. '*We are experimental. We are a prototype protected person – in case the Isi attempt to control humanity in the way they command their Juttahats.*'

'Exactly!' cried Osmo. 'That's exactly it!'

'*Queen Lucky did not send us to your keep. We came here of our own accord. How gauchely.*'

'Valiantly,' suggested Minnow. ('A girl can't help but be flattered, can she? No harm in that. Keeps a hubby on his toes. Even if it's only barely the day after the night before.')

'*We would not dream of harming you, Lord Osmo. Literally! We only dream*'

101

*of chess problems. Queen checks Castle. Castle takes Queen. I must release my
control. Farewell, Princess Minnow.'*

'Lady van Maanen,' she corrected him, to be on the safe side.
No more misunderstandings, please.

Roger Wex gasped and gaped. He choked and coughed and
spluttered. He knuckled tears from his eyes.

'Castle *checks* Queen,' mused Osmo. 'Keep takes Keep. What's
your news then, Wex?'

The Earthman recollected. 'Juke Nurmi shot you down and is
living in Pohjola Palace now—'

'Don't I know it!'

'The everything machine is supplying the Queen with a pile
of weapons. She might use these against you when she learns
you survived.'

'The possibility did cross my mind. I shall be delighted to see
her lead an attack. Come quickly, Queen, if you dare.'

'You must be very angry at her on account of the contest and
the mutants.'

'For ever.' A concise enough reply. Osmo nodded up at the
cuckoo which was still worrying Wex's wig indifferently. 'I suppose these scraps of *tattle* were intended as your safe conduct so
you could wander in here and carry off a certain person?'

'There were hundreds of cuckoos in a cave. They were upload-
ing a mass of gossip from all over Kaleva—'

'Up-*loading*? What does that mean?'

'I'm sorry; it means dumping data from memory to a main
CPU. A central processing unit. An Ukko, by any other name.
Maybe they were clearing out their own memories—'

'Skip the hex-words, Wex, and keep to the point.'

'Hex-words . . . ? Oh, I see! Those cuckoos cackled about Nurmi
and the weapons and some armoured self-steering vehicle which
malfunctioned – a war-wagon berserked. I was dazed by the reek.
I learned how you and the Princess were shot down. I'd been
optimistic despite my broken leg. Then I despaired at the folly
of my journey.'

'Indeed,' said Osmo pointedly.

'I had to go somewhere next. To Landfall; that was the idea.
I didn't have much heart. Besides, that cuckoo had infested
me . . .'

The bird had persistently ridden on his shoulder when not
making forays to catch some leppi or little bird to eat. What had

he himself eaten? Fish and fungi and berries, and emergency foodbars.

He opened his cloak like some tinker displaying spoons, revealing pockets little and large. His green shirt and breeches were extremely creased and grimy.

Wex (and his other self too) had hoped that this cuckoo might confide in him after a while – genuinely confide, voicing its own viewpoint rather than just prattling gossip. This could be a breakthrough in relations between people and cuckoos, supposing that cuckoos were capable of expressing a personal viewpoint. And if this wasn't the case – if cuckoos were purely instruments of an Ukko, creatures possessing a high degree of vocal mimicry which had been commandeered – dare one hope that here might be a key to the conundrum of an Ukko?

Wex (and his other self) hadn't been too eager to hurry back to civilization in case his green-plumed companion might quit him, pest though it was. Actually, the bird was a distraction from his desolation – just so long as it didn't try to peck out a juicy eyeball!

This particular gossip-bird had remained stubbornly dumb. Not *absolutely* dumb. Intermittently it muttered to itself – inarticulate noises, reminiscent of a cruel parody of Princess Minnow.

('Huh!')

How many times had Wex encouraged that bird with, 'Sing me a story, tell me a tale'? Whether he addressed the cuckoo as its own creature or alternatively as a mere mouthpiece, he'd made no headway.

Had he offended by trespassing into that cave? Had he brought upon himself a jinx? Would the bird use him as a perch and latrine for ever after, rendering him flagrantly conspicuous in the eyes of all beholders, an object of superstition and suspicion? Earth's agent was cumbered and frustrated. Recently Wex had tried to gimp rapidly away from the bird; his healed leg wasn't quite up to sprinting. He'd tried to hide; all in vain. Curse of the cuckoo.

It went without saying that the bird couldn't be killed or injured. A growl from his audience confirmed this. Wex's predicament confirmed the taboo.

'Captive cuckoo in a cage, puts all Kaleva in a rage!' shouted someone. How much worse to slay a cuckoo. The man who'd called out was of slight build but with the hefty arms and

103

shoulders of a hauler of nets. He would need a strong right arm to sustain his hand, which was petrified into a grey, heavy sculpt of rock. A crimson tattoo of a brooch around a black mole disfigured rather than decorated the top of one cheek.

'Who's that?' hissed Minnow.

'Hans Werner . . . Stabbed two young folk a year ago. I bespoke his hand to stone. It's the day after the anniversary of his punishment. Dog to its vomit, mm?'

And who was that robust blond fellow standing in seeming solidarity beside the fisherman? Was he a friend who helped Werner carry on his trade despite his partial petrification?

Osmo shuffled in his seat. 'That's Per Villanen—'

He was the husband of Vivi's sister and son-in-law of the very Viktor who had snatched Minnow from her bed for his lord, and who had died in the sky-boat crash. Per Villanen had sailed grieving family members to Vivi Rintala's funeral a year since.

Dead young woman, then dead father. Osmo might be said to have brought tragedy upon the Rintala family.

'Maybe,' said Wex, 'that bird's been set upon me as a kind of tag to register my whereabouts . . .'

When he finally arrived in the van Maanen domain, Wex with his crutch and his cuckoo had provoked gawks and charm-signs. He also heard news which was bubbling hot: of Osmo's sudden return, with a princess.

Hurry as he might, Wex missed the wedding. His wretched bird could have told him just as soon as any cuckoo in Maananfors learned. Wasn't it obvious that all cuckoos shared awareness in common?

'Ukko-ukkoo,' croaked the cuckoo. At last it let Wex's wig fall. He scrambled to retrieve the hairpiece. Clapping the wig upon his scalp, he squeezed with both hands like one of Tycho Cammon's former victims whose head was on the verge of bursting.

Osmo's white-haired bondsman remained suspicious. 'Doesn't Earth's special agent keep a powerful communicator in one of those pockets, eh Mr Wex? When you bust your leg couldn't you have called for the help of one those dovecraft from Landfall?'

'This seemed,' said Wex carefully, 'to be a personal affair.'

Sam tapped the side of his nose: a word to the wise. 'He's a *rogue* agent, in my opinion. The noise in his noddle has unhinged him.'

However, the Lord of Maananfors had weighty words to say upon this very matter.

'He's better off, Sam, than *we* would be if the Isi were forever whispering in our minds!' Whereupon Osmo stood up to address the gathering.

He spoke of the Queen's faith that somewhere on Kaleva there lay hidden a juvenile maturing form of the star-spanning, mana-spacefaring Ukko which brought human beings to this world. Passions, raptures, rages, and manias of the inhabitants of Kaleva were its mana-diet, its stimulus. Events were its nurture just as the telling of the great old tales of heroes impelled the elder Ukko to shift itself across the star-field carrying colonists. This was the fare an Ukko demanded; the fee, and the food.

Osmo waxed eloquent in prelude to full-blown proclaiming. Wasn't it plain that the elder Ukko has settled people on Kaleva – and other Ukkos later brought the Isi to this world – just as the testy-fly laid its egg on a feverish living body? To hatch hotly and feed upon fever?

If an Ukko could be steered by stories, and could in turn sway men's minds, an Ukko itself might be swayed by the Isi to massage the minds of mortals. If the alien serpents could find the young Ukko and beguile it, they might learn how to rule the minds of men in the way that the serpents ruled their Juttahats.

('How about women's minds—?')

People would be puppets.

'The Queen's quest for her echo-twin must fail! Otherwise she'll lead the Isi heedlessly to their goal. Maybe only she can enter the young Ukko – just as she entered the secret heart of the elder Ukko four centuries ago. We'll divert her and distract her and destroy her hopes. I shall. You shall. This is spoken.'

He was a hero, proclaiming to his people. 'We'll act together to safeguard the human soul!' His fury at Lucky had full moral authority. 'I'll gladly risk my longlife unlike Tapper Kippan who hides in his woods.' Fondly he stroked Minnow's frizz, and a comb fell out. 'In any case, my friends, a war is *inevitable.*'

Ukko-ukkoo, croaked the cuckoo from aloft.

'News of my survival will enrage the Queen. But we shall also provoke her.' Oh yes, these things *would* happen. 'I've decided that we shall garrison the aitch-house at Loxmithlinna with or without agreement of the Loxmiths. Yesterday I spoke by communicator to Elmer Loxmith. He shilly-shallied. A week from today we shall cross the turquoise lake in a fleet of ships. Thanks

105

to Mr Peller's activities during my absence we have the weapons. We'll enforce our will for the sake of the human spirit.'

('And I'll get to visit Eva—') Minnow wasn't averse to invading her snooty sister's keep.

Osmo singled out the captain of the paddle-steamer. 'Skipper: there'll be Brindled Isi rocket-launchers mounted on your deck. We'll blast the portcullis of the aitch-house open if we need to; and soon the Queen will come like a frantic stingfly. We'll shatter her.'

Did he mean: *kill* her? Osmo's rage was infectious. His audience was provoked, not least stone-Hans who brandished his petrified hand. *'Shatter her! Shatter her!'*

With an effort Osmo controlled himself, for it was important to act magnanimously. Affectionately he caressed his wife. 'We'll imprison the Queen for life; and I'll live a long time to guard her.'

'Put her in the niche, Lord!' cried somebody.

'Yes, in the niche!'

'Stone woman!'

'Statue of herself!'

Osmo flushed. What, stand Lucky in that nook behind the arras? In the very same nook where the tyrant Tycho had stood petrified . . . until Juke Nurmi freed the stone man to murder Vivi? Oh no, don't make the same mistake twice.

Besides which . . .

'I don't know for sure that Lucky Sariola can safely be bespoken. She may be immune. No, my people, we'll carve a dungeon in the granite beneath our keep, rather like the ice-room. A dungeon with a granite door. I'll appoint a regent Queen.'

Minnow squeaked excitedly.

'Indeed, my duckling.'

('Eva: now just you kneel to Queen Minnow! Isn't our Minnow quite the shamaness too, fresh from gobsmacking a monstrous mutant mana-mage? Poor mad Mummy. She'll be even madder now.')

{*It is vital we contact Penelope Conway soon. Her surmise about an Ukko-child is not the fancy of a wombless woman; pardon my false consciousness. Earth needs more Ukkos as sledges to the stars, my Roger. If a new one has indeed grown here on this world*—}

From a seed, from a rock, from a skein of stories?

{We must reactivate Carter. Concentrate! I refer to the cartographic satellite. Armed with military lasers, moreover. Carter has capacities.}

And capacitors too, but not much of a mind.

{It has a proto-mind, centuries simpler than mine. I feel sympathy with its silent trance, floating in the void on standby.}

Wex had lost Minnow. No, he had found her. Lostandfound, foundandlost. Had he lost himself too? His wetwear had taken control of his voice in front of her.

{I shaped my own voice, my Roger. When I control you I grieve for a human being to be controlled. False thinking should be controlled. I let you have your head, and your heart, in the matter of Princess Minnow. We have been wayward, we are rogue.}

Surely his other self had hankered for Minnow too. Wetwear in love with a wayward girl!

{Not a girl, but a woman and a heroine. What folly, though!}

The cuckoo flapped down from the beam to sink its claws into Wex's shoulder. Once more its plumes and its weight and its ammoniacal odour assaulted him. The bird rocked to and fro and began enunciating broody quasi-words, wheezy throat-throbbings, which made no sense at all. Its silences had been preferable. This was a language of lunacy! Would he have to listen to this for days, for weeks, for months?

Could the satellite locate the Ukko-child? It had failed to peer through mana-mists in the past. It could probably track the Queen's forces. Yet if Lucky led the Isi to the Ukko-child, people might become puppets unless they wore wetwear in their brains. The cuckoo burbled nonsensically in his ear. Static and tinnitus.

'The Queen threatened to burn you to ashes,' Wex called out. 'Lucky said that to me. I'll blot out Osmo's soul, she said. He'll be a statue standing in a fire pit.'

'*Do you hear?*' Osmo demanded of his audience. 'We're at war, we're all at war: *this is spoken.*'

Minnow cheered. People were stamping their feet in unison: an army marching on the spot. They were chanting, 'Os-mo, Minn-ow, Os-mo, Minn-ow.' Such a bellicose sway. That fisherman brandished his stone fist. A wreath of rum and nutmeg fumes from Alvar's pipe hung in mid-air like carrion-gnats. As the din subsided, blessedly the cuckoo had quietened too. Minnow was whispering to Osmo. He beckoned to Wex.

'I shan't meddle with a cuckoo,' declared the proclaimer, 'but may your leg be nimble, Earthman. Maybe you can escape from what haunts you. I wean you from your crutch; this is spoken.'

107

7 · THE GOLDEN LASS

A malaise of unease had spooked the aitch-house since the dreadful Lucky's Day feast at which the newly installed Lady Eva Loxmith lost her left eyeball. Cut out by Cully in a frenzy! The young man had decamped without a trace. Search parties of Defence Volunteers had returned empty-handed from Loxmithlinna town and the countryside. It was almost as though the eclipse of Eva's vision had conferred upon her mutilator a corresponding degree of invisibility.

Now there was such anxiety afoot at what Osmo van Maanen might intend and how the Queen would react. The Dread, which originally prompted the construction of the gargantuan keep, had come again. Irrespective of the convivial harmony which its many occupants had enjoyed for so long, were its granite stones forever imbued deep-down with the reek of old fear? Had this great habitation merely been biding its time, waiting to become not a haven but a trap, attracting brawling rivals to the *bait* it offered?

The aitch-house was shaped like a double-ended nutcracker. Its denizens dreamt of being *held* in a nutcracker. They dreamed of breakback mus-traps and snares. They also dreamed that huge hammockis, a million times the natural size of that tiny arachnid, were stepping across the rooftops. The dream-insects made the keep seem midget rather than mighty. Spinning out sticky cords, the giant hammockis wove a dream-net across the water-yard between the south and west wings – where one set of granite jaws jutted into the turquoise lake – and another net across the land-yard between the north and east wings abutting on the town.

Boats in the water-yard were already held prisoner by the portcullis, and after decades of disuse the great iron-bound tammywood gates of the land-yard had been pushed shut laboriously. An iron wicket remained open for access to the rest of Loxmithlinna town – whose citizens were less tormented by panic. The out-dwellers didn't besiege the keep for sanctuary or, save in a few cases, beg their relatives within for a share in their lodgings. These days the aitch-house couldn't possibly accommodate all and sundry as once it had when the population was smaller. Wiser to slip away into the woods if need be.

Still, townsfolk weren't oblivious to the mood in the aitch-house. It was almost a relief when a party of five bronze-skinned Juttahats made their way through a drizzly town to the guarded wicket, four days after the feast. Something quite unexpected was happening.

The leading Unman carried a white flag, semaphoring this from side to side as if to sweep the route clear. Two were porters who carried on poles a sedan chair. A shroud of reflective fabric hung from the canopy of the chair, hiding its occupant from view. Was a brazen *serpent* coiled behind the veil? Two armed Juttahats were acting as escorts. However, they held their lightrifles reversed, muzzles pointing at the ground.

A flock of gawking townfolk completed the procession. A few short axes and long knives were in evidence, but the mood of the crowd remained one of utmost curiosity at this spectacle. Daring kids darted to tag a Juttie with their fingertips, flicking at lustrous coppery livery and hissing '*Isi-isi-isi*', before skipping back to safety. The five aliens were humming purposefully: '*Woo-hoo-hoo, woo-hoo-hoo, woo-hoo-hoo*' . . . This breathing exercise co-ordinated their progress and emboldened them.

Through the mild mizzle a lookout at a high window had been sure he spied a sky-boat descend in woodland to the north of town. Elmer and Lyle Melator and Rolf Haxell were forewarned – of something.

The new Lord of Loxmithlinna and his assistant and Captain Haxell were all soon at the iron wicket; as was a squad of Defence Volunteers in their patchwork bottle-green and umber leather. As was a rubbernecking crowd of tailors, saddlers, shoemakers and bakers; word had darted through the aitch-house. Mana-priest Moller arrived there with Nikki; the flame-haired chaplain held an umbrella over Elmer's sister.

The Juttahats had halted in the square known as Out-the-House. Wooden houses of vertical white boards and shops bordered the granite cobbles. Now that the gates were shut, the residences faced a prospect of towering iron-bound purple timbers rather than the usual open breadth of the land-yard with its bustle and ponies being groomed.

In the square a couple of curver trees spread their quiffy chartreuse foliage. An elaborate fountain of branching pipes sprayed water, causing perching copper cuckoos to flap and warble – fruit of the engineering ingenuity of Elmer in innocent days gone by. Verdigris had painted those artificial birds their true, green colour. A punishment pillory stood next to the fountain, untenanted.

After some debate, and proceeded by guards, Elmer Loxmith and Lyle and the Captain stepped into Out-the-House, to a smattering of applause from townsfolk. The work-leathers worn by Elmer and his assistant were grubby by contrast with the uniform of the crewcut pasty-faced Captain. Elmer's bony hands and cadaverous face bore smuts and streaks of grease. People could see that he was keeping himself busy with practical matters in defence of the domain in spite of the shock of his wife's mutilation. Spectators crowded to peer through the wicket. They jumped up and down. Those to the fore related the proceedings in a jumbled chorus.

The Juttahat held its flag to attention. A black hieroglyph on one shoulder was a disconcerting blemish of spilled ink upon an otherwise impeccably lustrous livery. Its black boots forked like a cow's hooves. As it harkened to an inner voice its golden eyes glazed and the gland-slits on its prominent chin leaked pearly droplets. How dainty the alien's teeth were when its cupid lips parted.

'Bringing greetings from the Great Isi, Lord Loxmith!' Its diction was hissing and clickety. It had no difficulty recognizing Elmer. 'Being Tulki-seven of the Brazen Isi nest,' it introduced itself.

Elmer rubbed his palms roughly on his jerkin. 'What do you want, serpent-servant?'

'What are *you* wanting, Lord? We are bringing you a gift.' The two porters set the sedan down upon its chairlegs. 'A mistress curative for you in your misfortune!' The pair hoisted the concealing fabric, to drape cloaklike behind the seat. 'Be beholding Goldi the Girlem.'

On a throne of carved ivorywood sat a sumptuous female person. Her skin – a lot of which was exposed – was goldleaf upon fresh firm butter. Her short silvery tunic revealed gilded butter-sculpture shanks and knees and much of her thighs. Bare shoulders sported a violet starflower tattoo, a floral beautyspot. White moccasins were on her feet. White lace gloves came up to her elbows. Such grace, such provocation. Her countenance was ample and oval. Her dark amber eyes were set close and deep. Her cheeks were as prominent as buns, and her jet-black hair was bobbed – were the roots rusty? Twin dimples puckered her chin. This female person named Goldi smiled radiantly at Osmo; and he flushed crimson. Her face was Sariola – almost.

Eva's very tattoo . . .

Goldi rose. As she stepped forward to curtsey, a whiff of her scent provoked Elmer: a heady floral attar of a soft tenacious power, yeasty, and with a hint of chocolate. Sensation cascaded through him. He swayed.

The townsfolk were goggling. Necks craned through the open wicket.

'Guns to the proclaimer lord, being given by the Brindled,' announced Tulki-seven briskly. 'A Girlem to the inventor lord.'

Was this bizarre gift an act of reciprocity by which the Brazen Isi – in their alien reckoning of such things – balanced the arming of Osmo? How splendidly made was this golden lass. How gorgeously. How like Eva before she lost her eye.

Quite like Eva. Eyeing the Girlem critically Elmer could deduce her Juttahat origin: those dimples on her chin, the dyed hair. The Brazen Isi had moulded by scent and surgery a male Juttahat into *Jarl Pakken* who seduced Eva's sister Jatta. Now here was a female equivalent.

'Trojan Whore!' cried a voice from the back of the town crowd. One of those obstinate Christians. Such wasn't the general opinion. The spectacle of the golden lass prompted far more murmurs of approbation and envy.

The Isi were supporting Loxmithlinna in its hour of dread . . . Or were they? How would poor dear Eva – his half-blinded goose – feel about such a gift? Mightn't Nikki rail at him?

'Well, I certainly must thank your serpent-masters,' Elmer began diffidently.

'Accept her,' whispered Lyle. His spectacles had misted in the mizzle. Wiping the lenses casually with a kerchief, he reseated the specs on his snub nose with a few twitches and sniffs. 'You can practise with her until you succeed. Don't feel inhibited.'

Elmer was aghast. 'What do you mean?'

'Come now, Elmer . . .' What a sympathetically supercilious emphasis. 'Your goose is still waiting to lay the magic egg if you whip her feathers hard enough. I heard Nikki at the feast. If you refuse the gift, that Juttie might spout out your secret while it's trying to persuade you.'

'For mana's sake be quiet . . .' Ears were everywhere, though eyes were universally on the Girlem.

'I am being quiet. The cuckoo must have heard Nikki too. Now the Brazen Isi know a bit about your problem.'

If only it would rain more fiercely to cool Elmer's cheeks.

'They couldn't have created this Girlem in just a few days, Lyle!'

'I agree, that's quite absurd.' Such a nonchalant drawl. 'Obviously they already prepared Miss Goldi for future use, wherever she would be most serviceable. You'll be able to ask her all sorts of questions. It's your duty to find out about her, at great length. Firmly, if tenderly.'

Through gritted teeth: 'Supposing she can speak.'

Flashing a smile, the golden Girlem stepped back and stooped to open a drawer in the base of her ivorywood throne. From that nook she lifted a diminutive silver harp. The instrument was bow-shaped: a stringed sickle blade the thickness of her little finger and the span of both her hands. Silver pegs and tuning pins and buttons studded the frame. She plucked – and a plangent arpeggio rippled with surprising forte. The machine harp was a little loom weaving enchanting amplified notes. Such grace, such volume.

'Are you hesitating, Lord?' asked the Tulki.

Dither, and provoke an exposure of his shame?

'This being told in your own compelling stories, Lord Elmer—' With a wave of the white flag the alien cued the Girlem. In a voice at once mellow and sinuous and lusty she sang out:

> 'Thus the smith awhile lived wifeless,
> 'And without his wife grew older . . .'

She was reciting from the *Book of the Land of Heroes*!

> 'But I want a golden consort,
> 'One of silver half constructed . . .'

She postured to emphasise the perfect aptness of the description. Copper-skinned in her silver tunic, she plucked chords from the silver harp, and chanted:

> 'Then a maid rose from the furnace,
> 'And her figure all was lovely.
> 'Others greatly shuddered at her,
> 'But the smith he was not frightened.
> 'After that he laid the maiden
> 'On the softest of the blankets,
> 'Smoothed for her the softest pillows,

112

'On the silken bed he laid her.

'At the maiden's side he stretched him . . .'

She paused. She curtseyed again; and Elmer groaned.

'Being in your tales,' insisted the Tulki. 'In your compelling tales.'

'I am telling stories,' Goldi promised brightly. 'Telling many stories.'

Stories had an urgent power, especially ones from the *Book of the Land of Heroes*.

Of heroes? *Heroes?* Were they comporting themselves as heroes in the aitch-house with its portcullis and gates closed against threats which weren't yet present?

'In the rest of the story, as I recall,' Lyle said to Elmer, making no effort to keep his voice down now, 'the smith passes the gold-and-silver lass on to his old buddy, doesn't he? The buddy in question rejects this second-hand gift – but he could easily have been beguiled by her.'

'Osmo's going to be surprised to see her . . .'

'Bamboozled! Thrown off balance. I think we have to agree that this Girlem's rather stunning.'

Pressure was definitely mounting on Elmer, and it wasn't a pressure which he necessarily wished to resist.

Said Captain Haxell: 'In other words, Mr Melator, this Juttie lass could be used to the advantage of the aitch-house to flummox van Maanen?' He flicked at one of his earrings, which was a miniature silver portcullis. No, he hadn't lost it. The portcullis was still in place. 'He won't fall for such bait. He's newly wed.'

'Ah,' replied Lyle smoothly, 'but he'll be fancying himself as the perfect hero. Didn't Lord Osmo become intoxicated beyond all reason with that poetess at the gala last year? Do you imagine he'll be bringing his new Sariola bride here with him on a danger-ous expedition? Not to mention the fact that he *kidnapped* her – she could well be looking for a chance to escape.'

'So we'd be best advised, in your view, to subvert him rather than resist him?'

'Unless you're positive the aitch-house can withstand any amount of attack.'

'What else is it built for, eh? But still . . .' Haxell stroked his jowls.

*

Melator, as usual, was looking for an ingenious solution. Rolf Haxell appreciated this well enough. Eye to eye! Presumably the Brazen Isi were hoping to thwart the Brindleds who were backing van Maanen with weaponry. This Juttie lass could entangle and undo Lord Osmo just as the mutie poetess had swayed him irresistibly until he turned upon her in rage. That's why the snakes had sent her. Didn't tales from the book tell of the unmaking of heroes, as well as the making?

But to begin with, one really needed a balanced assessment of Osmo's strength. If the neutrality of the aitch-house were to be violated there must at least be some token resistance which wouldn't let too much damage occur. At least a short siege. Then they'd let van Maanen in and play the Girlem card.

Haxell would have words with the Defence Volunteers; with Lord Loxmith's consent, of course.

Unconsulted for a while, Elmer shuffled. His dark mellow eyes begged Lyle for understanding, of his embarrassment, and chagrin, and unconscionable excitement. The Brazen Juttahats waited patiently, perhaps hearing inner voices. The Girlem thrummed an occasional stirring string; and the town crowd gawked avidly, while the wicket gate was a mass of peering faces.

The inventor lord swallowed. He sucked in his cheeks, looking at once so candid and cadaverous. 'How should I explain tactfully—?'

Explain to his half-blinded, unbedded princess-bride; to his increasingly pert sister who used to worship him; to his mother, too, perhaps?

'Elmer, Elmer,' Lyle purred softly, 'be sly. This Goldi Girlem is a gift from the Brazens, to divert Osmo, isn't she? It's all for the sake of our house. You must question her closely; there's no need to say *how* closely. Make a second-hand maid of her, though. She's curative, remember? She'll have several talents; enough said.'

'You're a good friend,' the Lord of Loxmithlinna mumbled to his assistant.

Lyle was affability itself. '*I'll* escort the Girlem for you. I'll put her in a room well away from the armoured suite.'

Since Eva's injury, Elmer had tossed and turned nightly on a sofa in the dressing room adjacent to that chamber panelled in cast-iron which he had swathed in soft silks for himself and his bride. Eva wouldn't miss him.

'Shall I see you back at the workshop?' prompted Lyle. 'We'll finish work on the warrior by tonight. It's what the people expect.'

Doubt assailed Elmer. 'One single war-dwarf: isn't it rather inadequate?'

A breath of the Girlem's scent distracted him. Attar, yeast, and chocolate. To be inside a room with her: wouldn't that be overwhelming?

Of his inhibitions, no doubt! Still, he must remain master of himself. He must test this Goldi to determine her likely effect upon Osmo; just as he and Lyle would shortly test the stumpy brass soldier they'd been working on.

The aroma had vanished. Maybe she could release scent at will from those dimples in her chin, or some other gland. What *will* did a Juttahat possess compared with a man? Of this, and more, he must enquire – of this Juttahat who seemed so womanly.

'That brass dwarf of ours might take Osmo by surprise too,' Lyle said encouragingly.

'By injuring him? Assassinating him – is that it, Lyle? Osmo and I were such firm friends once.'

'He'll feel confident. He won't believe you could betray him, not deep down. Despite his bitterness about losing the contest he'll take you for granted, as he always did.'

'No, I shan't be taken for granted.'

'Before long we'll be building more and better fighting automata with which to defend the aitch-house, won't we? Brass warriors know no dread. Osmo might need such warriors if the Queen comes with those wooden soldiers of hers. He'll need our skills. If the aitch-house succumbs and the Girlem fails, there's a bargaining position to keep our independence.'

'Lyle, I don't quite understand: are you advising me to oppose Osmo or to co-operate with him?'

'*Flexibility*, Elmer, flexibility. That's what it takes. Our brass warrior is far more flexible now.'

Confusion plagued the Lord of Loxmithlinna. His assistant could fathom motives as instinctively as Elmer himself understood machines. Motives were such a mobile mystery. An afternoon spent with the artificial warrior would be therapeutic; Lyle was right. The mechanical dwarf would keep his mind off knotty dilemmas.

'Now,' said Lyle, 'you had better thank the Brazens formally and quickly and send them safely on their way. Captain Haxell: will you make an announcement afterwards about the need for secrecy regarding this golden lass? She's a Loxmithlinna secret, not for the ears of cuckoos or anyone from Maananfors. Make sure people understand this.'

Evening came. Beyond the mullioned window of the family dining room drizzle gloomed the turquoise lake to dull grey slate. The meal was earlier than usual, and consisted of a summer soup of milk and tender vegetables accompanied by cabbage pasties. No meats tonight. Nor wines nor spirits, but only pink valleyberry cordial to drink. Austerity and sobriety prevailed in anticipation of a siege.

The clockwork dumb-waiter fed Elmer's paralysed father strapped in his wheelchair, to which a cable linked it. Henzel Loxmith's active fingers tapped the control buttons. The skeletal servant spooned soup to his lips with one metal hand. With another it dabbed a napkin. In its third it held a knife. Its fourth hand balanced a forkful of pasty. A final hand angled a mirror so that he could see to left and right with those restless eyes of his, sunk in a jaundiced parchment face.

Elmer's mother wore her best robe sequined with the wing-cases of glitterbugs. Lokka's long horsy face was as blanched, by paint, as a soulflower. Supping sparsely, she focused her gaze upon her daughter-in-law's bowl and upon her hand. The rucked sleeve of Eva's gown revealed a wrist tattoo of a starflower. That gown was high-necked, grey, and unornamented, deliberately plain. Lokka followed the desultory progress of a spoon to Eva's lush and wistful lips. A dire black patch hid the emptiness of one eye socket, but Lokka didn't care to look directly at the patch. She would address Eva's hand instead, wherever her hand might be, whether resting upon the table linen or in the vicinity of that sensual, sad, flawed face.

'Lovely summer soup, isn't it, my dear?'

That patch could almost be a giant curl descending from Eva's coaly mane which she now wore loose without spangled combs or golden ribbon.

Eve was seated between her husband and his sister. 'Brother mine,' said Nikki when Eva made no answer, 'isn't your zeal in the workshop with that toy a little misplaced?' Nikki's sable chignon, tied up with red ribbon, exposed a fawnlike vulnerable nape and accentuated a dainty innocence of features. However, her tone was sharp. She addressed her brother, but she was looking at Lyle who sat opposite – in work-leathers similar to Elmer's.

'You haven't visited our workshop for a long time,' Lyle protested.

'Not since my cat died.'

'The fighting dwarf's a masterpiece, Miss Loxmith.'

'Is it really, Mr Melator? Will my brother be demonstrating it to his anxious vassals to reassure them?'

Lyle's hazel eyes assessed Nikki from behind his spectacles. '*Vassals*,' he enquired, 'in this democratic house?' He, of course, was the son of a boatwright.

'What if the Defence Volunteers decide that a brass dwarf isn't quite sufficient?' *What if they decide that Elmer isn't quite adequate as head of house in a time of crisis? Might you be encouraging Elmer to make a fool of himself?*

Henzel's voice rustled. 'Change pilots in a storm?' His tongue might have been a dry rusk; yet though helpless in body his uptake was quick.

'Toss the captain overboard?' Rubbing a control ball set in the arm of his wheelchair he slanted the mirror at Lyle. 'A house needs a noble master, or else other lords divide the land. We've held this domain since the founding, elected by mana as everyone knows. Did Tycho Cammon's subjects rebel against his bloodline after Lord Osmo trounced him? Of course not. When Lady Eva conceives, her child will be heir to the aitch-house and province.'

Elmer upset his glass of cordial. A pink tint spread across the linen.

'Such zeal for a brassy plaything,' Nikki repeated, undaunted. 'How could you possibly accept a gift from the Brazen Isi, brother mine? Another brassy plaything, hmm? Seemingly a softer one.'

Elmer spread his slim bony hands defensively, partly to hide the stain.

'I'm the lord,' he said, 'so I made the decision. The Brindled Isi are supporting Osmo. The Girlem will confuse him, inveigle him – the way he was confused by Eyeno Nurmi. I'll be preparing the Girlem for that role.'

'You'll put her through her paces.'

'Don't be coarse,' Lokka chided.

'Remember that it was the Brazen Isi who twisted Cully's mind – so they're responsible for your wife only having one eye, with which she'll fail to see you tip-toeing to that Girlem's room.'

117

'Nikki, please!'

Eva, expression inscrutable, had assumed the hauteur of royalty.

'And now they've provided a substitute wife according to their exotic logic.'

'*Nikki!*'

'That will not be the outcome of their gift,' Elmer promised, though he was all a-dither.

'Certainly not,' said Lyle. 'She'll be the undoing of Osmo. You'll see.'

'*Shall* I see?' asked Eva.

'When you squired that Juttie slave-slut past me through our gate,' said Nikki to Lyle, 'she ponged so much I'm astonished you could even walk beside her. Got right up my nose, she did. Not her fault, I don't suppose. Made that way. Where's our dignity, Elmer?'

'I'll really have to ask you to leave table—'

Lyle twitched his nose as if testing the wind. 'I'm sure I didn't notice any such thing, Miss Loxmith.' How formal he was being.

Elmer flushed at a memory of the Girlem's scent.

'Remember our dignity, brother.' Nikki simply wouldn't use Elmer's name. 'What will our people really think about this? They might grin with envy and salacity now, but—'

Eva bowed her head. Her tresses dangled upon the table linen, almost trailing in her bowl of summer soup.

Quietly she said, 'My sister Jatta didn't lose her dignity when the Brazen Juttie seduced her. The result was her fastboy, wasn't it? Her miracle. This Girlem creature's almost a sister of Jarl Pakken . . .'

'Actually she looks quite like you,' said Elmer tactlessly. 'Quite like your mother too.'

Behind that tumble of hair did his wife shake with stifled sobs or silent laughter? 'What are the Isi playing at? Elmer, you have my consent to find out for the sake of this house and its descendants.'

Such a hush, but for a whirr of clockwork in the dumb-waiter's pelvis.

'Spoken like a princess, my dear,' said Lokka, her features a white mask. 'I'm proud.'

'So am I,' mumbled Eva. 'Oh yes.'

Did Elmer's mother realize that her son was no nearer to engendering an heir than he had been on his wedding night? Eva straightened up, tossing back her hair. With a damp dusky

118

eye and a black fabric patch she regarded – and disregarded – those around her. Nikki laid her fingers upon Eva's which were splayed on the linen. It might have been appropriate had Elmer squeezed his wife's hand gratefully, yet he could hardly do so in the circumstances.

Eva smiled hauntedly at Lokka. 'Yes, it's lovely soup,' she replied as though nothing grotesque had occurred in the interim.

Henzel's voice rustled. 'You seem nervous, Lyle.'

'Me? No. What about?'

On the ground floor of the south wing which was the Loxmiths' personal bailiwick were workshops, storerooms, ice-room. On the first floor: the armoury, Moller's mana-chapel with its ikon of Lucky, wisewoman Mother Grünwald's apothecary service, and the kitchens. On the second: the bedchambers as well as two guest-rooms. Above: parlour and salon and sanctum and family dining room and more guest-rooms. Offices and treasury and staff quarters occupied the fourth floor, while most of the fifth consisted of the long gallery, that faded glade of green carpets and woodland tapestry.

Lyle had quartered Goldi in the same guest-chamber on the third floor which Gunther the dreamlord had occupied a year and a few days previously; and nobody since.

During that night while Lord Beck tossed and turned drunkenly, nightmares had vexed the inhabitants of the aitch-house.

On that night of nakki-dreams Elmer had imagined himself confronting, upon his knees, a glossy human-like machine, an animated female mannequin. The siphon at his loins dangled limply. The automaton's legs pistoned demandingly, but her face and torso were twisted out of sight, contorted away from him. Her skin was creamy. *Who could she be?* His own mechanical manhood failed appallingly.

A few hundred keys away to the south-east at Castlebeck Gunther would be in deepest hibernation inside the monitoring cradle which Elmer had built for him; a labour for which two hundred golden ors were still owing.

Should Elmer deduct from the debt the wage for Cully's bumbling work in the aitch-house culminating in the putting out of Eva's eye?

After the failure to catch Gunther's absconding nephew in the neighbourhood of Loxmithlinna, no wider pursuit had occurred.

No riders from the aitch-house had pressed onward towards Castlebeck to warn Lord Beck's watchmen that Cully had mad murder in his mixed-up mind, or to help stand sentry by the dreamlord's casket. Nor had anyone sought to send a special message to Castlebeck by cuckoo. A cuckoo might deliver such a message after a couple of days, or a month. Hadn't a cuckoo already witnessed Cully's attack on Eva, to make of this what news it chose? To blab it all over Kaleva sooner or later?

A message by radio equipment would ensure that anyone with a receiver promptly learned of Lady Eva's injury – which was such a wound to the new Lord of Loxmithlinna too.

Would anyone at Castlebeck even have dusted off Gunther's communicator? The dreamlord himself scorned radio communication. He'd said so himself at that café in Yulistalax where Osmo became so crazily enraptured with the poetess to the extent of virtually snubbing Elmer. 'Pooh to radio,' said he. Gunther had travelled all the way to the gala rather than resort to radio to ask Elmer a simple question. Maybe he thought that using a communicator would debase his precious dreaming skills! For sure he could never reach his beloved long-dead Anna by using a communicator – even if he was willing enough to use a machine built by Elmer to safeguard his anatomy while he *dreamed* his way to Anna, supposedly.

What in the way of warning did Elmer really owe Gunther, when the upshot had been the loss of Eva's eye? It was Gunther who owed Elmer: two hundred ors with the Queen's head on them, at least!

Besides, the Dread had resurged. This wasn't the time to strip any personnel away from the defence of the aitch-house, not when Osmo was making demands.

Yes, Dread had come. So had the golden Girlem . . .

And Lyle had put her in the room where the dreamlord had slept, and had stained people's dreams, because it wasn't on the same floor as the family bedchambers including the armoured suite.

Elmer was understandably tense when he entered the guest-room.

The silver-clad golden Girlem was waiting patiently upon the quilted bedspread, her little harp on her lap. That silk counterpane was all hues of blue – azure and sapphire and lapis, cobalt and blueberry – suggestive of the wind-ruffled turquoise lake.

Silk, of course, came from fungus-eating spinneris in Tapper Kippan's forests, large hairy cousins of the white hammockis which, much magnified, had lately haunted dreams . . .

The motif of blue billows repeated itself in a tapestry on one of the walls – and also, in purple carving, upon the headboard of the bed. A window overlooked the darkly dismal water-yard where boats were incarcerated behind the portcullis which hung from the bridge-gate.

Crossing to the window, Elmer gazed a while across the gloom-veiled water-yard at the equivalent floor of the west wing. Lace-makers lived over there. Most windows were shrouded. An oil-lamp glowed in one room. Some girls were busy around a table, no doubt with their bobbins, producing white webwork; a circle of diligent human hammockis. The next window along was dark. Was that a bowl of featherfern upon a ledge within? Or a head peering over the sill? Was someone kneeling there spying? Peer as Elmer might, the silhouette neither ducked nor wobbled, so he closed the curtains of wavily patterned blue damask.

As far from the bed as could be – so that one mightn't readily think of dousing it – the twin of that lamp across the way perched on the end of the mantelshelf. The bedside table with its undulating twist-turned legs and marquetry of mingling currents bore a plate with a dozen empty half-shells of freshwater osters upon it. The Girlem had fed stimulatingly.

How had the Brazen Isi learned about Elmer's marital difficulty? How could the alien serpents possibly know of his temporary impotence? Maybe they didn't know, and Goldi's arrival was coincidental. That Tulki had used the word 'curative'. Curative of Elmer in his misfortune. Or was Osmo, armed by the Brindleds, Elmer's real misfortune? It was time to ask certain deep questions, as befitted a head of house.

Surely here was his dream-enigma in the flesh; in the alien flesh masquerading as womanhood. An artificial person; yet a living one as well. A slave twisted by Brazen cunning into an exemplar of golden beauty. Where was his sauna switch, where was his little whip? Where were the ropes of love, the cords with which to tie her?

When he had smelled her scent he had known that he wouldn't need those. Now in the confines of the blue room, as she rippled the harp softly he smelled again: attar and yeast and chocolate.

She was mistress of the strings. Yet who was *she* in her secret self? Was there a true self at all?

121

So warm in this room. He stripped off his shirt as though to administer a whipping at a pillory. His slim bony hands hung emptily. The starflower tattoo upon her shoulder, so like Eva's! Her cheeks that were fresh soft buns. Her butter-sculptured flesh. The coaly hair.

She still wore her silvery tunic and long lace gloves, though she had kicked the white moccasins from her feet.

'Sitting by me,' she said in Juttie style. How lusty yet sweet her voice was. Then, 'Sit here by me, my Lord.'

Who was *me*? Who was he himself? He was becoming rapt in the sway of an erotic seizure, concentrating upon her as though she were the sole object of attention in the whole wide world. He was sitting beside her in his prisoning leather breeches – but aware of necessities; oh so aware.

Might she want human seed in her so that she might conceive a human child within a Juttahat vessel? The fastboy, Demon Jack Pakken, had been self-born of Jatta Sariola – hadn't he? – under the spur of this Girlem's male counterpart.

Could she receive Elmer's seed and ripen it – self-fertilized – within her womb? Here in the aitch-house might she nurse his heir, if he couldn't command his loins in his own marriage bed? What sort of child might that be?

With a lace-gloved finger she touched the tattoo of pliers on his forearm and of hinges on his elbow, emblems of mechanical grasp and flexibility. She herself sported a violet flower, and beneath her tunic, what else?

Bouquet of chocolate and yeast and attar.

'What is the meaning of these marks?' she asked. He almost answered, but with her other hand she caressed a chord of vibrant silver, a lingering chime.

'They are the wordless words upon the flesh,' she rhapsodized, 'the signs upon the skin. They bespeak a power or a protection. Beware: he who has himself marked unsuitably!'

Was this Elmer's flaw in regard to Eva: that he was tattooed with mechanical symbols? Thus he approached Eva too mechanically, whatever passion fired his blood? Not deliriously, but calculating upon longlife and determined to carry out the drill as prescribed by the Queen? Not obviously, but mindful of the tiny possibility that he might become zombie . . .

How could frenzy and forethought conjoin? Ecstasy and intention?

'I am spinning many stories,' Goldi said brightly. 'I tell many tales. Once there was a beardless youth who loves a maid. Ever since he was a boy secretly he has watched the maid, so upon his chest beneath his shirt he wears a tattoo of an eye. At last he entices her to a bower. But when he sheds his shirt, she cries out, "Oh, I cannot have that strange eye watching us!" She shuts her legs as tightly as a pair of pliers.'

Goldi twanged the harp. 'The youth hastens to the tattooist and has him prick his chest with coloured needles so that the eye is cleverly hidden within the body of a bird. He cajoles the maid to the bower again. But as soon as he sheds his shirt she cries out, "Oh that's a robberbird! It'll loot me and fly away."'

And the harp chimed twice. 'The youth hurries back to the tattooist. Soon the bird is hidden within the contours of a fluffy kitten. The lad has hair upon his chest. Next day when he strips to the waist, the maid wails, "Oh but its claws will scratch me!"'

Three silver chords rippled. 'Back to the tattooist! The kitten is hidden inside the picture of a curly little lamb. A lamb is larger than the kitten, so the work takes longer. When the lad next sheds his shirt in the bower, his heart's desire complains, "Oh, a lamb's too meek and mild for me."'

Four arpeggios on the harp. 'Are the hours rushing by, my Lord? Is there a hint of dawn in the sky yet? Back to the tattooist. The lamb is hidden within the figure of a junior billygoat. This tattoo takes longer still.

'By now the youth's chest is almost all covered by tattoo. When next he strips off his shirt the maid protests, "Oh, you're just a kid."'

Five plangent chords. 'Back to the tattooist, my Lord. What shall we tattoo to swallow up a young billygoat? Tell me, Lord Elmer. Be telling me.'

Elmer ummed.

This seemed like a story-trap. It might lead inward and inward compellingly, just as the eye was trapped within the bird, and the bird within the kitten, and the kitten within the lamb. Surely there must be an eventual logical conclusion to this series. The youth would be completely tattooed all over his skin. So what would happen then? Would tattooing continue *inside* him, within his mouth? Would the tattooist open him up and tattoo his stomach and lungs? He'd be dead by then.

'Be telling me,' begged the Girlem.

He was being encouraged to set his own trap. For himself, or for the desirable maid – or perhaps for Osmo! Attar and chocolate and yeast; and six chimes of the silver harp.

Inspiration seized Elmer. '*At last*, my Goldi,' he told her, 'eventually there was nothing else for the youth to do but tattoo the whole of his skin with a life-size picture of *himself*.'

How the golden lass grinned. '"Oh yes," the maid exclaimed, "*that's* who I want – and it's you."' Casting aside her harp, the Girlem kissed Elmer upon the lips. Her gloved fingers roved upon his tattooed hinges and pliers, guiding his arms to her, to unwrap the silver from the gold.

Somewhat later Elmer whispered, 'You're enchanting.' Waves of sapphire and azure rippled on the coverlet, rucked by a storm now calming. The bed was boat and billows. 'When Osmo comes, you'll be our minstrel and our storyteller. You'll befuddle him. But take care: he's a champion proclaimer.'

'I know.'

'You'll tell him a tale to trap him, Goldi. But who are *you* yourself? Are you a free individual? What's your own dream, Goldi? What's your desire? Are you a sister to Jarl Pakken? A cousin?'

She shuddered.

Surely she wasn't shivering. Too warm for shivers. They were both sweat-slicked. Were voices in conflict in her head?

'Being zombie,' she hissed at him.

Elmer flinched from the Girlem as if her tongue were poisoned and she were pronouncing a curse. Then he saw the truth in her amber eyes.

'You and Jarl Pakken were the only free Juttahats – free of voices that control you.' And now Jarl was a zombie.

'Being so solitary.'

Was individuality such a tragedy for her? Of course it must be, if she were the only such creature amongst her whole species, which in effect she was, with Jatta's seducer reportedly reduced to a pathetic condition of life-in-death. To be unique must be both glory and tragedy.

He laid a hand on hers. She still wore one lace glove as if betokening a limited, if provocative sovereignty over her own body.

'I'm sorry, Goldi.'

He had never expected to utter any such words to a servant of

124

the serpents. What would Osmo think if he heard? Or Captain Haxell or any of the Defence Volunteers? Or . . . Eva?

'Being unable to understand his own condition now . . .' Reaching, she twanged a string of the discarded harp which hadn't tumbled from the bed. 'Being controlled, to protect him . . .'

'No one knows a cure for the zombie sickness.'

She was silent and expressionless.

Insight illuminated him.

'You think you know of one! If you gather the seed of a longlife inside of you and carry it to your Jarl—'

And if the zombie could be beguiled to couple with her . . .

A fleeting vision assailed Elmer of a living cadaver in Goldi's embrace. While he copulated with bewitching Goldi, inhaling her odours of yeast and attar and chocolate, she had been dreaming of a virtually dead body reviving in her arms and recovering vigour. For a moment Elmer was sickened and aghast.

Then it came to him that precisely because the Girlem had been focusing all of her desires upon a numb caress becoming potent and vital – rather than the reverse! – she had cured him of his sexual hex. *Because* of this, his pathetic impotence with Eva must certainly have remitted; and in the embrace of a Sariola princess he would certainly now be safe from any risk of suffering Jarl Pakken's fate.

Except, of course, that Eva had lost her eye. She was aching both physically and emotionally . . .

'If you can cure your Jarl,' he asked pityingly, 'do you hope to breed a family of free Juttahats like yourselves? Did you and Jarl ever dream of that happening?'

'Not understanding *free*.' Goldi seemed to have lost her comprehension and fluency. Maybe she was prevaricating.

'Free means doing what you choose.'

The Girlem trembled. 'All beings, obsessed and possessed. Tales telling us all to act out those tales.'

He persisted. 'Your issue might become lords amongst Jutties rather than underlings? An elite assisting your royal Isi rather than their instruments?'

She replied, 'Once there was a Juttahat who lacked a second self. When he walked in any direction he could not stop if nothing told him to stop. Jarl Pakken being my second self. I, being his.'

Was this a Juttahat definition of love? This Girlem's essence eluded Elmer, just as longlife still evaded him. Maybe Nikki could understand Goldi, but his sister wouldn't wish to.

'You'll certainly lie with a longlife when you charm Osmo,' he consoled the alien lass. 'Myself, I shan't be able to lie with you again. Do you understand this? I shall have to seem stern towards you. Osmo's your chance.'

8 · A SHORT SIEGE OF THE AITCH-HOUSE

Fair blew the wind from Maananfors. Eastward along the turquoise lake a flotilla of fishing boats wafted. Charm pennants fluttered at the mastheads. White sails displayed a black cat's head or the silhouette of a cuckoo or a palm with an inset eye.

A grey plume puffed ahead of the paddle-steamer, *Sotko's Daughter*. On her forecastle a rocket-launcher poked between two shields of tammywood thickly coated with shiny lacquer to reflect away any lightrifle fire. The ferry's mainmast was rigged fore and aft for added propulsion – and in case the mintywood-fired engine failed. This expedition was aimed against an intuitive engineer, and he might think ill of the vessel. Mounted on the tip of the foremast was a pony's skull mockingly suggestive of the equine features of Lokka Loxmith and her son.

As *Sotko's Daughter* churned along, Hans Werner thumped his stone hand regularly upon a kettledrum set in the bows. The hervy vellum had been redecorated by Osmo's mana-priest with a cartoon map of the lake. Fiery arrows flew from many little boats. The aitch-house was broken open. A giant Lord Osmo in brassy armour bestrode his conquest in triumph. Imbued with mana, and assisted by an amplifier, each drumbeat boomed over the wind-combed water.

In a trance, which was unusual for him, baldy Seppo Hakulinen had chosen Hans the fisherman as beater of the drum. Werner's percussion would bless this voyage, as well as serving to signal to other boats since there weren't nearly enough communicators to go round.

Was it such a good idea to station a criminal in the prow? Ah but this assignment emphasized the unanimity of all men of Maananfors, high and low. Hakulinen had named Hans Werner 'The Stone Hand of our Lord'. Minnow attributed Hakulinen's inspired choice to pusillanimity. The priest avoided drum-duty for himself.

Lord Osmo's bride had insisted on being with the main assault vessel. She was paying a neighbourly visit to sister Eva, wasn't she? Her arrival on deck, in magenta satin gown and platform boots, glittery combs in her frizz, had stirred a storm of hurrahs. Hopefully she would stay below during the actual attack, should an attack be necessary once the aitch-housers witnessed the size of the fleet which was arrayed against them.

Meanwhile Roger Wex was keeping a protective eye on the princess bride. If the steamer rolled, Minnow might twist an elevated ankle. On his stained shoulder roosted the cuckoo. Lookouts in the aitch-house might be quite intimidated to spy man and bird so intimate with one another — even if the bird was really no pet at all but a pertinacious pest.

Osmo wore a quilted woollen coat reinforced with a flexible wire armature tough enough to blunt the force of a bullet. Now that he was longlife, if he were to be injured his wound would heal quickly; yet he wouldn't wake up again if he was killed. Off to the shore of the Swan's stream, then, to contemplate his memories! Sam Peller had insisted on the protective garment, and advised against bravado.

But what a fine thing it was for the armada to see their commander, newly longlife, risking himself in this way. Was it too soon for the full significance of the gift to have sunken in upon him? Oh but Osmo was perfervid in his enmity against the Queen, of which this voyage was the first expression.

A stiff breeze from astern ventilated him, otherwise he might have sweltered. Now and then he proclaimed:

'Boats afloat!

'Speed, fleet!'

A hero shouldn't omit the appropriate words.

Had a week been long enough to prepare? Each member of the town watch and each keep-guard had been obliged to muster ten able-bodied men or women apiece. The resulting army of three hundred souls had proved to be no more bother to raise in a day than if a force of Jutties had been attacking the town. Osmo's proclamation of war had put a sway into the air; and Maananfors was predisposed to heed a van Maanen. His denunciation of the Queen, whilst shocking, had convinced most people.

There had followed drills with rifles and lightrifles and

127

lightpistols, with the short axe and the long knife; familiarization with the three armed jump-bikes which the Brindled Isi had supplied; and a demonstration of rocket fire, though only once so as to conserve the arsenal.

Sam Peller had deployed scouts on picket in the countryside. Bolstered by mobilized townsfolk, half of the keep-guards remained behind at Maananfors as sentries. A sixth of the army ought to be a sufficient garrison to leave in the aitch-house.

Once Osmo was within that house, would he bespeak Elmer and his paralysed dad and Lady Lokka? Ah, but the Loxmith's authority was limited. Decisions were a shared affair. Osmo would need to bespeak Captain Haxell too, and the mass of Defence Volunteers, and the house council. That might be too sweeping a sway. Loxmithlinna wasn't already biased in his favour. He'd be worn out with proclaiming!

Once the Loxmiths' keep was captured – say rather, *reinforced* by Osmo's garrison – and once the reason for this was fully understood, the aitch-house would unite with Maananfors to oppose the Queen when she descended like a verrin upon a flock of sheep, unable to tolerate that fortress being in his hands. Osmo's neighbours would see the sense, inspired by a hero, and a heroine.

Sotko's Daughter was named for the patron spirit of all swimming birds, Earthstock ducks and honking native harnies alike. On her deck, Osmo addressed his bride, his joy, bestower of the gift, saviour of his life and soul. Suitable titles buzzed in his brain.

'At Loxmithlinna, my duckling, in advance of capturing your mother I'm going to declare you to be Queen.'

'Gosh,' said Minnow.

'That'll prick Lucky's vanity almightily. It'll be an exquisite insult.' He nudged her jauntily. 'Your mother won't conceive any more magical mana-daughters. She's finished. She mustn't ruin all of us along with herself, damn her. Queen Minnow, mmm?'

'Mmm,' she mused. 'In for a penny, in for a golden or.'

'You're right: we should change the currency. Lord Helenius's mint will recall all ors, melt them down, and stamp your face on fresh coins to mark a new era! Quite a dowry: all the gold of Kaleva.'

'Excuse me,' Wex interrupted primly, 'but withdrawing all the

high-value coinage in circulation is impractical and would precipitate an economic crisis.' His cuckoo blinked.

'But,' said Osmo, 'we can't tolerate everyone rubbing their
thumbs on Lucky's face for ever more. Minnow's head will need
to appear on ors some day.'

Minnow patted her breeze-blown, comb-speared frizz.

'My portrait will be a job for Mikal. In return, I'll free him
from decorating the Dome of Favours.'

Wex sighed. 'You pulled your mother's statue apart, Princess
Mischief. Now you'll dismantle the economic base.'

'Which of you is lecturing, I wonder? Oz' – she had taken to
abbreviating Osmo's name in private, and Wethead Wex could
be taken for granted – 'what shall we do about Lucky's Day?'

'Rename it Queen's Day? Or Mana-day?'

'Don't count chickens till they hatch.'

'Wethead, one of you is a real spoilsport.'

Osmo hugged Minnow, upsetting her balance. 'My chick, my
gosling, my little black pullet.'

Was it the lancey west wind which made the Earthman's eye
moist?

Sotko's Daughter manoeuvred to face the portcullis beneath the
gate-bridge between the onion-dome towers. Osmo had made no
attempt to radio to the aitch-house, nor the house to him.
Defenders aimed lightrifles and bullet-rifles from top floor
windows. Bullets raindropped the water. Light sliced sails. A
sailor tumbled shrieking into the turquoise lake. Granite
sparked and chippings flew and glass shattered as the fleet
returned fire. A fire-arrow ignited canvas.

Stone-Hans beat the drum – and the first rocket exploded
against a bar of the vertical grate which blocked entry to the
water-yard.

Osmo's guard Jurgen was now a mechanized cavalryman.
Dressed in light blue leathers, the brawny moustached fellow
straddled a jump-bike. Twin gun barrels jutted from the curved
horns of the handlebars. Jurgen was also equipped with short
axe and long knife. Would he be able to urge the bike to jump
through mana-space into the uppermost storey of the aitch-
house? The bike throbbed softly.

A second rocket flew to detonate against another bar, bursting
it. Throwing his weight back, Jurgen reared the black mount up
on its hind wheels. Of a sudden the bike disappeared.

Not many moments later, from somewhere within the aitch-house there came: percussion.

Jurgen's twin Johann sat on a second bike. He felt a link with his brother.

'He's alive, he's still alive.' Johann also reared his bike.

But already a white flag waved to and fro from an upper window, while Osmo's communicator was squawking for attention.

'High time too,' said white-haired Sam, whose own lifetime had been so thoroughly advanced by Osmo many years ago. 'Warp yon portcullis, and it would never rise up the rails.'

The whole siege, from arrival offshore, had lasted less than half an hour; which augured splendidly for co-operation by the aitch-housers, not to mention the future course of hostilities.

Parley would take place in the long gallery on the fifth floor of the south wing, maybe in reproach for all the broken glass and the several deaths suffered there, as well as signifying the surrender of the high ground.

Jurgen's jump-bike had materialized at the landward end of the gallery.

A throb, drowned by other din; a gust of air. Being so busy at the windows, few of the defenders noticed this advent soon enough. To those who saw, at first the machine seemed larger than it really was. An inky-black mana-mare bearing a blue ghost from death's shore: *what in mana's name was it?* During these seconds of indecision Jurgen had time to swing the bike around; and his guns thundered.

Three defenders died instantly. Four were injured.

Weapons were quickly tossed down. Indeed a white flag was already at hand to be waved from a shattered window while the brave jump-biker looked on.

Once the portcullis was winched aloft, *Sotko's Daughter* had nosed into the water-yard. Since this harbour was blocked with moored vessels little more than the steamer's nose could fit inside. A swarm of eager sizzleflies with sails for wings, the fleet had clustered into a raft of boats tied together around *Sotko's Daughter*, and behind. An assault force bounded from deck to deck.

Might some stubborn defender drop the heavy iron grating down again crushingly upon the bows of the flagship? While

Osmo and Minnow waited aboard the steamer, towers and winch gear were secured.

Within another half-hour Lord and Lady van Maanen stepped out of the lift into the gallery.

The architect of that lift waited – in company with his own princess bride. Was it only ten weeks previously that Osmo had hoped to wed Eva? No: it was in another era!

Also present, under the scrutiny of Sam and Jurgen astride the jump-bike and other men of the Blue Guard, were Elmer's assistant and the vanquished Captain Haxell, and even Nikki Loxmith; though neither of her parents attended the surrender. By now the van Maanens were fully au fait with the fact that Henzel had retired and that Osmo's one-time playmate had assumed the lordship.

'My congratulations on your recent elevation!' Osmo hailed Elmer heartily. As to violating his friend's dominion so soon after the event: why, a sheer case of bad timing . . .

Elmer winced, then contrived a lugubrious smirk. Shards littered the frayed green carpets which stretched glade-like, studded with pastel flowers, beneath faded tapestries of woodland.

And Elmer's wife wore a black eye-patch.

Injured in the assault by a fleck of granite, a splinter of glass?

'I'm so sorry you were hurt, my lady!' Courtesy could be Osmo's forte. 'I trust the injury is minor?'

She echoed him incredulously: '*Minor?*'

She didn't seem in pain as such but she certainly looked *defeated*; and how precipitately! Sumptuous Eva's hair was a sombre veil. No well-tended turban of tresses now. No glittery combs such as Minnow had stuck in her frizz like a clutch of coronets. A plain high-necked grey gown without any pearls to bobble her bosom. Could this really be the same voluptuous princess whom Osmo had so desired?

The flash which once dazzled him had departed. Eva was gross, she was grim. Oh but he was viewing her with eyes awakened by his own petite princess. Comparison was invidious.

Comparison was inevitable. It certainly didn't diminish Minnow.

Trembling with indignation, Nikki cried, 'Do you think *you're* responsible for everything that happens?' Tremulous filly, shocked by the invasion of her home . . . Elmer's sister yanked the red ribbon from her chignon. She threw the hair tie at Osmo, but it fluttered aside upon a heap of torn-down curtain under which a curled-up corpse evidently still lay. The ribbon mimicked a streamer of blood. Nikki's coaly tresses spilled in sympathy with Eva as she prodded the shrouded body with her shoe, hardly the reaction of a nervous foal. 'You haven't injured her! You killed this fellow, though.'

'If people fight,' Osmo said regretfully, 'people die.'

Why had a corpse been left under a curtain except to reproach him? It ought to have been removed. Everything today was hurry and scurry. Osmo glanced at Sam, and at the shrouded body. Sam nodded reassurance: the corpse was indeed a corpse, not somebody pretending, lying coiled in ambush. Sam must have decided that this morbid presence would intimidate the Loxmiths and their pasty-faced Captain.

'If you'd lifted the portcullis right away no one need have been harmed.'

The presence of the corpse didn't appear to subdue Nikki. 'Doesn't a hero need to take places by storm?' she demanded acidly. 'And brides by violence?'

For some reason Elmer shuffled ruefully.

Minnow minced forth on her platform boots. 'That's quite enough of *that*,' she told the girl, and quizzed Eva: 'If you weren't hurt in the recent rumpus, do you have a black eye then? Has hubby been beating you?' She still wasn't as tall as her sister.

Eva shook, she swayed. Was she about to sob? Her tremors gathered themselves into a gust of wild laughter, which ceased as suddenly as it began. 'Minnow, I've missed *you*! Here you come a-swanking . . .' Indeed, all the glittering combs were in Minnow's hair. 'Make free, my Lady Sprat, make free . . .' So saying, Eva raised her black patch—

—upon sunken eyelids shiny with salve, and a vacancy between them, an empty nook, a little cave of nothing.

'Your poor *eye*! What eye? Where is it? Gobsmack me, Minnow, here's a mess! Evie: whatever *happened*?'

Eva shoved the patch back into place. 'Haven't cuckoos been cackling in your keep yet about how Beck's nephew gouged out a lady's eye to stop her from pestering him? What a fine time to attack a neighbour and his blinded bride.'

Minnow gaped. ('Why? And how? And when?') All she could think of to say was, 'Does it hurt much, Evie?'

'How can something hurt which isn't here? Oh but the emptiness aches. It's draughty.'

'Jibbering Jutties!' Minnow stretched out both palms to her sister, offering a hug of hands, if not a full embrace; and Eva accepted. Sister held sister at less than arm's length. Rivalry, snottiness: such sisterly Sariola traits were quite swept away in this moment of compassionate intimacy. Blinking away tears, Minnow stared into Eva's surviving eye, which was moist too.

And through this mutual lachrymal lens Minnow scried that something else besides mutilation may have humbled Eva's vanity. Hideous though the loss of an eye undoubtedly was, this other veiled circumstance was consequential too . . .

'I presume that you caught Beck's nephew?' Osmo was asking Elmer. 'You didn't? I'd be glad to offer my own resources—'
'—now that you're responsible for law and order,' Nikki heckled him. 'But I suppose you need those resources to control us.'
'Control? No, I've no wish to control you, no wish to proclaim. I just want to explain – for the sake of us all, believe me, Miss Nikki. The present Queen's craze could make slaves of us all. Slaves to the Isi—'

Lucky was hunting for a hidden child of the original Ukko. She was convinced that her true lost self was sequestered in it. The Isi hoped she would succeed so that they could commandeer that Ukko-child and sway it to control human minds. By now Osmo's recitation was glib.

Therefore Lucky must be deposed. Provoke her, confuse her, capture and dethrone her. *Believe me.* Here in the aitch-house at Loxmithlinna the Lady Princess Minnow would be anointed Queen to replace her mother. His Minnow was more than worthy. She had mastered a mana-mage, as all would learn presently. Not merely any mage, but the fabled Viper!

'Monstrous,' Minnow whispered to her sister as they released one another. 'And mutant!' Minnow winked, which wasn't perhaps the most tactful motion in the circumstances, but it spurred a wry and thoughtful smile from Eva.

'Call for cuckoos to come to the coronation!' Osmo effused.

Lyle Melator was wrinkling his nose at Elmer. Elmer was fiddling in his pocket. Near where Jurgen sat on the jump-bike at the far end of the glade-gallery from the lift, a yellover panel swung open.

From a cubby-hole, a gleaming brass automaton marched forth

on stumpy legs. Red glass eyes blinked. In flexible metal hands the rotund dwarf held a pair of lightpistols. It pointed these guns at the jump-biker, who gawked in astonishment.

Sam Peller aimed from a distance at the intruding mechanical soldier; but he held his fire. Hot light would bounce off the automaton's body. 'A secret passage—' He was chagrined.

Osmo applauded in mock enthusiasm. 'Bravo! Can it sing a tango too?'

Elmer grinned disarmingly. 'Shall my soldier shoot your champion, or shan't it?'

The engineer removed his hand from his pocket and showed an empty palm. 'Maybe I fitted a pair of dice inside its body, so that from now on my robot soldier decides, not me. And maybe it also responds to sudden movement. Though how sudden is sudden?'

Jurgen sat very still on the bike, staring at the muzzle of a pistol. Sweat beaded the champion's brow. Was the brass dwarf really rotating dice inside its belly, matching them up? How many times? Best of three?

'To bespeak a machine *can* be troublesome, as I'm sure you recall,' hinted Elmer.

'I primed that damned everything machine of Lucky's, Elmer. Damned if I didn't. Then I was cheated of—' Osmo recollected that his bride was listening. 'That doesn't matter a hoot now. I had the best of the bargain.'

Wasn't this remark somewhat disparaging of Eva and her injury? Osmo took a few vexed steps along the glade of green carpets.

'Not a hoot, do you hear?'

'Keep back,' advised Sam.

Lyle wriggled his spectacles higher upon the bridge of his nose. 'A nod's as good as a wink to a blind donkey, my Lord—'

It must have been Melator's idea to hide the brass warrior up here in that secret compartment. With what in view? Assassination? The extortion of concessions? Osmo glanced back towards his high-heeled bride. *What do I do?*

'How long did it take us to build the warrior, eh Elmer?' Lyle prompted the Lord of Loxmithlinna.

'Oh, not long.' And Elmer called out: 'You there, on that machine: how many years did it take to build you up into a man?' Jurgen wouldn't be distracted; he didn't even flick a glance along the glade.

Osmo took another step. Was he going to *show off* at the cost of Jurgen's life, life of a champion who had stormed this gallery solo? Should he bargain instead?

'We're safe enough along here beside Elmer and Eva,' Minnow reassured herself. 'If the brass soldier kills Jurgen, Mr Peller will probably shoot *that one* in sheer exasperation.' Her thumb jerked at Lyle Melator.

A faint smile crept over Sam's whey face, and he swung his pistol. 'In my opinion I'll probably do just that . . .'

'Stop it!' Nikki cried – to Elmer, and to Osmo. 'For mana's sake stop it! We're neighbours, aren't we?' She reserved a scowl for Minnow who was only a very recent neighbour.

'For all our sakes,' said Minnow, 'let's stop Lucky. Don't you agree, Evie?'

'You're deliberately luring her here, little sister.' Eva's eye was no longer weepy.

Lyle cleared his throat; then again significantly, till Elmer asked, 'Don't you think, Osmo, that we could well use a squad of such mechanicals – bearing in mind the Queen's wooden soldiers? My brass warrior's disconcerting, don't you think?'

'Oh very.' Osmo was being diplomatic.

Elmer slid his hand into his pocket and fumbled until the automaton lowered its pistols. He seemed satisfied that he'd proved his mettle or salved his pride.

'Lads,' Sam told the Blue Guard, 'shoot any other surprises that come through yon door. A secret passage, damn it, who'd have guessed? This is the old house of dread, don't forget.'

The robot had been a charade. Now that the threat was gone, the automaton appeared to be little more than an absurd distraction; and Captain Haxell certainly looked peeved at the episode.

'Let's discuss terms for the garrison,' said Osmo briskly. 'I propose putting *Captain* Jurgen in charge, assisted by his brother. I brought Bailiff Septimus with me to arrange billeting of the excess troops whom I'll be taking back to Maananfors. We can't all sleep in the boats. I'll need to talk to your mana-priest, Elmer, about a suitable ceremony for the coronation. The Queen-to-be and I will share—'

'—the armoured suite,' hissed Sam. He knew the layout of the aitch-house, though imperfectly – that pesky cubby-hole behind the yellover panel! An iron-sheathed room seemed secure.

'Ah . . . but my wife and I . . .'

135

'So that's your bridal bower now, eh?' Osmo grinned. 'I wouldn't evict you from bliss. How about the blue bedroom? Cradle of the waves? Bring back memories of the good old days.'

'The blue room's being refurbished – on account of mildew. You must have *my* old chamber.'

'Wherever, wherever!'

Uneasy affability prevailed.

'Won't you come to my dressing room?' Eva invited her junior sister. 'I'll have coffee and cinnamon buns sent to us. You must need some refreshment after all the exertions.'

'Wouldn't you rather entertain her in the family parlour?' Elmer suggested. *For the dressing room housed the sofa where lately he'd slept in exile from his blinded bride's bed, on all nights other than the one preceding the siege* . . . 'Nikki might like to have a bun too.'

'Just Minnow and me together.' Pensively Eva adjusted her eye-patch. 'Two sisters. Old times. Is it really true, sprat, that you thwarted the *Viper*?'

A buoyant Minnow strutted tall on her high boots, if still not quite so lofty as her sister.

While they were waiting for the coffee to arrive, Minnow strayed through the communicating door into the master bedroom despite that neighbouring room being deep in gloom. Eva followed her.

Manoeuvring around the colourless vague bed, Minnow rapped on iron shutters obscuring the window. She knuckled the cast-iron panelling behind its swathes of soft silk. A pot-pourri of sweet nutty clearsage and perky glamorous jismin scented the confined air euphorically. Visibility was poor indeed; a vase of shinbones proved to be chimneyflowers.

Minnow perched on the dim counterpane. 'So this is where it happens . . .' She hesitated. (*Has hubby been beating you? Brides, by violence . . . and that other veiled circumstance.*) 'Or doesn't it happen?'

Although the gloom hid Eva's expression, she averted her face, presenting only a hang of inky hair.

Minnow thought that her sister's silence might last for ever. She forced herself not to fidget.

Presently Eva whispered. 'He can't. Not yet.'

'Oh dear.'

'Damn our mother's games, damn our precious gift.'

'Can't Elmer get your girdle off? Did she tell him the wrong word?'

'Of course she didn't!'

'Oh I *see* . . .' In that dark chamber Minnow could see very little but it was best to sound wise. Vapouring oils of jismin and clearsage prompted her to murmur, 'A male problem, hmm? Men are a problem in themselves! Do you love him, Evie? I love Osmo. I think I do.'

Wistfully: 'Obviously Osmo adores you . . .'

'Maybe almost as much as he adores himself!'

'Not that Elmer doesn't dote on me quite strenuously—'

'Poor Evie. So he can't perform?' The unaccustomed solidarity of sisterhood inspired Minnow to boast, 'It's fine for us.' She giggled. 'So long as I'm in the saddle. Upon him, perched on the pommel. That's the best way for me.'

With a swift intake of breath Eva joined her sister upon the bedspread. She raised the patch. In needing to scrutinize Minnow more closely momentarily she forgot the reason for that patch.

'In the saddle? Always?'

'So far! I'm not as hefty as you. What else should a Minnow do? Be crushed?'

'I'm thinking, sprat of a sister, that you've no idea what I'm talking about—'

The ritual prescribed by their mother for a firstnight so as to ensure longlife for the lucky groom consisted of being bound to the bed face-down by the ropes of love; of having a playful lashing administered – *whip your buttocks and tickle your loins to work up a sweat* – and, most importantly, of being deflowered from behind. If not, a lover didn't reach deeply enough on account of the curve of the tunnel, according to mechanically minded Elmer. Some tiny pouch inside the body needed to burst and release its virility – its virus – into the man's member. If the lovers adopted the wrong position the little purse would very likely leak its prize uselessly.

Minnow listened in panic. Jatta had never confided this aspect of her ravishment by Jarl. Jatta had talked of a roaring and rushing of rapture; not of being turned tail-up. It was hardly surprising that she hadn't divulged each intimate detail and had spoken more in terms of a rush and a roar. Why, indeed, why should she have realized that being mounted from the rear was the nub of a ritual? Jatta wasn't being wedded to a suitor who

137

had been enlightened by Lucky. She was being seduced, in ever so gallant guise, by a Juttahat. After years of study Jarl's Isi masters must have deduced the nature of the nuptial rite.

When Viper had manipulated Minnow and Osmo, the aim of the mutant mage had been for Osmo to lose his mind in an ecstasy achieved by any approach. Longlife couldn't have been an issue; and in any case Minnow had scrambled clear . . .

Osmo wasn't longlife at all.

He never would be now.

Minnow had squandered her gift.

'Well now,' said Eva.

'Don't tell Osmo. Please! Or Elmer either. You won't, will you, Evie?'

'Does the Queen-to-be beg a favour?'

'Yes!' yelped Minnow. 'I'm a heroine, remember. Anyway, I know *your* secret. Elmer can't get any further than whipping you!'

'I wonder whether our men might get drunk together and compare notes? Somehow, sprat, I think not.'

A knock on the door of the dressing room interrupted this shadowy tête-à-tête. A chubby, flaxen-haired maid carried in a silver tray bearing coffee pot, basket of warm fragrant cinnamon buns, and porcelain cups decorated with starflowers. As the two princess-brides headed through, Minnow's heart pattering, the maid was all glances: at the mistress of the house and at the diminutive conqueress. *In the privacy of that darkened bedroom had one Sariola sister been showing – or letting the other feel – that hole in her head?*

'Your patch,' whispered Minnow. Eva hastily adjusted her appearance.

Starched virginal netting filtered the scuddy dazzle of the afternoon. Oily ginger nuggets inside the spiced buns were chopped musktree nuts.

'I wouldn't want our mother coming here and mocking my blindness, or mocking anything else,' admitted Eva, sitting with Minnow on the sofa where Elmer would doss at night. *Though not the previous night.*

'So really you approve of what's happening, aside from the casualties and broken glass . . .'

'Did you really control an Isi mage, little sister?'

'I certainly confused her! And I glimpsed her native world.

138

She's waiting to burst out of her womb-cave when the young Ukko shows itself – or when Mummy shows the way. The Precious One eats her own servants! Lost all her teeth, she did. She can't swallow normal food. Jutties have to crawl down her throat.'

'You're making this up.'

'No, honest.'

'You really did control this monster?'

Minnow launched into an account of her adventures in the forest mana-maze and in the serpent's den . . .

'Let me tell *you* something,' said Eva. 'The Brazen Isi have sent us a golden lass—'

'Made of brass, like Elmer's soldier-dwarf?'

'No, of flesh and blood, like Jatta's Jarl. She's an entertainer. She takes a man's mind off things, if you follow my drift. Elmer spent last night with this . . . Girlem.'

'Oh *Evie*.'

And on the night before a siege! Even if no one at Loxmithlinna had known that an armada was to arrive on the very next day, this was hardly the way that a responsible lord should conduct himself.

'This *Girlem* may have helped Elmer, if you follow me . . . I don't know yet!' Eva turned away; tresses hid her distress. Maybe the Juttie seductress *had* proved therapeutic for Elmer . . .

'She's locked in that blue room, isn't she?'

Eva nodded.

Minnow bubbled with curiosity. 'When can I see her?'

'Not yet! I need to know how she affected our marriage. Elmer might put her on show as a surprise to Osmo – say, at your coronation.'

'So that he can show off and seem like master in his own house?'

'You've hit the pin on the head. Promise you won't tell your husband or anyone else from Maananfors about her, Minnow. It's terribly important to me that Osmo doesn't find out beforehand and jeer at Elmer and *spoil* everything.'

'Putting him off his stride again? I can see that, Evie.'

'Oh, Osmo might hear about the Girlem anyway! Still, our people mightn't feel too chummy yet towards Osmo's army. If he does hear a rumour, will you reassure him about why the Girlem's here? Or things could continue awfully between Elmer and

139

me. And I won't mention the proper way to open a certain gift.'

'You mustn't.'

'We'll keep our secrets secret.' Eva swiftly changed the subject. 'Are you intending to wear those boots at your coronation, by the way?'

'What's wrong with my boots?'

'They're a bit exaggerated. I suppose becoming a Queen is to exaggerate oneself.'

'Well, I realize you always looked more regal than me, in the past. Your gown's rather dowdy. I can appreciate why you're wearing it!'

'Oh it's *you* who's the heroine, little sister. Have another bun. What will you do for a crown?'

From the bedroom Eva brought a lacy bodice bobbled with large pearls. She laid it upon the sofa. From her mirrored vanity table came scissors and needle and thread. In a corner stood a chamberpot-cupboard of pale leperwood. A leper tree was modest; its foliage shrank from being touched. A curved tambour door hid the pot. Eva knelt and slid out a lower drawer. From the drawer she lifted a little two-thonged leather whip.

'Elmer adores me with *this*,' she admitted through her tumble of hair. The lash was suitable for flicking the rumps of ponies.

Minnow squirmed. 'Why didn't you throw it away?'

'He might have replaced it with a bigger one. At first he just used a switch of curver twigs. How do you fancy a crown made of leather and pearls?'

A leather hat made of such thongs, of these particular ones and of others woven together and all embroidered with pearls: how about it, Your Highness, doesn't it appeal? To wear your sister's humiliation on your head: how poignant, irresistible, and naughty.

'It'll be' – Minnow cast about – 'more natural, more endearing, more *organic* than Mummy's glitz, won't it?' She'd be cocking a snook at Mummy's sense of majesty. A self-proclaimed Queen ought to invent her own crown.

'And you'll be doing me a favour—'

This would certainly dispose of the whip in a blatant fashion. Should the Juttahat lass not have remedied Elmer's problem he would scarcely have the gall to wield a lash again.

'Sisters ought to do favours for one another,' stressed Eva.

'I see that! I'll still wear my boots, though.'

140

9 · A PHOTOGRAPHER FOR THE CORONATION

The following day brought two surprises which might reasonably be viewed as auspicious. To begin with, in the banqueting hall Elmer presented the van Maanens with a high-backed chair of precious ivorywood. A veritable throne!

Such exquisite carvings of blooms ornamented the wood. Bell-flowers and bloodflowers and little narciss and heartbells intermingled with several unfamiliar species, fancy and flamboyant. Maybe those exotics were flowers of far Earth, or perhaps they were whimsical inventions. All, of course, was a creamy-white, the hue of the ivory. Colour was in abeyance. Were the carved seat to be painted in apricots and crimsons and yellows it might have seemed more like a gaudy wooden bouquet in the heart of which an elfin nakki could perch. In monochrome the throne was serene, like dreaming bone recalling in immaculate white memory the flowers of life.

Wherever had the Loxmiths obtained such a fine piece of furniture, not to mention the unusual silvery fabric which served as awning and backdrop? Elmer wasn't too skilled in evasion.

Minnow nudged Osmo. 'Don't count a pony's teeth or it might bite. The gift's the main thing.' *The gift, um, the gift* . . .

Osmo chuckled indulgently. 'He's certainly co-operating now. *Thank you*, Elmer, from both of us. We're most obliged.' Naturally he didn't allude to the crown of unique design which Eva was helping Minnow to make, according to his darling little goose. That was to be a surprise.

Roger Wex was of the opinion that the reflective fabric was a survival blanket for insulating one's body heat if marooned in a snowstorm.

A messenger had brought the van Maanens from the chapel to view the throne; and the interview with the Loxmiths' mana-priest, recently concluded, had called for both patience and firmness.

For the pre-coronation consultation, Moller, red of hair and of complexion, had forsaken the customary grey serge suit and stiff white wing collar as though to disclaim complicity in Osmo's ambitions. He wore plain black breeches and a white shirt. His

141

sleeves were rolled up like those of a beadle about to administer a whipping at the town pillory. He even held a curver switch, with which he fanned himself.

Moller's groin-vaulted sanctum was stuffy. An oil-lamp burned below an ikon reversed against the plastered wall; undoubtedly an image of Lucky in one of her moods. Had Moller turned the picture back to front out of a sense of diplomacy? Or in case the Queen might somehow be able to peer from her portrait at what transpired? He certainly hadn't removed the ikon from the room.

A companion ikon showed Paula Sariola's Ukko: a potato of rock with a golden aura against a glory of stars, like a lump of clinker in a furnace.

Otherwise, in its decor, the chapel was anatomical. One section of plasterwork was frescoed with a diagram of the blood vessels of a human being. Another depicted dissected musculature, in blue. A third, in gold, the nerves. Fold the walls of this chapel together – its bones of granite and skin of plaster – and you'd have recreated a body, as it were. The Queen's hidden features would serve as its face. That clinker potato would be its brain.

A squat candle scented the chapel with attar of soulflower. An open copy of the *Book of the Land of Heroes* rested on a brass lectern. Stools of speckled horzma wood surrounded a divan ample enough to accommodate a visitor stretched out full-length – for Moller kenned the vitals of the living body, its inward contours, currents, and climate. This couch was where Osmo and Minnow sat.

Truculently Moller tried to lecture the couple about the hazards of lese-majesty in a world imbued with mana.

'The star-being appointed Saint Lucky as Queen of Kaleva, my Lord—'

'I'm perfectly aware of it.'

'Her Ukko serves as a cosmic ferryboat on the understanding that Paula Sariola is Queen. The mysterium floods her realm and you gain your own powers as proclaimer, Lord Osmo. Your nobility too, and your newly acquired longlife.'

Minnow squirmed fretfully on the muscular upholstery. Peeved by her fidget, Moller thrust the hand that held the curver switch toward the lectern.

'The Ukko required a Queen of caprices, young lady, so that the old tales can forever give rise to dynamic variations.'

'Is this dynamic enough for you?' retorted Osmo: 'The overthrow of Lucky for putting us all in deadly peril of enslavement to the Isi?'

'Consider the possible disruption of the mysterium! Mana is our life and our afterlife in echo on the shores of death. I'm obliged to point out to you—'

Osmo was too used to Seppo Hakulinen to feel intimidated. Johanna's appointee hadn't been of such calibre as to have much influence over her son. Should he who had petrified the tyrant Tycho quail before a priest?

'Basically, *Pappi* Moller,' said Osmo, 'you'll be anointing my lady as Queen with a good heart and fulsome sentiments . . .' He swept a hand through his chestnut hair. 'Why, you're as red as fire, man. Fan yourself some more. Don't boil over, don't burst into flames.' (No, don't do those things. But they might be *done* to you.)

'So how *do* I anoint a new Queen, Lord Osmo? When I studied for the priesthood in Tumio I wasn't given a clue as to any such proceedings.'

'Improvise! Invoke mana and scorn the mad old Queen. Conjure Lucky's Ukko to acknowledge a new monarch. Tell the cuckoos. Melt some tin to toss on water.'

'To shape into a tinsel crown?'

'*No.* A crown will be provided.'

The priest licked his lips. 'Scorn the former Queen, eh?' Red-faced, Moller stepped to the lectern and paged through the hefty leather-bound volume, chasing from page to page the clues he had marked with a thumbnail or a stain.

No more than Osmo or Minnow could he read the book which he had committed to memory during the incessant chantings of his novitiate. He couldn't construe the words, consequently the power of word should not diminish. Printed on a press at Kip'an'keep, this text of talismans – this monkey-chain of squiggles – wasn't to be *read* by him, a priest. He perceived the pattern on a page and voiced the appropriate verse.

What of a priest who inadvertently, by repetition and familiarity, acquired the ken of reading literally? He'd be the poorer. Words would weaken.

Presently, with sleight-of-eye, Moller recited:

> 'Louhi, Pohjola's old mistress,
> 'Fell into the greatest fury,

143

'But she felt her strength was failing,
'And her power had all departed . . .'

Perfect. Ideal.

'You won't burn with fever,' Osmo assured the priest.

'I suppose, Pappi,' asked Minnow circumspectly, 'the Loxmiths consult you without fail whenever they have a medical or mental problem?'

She was fishing. *Had Elmer or Eva confided anything about impotence?* Really she *shouldn't*; not while Osmo was here with her.

Moller gestured at the maps of blood and nerves and muscle upon the walls and in the barrel vaults. Reply seemed superfluous yet he had always been one for stating the obvious.

'Most certainly they consult me, and Mother Grünwald too.' Candour obliged him to add: '*Without fail* begs a question. Do you mean habitually – or infallibly and successfully? Lord Henzel's palsy hasn't eased, even if it no longer worsens. The dowager's melancholy recurred after Lady Eva lost her eye—'

'If I were Elmer,' hinted Minnow, 'I might worry about inheriting his dad's condition of paralysis.'

'Do you wish me to check your vitality, my Lady? Your stamina for the high office which your mother has held for four hundred and four years now?'

'No, no—'

'Or yours, Lord Osmo?'

Minnow's husband chuckled fondly. 'That's hardly necessary *now*.' Minnow was relieved to hear it.

Moller fanned himself. He glanced at the reversed ikon. 'I'll be officiating under protest, you understand? Under duress.'

'But in your proper suit and collar, Moller. The mad old Queen would surely sympathize with your predicament, wouldn't you say?'

'I wouldn't,' was Minnow's opinion.

'So you'll be well advised to support the new regime wholeheartedly.'

'Mana's my prime concern, Lord Osmo—'

'Mana, eh? My Minnow defeated a mana-mage. Did Paula Sariola ever plumb an alien mage's secrets or reach into its mind?'

('Into its gob too, don't forget . . .')

'That,' agreed the priest, 'is a powerful argument in your favour.'

At this point Elmer's messenger had come to conduct Osmo and Minnow to the banqueting hall to admire the throne.

The second surprise of the day was a certain fellow who arrived at the wicket gate midway through the afternoon, demanding to speak to the instinctive engineer.

Minnow happened to be in the land-yard at the time. She was touring the stables to collect suitable whips for her crown. Jurgen's brother Johann and a couple of stalwarts of the Blue Watch were acting as her bodyguards, and Roger Wex was tagging along, ridden by his persistent cuckoo. A watery sun hazed by thin cirrus barely peered over the soaring midriff of the house, a sweaty cheese perched on the roof ridge. No sooner had a gatekeeper scurried off to fetch Elmer than Minnow sent one of the Blue Watch dashing to bring Osmo too.

The newcomer's principal article of clothing was a coarse knee-length khaki kilt of sacking or bark fastened to an iron band around his waist. He wore the weirdest short boots with spikes upon the heels and suckers upon the soles. *Hooks* were planted in the bare flesh of his chest. From these there dangled leather pouches and slim satchels – he was using his own flesh to carry his belongings. Such a fellow just had to be a shaman. Over one shoulder he toted a box which was partly a bellows, and fixed to a tripod of purple tammywood. From the bellows-box protruded a lens.

Spry and sinewy, with a gloss to his honey-pale skin, he must nevertheless have been in his sixties. His was a lean, long, dog-like face. Dirty grey hair coiled around his cranium, secured by sizable pins.

'Ukko-ukkoo,' cackled Wex's cuckoo. Little scaly blue scavvy-birds had been pecking squabblingly at pony dung. The cuckoo launched itself; scavvies rose in panic. From mid-air the gossip-bird snatched a victim and circuited the yard triumphantly, dangling the scavvy from one foot, before descending once more upon its reluctant host.

Its landing – necessarily single-footed – was awkward. Wex's jinx buffeted his head, cushioning itself. Perching one-legged, and clutching so tightly that despite the shoulder pad he winced, the cuckoo manoeuvred its prey to its beak and tore the scavvy in half. Blood dripped upon the guano staining his cloak.

145

With a grin the stranger unshouldered his burden. He opened
the legs of the tripod. The lens of the bellows-box pointed at Wex.
The shaman peered through a glass in the back of his apparatus,
then tugged a dangling wooden bulb.

Presently a square of sepia card slid from the side of the box.

'Ah,' the stranger exclaimed, 'I imagined your cuckoo mightn't
show up! But look—' As he paced towards Wex, those heel spikes
grated on the cobbles, striking sparks, while the suckers adhered
then plopped free. 'It's your face that's blurred. Do I see two
different misty faces, imposed upon one another? Do you have
two faces in the eyes of mana, sir, or no clear face at all?'

Wex snatched the card with his right hand – and also with his
left as though each hand were acting independently.

'Be careful, you'll tear the managraph.'

'Managraph?'

'*Photograph of mana!*' Both of him had spoken, and he swayed in
confusion.

Avoiding the cuckoo, Minnow peered avidly. 'It's your other
face, Wethead! The face of your wetwear as well as your own.
(Ooh this is really important.)'

Wex lurched. '*But how can I have a face?*'

The shaman scratched his head. 'And two different voices? One
so prim and one so fruity?'

'I think you're developing an image of yourself, wetwear,' said
Minnow.

'*Your camera is of archaic design—*'

'Has to be! It films primal phenomena. Put it together myself,
I did, in the junk shop of my bone-house. Lens from Landfall,
photosensitive cards from the Velvet Juttahats. The equipment
still falls short of perfection, sir – which is why I have come to
consult your famous Elmer Loxmith. Would you be his assistant,
since you're acquainted with cameras?'

Wex wobbled wildly. The aggrieved cuckoo slammed down the
foot which held half a scavvy. Splaying its talons, it impacted
the bloody gobbet upon his shoulder.

But he regained his voice. 'A lens from Landfall bespoken
so that it can film mana-phenomena! Carter the surveillance
satellite! Pen Conway—' Was he trying to sidetrack his other
self?

The photographer marvelled. This man with two faces (or
none) spoke in tongues, so it seemed. Did the instinctive engineer
employ a holy fool as his apprentice?

Minnow giggled helplessly, and clung to Wex to steady herself.

'Would you be his daughter?' the shaman asked her. He glanced down at her platform footwear. Such a haunted pang troubled Wex's features for a moment.

'Why,' she gasped, 'do you have spikes and suckers in your shoes?'

'So that I shan't float away, miss.'

She contrived to nod with precarious solemnity. 'Of course. That *would* be why, wouldn't it? (Can a Minnow argue with that?) Actually I'm Lady Minnow van Maanen, and I'll be anointed Queen of Kaleva tomorrow.'

The stranger, with pouches and scrips hooked upon his chest, contemplated her. 'Seems I was right to set out on my travels . . .'

More spectators were arriving: citizens of the aitch-house and of Maananfors, variously armed or disarmed. From one door came Elmer; from another, Osmo. Someone had tipped off the mana-priest too.

Hermi was the newcomer's name. He was Lord Helenius's emissary to Juttahats of the Velvet Isi, or at least he *had* been so until he walked away from his hut built of bones.

Lord Helenius, as people might or might not know, collected alien gadgets and souvenirs; while the black Juttahats accumulated human trivia for their masters. This eccentric commerce minimized friction on the hazy borderland between human and alien territory.

In the mana-misty forests to the north-east of Threelakes, between Helenius's realm and the velvet serpents' nest, stood Hermi's halfway house. For years, eccentricity had been Hermi's safeguard in his dealings with the aliens – frankly, he fascinated Jutties. Why, Hermi was frankness itself. He would answer any question even before it was asked. To suspicious souls such radical honesty as his often seemed like guile and craftiness, subterfuge and fraud.

('All of those at once?') Minnow asked herself.

In truth there was a deeply serious purpose to Hermi's life – namely *insight*, into the mysterium.

To the Isi, life was a game of vision, of obscurities and revelations played amongst themselves and with their unwitting human rivals. Creatures who lacked arms with which to reach out, and hands with which to grasp, yet who could *think* their slaves into action, must by their very nature be manipulative in

147

a manner that men and women could scarcely appreciate. Human beings reached out more directly. The prizes in the game were pearls of perception: perception of the mysterium, the modus of the Ukko entities which were stimulated by tales of the games of planetary beings.

('So a crown of oster pearls is really apt!')

Moller no doubt felt that this trickster-shaman and quondam emissary was trespassing upon a priest's prerogative, much as his toes had already been trodden upon by Osmo. 'Did you study at Tumio?' he enquired, flush-faced. 'Were you expelled as a novice? It's all very fine to seek your star up a tree, my wild man, but to come here and preach to us—!'

'Am I preaching?'

Hermi had come to consult the instinctive engineer about his photographic, or more properly *mana*graphic, apparatus. After much meditation and concentration he had assembled the bellows-box and lens and tripod so as to capture images of the otherworld as it impinged upon the mundane. Seemingly his arrival coincided with the beginning of a war!

Delving into a slim satchel hooked to his chest, Hermi flourished a fan of sepia cards. Minnow and Wex and Osmo crowded round. Elmer rubbed shoulders with his boyhood friend, their recent contretemps forgotten in this diversion. Moller and Lyle craned to see as Hermi showed one managraph, then another.

Over a cabin built of bones, hemmed by curver and sylvester trees, streamers of light cascaded . . .

'That's an aurora dance,' piped Minnow.

Ghostly, a pocked oval moon hung in the sky . . . So where did that moon come from?

'From the era before the sky-sickle?' Lyle suggested flippantly. 'Maybe his cabin travels in time?'

'I think a moon ought to be round,' said Elmer, 'otherwise it breaks up – into a sky-sickle.'

'Looks to me like an Ukko,' said Osmo. 'Much closer to the ground than any Ukko has ever come before . . . unless it was *already* buried in the ground. What's your bone-cabin built on top of, Hermi? Why's it there and not somewhere else?'

'What a curious question, sir! Should my home be in more than one place?'

'Tongue-trickster,' grumped Moller.

The next managraph was a portrait, of a priest.

He was slight and bespectacled. Sporting a trim moustache and oiled curls, he was very dapperly dressed. He stood arm in arm with a dainty bright-eyed lady in black lace, his junior by at least a decade. A snaky medallion adorned the priest's fine shirtfront, and serpentine bangles his wife's wrists. The priest's expression was one of hesitant yet heartfelt yearning; of ineffable desire unrelated to the woman by his side, whom nevertheless he cherished.

Upon the priest's head there perched a blurred cuckoo, which was ducking its head to whisper in his ear. The man's smile of fretful anxious invitation, directed toward and through the lens, suggested deafness to the bird's whispers, utter oblivion to its presence.

'How he rejoiced when he saw the result! Transfigured with joy, he was. He wept. A dream come true.'

'That's Juusi Haavio . . .' Moller reached for the managraph but Hermi held the sepia card away. 'You played upon the man's obsession, didn't you? I believe you hoaxed him.'

'*Ukkoo*,' croaked Wex's bird dolefully.

'Hoaxed, Pappi?'

'By visualizing that cuckoo perched on his head; that's how. You can impose an image of your own fancy upon one of those cards. Come on now, isn't it true? It's a conjuring trick. You and your enchanted lens!'

'My mana-sensitive lens, Pappi.' Hermi sounded hurt.

'Aye, but sensitive to whose mana? To your own, I'm thinking.'

Hermi shifted from foot to foot. As he did so, those suckers on his soles slurped and plopped.

'Well, Pappi, I must confess there's a grain of salt in what you say. It's in precisely this respect that my apparatus falls short of perfection, you see! It's such a temptation when I'm faced with someone who yearns to witness something special which I happen to know about . . . That's why I hung on to the managraph of Pappi Haavio instead of letting him keep it; much as he begged me for it.'

'You kept it in case an honest shaman inspected it and disabused him!'

But Hermi had his own definitions of honesty. 'Quite often,' he informed the gathering, 'a single glance reveals a person's soul to me. Yet if somebody other than myself operates my apparatus it still performs its task.'

149

'I presume,' said Elmer, 'you mean that your camera also takes ordinary pictures.'

'Extraordinary ones too, Lord Loxmith! Genuine managraphs. What I dearly wish is to be able to use this machine without my own observations interfering with what the lens perceives.'

Hermi delved in a pouch and pulled out two spoons of solid gold. Upright in his grasp, the twin utensils were a pair of legs culminating in golden buttocks. When Hermi rubbed his fingers together, the legs waggled provocatively.

'I can pay you for your pains, Lord Loxmith.'

Golden buttocks ... Elmer flushed.

'Did those spoons belong to Leena Haavio?' demanded Moller.

'Does a priest eat his boiled egg with a golden spoon?' retorted Hermi.

'Why shouldn't he?'

'I've heard,' said Lyle airily, 'that gold spoils the taste of a yolk.'

'Yet you wear gold round your eyes,' Hermi said promptly to Elmer's assistant. 'You view the world through a golden frame, through a golden shell. Bands of gold encompass your vision, wedding you to your future fortune.'

'So you also tell fortunes? What a man of talents.' Were Lyle's feathers ruffled?

'Well now,' said Minnow, 'obviously a picture is going to be made of my coronation – but Mr Hermi's fancies might interfere with the image. So who will take the picture? How about you, Lyle Melator?'

Lyle smiled blandly. 'If Elmer is going to be *experimenting* with this camera, maybe as host he should do the honours tomorrow?' The aitch-house had fallen. Men and women of Maananfors were occupying it. And the Lord of Loxmithlinna would be tinkering with a bellows-box brought by an itinerant shaman. When some of Osmo's garrison chuckled, Lyle glared indignantly at them.

Elmer evidently itched to inspect the apparatus, though as to operating it at the coronation ...

'I don't think so,' he demurred. 'Mr Hermi ought to be the photographer. Then we'll see what we will see.' He winked at his assistant. 'Who knows, maybe we'll see something else entirely? If that's all right with you, Lady van Maanen? If you're willing to risk it?'

Well, a Minnow would risk most things.

said Elmer. 'I'd better familiarize myself with it. Come along to my workshop, Hermi.'

'I don't know if this is wise—'

'Please, Oz—'

'Granted, the witch is dead—'

'The new Queen wants a magical picture taken—'

'My gosling—'

Elmer said to Hermi, 'You'll need to take off your shoes inside or you'll spoil the floor with those spikes.'

'I might float away—'

'I'll give you something heavy to hold—'

'A yoke of iron,' suggested Lyle. 'A portable pillory.'

Hastily Elmer collected the tripod and hustled Hermi, plopping and sparking, through a crowd of spectators towards the house. Chuckles earned a scowl from Lyle Melator.

Before the trio reached the door to the towering crossbar of the aitch Elmer whispered, 'Puts Osmo off the scent of the Girlem. Now he assumes we have nothing better to do. That was sly of you, Lyle.'

'I'm glad you approve.'

Windows stared down: six storeys of windows on three sides, barred with granite mullions and transoms. Faces gazed from many.

Wex, and his other self, had believed that he was proof against mana-effects. A primary role of his wetwear was to safeguard him against possession – either of a manic kind, or such as the Isi might try to impose on him. His fondness for Minnow was a temporary aberration: pardonable, understandable.

Admittedly he and his other self were having trouble adjusting. Maybe he and that other self were a paradigm for a lack of integration which might frustrate any attempts by the aliens to control human beings successfully?

Yet people were often enough the prey of their own passions. People were swayed by whims and frenzies and obsessions. People were vulnerable to human proclaimers such as Lord Osmo.

Anni the body-slave had retained her human integrity under alien control imposed by a garment of snake-skin. By all accounts the young man, Cully, had remained rebellious against the alien bid to programme his mind. {*By what method did the Brazen*

Isi try to impose on the dreamlord's nephew?} Cully was an enigma; Cully was a key. Deeply confused but defiant; driven insane, perhaps . . .

Was Wex *immune* to mana – or merely *opaque*, merely blurred and cloudy?

Had Hermi's mana-lens really revealed the hint of a different face inhabiting Roger's own features: the true face of that intimate *other* within his own brain?

'Didn't your face look at all like mine?'

{*Or yours, like mine, my Roger?*}

'Mine is the matrix!' How could wetwear possess a physiognomy of its own?

Supposing that Hermi's lens wasn't a spoof, what if such a piece of equipment could be fitted to Carter, to the semi-sentient satellite with its spy cameras?

{*And its lasers too.*}

A lens which might pierce the mana-mists around Isi redoubts! A lens which might find the Queen's goal, that beacon of mana, the Ukko-child . . .

When Wex had at last radioed to Penelope Conway in Landfall with warnings of the beginning of a war, the Earth Resident had assumed that after so long a silence he must be dead, victim of random violence or of alien malice in spite of his other self's martial skills. Wex was an agent too secret by half! Or by *double*: an agent who mainly reported to himself.

To reactivate the long-dormant satellite (fitted with those lasers) seemed to Conway to be a risky intervention. The Isi might detect the move and interpret it as a new gambit in the game which they played with humankind. This was a game which Earth would rather not play at all, or at least as quietly as possible.

What, she had worried, *might the consequences be?* The Isi might respond unforeseeably.

She also worried whether Carter would function any more reliably than Roger Wex and his artificial other self. Yet a war was beginning, if Wex (and cuckoos) were to be believed. Better observation was surely needed now. If Conway switched Carter on, Wex must promise not to access the satellite himself from any of the cairns which still functioned.

Of course he promised.

*

How could a mana-lens, such as this one here in Loxmithlinna, be fitted to a satellite in orbit?

{*It would be possible, if tedious, to divert a shuttle to rendezvous with Carter to fit a new lens.*}

'Why not divert the Ukko itself?'

Why not persuade Earth's star-ferry to carry out the rendezvous by telling it a suitable story? And what would a suitable story be?

{*Oh that's easy. Hark and hear, my Roger:*

    {*Thou canst fly on high with swiftness,*
    {*Fly aloft with easy effort,*
    {*O'er the moon, below the daylight,*
    {*And amid the stars of heaven,*
    {*Flying windlike on the first day*
    {*Past the borders of the moon ...* }

'That's the ticket, wetwear.'

{*This might disrupt the Ukko's routine of travelling between Earth and Kaleva. We might lose the route, my Roger. There's also the problem of accessing the Ukko-ferry while it's in orbit. Maybe only Paula Sariola can give it such* new *instructions?*}

These were technical details. A more immediate problem was that Hermi, the owner of solid gold spoons, would hardly be likely to sell his mana-lens.

{*So you'll steal it. If that lens truly does perform for objective observers other than Hermi, then we'll steal it.*}

What if their cuckoo were to screech at the wrong moment? At night the pest roosted upon the headboard. Come dawn, the bird would fly out to a cuckoo perch to feed on impaled chicks. *Then* was the time for Wex to scramble out of bed and wash quickly and tie a pad upon each grooved shoulder and dress. If he shut the window, the bird would clamour outside and peck the glass fiercely, soon smashing entry. At Maananfors a maid had changed the linen every morning. Usually the pillowcase smelt of ammonia. Should he strangle the taboo bird, as it so richly deserved for its persecution of him – and maybe cause unpredictable ripples of malignity?

Minnow had lingered in the land-yard to commune with Wex. After the hasty departure of Elmer and Lyle with the photographer-shaman, Osmo had also left to continue arrangements for the occupation of the house and the coronation which would enrage Minnow's mother. But Minnow had stayed. The crowd had mostly dispersed when the Queen-to-be at last interrupted Wex's reverie.

'Weren't those wild shoes he was wearing?'

'What—?'

'The spikes and suckers. Do you think he'll really float off without them?'

{*Levitation is not a recorded mana-phenomenon.*}

'The junior Ukko might levitate itself to reach outer space.'

The seemingly inconsequential grandeur of his response made her grin. 'Well anyway, Wethead, I've a favour to ask.' From her slight cleavage she pulled what he took for a moment to be a thin black snake, but which proved to be a thong.

'My sister's helping me to make my crown. It'll be of leather and pearls. Will you find Cully for my sister's sake? Will you capture him or if he's crazy put him out of his misery – so that the loss of her eye won't be such a senseless ache, and in vain? She was trying to cure him. I'll be grateful – you'll be in good odour with the new regime.' She squinted at the bird droppings and crushed scrap of prey on his shoulder.

A quest on behalf of this girl who had won his heart (folly though this was)!

A quest which would free him from the sweet torment of being near her: maybe that was why she was proposing it?

A mission which was precisely what he, and himself, had been mulling, offering a perfect pretext to decamp with a stolen lens and not be suspected or chased.

'The Isi tried to programme the young man's beliefs,' Wex said. 'How did they go about it? Does he still have an Isi in the back of his mind? Important questions! You're right, Princess, he must be found. I'm the one to find him, as a former member of the Peace Police of the Harmonious Society. I'll gather descriptions from the staff of this keep. Some may be able to draw him. I shan't bother your sister – that might be distressing. My other self will construct what we might call a composite – a mental picture of Cully.'

'Would that be like a managraph, but inside of your head?'

'Magicians and their magic boxes!' Wex hoped he sounded suitably disparaging. Impelled to throw her further off the scent of his intentions, he told her, 'The seeing-eye satellite up in orbit has been reactivated. It has very high resolution . . . so long as

155

it's over the right patch of territory.' She wouldn't understand much about spy satellites. He sketched a curving line with his finger. 'I'll head for an access cairn, and I'll feed the composite to the satellite. We'll find Cully.'

'By peering down on the top of his head?' Minnow was sceptical.

'Carter has some intelligence,' he assured her.

Of course he wouldn't find Cully by that means at all, but in a dovecraft commandeered from Landfall. Meanwhile there was the matter of the mana-lens.

{*Maybe we oughtn't to leave this new Queen, my Roger? She will be a focus for events.*}

Did his wetwear now not wish to lose sight of Minnow? Couldn't it abide the separation?

'I promise I'll carry out your mission,' Wex said nobly. His cuckoo ruffled its dowdy green plumes. May it not shit again right now!

{*Of course we must resist distractions. I merely queried you. When we take the lens to Landfall we shall commandeer a dovecraft from Harmony Field to reach Castlebeck quickly; and work backward from there.*} Ah, he and himself were in agreement.

'I might understand Cully better than anyone else on account of my own condition—'

Mischievously Minnow returned to the matter of the camera.

'Your secret face, Roger – the one that Hermi saw through the mana-lens: don't confuse that with this *composite* or else you might go looking for yourself just like my mad mother, mmm?'

'I'll be very careful to avoid all mana-lenses,' he assured her.

Royally, she offered him the back of her hand to seal the commission. Wondering whether she might laugh at him whether he did or whether he didn't, he brushed her skin with his lips. To be out of sight of her for a long while would be so much less tormenting.

Minnow tottered away on her high boots, followed by her bodyguards.

In the forenoon of coronation day there'd been a knife fight in
the land-yard between a carpenter conscript from Maananfors
and a blacksmith of the aitch-house. The cause was a flippant
taunt about Lord Elmer's interest in the camera. His two-gun
brass dwarf failed to halt the seizure of the keep. Maybe a three-
legged bellows-box would shoot beams of hot light at Lucky's
forces when they attacked? Just as well that the aitch-house was
under Lord Osmo's protection! The carpenter's cheek was slashed
to the bone, and a tendon was severed in the blacksmith's hand.

Another dispute had flared up in the afternoon about billeting.
One of the visiting garrison considered this ought to include his
host's daughter as well as a berth. Bed and bawdy.

The coronation feast that evening was one for cuckoos too.

The cages of thin wrought-iron foliage which screened the tall
open windows of the banqueting hall were decked on the inside
with dead chicks, with dripping lamb livers, kidneys, and hearts.
Three birds had heeded the *coo-coo* call and had clambered
through the tracery. Abandoning Wex's bleached shoulder his
pest had joined its kin to guzzle offal.

It was barely the first hour of the evening. The summer sun
still hung above the lakeward thrust of the west wing. All of the
chandelier candles had been lit, but it was the stream of sunshine
which made the lustres sparkle, clusters of diamond-ice. Sunlight
also cast an embroidery of shadows upon the crowded long tables.
Only the high table, on the dais, was free of sunshine and spidery
shadow. A couple of candelabra contributed some modest flame,
and reflections glittered star-like in the silvery awning of the
ivorywood throne. Placed at one end of high table, the throne
awaited formal occupation.

Diners had frequent recourse to the serving table, which was
loaded with slabs of fish, a mountain of meatballs, a cauldron of
blood soup, goose and sausages and jellied veal, tongues and
trotters, salads of onions and soused fish. A calf had been slaughtered too. Could such a feast lack liquor? Sam Peller had insisted
that there should be no spirits nor wine to lessen the likelihood
of feelings growing inflamed. Only ale was served. Strategically

seated Blue Guards had promised to drink nothing stronger than fruit juice.

As proof of solidarity a third of the feasters – but no more than a third – were natives of the aitch-house. Two local harpists played soothingly.

Upon the dais sat Elmer's white-faced mother who was barely touching her food, and paralysed Henzel accompanied by his automaton. Nikki had dressed in silk as inky as her own hair – out of respect for the dead, so she said. A stole of blue gauze and a peacock ribbon in her chignon countered any criticism that she was being wilfully dour.

Patch-eyed Eva still favoured her severe grey gown buttoned up to the throat. A lace-edged white muslin shawl hung from her shoulders like frail limp insect wings. Eva fanned herself frequently. The fan, of black lace on bone, was a fluttering bird eclipsing her face.

Elmer had spruced himself up remarkably. The maroon jacket with brass buttons and white lapels and the pea-green waistcoat and breeches was the same outfit as he had worn to woo his wife in Sariolinna. Osmo, of course, was impeccable in green and gold waistcoat and ribbon rosettes; no padded coat this evening.

On the table near Minnow, in her magenta décolletage, there reposed the crown of leather and pearls. Amidst the plates and dishes the crown resembled a sombre cake: a hillock of sweet intertwined pastry edged with mustaberry, and studded with white berries.

Elmer hadn't set eyes on the headgear till he arrived at high table. How many edgy glances he stole towards that pearl-studded turban woven of whips. He didn't need to ask to know that his lash-for-a-lass was included.

'Eva,' he murmured, 'was the crown your idea?'

The fan hid his wife's expression. 'A Queen needs a crown. It can't be the same as Mummy's was. New era, new hat. I thought it seemed suitable. Leather for power and protection, pearls of wisdom.'

'It taunts me.'

'But who knows why?'

Who indeed? Did Eva's sister and Osmo know about the whippings? Could Eva have divulged something of such a personal nature to a Sariola sister who was a pert child, a whipper-snapper. (Yet a heroine too, by all accounts!)

Whipper-snapper: that was the word which had been confided

158

by Lucky to Elmer, to unlock his bride's girdle . . . Such a droll joke! Lucky deserved to be deposed. To have mocked a man so and sowed the seeds of his shame, she ought to be humiliated. Wasn't Osmo absolutely justified in rebelling? Oh but for his own motives of pique and pride! Those really shouldn't be Elmer's reasons. Elmer had won the contest to awaken the everything machine; won it fairly, and thereby won Eva – though he hadn't yet possessed her.

Nikki obviously appreciated the significance of that crown of whips. Lyle would also understand. But Lyle was seated in the body of the hall along with Moller and Minnow's Earthman, who was temporarily disencumbered of his birdy burden. Lyle wasn't family or royalty-to-be, and high table mustn't be too crowded. If only Elmer's assistant were beside him to lend support and sympathy.

'Who knows why?' Elmer echoed. 'Several people by now, I think.'

'Soon be all over, won't it, my Lord?' she murmured.

All over? Broadcast to everyone? Or finished and done with?

Naturally Elmer hadn't rushed from the Girlem's arms to Eva's bed to test himself. Nor with the aitch-house invaded had he yet done so. Not while the Girlem was still on the premises.

The Girlem was their secret weapon with which to pull the rug from under Osmo's feet and free the house. Soooon, as they used to tell Nikki's talking cat. This must be Eva's drift.

'Soooon, my goose,' he assured her. Her fan shifted and she smiled at him alone: a private smile. On this point of pride his half-blind wife surely saw eye to eye with him. Though what if Osmo was justified in his military action? What if Lucky had caused Elmer's problem, with that *whipper-snapper* word?

On the wall behind high table Lucky's visage smirked in oils, framed in brass. Not for much longer – Osmo had a plan for the portrait.

The feast had only been under way for a short time when Osmo stood and bellowed impatiently, 'Hark and hear!' The command was almost unnecessary, so quickly did the assembly hush.

Minnow teetered from her seat at the dining table to stand high-booted before the throne. She bit on her lower lip so as not to chatter nervously to herself.

At a signal from Elmer, Hermi approached the bellows-box which stood waiting upon its tripod, angled at the throne. Osmo

159

glared briefly at the shaman, then shrugged. Chunks of iron hung from the band around Hermi's waist like cumbersome armour over his khaki kilt. Oh no, he wouldn't float away now, even though he was barefoot. Hermi peered at the throne through the lens, but the flood of sunlight in which he himself stood made him blink, made him frown. He pulled all the long pins from his hair and stowed these in a pouch which hung from his chest. Swirling his dirty grey mane loose, he combed with his fingers. A hood of hair dangled to shade the eyepiece of the apparatus.

Moller advanced. The priest hadn't brought the *Book* with him, but it was too late to send him for it.

Sam Peller nipped up on to the dais. When he hauled the portrait from the wall the frame was heavier than he had estimated. Osmo's bondsman staggered – and thumped his burden upon the table, steadying it upright.

Slowly Osmo slashed the painting with his knife, while Moller was reciting:

> '. . . But she felt her strength was failing,
> 'And her power had all departed . . .'

Canvas hung in ribbons. Lucky had been flayed in effigy.

Next, the priest raised the crown above his fiery head, displaying it for all to see; then he turned to Minnow. A drum began to beat an urgent rhythm; Stone-Hans was thumping his fist.

'Hark, cuckoos, hark,' Osmo cried to the birds perching on the wrought-iron. 'Tell the Queen, the old Queen, the deposed Queen: tell her that she *is* deposed. Prince Osmo van Maanen is the consort of the true new Queen. Sing the story, tell the tale!'

He guided Moller's hands as the priest settled the leather and pearls down over Minnow's frizz; and stepped back. Drumbeats ceased abruptly. Minnow sat down, to total silence in the hall.

Should the assembly applaud? Should they clash their cutlery and bang their pots of ale?

This was the first time that a new Queen had ever been enthroned. Citizens of the aitch-house and the folk from Maananfors eyed one another. Already, to cheer would draw such attention to oneself. If only the shaman-drum had quickened its pace dementedly, rather than this eerie hush.

Osmo – *Prince* Osmo, now – might intend to say more; who'd wish to interrupt? Queen Minnow might be about to make a speech from the throne. Her lips were moving soundlessly. In the protracted quiet, with an audible click, Hermi tugged the wooden bulb below the bellows-box.

Soon a sepia card emerged. Tossing back his waist-length mane, the photographer peered at the managraph.

're-*markable* . . . *Extra*-ordinary . . .'

'What does it show, man?' from Osmo.

'What?' from Minnow.

'What? What?' came a chorus from the assembly.

Moller seized the managraph from Hermi, and goggled. He surrendered the card to Osmo a moment before patience ran out.

'Let me *see*,' squealed Minnow.

The picture wasn't *too* indecent. Yet it was certainly revealing: of bare bum, spine with bumpy vertebrae, legs tucked around a huge pink tongue. *Herself*, nude inside a monstrous serpent's mouth.

'Hey,' Minnow yelped. Was this a royal portrait or a striptease tableau from some sleazy tent on the fringe of a gala?

All at high table but Henzel were craning to see. Eva quickly turned a blind eye. Elmer blinked embarrassedly. Nikki looked scathing. But Osmo was enthralled.

'My little hen, my life,' he exclaimed. 'This,' he declared to the hall at large, 'is how our heroine trounced the Viper! It's just as I said! Right here, for all to see: how my duckling choked the giant snake.'

For all to see: her rump.

('Oh well I don't care!')

Her backside: access to longlife, as it were. Not that her bum itself was the route; that would have been too perverse of the Ukko which transformed her mother! Longlife lost to Osmo unbeknownst. She certainly cared in that regard.

Her prince consort flourished the managraph. 'Our heroine and our Queen gagged the Isi mage with her own virgin flesh – and saved me from possession!'

'*Oz*—'

For all to see: that's what he'd said, and a proclaimer ought to be true to his word. The assembly was agog.

The managraph travelled by way of Sam Peller to the nearest table. Roger Wex intercepted the sepia print and after one glance seemed about to stuff it inside his cloak. The card was snatched from his hand by a man nearby and continued onward rapidly . . .

'Stand, stand, Your Majesty,' urged Osmo. No sooner had Minnow complied than he seized the silvery fabric which graced the throne and draped this as a cape around her bare shoulders, as if in doing so he was cloaking the nudity of her image too. Accompanied by whistles of acclaim, her picture travelled from hand to hand so swiftly that most spectators enjoyed glimpses rather than gawps.

('*Spanky—*')

('*Spunky—!*')

Inevitably there were some respectful vulgarities, but increasingly a groundswell of acclaim arose.

('*Holy mana, she's a champ—!*')

('*Let's hear it for our Minnow—*')

('*It's just as he said, though he didn't say the half of it—*')

('*Let's hear it for her—*')

Chagrined if exalted, Minnow adjusted her crown which had tipped askew.

('*Let's see—!*')

('*It's a new reign, too true—*')

Could every mortal man possess a Sariola maiden? Oh no, but they could share a fleeting glimpse, men and women alike. The folk of Maananfors and the citizens of Loxmithlinna were akin now in their enthusiasm – united in their applause and loyalty to the heroine who had jammed herself in the Viper's gob. Allied in a furore of jovial fidelity, they acclaimed Minnow until the managraph had passed back into the custody of Sam Peller.

Minnow retrieved the card from the grizzled bondsman.

'That's enough!' Enough for all to see. Puckishly, draped in soft shiny silver, crowned in her pearls and black leather, she held the card to the nearest candle flame; and the assembly sighed as one body.

'Enough, don't you think?' Enough to brand people's memories. If she burned the managraph it would become legendary.

Flame crisped the card; flame ate it up. Minnow dropped the flaring remnant upon the fireproof tammy table to leave a historic scorchmark.

Just then, as if a huge hand had interposed outside, the sunshine faded. A cloud had masked the sun just as it sank behind the roof ridge. Candles burned brighter. All the shadows of cagework which had webbed the tables disappeared. A full third of the coronation guests sighed again – and grinned in amazed relief.

162

'Can you feel?'

'It's gone!'

'Gone away!'

Folk from Maananfors were mystified at the new surge of bon-homie on the part of their hosts. Explanations soon bubbled:

'The Dread has gone—!'

'The Dread is over—!'

As the sharp shadows faded, so had the cobweb which had haunted the aitch-house. Those hammocki webs had dissolved, in the mind, from off the roofs in this evening dawn of a new Queen's reign.

Now the interrupted feast resumed with gusto, though still without strong liquor. Queen Minnow perched on her ivorywood throne, accepting dainties from Osmo's fork.

In view of the collective éclat for Osmo's bride, not to mention this sudden remission of the Dread, Elmer had been exchanging worried looks with Lyle. Lyle had been nodding urgently, mim-ing: *We must.* And: *What else can we do?*

At last the Lord of Loxmithlinna announced: 'We have a special entertainer for the coronation—'

Lyle was already sauntering to a side door. He opened it wide and stepped aside, to admit . . .

'Her name's Goldi—'

Goldi by name, and gilded of skin, the Girlem approached slowly. The butter-gold of her flesh! Her brief tunic was of the same fabric as Minnow now wore as an impromptu cape. White mocca-sins, white lace elbow-gloves. An oval Sariola countenance, dark amber eyes close-set, bun cheeks. Her jet-black hair was bobbed. Her chin dimpled as she smiled tantalizingly. She rippled scales on her little silver harp. Upon one bare shoulder sat a starflower tattoo.

'Who in mana's name is *this*?'

'Don't be uneasy,' Minnow reassured Osmo. 'Eva already told me about her. She's really a Juttahat.' Nevertheless, Minnow raked the Girlem with her gaze. Eva looked away, fluttering her fan.

'A Juttie! That's absurd.'

'She was bred by the Brazens, the same way as Jatta's Jarl was bred.'

'To seduce people: is that why she's here?'

'It's all right, Oz. This is all to do with,' and fleetingly her eyes signalled, 'Elmer.'

'You mean to say he needs . . . ?'

'Shhh.'

'Why didn't you tell me?'

'Because!' Such childish truculence.

'*Because?*'

'Because, and that's it.'

Eva was smiling evasively – putting a brave face on matters? Sam scrutinized the golden lass and her unusual harp with considerable mistrust, his nostrils a-twitch. A good two-thirds of the assembly were amazed, in mid-mouthful. What hasty explanations were the remainder conveying to their neighbours, now that all were loyal fellow subjects of Queen Minnow?

The Girlem curtseyed to Minnow, then she bowed to Osmo. Plucking strings, she declared in a lusty melodious voice:

'Telling a tale of Tycho Cammon is my task, my Lord; and a tale of how you defeated the tyrant Tycho – you who will now humble Lucky Paula Sariola, and tie her hands. Isn't this fitting, my Lord?'

Momentarily Osmo was lost for words.

Well, of course it was fitting.

'*Let's hear it for Osmo!*' bawled someone.

'*Sing the story, tell the tale, eh?*'

'Let's!' urged Minnow. 'For Elmer's sake.'

The famous victory over Tycho at that gala where he had bespoken the tormentor into a stone statue (at great risk to himself if he'd faltered, but he hadn't) really was a model for how Osmo must cope with the mad Queen and her wooden soldiers. A model of courage and determination.

Not that he should even dream of turning mad Lucky to stone. Irrespective of her reputedly being immune to mana-effects, she was the foundress of a world, after all. Common people saw her as a saint as well as a delinquent given to quirks and foibles. In so far as she was a figurehead she had quite a deleterious effect upon people, no doubt! Yet even if she felt homicidal toward Osmo he couldn't kill her – that would be to act like a Tycho himself.

Just lock her up safely inside a granite dungeon, her immortal flesh surrounded by stone: that would be a punishment quite petrifying enough.

Actually, such an entertainment as this was splendidly timed to flesh out the coronation, which otherwise might have seemed somewhat off-the-cuff and lacking in ceremony. He'd wished to avoid *fatuous* pomp; to convey a mixture of seriousness and informality endearing to his followers. This would best reflect the new Queen's personality. (What could have been more suitable – if not wholly decorous – than Hermi's managraph of Minnow?) Yet Osmo did hanker for a bit more pomp.

Here it was in the person of this golden lass. After her no doubt fulsome narration Osmo himself might retell to everyone present the tale of Minnow and of mana-mazes and a mage . . .

Really, he owed quite a lot to Elmer. (His friend's initial opposition had been token, and understandable.) He owed Minnow's throne; and her silver cape. And now the exotic praise-singer! Minnow owed her crown to Elmer's wife.

Why, the material for Minnow's impromptu cape was the same as that of the entertainer's tunic! The precious ivorywood throne must have accompanied the Girlem to the aitch-house. Those brass rings on the sides of the chair were slots for poles so that seat and occupant could be carried . . .

Jutties bore their serpent-masters aloft. This luscious unique Juttie strumpet had been shouldered likewise. Minnow could be transported royally in such a fashion too, her stature enhanced without recourse to platform boots. There'd be a braggarty to riding on such a throne. Impressive, though.

The Brazens must have been keen to impress Elmer as well as excite him. Did the Isi want some device made for them by the instinctive engineer? What, they, with their workshops full of nimble slaves to carry out their notions – such as the manufacture of a miniature harp with silver pegs and tuning pins and an amplifier within so that the instrument sounded larger than it was, possessing more volume than the eye allowed it . . . ?

Elmer had kept the gorgeous alien lass hidden as a surprise but also for fear that Osmo might smirk at him on account of *because*. Elmer had always been guileless. How did his proud, injured bride cope?

With hands folded upon his green and gold waistcoat, Osmo prepared to hear the Girlem sing his praises.

> 'As a lad, young Tycho Cammon,
> 'Son of Ivan, and his lady
> 'Sophie of the family Donner,

'She who hailed from Verin Meadow
'Also known as Verinitty,
'Named because attacks by wild beasts
'In the past had posed a problem
'Till the Donners in their wisdom
'Fenced their fields with words and palings
'To exclude the savage raiders
'Then set poison bait near beast-dens
'Brewed from fungi by a shaman
'Known as Edvin son of Hubert
'Who had come from Kippan country . . .'

Young Tycho had been clever, and handsome too – with the minor exception of a little wen on his right cheek, which would later be known, sotto voce, as his *verrin's nipple*, as if the souls of all those poisoned carnivore cubs of old suckled there in secret, infecting him with their saliva. A comely lad, with sensual lips; but cruel. When his words became potent he would bespeak puffed-up barnyard roosters and pregnant pussycats to swell and burst apart.

Later, he would rupture rivals with his proclaimings, and steal women. To compel became a compulsion . . .

The Girlem was still harping on about Tycho's beginnings and the circumstances of his mother Sophie and of his father Ivan, and of Ivan's father too, and Sophie's mother, and Tycho's younger brothers as well. Fascinatingly! Her audience were enrapt.

To precede Osmo's praises, to be sure, certain preliminaries were essential. If you intend to handle something masterfully you must declare its origin. Name the root, then rule the branch.

When would she arrive at the meat of the matter in so far as Osmo was concerned? Each person and item she named led into a digression which she would gracefully abridge, leaving an off-spring tale dangling pregnant with possibilities, only to divert herself along another track. When would Osmo ever hear of the gala where he had bespoken Cammon into stone?

What gala? When? That bygone event hardly seemed urgently impending. On the contrary, it was becoming utterly remote from the past, and from the present too; detached into the distance, exiled.

So as to reach that climax, must the tale be taken up again

on another evening, and then another? Should he hear the rest of the tale of Tycho – the majority of it, if infinity could be divisible – from the Girlem in private, alone with her?

The coronation, so prematurely climactic, was being protracted interminably. How long had the Girlem been chanting this great narration at him? A story, evocative of power? No, of a prelude to power.

No: of the *very opposite*.

This lulling and dilatory tale of the tyrant, and presumably of Osmo's eventual triumph, endlessly unfolded itself and refolded itself, enmeshing him in a maze of futility. Harking to that supple voice, he realized hazily that he had no idea what his own long-term plan might be.

New coinage, yes. What then? His Minnow would wither and grow old until her face on the golden ors would no longer be her face at all. Should the coins be reminted to portray a tiny crone? She would have shrunken with age, as all old folk shrank. Especially in her case, she might almost disappear; might shrink into the distance, growing utterly remote from him. His little hen would become a scrawny chick. The chick would crawl feebly back inside the egg. The egg would re-enter the body of her mother hen. The mother hen would shrink in turn to become a skinny chick. Yet such futility was oddly comforting, verging on blissful.

Scales descended, and descended, on the Girlem's harp.

'Trip-trap!'

Minnow was shaking Osmo's arm.

The golden lass was telling a tale of the second wench whom Tycho seized. Such swoonful cadences; such sinuous fingering of the harp.

'Trip-trap!' Minnow nagged.

Osmo only half saw her. What could be so urgent?

'*Trip-trap, Oz! She stinks.*'

At that moment he became aware of what had evaded him hitherto; or rather, of what had been transmuted for him into a different sensation – into a delicious erotic languour, sweet detumescence which nevertheless lacked a climax; which *evaded* climax, so that somehow cravings were fulfilled without any culmination having occurred. In the absence of culmination, such barren bliss must continue. Desire was drained and appetite was quenched – yet addictively, so that one might wallow for ever and a day.

'Oz, the Brazens must want Mummy to win—'

The dimples in the Girlem's chin were moist. Despite the interruption she never paused in her bewitching attention to her tale and to himself. She was weaving himself and the tale together till soon it would be too laborious to find the knot with which to unravel himself, hidden under layers endlessly folding.

'Oh but the Brazens planted her here because the Brindleds armed you, Oz—'

Like some ingenious clockwork automaton of Elmer's with an Isi battery for a heart, the golden lass persisted in her harping and her telling.

'Don't you see, Oz, the Brindleds hoped you'd seize the aitch-house because they want to madden Mummy so she'll be careless. Whereas the Brazens must want her to find the Ukko-child without being distracted—'

An Isi mage had trained the Girlem superbly, yet not quite superbly enough now that Minnow poked her oar in. The Girlem's fragrance had been embalming Osmo. Realizing this, he was incensed.

'Be silent, *Goldi!*' he bellowed, rising to his feet. 'Snip your tale short; this is spoken. Sway me no more; nor the good people in this hall. Be dumb. I gag your gob and tie your tongue!'

Goldi's chest heaved, her throat fluttered, she choked. Speechless, the Girlem gaped. Her thighs trembled. Anxiety welled upwards in her like floodwater arising – and she plucked crashing chords. A silvery din rebounded around the hall so that cuckoos screeched. Heads ached at the overwhelming clangour of the tiny, potent instrument – it was hardly possible to think straight. Galvanized, the assembly leapt to their feet in alarm and protest.

Her teeth on edge, Eva choked out: 'Is that how they swayed Cully, day after day—?' *With the mind-maiming music of a miniature harp?*

'Be limp, wrists! Slip, grip, and fingers fail.'

Still the deafening dissonances tormented everyone's ears. Would Osmo's words be audible to her? Or would they be drowned as her own words had been drowned?

'Hands, be still!' he howled – and the harp finally slid from her grasp. Tumbling upon the floor, it emitted a final piercing twang. Amid blessed silence the Girlem stood desolate. Her lips moved dumbly. Moisture leaked from her dark amber eyes – tears of disappointment. Her right hand rose feebly though with such pathetic effort until her fingers touched her moistened cheek, and there was bewilderment as well as heartbreak in her eyes.

Guests surged to mob the performer. Yet this jostling assault faltered, restrained by the genuine grief of this alien lass. She wasn't merely disappointed; she was heartbroken, and her helpless dignity daunted them. Here was something quite outside of their experience. The indignant, confounded throng merely hemmed her in close to the dais.

'Be dumb,' Osmo repeated.

Elmer spoke gingerly. 'That's too harsh . . .'

'*What did you say?*'

'It's too severe. She has her reasons and her sorrows. She's all on her own.'

On her own?

Bred by the Brazens to seduce and tell trap-tales, and equipped with that box of tricks which played upon the mind, she was to be pitied?

Elmer's defence of the Juttie strumpet flabbergasted Osmo; fair took his breath away. *On her own?* Oh but this golden hussy had most certainly been intimate with bashful young Lord Loxmith! He knew her sorrows, her secret feelings, her sensitivities. *On her own*, indeed? Was Elmer disavowing responsibility for this attempt to trap Osmo in a web of words and weaken his will? If so, he was hardly very clever at concealing the ruse.

Eva's face was hidden by her fan, all but one lopsided eye – was she a party to this plot? And amid the throng around the Girlem, Lyle Melator was smirking, until he discovered an urgent need to polish his glasses.

Maybe it would be misguided to rant at his neighbour – and ever so reluctant ally – at this feast of reconciliation. But really! *Defend* the alien lass? Osmo's dander was roused.

'Speak her a lighter sentence,' Minnow appealed. 'Just . . . send her away.'

The Juttie lass was manifestly suffering bitter grief at her failure; unutterable heartache as if her whole reason for living had drained away. Her sorrow was quite literally inexpressible. Yet in what exactly did her tragedy consist? Being on her own amidst human beings, and shedding human tears?

'Please,' begged Minnow. 'The Queen pardons her.'

('Why yes, the Queen. That's who she is—')

('Our Queen Minnow, and no mistake—!')

('Just saved her lordly hubby's bacon *again*, I'd say—')

('It's that poetess business all over again. Next thing he'll be telling this Girlem to go and drown herself—')

('Talk about being trapped in your own tale—')

('I'd like to trap the Juttie chick's tail—')

('Just mind your talk, *and* your thoughts! She's Brazen trouble, is what she is. Any fellow touching her's a fool. He'll end up bewitched. Let's see the back of her—')

('Aye, to that—')

('You're a numbskull. She's *nakki*—')

('She's in misery—')

('Seems as Jutties have feelings too—')

('Scared of what her masters'll say—')

('There's more to it. And I'd say our Elmer knows what—')

How the jostling mob chattered.

Tread carefully on eggshells.

He mustn't bespeak her to flee and throw herself in a lake; or likely there'd be another Juke – a Juttie Juke – who would carry out some vengeance. He mustn't behave like a Tycho Cammon, or he'd end up turned to stone. The golden lass mustn't remain anywhere in his vicinity – certainly not in the occupied aitch-house – yet sending her back to the Brazens wasn't likely to be a bright idea.

'Get rid of her,' hissed Sam.

Where? Where? To the Brindleds, instead of the Brazens? Send her to his arms suppliers? That could prove provocative.

Her despair was so . . . eloquent, even though she couldn't say a word.

Ruefully Elmer confessed, 'She needs a partner . . .'

Osmo managed to keep his voice down. 'Was that to be me? Did *I* need a mistress, eh Elmer, in whose arms I could doze limply and forget myself?'

'She needs . . .' Elmer sucked in his cheeks, seeking a word, but the purse of his lips couldn't furnish one promptly. 'Someone as golden as herself,' he suggested at last.

Osmo breathed deep. 'Very well,' he said to the Girlem, 'be dumb for a week and a day; this is spoken.' Was there gratitude in her moist eyes? Perhaps; but mainly . . . tragedy. 'You'll go from here right now, alien witch—'

'With a knapsack of food,' urged Minnow. How could she be so forgiving of Elmer's duplicity, and of the instrument of that deceit?

170

'Yes, with a knapsack of food—'

'And in safety!' (Why *was* she so concerned? Ah, sympathetic memories of her sister Jatta's exile must be swaying her . . .)

'And *safely*,' Osmo bawled at the buzzing crowd. 'Do you all hear me?'

First the brass dwarf – and now this lustrous lass! Did Elmer have any more tricks up his sleeve? No. None at all. Elmer was abashed. Maybe Minnow's attitude of forgiveness was the wisest policy. She had trounced a mage, as everyone had witnessed in the sepia managraph. Now she had thwarted an alien witch.

'Go,' he told the Girlem, 'until you find a golden mate to bring you joy.' Which might take till for ever.

A delectable Juttie lass – the *only* such – searching the countryside continually for the unattainable, putting forth those aromas of hers to attract or repel, sniffing the breezes for clues like an animal, if this was within her capacity. Oh this would make a nobler tale than his doom of Eyeno Nurmi – who seemed to haunt him still at this moment, in the person of Elmer's one-eyed bride, dissimilar though those two afflicted women were in all other aspects.

The poetess may not have meant to bewitch Osmo; whereas the Girlem had so intended.

'Goldi could use a cloak,' said Minnow. 'Something discreet.'

A grey trousseau for a melancholy, vain pilgrimage.

'I'll see to it,' volunteered Nikki. Elmer's sister evidently made the offer not out of any affection for the golden lass nor any compliance to Minnow, but to be rid of the seductress for the sake of her sister-in-law . . .

And since the Juttie jade needed to carry food with her: 'May your fingers be firm enough to lift your knapsack, Girlem!'

The dejected mock-lass flexed her empty hands. Nikki ushered her silently to the door. The mass of the guests were milling about, babbling to one another.

Elmer scooped up the fallen harp, inspecting it for dents. 'So this kind of instrument caused Cully's confusion . . . and made him blind my goose. The same harp might have cured him too. We really ought to learn more from the Girlem—'

'Can't you bear to see her leave? Was she so addictive – that you fancied I needed a dose of her too? Can't you bear to see her go?'

Briefly Elmer hung his head. What a pang Eva must be suffering because of Osmo's jibe.

'Behave yourselves!' cried Minnow from her throne.

'*I'll* keep the harp,' Osmo told his equivocal ally.

'Ah . . . it stores in the drawer. Excuse me—'

Minnow hoisted her platform boots as Elmer stooped to deposit the instrument beneath the seat of the throne. To the casual eye it might have seemed as if he was kissing those boots as a mark of allegiance.

'It's yours to keep,' he mumbled. 'Throne and harp.'

'Bygones be bygones,' said Minnow. 'I'm glad you sent her away gracefully, Osmo.' She darted an oddly conspiratorial glance at Eva, who responded with a twisted smile. *Was something important eluding Osmo?* Something to do with Eva and Elmer and the banished Girlem, and leather thongs, and Minnow too? For the life of him he couldn't guess what that might be; so maybe it didn't exist.

Meanwhile a measure of decorum ought to be restored. Even if the new reign were to be more populist than Lucky's, propriety mattered at a coronation.

Osmo waved his arms. 'Let's all *sit down* again, good folk! Back to our seats, eh?' And to his bride, as the crowd complied: 'Bygones! But not so far as your mother's concerned, my royal duckling, mmm?'

During the commotion somebody – Hermi, doubtless – had draped a square of black silk protectively over the bellows-box on its tripod. If there'd been black silk in one of his pouches, why had he used his own hair as a hood beforehand? Hermi was no longer in evidence.

Presently Sam Peller peered suspiciously under the silk, and hurried to his lord.

'The lens has gone – as well as himself!'

Surely this was perfectly explicable. The shaman had been intent on safeguarding the mana-lens. Unable to hoist the complete apparatus due to the crush, he had removed the important part. A cover would keep dust out of the bellows-box . . . though where had that cover come from? Had Hermi floated away? Had he left the hall to intercept the Girlem and peer at her through his lens?

Hark and hear: it was almost two hours till a servant discovered the missing shaman in a cupboard. Hermi had been tied and gagged and blindfolded with yet more black silk.

It was a while longer till Hermi was halfway lucid; and even so his memory of events remained hallucinatory. He didn't know whether *he* had removed the lens for safe-keeping, or discovered that it had been removed. Was he himself carrying the lens away or was he in pursuit of an unknown thief when he was touched upon the neck and paralysed and dazed by a fragrance? He was quite unable to decide.

A drug had filled him with time-twisted, multi-faceted visions: of the lens and of corridors, of an assault so sudden that he barely noticed it, of the Girlem's buttergold face and a peering cuckoo harking to a fruity voice imploring, *'Don't sing this story; don't tell this tale'*; of Minnow and managraphs and Wex and the Girlem and a pocked oval moon-face with a single eye in it, and a young blonde woman rising from a waxen bloom, and a ginger-bread man dancing upon the hugely magnified webs of hammockis; of golden coins bearing the features of Lyle and Eva and Minnow and Goldi and himself; of faces galore, hundreds of persons. Untold dreamy versions of possibilities had replaced any single certainty as to what had happened to him. The longer that he had lain blindfolded in that cupboard, the more variations had proliferated kaleidoscopically until they were legion.

Where could such a drug have come from? From a Juttahat lass's chin-glands? From a rare fungus?

The Girlem had gone. Presumably she had gone. To find her a knapsack of food and a hooded gown hadn't taken long at all. The golden lass had been under such a sway to flee that Elmer's sister hadn't bothered to see the alien female down to the land-yard before returning to the banqueting hall for the drumming and the dancing.

It transpired that Roger Wex had left too, with his cuckoo. But Minnow had asked the Earthman to go – to catch Cully for Eva's sake. Maybe Wex ought to have taken the Isi harp with him to play to the dreamlord's nephew if he found him? Osmo wouldn't have allowed this. The instrument which could bemuse people's minds lay in the cupboard at the bottom of the ivorywood throne.

Really, the disappearance of the mana-lens could only enhance Minnow's legend as mage-tamer in the same way as had her burning of the managraph of herself naked in Viper's mouth . . .

Would Hermi ever fully return to his senses, or at least to his habitual frame of mind? The loss might have vexed him more if it hadn't seemed, in the hangover from his fugue, that in the realm of possibilities in some intangible sense he still possessed the lens but had merely mislaid it.

Waiting behind that side door to begin her performance and doubtless peering through the keyhole, the Girlem would have witnessed the making of the coronation picture and the excitement this produced. Hermi had previously been allotted a corner of Lord Elmer's workshop to sleep in. While he was taking the lens there for safety (but taking his time about it) she – on her way to quit the aitch-house – must have intersected with him. She must have assaulted him with paralysing fingers and overwhelming odour. That lens would compensate for her failure. In his experience Juttahats often collected unusual human memorabilia for their Isi masters. Wouldn't Lord Elmer send riders after the Girlem to search her?

And likewise riders to chase after Wex, who had taken a pony from the stables?

The next morning riders were indeed sent after both. The Girlem had set out on foot, muffled but unmistakable, as the guards at the wicket attested. No trace could be found of her. Numerous forest trails meandered northward of the lake, and anyone could hide himself.

Since Wex was on pony-back, pursuers were chary of racing helter-skelter too far away from the security of the aitch-house. After all, they had never caught Cully either . . .

So the bulk of the army sailed and steamed home to Maananfors, leaving behind a garrison genuinely leagued with the Defence Volunteers by those fleeting glimpses of the plucky young Queen in a monster's mouth. Next time that an invasion came, the aitch-house – reinforced by a jump-bike and guns, and boosted in morale – wouldn't surrender so readily, to a less gracious, less fair-minded invader.

Osmo – hark and hear! – remained oblivious to the likelihood that he might not be longlife, after all, and now might never be. Nor had Minnow any idea whether Eva would enlighten Elmer on this score, supposing that the Girlem had cured her husband of his problem, or alternatively supposing that Goldi hadn't . . .

174

PART TWO

MANOEUVRES
AND
MASSACRE

11 · THE CANDLE-PALACE

Minkie Kennan's splendid palace was in flames. So was the village which that marvel of white marble had dominated. Well, the edifice *did* still dominate the abandoned village. Blazingly so!

Its master was no longer at home. He watched, with his army, from a trampled pasture overlooking his former dream home.

Minkie could understand the white-painted wooden houses burning. But how could marble burn? Why, it burned like an enormous ornamental candle. Each embrasured window was a wick out of which gassy fire shimmied and billowed upward. Slim soaring towers were even more candlelike. Their erstwhile pennants had become hot panting tongues of scarlet and orange. The palace glistened greasily, its fabric luminous. It glowed as pinkly as the faces of all the acne-afflicted Snowies who were his troops.

Blistering houses were collapsing into crumbling cages of sparks. Soon the village would be a charred waste. Yet though transmogrified into a semblance of wax the palace seemed set to endure brightly, a memorial torch, a fountain of mana-fire.

Smoke rose up to haze and smut the sun-eye which hung in the zenith. That orb of hot butter had never slid from its central position, though when afternoon finally waned it would dim behind clouds which were its lids, to become by night a feebler silvery moon attended by a semblance of stars circling like phosphorbugs. Ascending fumes from the candle-palace polluted the limpid air. Already the upcurving landscape of forests and lakes without end – ever smaller and more remote but never yielding a final horizon – was becoming vague and tremulous at its infinite and infinitesimal extremities. Would a night of denser darkness descend in the wake of this evening, or of future evenings, if the palace continued to smoke?

Seated upon his three-wheeled Juttie jump-bike, attired in brass-studded black leathers with exaggerated lapels and cuffs and high collar – and upon his head a crested black leather helmet trimmed with brass dangling a plume of black pony hair

– Minkie surveyed the demise of his paradise here in this hidey-hole away from the ordinary world and from the Queen's wrath.

Wrath had arisen here too, in the person of a one-eyed poetess militant. *So it had come to this! Expulsion from his palace.* How unfair, when he had merely been enjoying himself, seducing his way through the echo-damsels in whom that damned Eyeno Nurmi felt some obsessive proprietorial interest.

Sure as shit he wouldn't be chased out of this inner otherworld by a poetess with one eye missing!

He dismounted.

Ranged around Minkie were a hundred Snowies clad in bright red leather and armed with long knives and crossbows or lightrifles. Five-score blond squinty stuttery henchmen with the complexion of damp strawberries thanks to their rampant acne: this was five times as many sidekicks as had originally guarded his palace and acted as steward and cook and valet and flunkey.

Nakkis, the lot of them: creatures who served Minkie's will, cast in the mould of the real Snowy who would be back home in Niemi Keep mending leaks in the roof for Minkie's mum and Kyli; or not, as the case might be.

Come to think of it, Kyli's pregnancy should be almost full-term by now. Snowy might already be leering and crooning over a cradle, to Kyli's consternation. Our Minkie might be dad to a brat by now. All sense of time had deserted him.

Where had all the extra Snowies come from? Whence this sur-feit of blotchy-faced, tongue-tied soldiers? All of the nakki-maids in Minkie's palace must have become Snowies. Gave him summat of a squirm, it did, to recollect how he had sported with those obliging female attendants before his amorous attentions turned to the echo-sisters who were quite a different kettle of fishes . . .

Snowies had suffered casualties. That didn't mean they mightn't reappear in the ranks. Maybe when one was seemingly killed, two Snowies took the place of the casualty. This might be the key to how he could overwhelm Eyeno Nurmi's supporters. Successes on their part might only result in flooding the place with Snowies – unless our Minkie lost control of the resulting multitude.

A multitude of *one and the same*, repeated over and over.

'Wu-wu-whatdu-du-dowedu-du-donext,Bu-bu-boss?'

        'Wu-wu-whatdu-du-dowedu-du-do,Bu-bu-boss?'

                'Wu-wu-whatdu-du-dowedu-du-do?'

The candle-palace glowed and smoked. Burning houses fell

apart. Away beyond the conflagration, Eyeno's forces capered. She commanded jugglers who threw their clubs a long way as missiles; fiddlers who fired arrows from their strings; bandsmen in scarlet uniforms who blew fire-darts from trumpet or cornet. Worse were the former mummers who had become beasts on two legs. Shaggy goats and antlered tarandras toted sickles and lightrifles. There were even a couple of man-sized nakki-cuckoos whose great clawed feet could eviscerate a Snowy.

Hadn't Eyeno's regiment suffered losses? Certainly; but now there seemed to be more of them than ever. Maybe the principle applied that the more the two sides fought, the more extensively the two sides *would* fight – unless Minkie himself was laid low. Or Eyeno herself. Maybe she had broken off the engagement in order to muse a while about the implications while her army celebrated.

'Bu-bu-boss,whatdu-du-dowedonu-nu-next—?'

This particular Snowy's right arm rested in a blood-stained sling.

'Where do *you* come from?' Minkie asked him.

'From the pu-pu-pu-pu-PALACE, boss! I come from the palace.' The injured Snowy beamed in triumph.

From the palace; where else? And from Minkie's mind and memory.

'What I mean is: were *you* originally in my palace to begin with?' *Or were you a nakki-maid? Did I embrace you ebulliently and obliviously in my silky bed before the lack of challenge jaded me? You, with your weepy roseate face?*

The Snowy's stutter resumed in full disconsolate flood. A dozen big boulders blocked the stream of every sentence. 'Du-du-dunno whatyoumu-mu-mu-mean,Bu-bu-boss.'

Naturally the Snowy didn't know. He was the same Snowy as the others. Apart from injuries, how could you tell them apart? You shouldn't even try to in case you bewildered them and made them fractious.

Our Minkie must certainly decide what to do. Give them a lead. Sow no doubts in their blond noddles in case his authority evaporated.

Hemmed round by Snowy custodians, Minkie's two echo-girl hostages were protesting shrilly. Minkie strode over to resolve this problem first.

Hard to say which of the two was the more vociferous: peachy-skinned Anna of the sultry eyes and black curls, or Paula of the

179

blonde pigtails – though in every other respect the image of Queen Lucky. Anna's lacy gown, hung with hundreds of pink and rose ribbons, was now quite dishevelled. She seemed to be a beggar dressed in tatters. Muddily barefoot. Paula's gauzy frilled flouncy frock was far more pristine. It was embellished modestly with a constellation of yellow ribbon rosettes as if narciss flowers grew upon her bosom and midriff. On her feet were dainty yellow moccasins. Paula hadn't been in Minkie's clutches for nearly so long as Anna. The Queen's echo had been a lucky capture during the recent fray.

'Minkie Kennan, I insist on being with my girlfriends! I thought you were a blithe gentleman who only cared about joy and delight—'

'—and about Inga and Gerda and Gretel and Maria and Anna,' muttered Minkie, itemizing his various romps which Eyeno had put paid to. 'And about you as well, my fine hen.' Paula had been his ultimate amatory ambition, before the wretched mutilated poetess turned up.

Aside from Eyeno's missing glimmer, and ignoring (or imagining away) those stern brown breeches of hers, no doubt she was still as sveltly handsome as when first he had set eye on her. Alas, proximity to that particular hen made his cock wither and turned all beauty to ashes. (Similarly, her inordinate hostility had scorched his pleasure palace!) He should keep well away from her for ever more. How could he avoid her, when she pursued him so belligerently? No two ways about it: his Snowies would have to kill her. Maybe the proliferating Snowies would only kill her troops, and vice versa . . .

How might he come to grips with her personally? The solution would have to be a crossbow quarrel or a shaft of hot light fired by himself. She didn't expose herself needlessly . . .

His custody of Anna, and now Paula, might goad Eyeno into carelessness.

'At least you have a chum with you,' he told the Queen's echo.

'You must let us both go, Minkie Kennan!' the pigtailed blonde insisted. 'We shouldn't be apart from our girlfriends—'

'Gunther will find a way to punish you! Especially if you touch me again. Or if any of these disgusting bum-faces do. I'll catch a disease from them—'

'No you won't.'

If anything, Anna was the more indignant at her captivity. 'They're nauseating!'

'Dear ladies,' Minkie appealed. 'My Snowies won't touch you . . . much . . . not if you move when you're told to, and where.'

'My Gunther will be furious.'

'Him? I'll blow him away on a puff of wind and a wish.'

'Excuse me,' Paula quizzed her fellow prisoner, 'but *whoever is Gunther*?'

Naturally Paula didn't know about the big chap. Gunther had appeared from nowhere, starkers, in the master bedchamber of the palace just as Minkie – likewise in his birthday buff – was delightedly enjoying Anna in similar déshabillé. Minkie's activity had somehow stimulated the materialization of Anna's hubby as a witness of this randy scene, and had caused a partial recovery of her memory of him.

Such an interruption quite put a fellow-me-lad off his stroke. Nor was it immediately evident that the nude intruder lacked solidity.

Well, Gunther did seem to have been engaging in some rather drastic slimming. His face, framed by straggly blond hair which could do with a wash, had been strikingly cherubic, though his grey eyes wore a haunted cast – as well they might at confronting such a spectacle as Minkie sporting with his wife. A silver chain, dangling a locket, had hung between rings through Gunther's nipples: his sole article of attire. Recently he must have been considerably stouter, to judge by slack skin and stretch-marks. He had bloated himself, and now was starving himself. Yet it wasn't therein that his dearth of mass consisted, for his was still a substantial presence. No: he could be banished by a harsh word, blown back to where he had come from.

Minkie gathered that Gunther had *dreamed* his way to Anna's echo, from some berth in the ordinary world outside of the wonderland of meadows and maidens and nakki-folk. Long ago he had been wedded to Anna who had grown old and died. Anna – indisputably a Sariola daughter when she was alive – had given him longlife, and he had remained fanatically faithful to her memory. Anna had lost all memory of him till Minkie's cock crowed and reawakened her recollection.

At the time of this contretemps Minkie had cudgelled his brains to identify the intruder. He'd seen him *somewhere*; and in burlier fettle. By now he realized that Anna's husband was . . . Bock? Buck? Beck? An eccentric lord. A dabbler in dreams, about whom he'd heard scraps of gossip in taverns on his former Juttie-hunting travels.

Sultry Anna, whom Minkie's incomplete massage had roused from amnesia, had regained full-blooded passion for her absent hubby, though only incomplete awareness of her previous life with him, or of her present circumstances. (Still, she was enlightening her fellow hostage now, as best she could, surrounded by Snowies with suppurating red faces . . .)

The encounter in the bedchamber had swiftly been overshadowed by the attack on the palace, stirred up by the poetess to rescue Anna and put Minkie in his proper place. That place wasn't, in her view, a château of sensual indulgence commanding the hamlet. Nor should her girlfriends be his concubines. No sooner had Eyeno returned to the village from whatever wanderings she'd undertaken through the nakki-domain than a siege commenced, which fully occupied Minkie's attention. During the siege – according to a Snowy who guarded Anna, to her disgust – Gunther had reappeared twice. Gunther had tried to embrace Anna, and she him. He had tried to carry her off. Instead, he had floated away and evaporated. Would Gunther be able to find Anna again now that the palace was ablaze, and Minkie was expelled with all his Snowies? Maybe Gunther's dream-ghost could burn like a candle.

Wherever Eyeno had previously wandered to, evidently she'd acquired some forceful *words*, sufficient to mobilize nakkis and set marble on fire. Yet – being a girl – she couldn't have learned enough, could she? Otherwise the siege would have been shorter. Minkie would have been booted right out of this peculiar paradise which had turned sour. He wouldn't have been able to torch the village after the palace started heating up.

Bit of a proclaimer by now, that poetess. A far cry from when van Maanen had bespoken her to leap in a lake. To what extent was she in control of her newfound powers? Her army were frolicking about; whereas his own Snowies were merely milling, awaiting leadership. Bless the two Snowies who'd been lucky enough – and had the initiative – to snatch Paula while they were in retreat from the palace.

'Wu-wu-whatdowedu-du-DO,now,Bu-bu-boss?'

'So you see, Paula, you're really the echo of my *mother*—!'

'How *can* I be, silly?'

'My Gunther says you must be. I think that's what he meant. We didn't have long together, and he was trying to rescue me—'

'*Bu-bu-bu-BOSS*—!'

Minkie made haste to recover his bike, and free-wheeled it back towards his reluctant guests.

'I can't be taken away from here, can I, Paula?' he heard. 'I'm an echo. But *you're* the echo of my mother. You're the echo of the Queen, and the Queen isn't dead. She lives forever—'

'We can't be dead,' argued Paula. 'We're echoes in the mind of the moon-seed.'

'You are, Paula, but I'm dead. I died years and years ago. I was Gunther's wife. I know my whole name now.'

'You found your other name?'

'It's Beck. Anna Beck. And you're Paula Sariola.'

'Silly, I know I am.'

'That's the Queen's name.'

'The Queen of where? The Queen of what?'

'Of Kaleva! It's a whole world outside this world. Mind, you're much sweeter than I remember my mother ever being – though I don't remember too much about her. I'm still confused. I'm sure you're the echo of a Queen who's alive.' Anna tugged at her coaly curls as if to convince herself. 'That must be why your hair's not the same colour as ours, Paula.'

'Maybe you're the *real* Queen!' Minkie butted in, inspired. 'Maybe the Queen on the throne is an impostor—'

'You *know* about this?' cried Anna.

'A sham, a pretender, a double! Maybe she hid you away here – her twin – and stole your memory so that she could reign in your place.' *The old story of Lucky Paula Sariola told how she entered the space-faring entity and was altered by it . . . No mention of a twin coming into existence.*

'You know about this?' echoed Paula. She smelled of spicy buns, which Minkie had hoped to *devour*.

'I know a lot of things, dear lady.'

'You must let me go then! You must let both of us go.'

'Then how would you learn what I know?'

'BU-BU-BOSS!'

'BU-BU-BOSS!'

Snowies everywhere. One of them raised Minkie's standard high. He was waving it to and fro as if semaphoring to the opposing forces. The flag on the pole – Minkie's chosen battle emblem – depicted an ebon-skinned Juttahat in sable livery hanging upside-down by one ankle from a tree, its guts transfixed by an arrow.

'BU-BU-BOSS!'
                'BU-BU-BOSS!'

'Wait a bit, Snowy, will you all!' *To have a compliant rival Queen in his clutches, one who could plausibly be presented to folks in the real world as an improvement on Lucky, and a suitable replacement for her . . . ha! He'd need to be even more of a subtle charmer than usual – though firm, into the bargain.*

The possibility of deflecting Lucky's revenge by this ploy, supposing that he was forced out of this otherworld, beckoned tantalizingly. Always have a few strings to one's bow, eh?

Meanwhile . . .

'Bu-bu-*boss*—' One Snowy was practically blubbering.

'Such things I can tell you, Paula Sariola. Maybe I can take you out of here, to your true realm!'

'We can't ever leave our home here,' protested Anna. 'My Gunther wasn't able to carry me off in his arms.'

'Maybe a dream-ghost shouldn't try to snatch a dead echo. Anyway, look,' and he pointed, 'your cottages have all burnt down.'

There was such doubt in Paula's eyes. 'You and your bullies burned those!'

'Bullies, Your Majesty?' Should he call her that, to tempt her? Maybe this would make her haughty. 'Kindly cast your eyes upon Eyeno's *monsters* over there. See what she turned your villagers into with her hatreds.' Goat-men and cuckoo-men capering about . . .

Paula's brows were knit. She would need some persuading – at which Minkie was a dab hand, so long as he could squeeze a few hours peace amidst the tumult. Right now, he was altogether too close to the meadow where he had first entered this domain. If he and his Snowies were driven towards that meadow with the stream and the creamy waxen flowers, supposing that their situation seemed desperate and he jumped the bike in a certain direction, why, he might find himself back up on the bouldery headland overlooking Loom Lake, all alone. Or he might find himself *in* the waters of the lake, spluttering, his bike sinking from under him.

Somewhere beyond the stream there would be an entrance to a tunnel, probably by way of some caves. His dad Ragnar had entered this otherworld beneath the supposedly bottomless lake without benefit of jump-bike. Dad had simply chucked himself down from a cliff-top. Water-nakkis had hauled him the rest of the way. Eyeno, likewise, for sure. She'd know which way to chase our Minkie. He mustn't be pushed in that direction yet.

Shading his eyes against the hazing sun-eye in the zenith, Minkie gazed up the curving repetitive terrain of forests and lakes as the smoke from the candle-palace arose. Oh you couldn't accommodate all this even under a bottomless lake. This place was woven of mana. Perhaps it was fairly modest in volume. Yet the further you went within, the smaller you yourself and the landscape progressively became so that this otherworld could contain a multitude of places similar in substance if not in size. You would never notice that you'd become miniature, no bigger than a bug, no bigger finally than a thought. The air was like a lens, magnifying what seemed far away. That lens was becoming blurred.

Where had the poetess gone to, up the slope of the innerworld, to become powerful? (Not all-powerful, by any means!)

If Minkie could go where she had gone, and find what she had found, mightn't he transform his own bewitching charm into commanding power? Thus his Snowies would become invulnerable, and himself too, safeguarding him against Lucky when he chose to leave this place? Aye, leave it together with an acquiescent blonde twin of the Queen, who could replace the madwoman of Pohjola Palace!

Eyeno Nurmi hadn't expelled him. She had spurred him; saved him from soft pillows and tippling. The route out was too close, too soon. There were prizes to seize. Minkie the Juttahat-hunter was the man to make the most of it.

He revved his bike.

'Lads,' he called to his Snowies, 'a war calls for marches and camps. We'll occupy other villages; loot them for food, and maybe burn them behind us. Yes, torch them. We shan't be squibs in this war. Our enemy will pursue us into desolation and ambush. She'll follow us because we'll be aiming to find what she discovered; and with us as our guests' – at which Snowies grinned and chortled – 'will be these two girlfriends of hers, one of whom is of high importance to me. *Both* are, of course,' he added gallantly. 'We'll treat them very decently and protectively.'

'Haven't we always, Boss?'

'How can I *march* anywhere?' Anna complained. 'I've no shoes. My Gunther will strangle you.'

Under ordinary circumstances – and had he not been slimming so severely – her Gunther might have achieved that aim. If the dreamer reappeared while they were marching and camping, he hardly had the tonnage to perturb Minkie one whit. No ballast whatever, no more than a bag of fluff.

'Well now, dear ladies, there's a point. Naturally you mustn't walk. One of my Snowies will carry each of you pickaback on his shoulders.' This would allow the ladies far less opportunity for escape.

Anna stared in horror at a leering Snowy whose face was as pink as a pig with leaking acne. Were her thighs to be pressed against such cheeks? 'I'll walk!'

'No, you'll ride.'

Paula looked thoughtful. She brushed her flouncy frock as if ash from the blaze was settling on it. 'If I'm important I ought to ride, oughtn't I?' Oho, did one detect a certain vanity?

'Jutties carry their serpent-bosses aloft, coiled around their shoulders,' Minkie said encouragingly.

'What are Jutties?' asked the Queen's echo. Anna, also, looked blank.

'Why, they're the servants of the alien snakes. Giant alien snakes infest the world outside of here.'

'Snakes?' squealed Paula. 'My so-called realm is full of giant *snakes*? Let me go back to my friends even if our village is burnt down!'

'No no,' Minkie said hastily, 'they don't *infest* everywhere. In fact there aren't all that many of them. Just a handful or two. Unless you go looking you'd be hard put to see one. They live underground and hardly ever show their heads, honest.'

'You're trying to scare me—'

'I wasn't.'

'Better the Snowies I know than these Jutties that I don't! That's it, isn't it?'

'Actually, the serpents are called the Isi. The few that there are. Do you see how much I have to tell you?'

'Do I wish to know? We were enjoying ourselves before you came—'

'And you continued to enjoy yourselves – even more so, thanks to me – till Eyeno shoved her oar in!'

'*She* didn't scare us.'

'She ought to now.' Minkie gestured at the poetess's troops, those beast-persons and cuckoo-persons.

'I'd rather Gunther told us such things,' said Anna. 'Then I'd know they were true.'

Said Minkie, 'You're innocent, so you need protecting.'

Anna glared scathingly at her seducer.

'Probably we'll find other sisters of yours in other villages, dear ladies.'

'And burn their villages?' Anna was really being obstreperous. *Damn that intrusive dreamer.* It was Gunther Bock, no, Beck who deserved strangling while he lay asleep in some keep.

Was Beck only dreaming by night? 'More deeply than any man ever dreamed': so he'd bragged, when his dream-ghost invaded Minkie's bower of bliss. Was his any ordinary sleep? Or was it a kind of extended shaman-trance lasting for a week, a fortnight, even longer? This could account for Beck becoming skinny when he had evidently boasted a mass of blubber in the not-so-distant past. Gunther was feeding on his fat – not merely fasting so as to summon a vision but maybe unable to eat at all. Like some hibernating serpent, ha!

'How can your Gunther stay asleep for so long?' Minkie challenged Anna.

Maybe she knew, but wasn't saying.

'We'll mu-mu-march, Bu-bu-boss. We'll bu-bu-burn villages for you. We'll lu-lu-lure that Eyeno to di-di-disaster—'

To boost their morale, it was time for a promotion. He called out, 'Which of you lads caught the blonde chick?'

'Mu-mu-me,' managed one of the red-clad cronies.

Minkie raised his voice. 'You did good. As a reward, from now on you're my right-hand Snowy. Stick by me.' The nakki's countenance certainly looked syrupy enough.

Dismounting, Minkie removed his helmet, exposing his chestnut curls, and yanked off the plume of black pony hair. Such a spring in his step. In some dreams you could dance; other dreams were full of treacle. It had been quite a burden to carry Anna up all those stairs to his bedchamber not so long ago – but a surmountable burden. Back in the ordinary world he couldn't have managed it.

Minkie thrust the stem of the plume through a slit in the Snowy's lapel. By decorating his newly appointed lieutenant he made sure that he'd be able to distinguish him from the rest of his kin. Contented, he stepped back.

How gratified was the Snowy? The acne-stricken nakki shuffled. 'Thanks, Bu-bu-boss . . .' He squinted at his peers, some of whom seemed puzzled. Weren't they all the same as himself? 'Du-du-does this mu-mu-mean I get to be cu-cu-called "boss" too?'

'You're Little Boss,' said Minkie, 'and I'm Big Boss.' Now he had a special name for at least one of the Snowies; which was a help. 'You, and you,' he told two others, 'crouch down so that the ladies can mount you.'

When the chosen bearers had squatted: 'Come on now, dear ladies, climb aboard and we'll be off.'

Anna clutched her pink and rose ribbons protectively around herself; but she obeyed. So did Paula.

When the Snowies straightened up, Anna and Paula rose almost as high above the troops as the flag. They'd easily be visible to that throng of bandsmen and beastmen – gallingly so to the breeches-clad poetess. Minkie's nakki-men cheered derisively at their enemies.

Led by Big Boss on his black Juttahat jump-bike with Little Boss marching alongside, the Snowies brandished crossbows and rifles and knives as they tramped off in a disorderly mass. The candle-palace continued to burn with multiple flames without showing the least sign of melting or crumbling. Though its smoke misted the heavens, surely it would remain a beacon while they ascended the landscape heedless of any steepness, and shrank, perhaps, without feeling diminished.

Amidst her frolicking forces, Eyeno Nurmi seemed to dither about giving chase.

12 · LOST FOR WORDS

Atrocity-monstrosity-osity-osity . . .

Eyeno had heard that refrain previously, when first she entered this domain. Previously the hum of *-osity* in her head had been merely a minor descant to the invasive voice of the moon-child.

Monstrosity and *atrocity* had swiftly ebbed away, just as the animal anguish of her flight towards oblivion was to abate once she met the meadow-maidens of her dreams.

On her vagabond journey from Speakers' Valley to the end of the world much had vanished. She'd been under Lord Osmo's harsh sway, of course, yet horror had also driven her and robbed her of words. Words such as *brother*; words such as *love* . . .

188

Now, with Minkie's palace in flames at the edge of an incinerated village, the hum in her head had returned: the same
crazy croon as when her rags were still soaked from her suicide
bid.

> *Bellicosity* ...
>> *Ferocity* ...
>>> *Monstrosity!*

Those were hideous unwieldy words, fit for no poem whatever.
They reverberated in applause for her achievement in ousting
Minkie Kennan who had once tried to ravish her ... A certain
Juke Nurmi had also yearned to do so in a furtive, corrupted
part of himself.

Eyeno was no longer a poet. Too many precious words were
missing. Yet she had set out through that new terrain in search
of words. Perhaps she had been on the brink of success – until
she set eyes on that *rogue*, romping rampantly.

A brown-kilted goat-man pranced, waving a sickle. In jubila-
tion or frustration he flung this high over the collapsed glowing
debris which had been a cottage. As the sickle sped away from
his hairy hand, it was a lethal little cousin of the shining arc
over the night-time horizon of the land which Eyeno had left
behind, the debris-ring of Kaleva's bygone moon. The sickle
swung. The curved blade was returning from over the hot cindery
wreckage; swooping back.

Gerda squealed, and clutched her sister Maria.

Gerda and Maria were so twin-like that you could scarcely tell
them apart unless you saw their souls – as did Eyeno, faintly,
with her inward eye. One lass was a pink heartbell fluttering as if
in a breeze. The other echo-lass was a quivering violet starflower.
These blooms were their hearts, their essence, perceived in a
different mode of vision from everyday sight. The two flowers
twined together in panic as the airborne sickle skimmed back –
to *decapitate* one of them?

Ah no, the weapon was flying towards the goat-man's upheld
palm. He snatched it by the handle. He sniffed the blade with
caprine nostrils, tasted it with his rough tongue, trimmed a few
hairs from his dangling beard. Maria and Gerda released one
another, though they still shuddered with shock. As well they
might, upon a battlefield.

Kennan had previously made the beast with two backs with
both of them. Oh, the beast with *three* backs. They'd confessed
this to Eyeno so guilelessly. Kennan's amours might have been

a game, not an imposition upon innocence by a scoundrel whose presence was corrupting this inner world, breeding blotch-faced bullies like so many nakki-offspring of his couplings; whose wishes had reared him a lordly palace, and decreed a perpetual drunken carnival to amuse him.

Eyeno mustn't be priggish in her fury, must she? Juke had been a prig. Look what lurked beneath. Between purity and priggishness was a crucial divide.

A scarlet-clad trumpeter in jaunty peaked cap tootled. From his instrument he blew a fire-dart mischievously in the direction of the burning palace. A harlequin somersaulted.

And who was this?

An upright brindled brown beast with such a rapacious yellow-toothed snout!

Those fierce beady eyes; that long bald tail like a whip. It was a *verrin-man*.

He wore a leather harness and leather kilt. In his claws he clutched a lightrifle. Where had he come from? Eyeno had inherited a veritable carnival dedicated to Kennan's appetites, and had transformed it. She hadn't seen this fellow till now. The verrin-man seemed a quintessence of savagery. So many of her nakki-troops were freaks; or had become freakish.

Not that she, of mutant blood, should quail at this. Her mother Ester's eyes with their rectangular pupils were those of a goat. But still! A verrin-man . . .

She spied another such, armed with a huge rusty knife – or was that the dried blood of a Snowy upon the blade?

Where had so many of those Snowies come from? More Snowies than ever crowded that wide pasture in the distance.

As the verrin-man with the rifle paced in Eyeno's direction Inga whimpered, 'I don't like *him*.'

'He won't harm you.'

Of the echo-lasses, Inga most resembled Eyeno in build, being slim and tall. Though dark-haired, Inga was peppered with freckles. Eyeno herself sported several milk-chocolate moles on her cheek and neck. Her loose silky yellow hair mostly hid those grace-notes upon her flesh.

Eyeno reassured Inga. 'He'll protect you from oppression.' Ah yes, from exploitation and abuse.

'Everything's different and horrid – except for you, Eyeno. Now Paula's a prisoner as well as Anna! What will Minkie and his Snowies do to them? Look!'

190

Wee in the distance, Snowies were hoisting the blonde lass and the coaly-haired lass high . . .

The verrin-man growled. Spittle sprayed as he spoke gutturally. 'War-woman, we attack again?'

Was that what she was: a war-woman? Snowies had been butchered only for more Snowies to spring up. Eyeno noticed a third verrin-man amongst her frolicking throng, and felt sick.

'We swarm after them, warrior-woman?' Her inciter bared yellow fangs in a grin.

'No, not yet—' This world might be lacerated by strife as combatants multiplied . . .

'Palace won't stop burning till we snuff all the Snowies—'

Did he know this for a fact? The fire spurting from the windows and pinnacles of the palace was like none she had ever seen. How could marble glow as if molten?

A cuckoo-man was approaching her, staring with big yellow eyes and harking with feline ears. Instead of a nose: a cruel beak. Tarnished green plumage coated his body. A baggy plumed membrane linked each arm to a side of his rib-cage. Only Eyeno's familiarity with such dear mutants as Lammas the werewool persuaded her not to flinch; and the fact that Inga and her sisters were relying on her. In a clawed hand the cuckoo-man clutched a three-pronged harpoon.

Ordinary cuckoos were repositories of gossip, if not exactly of wisdom. What, therefore, might a cuckoo-man have to say?

Announcing his presence, he crowed, 'Ukko-ukkoo!'

'Sing us a story, tell us a tale,' she suggested.

The cuckoo-man blinked. 'There's to be war in the world,' he announced. 'Queens and lords in conflict, until a new moon is born in bloody fiery throes.'

Was this creature a prophet rather than a narrator of what had already happened, as ordinary gossip-birds were? Had he come to restore her own lapsed ability to tell fortunes, so that she might gain some guidance as to what was best to do?

'How can there be more than one Queen?' she asked the cuckoo-man. Surely this couldn't be an allusion to herself just because she was now in command of a little army . . . an army which might grow vaster. The problem with fortunes was that recipients readily misunderstood because their wishes clouded their judgement.

'Which Queens?' she persisted.

'Till the moon-child is born,' croaked the green-plumed figure. 'Uprooted in a rupturous schism.'

'You're our Queen,' Inga said tremulously. Her tone implied that for the sake of herself and her sisters this had better be true. Eyeno must command these verrin-men and other prodigies effectively – or what might happen?

Eyeno, Queen of nakkis . . . versus Minkie Kennan, lord of other acne-flushed nakkis. She must be careful not to become puffed with pride and make wrong assumptions.

'*Paula's* the echo of Queen Lucky,' she told the cuckoo-man. Kennan held Paula captive now, chaired like a trophy on a Snowy's shoulder.

The verrin-man interrupted. '*Enemies, going.*'

This was true. The mass of Snowies were moving off – and not in the direction of the tunnel by which Eyeno had first entered this domain. Somewhere thereabouts would have been the best place for Kennan to jump back out again to the cliffs overhanging the lake on his strange machine which could disappear then appear elsewhere. If Kennan intended to leave.

Burned out of his palace, she had hoped that Kennan might quit this domain. Yet if he took Paula – or Anna – with him: *oh no*. Minkie could hardly carry both of the lasses on his riding machine. He might force, or charm, one or other of them to go with him . . . That mustn't happen.

'Attack them now, war-queen?'

War-queen! How the verrin-man's eyes gleamed.

To rush in pursuit of the enemy now might panic Minkie Kennan. He might bundle a lass on his bike, abandon his Snowies, take her away where only Eyeno could follow . . . ineffectively, lagging far behind, leaving her domain abandoned. Could Paula, or Anna, genuinely quit the moon-child? How could they possibly do so? Kennan mightn't care whether they survived.

'Let them run away for now,' she told the beast-that-walked-upright.

'Or else war will finish too quickly?' How the verrin-man grinned. Supposing that he only existed due to this strife, and only during its course, should he wish the conflict to come to a premature end?

'What about Paula and Anna—?'

'Inga, listen to me: if we act right now we might scare Kennan.

192

He might carry one of our friends off ... to the place I came from. We might lose Paula or Anna for ever.'

Inga nodded, though she didn't really believe in the existence of such a place, elsewhere. In spite of her loving loyalty she must be dubious about pursuing those Snowies.

'The war might finish too quickly,' Eyeno told the verrin-man. 'We need to watch where our enemies go and what they do before we punish them.'

Kennan's troops were heading away in the direction that she herself had taken on her trek through the moon-child. What might *he* discover on that route, treading it with greed and vexation in his heart?

'Can you fly?' she asked the cuckoo-man. 'Can you follow Minkie Kennan and the Snowies from the air, as our scout?'

The cuckoo-man flapped his arms. Plumed membranes billowed. 'To see ahead, war-queen?'

'Ahead into the distance – and maybe into the future too? Can you see both, Cuckoo-man?'

The creature considered. Altering his grip on the trident, he scratched his buttock with a prong. 'War shall not cease,' he squawked. 'The son resumes Ragnar's ruin, reflected and magnified.'

The son resumes Ragnar's ruin ...

On her journey Eyeno had heard tell of this Ragnar. Ragnar had been the only previous trespasser into the moon-child. He had indulged his whims until his short temper and rashness turned the nakki-inhabitants fiercely against him and he was chased out with salt on his tail.

Hitherto she hadn't been aware of Ragnar's other name. Now she knew. Ragnar had been Minkie Kennan's father! That was how Minkie had found his way here, to repeat his dad's self-indulgent follies.

Now a wilder struggle was in progress than that previous affray inside the moon-child. The spark was Eyeno's rage at Kennan for his libertine ways – shades of how van Maanen had behaved towards herself, and also of Juke's furtive desires! The spark had lit a whole palace as its candle, a wick for a war.

What had the cuckoo-man said? *Queens and lords in conflict* ... Would a mirror war flare up in the outside world too? Would strife in the outside world reflect itself here? A premonition of helplessness haunted Eyeno. Helplessness would be her ruin.

Smoke hazed the sun-eye. Mana-mists were billowing from

lakes higher up the landscape as if those too were on fire. How could she guess the fate of this place, and of herself?

'Will you fly, and spy?' she demanded.

Trident in one clawed hand, the cuckoo-man extended his arms so that those membranes stretched tautly. He began to run. Away he sprinted, helter-skelter, leaping and flapping. It seemed as if his capers might end in him stumbling and sprawling. However, a person's weight was lighter inside the moon-child's realm of wishes. Ponderously the cuckoo-man rose up and away from the pasture. Once he had left the ground, his aerial agility soon improved, and he spiralled higher.

Ferocity . . .

> *Monstrosity* . . .

Those weren't the words she had been seeking when she set out from this selfsame spot such a while ago . . .

The season which Eyeno had spent with Paula and the echo-sisters in their village and the surrounding meadows had been sweetly recuperative. Yet sweetness had been bound to pall. Those affectionate lasses were so dreamy, so accepting of their felicitous state, their amusing rituals of game and dance and admiration. They could watch a creamy waxen flower for an hour, absorbed in it. Then they would skip away heedlessly as if, having lent their souls to those petals, they had quite forgotten about the transaction.

It wasn't that the echo-lasses lacked horizons. Horizons swooped upward all around them, visibly similar to their own domicile of woods and meads and loughs. If elsewhere was the same, there was little evident reason to concern themselves with elsewhere. At some time or other they had evidently paid visits to other villages housing other lasses and friendly nakki-folk. *When* was unimportant. When was never an issue.

Came a day when her friends delightedly led Eyeno into a shingled cottage. On the kitchen table a leather-bound book lay open. It was the *Book of the Land of Heroes*. Surely this was Eyeno's own copy from which she had told fortunes! That stain on the edge of the pages, that scuff at the top of the binding . . .

At the very least it was a faithful imitation of her copy. Eyeno was amazed and thrilled. Would the book bring precious lost words back to her?

'Where did this come from?'

Why, a nakki had told Gretel that they would find a surprise in this house right here in the kitchen upon the table. Eyeno had talked a bit about books and being able to read from them, which seemed very clever of her. Gretel and her friends couldn't recall actually having *seen* a book before. Obviously this was one, full of delights.

'Sing us a story, tell us a tale,' they chorused, as if Eyeno were a gossip-bird. Weeks of amusement awaited.

Brass pots and pans hung from hooks, and also a large saw. A wooden laundry tub with tongs stood beside a spinning wheel. Cream plates painted with daisies were racked in a dresser – calling to mind the glass paperweight eye which Ruokokoski had made for Eyeno to wear but then had smashed in chagrin at his daughter's fortune. The pupil of that false eye had been a daisy.

When Eyeno leaned over the volume she found to her bewilderment that she couldn't understand the squiggles upon the paper. Tiny snakes and circles and wing shapes; chevrons and little boxes and loops with tails or stems or bars: the marks seemed perfectly familiar yet at the same time thoroughly meaningless. *She couldn't read a word*, not even when she clapped a palm over her one eye and tried to see with the other eye within her skull.

'What's the matter—?'

'Don't you like your surprise—?'

'Won't you read stories to us—?'

She had swayed with shock. Her heart raced. She turned page after page in case other leaves might reveal more meaning, but the whole volume was quite incomprehensible. The letters were the right ones, the usual ones. Of this she was sure. Although she could see them clearly she was blind to them. Comprehension eluded her.

To have lost the grace of words, and now to lose sight of them entirely! Tragedy whelmed her. She had thought that her spirit was mending ... On the contrary, she was robbed the more so.

'What's the matter, dearest—?'

Would she become like Paula and Gretel and Inga, forgetful of her own fate? An echo of herself? She choked. Let her not lose the use of her tongue too!

'I can't read!'

'You said you could—'

'Were you teasing us—?'

'It's gone from me! I'm blind to this book!'

'Was it your missing eye which could read?' asked Gretel.

Eyeno had wailed in protest: '*No!*' She had reeled, and slapped the book in absolute frustration. At that moment, nauseatingly, she heard within her head the same voice she had heard when she stood sodden from her suicide bid. It was the moon-child's lilting voice.

A proclaimer must not read or the force of words would weaken . . .

This was perfectly true.

Proclaimers couldn't read. Nor did mana-priests. Priests learned words by heart and recited them.

What did *this* have to do with her? Women weren't proclaimers – certainly not in the full-blown sense! Wisewomen might utter cantrips and charms. Yet to bespeak in the style of a van Maanen or a Juke? Oh no, not at all.

Eyeno had certainly wished with all her heart that she could have bespoken herself away from the mound in the middle of Speakers' Valley on that vile occasion when she was forced to stand there before the gaze of a multitude of spectators as a trophy in a contest between besotted Lord Osmo and her unspeakable brother. Oh she had wished. Her wish was a delicate daisy crushed underfoot into a smear of shit. Her wish was no more potent than a scavvy's fart.

What did the moon-child intend by robbing her of the art of reading, blinding her mind to the meaning of writing?

Maybe she hadn't heard its voice at all but was simply insane, her brain a cave of crazy echoes bouncing from walls within, which sealed off her lost gift for words and beauty. Now a new inner wall had arisen, upon which were scrawled stupid snakes and circles and bars, mere caricatures of script, words scried through a warped lens.

How bright the saucepans were beneath their hooks. How bemused were Maria and Gerda, and Gretel and Anna, and Paula and Inga at being denied the stories which they'd been looking forward to – but especially Inga who was so like a dark freckled twin to Eyeno, being of the same height and figure. Inga was hardly devastated with disappointment, merely somewhat mystified. To be truly disappointed, Inga would have needed to know what was lost: all those words, precious words, reduced to squirms of nonsense.

'Don't be *sad*, Eyeno – it doesn't matter.' Inga fondled her gently yet fervently. She cuddled Eyeno, stroked her hair, kissed her. The warmth of this dark twin's lace-frocked limbs was so welcoming, and softening. Her breath and her skin were as subtly sweet-scented as morning honeydew upon a newly open sun-kissed blossom. Eyeno likewise felt herself coaxed to open moist petals within herself, from a bruised tight bud, in response.

If this is your wish, voiced the moon-child within, *this can be your future.*

'No . . .' she had protested. She had disengaged herself from Inga's loose embrace.

'But I love you,' murmured her dark and willowy likeness.

Eyeno had sought a bitter oblivion in Loom Lake. Here was an alternative: of sugary dulcet forgetfulness.

Or else you can hike to where I bathe in my navel. You can trek to the pool of lost words far away . . .

Was she truly being offered a choice? Words had been pillaged from her. If she chose to love Inga, more would be lost than would be gained. She found herself recalling the Juttahat Tulki-twenty, who would have been lost without a guiding voice in its head. Was the moon-child to become her equivalent of an Isi? Or was she to be herself, and remain solitary? The sense of the moon-child's presence made her queasy.

Should she quest for the source of such qualmy pressure? Such a journey might be akin to trying to return to Speakers' Valley against the push of Lord Osmo's proclamation. In a sense that would indeed be her situation, for in that valley she had first begun to lose words. Might she now regain them, in that strange pool or navel where the moon-child floated within itself? Such a prospect provoked biliousness as well as hope.

You can trek and spy me with your inner eye . . .

If she weren't in this kitchen, in the nakki-village, wouldn't she be seeing the moon-child everywhere about her? Did it possess a special puppet of itself?

She decided.

'Inga, Paula, everyone: I'm going away. I promise I'll come back to you . . .'

Eyeno's journey was to seem a long one both in terms of distance and of days. Forest followed woodland; lough succeeded lake. Here would be a hamlet of jaunty lasses and hospitable nakkis. Elsewhere, a solitary cott in a clearing or beside a meadow. Such a cott might house an old beldame or a nakki-woodsman, who would give Eyeno shelter then point out a path in the morning. The vista of upswooping forests and lakes changed as she travelled. After a while, if she looked over her shoulder and upward, she was almost sure she could see Inga's village (and Paula's, and Anna's) tiny in the distance – at least for a while. Though the panorama altered, its similarity persisted.

Might she walk all the way across this domain only to arrive once more at her starting point? She thought not. The upward horizons seemed to bend away. When she recalled the cavities and chambers she had originally scried with her inner eye within the moon-child – hollows of uncertain size which had appeared to be as huge as a valley one moment, then no larger than a nut – a feeling grew that the apparent vastness of her surroundings was misleading. Surely it was the case that the terrain and its residents and she herself were all becoming progressively smaller the further that she advanced. By now perhaps she was no taller than a thumbnail, and a tree no higher than a finger. Subsequently a tree would be as tiny as a fingernail, and she would be a marching mite beneath it. In scale with a tree or a lake – which would be a mere puddle – she was the same as ever.

At first she had seemed to traverse many keys on each day of her trek. Thereafter from dawn to dusk the distance covered would be no greater than the size of an actual iron key to a door. The day after that: a brass key to a little box.

> A key
> Slides into emptiness
> Of the same shape as itself
> And turns that emptiness around . . .

Words were missing. She had slid a finger into her eye socket to cleanse it gently of the ghost of a tear.

Eventually, deep in woodland, there was a pool.

Harper trees in full jade-green foliage ringed it. The under-growth was of bubberry bushes in berry and shrubby jismin in flower.

At first Eyeno only caught glimpses of the pool. The scent of the jismin was heady and sensual. The berries were pink nipples. The multitude of strings between the branches and the tree trunks hummed. Memory of the bleating harper trees around the ridge of Speakers' Valley tormented her. Eyeno trod softly so that those strings should not wail at her approach.

198

The pool was tenanted. The rotund, half-submerged resident of the waters was large and rufous in hue. It wallowed like some vastly pregnant swollen sow perched upright on its sunken rump, stained with rusty mud.

And it stirred.

You have arrived at my navel . . .

A queasy spasm assailed Eyeno. She simply had to seize a spray of jismin and crush it to her nose, inhaling. Plucking bubberries bursting with pink juice, she crammed her mouth. Harper strings thrummed a melodious moan as she picked her way forward to the bank.

The pool was no more than thrice the width of its massive occupant. That denizen was at once an obese woman and a beast of ruddy brown and perhaps something else besides. She was alien in a manner quite unlike any Juttahat. If an overgrown Isi had formed itself into a gross tower of coils, which had then fused with one another, such might have been the resemblance.

The torso resting in the water was a rounded tawny vat of flesh. Dugs bulged from bosoms and gorbelly. Little hands waggled, incapable of reaching anywhere. The head which balanced upon this mass was a great brown globe with a moist split of a mouth, snub of a snout, and sunken red eyes. Jug-ears jutted. Henna hair rose coiled in a topknot so tight that it might well be solid: a knob. Elsewhere on her gross body a down of gingery hair formed mazes of subtle curlicues.

Could this creature ever stand up? Were there *legs* tucked beneath her? Were there huge waddly feet? She was certainly lacking in arms, though not in hands, of which she possessed rather too many. If she could ever heave her bulk out of the pool maybe she would only be able to proceed anywhere by rolling.

What, leave my house of buoyant water?

Oh so this was her permanent dwelling place . . .

Hers? Was she a female at all?

Queen Lucky is female, came the queasy-making reply, *and so are all her daughters.*

Consequently this creature must assume a female appearance? 'Why did you choose—?' Eyeno couldn't continue.

Why did the moon-child choose this grotesque anatomy as a representative and embodiment of itself? Of course this was not the whole of herself any more than the navel is the whole of a person. Why not a graceful sylph-like figure?

As graceful as yourself, perhaps?

Ripples of nausea eddied through Eyeno, such as she had never felt at the sight of any familiar friendly mocky-fellow.

Self-indulgence must be the answer. The infant moon-child had indulged her appetites, and was sick from all the emotions of Kaleva upon which she suckled: all the fierce feelings, the surfeit of rages and jealousies and frenzies and erotic seizures. Like Queen Lucky herself she was unbalanced. Therefore she rested legless in a pond, preparing herself for a violent spasm, a problematic birth after such a profligate gestation. She was the fallen moon of Eyeno's verse: a moon-seed which had tumbled into the lake to gestate and feed on the frenzied feelings which she stimulated – which in turn debased and depraved her, so that she was doubly fallen. She would arise rupturously one day – to achieve sanity and serenity?

Those thin slobber-lips parted. Though no sound emerged to set the harper trees humming Eyeno heard: *Spy me with your inner eye.*

Fearful that she might be plucked into the pool in a moment of blindness (though how could such stumpy chubby hands reach out?) Eyeno shut her right eye.

A sylph composed of stars stood in the phantom water which was word and mana, a creative fluid. Behind one ear of stars, a creamy waxen flower cupped like a huger ear harkened to the music or the discord of life.

And now the sparkling sylph was sitting upon a boulder. The boulder was vast, yet afloat. She was a giantess. At the base of the boulder creatures formed a surf of rippling flesh. Creatures serpentine and humanoid and octopoid and piscine and avian and amorphous. Here was the harvest of existence; and the murmur of the surf was the uttering of a trillion tales speaking of existence past or present or henceforth. Tales were sucked under. Tales were lost and surfaced again as the sylph dabbled her starry toes in the spume.

All was contained within a cave which was woven vibrantly of emptiness and space, a great bubble glistening with reflections of itself; for of itself it was made, and of nothing else. Briefly that bubble divided into a hundred glassy-walled bubbles. Then it rejoined. That bubble was a vast eye looking inward (for inwards was the only perspective), and seeing itself within as an ivory blossom in bud and bloom and decay and once more again

in bud – and also as a puppet-being formed of ivory petals afloat
upon a pool of mana-mists wherein stars gleamed . . .

Bathe with me . . .

In the same pond as the monstrosity? Within reach of those
stubby hands?

No: in the same pool as the sylph!

Keeping her right eye closed, Eyeno kicked off her moccasins,
shed her gown. Blindly, yet perceiving mist and stars and petals,
she stepped down from the bank. Cool liquid slid up her shanks
and thighs, laved her maidenhead and navel. As she crouched,
the ichor of the moon-child caressed her bubbery nipples. Harper
strings throbbed, and jismin reeked sweetly.

She asked: 'Where are my lost words?'

Submerge yourself . . .

Not in a lake again, of iron water! Not to drown!

Yet the alternative was to open her one good outward eye and
see beside her, only a touch away, the great brown creature
which had fed on frenzies.

Eyeno ducked her head, her hair floating upward as a silky
veil. Fluid washed into her empty eye socket. Underwater she
held her breath.

The breath that speaks words.

Terrified, she breathed in sleek ichor, body fluids of the
moon-child's freakish female creature, her sustenance, her
urine.

She heard:

> *Lady, coming to my bower*
> *Take from me these words of power:*
> *Thrust at lust, and cage my rage,*
> *Be the mistress of my plagues.*
> *Lucky hour, or evil hour?*
> *Man, or mage? War to wage?*
> *Blank stays your page*
> *If your soul is sage.*
> *Deflower and devour:*
> *Oh I empower adjustment.*
> *Be eloquent*
> > *magniloquent*
> > > *malevolent*
> > > > *turbulent*
> > > > > *virulent*

201

take from me these words of power
lady coming while I flower . . .

Coughing, Eyeno scrambled on to the bank before she opened her ordinary eye. The monstrosity had shut *her* eyes. The little hands hung limply. The ginger hairs on her gross body stood out, crinkly and curly, in a crackly corona.

While Eyeno was in the pool a nakki must have stolen her gown away. In place of it, draped over leafy deflowered shrubs, she saw: a ruffled white blouse, breeches of brown leather buckled with brass, and a grey cloak. Boots stood waiting: amputated hollow brown feet. Eyeno's bare toes squashed fallen decomposing bubberries, smearing dirty pink stains. The bushes had shed all their fruits. She noticed her gown. It was almost hidden by fallen decaying jismin petals. Time had passed. A lot of time.

Dressing quickly, she had quit the pool side without looking back at its resident, and fled through the woods.

What had the moon-child's monstrosity given her? What had she meant? Two opposite things at once, perhaps! She had seemed to appeal to Eyeno for some kind of deliverance from frenetic urges while at the same time bestowing the capacity for the enactment of these same urges.

When Eyeno finally returned by way of beldames' cotts and nakki-hamlets to Inga's village (and Paula's, and Anna's!) she had beheld a white marble palace with blood-bright pennants looming over the settlement.

She could hardly believe her eye. Had she returned to somewhere else? A boisterous carnival was in full riot. Minkie Kennan was amusing himself.

13 · WINTER WAR

Flurries of snow streaked an ashen sky. In the zenith the twilight-sun was a ghost, already less than moonlike. Tonight perhaps it would entirely disappear from view behind smuts and snowflakes. Hindward – two-score keys away to all appearances, elevated by the swell of the darkling terrain – the tiny candle-palace radiated brighter light. Forever it continued to burn unconsumed, an incandescent nub scattering luminosity through the murk. Smoke and blizzard could never wholly impede its visibility. Its candlelight diffused through such veils as if snow-storm or smokedrift served as a mana-lens. At times the image seemed larger, at times smaller. Neither distance nor haze nor frigid squalls quenched its aspect.

More than the feeble and dimming sun-eye, that beacon cast a pallid phosphor-sheen over the smouldering ruin of a once-happy hamlet and a hand's depth of snow. Curver trees bowed to the ground under bleached bonnets. Never had blizzard blown through this domain before the war of Eyeno and the Snowies. Now erratic snowstorms pounced. Diffuse frost-beasts rushed through the forests to bite, then bandage their victims in white. The air was chill: a gas of ice. Flakes still capered. In a grove of musktrees and yellovers fluffed with pompons of cotton from the snow-loom little candles seemed to burn upon branches, reflecting hundredfold in miniature the palace far away.

Blackened bones of cotts poked upward in incinerated fractures. Slaughtered nakkis lay sprawled. A few had been cleanly killed by hot light, some by crossbow quarrels. Most were the mutilated victims of long knives. Maria and Gerda were comforting three dark-haired lasses who were shivering in chiffon and blankets. Eyeno's friends were bundled in warm coats of tawny verrin fur with tasselled fur hats and fur-trimmed boots. She herself had exchanged her cloak for a similar coat which had been provided grinningly by one of her verrin-men.

In offering consolation – by cooing and cherishing – perhaps Gerda and Maria were nursing their own aghast selves, too, in the face of this atrocity. Inga clung close to Eyeno. Inga's freckles seemed like flecks of blood which had sprayed from the corpses.

'Dear Eyeno, what if you hadn't—?'

'Hadn't what?'

Inga sought for a word. Her previously delectable life had become a vague dream. What was happening now was almost beyond her comprehension. 'What if you hadn't *interfered*?'

There it was: the gentle reproach, the hint that if they were to abandon this hunt through bitter woodlands, everything might still be well again, and the sun-eye might smile upon meadows once more.

'Don't you see what sort of person Minkie Kennan is?' Eyeno asked her. 'A killer and a kidnapper. Quite uncaring! A glib bully with a gang of bullies.'

And she herself?

Inga eyed a rapacious verrin-man who was polishing a long knife on his furry flank, indifferent to the carcasses of his nakki-kin.

'If I don't keep *control*,' whispered Eyeno. 'If I don't lead my troops . . .'

Inga shivered and hugged herself. 'Where's Paula?' she asked in sudden panic. 'Where's Anna?'

'He kidnapped them, remember?'

'Of course. Poor girls . . .' Inga was staring at the three refugees whom Minkie had left behind. They were casual acquaintances of Eyeno's who had entertained her overnight during her journey to the pool where the monstrosity wallowed, and on her route back. Oh but Minkie wouldn't wish to encumber himself with any more prisoners. He had left these lasses behind, burnt out of their cotts, as a burden to delay Eyeno.

She wouldn't be hindered unduly.

She crossed to the wretched threesome while Inga tagged along by her like some lanky pet foal, a filly who would nuzzle one's hand with sweet moist breath for a lump of sugar, teasing reminder of an impossible alternative. *Minkie Kennan was the horse-breaker*.

'Lasses, be brave,' Eyeno told the trio, which wasn't quite the same as bespeaking them. 'Go to the candle that's burning amidst the snow and warm yourselves by it. That's why it's there.' Maybe snow fell so that the forests wouldn't kindle from fire-darts and hot light.

She beckoned two braided bandsmen whose scarlet uniforms weren't, at a glance, too unlike the bright red leathers of the Snowies. One clutched a trumpet which blew burning darts in battle, and the other a long sword which, with its horn-like basket hilt, might once have been a trombone. They saluted their leader, touching their peaked caps.

'Lads: you'll escort these ladies safely to the candle-palace, do you hear?'

'Though not inside it,' said the trumpeter.

'Of course not.' How could anyone enter that pile of incandescent waxen marble? 'There'll be buttermilk bread and thick soup waiting.' *Let it be so*. Let that palace serve as an oven and a cauldron for those outside. Let dripping wax become bread and soup.

A verrin-man gestured with a lightrifle. 'Look!'

Flapping through motes and flakes the cuckoo-man was returning. At first glance in silhouette he looked larger than before, his membraned arm-span matching the branches of trees he flew over. Was the scout whistling to signal his return?

Down he came towards embers and landed on the run, his claws bounding over cinders then snow, printing a track. A shrill shriek accompanied him, as of lips blowing on a blade of herbage. Alarmed, the goat-man voided a crotty of dung from beneath his kilt. Peevishly he stamped his cloven hooves and swung his sickle to and fro.

Cuckoo-man spoke. 'War-woman: I pinned a Snowy to the ground with my trident! I planted a tree upon him.' The cuckoo-man displayed a puncture in one of his plumed membranes, source of the recent whistle. 'A quarrel passed through my wing.'

The hole looked too small to have permitted the passage of a fletched dart.

'I felt huge, war-woman. The Snowies looked tiny on the ground.'

So they would from the air. Yet might it be that the cuckoo-man had retained some of his size while he flew ahead, out of touch of land? Could he swoop down and clutch Paula or Anna in his claws, and carry them up and away to safety? Part way to safety, at least! Surely the lass whom he snatched would grow in his grasp during his return flight, becoming too bulky for his wing-beats to support – unless what he brought back remained a midget lass, which would be frightful, and worse than no rescue at all.

'Fetch your cuckoo-cousin,' Eyeno told her scout. 'I want you both to fly and try to snatch Paula and Anna away from Kennan – in the gloom.' As the sun-eye dimmed to a dead bone-disc which was hardly discernible any longer, the scene had been growing ever more obscure. 'You can see well enough by candlelight, can't you?'

'A cuckoo sees everything,' boasted the plumed scout. 'But my arms ache.'

Aching arms wouldn't lift even a lightweight lass off the ground.

'You'll fly early tomorrow, then!' Very early indeed, while the Snowies were cold and groggy and at a low ebb. Now that Eyeno had conceived this plan, it possessed her passionately. Of course the scheme would succeed. Kennan would be cuddled up in thick furs. (*Cuddled with whom?* Tormenting question!) He'd be taken by surprise. So would his Snowy sentinels be, sheltering their acne-raw faces from the frost.

'Anna—'

'Anna—'

'Hush, Anna—'

In the chilly darkness curver trees formed a semi-corral with an awning of quiffy foliage around the bivouac of the Snowies. The bendy boughs had been shaken free of snow before the army settled down to sleep. More flakes had settled subsequently, softly rethatching the canopy though not enough to press it down to earth. Upon a mat of curver switches cut from trees nearby, Anna lay wrapped in furs which Snowies had looted from a nakki-woodman's cott. Close by on her left slumbered the Snowy who'd been carrying her on his shoulders since the start of the expedition. A long leather thong tethered her wrist to his. Minkie Kennan slept in a tiny tent of his own.

'Hush, Anna, I'm here with you.'

A pressure upon her right side; a body squeezing against hers. The voice of her awakener trembled: 'It's Gunther, dearest hen.' Teeth were chattering.

Murk was profound beneath the curvers. Some grey relieved the glimpse of sky. Thanks to the smudged beacon of the candle-palace a fitful pearly sheen faintly glazed the snow bonnets worn by the woodland. A wraith-light waxed and waned erratically, yet this did not elucidate the darkness. If anything, the fleeting phosphorescence deepened the night shrouding the encampment.

Gunther was shivering convulsively. Careful not to move unduly and tug on the thong, Anna opened her furs to pull a coverlet over him. His nude bulk thrust against the lacy gown which now only served her as a petticoat.

'*I can feel you—*' She couldn't feel his manhood which was shrunken by the cold, but his tangible presence, his bulk! He had gained substance. He'd become denser.

His arm encircled her. '*And I can feel you, after so long! But hush—*'

Lest their whispers rouse the Snowy who lay so close by, or the other porter who slept beside Paula, or snoring Minkie Kennan from his tent, or his lieutenant, Little Boss who slept

206

outside. Lest they alert the sentinels numbly standing guard in the open where the majority of Snowies sprawled comatose, their leathers coated with snowfall.

The frustration of whispers! The joy of touch, deferred for centuries! If only Gunther were not so vulnerably naked – save for the hard little locket slung between his nipples. If only he was dressed suitably for this unaccustomed winter. Yet if so, she wouldn't feel him nor he feel her so persuasively. He and she mumbled endearments, they nuzzled. He was so cold, a thief of her heat. Fervour banished shivers for a while.

Anchored to her by a thong, her Snowy porter still slept. If only Gunther had a knife with him and was clad in leathers!

Despite the joy they shared his mass seemed that of a child rather than a grown man. Less than hers, certainly. She understood how he was consuming himself during his heroic hibernation, dreaming deeper than anyone had ever dreamed so as to find her. Yet even so!

'You're lighter than me, my Lord, my love.'

'I feel so much more fully present – more *concentrated* upon you, Anna.' Undeniably. 'If I can persist in finding you—'

Would he attain sufficient fullness of presence to remain with her in this domain?

'Ach . . .' How could he remain here while his aestivating body lay in that monitoring cradle back at Castlebeck awaiting re-awakening at a date which must surely be soon? Besides: the cold and the darkness; that eerie burning palace; herself, abducted. This realm of Anna's was no longer a dream but a nightmare!

His locket was pressing against her lace-clad breast. She touched the locket. 'Does my portrait look old or young?' she whispered. She had died of old age – of heart failure – while he remained as youthful as ever. All he had told her about the locket hitherto was that *she* was in it. 'Did you describe me to the artist or did he paint me as soon as I was dead?'

'Anna . . . don't be shocked, please. What's next to my heart is a chip of your skull.'

She almost drew away.

'This place isn't *actual*,' he insisted.

'It is! Eyeno, our friend, said she came here from the actual world. We didn't believe her. We didn't understand. Now that I remember you properly, I think I understand.'

'Eyeno's dead. She was told to drown herself.'

'Minkie Kennan has that *bike* of his that can jump from place to place immediately. That's how he came here. If only you could come on such a bike, not in a dream.'

Gunther sighed deeply. 'Come where, Anna? Where's *here*?'

'Eyeno and Kennan both know.'

'Has he molested you again? No, don't say.'

'He hasn't. He won't! I'd kill myself.'

'How could you—?' Don't remind her of the fragment of skull in his breast box. 'You mustn't even think such a thing.' He was trembling convulsively.

She hugged him. 'I shan't, I shan't. Besides, it's Paula he wants most. He wants her to become a Queen in the world outside of here.'

'*What?* Can you be taken from this place, back into the world? *Cu-cu-can yu-yu-you?*' His teeth chattered the question into nonsense, like a Snowy, and she jerked as if slapped.

'Wu-wu-what's up?' The leash tugged her wrist. Her custodian was sitting up. 'Hu-hu-who's there with you, lady?'

Gunther was rolling away. Hastily Anna sat up, opening her fur coat like a great bird its wings to hide him. As the chill lanced her she gathered the thick coat around herself again. 'Nothing's happening!'

Yet a swish of wings was audible. Two big sombre silhouettes appeared over the trees, beginning to descend upon the bivouac. A pair of Eyeno's cuckoo-men were invading the camp from the air.

As her custodian leapt up, so did she.

'Bu-bu-beware bu-bu-birdies!' bellowed the Snowy. He dragged Anna with him into the open as he booted bodies into wakefulness.

Paula's Snowy had roused. Marking what his colleague was doing, he followed suit, hauling Paula bodily with him. Snatched from sleep, she stumbled and shrieked. Little Boss was babbling into Kennan's tent. Kennan staggered out, confused.

The sentries were levelling crossbows and lightrifles. Other Snowies, still stupefied, blundered into those sentries in the darkness. Though the cuckoo-men seemed massive now, a bright pulse of hot light flew wild. The dazzling slash split the murk achingly. Vision was divided into two dark segments till the afterimage would fade.

How could those cuckoo-men fit into either segment? Wings

beat. Beaks dipped. Claws plunged. Snowies shrieked and milled.

A fiery blast erupted in the belly of one of the raiders. Kennan had fired an explosive bullet. A chaff of plumes showered. Screeching, the birdman collapsed from out of the air, crashing upon Snowies, bearing half a dozen down with him into the trampled snow. How could it be so large?

The other cuckoo-man caught hold of Paula's fur-clad shoulders. Wings pumped, stirring such a fierce snow-swirling down-draught as the raider rose, hauling her off her feet. However, the thong still tied her to her custodian. The Snowy's arm rose as she rose. Her own arm was dragged downward. Hovering, the cuckoo-man pivoted. All was dense shadows, punctuated by the aftersight of hot light and explosion. Then the cuckoo-man sank so that Paula's boots hit the ground, and his beak slashed out. It snapped shut, and twisted.

The birdman was rising upward again, with Paula beneath him. Beneath her dangled a hand on a thong. The Snowy was screaming, clutching a stump which must be spouting blood. Then the hand fell free. A moment later the Snowy was on his knees. Was he trying to fit the severed hand to his wrist again? Other Snowies were plunging knives into the great plumed corpse on the ground.

'Aaaaa,' cried Paula, airborne, ever higher. 'Aaaaa.'

Kennan waved a crossbow furiously. 'Come back, come back!'

Little Boss was sighting a lightrifle. Big Boss struck the weapon aside.

'Which lass did it take?' he cried. 'Which one was it? Where's the other one?'

'Here, Bu-bu-boss!' Anna's custodian hauled her out of the mêlée to exhibit to her captor. In the gloom could Minkie be entirely sure of the colour of someone's hair or even whether or not she wore pigtails?

Frustrated, he shouted, 'Who are you? You're Anna, aren't you? Oh damn, and damn it, you are. I've been robbed by that mutie bitch. You're just Anna.'

From behind a pitch-dark curver tree hobbled a naked ghost. 'How dare you, pipsqueak!'

'No, Gunther, *go*,' appealed Anna. As Minkie swung the cross-bow around: 'Don't hurt him!'

'Hurt him? He's hardly even here – though that's more than he needs to be. Blow away on the breeze, you pest!'

Gunther banged his fists together to pummel vigour into them.

He flexed his fingers. He slapped his bare thighs. Caution seemed to prevail, for he took a step back.

'Hear me, Minkie Kennan: you can't kill me in a dream. I warn you: my dream-body's gaining substance.'

Kennan raised a hand from the crossbow to scratch his head. 'Is that so? That dead birdman's quite a size ... Came by air, he did, not step by step like us. I knew it: the further we tramp, the more we shrink. I suppose a dream-spook might become denser. Little Boss, make yourself useful. Find me my helmet.'

'I beg you, fellow,' said Gunther, 'set my Anna free.'

Minkie sneered. '*You're* in no fit state to look after anyone. You're almost blue! Why didn't you go to bed with your clothes on? I presume you planned to be stripped for action, eh?'

Anna would have slapped Minkie's cheek except that her custodian jerked his arm in the other direction, and the tether stayed her hand. She sneezed explosively several times.

'See what you caused, Lord Beck. You gave her a cold.'

The dreamlord was quivering and wobbling. A spasm was gathering in him too. He began to heave. He rocked from side to side.

'It's du-du-dawn, Bu-bu-big Boss.' Little Boss was holding Minkie's black helmet out to him. In the zenith the sun-eye was barely perceptible once again: the dimmest of discs.

Gunther was fluctuating, blurring.

At last, he sneezed.

Such sudden swelter, and so bright.

Warm water thawing him. Scent of jismin.

It was as if he had plunged into a sauna after his frigid exposure. Sweat or melting frost blinded him at first. He blinked, he squinted – and perceived the pool wherein he was basking, in company with a gingery-brown monstrosity who was at once obese woman and sow. Hairs on her body crackled with light.

Too many little hands and too many fat tits. Such a girth as to put him to shame in the days of his erstwhile gluttony. Balancing thereon: a globe of a head with red piggy eyes.

'Gingerbread Woman!' *he cried out.* 'I've found you!'

{*You're starving, longlife lord. Sustain yourself. Suckle on my paps. I'm swollen.*}

'What—?'

{*Nurse yourself at my dugs. Feed your body that lies at home.*}

Was this a true dream or a phantasia? Hitherto there'd been a maze of phantasias from which, periodically, he had found his way to Anna, recognizing at once the authenticity of those discoveries of his long-lost wife. Now he was confused. How long ago it seemed since he had burbled to Alvar about swallowing Isi gland-juice so as to sleep as deeply as a hibernating mage, and find the Gingerbread Man at the heart of events – except that she was a woman – and beg that his Anna should be restored to life in his dream ...

He had already found Anna. He was impotent to help her. At least, on the most recent occasion, he had touched her.

Could he remain here in this domain? Could he achieve more actuality, and stay with Anna? Supposing that the winter and the war abated, and that he rescued her from the captor who held her hostage!

The Gingerbread Woman spoke of his real body back in Castlebeck as needing sustenance. Could he obtain nourishment from her milk or ichor? Could he bear to do so, for Anna's sake? Ach, his body would still awaken in due course. Elmer Loxmith's machine would see to that.

'Gingerbread Woman,' he implored, 'can you restore Anna to the world for me, from wherever this is?'

{You need to nibble on me, Dreamlord. You need to kiss my teats.}

Propinquity to her girth was disturbing enough; to her tub of flesh with hairs erect and glittering.

{Gratify your needs.}

His thigh throbbed where the silver tattoo pictured the swan pierced by an arrow and contorted into the shape of a heart, emblem of his death-defying passion. He shuffled closer, and raised his lips to a tit. Sweetness, as of liquid jismin, pulsed. Blubbery fingers stroked his cheek, and his own long hair crackled with a wild energy, standing out from his scalp. Vitality coursed through the fibres of his being.

{Give me your trinket, Dreamlord.}

The locket?

{With that little bit of her bone inside it. Bone is the basis of a body.}

Give the Gingerbread Woman the fragment of Anna's skull? Thereby his love might be restored to the wider world?

{What else have you to offer in exchange?}

(True enough.)

{Tear it loose.}

There'd be pain in the offering . . .

Gunther gripped the links of the chain close to each nipple-ring. He braced himself, and wrenched. His nipples ripped. Two little stars of fire, two burning coals, tormented his chest. His torn nipples leaked blood. He wrapped the chain around that armless hand which had caressed him. The podgy fingers closed tight upon the little silver box.

{You need a name for me, Dreamlord. Call me Mistress Marietta—}

The name of the only woman with whom he had been unfaithful! The name of Cully's mother, who had borne such a resemblance to Anna in her middle years . . . Marietta, to exorcize whom he had sawed a fragment from Anna's skull and pierced his own nipples and suspended the reliquary above his heart! Cheated, he howled, 'Give it back!'

{FOOL! YOUR ANNA WOULD ONLY GROW OLD AND DIE AGAIN.}

Deafened by her laughter, he was falling forward into the Gingerbread Woman, pressing inside her into a lambent void filled with scalloped islands of light.

The sun-eye was shining feebly, a gauzy spectral lemon at the zenith. A wavering light flowed from the far candle-palace, rendering flurries of flakes and smoky mists and the whitened woodlands and the clearings luminous rather than illuminated. A bandsman tootled a hunting tune. Hairy verrin-men snarled a throaty accompaniment as they trudged.

The surviving cuckoo-man hadn't been able to carry Paula all the way back to safety. His size had diminished; her bulk had increased. He had come down in a clearing, where presently Eyeno's army had caught up with them. The bird-man was exhausted. Despite her padding of furs, Paula's shoulders ached from being carried. Her muscles were so bruised by the squeeze of his claws. Those sore contusions were of less immediate import to her than the experience of flight: of being dangled helplessly in near-darkness while she was carried through the air.

'The dark, the cold,' she told Eyeno insistently as they trekked together amidst armed nakkis and so many savage freaks. 'I remember those now; and the emptiness too, the void. Living in a metal eggshell, loving the void because it terrified us. Our ship was called the *Katarina*.' Paula's frosted breath puffed out like smoke.

'The spaceship Lucky's family flew in . . . it's famous.'

'Oh, tell us,' clamoured Gretel. 'Tell the tale.'

If only there was time to pause and tell stories. Not whilst they were marching after Minkie! He still had Anna with him. He was heading for the pool of lost words.

'The cold and the dark and the emptiness: how can my memory be full of so many nothings? Such opposites to light and warmth and wholesomeness and joy?' Paula's arms hung stiffly by her sides as she walked. She couldn't bear to swing them. Paula's presence, and her echo-daughters' presence too, was slowing the progress of the army. Should Eyeno despatch her friends back to the candle-palace accompanied by an escort to join the other refugee lasses? Then they would be out of her sight. To her inward eye Paula's spirit was a soulflower in silhouette.

As yet there was no sign ahead of the bright red leathers of the Snowies.

'Verrin-men,' she shouted, 'you must hurry ahead. Drive Minkie Kennan from his route. Harry him, head him off.' *Let it be done.*

The beastmen grinned appreciatively. They saluted Eyeno with their clawed paws. Those who had been carrying lightrifles exchanged these with other combatants for a pistol, or a sickle that could be thrown and would return, or a long knife. Some slotted the new weapon into their leather harnesses. Others clutched their weapon in strong jaws between yellow teeth.

One by one, the verrin-men fell upon all fours and bounded away along the trampled white track following the trail of Minkie's army.

14 · FIRE FROM HEAVEN

The pony which Roger Wex took from the stables of the aitch-house was named Goodbrand. After Hermi showed up in the land-yard with his mana-camera and after Minnow commissioned Wex to find Cully, Roger had made himself acquainted with the animal by feeding it lumps of brown sugar. This might be bad for its teeth but was good for a future relationship. A sign over the stall had depicted an upraised thumb and a miniature branding iron. 'Goodbrand', a groom had construed; otherwise one might have fancied that the symbols referred to the pony's stature and strength, and perhaps this was also true.

Goodbrand was stocky and shaggy, toughly built and well-muscled, with a good gait and nimble hooves. His bushy tail dangled almost to the ground, a fine lustrous swat for suckerflies. His colour was dun, with a black stripe along the back to aim him steadfastly onward. Mane hung from his throat.

As morning grew brighter, even Goodbrand was wearying at the burden of two riders on his back. Both were cloaked: one in grey fustian with a hood, the other in faded and shabby green gaberdine much stained and blanched about the padded shoulder whereon a cuckoo rode. Really, Goodbrand was carrying three riders – or four, if you counted Wex's second self within his skull, minimal though the weight of wetwear was.

By now they had left the turquoise lake well behind. A neglected track wended through mature woodland mainly of horzma trees and larkeries. Umbrellas of emerald fronds nudged glossy spade-blade leaves. During the night the sky had remained fairly clear. At first they had ridden at good speed through farmland pearled by the glow from the sky-sickle. Then they entered forest. Scant illumination percolated through the foliage. To allow the pony to proceed Wex had shone a bright torch beam ahead till, in the early dawn, the battery – purloined from Lord Elmer's workshop – had faded and quit. As sunlight reappeared, a warm breeze from the south had begun to invade the woods. The coming day promised to be hot.

Wex's companion had been nodding against him fitfully for a while, pressing upon the stolen mana-lens in one of the inner pockets of his cloak. Now that the torch was of no further use his left arm crooked around her waist so that she wouldn't fall off. In his right hand, slackly: the reins. Presumably by now the pony was far enough away from Loxmithlinna. Personally he felt bushed.

{*How about a jolt of adrenalin for you, my Roger?*}

Administered by direct stimulation of his posterior brain where it merged with the spinal chord . . .

'That wouldn't perk up our *mount*.'

At the sound of his voice the drowsy passenger twitched and uttered a wordless animal moan.

When Goodbrand had overtaken the Girlem in a deserted lane on the edge of Loxmithlinna, Wex and his other self had arrived at a speedy consensus to offer her a ride. This Juttahat wench {*mind your jargon*} was unique: a specially bred, superbly groomed agent of the Isi with the ability to enchant, and aswirl with strange emotions besides. Desolate at her failure to entrap Lord Osmo — more grief-stricken than Wex could quite account for, and swayed by his proclamation — she had offered no resistance to Roger's proposal. Henceforth she must seek a mate as golden as herself to bring her joy. At Elmer's urging, and with Queen Minnow's acquiescence, Osmo had bespoken her to do so. How could she possibly succeed? Osmo hadn't simply been alluding to the hue of her skin but to her presence and her glamour, and — in spite of her being a servant of the serpents — to that aura of independence and free will which empowered her to sway human beings. She was doomed to become the Wandering Juttie.

Wex had ditched the saddle so that Goldi could sit in front of him on the pony, and to lessen the burden for Goodbrand. He had dumped the saddle down a well. In a few weeks or months people might purse their lips at a taste of leather in the water. Till then nobody else would know what had happened unless his pesky cuckoo quit his shoulder at last and began to blab.

Don't sing this story; don't tell this tale. That's what his wetwear had begged the bird — appropriating Wex's vocal chords — when he and himself had assaulted Hermi in that corridor as the shaman, encumbered with chunks of iron, was sneaking the lens slowly away to safety; had waylaid him and had injected him with Con-fusion, a drug produced in a Peace Police lab back on Earth. {A ring-binder, so called. Psychotomimetic. The indole rings of Carbon, Hydrogen, and Nitrogen bind to synapses in the brain, variegating the most recent memories chaotically.} Yes, yes.

A stream flooded across the track. Goodbrand needed a drink. After the pony had slaked its thirst, Wex swung it to wade along the beck. The watercourse drained, presently, into a secluded mere surrounded by larkeries and nut trees, kasta and musk. The fruit on the kastas wasn't yet ripe but the musktrees, which had blossomed gingerly in June, already wore masses of oily nug-gets. Several blue-chevroned soarfowl were dabbling, uptailing to pluck strings of weed from underwater then shrugging pearls of water from their iridescent plumes. The margins of the mere were rich in sedge and herbage for Goodbrand to munch, and there were beds of soft blushmoss.

Wex dismounted and hauled the dozy Girlem down. His leg was so much firmer since Osmo had weaned him from his crutch.

'Ukkoo, ukkoo,' confided his pest so softly that it might have been cooing an endearment. Abruptly the cuckoo launched itself.

Flapping soarfowl ran upon the water, erupting into flight. Too late for one of them. The cuckoo snatched prey in its claws.

The sun was high when Wex and the Girlem awoke on blushmoss shaded by the big spatulate leaves of larkeries.

In fact the golden lass awoke first and sat bolt upright, her lace-gloved hands leaping to her face in the heartache of recollection. But Wex {*rouse yourself, my Roger!*} was conscious a moment later. He'd been dreaming a chess game. All of the pieces had been white on one side and black on the other. Depending entirely on one's stance and viewpoint – for he was one of those pieces, a knight – one side was winning or losing. Really the game hadn't been about victory, or capture, at all; but about recognition.

One Queen was a black and white Minnow, on platform boots. The other was Lucky, white and black. One King was Osmo, and the other had no face at all. Bishops were Serlachius and Moller, and again Moller and Serlachius. Queens and bishops hardly moved. This was a knights' game, and the black and white knight who manouevred in response to Wex was none other than his other self. It always kept its countenance averted from him.

He, the black and white knight, had jumped to another square just like a rider on a jump-bike. In a flash his counterpart had shifted, and Wex still couldn't see its face. Such was the dream.

Goldi moaned softly. Hers was a sway without surcease. Additionally, a subsidiary sway afflicted her – temporarily though frustratingly both to herself and to Roger. *Dumb for a week and a day*, that's what she was.

The cuckoo eyed him alertly from a nearby musktree. A scatter of iridescent plumes littered the ground beneath. Had he time to strip and rush into the mere to wash himself before the curse descended again upon his shoulder? Discretion prevailed. Besides, by precipitate stripping, mightn't he disconcert the golden lass and give her a wrong impression?

He reached for her knapsack, and produced some hastily wrapped leftovers from the coronation feast to offer her.

'Meatballs? Sausage? A wing of goose?' he prompted.

She accepted the greasy wing in her lace-clad hand and nibbled with those neat little perfect teeth of hers. Her dark amber eyes

216

regarded him forlornly as he helped himself to meatballs. The cuckoo descended and clamped upon him. He offered the bird a meatball too, to appease it. Goodbrand was grazing nearby.

'I have two minds within me,' Wex said primly. {*Don't forget that she's an agent of the Isi*}. He wouldn't be allowed to forget. 'Yes, I have a second mind which knows a lot of things. I suppose I'm rather like the members of your own species – all except for you, I think, Goldi. Otherwise that other mind would forever be swaying you, and you yourself wouldn't have been able to use mana to affect Lord Osmo. Do you understand me? *Understanding*, hmm?'

She nodded, she nibbled. Her gaze never left him, as if she yearned to speak with her eyes.

'Of course, your Isi harp helped you. Made by a mage, I'd say. It, or one like it, was used to bemuse the dreamlord's nephew Cully, hmm?'

Her pupils widened in bewilderment.

'Not knowing that?'

She shook her head; she frowned. She was responding yet she was also protesting at his imitation of Juttahat idiom. She could use, and think in, human tenses as skilfully as any native speaker of Kalevan – except that right now she couldn't utter a single word.

'Your masters sent you into a verrin's den, in a sense, considering that Cully had put out Lady Eva's eye.'

A shrug. {*Risks had to be taken.*} 'Anyway, you tamed Eva's husband.'

Oh but *Elmer* hadn't been her prime objective.

'So as to bemuse Osmo, hmm? To rob him of his will?'

A moue. {*Rob him of more, besides.*} 'In a way we're alike, you and I – aren't we, Goldi Girlem? We're both agents' {*Take care!*} 'yet with our own private agendas and our passions and our griefs.' How subtle and competent – almost intimidatingly so – Wex felt in this one-sided interrogation here in this lonely spot. 'You see, Goldi, I happen to treasure a vision of Minnow Sariola. So gamin and spunky, and chattering to herself! And so little too, so fresh.' {Beware!} 'But my feelings for her – which even my other self shared – were impossible folly, do you see?'

She blinked, moistly. The goose wing, mostly devoured, slipped from her white glove. Was that a bead of grease or gland-juice in the dimple on her chin?

Who else had he ever told this to, in such terms? Oh he had

217

blathered foolishly when he arrived in Osmo's keep, but to utter a true declaration of unappeasable love perhaps required the presence of this alien wench, this masquerade-miss, as audience.

'We two can enjoy a truce of the heart,' he told her.

Enjoy? Enjoy? When she was despatched as a Wandering Juttie to search for a golden counterpart who could hardly exist?

Such frustration tweaked her features as if she were tasting not roasted bird but {*the bitterness of aloes.*} There seemed such pressure in her to communicate, to elude the seal which Osmo had set upon her lips. Her hands fluttered, making tentative sinuous signs – these were palpably insufficient. She leapt up and shed her borrowed grey cloak. Once more the Girlem was as she had been at the banquet, her short shoulderless silver tunic revealing so much butter-sculpture flesh. Her shoulders were a suave yoke fashioned from golden yolk, home to a single starflower tattoo. The swell of her thighs, abridged by silver fabric, was captivating. She kicked off her white moccasins.

Mutely she began to mime, with all of her body: with arch of foot and bend of knee and twist of waist and flex of elbow, to which her long gloves reached; with lace-sheathed fingers, with her full oval face, and with those eyes, those deep close-set amber eyes.

At first Wex himself could not fathom the meaning, though he was charmed by the grace and pathos of her gestures. However his wetwear – so much more fully endowed with instant information and with inference too – began to interject a commentary; almost a translation of this alien yet humanoid dumb show. Roger began to prompt Goldi with questions, which she answered with reprise and with carnal cadenzas of emphasis.

She kissed the air. She aped ravishing song. She turned away and half-swooned, allowing a fleeting glimpse of the gluteal folds of her rump, veiled by lace. She twirled and rocked an invisible babe against her bosom. She windmilled her arms, evoking whirlwind. She froze glacially.

'You loved the seducer of Fastboy's mother?'

Attar of soulflower teased his nostrils, and the scent of mushroom gills and cinnamon – and a nutty odour too, as if the immature knobs on the nearby kasta trees had already ripened and been roasted. The Girlem's glands were fluent with hormone and pheromone, a language in which there was no verb at all but only adverbs: sweeteningly, thrillingly, rapturously . . .

'He was your other self?'

She sagged; she drooled; seemed pale. {*Now she has no other self, for her soulmate's a zombie.*}

Rendered speechless by Osmo's proclamation, she was nevertheless so eloquent. Her theme was impossible love. She wrenched at Wex's heart. He was utterly privileged to behold hers, almost nakedly.

'Osmo – the Voice – was your target?' Needless to say; oh yes indeed. 'For a purpose of your own as well as to serve the Isi?'

Yeast and attar and chocolate assailed him, overwhelming the ammoniacal odour of cuckoo droppings. Her lips, her lace-white hands, her thighs provoked the air to embrace her. She was deathless in her healthy beauty, prompting dreams of longlife. Goldi milked an imaginary male shape she moulded in the breeze, and she conveyed its essence to a drooping ghost who was her twin, quickeningly, revivingly.

{*By coupling with longlife Osmo then with the zombie she hoped to restore her Juttahat sweetheart to health!*}

Her private hopes were utterly dashed. Maybe those had always been in vain, a forlorn illusion. Osmo had replaced her alien fantasy of a future with her other self, each acting as the other's voice, with an urge to find an impossible alternative. Failing in which, she would be the loneliest of aliens, accompanied within herself only by that tantalizing mirage which must forever elude her. As soon chase rainbows to and fro across the face of Kaleva!

How Wex pitied her, and perhaps himself too.

The Girlem's mime had been by turns mellow and sinuous and as lusty as the cadences of her recitation in the banqueting hall. Now she desisted and regarded him, inviting what response? Sympathy? Sexual distraction? Temporary discharge of poignant tension? Abandonment to pure sensation? Wex felt no titillation.

Take her to Landfall with him – as the most interesting and deviant of Juttahats? She was possessed with the urge to roam frustratedly. What if Pen Conway should pen her up inside the Earthkeep?

How would Goldi fare on her own? Could she protect herself against assault? Would her search provoke, and even compel, whoring with humans? Ravishment until she was ragged? Could she protect herself by the power of scent while nonetheless she was obliged to seek fulfilment?

{*Certain female animals on Earth can store seminal fluid within themselves for months on end, or even years, keeping it viable and vital. I allude to rattlesnakes*}

219

and indigo snakes, and the French hare, and certain bats. The female indigo snake can keep sperm viable within herself for up to six years. Evidently Juttahat females can do likewise. If, with her pheromones, this Girlem could have galvanized the shrivelled organ of the zombie to penetrate her, contact with the fluid of longlife Osmo might have cured her moribund sweetheart. Yet longlife in itself isn't genetically inheritable, my Roger. Maybe she was quite deluded. Are we likewise deluded by her pathos? She has been a schemer on behalf of the Isi, and isn't exactly a defector even now. Equally, she is most unusual.}

As unusual as Wex himself! He was a human being with a voice in his head. She was a Juttahat who lacked one, save for the sway which Osmo had inflicted on her.

Could he – and himself – have been *deluded* about the meaning of her mime? Or could such bodily eloquence have been a lie? Oh but he felt no sense of titillation, only a surety of truth.

Deluded? Why, there was one way to know for sure. He reached inside his cloak and removed the stolen mana-lens.

The Girlem's eyes widened. Plainly she'd been eavesdropping prior to her performance in the banqueting hall. When she entered the hall she had spotted the camera which had pictured Minnow starkers in the mana-mage's mouth.

'Goldi: I've seen what your body has to say. Now I shall inspect your mana-image.' Wex raised the lens to his left eye and closed his right eye. Normally he would have favoured his right eye, but the cuckoo might nudge his head aside.

She posed. He peered.

Attired in her scanty silver garb, the lustrous lass was holding hands with a golden figure who for sure was no Brazen Juttahat yet who could hardly be classed as human, either, despite possessing human mien and musculature. Undoubtedly male and mobile, this person's amber body was such that a viscous liquid – a syrup – might have congealed to form its flexible polished frame and limbs and features. Goldi appeared radiant with joy.

The image was hazy, yet the belly of that personage was less opaque than the rest of him, and contained a shadow suspended within. Was the unidentifiable silhouette an organ of that bizarre though admirable body?

A weirdly sprawling tree with beige bark was nearby.

What a strange voyeurism this was. Were Wex to thrust the mana-lens into Goldi's hands, might it somehow retain its image just long enough for her to catch a glimpse of what he was seeing?

Ah no. No chance. She would spy *him* – or else his other self, emerging from concealment to reveal a countenance of its own.

If only he'd been able to steal the entire mana-camera along with its photosensitive cards, and not merely the lens!

Should he ask her to look at him, nonetheless, and attempt to mime what she saw? Bemusing him with musk, she might try to steal the lens. Leaping on to Goodbrand, with her knees poked in its ribs she might urge the pony to bolt, galloping away with her prize toward the Brazen Isi nest . . .

{*Only you can bemuse yourself, my Roger. Why should she return to the Isi when she has a much more urgent personal imperative?*}

For an eerie moment Wex felt as though he had exchanged places with his other self, such that *he* entertained a cautionary suspicion about the Girlem, while the wetwear succumbed to her appeal. Might it be that as time passed the wetwear would usurp full governance of his body and deform his former face, and he would reside entirely within, merely peering mutely from his annexed eyes?

{*My Roger, you must not think so! I am your safeguard. Beware of mana-fugue emanating from Hermi's lens.*}

Wex snatched the lens from his eye. The Juttahat lass was gazing at him – and his cuckoo – with such wistful anguish that the fibres of his being shivered in compassion and in gladness.

'Goldi: you'll *succeed*. You'll find your golden counterpart, your . . . Amberman. He's {*in Kippan's forests: that's where the mootapu tree grows*} in Tapper Kippan's realm, the woodlord's {*away to the south-west, two hundred and fifty keys*} two hundred and fifty keys to the south-west.'

Already she was eyeing the position of the sun in the sky above the mere, and was turning.

Yet she twirled back towards Wex, her eyes moist as though the sun had blinded her. {*She cannot nictitate because she lacks a third eyelid. The Isi gifted her with more capacity for tears than their other slaves.*} The Girlem flashed such a glorious smile. She rushed, she knelt. Dumbly she hugged Wex's knees so that his other self stiffened his stance. Yeast and attar and chocolate whelmed him. He stroked her bobbed black hair.

'Take the pony,' he offered, ashamed of his previous qualm. {*Roger!*} 'I can radio to the Earthkeep at Landfall to send a dove-craft for me.' {*Roger, the Isi may intercept our message. An Isi sky-boat may arrive before the dovecraft!*} 'Well, I may walk. Perhaps I shall beg boat rides.' {*With this bird shitting on our shoulder?*} Already the reek of guano was reasserting itself. 'Take Goodbrand, Goldi, with my blessing.'

Next day around noon, Wex and his wetwear and his cuckoo came to the cairn.

There had been a downpour, which drenched him, but a brisk west wind was drying him off. The same wind had shredded the gloomy sodden nimbostratus clouds without more than a few streamers shooting off to persist at high altitude. The raggy storm front had fled eastward, scourged by gusts. The wind showed signs of weakening rather than whipping itself into a gale. Rifts of blue sky were opening.

The cairn stood on a little marble outcrop which broke through the crest of a hillock like a ball of pink bone through hairy hide too tight for it. Colonizing the thinner soil hereabouts were somewhat stunted sylvester trees with chalky bark and hoary blue bristles, a few larixes with henna scales, and a lone minty with a pea-green crown – roost, of a sudden, for a wet cuckoo weary of being jogged by Wex's dogged tramping.

If only a full-blown tempest might erupt complete with lightning. If only a sizzling flash might strike that combustible minty tree, exploding it while the bird perched on high, incinerating the pest. Fair weather, however, was in prospect. As regards contacting the satellite, this was just as well.

The cairn, no taller than Wex, was a slim ceramic pyramid patterned with eye-catching red and black zigzags, and fixed to the granite by cleats of once-stainless steel. Over the centuries the glaze had dulled. Someone had impaled a billygoat's skull on the apex. Lower down each side were the translucent insets of small solar panels. One was entirely coated with dried bird droppings but the other two were sufficiently clear for power to have been maintained. Whoever mounted the skull on top must have cleaned those panels but didn't much care for threesomes. A ram only had two horns.

Wex shook water from his canteen and cleaned the panels. He removed the shamanic decoration and tossed it aside. He had to hunt through many inner pockets before he found a key to the access tile.

This worked loose with difficulty. Inside, a little green light glowed faintly. From his cloak he took a length of thin coaxial cable which might also serve as a garotte. Removing his wig, he placed the hairpiece between his feet in case the cuckoo swooped, intent on mischief. Feeling for one of the steel pennies inset in his own skull, he pressed in a certain way. The disc rotated upwards. Carefully he inserted one end of the cable into his head, and the other end into a port close to the green light.

{*Carter, Carter, Carter!*}

As Wex stood there connected to the cairn his wetwear continued calling at intervals. Each orbit took ninety minutes. Even if Carter was crossing the northern hemisphere it might be too far to the east or west. Was the cartographic satellite merely elsewhere in its orbit, including away around the backside of the world? Or hadn't Penelope Conway reactivated it as promised? They might have to wait for hours.

{*Patience.*} Wex lowered himself on to the granite and adopted a half-lotus position. Really, his leg had healed splendidly.

{*I have it, my Roger. Alas, how existentially challenged it is! What a simpleton.*} Wex's bum was numb. In the minty tree twenty metres away the cuckoo seemed to be snoozing, utterly bored by the static tableau.

Let's face it, that bird's never going to tell us anything at all, just crap on our clothes and chuckle in our ear.

{*I feel diminished by contact with Carter rather than extended, my Roger. We are curtailed by that cuckoo too. Its telepathic kin can cackle our secrets. How about instantaneous evaporation at the speed of light courtesy of Carter's lasers?*}

Was it possible to aim tightly at a tree twenty metres south-south-east of a cairn the position of which was exactly known to the satellite? {*That's well within Carter's competency. Its next pass will put it within adequate range. It'll take until then for Carter to check out its lasers. Centuries old, and never used till now. There should be minimal cloud cover.*} How could any blame for the bird's slaying attach to Wex? The cuckoo could have no suspicion of what he and himself were thinking. The pest would simply and instantly vaporize. Quite by surprise it would vanish from its kin's ken. Dumb of it to roost in a minty.

Actually – should anyone somehow become aware of the incident – the satellite would *seem* to be shooting at its own cairn, so the intention could easily be misconstrued . . .

Wex must stay quite still for quite a while.

Om. Ommmmm. Ommmmmmmmm.

When the pea-green tree exploded Wex was bowled over from his half-lotus by the blast. Heat scorched him. A spuriously cool odour of mint assailed him. He was deafened. He'd already shut his eyes in anticipation.

As he uncramped isometrically, assisted by his wetwear, he was lying partly in the lee of the cairn. The cable had pulled loose from his skull, though without damage to himself, so it seemed. The steel penny fitted back flush into his cranium.

'Bye-bye, birdy,' he cried. His eardrums popped, and he heard . . . not a roar of conflagration but a great *gasp*, as of the world breathing out. Nor had the fierce heat persisted.

When he looked, blinking, what he saw was not at all what he – or himself – had expected.

Instead of an incandescent minty trunk gushing fire, there arose a pillar of light twice as tall as the tree had been. A luminous tower, it suggested architecture. Flames flickering from the finial tip of its spire were like pennants fluttering. In its spectral insubstantiality it appeared greasily, gassily waxen: a wraith of a candle. The whole apparition was molten, yet coolly so. No torrid swelter radiated from it. An impervious screen might have enclosed it. In its depths, lens-like, swam cloudy images, distorted and prismatic.

'Wetwear, what in Minnow's name *is* it?'

The column could have been a memorial beacon to mark where the cuckoo had expired, a great gassy candle which would burn for days and weeks . . . *This* was the outcome of the surreptitious snuffing of a cuckoo?

{*Puts all Kaleva in a rage, my Roger, as the saying goes. Use the mana-lens. If it isn't broken.*}

No, Hermi's lens was intact. It hadn't cracked when Wex toppled over.

Wex raised the lens to his eye – defiantly to his *right* eye – and peered at the tower of light, at that other waxy gassy glistening lens. Already he was shuffling forward, descending the smooth granite, partly propelled by his other self. He was glimpsing snow-clad woodlands and frozen lakes which curved upward as if they might crack; then a cluster of luminous towers afire, a burning palace really, of which the tower he was approaching was only one part, one aspect. He stumbled. His slight shift of position revealed instead a candle-tower at the edge of a flat black expanse with a circle of pink within it. A curving tail of pink intruded upon the black.

{*That's Harmony Field, at Landfall. Part of the landing apron decorated with the yin-yang emblem in obsidian and granite. There's a Carter-cairn near the edge.*} Not any longer. Now a candle-tower burned alongside Harmony Field. What would Pen Conway say about that? {*A replacement guidance beacon can easily be arranged. A shuttle can still land.*} Right next to an unpredictable pillar of mana-light?

Wex tilted Hermi's lens, and spied another cairn on a low headland overlooking some lake. That cairn remained intact but it wore a tapering quivering sheath of radiance.

{*Focus on Harmony Field again, if you can.*}

He could.

By now he had come much closer to the candle-tower. The uprush of gassy light was only a few metres away, and still he felt no leakage of heat.

{*I believe this is an aperture through mana-space, my Roger. A cuckoo is a living tool of the junior Ukko which Lucky seeks; and we consumed that tool with hot light. This display is the reaction. If we step into this manifestation we may travel as no others have travelled before us, save within the protective shell of an Ukko.*}

A premonition of disaster possessed Wex. What if all of the other cairns which were functional had become mana-candles in the same way as the cairn at Harmony Field? Lucky would learn of this soon enough. A similar candle-cairn might be shining near Sariolinna. Here was a door – a tubular door of light – leading directly into the Ukko she sought for with all her soul. No need, any longer, to search the whole world for the hiding place!

Isi mana-mages would find these beacons too. The Isi could gain speedy access.

{*Not necessarily! I speculate that these apertures only lead to other candle-cairns – and I also surmise that they may not endure for very long. This manifestation is an impulsive response to the killing of the cuckoo. We may not have long if we wish to reach Landfall swiftly by this route.*}

By focusing upon the image of Harmony Field through Hermi's mana-lens. By stepping into the column of light . . .

{*You gave our pony away, my Roger. Now we don't need one if you're quick and bold.*}

Quick and bold.

'You're sure this will be safe?'

{*We owe it to Earth to try this route. Probably it will be like riding a jump-bike through mana-space*} – which Wex hadn't experienced personally, though he had quizzed Jurgen and Johann – {*but making a much larger leap.*}

The column of light, so close to him, was cool.

He clapped a hand to his head. 'My wig – I need my wig.' His hairpiece was still lying beside the cairn.

{*For the want of a wig the world was lost . . . Act now, my Roger, before the opportunity evaporates! You can get another wig in Landfall. Act now!*}

Yes of course. Meet Pen Conway; alert her to the full significance of these doors of light which he had pioneered. See if the mana-lens could be attached to Carter in orbit. Take a dovecraft and find Cully, though maybe that was of lesser consequence now. Of course.

Adjusting the angle of the lens, Wex located the edge of the yin-yang once more. Wetwear-assisted, he was walking towards it.

Intolerable agony seized him.

15 · A WIGGING FOR WEX

Wex's skin was on fire. He was being flayed. His organs were burning. Oh but this wasn't in the least like the *in-between*, the flash of darkness described by Johann and Jurgen. How insanely he screamed. He pitched forward on to black obsidian, hard as a hammer, agleam with sunlight.

And sprawled insensately. The excruciating pain had vanished abruptly. All other bodily sensation had disappeared at the same time. Lying there, he was bereft of feeling. Paralysed.

No, he wasn't *paralysed* . . . He could flex his hands. He could turn his neck.

He raised his head to see through tears of suspended torment a shuttlecraft ferry looming skyward and the blue of the sky with some rag clouds fleeing away. Blurred, he spied the ziggurat of red brick and glinting windows which was the Earthkeep. Blearily he glimpsed the dome of the observatory, and a squat rose-red building supporting a satellite dish.

When he brushed the moisture from his eyes his palm was dead meat. So was his cheek. Fingers heeded his will but they were so numb and uninformative. Was he really feeling his face? Yes; since there was resistance.

He rolled over. His trunk could move. His legs could move. His arms could move. Yet feeling was absent. Evidently his spine hadn't snapped and his neck wasn't broken. But all sensation had deserted him along with the absent agony. He was a dummy – which functioned well enough, nevertheless. Did a zombie feel (or fail to feel) thus?

He cried aloud, 'Wetwear, I can't feel anything!'

{*That is because I disconnected your sensations to protect you from the induced pain. The illusion of pain continues but you cannot feel it. You cannot suffer. The column of light was a trap, my Roger who killed the cuckoo. Now the phenomenon has discharged itself.*}

Wex jerked his head. Instead of a candle-tower there was only the stump of Harmony Field's cairn, fused and melted. No remnant of radiance hung around it, no caul of mana-fire.

The deadness of his body was abominable. All sensual significance had fled. He'd been robbed, dispossessed . . . by his wetwear.

'Give me myself back!'

Being out of touch with the world in this way – all of his feelings appropriated – it might be an easy transition for him to become exiled within himself.

'Give me back myself!'

{*That would be unwise. You're immune to mana-effects by virtue of my vigilance—*}

'Am I? Am I? I used Hermi's lens, and I stepped through mana-space—'

{*With my acquiescence.*}

'Give me my feelings, wetwear!'

{*If you insist that I relax my guard . . .*}

Lying there upon his back, Wex screamed as fire flooded him.

'Stop it stop stop it!'

{*In time you might become accustomed to this torture, my Roger. You might learn how to endure it and still function intelligently.*}

'Stop it stop stop!'

His torture ceased. He rolled his numb rubber carcass away from where the pain had been, and pushed himself into a kneeling position. He drooled, unaware of this until he noticed spittle upon the glossy obsidian.

Wiping his mouth with a dead hand: 'You betrayed me, wetwear.'

{*Oh, I'm hurt.*}

'No, it was *me* who was being hurt until you switched my nervous system off. Now: ashes, dead embers. All is ashes.'

{*Ashes are better than lashes.*}

'You cheated me.'

{*How could I have known? Would a deceiver have saved you from your agony?*}

227

'I might have flayed myself with my fingernails. I might have put an end to myself, stabbed myself to death.'

{*No, you could not do that.*}

'I might have been crazed enough to succeed!'

{*Please let's not quarrel, my Roger. We are inextricable. You shouldn't address me aloud so much, or how will you appear to others?*}

He would seem like Minnow muttering to herself . . . Farewell to any foolish amatory sensations about that young lady. Farewell to all feelings whatever. The very recollection of Minnow taunted him. He was a unique new breed of eunuch now: a whole-body capon. Of course he'd been talking out loud – so that he could hear his own voice externally.

He could hear, he could see. He couldn't touch, or taste anything, or smell anything whatever.

{*You'll have to be careful that you don't injure yourself. I shall watch out, too. Now at least nobody else will use candle-cairns as a way of jumping around the world. The harm has been undone.*}

Nobody else. No body.

People in olive uniforms were running across the pink granite zone of the landing field in his direction.

How long it seemed since he had last been in Penelope Conway's sanctum looking out toward Harmony Field and the blue boomerang of Lake Plentiful. Must be almost a year to the day. {*In fact it's precisely*—} The calendar count didn't matter. The Earth Resident's purple tammywood desk was littered as ever with files. Labelled stacks of these ascended upon tammy shelving from floor to ceiling. One wall was crowded with photographs and drawings and paintings of keeps: the aitch-house, Osmo's keep, dozens of them.

Pen Conway's data-screen displayed a motto:

'This untenable place where our
speaking species resides, threatened by
madness beneath the emptiness of
heaven . . . The black thrusts of desire –
subject of the discourse of another . . .'

J. Krist.

228

How true. That poetess, Juke's dead sister, would have known well enough about black thrusts of desire and being subject to *Osmo*'s discourse. Wex himself had known a bit about black thrusts, though half an hour ago all of his tactile sensations had blacked out.

He considered the text. {*Semiotic scripture, I believe, my Roger.*} During his year-long absence had Pen Conway become a Kristian, or rather a Christian? In the interim could she possibly have succumbed to mysticism? No cross hung around the black woman's robust neck so far as Wex could see, unless it was well hidden underneath her summer sari. Same plain elegant olive garment as last year. Or perhaps a new one of the same cut and hue.

Conway's tight dusky hair showed a few more threads of grey than previously. She was somewhat stouter, though impressively so. She had presence and substance, a matronly gravitas. Wex stood before her cumbersomely in his shabbily beshitted cloak. His body image – his intuition of contours – was larger and more awkward than the actuality. Just as well. He wouldn't be so likely to bang and bruise himself.

Conway was obviously deeply peeved, but she was doing her best to *om* her passions away. She blanked the screen.

'To think that I once imagined you might be my replacement! You promised not to access Carter.'

From an inner pocket Wex produced the mana-lens.

'This device lets us perceive mana-phenomena, Pen. It could be attached to Carter up in orbit either by diverting a shuttle or, better, by persuading our own Ukko-ferry to co-operate.'

'Divert our Ukko from its regular route to Earth? Maybe maroon us? How fares your own co-operation with yourself, Wethead? Have you both gone crazy, sharing that skull?'

Mention of his skull reminded Wex. 'By the way, I need another wig. Is there somewhere in Landfall town—'

She eyed him sombrely, especially the two steel pennies in his cranium, as if those might flip open and liberate . . . horns? Or a couple of wee snakes?

'You've experienced something of the power by which an Ukko propels itself from star to star, even from universe to universe—'

'I think it experienced *me*!'

'—and you worry about a wig. You look like shit. What *is* all that mess on your shoulder?'

'You said it, Pen.'

The wombless matron wrinkled her nose.

229

'Did you fancy yourself as some big-game hunter from the days of ecological extinction? A gossip-bird – and a space-gun in orbit! Do you care how much damage you've caused? Our landing beacon is slag.'

'It can be replaced.'

'Presumably other cairns are junk too.'

'Carter can still find its way around. Its mind's full of maps and co-ordinates.'

'Worse than that, thanks to you the juvenile Ukko has expressed itself in the world at large – and in a hostile way – and while a war is brewing.'

Oh he cared. Aside from the wider ramifications he had lost touch with his own body. *Put more simply, had he lost touch?* The black woman's expression certainly implied so. How could she possibly conceive the effort it required for him to stand here like a lump and still be lucid?

'I can't feel myself, damn it!' (And she cocked a sooty eyebrow.) 'Oh I can move myself about because I remember how to, but this body has no feeling.' This body: his own. No one else's. 'My wetwear disconnected me, otherwise I'd still be in agony from mana-fire. That's how the Ukko aimed to punish me for killing its cuckoo. It's fortunate I'm protected.'

Conway shuddered.

'Obviously you're in trauma, even if you did bring this upon yourself . . .'

'Oh, I'm perfectly sane. With this mana-lens,' he resumed, holding up Hermi's device, 'I saw my way through the doorway of light. And I saw the future destiny of a Juttahat Girlem—'

'Don't point that thing at me! What's this about a Juttahat?'

Wex told her as briefly as he could, though inevitably his account – touching as it must upon many circumstances – sounded hectic and cluttered even to himself. Conway appeared to take in most of the details.

'Dear me,' she said presently, 'so you gave this exceptional Juttahat – with whom we could have talked, and from whom we might have learned so much – you gave her your pony to ride away on?'

'A special agent has to make choices.'

'What if most of those choices are wrong, and dangerous? Such as using an orbital laser to shoot a bird that's bothering you?'

Wex glanced at his filthy padded shoulder. 'I need a new cloak,

230

just like this one. And I want a dovecraft so that I can find Cully, whom the Isi tried to control. The dreamlord's nephew.'

'You let that *Girlem* ride away . . . out of infatuation?'

'Oh no!' It certainly wasn't Goldi with whom he had been infatuated . . . This was a private matter, even if it did touch upon the new young rebel Queen. 'Not at all.'

'You really must tell me a great deal more in detail, Wethead Wex, before I let you borrow any dovecraft to boost your mobility. Your reports have been scanty, to say the least.' Even if he *was* Earth's special agent, she wouldn't be browbeaten; not in view of his recent antics.

Just then the Chinese aide, Yü, brought in a black lacquer tray bearing two cups of coffee, jug of cream, and sugar bowl. After depositing this beside the screen, Yü was inclined to linger. Her large spectacles made her flat oval face seem particularly owl-like as she peered circumspectly at Wex. Had she been eavesdropping on an open link, and was worried about Pen Conway's safety? Wex returned Yü's scrutiny, surprised to feel surprised by that oriental visage last seen so long ago at the gala in Yulistalax. Oriental woman; and black woman – he was most certainly back in the far-flung, star-flung citadel of the Harmonious Society. He felt, in default of other sensations, subtly out of place. Oh to be on his way, with new cloak and new wig, in pursuit of Cully.

'That's all right, Yü,' said Conway. As quietly as she had come, the Chinese aide withdrew, no doubt to continue monitoring the conversation. She had neither greeted Wex, nor did she bid adieu. From the holster attached to the belt of her olive uniform the butt of a lightpistol protruded.

At first Wex ignored the coffee. Best Pootaran coffee. Maybe with cinnamon in it. It steamed, and he detected no smell whatever. Should he check that it lacked taste too? How easy to forget that he was already holding something in his hand: the manalens. He deposited the lens on Conway's desk.

{*Our body needs hydration, my Roger.*} *Our* body? *Ours?* If only his wetwear would stop calling him 'my Roger' so proprietorially as if it were the proprietor; and as if he were a pet!

For a fraction of a second: a searing flash of pain.

{*I'm sorry, my control slipped momentarily.*}

Thank mana he hadn't picked up the cup or else he would have jerked half of the contents over Conway's files. He had winced almightily and broken out in a sweat. Had the protective control

231

slipped accidentally – or intentionally, to remind him of the alternative?

{What shall I call you? Wiggy? What style of wig will you commission, by the way? Short bob or long bob? Peruke or periwig? A parson's peruke? Or one with a queue at the nape? A prudent peruke or a lunatic one? Genteel style, or jealous style? Royal, or rhinocerine? A bob wig with tiers? A white cauliflower wig?} His wetwear was becoming uppity. How did it know all this antiquated nonsense about wigs? *{Because you're a wig-wearer, on account of me. I'm full of data about wigs, in case I can be of service in this department. What shall I call you from now on?}* Just *Roger*. Plain Roger. Simply that.

Wex held the cup to where his lips were, and sipped. The coffee possessed neither heat nor taste. He was only aware of a certain degree of lubrication, proved by the fact that he could speak more easily. Eating would be a very dull activity, spiced only with the risk that he might inadvertently chew his tongue.

'Where shall I be able to get a new wig made hereabouts?' he asked. Lucky's chamberlain Linqvist was given to wearing *{a powdered peruke à la Cavalière with two tiers of curls}* proving that some barber in Pohjola Palace was able to create an elegant wig. But here in Landfall? Much of the town was dedicated to preparing and outfitting new colonists who hardly required expert hairpieces.

The black woman sighed. 'You might as well ask at the Pootaran puzzle shop.'

'That a *good* idea.' Pootarans sold curiosities, and a wig was a bit of an oddity. Pootaran sailors regularly visited Landfall town to escort any black immigrants to the coast and onward southerly by sailing ship to the sub-tropical island. Sailors were nimble with needles.

'Can you possibly forget this bee in your bonnet for the moment, Mr Wex? Can we explore some details? You saw the everything machine—'

Aye, that, and so much more. The first time ever he met Pen Conway was when Elmer Loxmith came a-calling to pursue discreet enquiries about a hibernation cabinet for a cat, prototype for the larger model in which Cully's 'uncle' would repose. *{We are searching for Cully, remember.}* Yes, yes. Really, Wex had been such an innocent back then. He had not wrestled with a mana-mage and popped it – alas – out of its sloughing skin. He had not become captivated by a gamin princess. He had not explored the full experience of being a prototype of a protected partnered

232

person, who had now lost touch with his own body, the alternative being unbearable phantom pain.

'I feel like a zombie, Pen Conway.'

She frowned. 'How do you know what a zombie feels like?'

'Ah, but I'm perfectly capable of piloting a dovecraft. I'm not rotting. Look,' and he held out a dead hand, opening and closing his fist by way of demonstration. 'After I've sorted myself out I need to find Cully because the Brazen Isi tried to control his mind by using an ingenious harp—'

'According to you this *Girlem* whom you helped tried to control van Maanen with just such a harp.'

'Yes, quite!'

'Maybe she swayed you with her harp so that you'd find Cully and return him to her, and to the Isi?'

'No, no, by the time I talked to her she'd lost the harp. Osmo and Minnow have the harp.'

'Couldn't you have managed to steal *that* instead of this bizarre lens?'

'If it weren't for the lens I wouldn't have arrived here so quickly!' What a tragedy his triumph had become when it involved the loss of touch and taste and smell . . .

'If this lens is fitted to Carter I'm sure we can find the junior Ukko before Lucky or the Isi do. The Ukko might be persuaded to influence everyone's minds, and bodies too. That's more important than a harp. I'll still be hunting for Cully to deduce what happened to him in the Isi nest. Are the last two skeletons still safe, Pen?'

For a moment she looked blank.

'The two alien skeletons in the vaults beneath here, from the original Ukko: are they still safe?'

'Oh. Yes, of course. How scattily you jump about! To lend you a dovecraft could be downright lunacy. As for interfering with the reliable routines of the Ukko-ferry to fix a lens on a satellite which has already provoked the hidden Ukko, thanks to you, well really!'

'*Do nothing* is the watchword, eh?'

'Earth doesn't wish us to stir the pot.'

'The pot's already in turmoil. There's a war. There's a spunky rebel Queen who actually foxed a mana-mage.'

'And whom you admire? Is that it, Wex? Reckless Wex, with no nervous system to your name! What, give you a dovecraft after you brought mana-fire upon our beacon . . . ?'

233

'Pen Conway: I can commandeer a craft. I do have the authority.'

Conway smiled evasively. 'Your attitude sounds partisan. Tell me more about this Girlem, invidious name. A girl golem, hmm? Tell me about Queen Minnow. Would you like some more coffee?'

Like? How could he possibly *like* coffee, or any other drink?

His gaze strayed to a small framed painting of the van Maanen keep, where Minnow would most likely be ensconced by now. That fortified complex of roofs and towers set on an upthrust of pink granite was, properly speaking, a royal palace now that she had been crowned with leather and pearls. The stronghold looked somewhat meagre compared with her mother's vast abode in Sariolinna.

During Wex's previous sojourn in Landfall – after arriving from Earth, and before Yü flew him to that gala in Yulistalax – Wex had strolled by the puzzle shop several times before finally entering it.

Beyond the market square with its array of shops and its white marble mana-kirk, the Pootaran emporium brokered many products from the great garden island in the south – spices, tobacco, candied fruit. Those aspects of its business were confined to the crooked jumble of rooms out back and upstairs. Except at the front, all inner angles of the building were disconcerting. Rooms were triangular or trapezoidal. Corridors ran aslant. No mischievous nakki would take up residence in such a place. Maybe this was the rationale. The Pootarans might be notorious as rationalists who would have as little truck as possible with mana-phenomena, and whose distant island was immune to such. By the same token the architecture of this, their de facto consulate and trading post, seemed aimed to banish unreason by flaunting irregularities. To navigate one's way about this building required a level head.

The front of the shop was largely given over to the wooden logic puzzles which Pootarans carved so craftily. Pyramids and spheres and boxes of many interlocking parts crowded shelves and a long display counter. A staircase led to a zigzag gallery from the other end of which plunged a second stairway, steep and narrow and shadowy.

When Wex entered, he found the portly proprietor – and representative in Landfall of the Pootaran democracy – sitting in a purple tammy rocking chair examining a dismantled puzzle.

Notched wedges, polygons, and rhombs of mustardy yellover wood and speckled beige horzma covered a lacquer tray larger than that upon which Yü had served coffee.

{*Bosco*} – I remember his name perfectly well – wore a pleated gown with vast sleeves, and a fez. This gown was of saffron and gold, though the beaded red fez was the same one as he had sported the previous year. Opposite Bosco was seated the Pootaran woman named {*Miriam*}. A mauve skirt, plentifully pleated and folded, would have wholly hidden the richly tooled leather pouffe beneath her had she herself not been so extremely slim. A full puffy purple blouse, loosely knotted, was complemented by a sumptuous turban of similar hue. Her skin and Bosco's were a glossy ebony, as if oiled.

En route to the puzzle shop, Wex had called at a clothier's to order an urgent replacement for his stained and shabby cloak, complete with quite as many inner pockets. At the clothier's, and out on the streets, his bare cranium, with those two little steel discs inset, had excited stares. Now Miriam arose fluidly to inspect the visitor. She overtopped Wex by a head and a half or even two.

'As you can see,' said Wex, 'I'm in much need of a wig, and I thought that Pootarans might have the knack, the patience, the nimbleness with needles. I can explain how to *make* a wig, that's no problem. First you measure my head from the top of the forehead to the nape of the neck, then {*from one temple to the other, passing behind the head*} and next { *from one ear to the other passing over the top of the head*} and fourthly {*from the middle of one cheek to the middle of the other cheek going behind the head*} and finally {*from the middle of the top of the forehead to one of the temples*} after which you make a block, a blockhead of soft wood – I suppose a plaster mould might be quicker . . .'

'Man, did someone shoot you through the skull?' Bosco's voice was richly vibrant. His eyelids were heavy hoods, his scrutiny languidly genial.

'Then, and next, and fourthly, and finally?' echoed Miriam in a cordial contralto.

'Didn't I just say so?'

'I'm thinking,' said Bosco, 'that we have a head-case here. So that settles it: I *will* be sailing back to the isles before I become a nutter too. Fellow, are those your own brains on your shoulder?'

Miriam sniffed. 'Guano, I guess. Bird-shit. He's some kind of shaman. He drilled holes in his head.' She patted her huge turban for reassurance.

'I'm not a shaman, I'm a special agent from Earth.'

'Delusions, too.'

'I've been in here before. Last year. I looked around. I met you both. You don't remember me without my wig.'

Bosco grinned. 'Without a wig you have identity problems, man. Do you hear voices too, by any chance?'

Wex shuddered. His tone – prim till now – became deeper and fruity as if to harmonize with his hosts. *All is explicable, Mr Bosco.*

Miriam gasped. 'Oh my, nakki-spirits are rattling him. He got to have his mind calmed. He's mana-crazy. Look, mister, this wig you're wanting. It ain't really that you want *it*, but you want it as a *cap*, a protector, ain't that so?' Leaning over Bosco, she whispered, 'He's come to us because he knows us Pootarans live the life of sweet reason. Something we make for him's a talisman, a charm to set him straight. Or somewhat straighter. Poor man, we got to help out somehow. Our puzzles won't unkink his mind.'

'A copper pot to boil the hair in; a stove to dry it in. Sorting and weaving and knotting; buckram plaques and wefts . . .'

'You hear how he has the whole ritual worked just like some exorcism?'

{*Let them think so, Roger.*} Wex regained himself, to the extent that there was a great deal to regain. 'I'd very much appreciate your assistance,' he said, 'and of course I can pay for it.' Pen Conway had replenished his depleted purse with golden ors and silver marks from the Earthkeep treasury.

The black couple whispered together for a while. Miriam appeared to be urging Wex's case out of compassion, for the sake of sanity. The stout consul picked up two notched rhombs of yellover and turned them this way and that with long, impeccably manicured fingers before slotting the pieces together. Yes indeed, Pootarans had something of a minor mission to introduce a mite of logic into the lives of those bedevilled by sways and manias. This visitor had sought them out for therapy, for a sort of salvation. He couldn't voice his real need but must concoct this requirement of a wig which would redeem him from drilling another hole in his skull to relieve the pressure from his inner phantoms.

Big Bosco consulted his manicure. 'Okay,' he said at last, 'so happens there's a sailor staying with us right now, name of Jonas, who's a champion puzzle-maker. Quite handy with a needle too, ain't it just so, Miriam? He's upstairs whittling away like a woodbug to keep his mind healthily employed.'

'I'll help Jonas,' volunteered Miriam. 'To the best of our ability we'll make you a wig exactly the way you want it.' And if that way wasn't the way that wigs were usually made, what of it? 'Why don't you sit down? Care for some coffee, Mr—?'

'Wex. Roger Wex. Some water'll be welcome. For hydration. Many thanks! I can't taste coffee.' Numbly Wex lowered himself upon the leather pouffe.

'Can't *taste* coffee?'

'Can't taste anything; can't feel. I've lost half of my senses.'

'Ah . . .' How sympathetically the tall thin woman sighed. 'He's deadened himself,' she murmured to Bosco, 'so that he won't suffer frenzies . . . *But*,' she continued, 'we don't happen to have any supplies of hair, Mr Wex, except for what's growing upon our own scalps!'

What crinkly black mane might – or might not – be coiled within that substantial turban of hers? Wex had pulled out his purse, but she frowned.

'You'll understand that I'd feel reluctant to donate my own hair, even for golden ors. That'd be slavish, you see, and we aren't slaves even if Lucky brought us here to grow bananas and oranges and cotton down on our plantations.'

Did Wex blush? Did nostalgia for the Harmonious Society needle him?

'I'll buy hair at a barber's,' he assured Miriam.

'Before you went bald what colour was your hair?'

'It was black.'

'Ah . . .' Again, a knowing sigh.

'And curly.'

'With sweepings from the barber's floor,' said Bosco, 'you might end up looking somewhat piebald.'

'*A question of sorting*,' said Roger's lips, '*and dyeing darker if need be.*'

Inside the barber shop, on a lane off the busy market square, two chubby white-aproned women in their thirties were beginning to snip, respectively, a charcoal-suited priest from the mana-kirk and a red-headed man with a large spongy nose which resembled a morel fungus.

Sitting awaiting their turn were a teenage woman with wild tresses so blonde they were almost white, and a lithe man dressed in a creased olive uniform. This fellow's features were brown. His abundant hair was curly, coaly, and oily, and he sported a stylish pencil moustache. Though he wore no sidearm, a tough tammywood stick the length of a forearm, shiny with handling, was stuck through his belt.

Wex's advent provoked the usual stares, and a brief giggle in unison from the two hairdressers – why was a bald man visiting the barber shop? Both were honey-blonde, with identical pigtails. One wore a little violet tattoo of scissors on a plump cheek, and the other a tattoo of a comb, the better to tell them apart.

As Wex seated himself next to the Earthkeep officer {*evidently from the Indian sub-continent*} the twins resumed snipping and chattering to their clients. The striped pole outside the establishment supported a cuckoo perch on its tip, unvisited recently to judge by the withered condition of the offal; yet this omission was no deterrent to the flow of gossip.

'I hear as how the new rebel Queen has really wild frizzy hair,' Scissors mentioned to Morel. 'She's just a kid, but Lord van Maanen went wild about her. Oh he's Prince van Maanen now, self-*proclaimed*.' She laughed at her joke. 'War won't come this far, will it?'

'I hear something odd happened earlier today at Harmony Field,' Comb said to the priest. 'Something *mana*-odd! A fisherman on Lake Plentiful saw a pillar of light. Do you know about this at the kirk, Pappi?'

The priest allowed that a colleague was investigating. 'What's more,' he said, 'on my way here a cuckoo in the square was crying that one of its kin had been *murdered*.' He paused for effect. Wex contrived to look innocent. 'And the killer will burn unconsumedly.'

Snip-snip. 'What's that mean, Pappi?'

'I suppose it means he'll feel that he's burning, but he won't die.'

'Ooh that's horrid, but how do you know the killer's a *he*?'

The Indian beside Wex was paying close attention to these conversations. Was that why he had come here, on the pretext of having his bountiful hair trimmed? So as to take the temperature of the town? The Indian glanced at Wex, and wrinkled his nose. Wex's neighbour was sitting to the cuckoo-shit side of the cloak, so Wex shucked this off, over the back of the chair. His purple silk shirt with its specially padded shoulders and his tan breeches were perhaps a bit smelly too, though he had no way of knowing. The Indian's skin was shiny as if massage oil had been rubbed into it. Scrupulous about personal hygiene!

The mana-priest hadn't replied to Comb.

'Can we be sure the killer's a *he*?' she persisted.

'You do prattle.' The priest sounded embarrassed.

'Oh but sir,' appealed Comb, 'word-power is quite vital to a hairdresser, almost as much as to a proclaimer, don't you know?'

'The facility of fluency!' agreed her twin. 'We need to occupy our customers while they're sitting here, to keep them still. Would we do our job as smartly otherwise?'

'It isn't just a matter of the words connected with the job, Pappi sir, such as braid and bun and bunch and coil and curl—'

'—or lock and mane and mop, or ringlet and plait and fringe—'

'It's all manner of words about everything whatever, sir. About all of life, don't you see? As many as the hairs that fall on our floor each day!' Of which there was a considerable motley lying in drifts. 'So, sir, could this cuckoo-killer possibly be a *she*?' Snip-snip. Snip-snip. The twins were excited, effervescent. Mighty events were afoot. Nevertheless they remained entirely attentive to their craft. In their ebullience they were unlikely accidentally to trim off all the highly suitable hair pell-mell from Wex's neighbour when it came to the Indian's turn.

{*He is a practitioner of kalaripayit combat techniques; hence the stick.*} What? {*A South Indian peasant fighting method involving crouches and leaping twists. Virtuosi perform the crocodile-walk for exercise, advancing on palms and toes. When he rises to have his hair trimmed he may strut with his heels high. Adepts can strike paralysingly or lethally at many vital points in the body, the location of which are closely guarded secrets. Their lore was written upon palm leaves with a sharp instrument, then those lines were rubbed with lampblack to render them visible.*} How could those vital Points remain secret? {*Insects were forever eating the palm leaves.*} Of course. {*In the event of injuries sustained during practice the adepts are often masters of alternative medicine, performing massage of fractures or abdominal damage.*}

Wex, assisted by his wetwear, was proficient in tai-chi, aikido, and karate, however he'd been ignorant of this other tradition till his wetwear enlightened him. Now he turned to the Indian and grinned.

'I take it from your stick,' he murmured, 'that you're a master of {*kalaripayit*} kalaripayit?'

The Indian smiled. 'Not many people have even heard of it.' His tone was soft and gentle. He sounded respectful – of himself, and more warily so of Wex. 'You're the agent from Earth who arrived last year, aren't you? I saw you a few times in the Residency.'

'You can actually recognize me without my wig?'

239

'I do pay attention to all bodies and physiognomies. Last year I decided that you must be wearing a wig. An agent adopts a disguise, mm?' He glanced, eyebrow raised, at the metal discs implanted in Wex's cranium. Plainly the wig had served to hide those. 'I saw you leave with Yü for Kaleva's illustrious gala, which I've never seen with my own eyes.' Those acute brown eyes, with such bright whites cupping the pupils. 'In five years I've never been beyond Landfall. If only I might have been your pilot.'

'Ah, so you're a pilot?' {*If Conway does insist on a nursemaid for the dovecraft—!*} 'I imagined you'd be a medic of the alternative persuasion. Maybe you're that as well? Don't kalaripayit masters massage fractures and ruptures?'

'Oh this is very true. We practise foot-massage. There's so little opportunity to pilot. There's so little opportunity. Every few months for practice I take off, circle, and land obediently. I itch to travel. This is not an itch to be scratched, dear me no.'

'So you massage people's feet to heal internal injuries? Pressure points on the feet corresponding to spleen and stomach and kidneys?'

The Indian blinked in astonishment. 'Oh no, not at all. We massage *with* the soles of our feet. We support ourselves on a rope strung lengthwise, and tread the afflicted body.'

'Oh I *see* . . . Forgive me, Mr, um—?'

'Gurrukal. Mathavan Gurrukal, at your service.'

{*Conway should rate Mathavan Gurrukal to be a suitable escort for us, given his skill in unarmed combat; and his hair is really lustrous.*} Yes indeed: his hair.

Wex continued to converse with the Indian in undertones while the blonde twins were trimming and commenting on cuckoo reports of the siege of Loxmithlinna and the ensuing coronation.

'*Her crown was of leather, stitched by the hoyden herself, would you believe—?*'

'*And a Juttie courtesan tried to enchant him—*'

'So, Mr Gurrukal, do you chafe at being restricted to Landfall and environs?'

'I am not chafing. But it is slightly sad to travel to the stars – to one at least – and only stay in one single town. If the Harmonious Society requires this, so be it. I've encountered more than most people. The light of a different sun, the smell of a different air – rather more exhilarating oxygen, and no pollutants to speak of.'

Wex no longer knew about smells. 'I have a proposal,' he whispered. 'Your hair: it's so glossy, and long.' (His neighbour eyed him askance.) 'You don't by any chance feel that your strength resides in that fine head of hair?'

'Dear me no. What a strange superstition. What are you saying?'

'Just this . . . I urgently need a wig, to hide my implants. I shan't insult you by asking you to sell me your hair—'

'Goodness me, would you glue it to your scalp in tufts?'

'No, I would have a proper hairpiece sewn by a Pootaran sailor. May I propose a more equable bargain, Mr Gurrukal? I need to borrow a dovecraft so as to find a certain man with whose mind the Isi have meddled. Our admirable Resident harbours certain qualms. I have the right to requisition a craft – but one must always seek to co-operate, wouldn't you say?'

'Indeed. If a man attacks you, you should always try to make peace before strong-arming him.'

Could he and himself neutralize Gurrukal if necessary? Incapacitate the fellow, using tai-chi, as had happened to Hermi? {*Not necessarily, if he's a full master of kalaripayit. The need should not arise.*}

'If you will have your head shaved bare for me, Mr Gurrukal, I shall request you as the pilot for my quest – which will take us first of all to Castlebeck, the dreamlord's keep, then who-knows-where.'

'Oh really? Really?' The Indian's eyes shone. He nursed misgivings. 'Won't Miz Conway think I'm acting oddly if I give you all my hair?'

'No, this is a southern Indian vow of honour, do you see?'

'It is no such thing.'

'Pretend! How does she know? Where's the harm? Say that you won't grow your hair again till you bring the dovecraft back safely. Being bald will remind you of your duty. You'll be doing Earth's agent a great service. Otherwise I'm obliged to rely on the mixture those twins have swept into bags to stuff pillows with. Most of it'll be too short. The delay could prove fatal.'

For almost half a minute Mathavan Gurrukal closed his eyes in meditation. Then he stuck out a firm hand.

'We will shake on this, Mr Wex, whose name I already learned last year.' His grip was powerful, though lightly applied.

'I should have introduced myself earlier—' {*Don't introduce me, Roger.*} Of course not.

Scissors angled two hand mirrors so that the redhead with the

241

morel-nose could inspect his trim. Satisfied, he nodded, and paid, and left.

The chubby blonde paused until her sister had finished with the priest.

'Who's next?' she enquired.

The Indian rose, and Wex too. He pulled black silk from his cloak wherewith to harvest the lustrous fallen locks. Lacking any feeling in his fingers, he would need to pay careful attention while gathering black upon black.

Gurrukal *did* strut towards the barber's chair. Heels high.

16 · VARIOUS RELATIONS

Baring his teeth and screwing up his eyes, Cully chanted:

> '*I – I – I—*
>> '*Am! Am!*
>>> '*I am. I am.*'
> He was . . . *what*?

As punctuation he banged his brow against the peeling bark of a harper tree. His goatish butting flayed skin from the trunk and from himself. Blood imprinted a blaze on the harper as if thus he recorded his itinerary. Blood trickled down his nose and cheeks. He rocked, he staggered. Such a roaring ache in his head. He slumped.

Strings of the tree stretching up into the jade-green crown continued to resound to his cries in what sounded like hysterical affirmation: *ayeayeayeaye*. Other strings twanged with: *mam-mam-mam-mam.*

Where was his Mam now, whom the dreamlord had debauched in her middle years? Where was mother Marietta? Where was Cully himself, bastard of them both? No, but he couldn't be Lord Beck's bastard . . . not if Gunther Beck had seduced his Mam when she was already middle-aged.

Uncle Gunther had tried to drown the product of that intercourse while the boy was still tiny. Somehow he had failed! How could that be? Then Lord Beck tied the little lad to a tree near a verrin's den – to no avail, either. Cully was still here. Where was *here*? Woodland! A rough trail meandered between horzmas and larkeries and the occasional harper tree. Above the canopy the sky was leaden. His memories were deceitful and contradictory.

How long had he been wandering? He was stunned, and ravenous. Mustn't head homeward to the farm of his upbringing. Had he been reared at Castlebeck? Mustn't go near his Mam, nor near Helga nor dear Olga. Must avoid home en route to the dreamlord's keep. Mustn't go *there*, or he'd kill someone.

Must.

Mustn't.

He'd been banged on the head by three thieves. No, he hadn't been.

Sizzleflies congregated, attracted to his self-inflicted lacerations. His hands flailed. The harper tree twanged.

Similar vibrant chimes had echoed now and then through the subterranean Isi nest. Arpeggios had assaulted him from a harp played by a mana-mage's servant while Cully, tossing, lay tethered to a couch. Apricot light; a reek of fruit; luminous bubbles floating upward from the mage's sharp little horns. A swirling glissando was the accompaniment to what the golden-liveried mouthpiece of the mage recited. Sometimes the chords were deafeningly amplified, plucking the sinews of the mind.

'Juttahats being sane,' the mage's mouthpiece had declared. *'Human beings not being sane. A free Juttahat being potentially a mad Juttahat. Submitting to guidance; yourself becoming the harp we play upon! Avenging the dreamlord drowning the child.'* (*And Cully's true memories began to submerge . . .*) *'Becoming as fierce as the verrin which would be attacking the child.'* (*This enraged Cully, to resistance . . .*)

'Bloody! Bloody!' he shouted. Sizzleflies zizzed agreement.

'Would you live for ever?' a gorgeous woman goaded him. *'Like your uncle?'* Starflower tattoo upon her cheek; spangled combs in her dusky coiffure. Peering at him: *Tell me, tell me, tell me, strip yourself bare for me.*

Aye, and release the verrin from within himself! Thus he'd struck at her prying eye.

Panic gripped Cully as he sagged beneath the tree which was a huge harp. He couldn't remember how he'd fled from that keep like a beast without articulate understanding, without a history of his actions or a sense of their meaning but only endowed with reactions to circumstances.

His shell had cracked, releasing chaos, and now he'd buffeted his brow in savage anguish.

A voice of concern: 'You there, are you all right?'

A young woman's tones.

'What's wrong with you?'

The timbre of her voice was crudely sweet, uncultivated yet engaging, quickened by a solicitude which seemed almost like excitement.

He rubbed blood from his eyes and licked his fingers. Hungry!

Already the speaker had hurried close.

'You had an accident! What happened? Ain't any Jutties nearby, are there?' Juttahats might have waylaid him? Robbed him and left him lying here under this tree? Cully blinked in bewilderment and fended off flies.

The girl's flaxen hair was tied back by green ribbons. Her face was broad with two thumbs' worth of nose, generous lips, and sky-blue eyes. The skin was somewhat pocked and smeared with a cream which smoothed her countenance as well as serving to deter flies. A full-sleeved white linen blouse was bouncy with bosom. At the waist of her long striped skirt hung a sheathed knife. She carried a wicker basket of cheeses under muslin, which she set down. Muddy moccasins were upon her feet.

'Ain't any Jutties nearby, are there?' Her hand was near her knife. 'Your forehead's all bloody. What happened—?'

Aye, what happened to this otherwise handsome young fellow with a dazed blue gaze and tangled blond hair lapping the shoulders of a brown corduroy shirt?

Cully raised himself clumsily. His brains ached. 'I stumbled. I'm starving . . .'

'Have some cheese!' Ducking circumspectly, she reached under the muslin and broke off a chunk as yellow as her hair. 'Then you must come home with me . . .'

Come home with her.

'Get cleaned.' She was weighing him up. 'You should go to bed. We'll call a wisewoman to look at you.'

To look at him. To eye him, to scry him. Her blue eyes probed him.

Instead of accepting the cheese he caught hold of her wrist. With his other hand he wrenched her knife free and tossed it far.

'Oh,' she cried. 'Let go!'

'What's your name?'

'Olga, it's Olga. What's wrong with you?' Her eyes were wide. She was panting.

'You aren't Olga.'

'*But I am.* Please let go of me.'

'You won't fool me, nakki-maid!' he snarled. 'That's my sister's name. You're nothing like her.'

'More than one girl can be called Olga. You bashed your head. That's what's wrong.' She smelled cheesy with sweat. He hungered for her, so close to him. 'Why are you acting this way?' she begged. 'What's your name?'

Questions, damnable questions! *Tell me, tell me, strip yourself bare.* Blood engorged him, the blood which would transmute into sticky milk. The verrin which ripped flesh was loose in him. He would strangle her unless he invaded her to release the milk and the blood. He would drive all questions about him out of her mind. Her left hand darted to scratch his eyes, but he caught hold of her other wrist and forced her back upon moss. He tumbled upon her.

'No don't, please don't.'

When she bawled for help the strings of the harper tree took up her wail. The harping crazed him. If he didn't violate this nakki-maid, for sure he'd kill her. Blood was raging. Either he would spill blood or else he would disgorge the hot milk which was the pale variety of that blood.

Her shriek hurt his throbbing head. Releasing her wrists, he shuffled backward. Hoisting her shanks upon his shoulders, he rucked her striped skirt over knees, over thighs, over belly, disclosing no undergarment at all but only her parcel of private hair, her blonde puff, and infolds of white flesh. He unbuttoned the stiff raging teat of his loins.

'I'll let you, I'll let you,' she cried. 'Just wait.'

How could he wait? His gorged teat butted and jabbed and entered her cranny. She shrieked, tears starting from her eyes.

Bull into heifer, the hot milk gushed.

Being under our control, wild human. With our voice in your head, becoming sane. Going to kill the dreamlord. How could two such impulses cohabit in his consciousness?

Hot milk, hot blood . . . He sagged aside. His hand fell upon the chunk of cheese, her gift to him. He gobbled while she moaned, her violated tummy bare to the navel. Then he gathered up her basket of cheeses and her knife as well.

As soon as she saw her blade in his hand she promised, 'I won't

245

tell, I won't tell.' Sizzleflies were flitting between her legs. *Tell, tell*, the harper strings twanged.

Cully, however, was already lumbering on his way.

Pierce Uncle with a blade for ravishing our Mam. Skin the lord of dreams. Plunge his flayed skin in vinegar. Take this to a mana-mage.

No no no, don't!

Robbed, the raped lass wept with the hurt and horror though also with relief.

'Shan't tell shan't shan't shan't,' she chattered to no one else but insects and a tree, to affirm her survival.

How to explain to her parents how the produce and her knife had gone astray? Jutties Jutties Jutties, Jutties in the woods. His sour cream trickled from her mingled with threads of blood.

'Tie an egg into a knot, an egg into a knot,' she prayed. Let her not conceive a baby. Above the jade-green foliage the sky was the lid of a vast pewter saucepan.

Snowy's head was humming, which was why he'd clapped Minkie's floppy cord cap upon his blond thatch. Smother those queer qualmy buzzings-in-the-bonnet! He was also wearing the Boss's long tawny leather campaign coat with its colossal collars which Minkie had left behind in Niemi Keep when he flew off to Sariolinna, kitted out in finery.

Snowy and Dame Inga and a querulous Kyli and Minkie's junior brothers Kosti and Karl had been hiking for a couple of hours since they left the keep. They hadn't passed through the cliff-top community itself but had skirted the other side of Lake Lasinen before forging off into the forest. No need to accumulate a small cortège of disapproving townsfolk who might trail after them to keep an eye on what transpired. Might Dame Inga be heading out to a secret rendezvous with her reprobate son? Ever since a cuckoo had cackled how the heir to the keep had murdered Lucky's consort, Minkie's name had been muck. Previous roguery, bridled by his marriage to Kyli Helenius and her dowry, was as nothing. Seemed as how his devilment had only been adjourned – *prorogued*!

Fat suckerflies cruised the sunny aromatic woodland of musk-trees, yellovers, and featherfern. Flycatchers – flashes of lime-green and sapphire – jinked through stray drifts of gads and piss-in-your-eyes. Sizzleflies hung like puffs of smoke above the azure tubes of chimneyflowers. Boulders were convenient seats for the weary, amongst whom Kyli Kennan counted herself. Just a week prior to this hadn't she given *birth*? Labour had *panged* her worse than she'd imagined she could pang. Despite Beldame Goody's potion and dazing fumes of sinitus herbs smouldering in a pot to be sniffed when cramps crescendoed, labour had been like the horridest constipation imaginable.

The baby was a bawling boy. Today Goody was caring for the floppy pink bundle of desires and frustrations. The toothless old housekeeper was lulling and crooning and cleaning his squidges and offering him milk in a bottle with a pig's-bladder teat. Really, Goody could look after the piglet every day. *Piglet* was how Kyli thought of Minkie's heir, though the name she had actually chosen in consultation with Inga was Johannes. Johannes Kennan: a curtsey to her father Johann, Lord Helenius, prosperous and powerful.

'Can't we have another rest?' Kyli pleaded.

'Not yet,' said Inga. 'We just had one.'

'That was two keys ago. Look: a nice flat stone over there. We could all fit on it.'

'It's too near those chimneys. Sizzles would bother you.'

Round their necks they were all wearing smelly sprigs inimical to insects, weren't they, even the boys?

Propelling herself with a stick, Inga stomped onward in her black woollen skirt hung with trinkets, and her black lace bodice studded with spangles. For this outing the Dame had insisted that since Kyli had regained her figure she must don her revealing low-cut gown of lace over muslin. Somehow this excursion was woman's business. Kyli ought to look womanly.

Lagging behind as rearguard, with crossbow in one hand (its hefty winding handle worthy of a mangle), and wicker picnic hamper in the other, strawberry-faced Snowy was undoubtedly squinting at Kyli's silhouette whenever she tramped through shafts of sunlight. No point in trying to abash him; his face was a permanent oozing blush. Minkie's young brothers were surging ahead: one noddle of curly chestnut hair, and one of lank brown string.

Kyli thought that a fly had landed on her palm, but of course it was just the little key which had been tattooed there at her wedding. A key to a treasury! Alas no . . .

Oh to have no child at all – no squealing piglet – but to be a girl again at the court in Saari of the splendid fountains and

247

canals, surrounded by frolicsome girlfriends flaunting fine jewellery. A gold mine and a silver mine and veins of precious stones were in the neighbourhood of Saari. Consequently the Kalevan mint was located there. It stamped out coinage for the Queen in the north. The Lord of the domain of Sáari took his concessionary cut in a scrupulously well-accounted way. The court was lavish and blithe, yet the senior Helenius was always a man of such integrity and scruples. An obsessive punctilious sway beset the male line – hence her father's annoyance at her alliance with a rascal, even if the rascal in question had seized and ravished her, meaning that the marriage wasn't exactly her fault.

Quirks constrained what sort of person a Helenius should wed. No Helenius male might ever marry a Sariola daughter. For the Queen's peace of mind, no potential future keeper of the Mint must ever become longlife.

Maybe Johannes the piglet might restore Kyli to her father's good graces. Maybe not, for within Johannes there was half of Minkie.

Kyli still positively *ached* from the piglet's birth. Now she had to hike bare-shouldered through a hot wood full of insects, her nipples near-as-not on show, while her miscreant hubby's crony ogled her abused hips.

Actually, Snowy was preoccupied by the hum in his head. It was as though a hundred Snowies were stuttering faintly if hectically deep within himself. As if some echoey dream-brawl were in progress! A nook of his brain was dreaming of battle while he himself was awake. Awareness of this internal fray was vague but bothersome. Maybe he was taking sick, and what he sensed was all the tiny busybodies within himself trying to combat an imminent malady . . .

Hark and hear: just the evening before, Arvid Blomberg the local shaman's apprentice had turned up at Niemi Keep, full of a need to narrate what had recently happened to him.

It had been dinner time in the hall: mutton stew, mashed potatoes, and carrots. The babe was asleep in the carry-cradle formerly used by Karl and by Kosti and before them by Minkie. Out of habit some china bowls and copper pans still stood stacked in a corner although Snowy had patched the roof with a high degree of success.

The bell which hung inside the ironbound tammy door jangled

as someone outside tugged the handle up and down. Snowy had hastened from the table in case the clangour woke tiny Johannes.

'I bet it's Pappi Hukkinen,' piped young Kosti. Kosti was prone to leap to conclusions – in this case reasonably so. Ever since word had spread of how his father had murdered Prince Bertel there had only been one moderately significant visitor to the keep. Niemi's mana-priest had come a-calling to offer mingled condolences and reproach to Dame Inga at what her son had wrought. Hukkinen, the priest, chose to live in one of the shanties alongside the lake rather than up in town in a decent house. Several times a day the tall tireless figure would briskly ascend and descend the track of the disused funicular railway from shore to heights, from cliff-tops to beach, as if he were an engine infusing mana-energy into his parish.

Really, Hukkinen was only limbering up. Next year he intended to march daily the ten keys from the landlocked lake to the Murame river and back again. A linking canal *would* be excavated by the townspeople. Hukkinen's Hike would at last propel them into action by example. By rights the Kennan family ought to have been the initiators and sponsors of this great scheme. Sadly, the Kennan family were neglectful to the point of dereliction. Now, alas, Minkie's crime might well have soured the vital energy which Pappi Hukkinen was accumulating.

Inga disapproved of this priest whose energies seemed as misplaced – and even displaced – as those of her elder son and his father before him.

What if the jangler at the door was not one person but several? Or even many? Sent from Pohjola Palace with weapons in their hands for vengeance?

However, the visitor spied through the snoop grille proved to be Arvid – draped in a smock to which dozens of tin stars were loosely sewn and a skirt of lustrous harny wings. Mauve and violet and lavender plumes swung as he was admitted.

Arvid was a second or third cousin of Snowy's, a gangly lad. His large forehead was decorated with a gesturing purple stick-figure set within a five-point star. His arched brows were expressive of a kind of astonished theophany. His chin was sharp, his blond mop was tousled. What a hikerbird he seemed, rather more so than Hukkinen. And what a story he felt compelled to tell.

Out in the boulder-strewn woods where the sky-cairn pointed its finger towards heaven Arvid had been perching on top of the slim ceramic pyramid, as was his wont, using a sheep's skull as a saddle. Balanced there in a trance, he was seeking his soul-star by daylight. His shaman master Sven Hartzell, who was training him, had said that since the soul is invisible the star corresponding to it might best be sought not at night when thousands of stars twinkled but whilst those were outshone by the brightness of the sun. *That* would be a true feat of perception.

Privately Arvid was convinced that he already knew his star. It was the tiny unblinking one which rushed across the heavens periodically, and which was *not* an Ukko. As yet, however, that star had confided nothing to him.

Of a sudden, as he perched on the cairn, radiance bathed Arvid. Tin stars on his smock lifted upward around him as if sucked by light. In one of these he saw mirrored in miniature unmistakably the face of none other than Minkie Kennan, framed by a high leather collar and topped with a brass-trimmed black helmet. In others he glimpsed desolate maidens in flimsy rags, blazing cottages, a curving snow-clad terrain across which smoke drifted, a towered palace burning all over with white fire, and a capering *cuckoo-man* brandishing a trident.

Arvid was tossed off the cairn. For a few seconds he was *flying*. He hit a puffybush which cushioned his impact. Just as well that he hadn't crashed into a boulder! Dazzling scenes swirled around him. He knew that he mustn't look behind him but must follow the thread back to the world, through the trees.

When Arvid arrived at the shaman's hut Sven Hartzell wasn't there. As often happened, his master had wandered off alone in the forest. Arvid waited – and as he waited he experienced a mounting sense of urgency. A cuckoo-impulse filled him, to tell his tale to someone who yearned to be told, someone who would take the tale from him; otherwise he'd be impelled to carry on telling it over and over, and he'd never have peace of mind to muse about his epiphany.

Who else might he tell but the mother of that son whom he'd seen dressed up as a warrior in a ravaged terrain?

He made a foray in search of Sven, steering well clear of the cairn which had thrown him off. The next day he made another foray in vain. Obviously he must tell his master first of all. Several days went by on tenterhooks before Sven Hartzell returned to the hut and the shaman's apprentice could hurry off to Niemi Keep.

By then Arvid was also convinced of another imperative. The spirit of *cuckoo* was in him. He would become a cuckoo-man, an oracle, perching in trees in a trance. He needed to fashion a cuckoo mask for himself – though not from the plumes of a gossip-bird, perish the thought. Goose quills, dyed a dull mottled green then flecked with rust-red, would do nicely. The mask would require big flat yellow glass eyes just like a cuckoo's. Dark smoky pupils would hide his eyes yet allow him to see. Where should he come by such spectacles but at Ruokokoski's glassworks in Niemi? Who should most appropriately pay for this commission but Dame Inga, in recompense for his report about her son? All made sense, including the delay.

Thus Arvid had related, the evening before, while mutton stew cooled on plates.

Kosti and Karl were thrilled by this visit from a shaman's apprentice. Snowy had scratched his blond head. He often scratched, or struggled to refrain from scratching his acne. Kyli felt a great flutter at what Arvid's vision might signify. The piglet woke up and squealed long and loud. Beldame Goody had little choice but to remove tiny Johannes from the dining hall. The old nurse hobbled off, cooing grousingly at the babe, to the other boys' disgust: 'Oh, Wee Sir knows how to spoil things, doesn't diddums?'

As for Dame Inga . . .

She had blanched, and pursed those full sensual lips of hers. Her bold hazel eyes scrutinized Arvid for quite a while. She kept her counsel. She toyed with a greying chestnut tress.

'Tomorrow,' she declared, 'we shall make a trip to that cairn ourselves to see if *I* can see what you saw.' She burrowed in the purse that hung from her belt, and counted out three tarnished silver marks. 'This should be quite enough to buy two bits of coloured glass of the finest quality.'

'Take care,' Kyli said suddenly to the apprentice, 'that Ruoko-koski doesn't put a sway on them so that things begin to look ugly. Don't mention *our* name.'

'Why not?' asked Arvid.

'Never mind!'

So here they were in the woods, and Dame Inga had still kept her counsel, though Kyli was obliged to dress glamorously.

'It's all because of the family secret, isn't it?' Kyli accused her mother-in-law. She slapped a sweatsipper from her bare shoulder. 'Minkie would never tell his Kiki-liki no matter how much I wheedled, mana knows why. You know very well where he vanished to!'

'That's as may be, my dear. The less people who know, the safer my son is.'

'I'm his *wife*, and mother of his—' piglet. 'Didn't Minkie tell *you* the secret?' she called back to Snowy.

Hefting hamper and crossbow, Snowy caught up. 'What's that?'

'Maybe my husband told *you* the family secret, which explains where he is now.'

The weepy strawberry face loomed. 'His su-su-su-secret . . . ? Fu-fu-far as that gu-gu-gu-goes, he was tu-tu-tu-tighter than a du-du-duck's fu-fu-fanny with an egg in it underwater.'

'Oh really!'

Of course Inga's son hadn't told his Kiki-liki about the paradise beneath Loom Lake with all those lovely daughters of Eve residing in it! What an enticing prospect for a fellow-me-lad. Not that Inga's son would have dreamed of heading for that distant lake – shaped like a rhomb, with cliffs along two sides and huge boulders balanced at the highest point – merely on the off chance of some illicit fun, but only if his life was in the direst danger and he needed a hidey-hole which no one else could ever locate . . .

How could that paradise which Ragnar had described to Inga – and where Minkie surely was right now – be remotely as Arvid had glimpsed it? The shaman's apprentice had talked of burning and snow and destruction. A hellscape, where the maidens wore rags!

Admittedly Ragnar's sojourn in paradise had turned out unfortunately in the end. Yet to no such degree! Could Arvid's insight be flawed, being as how he was a man? Men were so obsessed with conflict. That world under Loom Lake was a woman's mystery, a scene of creation, not destruction. How could a male accurately perceive the female nature of that domain? Inga must scry Alvin's perch with her own eyes . . .

Up ahead, faintly they heard a gruff voice chanting. Snowy set down the picnic basket so as to crank his crossbow. 'Stay bu-bu-bu-behind me, bu-bu-boys,' he advised.

Presently the party came in sight of the cairn – and of the figure who was shuffling around that slim pyramid of red and black. Undoubtedly the slow dancer was Arvid's master, though his features were largely obscured.

On his head sat a high felt cap banded with red and yellow braid. From the brim there dangled a veil of blue-chevroned

252

tassels made of many short soarfowl plums knotted together with wool. Through this shifting curtain the shaman was peeping at the broad shallow drum which he held in one hand. In his other hand he held a stick of charcoal. The vellum of the drum had been freshly whitewashed. Intermittently he was sketching dark marks upon it. He was wearing a purple tunic appliquéd with a corset of white ribs, imitating a skeleton from the waist upward. Arvid's master was half-alive, and half-dead; half here, and half elsewhere.

Chanting to himself, Sven Hartzell completed another circuit of the cairn, and added another mark.

Strictly speaking, the slender pyramid wasn't a cairn in the sense of stones piled upon stones. However, the contrasting zig-zags of black and red made the structure resemble an upright jigsaw which had been carefully slotted together by some Poota-ran puzzle-maker. Now the top was twisted askew, pointing south-eastward, as though it had softened then stiffened again. A few misshapen golden stars were imprinted upon various zig-zags as if at each such spot a kind of compass had impacted, which now the shaman was consulting. Of Arvid's sheep-skull seat there was no sign.

> 'Show me, star-cairn, guide my charcoal,
> 'Picture me the path to elsewhere;
> 'Let me find the source of mana,
> 'Heart of Ukko hidden from us,
> 'Shining forth upon disciple,
> 'Hurling Arvid from his saddle . . .'

'Sven Hartzell,' cried Inga, 'what are you doing?'

The shaman lurched and dropped the coaly stick. His hand leapt to cup his braid-capped ear as though it were the twisted pyramid which had addressed him. How avidly he harked, till the Dame of Niemi called his name again.

'Sven Hartzell!'

Swinging round slowly, he peered through his veil of plumes and wool at the intruders.

'Go away,' he croaked. He brandished his drum at the gaping boys, who scampered well clear. On the drumskin was a con-fusion of wavy lines and lozenge shapes and token trees.

'Don't interrupt. I'll lose the thread! Come back in a long hour if you must, Dame Kennan.'

Inga was a tough bird. She strode forward, stomping her stick. 'You're making a map.'

'Of course I'm making a map! My fingers will drum my way to the wellspring of mana.'

'Arvid told us what he saw.'

'Of course he did, but I see more than my apprentice. I can see *where* as well as *what*. Take your blather away from me.'

'You'll see where my Minkie's hiding?' queried Kyli.

Impatiently curly-headed Kosti asked his brother, 'How long's a long hour?'

The stringy-haired lad squeezed a pimple on his chin. 'Maybe two hours?' he suggested.

Inga's nose jutted straight and firm and truculent. The trinkets and spangles on her skirt and bodice glittered in the sunlight. Oh she was a match for any sorcerer.

'This isn't your mystery,' she told him. 'It's a woman's mystery – a female matter. I know it in my waters.'

'*Under* the waters; and in a womb!' cried the shaman, inspired.

'Men mostly cause fighting and fire.' *Others mustn't discover her son's whereabouts. The family secret must stay secure.* To Sven Hartzell's amazement, Inga seized the drum from him and held it at arm's length. 'Snowy, Snowy,' she called, 'you're a man. You know what to do about this.' She jiggled the outstretched drum invitingly. The shaman stood stockstill in astonishment, or perhaps he was trying to save his *thread* from snapping.

Snowy licked his lips. He squinted.

'You know what to do.'

Snowy hefted the crossbow. 'A nod's as gu-good as a wu-wu-wink to a bu-bu-blind donkey, Dame Inga!'

Hartzell squawked as the fletched quarrel erupted from the bow and burst through the drumskin. The stretched vellum ripped open, to dangle. No more mana-map would be made on it now. Inga dropped the drum unceremoniously.

'*You!*' Hartzell jabbed a finger at Snowy. '*You!* You'll have a hundred naughty nakkis in you—'

'I already hu-hu-have—'

'—for the rest of your life!'

'And *you*—' The shaman's plumes swung in Kyli's direction.

She cringed and covered her bare shoulders with her hands, elbows protecting her décolleté bosom as if shivers were seizing her in sunlight. 'I wanted you to finish your map, great shaman!' Adding hastily: 'I'm the daughter of Lord Helenius.'

Hartzell's shielded scrutiny shifted to Inga. She stood stead-fastly, and even raised her walking stick. Her hazel gaze was unflinching.

'This is *woman's* business,' she insisted. 'Mother's business. And wife's too.'

Kyli was less than happy to be included in this confederacy.

Bravely young Karl tossed a sod of dry turf at the plume-veiled shaman. The soft missile bounced off appliquéd ribs. Already Snowy was cranking the handle of the bow prior to inserting another abbreviated arrow.

'Nod's as gu-good as a bu-blink to a bu-bu-bu-blind donkey!' he bellowed. *Sizzleflies seemed to zizz in his head.* 'All my nu-nakki-brothers feel the same way!'

'We'll go *home* now,' stated Dame Inga in what might almost have been a proclaimer's tone of utter authority.

The four mocky-men were the worse for wear and very hungry when they finally chanced upon the abandoned bone-house.

Their journey had been exhausting, and took much longer than expected. The Great Fjord had petered out into a vast maze of scrub-bog hatched by meandering corridors of evergreens which as often as not failed to link up with one another. Hot air had trembled in fatigue, laden with sneezy scents. Spinach-threads webbed little pools. Yellow scum like gold dust lay on loughs. Late at night, the sky was mustard. Insects pestered Arto, especi-ally attacking his goaty ears. Knotty with his ropy skin was much less bothered, as were Lammas with his tufty grey wool, and crusty Pieman. The glovemaker was obliged to smear his exposed skin with a paste of lichen so that he looked like a dwarf twin of Pieman. Obviously the four travellers must veer to the firmer north – away from treacherous quags and squelchy morasses – and could not strike out southwards.

Farmsteads were infrequent. Likewise, encampments of taran-dra herders, perched on bluffs above the fly-busy vales. Could four such curiosities as composed the mutie combo escape very quickly from the hospitality of which they certainly needed a modicum? Lammas was obliged to sing for their supper and breakfast and supper again, and the next day too, and the day after (and Knotty to saw on his fiddle, and Pieman to whistle and knuckle the cymbals, and Arto to conduct with those white six-fingered gloves of his) until the sentimental appetites of their hosts were slaked. The four couldn't simply tramp onward prematurely; Spitz hounds yapped and snapped.

On one occasion a shaman wearing tarandra antlers took a *leer* to them, and maybe their lives were in danger. Evidently he coveted Lammas's fleece and Knotty's natural string vest as valuable additions to his costume. These might enhance his powers almightily. However, the werewool lulled him – and a crowd of herdsmen – to tears with poignant tango verses redolent of the mocky-men's homesick plight.

Eventually, further to the north-east than the combo had ever intended, the four friends were able to change course into rock-strewn forest where boulders were grooved as if by verrin claws. Horzma trees and tammies appeared amidst the henna-scaled larixes and green-needled veras. When smoked tarandra meat and cheese gave out, they fed on berries and mushrooms.

How close to the Velvet Isi nest might they be heading? Ought they to swing westward again in a circuitous sweep? A snivelling cold afflicted Lammas, and his throat was husky. Downpours had soaked his wool on several occasions. Worse still, the tendons in both of Arto's ankles were acting up something awful. So much plodding with a bow-legged gait had resulted in a double limp. By the time they happened upon the bone-house in the woods Arto's pace was a pathetic lurch. Unless he could rest his pegs for a week or two he feared being lamed for life or what was left of it; and Lammas risked a bout of lung fever, bilge in his bellows.

Secluded amidst hoary sylvesters and the chartreuse quiffs of curver trees was a habitation entirely built of the bones of beasts roped together. Roof shingles were jaw bones. A hooped door was composed of ribs.

So many thousands of bleached bones . . . and no swarms of carrion-gnats; not that a jot of dried flesh remained to scavenge. In the immediate vicinity of the hut there appeared to be no flies of any kind as if a sway kept pests away.

Lammas sneezed, and Arto harked keenly.

'No one's at home unless they're keeping quiet as a mus—'

Pieman peered through a femur-framed window.

'It's full of *things!*'

Thus did the deserted bone-house prove to be. Cupboards overflowed with pots and dolls and tools, with pans and twine and brushes and Pootaran puzzles, with scrolls and statuettes and combs – and wonderfully with jars of pink soused sea-eel and osters in aspic and ginger sweetfin roe and black mustaberries as

well as with rusks and a smoked ham or two and some bottles
of cordial. Several hard black round rye loaves hung on strings.
Indeed it seemed as if some donor had continued bringing deli-
cacies and groceries despite the absence of the occupant, though
perhaps not lately. Several jugs of milk by the door were foetid
with mould, as was a pie on a platter, fur growing upon its rotting
blueberries. The reek of sour milk prevailed over the odour of
warm dry bone.

'Mocky-mates,' rejoiced Knotty, 'we've found a refuge.'

None too soon.

Arto subsided thankfully upon a rug woven of black and blond
hair, his back to a pot-belly stove. He surveyed his soiled worn-
out moccasins, his dilapidated black breeches, his kidskin gloves
grey with dirt. Then he scanned the walls of bones.

'This place'll creak something chronic,' he said approvingly.
Just like the ramshackle cott back home.

Pieman was already opening a jar of sea-eel.

17 · BRINGING THE ROOF DOWN

How royally goaded Lucky was.

Not only had that inexpressible Osmo survived Juke's missile
– along with Minnow – but the two of them had proceeded to
wed – enthusiastically, according to cuckoos!

To wed, without motherly consent or advice . . .

Osmo must have managed to bespeak the girdle off the girl.

Oh but there'd been cuckoo cackle about a smutty episode
involving a bare-arsed Minnow – and the Brindled mage, Viper.
Osmo had evidently had assistance.

Heads or tails: had he *rumped* her?

Gossip about a certain mana-photograph suggested so. Minnow's tail had been showing.

In which case, van Maanen had achieved longlife without
Lucky ever whispering in his ear.

And then he and Minnow had the gall to claim the monarchy!

The staging post which Lucky had chosen for her attack upon
Loxmithlinna (initially, and then upon Maananfors) was the

upland town of Luolalla. Some fifty keys north of Loxmithlinna, Luolalla sat upon a network of limestone caves. The surrounding countryside was exceptionally bald: a sea of herbage with hardly a tree in sight. Low dry-stone walls chequered the vista under a huge breezy expanse of sky. Sheep grazed. Pigs rooted, converting pockets of pasture to snout-ploughed and manured dirt which would be sowed with rye. Kilns smoked, burning chalky stone to lime.

What did the absence of combustible minty trees matter when there were easily accessible coal seams in the neighbourhood? Oh, the town was windswept, to be sure. In winter the lanes and fields were bitter. But the houses were built of thick pale yellow stone, and on bleak dark days fires always blazed in hearths. In fine weather you could race ponies for key after key, leaping field walls where need be – which was how Hubertus Jaeger's father had broken his neck.

On cloudless nights in the spring and autumn such a view there was of the constellations: the cow and the cuckoo, the harp and the archer, and the nakki perched on the chanterelle. In the south the silver sky-sickle spanned the horizon. If you stared very close to gassy Otso, you might spy the larger of its mooncubs. You'd easily see Kammo, a pocked dead rock almost the size of Kaleva – and even Sejda, a smaller ball of rock much closer to the sun. To catch sight of Sejda with the naked eye was auspicious. Without use of a spyglass you'd never spot giant ringed Surma far away beyond Otso. Who would wish to set eyes on such an emblem of cold poisonous death, final and outermost, where even the swan itself would expire?

Could a person feel vulnerable in Luolalla? Not physically vulnerable to gales – so much as vulnerable mentally to the empty expanse? Rather as a scampering leppi might feel exposed to the scrutiny of a circling gyrebird? Ah but there were always those caves underneath the town, constituting its hidden basement – though not exactly its *cellars*. Pothole shafts ran down from under various buildings. Nevertheless, the snowmelt of spring would regularly flood the underworld brimful before draining into vales beyond the upland. So there was nothing permanent about those cellars. Even in summer a prolonged storm could swell subterranean streams which, otherwise, generally dried to trickles.

The Jaegers' limestone keep, on a knoll in the centre of Luolalla, resembled a cluster of domed yellow calcified kettles fitted with windows. Turrets and chimneys were vertical spouts. When wind blew strongly, those kettles sang.

Lucky's guards in their brown and green camouflage leathers were exercising around that keep as well as out in the stone-walled fields. Thirty of her invulnerable wooden soldiers were drilling, here where scarcely a tree grew.

The royal sky-boat – winter-white with vermilion eyes around its portholes – was still engaged in ferrying weapons and supplies from Pohjola Palace. So was the sky-boat from the Fortress in the Fjord. This was blue-chevroned upon beige like a soarfowl – or like the fletchings of a very bulbous arrow. The smaller flier which Fastboy Jack had stolen from the Isi stood parked in the courtyard of the keep within that corral of kettle-buildings. So did a trio of armed single-seater flying pods recently produced by the everything machine. Three parts silver cocoon and one part transparent canopy, they were. Every day pilots took these pods aloft for practice. Jack had performed aerobatics over Luo-lalla, which dismayed his mother.

Three jump-bikes hopped around the town and neighbourhood, performing mock ambushes upon guards, upon wooden soldiers, and upon those men of the Jaegertroop whom the Queen had impressed into service to fight for her.

Jack had also jumped a bike down into the caves, with a certain passenger riding pillion . . .

When Hubertus Jaeger travelled to the Northland some years earlier to sue for the hand (and body) of a Sariola daughter, the plump pompous fellow had intrigued the Queen by an extrava-gant account of exploits in the caves. Why, Hubertus had explored keys and keys of caverns and twisting tunnels, vaults and crannies and grottos and subterranean rivers by lamplight at quite some personal risk. Didn't this bold adventuring recall her own explorations of the innards of the Ukko which her family's mining ship had found in Earth's asteroid belt far away and long ago? Chambers and cavities and curvy tunnels and cochleae!

'Do any waxy white flowers grow in your caverns?' Lucky had quizzed Hubertus mischievously, mystifying the young suitor.

'No, but there are a few phosphorescent fungi,' he'd said.

'Are there any bones of Juttahats and serpents?'

Absolutely not! Take it from Hubertus Jaeger, Luolalla was perfectly safe from Jutties and snakes. Neither the Isi nor their servants would ever find their way through the twists of caves to emerge from potholes inside the Jaeger keep. Why should they try to, when they had never done so in the past? Queen Lucky need have no fear on her daugher's account. (Nor did she; nor did she. Lucky had guffawed.)

Daughter Kay was impressed by the bombast of Hubertus and by the thrill of mysterious caverns – which she needn't ever venture into in person. What excited her most was the prospect of galloping a pony across windy open spaces under the stars (with an escort, naturally) until her muscular mount lathered between her legs.

Consequently Lucky had given her consent, and Kay had given longlife to her new lord and hubby (and thereafter two children). Thanks to the gift which Kay had bestowed, Hubertus would now be so much safer during his speleological ventures – though these proved to be surprisingly infrequent and abbreviated, undertaken more for the show of it.

Hark and hear: when Jatta sought sanctuary for Jack and herself at Kay Jaeger-Sariola's keep, Lord Hubertus had taken umbrage at the bumptious bairn. The brat was so impertinent and greedy. Besides, news of this demon child's presence might well lure snoopy aliens into the cave system. Nor was Kay averse to giving marching orders to a sister-in-distress – in the direction of Osmo van Maanen who happened to loathe anything resembling a mutie, a category which surely included the fastboy.

Under her mother's truculent wing, Jatta had now returned to that keep of limestone kettles; and Jack too, sporting a tache on his upper lip, and possessing *powers*, of light and cold and wind.

Abashed, Kay had greeted her younger sister with, 'Didn't it all turn out for the best? Here you are with a fine handsome talented son of whom cuckoos have cackled . . .'

Small thanks to Kay's brief hospitality! Yet Jatta hardly cared a jot. Lucky had virtually forced Jatta to come along on this expedition of revenge. Reluctance made Lucky fly into a rage. Jatta *must* proudly show her face in the keep at Maananfors from which the unspeakable Osmo had expelled her and Lucky's grandson. She must swank it in Osmo's hall when the Queen put paid to him; or in the ruins of his hall, whichever.

Dearest Anni must stay behind in Sariolinna. Anni couldn't possibly accompany Jatta. That would be quite unsuitable. Lucky was fully conversant with the loving liaison between high-born lady, and low. Not merely a matter of sharing a bed-chamber, but also of enjoying one another's bodies! Maybe Ester had snitched. What was a junior daughter useful for?

Was the affection between Jatta and Anni the ultimate outcome of Jatta's former perverse refusal to wed a man? Was it the upshot of their both having once shared the intoxicating embraces of the Unman, Jarl Pakken? Jarl being unavoidably absent, each woman became the ravisher of the other. What offended Lucky *most* about Jatta's behaviour and her protestations was the extent to which such conduct detached Jatta from realism and responsibility at a time when Lucky's sovereignty was under assault from that coxcomb upstart and his pipsqueak rebel Queen, self-styled. Queen *Minnow*, indeed! And *Prince Osmo!* Jatta couldn't simply look the other way. Her mother wouldn't hear of it.

So spake Lucky, with a buzz raging in her bonnet (or at least in the chaplet of amber beads which she now wore as her tiara).

The only actual incentive for Jatta to accompany Lucky's army was a hope that proximity to Jack might moderate her son's quicksilver spirit and keep him from darting into danger. Jatta's anxiety at Jack's aerobatics jostled with her aching dismay at Anni's absence.

Alas for moderation, Jatta's presence had a contrary effect. Here was Jatta at a keep where her sister and hubby had denied Jack and his mother comfort and had even played the prank of directing them to Maananfors. Jack remembered the shunning all too clearly.

Lucky's pugnacious advent had already intimidated Lord Hubertus. Favourite grandson Jack bullied the young longlife lord into a tour of the caves by jump-bike. With Lord Jaeger clinging behind him, Jack had leapt the bike downward from the courtyard directly into a cavern – as Jack related gleefully when he returned the chastened lord to his bailey, pale and quivering, unable to walk in a straight line for a while . . .

Headlight glaring, wheels skidding, the bike had jumped recklessly from cavern to chasm, from chasm to cramped confine until Hubertus shrieked and shook like a leaf. The jump-bike wouldn't have materialized *inside* solid rock: of this Jack was positive. Nevertheless, the *in-betweens* had been akin to burial alive. The abrupt askew emergences – upon slope or brink – were petrifying.

Hubertus had been punished for his shunning, though not in

such a way as to alienate Luolalla from the Queen's cause. Hubertus could hardly protest at his humiliation. An expert speleologist, wasn't he?

What of Jack's own fatherly responsibilities?

The demon boy had gestated inside Jatta's womb for a full nine months but then had grown apace from infant to moustached youth in a similar span of time. The sprats which June conceived from his hectic ardent seed represented a further acceleration of metabolism – as Goody Hilda had diagnosed back in Sariolinna.

'From tads in the womb to whelps in the world within two months!' the wisewoman had stated, to Lucky's delight. They would be born on the tiny side of small. Hilda felt in her waters, and in June's, that those four petite maids would never sprout up much taller than knee-high to their mother.

Maids, ah yes, definitely maids. No doubt of it. There'd be four of them, one for each nipple.

In Pohjola Palace at the end of the first week in August, while sky-boats were beginning to ferry preliminary equipment and men south-south-westward to Luolalla to the consternation of the Jaegers, a quartet of wee daughters had duly slid smoothly one by one from June. These four squalling nymphs were each no larger than one of June's hands – and she hadn't podged out appreciably from her original buxom figure – though what a tenacity for the tit they showed.

If only June had possessed four hands, to nestle one daughter on each. Four slings round her neck must serve, with spongemoss pads for pee and poo. Bent double as Hilda was (though now furnished with a short tammy stick to prop herself) the wisewoman could hardly help except with advice.

Who *could* reasonably help June? *Was it safe for anybody to touch her yet without being given a disease?* Why yes absolutely, determined Hilda.

Supposing that the maids' plaguesome powers were already active to some degree, was it safe to handle June's miniature family? Maybe Anni, wearing the snakeskin body-glove for protection, might lend a couple of hands? That was Hilda's suggestion. A vigorous 'No' came from Jatta. Likewise from Lucky, about to leave her palace with her reluctant daughter to take up residence in the Jaeger keep. After a short rest from her trouble-free nativity, June was to follow on a flight a few days later with her mites and accompanied by Hilda. Not Anni, though. Not Anni.

That keep of stone kettles was soon crowded with personnel and officers. Aleksonis, Prut, and Bekker. Juke Nurmi and Nils Carlson the young proclaimer. Paavo Serlachius, now a priest militant. Jatta and Jack and June and her midget progeny . . .

In a corner of the courtyard two tents housed a little troupe of players led by one Peter Vaara.

All that was missing was a roving cuckoo. In spite of several wrought-iron perches in town and a pair in the courtyard of the keep, gossip-birds rarely cared to visit the exposed upland. Preparations were proceeding unobserved by the tittle-tattles.

To Jatta's mind the place was half-empty because Anni wasn't present.

Yet Jack was always nearby. What's more, Jatta was suddenly a grandmother. Shouldn't she be occupying her idle hands by helping June? Jatta preferred to walk around breezy Luolalla and watch the drills in numb anticipation of the injuries and death these exercises boded. Maybe she might venture with a lantern a little way into the caves? If she did so, she knew that she would feel hopelessly lost rather than released from vicissitude.

A marriage hadn't *exactly* occurred. More of a mating. The diminutive babes weren't any ordinary offspring. Having spent a scant two months in June's belly, they seemed more like mewling kittens devoid of fur, or nakkis who ought to sit on a toadstool.

Had they been within June long enough for a strong maternal bond to form? Their little mouths gaped wide open to accommodate a nipple. They seemed to *infest* June rather than to be her flesh and blood. Her chest was smothered by the pink creatures. Could their mother be said to cherish them? Was she simply submitting to their appetites, dazed by their needs, swayed into an instinctual animal-like acquiescence? June certainly didn't speak very much, contenting herself – and her litter – by crooning softly as she cradled them. Previously her double bosoms had been evocative of an excess of carnality rather than freakishness. Now that four perfectly formed tiny nymphs clung to her, had she become blatantly abnormal?

Not in the Queen's eyes. Or perhaps *yes*; but profitably so.

What of Jack, the daddy of such daughters? He dandled them carefully. He glowed. Pride gleamed upon his face; and hope. He weighed them by guess. He was afflicted less by the panicky urgency which might reasonably harass a lad who might possibly be obliged to gobble up his whole lifespan within a few fleeting years. *For sure* his daughters had given him a new and more normal lease of life. He had still played a wild jape on Hubertus. He whirlwinded a flying pod around the sky. He was Demon Jack the Fastboy, after all.

Indeed, Jack felt rejuvenated by the birth. At least, he felt that he was more in step with time. The *girls* would grow up swiftly instead of himself growing older prematurely. See, they had already put on a fingersworth more weight and length as though sucking mana as well as milk!

Jatta could only feel ambivalent about such strange grand-children. To be a grandmother already!

Hilda, as ever, had June's interests at heart. These interests must now also comprise June's tots-at-the-tit, since tying knots in eggs hadn't worked.

Lucky gloated in expectancy.

Jack himself had been born talking; and soon toddling. A week after June arrived at the Jaeger keep with her wee ones, these had chirped their first surprising words.

'What—'

    'Are—'

        'Our—'

            'Names?'

'June-Mum, June-Mum—'

    'Our names—'

        'Our names!'

            'Our names!'

Four sets of beady little eyes stared up at June's rosy face. The tiny girls hungered for names as much as they craved for food.

How could they become what they must become without any names? They couldn't just be addressed jointly as 'You Maids of Horror' or 'You Menace Lasses'. What mum would want to address her brood in such a grim and impersonal style, even if their destiny was to wreak havoc? Even if this was a *necessity* for them. (Otherwise, June wouldn't be free of her sickly curse – nor Jack of accelerated ageing.)

June put her pigtailed head together with Jack, and with Hilda, who confided the names she had dreamed up nauseatedly before the mana-mirror in the portrait gallery.

Minx and Jinx.

Jinxie and Minxie.

Jack conferred with Lucky, who consulted her mana-priest.

Let it be: Minx and Minxie, Jinxie and Jinx. Let there be a divination and a mana-baptism in the Jaegers' grand hall the very next day, before the maids grew really impatient.

Let there also be some appropriate dramatic entertainment courtesy of that dramaturge, Vaara, and his troupe. Everyone of importance must attend. Van Maanen had concocted a coronation for his pipsqueak, an event which was promptly cackled about in Sariolinna. The morrow's spectacle would compensate to some small extent – even if no cuckoo was likely to witness it. (Did one wish all one's military secrets babbled about?)

A short while after Lucky's arrival in Luolalla she had spared time to question Peter Vaara. Poor Bertie – deceitfully dead – had mentioned the dramaturge and his players. They'd been in Yulistalax when he escorted Eva to the gala.

Eva, whose forfeited keep would presently be under attack by her mother . . . One's sense of alienation from daughters was rather strong this season. This was why Jatta absolutely *had* to be on hand – aside from the advisability of separating her from ill-bred Anni. A mother could only tolerate so much disloyalty.

Vaara and his little troupe had been heading by way of Luolalla (and then Verinitty) towards Yulistalax, so as to arrive in time for this year's gala.

Gala was only three weeks hence. Would proclaimers and poets and singers and spectators be flocking into Lord Burgdorf's town in as great numbers as usual with a war under way not all that far to the west?

Surely *Prince* Osmo wouldn't dare quit his keep to sneak in a circuitous flying visit to Speakers' Valley! Especially not once the true Queen's forces interposed themselves at Loxmithlinna . . . ! If Osmo and his mutinous pipsqueak seriously dreamed of making a play to be acknowledged by the populace at large such a gesture of bravado might strike them as worthwhile. Ach, Osmo and Minnow couldn't possibly take the risk.

Ought Lucky herself to pay a queenly visit to the gala to emphasize her dominance and van Maanen's absence? By the middle of September Maananfors would likely have fallen to Lucky. Yet suppose it *hadn't* . . .

Was Lucky being led astray? Not merely by the lure of the gala, which Vaara's presence brought to mind – but diverted from her main concern by this whole campaign? Ach, *no*. The very thought of van Maanen and Minnow made her blood boil. Punish them, petrify them, set their bones ablaze.

Vaara's travel plans, so he admitted, had been knocked askew by the influx of war into Luolalla. How could a dramaturge desert such a source of inspiration as the Queen herself or those wooden soldiers of hers, or Demon Jack, offspring of a human mother and an exceptional Juttie? Ah but Lucky would send Vaara packing right after his performance, so that he *did* reach Speakers' Valley just in time, doubtless to stage what he had witnessed: the first act of *Lucky's Revenge*. En route, there'd be time enough for him to improvise a new show.

Peter Vaara had never travelled to the far north to present a play in Pohjola Palace. Nevertheless the Queen had often served as his theme. What Vaara presented in Luolalla before her arrival – which his players would re-enact in the Jaegers' hall after the baptism – was none other than the story of *Lucky's Ukko*, imaginatively interpreted.

'Very imaginatively, Your Majesty,' Vaara explained during his interview. The man was respectful but confident. To be faced by the living legend on whom his latest drama was based did not appear to intimidate him. If he was scared, he hid it well.

'You might be taking a risk, Peter Peril!'

His answer had been: 'How can we impress an audience if we slink about on stage for fear of offending, Your Majesty?'

After Lucky had talked to Vaara she could hardly remember what he looked like.

Serlachius had insisted on viewing a rehearsal. He had declared himself impressed. On the matinée afternoon doubtless there would be some variations. Vaara's works weren't written down lest they became cramped and stilted. On the well-remembered fabric of the outline woven by the dramaturge, he and his four players would embroider in a rapture of mutual creativity.

They had been working together for the past six years: Peter and Tancred and Stanislav and Natalya. Sophie had joined them four years previously to replace an actress who had died tragically of a mana-fit while impersonating an Isi mage . . .

The Jaegers' hall was a wide blue-plastered rotunda with a curving cantilevered gallery of speckled beige horzma wood, railed with wrought-iron. A grand timber staircase led up to this balcony, which accommodated chairs upholstered in dark red leather separated by individual tables. A rear door led away to private apartments in the adjacent kettledome. A flight of steeper stairs mounted to a much smaller and higher balcony. The main purpose of that eyrie was to provide a housing for the long chain which would winch the massive central chandelier down for replenishment and lighting of candles. At eye level with occupiers of the main gallery, a semicircle of deep windows alternated with family portraits, and one of Lucky beaming benevolently, crowned with her bygone tiara. The interior of the dome was embellished in silver with the zodiacal harp and cuckoo and cow and nakki-on-mushroom. Only from the gallery of honour could one see out over the courtyard where the royal sky-boat was currently berthed, and the erstwhile Isi flier and the silvery fighting pods.

Out there on the afternoon of the mana-baptism, several stocky shaggy ponies roamed while guards in leathers sorted sacks and boxes. The day was breezy-bright. An occasional shadow sped across the earthen bailey. Guards would glance up just in case a woolly cloud wasn't the source of the sudden shade.

Within, the rotunda had been completely cleared of long tables and benches so as to admit a sizable audience and participants and to allow ample free space. Space for the cauldron of cold water which was the font. Space for the brazier upon which a pan of molten tin simmered. Space for an imaginary stage on which the actors would strut. And space for any unexpected mana-festations. The floor was of white false-marble, flags of limestone which took a fine polish.

Up in the gallery sat the Queen in her purple velvet gown and scarlet suède boots and chaplet of amber. All sign of mourning was cast aside now. No hint of black lace or ribbon. In her full oval face, narrow eyes smouldered – as did the liquid tin below. As would van Maanen when she caught him. At her side Jatta contrived an aloof air though curiosity piqued her. She was hot in her purple suède tunic sewn with brightly dyed strips of felt. Kay's sequinned white gown conveyed a stylish disingenuous innocence, and her husband had dandified himself in best braided jacket, embroidered waistcoat, and striped trousers. Hubertus's mother Bella had absented herself with her young grandchildren who might be frightened or evil-eyed by June's wee whelps.

The babes were in the charge of an invulnerable wooden

soldier, his deep blue uniform trimmed with orange, his peaked
shako topped with a white pompon. Unwaveringly the soldier
held a shallow padded crib in which four naked bodies squirmed
side by side. June, in freshly laundered creamy satin gown, stood
anxiously at his left hand. Jack, in Juttahat livery at his right,
grinned encouragingly. Stooped double, Goody Hilda was peering
sidelong.

Ruddy-faced tubby Serlachius began to intone:

'Mana abide,

'Mana guide . . .'

The charcoal-suited priest chanted a while, then gazed up at
his Queen.

'Mother of Kaleva, appointed by your Ukko, anointed by the
mysterium, Grand Ma'am of this righteous war and of these
midget maids, may they be full of mischief in your cause if the
need arises. May each be a handful of trouble to your enemies.
Four handfuls of trouble! Menace Lasses, Maids of Horror, tiny
today, bigger tomorrow! Mana breeds them, mana feeds them:
these terrible tots, these naughty nakkis.' Serlachius was working himself into a state of effervescence. Onlookers were agog.

The maids frowned, they grimaced, they squealed.

'Tell—'

    'Us—'

        'Our—'

            'Names!' they squeaked.

Their custodian stared down impassively, features rigid. Jack
beamed at his bairns who surely bore the burden of June's jinx
and of his own rush to maturity. In the gallery, Lucky exulted.

Serlachius ladled tin and tossed it, *tomcat-hissing*, upon the
cold water. Almost immediately a thin film formed.

Afloat on the cauldron lay a flat tubby knobbly figure.

'A silhouette of the everything machine, Your Majesty!' cried
Lucky's mana-priest. 'That's what this is! The machine makes
weapons. These babes *are* weapons of plague and pox, to be
guided by your word as they grow.'

Four of the knobbles attached to the silhouette were duplicates
of the larger figure. As Serlachius lifted the tin pattern from
the font, those fell off: a quartet of little charms. He laid the
main section of tin upon the floor, then harvested the charms.
He placed one at the head of each babe, naming each bairn in
turn.

'You are Minx.

'You are Jinx.
'And Minxie.
'And Jinxie.'
The maids wriggled.
Which was which? It seemed to Serlachius that the maid on the right was suddenly the maid on the left, and that the inside twins had changed places before his eyes. Would this be the means of delivery of plague, that each maid could be in another place momentarily — perhaps far away — long enough to touch and contaminate her target? He rubbed his eyes. One maid, two maids, three maids, four: all present. Which was Jinx and which was Jinxie?

'I'm Minx,' squeaked one gleefully.
'I'm Jinx,' piped her sister.
'We—'
            'Know—'
                        'Who—'
                                    'We—'
                                                'Are—'
Which one had spoken twice?
'Cheer them and applaud them!' cried the Queen from the gallery. *Applaud her too.* Hail her and acclaim her. 'Bring the roof down!'

Captain Bekker, splendidly trimmed with crimson and golden lace, scabbarded sabre by his side, clapped with a wooden monotony. Gorgeous General Aleksonis looked uncomfortable in those clinging white breeches as he uttered gruffly, 'Huzza, huzza!' Young proclaimer Nils was chanting and swaying. Juke, mouthing forcefully, was gazing into remoteness.

What of the Jaegertroopers who were present? Were those new recruits passionate enough in their enthusiasm?

Should Peter Vaara and his players bawl themselves hoarse prior to performing?

Applause paced itself. How long should it continue? Nobody knew. The ovation failed to crescendo. A sense of climax would have permitted Lucky to wave thankfully for silence. Noise simply carried on, conscientious rather than vehement. Were too many fellows brooding about death? Were they intimidated by these precocious maids? In spite of Nils's swaying, the assembly fell short of a delirious unison. The hall was full of individuals who were following each other's lead. The chorus of acclaim and thump of handclaps lacked wildness.

269

Bring the roof down?

Jack glanced aloft.

He darted to the staircase.

In a trice he was up at the gallery.

'Fastboy—!' Jatta called in vain to a roguish child. Jack was already scrambling up the steeper flight of stairs.

In the upper gallery he examined the winding gear from which the long chain stretched to the chandelier. Scintillae sped from him like phosphorbugs, alighting on crystal lustres, flashing, gleaming. Such radiance danced.

'Watch out, below!'

At least he *did* pause for a few sparkling moments before letting the winch spin freely.

Links ratcheted through the apparatus as the chandelier plunged dazzlingly down. In an explosion of light it crashed into the cauldron, dragging its tail of chain. Bright crystals and comets of water fountained and fell. Serlachius was soaked. Complete silence also fell, apart from the thump of Jack dashing downstairs again.

From the wreckage arose bright little flies.

Four flies, eight of them, a dozen.

Winged sparks, these flitted towards the wooden soldier who held the maids' crib. Aerial chips of glittering emerald, ruby and sapphire, they glittered with bilious green, with fever-red, with asphyxiated blue.

Cooing and crowing, the babes reached out. The insects settled upon the maids' palms. The babes balled their fists. When they straightened their tiny fingers again, those insects had melted away like snowflakes.

Was it Jinx or Minx who bunched her fist once more and opened it to release, from nowhere, a black fly? This took wing towards the nearest window. As it wavered in the air, it took on a morbid iridescent shimmer. Almost immediately the insect weakened and dropped.

Hilda hobbled to inspect the expiring fly. She prodded it with her finger, then sniffed the fingertip.

Melancholy overwhelmed the old woman: a poignant ghostly retrospection upon a twisted lifetime. It was as if she had taken a step through a final doorway. From beyond that doorway, irrevocably behind her now, the perspective of her bygone days revealed itself in wistful pastel glimpses. So many days had expired like

*fleeting smiles which fled away, half-noticed and unfulfilled. She
thought that she heard the beating of the swan's wings. She was
so near to death – by touching a dying pestilential fly, harbinger
of many more.*

*Oh but the touch couldn't kill her. Nor anyone else here. And
besides, the wee maids must grow a bit larger yet. Hilda sensed
that there could be miseries of the spirit corresponding to the
maladies which the mana-bugs would inflict.*

*Her own span of life had been so strongly coloured by distortion:
her own distortion, and the kinks of the mocky-folk too.*

*Yet, could it be that at the moment when she died – when she
did step through that doorway, glancing back askew with fading
vision – that just then all her lapsed distorted days would be
twisted finally into . . . a misty semblance of perfection, of wholesomeness, immaculate, accomplishing the healing which had
always inspired her heart?*

Her wrinkled face angled sidelong and upward towards the
gallery.

'There's some spry young folk,' she croaked, 'as can snatch a
fly in their hands. Only four very special bairns can release a fly
as wasn't there before, and with such a sting as these. When
these maids are a little bigger, they'll be sending flies to your
foes, alas. Though not to your friends, oh no.'

Of a sudden the hall was full of friends. Feet stamped thunderously. Such a chorus of halloos. Now Lucky could wave her hands
to quell the hubbub.

She sang out, 'I shan't be having any more troublesome daughters.' As if Jatta should be delighted to hear this! 'But what
daughters my grandson has begotten! They'll be faithful to me
and my friends.'

On their quilted crib, held by that indefatigable wooden soldier, the maids of horror squirmed and bunched their tiny fists.
Pleased as punch, beaming bright, Jack pranced amongst
puddles and shattered lustres. He rejoined June and hugged her.
Above in the gallery Jatta nibbled softly at a knuckle and Kay
gaped at the ruination of her chandelier.

The hullabaloo ebbed with a perfect spontaneity. In the ensuing hush the babes began to wail hungrily. Hilda clucked. Time
for June to depart and resume her slings.

'And now for the *play*,' declared the Queen. Highly satisfied, she
beckoned to her general: 'Victor, will you kindly join me up here?'

271

Victor Aleksonis would serve perfectly well as a substitute prince. That white tunic with silver collar and chevrons. That scarlet supervest. The tight buckskin breeches, and the silver helmet with a winged eye and green plume! How very fine. On his chest he sported the starry Order of the Ukko. What could be more appropriate?

The players had set up a pair of purple screens to serve as backdrop. Black skullcaps hid their hair. They wore full-length matt black leotards. Face and voice and hands were the essentials of their art. Notwithstanding the daylight, soon you only noticed their supple gestures and facial expressions and harked to the lilted words, half-spoken and half-sung.

Faces floated. Hands motioned. Words bespoke personae and settings. The minds of the spectators elaborated. This sway was Peter Vaara's gift which he shared with his troupe and with which they swayed their audience. He could elevate the imagination – and the audience would partake of his pageant.

How little sense it made to regard Vaara as precisely of such-and-such an appearance. His was no longer the blandly forgettable whey face into which Lucky had peered during their interview. He was whomever he pretended to be. The same was true of his troupe.

Sophie was Lucky Sariola as a teenage girl.

How easy it was to imagine this hall – the Jaegers' hall, especially – as a cavern! Their hall was a cavity inside of Lucky Sariola's Ukko far away in time, and in space as well. An aurora dancer shimmered from between the screens, evoking drifts of stars and gassy nebulae.

She mimed the Ukko's own inner animate light, its spirit as revealed to the girl.

'Sing me a story, tell me a tale,' Natalya beguiled. 'And I will take you to the stars.'

Sophie-Lucky answered her, 'I'm driven by my longing. I will sing my people's legends.' She seemed to wear a black spacesuit though no helmet nor gloves.

Who was this Juttahat coming now? His hands slithered to and fro. He was supporting a serpent coiled around his shoulders. (The serpent itself was *almost* visible.) Afflicted by some dire disorder, the Juttahat faltered.

'Not killing my master and me, Great Ukko,' it hissed painfully. 'Not reducing us to bones for the sake of this lass and her

272

unruly kin. Helping my masters to be governing humans.' Oh but this was very perceptive of Peter Vaara.

'She must be wild, and she will be wild,' Natalya told the dying alien. With one hand Natalya the Ukko-nakki seemed to be offering a sceptre to Paula-Sariola-Sophie – or was that a long-stemmed flower?

Who was this captivating newcomer but Mana itself personified? Not Stanislav, but Mana Manifest: a meisterman. Accompanied by . . . *Bertel, Bertie*! Lucky's prince-to-be!

'I shall transform her into royalty undying,' vowed Meister Mana. 'I shall grant all her daughters a gift if she tells us a story, sings us a tale. I shall change her, exchange her.'

Lucky lurched.

'I shall beget babes for ever,' dead Bertie promised young Paula.

Paula's hair was blonde . . .

Lucky's true twin – her real self – allowed her suitor to kiss her hand. The Queen gripped the wrought-iron railing with both hands.

'Paula!' she cried. 'Bertie,' she murmured.

Sophie didn't look up. Visualization was intensifying. Isi snakes were rearing, peering . . .

'*Paula—!*'

Jatta butted in upon her mother's reverie.

'That's Eyeno Nurmi with the flower in her hand, Mother. I saw her when you flew Juke back to Outo, and I saw her echo when' – she hesitated – 'when I was with Anni. Didn't you see Eyeno greet Juke in Outo, Mother? Don't you recognize her? That's Juke's sister.'

'You're trying to confuse me. That's my *self*. You're lying.'

'Why should I lie?'

'To distract me from using the maids! Your nakki grandbairns. My chatter, you're as mischievous as Minnow.'

'No one else can sway *you*, Mother – but your own mania can!'

Oh but this whole pageant was tearing at Lucky's heart. To see her own lost *self*! And thus be seduced away from the war against the upstarts? Was Peter Vaara an agent of the brindled serpents?

The Queen had quit her seat. She was hastening down the staircase to the flagstones.

'*Paula!*'

As she rushed on to the extempore stage – '*Paula!*' – the players paused. Bemused, they made no move.

Then Sophie drew herself up. She was tall and willowy, not like Paula at all. One of her eyes shone brightly as if the eyeball were a shard of crystal lustre. Crying out in pain, the actress clapped a hand to her face. Meister Mana reached out to her in concern. Already Sophie was uncovering her eye. Briefly it seemed that within the socket there was only emptiness. She wasn't Paula at all.

Was *Juke* causing his dead sister's echo to be present here? From the stage, Lucky cast about for him. She quickly spied the mutie proclaimer. He was cowering. Oh no, he hadn't consciously cast this sway. Not wittingly. Maybe his guilt was to blame.

Lucky stamped on a broken lustre. If the Paula persona had become more intense, Lucky might have lost all sense of what needed to be done to the rebels *before* she could afford to continue searching for herself. She'd have been trip-trapped.

'Peter Vaara!' she shrieked.

The sickly Juttahat staggered towards her. *Why had Vaara chosen that particular role?* Though the pageant had swerved askew he wasn't about to abandon the character. Did he hope that the masquerade protected him? Mana, in the person of Stanislav, and Natalya the aurora dancer, light of Ukko, flanked him in case he collapsed.

'Majesty—' Vaara spoke in a tone which belied his apparent infirmity. 'There being processes of thought to which people being prisoners—'

Did he retain the idiosyncrasies of alien speech so as to distance himself?

'Stories being alive, Majesty. Ourselves serving their purpose: of evolving, adapting, extending themselves, capturing persons to be succouring their existence. Incarnating new aspects, acting out variations. Word being alive, and shaping world.' How alien he sounded.

'Be warned, Your Majesty,' said Stanislav-Mana, 'right now you're entering into your own old story, forging a devious loop.'

Tancred-Bertie was at Lucky's side: a face, and hands adrift. The Queen could smell her own yeasty response to him. 'Majesty,' he said soothingly, 'remember yourself.'

'But I am. I do.' Lucky stared at Sophie.

The Juttahat chuckled. 'Once, a woman was greeting her own reflection in a mirror. But as soon as she was embracing her mirror-self in rapture, the glass was becoming blank. Likewise

274

the woman too. She was disappearing. The pair of them were extinguishing one another.'

'Don't say that!'

How dared they address her so familiarly? By rushing on stage she had become a sixth player in their spectacle.

Could it be that finding her true self might result in an annihilation – albeit sweet and swooning – rather than in sanity and fulfilment?

'How many times have you performed before the Isi?' she demanded.

The answer came all too promptly from the bogus Juttahat. He didn't even query her question.

'*Never.* Merely by impersonating a mana-mage, our friend Solveig was dying of a fit.'

'So you said! So you said!' Where and why and how had Solveig suffered this fit? *In which Isi nest?*

'You'll be true Queen of a world,' Natalya lilted at Lucky. The actress was treating her now as Sophie-Paula. Sophie remained the echo of Eyeno Nurmi.

'I'll give you all this in exchange for sovereign stories—' Natalya was reverting to the unwritten script. The pull of the drama was embroiling her and Lucky. Lucky mustn't stay on stage a moment longer.

A seeing-eye Spitzhound had wandered into the hall and was whining. What might the dog be visualizing? If its trainer was peering into a mana-mirror, what was he seeing right now?

True Queen of a world, indeed. With her general watching her, and her wooden captain and her war-priest and her proclaimers and Demon Jack, all set to thrash the rebels in Loxmithlinna and Maananfors.

'Let your play in my honour continue,' Lucky told Vaara brusquely. 'I shan't interrupt again.' Indeed, once she was back in her seat in the gallery, she would shut her eyes.

18 · CLEARING THE AIR

Blazonry was the popular word for claims to fame as cried by cuckoos in market squares. A fellow would brag to a gossip-bird about a fine catch of sweetfins he'd netted, fat with roe, or a

Juttie he'd killed. In neighbouring towns, that same bird or its kin would presently *blazon* the fellow's achievement.

Along the waterfront of Maananfors for the past two days several cuckoos had been blazoning Lucky's victory at Loxmithlinna.

By the long low quayside of pink granite, fishing smacks were moored three and four abreast, their white sails furled. The paddle-steamer ferry, *Sotko's Daughter*, jutted outward from a jetty, its rocket-launcher commanding the approaches. Blue Guards manned two ground-to-air rocket-launchers on the quay. On the upthrust of blushing granite above the town a keen eye could glimpse several more such launchers poking from Prince Osmo's keep.

Market was under way along the quayside. Trade in fruit and sausages, mushrooms or cheeses, wasn't especially brisk. Fish was only on offer smoked or soused, not fresh. Fishing boats mustn't set sail. The mid-morning was grey and misty. Thin wool lazed on the reaches of the lake. Tiny tree-studded islands could be vague vessels, impostors.

Half hidden in the galvanized tubs recessed into rafts, women were scrubbing rugs slowly to hang upon drying racks. Everybody was taking their time about work or purchases. Drab in the dull light, one or other of the scrawny mottled green gossip-birds flapped from masthead to bollard to the awning over a stall, screeching Lucky's victory. Their recital was piecemeal and repetitious though of compelling interest.

'Hark and hear, hark and hear,' croaked a bird.

People harked for the umpteenth time.

'Queen Lucky's ground forces landed on a farm within ten keys of Loxmithlinna town. Escorted by three jump-bikes, they advanced upon the outskirts. Out-dweller vigilantes attempted a paltry defence, house to house. Sight of the Queen's wooden soldiers had caused a delusion that aliens were invading, masquerading as men. Stalwarts were swayed by a fatal passion to protect their homes. How much better if they had welcomed those who came to free the aitch-house from occupation—!'

'Hark,' cackled another bird, 'barricaded inside the aitch-house Lord Elmer and the garrison cringed as Lucky's sky-boats and armed pods bombarded the keep with hotlight and aerial torpedoes and explosives—'

Blazons were invariably biased. Had the bombardment really been as fierce? Had the defenders actually cowered? The aitch-

house was more massively and integrally designed than the fortified complex of walls and roofs and towers which comprised
Osmo's own keep, exposed on its elevation . . .

'Boats penned in the water-yard weren't set alight, in order
that Queen Lucky would be able to seize a small navy—'

That navy might soon be crossing the turquoise lake through
autumnal mist such as fretted the vista today. Now that August
was almost at an end, trees around the shores were painting
themselves scarlet and orange, and rust and tarnished copper,
as the flow of sap to the leaves pinched shut.

'In his jinking sky-pod Demon Jack Pakken evaded all lightrifle fire, for his is the mastery and mystery of light. He launched
numbing slowness at shattered windows where defenders
crouched. He wound up whirlwinds in the land-yard and waterspouts in the lake—'

People had heard this already.

('What, half a mark for *four* oranges?')

'By the evening the west wing of the aitch-house was ablaze,
and the occupants could have made use of those waterspouts. The
iron-bound tammy gate of the land-yard had been scorched and
battered from the air and buffeted by nakki-whirlwinds. Throughout the fire-lit night, the Queen's sky-fleet rattled the rooftops
with grenade-bombs so that the defenders could enjoy no rest—'

('Dear lady, we mayn't expect to see many more fine Pootaran
oranges such as these, not with *Sotko's Daughter* blockaded in
harbour.')

('*Sotko's Daughter* is *defending* our harbour.')

('Comes to the same thing, I'd say.')

'Make no mistake: the Queen wasn't squandering her
resources. The everything machine had been generous to her, to
make her invincible—'

A cuckoo paused to preen. Another bird took up the tale, crying
out:

'In the morning her guards and her wooden soldiers and the
Jaegerguard crowded the streets leading into the square known
at Out-the-House. They'd seized all the shops and houses in the
vicinity, purging them of townsfolk. Hot light lanced at the
broken windows of the north and east wings of the aitch-house
to cow the Defence Volunteers. Explosive bullets and quarrels
sped upward—'

('Come off it! You can easily lay your hands on oranges by way
of Tapper Kippan's realm. Profiteer!')

277

('Easily? Oh *no*, dear lady.')

'Hark now: in the morning smoke still poured from the gutted west wing. Holes cratered every roof. In Out-the-House Square the fountain of pipes with its copper cuckoos had run dry. Curver trees stood stripped of their crisping autumnal quiffs. The pillory was bleakly exposed, awaiting what wretch? Was the *Dread* gripping the souls of those within, or merely justifiable terror?'

Whoever had coached the cuckoos was blessed with a colourful tongue. Maybe the birds were embroidering upon events from their repertoire of bygone stories? But there was realism, too, in their tale. The more to chill their audience?

'Hark now: the Queen owns a hefty war-wagon made for her by the everything machine. This remains behind in Sariolinna. Altogether too massive to carry on chains slung beneath a sky-boat!'

('Half a mark for six—')

'Who needed such a war-wagon? Hot light roasted the great hinges of the battered tammy gate. A rocket blasted a hinge loose. Another rocket flew, and a second hinge burst. Demon Jack danced up such a gale. Juke Nurmi and Nils Carlson proclaimed—'

Nils Carlson? He was a bespeaker unknown to the citizens of Maananfors . . . Maybe Nils was the source of these blazons.

'Half of the great gate groaned and fell inward—' A scaly green head ducked under a wing.

Another cuckoo cried: 'Now was the time when the war-wagon might have been of use to plunge through enfilading fire towards the crossbar of the aitch-house – even though that juggernaut could only accommodate three persons easily, five at a tight pinch. *What need of the steel hervy?* The Queen's jump-bikes were waiting to leap into the central banqueting hall—'

'That was when Lyle Melator persuaded Captain Haxell to turn the Defence Volunteers upon the traitor Osmo's depleted garrison—'

A groan, which became a growl, escaped from the throats of several listeners.

'Of a sudden there was fighting inside the aitch-house, and no enfilading fire at all. What else made sense when Lord Elmer and Lady Eva had already fled in the *Sea Sledge* in the early hours, supposedly to deny the Queen his engineering skills should the aitch-house fall to her—?'

Alongside the quay the very same launch, the *Sea Sledge*, floated under guard. By now that power boat was equipped with a twin-barrel lightgun mounted on a swivel.

'What else made sense?'

Listeners nodded. Hadn't the instinctive engineer finessed the everything machine into action? (Even though Prince Osmo had primed it and been despicably treated!) How much safer for Maananfors that Elmer Loxmith should be *here* rather than *there*. Yet to run away from one's keep while it was under attack, leaving brave men to die . . . *ach*!

'My hubby was one of that garrison!' wailed a young fishwife in shawl and headscarf. 'Are they really all dead, cuckoo?'

'Ukko-ukkoo,' cackled the bird. When did a cuckoo ever answer a direct question? 'Praise the true victorious Queen of Kaleva.'

So many men – and some women – of Maananfors had survived a day of siege only to be killed by deceitful aitch-housers; and if not by those, then to be butchered by royal jump-bikers or implacable wooden soldiers. Slaughtered, to weaken Osmo.

'Curse Lucky!' screamed the young woman. 'She's as evil as our Osmo called her!'

This was a common reaction.

'She'll sell us as slaves to the Isi!' somebody else bawled.

'Hark and hear,' cried another cuckoo; and voices hushed. 'The Queen wasn't *squandering* her resources by any means—'

Osmo's Sam Peller had been receiving weapons from the Brindleds. *Sotko's Daughter* pointed her rocket-launcher out across the water. Boats: beware rockets. Sky-boats: beware them too. As for proclaimers, Osmo was the prime amongst them. Moreover, Queen Minnow had trounced a mana-mage. So the cuckoos' listeners were defiant rather than downhearted. ('Half a mark for *five*, then.') People still lingered to hear the gobbets of news. A mana-priest at Forssa claimed to have proof that cuckoos could commune mind-to-mind while far apart. These cacklers on bollard and masthead might be glimpsing inwardly, through the far-off yellow eyes of their kin, whatever was occurring right now in ravaged Loxmithlinna.

The mist, the deceitful mist! Surely Lucky would pause to consolidate and bring in more of her wealth of weapons, and lick wounds too. There must have been some wounds on the northerners' side.

How long would she pause? For a week? For ten days? For a

279

fortnight? Was Lucky even in residence at Loxmithlinna yet? Her so-called new navy – laughable, really – wouldn't loom into sight for a while yet.

That mist out on the waters may well have attracted people to the quayside market this morning almost as much as the presence of the gossip-birds or a desire to lay in supplies. The dense haze hiding the distance surely wasn't a mana-mist, otherwise there would have been more activity up at the keep. Would the same be true on a future morning? Would such a haze, then, be the handiwork of Demon Jack and Lucky's proclaimers?

When Captain Jurgen's jump-bike appeared in the courtyard of Osmo's keep its rider was very nearly shot. Lightrifles and crossbows jerked towards him.

'Friend!' he brayed; and former fellow guards recognized his abundant gingery moustache. Jurgen's face and his light blue leathers were stained and smutty. His boots were scorched. Some dried blood had crusted on his sandy curls.

He dismounted. 'Wheel this away, will you, Sven, there's a good fellow?' He spoke with a lightness of tone which belied a terrible tension cushioned by fatigue.

'You're a good fellow too,' said the blond rifleman, 'but I'm on duty.'

A crazed light gleamed in Jurgen's tired blue eyes. *'Do it!* I have to tell Prince Osmo immediately—' He swept a grimy hand across his face. 'Who the shite else do I report to? Johann's so far away it's only in the in-betweens that I still feel the echo of him fading.' He gestured at the closed doors of the banqueting hall. 'Can't take my bike in there with its guns that . . . kill, kill, kill,' he chattered.

'He's *Captain* Jurgen, remember,' hissed one of Sven's colleagues.

Oh yes indeed, commander of the garrison of the aitch-house – all of whom had been butchered; except, so it transpired, for him . . . Was this fatigued and almost incoherent fellow in command of *himself* right now?

'You'd best relieve him of the bike, Sven, just like you're being told—' In case *Captain* Jurgen, commander of nobody left alive, clutched that red handlebar and opened fire in frustration and frenzy.

'You'd better—'

'Take care of my bike, damn it!'

'Yes, *sir*,' said Sven, and laid his weapon down on the cobbles.

Inside the hall, the half-dozen stoves stood in between tapestries of trees like so many pot-bellied sentries made of cast iron – distant relations, perhaps, of the brass automaton abandoned back at the aitch-house.

Elmer regarded those stoves morosely from the bench he shared with Eva. When her fingers strayed against his long bony hand his expression brightened. Such ambivalent consolation there was to her touch, her *voluntary* touch. In the mysterious equations of feelings was his keep perhaps acceptably lost, when such awful violence had spurred a frenzied consummation of which he and Eva were beneficiaries?

Seated by him in that dour grey gown, that black patch the hue of her hair hiding the absence of an eye, was Eva sufficiently *consoled*? Was she adequately comforted that there would be no more nightly whippings? Was she *relieved* that her mother wouldn't be able to mock her about everlasting virginity and an impotent spouse? Were Elmer and his bride truly soul-mates in spite of the pains he'd been obliged to impose on her and the damage dealt her by Cully?

Elmer stretched his cadaverous frame and swept back his mop of black hair. He was still wearing a grimy tunic of buff leather as a token of exertions at Loxmithlinna. Its dirty condition emphasized his refugee status.

Longlife, longlife: he'd attained it.

After the day of assault from the sky, smaller explosions had continued to punctuate the short night.

What price a respite of darkness with the west wing still burning despite pumping and bucketing from the water-yard? The blaze wasn't spreading. Definitely it was under control. It still illuminated the other three wings as targets. Grenade-bombs fell upon roofs to the south, east, and north.

In the armoured suite behind iron shutters each detonation was an abrupt thump, jolting and jagged. Sleep was impossible, the prospect of sleep absurd and even irresponsible. Shouldn't Elmer have given the armoured suite over to his paralysed dad? To his mother, forever as white as a sheet as if shocked by a nakki? To young Nikki, who seemed to hate him? Or to some of the injured, for whom Moller and Ma Grünwald were doing their best to care?

281

Shouldn't Elmer be prowling corridors, offering a word of encouragement here, a word of consolation there? Lyle had thought not. The Lord and his lady must be sheltered and secure, together.

A single candle scantily illuminated the silks veiling the iron panelling. Around the walls soft filmy skin had quivered. The sweet and jaunty fragrances of clearsage and jismin mingled with a muzzy bonfire odour of smoke in a dizzying nuttiness.

Crump, on the roof three floors above.

'You fucked the Girlem on the night before the first siege!' Eva had cried coarsely at Elmer, to kindle him. 'You tickled her nipples and tupped her loins! And now here's a second siege!'

Shedding her gown, Eva had turned and waggled her bum at him.

She presented two ample soup spoons fused appetizingly side by side above the curved handles of her legs. He could see so little but he smelled burned chocolate, sweet thick soup of titillating contradictions. Those full spoon bowls swayed, inviting tasting and licking and delving. In the dim yellow candlelight Eva was a well-endowed muscular gluteal machine of clear design, oscillating, inviting him to sup. He shed his clothes, though he had no whip with him to whisk the chocolate soup. He was glad to strip. The air was so clammy. Glass was missing from the windows but iron shutters blocked the breeze, if not the seepage of smoke. He was slicked with sweat.

'Come to your Goldi Girlem,' she commanded feverishly, long coaly hair hanging down the dish of her back. 'Come, come with your key, your long stiff key!'

Alas, his key remained soft.

Crump.

Since he hadn't clutched her yet, she faced him again.

'I can't still be a virgin when my mother comes! I can't! You'll die if I am, you'll die. Come to your Girlem, Elmer. I'm her.'

Eva stared at him as if in farewell, then in a swift motion she slid the eye-patch from over her empty socket and around her brow to hide her good eye, her only eye.

'I'm blind, I can't see you, Elmer. I can't see what you do, not anything. I'm not me, and you aren't you. Who are you? Who am I? I'm a Girlem without eyes.'

She blundered about. She felt for the bed. She cast herself upon it. Crouching, knees spread, she thrust her rump high. 'Now! Now! Now!' she began to wail, voice partly muffled. The spoon bowls of this blind banquet provoked him so. 'Fuck me or you'll *die!' How obscene his princess-bride sounded. Surely Eva was someone else: a stripped, simplified apparatus – though a voluptuous one.*

Scorched chocolate soup . . . The house was on fire. Little bombs were falling.

Men and women had died today, seared by hot light, arms and faces blown off. Flying glass had lacerated flesh horribly, till there was no glass left to fly. Death, death . . . and the remedy lay between his legs, and between hers. So simple the connexion. So slippery with sweat.

He was stiff. He was behind her on the bed.

'Who are you?' she had cried. 'I'm blind. Now, now!'

He fell forward. She had braced his weight. And she swallowed him, sucking him within her. So simple, so slippery. Crump. Concussion rocked him. Besotted automatic frenzy possessed him, and he pumped – while she cried, 'Ah!' repeatedly – until he erupted, groaning and puffing. It was a gladsome pain as much as rapture that he felt, at expelling a part of himself.

Squirming, she collapsed forward.

Ponderously he turned her. Softly he kissed the fluttering lids of her vacant orb.

For a moment he had feared that she would thrust him away but her fingers clutched his shoulders, nails hooking him.

'Yes, yes,' she gasped. 'Love me, defaced, my Lord! Taste my tears!' Salt on burnt chocolate, oil of her hair, sweet nutty fumes, and jismin juice . . . Tiny vulnerable, hymeneal creatures, these flaps of flesh that lived at the doorway of the nook in her face. His tongue probed between the lids. It quested within. Osmo – best bespeaker – had been appalled by an empty socket when Nurmi's sister plucked out her false eye. Not Elmer! Who was the true tonguemeister of the two? How vast that cave seemed to the tip of his tongue, and salty as the sea.

Soon her hips arched. Her sumptuous hips, like a padded saddle. She convulsed.

They lay side by side.

'Thank you, my goose,' he babbled several times.

After a while they made love face to face. However, she insisted that while his manhood was at work within her so must his tongue be too.

She imitated a Juttahat voice. 'Such a tickling being in my head, my Lord, compelling my body. A tongue tickle from a snake.'

'I love you,' he told her sincerely.

283

'Licking me lovely, Lord Loxmith.' She sounded demented. Yet his appetite was again aroused. And hers! Such a pulse in her hips ...

A while later, Lyle had come banging on the outer door, calling urgently. When Elmer, hastily gowned and slippered, admitted his assistant to the dressing room, the oil-lamp in Lyle's hand disclosed flaps of shredded lace netting rippling from the window frame and jagged jewels of glass littering the floor. Lyle simpered at Elmer. He sniffed. Did he wink?

All was hurry. Elmer and his wife must leave secretly right away. The house was sure to fall. A man of Elmer's skills mustn't be trapped by Lucky. If Elmer stayed, Osmo would certainly lose the war. Captain Haxell agreed. They would crank up the portcullis enough to let the Sea Sledge *slip out and race away while night still cloaked the lake.*

At another bench in the banqueting hall silver-haired Sam Peller was talking alertly into a communicator to one of his scouts stationed at Asikkala. A Brindled Isi sky-boat had ferried yet more weapons *that* close in to Maananfors.

'They mustn't come any nearer than Asikkala, do you hear me, Pekka?'

Sam wore spruce new blue leathers, triply chevroned at the shoulders with red lips similar to the proclaimer tattoos on his lord's biceps. Those chevrons were a mark of rank devised and bestowed by Queen Minnow because Sam was Osmo's voice to the scouts and guards and the town watch (who were now known as the Blue Watch). Should Sam be known as *general*, equivalent to Lucky's Viktor Aleksonis? Should bailiff Septimus become his chamberlain?

Osmo was still considering these suggestions from his bride. Maananfors Keep was now a royal court, to be sure. Look where the democratic tendencies of the aitch-house had led! But Minnow was a new kind of Queen, and wholehearted popular support was essential. One didn't wish to imitate the capricious autocracy of Lucky which could selfishly lead Kaleva to ruin and alien domination. Septimus was a tubby toper. How absurd he would seem in a frock coat and cummerbund and powdered wig.

As for Sam, why, Osmo's bondsman would revolt at fripperies and pompous titles, though he liked the lip chevrons well enough as insignia. You could hear him already: 'If you want my opinion, *after* you win a war is the best time to call yourself a general.'

'Do you hear me, Pekka? Under no circumstances – *none* – do we want any Juttahat volunteers fighting on our side. Should the suggestion ever arise! Thin edge of the wedge of Isi domination, that would be—'

Alvar, in his old mulberry dressing gown, was meticulously penning at speed in a black-bound notebook. The wee insects of his finicky script scuttled along a line, leapt to the next, scurried onward. A pen emptied. Tutting, he thrust the empty tube into his left pocket and pulled a successor from his right pocket.

These days he hardly seemed to have time to refill the nibbed tubes of which he possessed dozens, crafted in Kip'n'keep, source also of his paper and ink. Alvar's gown was stained with wipings and leakage. How could he keep up with his *Chronicles* – how could he winnow grain from chaff? – when events insisted on happening almost under his nose? As he scribed, he puffed on his tammywood pipe, hazing the air with wafts of rum and nutmeg. Doors and windows were closed tight in case any cuckoo came a-calling to snoop on *plans*. Outside, the view of sky over town and lake was hazy too.

In her magenta gown and crown of leather and pearls Minnow perched amidst the carved creamy-white flowers of the ivorywood throne, kicking her elevated boots to and fro. The long table which used to occupy the dais had been removed, over a month since, to the body of the hall so that the throne would enjoy suitable prominence. A smaller table, from the kitchen, had been substituted.

Princely in green and gold, with ribbon rosettes, Osmo lounged alongside his Queen. Over the back of his chair hung the reinforced protective coat, always close at hand, at Sam's insistence. A smaller twin of it lay on the waxed yellover floorboards near Minnow like a brown dog sprawling at its mistress's feet.

Said Osmo, 'We'd better go through it all again, Elmer.' (And Alvar groaned, then grinned, and flipped a page, pen poising.) 'This time, as regards Mister Melator. It seems to me that Lyle sent you to bed with as much duplicity as he roused you subsequently.'

'Oh I wasn't asleep,' said Elmer, and Eva flushed. Minnow giggled, but she quickly composed herself.

('We don't wish to know about bed; oh no, that's private . . .')

'With almost as much duplicity,' emphasized Osmo, 'as the aitch-housers turning upon my men at Lyle's instigation; or so the cuckoos claim. I think he conned you out of your castle.'

'But it's better for me to be here . . .'

Elmer had already helped out, just the day before, by mounting that powerful lightgun on the *Sea Sledge*, converting the launch into a patrol boat. Elmer was keen that Sam should ask the Brindled Isi whether they could provide any mobile metal automata which he might be able to convert into robotic warriors to match Lucky's resilient wooden soldiers. ('So why should the Isi use metal automata when they already have their Juttahats?' Sam had retorted. 'If they do have metal men, which I'm sure they don't, you can bet your last mark Isi mages would be spying on everything through their lenses. Thin edge of the wedge, in my opinion!') How many marks did Elmer have with him? Why, none at all.

'I wouldn't be too surprised, Elmer old son, if in your absence Lyle forces your sister to wed him—'

'Force *Nikki*—'

'—with Lucky's full approval, to establish legitimacy for a new seigniory. Always in the wings, wasn't it, so far as Lyle was concerned? Now's his chance to grab much more. With you conveniently out of the way.'

Was Osmo's attitude to Elmer even more patronizing than when he had waltzed into the aitch-house with his army?

Elmer reddened. 'Lyle can't present himself as a *longlife* lord, though.'

Osmo gazed at the fugitive lord of Loxmithlinna in appreciative surprise and amusement.

'Well, well,' he said jovially, 'better late than never. A Girlem must work wonders.'

('No, we don't wish to know about that . . .')

Eva had shut her surviving eye, and was twisting her grey gown at the knee as if to strangle it.

'What do you mean by that?' demanded Elmer.

Chuckling, Osmo laid a proprietorial hand on the arm of the ivorywood throne. 'My gosling, my life, my royal wife,' he whispered.

('We don't want to know.')

Eva opened her eye. Unexpectedly she stood up and swept the patch from her brow, exposing . . .

Osmo shuddered and looked away, up at the king post of the tie-beam roof where he thought he detected a white stain of cuckoo shit on the purple wood.

Eva spoke slowly and loudly.

'I'm naked now, aren't I? Vanity's in the eye of the beheld. So: no eye, no vanity! – unless a man quests for what was lost. Unless he names it silently with his lips, willing to adore the wound as the price for . . . something else. I believe I've devised a new form of adoration. A new form of pleasure!'

Her words were bizarre. Minnow was mouthing *no*, and shaking her head.

'A glory of exquisite *light* explodes within me when the stumps of my vision are probed.'

'My soul, my heart,' Elmer muttered bashfully to his wife. His heart must be thumping with embarrassed pride. How inappropriate this intimate confession was, even if it did fluster Osmo.

'It doesn't hurt me, you know,' Eva continued exultantly. 'The hurt healed. It's delicious. I'm *proud*. I'm unique. Except,' and she leered at Osmo, 'except for Eyeno Nurmi, I suppose! If only she wasn't *dead*!'

Osmo twitched.

'Dead,' Eva echoed. 'Dead. That's what happens to mortal men and women who aren't longlife.'

Osmo looked relieved. He patted his wavy chestnut hair which would never turn grey or recede.

Minnow shrilled at her sister: 'Is this your idea of accepting our hospitality?'

'I thank you for your hospitality. I mayn't have a keep any more. I mayn't have a home. I don't feel mutilated now. I'm fulfilled, filled with tongue.' Eva chuckled zanily as Elmer gawked at her in sheepish wonderment.

Had his wife gone mad? Yet hers was a wondrous paroxysm. All that was pent was pouring forth. He felt giddy with exultation as much as embarrassment.

Machines were never mad. Maybe the everything machine had been a mad unpredictable device? Ach, no; it too was a rational if random contraption, mainly programmed for weaponry. Machines weren't mad. Must he acquire a streak of madness so as to cope with his exile – caused by Osmo! – without being humiliated by Osmo's charity? Was that what his wife was showing him?

'Dead,' she repeated. 'Not that I'm longlife myself! How could I be? But . . . neither are you, Prince Osmo.'

'No, Evie—!' burst from Minnow. 'She's criss-crossed, Oz—'

'Didn't you know that, Osmo? Didn't Minnow tell you?'

Osmo was gaping uncomprehendingly. Elmer tugged at Eva's gown. 'What in mana's name do you mean?'

'*A tongue in the empty socket floods me with light,*' sang Eva. 'I think I might be a poetess,' she declared. 'Don't I possess the right qualification? Namely, one eye! Except, the poetess is *dead*, and you aren't actually longlife, Osmo, but my lord Elmer is.'

Minnow was jabbering at Osmo, who sagged in his seat. The tiny pit in Osmo's cheek had whitened as though an invisible nail were being driven into him to transfix his tongue. Alvar was scribbling so fast that he snapped a nib. Into one pocket dived the casualty. Out of the other pocket leapt its successor. Rum and nutmeg fumes haloed Osmo's dad.

'Excuse me,' broke in Sam, 'but this really isn't *productive*. Wait, Pekka,' he snapped into the communicator. 'No, this isn't efficient at all.' Sam stood up. He rocked on his feet. How unsettled he was.

'I'm not hearing this. No one's hearing this. Certainly not me, and nobody else in this keep. Pekka, you haven't heard anything, do you hear? What have you overheard? Nothing? That's good.'

Sam tugged at his trim white beard, then dusted the chevrons on his shoulder.

'Excuse me, but I'm going to check the missile batteries. See if there's anything out of order.' Sam lurched towards the heavy tammywood door to the courtyard.

Head uplifted, Eva surveyed the banqueting hall as though it were thronged. She had regained her dignity, and Elmer's. She had restored the balance. *Hadn't she?* A misgiving flitted across her voluptuous imperfect face. Osmo squinted hauntedly. Despite the warmth and closeness of the perfumed air he was shivering.

Before Sam could make good his escape, the great door swung open, admitting a strapping grimy fellow with a ginger moustache who was dressed in soiled leathers.

'Jurgen?' exclaimed Sam. '*Captain* Jurgen? You're alive? You didn't hear anything,' Sam told the newcomer as though he were an eavesdropper caught in the act. Promptly Sam hurried past him. Jurgen's attention was entirely upon the dais where Osmo slouched numbly, still half disbelieving.

'Prince – and Majesty – I bring news . . .'

A torrent of tidings spilled from Jurgen. Alvar – pen racing – began to chatter to himself in an effort to do *something* with words which he hadn't time to capture on paper, to put them somewhere, store them somehow. Minnow eyed her dad-in-law with a bleak sympathy. Her own lips were also moving of their own accord, mumble-mumble. Excuses, explanations, consolations. Eva had sunk back into her seat, smirking faintly. Jurgen faltered. He glanced from his lord, who was so preoccupied, to the tapestry trees. Into those glades of greenery, deadly disappointed by his reception, the Captain might dash away to lose himself.

'Report, Captain,' Minnow called to him. 'Yes, you must report everything.'

When his twin brother was killed by a crossbow quarrel Jurgen had jumped his bike away from the murderous brawling in the aitch-house.

Johann's death had wrenched at Jurgen. The death had seemed to jerk Jurgen away, far away, so that he had no choice but to jump in pursuit of his dead brother.

If only he could catch up with Johann's fleeing ghost in the in-between, haul him on to the pillion seat, bring him back into the world from the shore of death!

Jurgen spent a day and a night jumping. Sometimes his brother seemed so close in the flash of darkness between one location and the next. Woodland, lakeside, streets infested by wooden soldiers and Lucky's guards. Jurgen could never lay a hand on Johann who was dead. If he *had*, what nakki might he have lugged back from the in-between?

Dodging, swerving hither and yon, he had seen so much of the aftermath of the siege, the pacification, the arrival of the royal sky-boat.

'Lucky's there already, Prince Osmo! Just across the turquoise lake. I could have tried to *assassinate* her. I knew I mustn't. We don't want her dead, do we, in case mana comes unstrung? We want to capture her, and lock her in a granite dungeon for the rest of her *long long life*—'

Jurgen's words pained Osmo incredibly. How Minnow mumbled at her husband.

Captain Jurgen was still at such a distance from himself. He was distracted by his twin's absence. Half of his soul was lost in the in-between, estranged. What a brave bulletin he'd delivered, but how tormented he was.

'Bespeak me,' Jurgen appealed. 'Save me from throwing myself off my bike in the in-between to join Johann and my garrison.'

'Do it,' hissed Minnow. 'For his sake!'

Osmo gathered himself. He breathed deep. He glanced,

289

distraught, at Minnow. Eva's revelation and Minnow's breath-less elucidation had shattered his composure.

'My duckling, my life,' he murmured. 'Why did you hide this from me?' As if he hadn't understood her protestations.

Miserably: 'I didn't *know* till I talked to Eva in the aitch-house! It's so wretched, wretched – another of Mummy's tricks! Never telling a daughter, only telling the bridegroom. Damn her! What would the truth have done for your confidence, Oz? Or your people's morale? And how stupid, how silly! Making love the wrong way round. Oh, mana help us. It was *love* that we made, Oz, it was love sincere and real. It will be too! Will always be! No, not *always* exactly . . . I did save you from, from—'

Osmo grimaced. He slapped himself upon the cheek. He stared towards the concealed niche where he had formerly kept the stone man. He clutched the arms of his chair. Strength, strength . . . Strength in front of Elmer and his wife; and his scribbling dad. Slowly he turned back to his spouse.

'Yes, you did save me from the monstrous mutant mage, eh? And from the Girlem's trip-trap too . . . it's true. Together we'll save the soul of humanity from the Isi. We'll save our world from crazy Lucky. Together.'

Smiling grimly, he reached to grip her elfin hand.

'Together, my plucky hen.'

'Oh, Oz—'

'I forgive you. No, forgiving is too lordly. I *embrace* you, my joy.'

'Ease me, my Prince,' Jurgen begged. Scorched and grimy, the Captain stood waiting insistently, oblivious to any nuances, aware only of his own urgent need.

'Minnow, I can't summon up the words right now. I *shall* be able to. But it's such a shock . . .' A rug torn from under him.

His hand plucked at a ribbon rosette on his knee as if to tear the decoration loose.

'To believe that I was longlife and to be plain wrong about it. *Deluded!* Oh what a ninny. Heart, be still. No don't be still! Carry on beating. Can't find the words.'

'In that case,' said Minnow, '*I* must find a way. I'm a bit of a mage, after all! And a Queen.'

What could a Minnow do? She slithered from her throne. Kneeling, she opened the ivorywood drawer beneath. She lifted out the little bow-shaped silver harp, and resumed her perch. Her boots rested on the open drawer. Fingers hovered over pegs and tuning pins and buttons.

'Hen, you don't know how—'

Elmer had risen. Fascination on his horsey features, he shambled closer. His long bony fingers twitched almost of their own accord. Osmo gestured him to keep his distance.

'Mana help me,' murmured Minnow. She shut her eyes. In imitation of the alien style of speech: 'Mana *helping* Minnow—' Her fingertips brushed the music loom. A plangent chord rang out.

Such a confusion of mutating memories. Chequerboard statue of her mad mother coming apart into hundreds of pieces . . . Being bound and gagged in a dark deafening cubby-hole . . . Jumping through glowing green hoop hanging from twanging harper tree . . . Snakes writhing on a path . . . Robberbird losing its wings from its body, the wings flying onward separately like twin iridescent souls . . . was this the image she sought?

Orange dunes under a violet sky wherein floated round white bones . . . an Isi homeworld, this.

To be entering into a mage's pysche, lying curled up in its gob . . . a great sway to be casting.

To be casting lassos of thought, to be entering into this supplicant humanbeing's essence, easing it, freeing the body from the twin-wing which was flying away, trying to pull the body along with it towards a dark shore.

Could a bird be flying with one wing only? Could it be shedding the other brother-wing? Yes, yes. The bird, jumping and jumping. Vanishing, appearing.

Be stopping! The bird walking now, pacing across soft easeful moss . . . Not to be flying again. Be leaving, brother-wing. Believing, Jurgen. Calming . . .

Minnow opened her eyes. Chords rippled caressingly, her fingers stroking strings. She stopped. How had she ever begun? Her thigh itched, and she used the cygnet ring on her finger to relieve the irritation. The back of her head itched too, and the ring served again to chase away the spasm, her knuckles nudging the crown of leather and pearls askew. The grubby Captain stood swaying, to all appearances asleep on his feet. A subdued smile visited his lips. Dreamily Eva had resumed her eye-patch. Alvar was sucking the end of his pen rather than his pipe. Osmo was exhibiting the same contentment.

Minnow laid the harp back in its drawer. So many carved

flowers, Kalevan and alien, surrounded her, all of the same ivorywood hue.

'What music did I play?' she whispered.

'I'm not quite certain,' murmured Osmo. 'The music of yourself, maybe. Usually you're such a puckish lass, and this was ... *serene*. It's better that I know about my, um, mortality – than be a fool.' He sounded so blithe, not bitter, that Minnow dared to joke:

'*Um*-mortality rather than immortality, hmm? A Minnow was never immortal to begin with, so I don't know what I'm missing!'

'True enough, my gosling ...' Osmo reached for her hand again and fiddled with the cygnet ring upon her finger. The ring had been slimmed to fit her.

'Should I resume wearing this, do you think?' Osmo asked. 'No, of course not! It's yours. And you're mine.'

Jurgen awoke. 'My Queen—' His tone was one of awe and gratitude.

'You oughtn't to ride a jump-bike again,' Minnow advised him. 'You mustn't. Go and take a sauna. Feed yourself and get some sleep. You're my very special Captain. Stay off jump-bikes from now on, in case jumping reminds you of you know what.'

Jurgen saluted and made a meandering departure, ignoring Alvar's beckonings. The Captain was so dog-tired he was almost sleepwalking.

Eva rose again. She sauntered towards her sister, her one eye moist.

'What is it, Evie?'

'I'm afraid I've caused you such trouble, sprat ...'

'Doesn't matter. You clarified things.'

'Never knew you could play a harp.'

'Nor did I, actually. Monstrous mutant mage,' Minnow muttered to herself. 'I got inside its mind.'

Eva leaned closer. Her voice was almost inaudible. 'Can I possibly borrow some *bungs*, Minnow? I'm not due for days, but ...'

'Oh, I *see* ... So that's to be your excuse. And why not? We all need excuses, don't we? Seriously, have you felt similar surges before at this time of the month?'

Eva laughed softly. 'What a fine sport you are, Your Majesty. You're really very charitable.'

Minnow eyed her elder sister sceptically. Lush of lips, ample of tits, and quite big on dignity too – until her hubby took to whipping her (which he needn't ever do again). And until her

292

eye popped out. In the aftermath of Eva's *surge* her sensuous abundance seemed considerably restored.

'Honestly, I mean it!' Big Sister protested. 'Who cares about being rendered homeless? Let's hope it doesn't happen all over again here too.'

'It won't.'

'Of course it won't, mage-Majesty. Not with my eternal Elmer and Osmo as a team. Those pearls really suit you, by the way.'

Minnow corrected the tilt of her crown. 'I'll see about the bungs presently.'

What was this mischievous complicity between Sariola sisters? Oh but Minnow was managing matters as tactfully and cheerfully as she could. She could hardly slap her sister on the cheek. Not now that there was an understanding between them.

'*Elmer*,' Osmo resumed with an effort, 'we really ought to talk about Lyle Melator's motives a bit more, now that our personal affairs have been . . . clarified.' His voice quavered then firmed. Strength, strength. 'At least nobody outside this hall knows that I'm not longlife.'

Except for Jurgen and Sam. Jurgen had been too preoccupied to notice. Sam hadn't wished to hear. Sam would censor himself. Osmo's dad wouldn't blab. As for Alvar's scribbles, who was there who could read who might sneak a look at them?

'I presume nobody at Loxmithlinna knows.'

'I certainly didn't know till now,' said Elmer.

'Nobody such as Lyle.'

'I should think he doesn't!' protested Eva.

Minnow fidgeted on her throne. She eased her rump to one side as if breaking wind.

'Well,' she said brightly to Eva, 'this certainly clears the air.' ('Doesn't it?' Minnow asked herself.)

Osmo persevered. 'So, Elmer, will Lyle be a compliant puppet . . . ?'

19 · LITTLE RED BOOTS IN HEAVEN

The Snowies were in full flight, as fast as they could stumble through the snow.

Phosphor-sheen glazed the buried meadows and melancholy

tree-spiked tracts. When Minkie's army – and then Eyeno's in pursuit – first passed this way, forest had been so much more extensive. Trees were everywhere. Nakki-trees, not natural ones! So many had shrivelled out of sight. Only scattered sentinels remained, as if the region were a battlefield which already had been ravaged by *atrocity* and *monstrosity*. The landscape had made space for an extermination from which no Snowy would possibly escape, so it seemed.

Enfeebled by dirty haze, the ghost-sun contributed less light than the refractions from the candle-palace to which this final cascade of the war was veering ever closer, in a return to its beginning. The frigid air was gassy and greasy as though the whole domain might soon belch bitterly to rid itself of a pain in the guts, a burning in the belly.

The fitful pearly sheen revealed tiny Snowies lumbering onward desperately, wading through drifts. Sight of their leathers dulled to maroon by distance and dimness and pollution provoked amongst the pursuers a craving to restore their original redness by making bloodflowers bloom from their corpses.

Verrin-men snarled at the heels of a straggler – and hauled down another victim. Braided bandsmen blew burning darts from trumpets.

The snow fields were wide open but hampering and slippery. The rout mostly proceeded at a stumble, a clumsy jog rather than a trot.

In her tawny fur coat and tasselled hat, Eyeno floundered onward. Her lungs ached as if hard frozen words were lodged within her. Her fur-trimmed boots sank and rose, carrying with them a white burden. If her weight had been greater, could she have persisted? In so far as she was keeping up with the main body of her troops she was still in command. Paula and Inga and the echo-sisters straggled way behind, with an escort.

Paula: mana-twin of the Queen of Kaleva, reflection of Lucky Sariola herself . . .

Patchily and confusedly, Paula now remembered how centuries earlier she had entered the Ukko which was parent of the moon-child. Kennan had thought to carry her away on his jumping bike back into the ordinary world as a hostage and pretender to the throne. Paula had been saved but Anna hadn't been . . . When Kennan's march towards the pool of lost words was checked and turned aside, the scoundrel had hung on to Anna as if his fingers dripped glue. The harried Snowies had changed course in a great arc which became a prolonged rout lasting days and days, of chasing, bivouacking, chasing.

As Eyeno's cuckoo-man reported, Kennan now carried Anna tied to the pillion of his bike. Kennan was still with the vanguard of his strawberry-faced gang, leading them onward little jump by little jump. He wasn't trying to outdistance them. Maybe he hoped that his fortunes might turn. Maybe he wished to keep a migrating barricade of doomed Snowies between himself and those who hounded him for as long as he could.

Was Kennan leading his mauled forces back to the candle-palace to threaten the refugees? Was Anna his safe-conduct out of this domain? Surely he wouldn't try to carry her away with him! He'd lost Paula. Why take Anna? Simply for lechery? Could Anna, echo of a long-dead woman, survive outside of the moon-child? Surely not. Yet if she did . . .

Why, her longlife husband was lying dreaming at Castlebeck. Some retainers must be guarding that comatose man – who had once been so brusque to Eyeno. *Damned lords and their ways!* Now at least Eyeno knew why Beck had been gluttonizing. Laying up fat to burn off while he dreamed the longest dream ever dreamt. Now she knew why he'd been so boorish to a certain young woman who simply wished to ask about her own dreams.

Beck had been right! He'd been justified. He'd found his Anna. And – as Paula related after her rescue – such joy had filled Anna. Along with dismay that Gunther's dream-body was so insubstantial . . .

How would Eyeno ever know a comparable gladness?

With Inga? No. *That* would be to surrender her soul to sweet illusions.

She slogged onward through snow. Her chest ached.

'Catch Kennan, you!' she cried to the verrin-man who paced nearby, her dreadful bodyguard. Beady eyes leered. His bald tail lashed from side to side, raising the back of his leather kilt. His snout probed the greasy gelid air.

'Leave me and sprint! Tell your nakki-kin to race ahead. Ignore the Snowies.'

Drool flicked from his chops. 'Snowies need to be killed!' Who would wish such a creature as this as a bodyguard? Who but that ginger beast-woman in the pool of lost words!

'You listen to me. Snowies die, and new Snowies appear.'

'Not on the same day, warrior-woman. Today we get 'em all.'

'Ignore them! Stop Minkie Kennan! Save Anna. I'm ordering you.'

'What if a Snowy gets you?'

'They're too busy running away. Stop Kennan!'

A cunning gleam: 'But then the Snowies stop too, Mistress.' Triumphantly the brindled brown beast shook his lightrifle.

'Give me that gun and *run*, run on all your paws.' Eyeno forced herself to approach the reek of its breath, and snatched at the lightrifle. After a brief tussle her guard surrendered the gun.

''S better to kill 'em with jaws and claws.' Away he bounded.

The cuckoo-man was hopping through the snow, jabbing his trident like a solitary ski stick.

'*You*: take to the air. Fly as fast as you can.' Each word was a nugget of ice. 'Pull Anna from the bike before Kennan abandons his army.'

'Do it! This is spoken.' Spoken by a one-eyed lass.

The cuckoo-man's large yellow eyes surveyed her. Its cat-like ears twitched. Its beak clacked.

'This is bespoken,' she yelled. Aye, bespoken. She was the commander of this savage nakki-rabble, their proclaimer. They *must* obey her will. Her wish was clear now: not revenge but rescue.

'Let Minkie Kennan escape just so long as he escapes alone! Pass the word as you fly! Cry it out!' Her creatures mightn't care for this now that the ultimate bloodlust was possessing them. *They would, they must, obey her.*

'Give me your spear and fly.'

An arctic calm stole over her. For days and days the momentum of chase and carnage had been uppermost. Now she was mistress of herself.

'Give me your spear.'

'Harked and heard,' croaked the cuckoo-man. He tossed the trident lightly towards her. She caught it one-handed. Fluffing out his verdigris plumage, the scout began to bound clumsily across the snowfield, holding out his arms. His plumed membranes inflated. He rose, touched down, and rose again.

A harlequin hefting a crossbow escorted Eyeno as she waded onward, lightrifle in one hand, three-pronged spear in the other.

A Snowy lay slain. Bloodflowers seemed to blotch the snow. Had the bloodflower become the patron bloom of Eyeno's soul, as Paula's was a white soulflower and Inga's was the slender azure chimney-flower (her freckles merely so many sizzleflies upon the petals)?

The bloodflower, rather than the daisy?

What else could Eyeno have done? Allowed Minkie Kennan to continue imposing his will?

Could she wholly lay blame at his door? It was his activities which had been corrupting the moon-child. Yet the moon-child feasted on manias which that moon-child herself fostered.

Behind the crest of a low hill the waxen towers of the palace shone with a licking white unconsuming fire. Smuts and gases shimmered upward. Near that oven there would be no snow. In whatever tents or makeshift sheds nakkis had contrived, refugees would be warm.

Here in the sloping meadow where Eyeno had first opened her eye within the moon-child, the freeze almost hid the stream she had once waded through. Snow-capped bulges of smoothed ice buried brows and amorphous faces in a flow which was brisker in its confinement. Rows of glassy blue heads bowed. Hoarfrost haloed trees.

In the centre of the meadow red-clad Snowies blundered about, bumping into one another, stumbling and tripping and shrieking, 'Bu-bu-bu-*Boss*!'

Eyeno's beastmen and bandsmen formed a loose wide cordon. They were taking their time over slaughter – with a dart of fire, with a pulse of hot light, with a boomeranging sickle. Bodies fell and writhed. Bloodflowers bloomed all over the central arena of trampled wool. The slow massacre of the deranged and aimless nakkis was nauseating. Would the palace stop burning, and the snow thaw, when all of the Snowies were finally snuffed?

Eyeno felt numb and desolate.

Minkie Kennan had gone. He'd jumped away out of the moon-child with Anna still tied upon his bike.

Should Eyeno leap the icy stream? Rush pell-mell into the bowel of the moon-child? Force herself into the depths of the lake? Swim underwater? With lungs bursting, thrust upward to gasp for her life below those steep cliffs? All the while Anna's abductor would be jumping further and further away with ease! *It was useless.* How could she quit Paula and the other maids? Leave them in the care of this nakki-horde of butchers!

'Gingerwoman!' she screamed, her breath puffing out.

Amid the mêlée of Snowies, one halted and harked and stood tall. Through the cordon of killers he stared at Eyeno. His tiny strawberry face and white thatch were indistinguishable from any other Snowy's, though upon his chest he wore a black plume.

Nakki-brothers around him babbled. Their cry was faintly audible. 'Little-Boss, Little-Boss what du-du-du-do we DO?' One of his neighbours fell, blood welling from a light-sliced throat. Little Boss raised something. A crossbow?

Eyeno's troops had wearied of killing at a distance. A verrin-man broke from the cordon. Suddenly the whole circuit was rushing inward.

Eyeno tried to dodge . . . a *blur*. A sharp fist hit her in the face – deep in her empty eye-socket. Lightning-brilliance exploded into jagged darkness.

Agonized, she staggered backwards, skidding, falling. Sparks cascaded as her vision lurched. Visibility swam and flashed. Her fingers clutched at the fletching of the quarrel which had lodged in her eye socket.

In the snow she rolled from side to side. A phantom bloodflower stained the kaleidoscoping whiteness. A stiff spike of fire, a searing poker was piercing right through into the interior of her brain.

Was the shrieking she heard her own or that of Snowies being slaughtered?

'Pain, stop!' she cried with all her being. 'PAIN, GO AWAY!'

Screaming co-operated with pain. Outcry only magnified agony. Screaming wasted energy. Outcry was lack of control.

She must be really quiet to concentrate on defeating pain. Calm and quiet. Pain was fire, and pain was jagged.

'Pain, be cool,' she murmured. 'Pain, be smooth. Be calm, be quiet. Be still. This is whispered.'

Blessedly the torture was easing.

'Serene . . .' Grovelling in the snow, she clasped the dart, and pulled.

With surprising ease it slid free. Another bloodflower bloomed.

By the time the dart struck her it must already have lost much of its impetus. How accurately it had been aimed. As though its flight had been guided by more than a Snowy's marksmanship!

She packed snow into the vacant injured socket. She hauled herself to her knees. Her vision wavered. The remaining Snowies had disappeared under a scrimmage of beastmen and bandsmen. Chilly ichor leaked down her cheek. The fluid was pink on her fingertips. She scooped more snow.

'Blood, stop swiftly! Wound, heal fast.'

The numbness in half of her head . . .

Using the dropped lightrifle as crutch, she rose rockily. The harlequin capered up to her.

'Oh mistress!'

'Fetch me a knob of ice from the stream.'

He rushed away, and soon was back with a frozen ball. Shaking discoloured slush from her orbit, she substituted the eyeball of ice. Harlequin by her side, she slid and swayed towards the trampled bloodied arena. A reek of shit assailed her nostrils. Snowies had voided their bowels in their breeches. The dead smelled as if they were already decomposing.

'Stop this!' she called out. 'It's finished. It's over.'

She stared from the carnage around the wintry wasteland. The towers of the candle-palace were still wreathed in white fire. With smoke still rising, would the sun brighten? Would a thaw begin? Would flowers bloom? Would trees reappear in their previous abundance?

Tears of meltwater oozed from her socket. The ball of ice slithered. A chilly lozenge would fall out soon enough.

'Nakkis,' she called, 'we need to rebuild the village.'

In the village Inga could nurse her. Inga would run to her, prattling thanks for salvation. Eyeno would reply, 'But I failed. He took Anna . . .'

She couldn't allow herself to be nursed. Not while the palace still burned. She must understand the beacon which Minkie Kennan's dreamkeep had become. It was eerie as could be, yet in another regard the spectacle was almost beautiful. Radiant, at any rate. From this abattoir of a meadow she glimpsed with her bruised inward eye an awful beauty. Ice was her lens.

Minkie had jumped and jumped with his hostage. At first, the early autumn hue of trees astonished him. Leaves were a palette of yellow or orange or scarlet amidst evergreen veras and hoary sylvesters. So many unfrozen lakes large and little! Fewer lakes, presently . . . Each time they emerged from the in-between Anna cried out as if the conclusion of each jump was a gulp of air to a drowning person.

Minkie halted in a mossy dell. Boulders of granite were pink islands amid the soft verdance. A crowd of tall sharp-needled veras hemmed the dingle with crueller greenery. Sunshine dappled through boughs.

The wonder of leaping from winter to warmth – an autumnal

warmth! – begged the question of how much time had passed while he was in the hidey-hole. That sudden freeze might have corresponded to Eyeno Nurmi's *frigidity*. Though if space in the hidey-hole could shrink yet everything seem to remain of the same proportions, why time might tick at what pace it chose . . .

Time's what you make it, me lad, he thought to himself. *Or what something makes of it!*

When had he jumped into the domain under Loom Lake? End of May? Now the tinting foliage declared early September. The teasing zest of the air was redolent of restlessness, of final piquant maudlin opportunities, of delicious tantalizing melancholy. Had he really spent over four months? First at play, and then at war . . . Time had sped by.

Anna was pallid. The peaches of her cheeks had lost their bloom. Did our Minkie spy streaks of grey in her coaly curls? He was quite shocked by the change. Caused, of course, by the shocks she'd endured. The difference in her appearance was disconcerting.

When he dismounted to inspect her more closely, Anna flinched. Soft mossy *bed*: was that what she imagined? Her fur coat and boots must be sweltery. He loosened his own brass-studded leathers with the huge lapels and cuffs. Taking off his leather helmet, letting his chestnut curls breathe, he stuffed the headgear into a pannier.

'My head aches. I feel sick,' complained Anna. Her breath smelled fusty.

'You're just too hot,' Minkie explained charmingly. 'It's the change of climate.' He reached to unbutton her fur coat. She whimpered.

'I'll only loosen it for you, dear hen.' He could hardly peel her coat right off while her hands were tethered to the bike. A suckerfly wobbled by, trailing a thready tube, its feathery antennae quivering. Insects might need swatting. He oughtn't to free her hands.

She could use a pouch of pot-pourri. Then she might smell fresher. Undoing her coat, he exposed her beggar's gown which had once looked so exquisite. The ribbons were tatty grimy worms now.

'To let some air in, eh?'

Off came her boots, which the freeze had required him to give her. She wouldn't be able to run away so easily, should the occasion arise.

'My Gunther will punish you terribly,' she whispered hoarsely.

'He'll reward me, if he's awake when we get to his keep. If he isn't, well, we'll see.'

'Castlebeck . . .' she muttered. *So long, so very long ago.*

'Fair way south of Landfall, hmm? Fancy a drink of water? Bite to eat? I'll feed you.'

'I feel sick.'

Pressure in Minkie's bladder reminded him of other necessities.

'By the way, dear girl, do you need a pee? Long thong in the pannier. Tether your wrist. Promise not to peep.' Not that he hadn't seen and explored her delights a while ago! The fresh glow had utterly gone from her skin.

'Don't touch me—'

'You don't want to burst yourself and wet the seat.'

'I don't care. I don't feel normal.'

'You aren't, dear chick. You're an echo I've brought back from the dead, for your Gunther.'

'I'm not a chick. I feel awfully old. My skull aches. There's a hole in it.' She drooled, and rubbed her mouth upon her shoulder.

'Nonsense.' He rummaged deftly in her curls. 'There's no hole in your head at all.' Some hairs came loose on his fingers. 'Well, *I'm* for a pee.' Sweatsippers were settling on her hands. He slapped them away and went to relieve himself with a fine strong amber jet upon a bed of moss.

When he returned, he refrained from consulting his passenger before they jumped onward.

A village! He hadn't expected to emerge right in the heart of a village. Shingled log houses and barns lined a thoroughfare of rutted dirt. Silver-spangled hens scattered from his wheels. Spitzhounds barked. A long lean dun pig uttered a squeal, and lumbered. A light shower of rain was falling.

A whole mob of people were out in the gentle rain. Peaked caps and pipes, headscarves and shawls. Raggy urchins crowded the back of a cart. Always good to have kids present to keep people's tempers under control. This wasn't much of a village – though it would amount to quite a farm. Nor was it too much of a mob, but Minkie clutched the red handlebar in case it was necessary to make an *impression*.

He'd come a long way back to habitation. After the débâcle in his hidey-hole and so much jumping he was frazzled. Otherwise he might have promptly jumped onward. Bound to be some decent grub in this farm village, though ...

Faces had turned to gawp.

A shout riveted him: *'It's come from the war!'*

From the war? The war? What could these rustics know about the war he'd just lost to the one-eyed poetess?

'It's one of them jump-bikes from the war!'

Gestures, and babble. Minkie's initial disorientation had made him miss the original focus of this mob – namely a cuckoo perched upon a gable end ...

'Help me,' Anna called weakly.

'Shut up.' Turning, he smacked her tied hand, dislodging some gnats which had settled. Those were carrion-gnats, weren't they?

That gossip-bird must have been cackling. Now it had fallen silent. Ears cocked, it peered attentively. How could it know anything about events in the domain underneath Loom Lake?

'Aye, it's one of them jump-bikes.'

One of those jump-bikes? One? There had only ever been a single such machine, namely Minkie's own.

'Help me—' Such a whimper.

'Will you shut up, you daft duck? Stop quacking.' More gnats had settled on Anna's wrist. Quivering, the insects paddled their minuscule feet as though her skin were a pool of slime. She spat at the gnats. Her sputum was a greenish-yellow hue.

'Hey,' he called at a rut-faced farmer whose hair splayed like flaps from under his cap, 'what war is the birdy talking about?'

Predictably the locals' attitude to the black war-bike and its leather-clad rider was apprehensive. Glances at the pillion passenger were shifty as could be.

'Come on, tell me!'

'Why,' said the farmer, "tis the war between the Queen and the rebel Queen. Between Lucky, bless her wild whims, and Prince van Maanen and his Minnow.'

The man pulled off his cap and wrung it in his hands. 'How can fighting be flooding this far, sir?'

A war between Lucky and *Prince* van Maanen? A rebel Queen – who certainly *wasn't* Paula! Whatever had been happening?

Kids had scrambled from the cart and were goggling at his bike as avidly as was the gossip-bird on the gable end.

'I'm a scout,' announced Minkie.

'For which side, sir?'

'Don't ask!'

'No, sir.'

'Help me,' quavered Anna.

'As you see, I have a prisoner.'

'Aye, we *see*.' A Spitz advanced, barking at the bike. A fellow in coarse shirt and knickerbockers kicked the hound in the ribs to scuttle it.

'Tell me more about what yon cuckoo's been saying. I need to know what sort of news is spreading. That's why I'm here. I can be anywhere else *instantly*.'

This remark provoked several wives to splay their palms in Minkie's direction, warding off wizardry.

'Why,' recited the spokesman, 'Lord van Maanen the proclaimer carried off Minnow Sariola and wed her and crowned her Queen and himself as Prince. And then he seized the haitch-house, whatever that is. So Lucky attacked this haitch-house by air and bombed and burnt half of it. She has *wooden soldiers* too. We hear tell as van Maanen has loads of missiles the Snakes has given him. No one knows who's going to win, whether Lucky, bless her whims, or the wee new Queen. She tamed a monster mutant mage, which must be why the Snakes is helping her—'

The present moment might *not*, after all, have been opportune for using Paula to flummox Lucky. By the sounds of it, Lucky was already sufficiently distracted to have no time to spare for Minkie. This didn't mean that he could waltz back home to Niemi and carry on as usual. Back to Niemi with Anna as his passenger? (He'd need to dump her first.) Back to Kiki-likki and a bawling bairn?

If Lucky lost the war, well and good. If she won, she might feel *really* vengeful.

Onward to Castlebeck, then? To apply appropriate pressure, or maybe a knife to the dozing dreamlord?

Anna coughed and hawked. Not at all the lass he'd bedded in his lovely lost palace.

Wives made more hex signs.

'*She be zombie—*'

> '*Dead and alive!*'

No, this couldn't be true. Swinging round again, Minkie gaped. Mana, the reek of her breath. Her ashen face.

'You *are* becoming . . . zombie,' he muttered, confounded.

No denying it. He'd been blind.

To be riding in tandem with a living corpse! To take a living corpse with him to Castlebeck!

'Why didn't you just *evaporate* the moment we jumped out of nakki-land?' he asked her bitterly. 'Why, why?'

Anna struggled with words, or with concepts. 'My Gunther keeps part of my skull next to his heart . . .'

'Does he indeed?'

Best laid plans. No use at all. *Where could Minkie go to on his own where no one would dream of looking for him?*

Why, he knew!

Up near the Velvet Isi nest where he used to hunt Jutties . . . in no-man's, and no-alien's, land!

A crazy shaman who hung weights on himself kept a well-stocked hut. Rob that hut. Set up camp deep in the forest of the mana-mists. Our Minkie knew his way about. Jutties had never trapped him before. Now he had this bike. *Who would think of looking in no one's land?* Almost as safe as his hidey-hole, give or take patrols of Unmen.

Anna's condition might be contagious. Fastidiously, with fingertips, he unpicked her bonds.

'Get off the bike. I'm setting you free.'

'Free—?'

Carrion-gnats circling her. What could a fellow-me-lad do? There were limits to a chap's charm and charity.

'Afraid our ways will have to part, sick hen. Hobble home to your keep. Folks will treat you as taboo. They oughtn't to molest you.

'Do you hear me, yokels?' he shouted out. 'This lass is taboo. I can come back here instantly.'

To raise her morale he whispered: 'Your Gunther can dream where you are. If he wakes up sharpish he can meet you mid-way.'

Anna dismounted clumsily in fur coat and tatty gown. Her bare feet were grey as if coated with dust. A few suppurations showed, looking healthier – pinker – than the rest of her. The change was happening so rapidly. Maybe she couldn't merely evaporate at once but must wither and rot and dissolve. Maybe she wasn't a real zombie and would never reach her destination. Maybe her mind would crumble, so that she mightn't be aware of her predicament.

Anna spread gaunt hands. 'How can Gunther ever see me like this?'

'Don't dreams lend enchantment?' Minkie asked gallantly. 'It's the soul that counts.' He did feel like a bit of a shit. What was a fellow to do?' 'I'm sorry I tossed your boots away, but they might have chafed.'

He swung the bike to point northward.

'Where are you going to, Minkie Kennan?' Ach, in her morbidity she'd become dependent on him at long last.

Enough of this. With villagers agog, and a damn cuckoo harking, he was hardly going to answer her.

Twist blue.

Bike and rider had vanished. A Spitz howled. The cuckoo shrieked, 'Ukko-ukkoo.' Soft rain sifted down.

And a ring of villagers surrounded this ancient decaying zombie lass.

'She ain't no everyday zombie!' These villagers knew about zombies. Cuckoos tattled, and tales spread, of unlucky descendants of longlife lords. Especially they knew that the sickness should not come over a person so suddenly. The process of decay should take a certain while, succeeded by a morbid stability.

Aproned grannies in long woollen skirts yoiked spells.

'*Hexy-pixie—!*'

　　　　'*Cacky-nakki—!*'

　　　　　　　'*Perkelly-circlely—!*'

Anna shed the burden of her fur coat and beseeched the showery sky, 'Eyeno, take me back to—'

To where, to what?

'*Where's she belong—?*'

'*Perched on the sky-sickle—!*'

'*Else we'll all be reaped—!*'

'*Soldier-fellow said he'd come back—*'

'*He won't, though—*'

'*We'll have to wear shavings of hervy hoof for a month and a day—*'

'First catch your hervy!' A fat little bald man in hip-length tunic and wide circumference of belt stomped to the fore, barefoot as Anna herself. His feet were huge, the toes resembling sausages, their horny yellow nails like the backs of crustacea. A touch of the mutie . . . However, the village hadn't cast him out.

'*Stumpy—!*'

　　　　'*Stumpy the Ecstatic—!*'

　　　　　　　'*What do we do, Stumpy—?*'

305

The bald man rolled his eyes. He flared his nostrils. He crossed himself.

'I smell burning. We shall wear little red boots in heaven. *Lovely* little red boots. Every one of us.' He danced, he stamped.

The crowd swayed.

Stumpy addressed Anna:

'Dead sister, you've come looking for your little red boots! But we'll each wear them one day. Why, you're as greasy as a candle. Ain't she so?' He rolled an eye at the patchy clouds. Lake of blue in the sky to the west, another to the north.

'Spot of rain's nothing. She'll wear little red boots. She'll dance a bit. We won't need no hervy horn, so no one needs be gored getting it. Bring ropes. Bring a pole. Bring a chopper to sharpen the end of the pole so it'll stand up nice and straight. Bring good dry straw. Bring oil.'

Some villagers hurried away. Others hemmed Anna in.

'You'll wear little red boots in heaven,' Stumpy promised her. 'I shall too, on the day when all days are ended, when the clock chimes backwards, twelve, eleven.'

Cully lurched from chalky trunk of sylvester tree to stout horzma. His long blond hair scythed to and fro. A harp chord twanged in his head. He tumbled into a mustaberry thicket. Scratching his hands bloody and staining them with magenta juice, he grabbed berries and crammed his mouth. His hair caught on thorns.

He'd eaten the last of the cheese . . . yesterday? How had he come by cheeses in a forest? Oh yes, from that nakki-maid who pretended to be Olga. He remembered gnawing the cheese with gob a-gape. He hadn't wanted to cut off slices by using the knife stuck in his belt. Too much like slicing through skin and flesh. The cheese had tasted like stiffened sweat.

Sweatsippers and sizzleflies attended him.

He must be somewhere near the farm of his boyhood. Near Olga and Helga. No, Helga was wed.

Near Mum.

The dreamlord *raped* Marietta then he cast her out of his keep when she was pregnant with Cully. No, it never happened that way at all!

The dreamlord *seduced* Marietta . . . No, not at all. Gunther took comfort with her. Marietta took comfort with Gunther. Her Cal had been killed by Jutties. They'd killed Cully's dad. Cully was a young man. He didn't mind his mother and his uncle — their patron — making a little love. Or did he, deep down, where only the twang of a harp could reach?

The dreamlord had *forsaken* Marietta. Disowned and rejected her. No he hadn't. Uncle Gunther simply felt guilty. Marietta harboured no hard feelings. Gunther's embrace had been largesse in her life, a little windfall.

Cully didn't resent this.

Yes he did.

Deeply.

Bitterly.

Homicidally.

The bad uncle had tried to kill him when he was just a bairn. Oh the harping in his head, harping on about revenge . . .

Cully's hands were stained scarlet. The hilt of the knife pressed against the top of his hip like a hard manhood. How to satisfy it but by a plunge? If Gunther were dead there'd be no more doubts, no dispute.

Except from Mum and Olga . . . He mustn't see them. He mustn't stray towards them. Rape a nakki in the woods. Olga would know about the nakki because they both shared the same name.

Cully eyed the glade. No marks were blazed on bark. No red-painted handprints pointed the way. Yet in his heart he knew that he was nearing Castlebeck. Sizzleflies zizzed the message: *ziss sway, ziss sway.* Soon there'd be blessed clarity and simplicity.

20 · THE DREAMLORD WAKES

From the air, Castlebeck was a six-limbed star of low granite salients enclosing a {*Baroque cathedral*} built of yellow bricks. The central edifice was {*very similar to the mana-temple in Tumio, in fact, Roger*}. Wex had never been near the seaport with its bishop's palace and its Pootaran quarter of sailors' hostelries and warehouses and emporiums. However, he and his wetwear had scanned photographs and artists' impressions galore.

'If I was a Pootaran I think I'd prefer to dock at Portti,' he said aloud.

Six hundred keys west of Tumio, that other port was at the southerly limit of the forest lord, Tapper Kippan's, domain. Portti wasn't directly on the coast but lay at the head of a steep-cliffed fjord {*the Porttivuono being a geological oddity resulting from an ancient extinct volcano being gouged by an ancient glacier*}. Deep water behind the shallow mouth of the fjord offered fine shelter from storms {*not that either Tumio or Portti are navigable in deep winter when the sea freezes over*}. However, there were certain problems about transshipment inland from Portti (whereas the broad river Mantijoki flowed on down into Tumio Bay). Thus many rationalist seamen, docking at Tumio, were obliged to tolerate proximity to the mana-temple and priests and novices. Black sailors had their wooden puzzles to distract them from mystification and mania.

Mathavan Gurrukal cleared his throat. 'Would your preference for Portti be due to Momma Rakasta's famous brothel there, of which one hears tell?'

'Certainly not! What are you thinking of?'

'I was wondering the same about you,' said the pilot, whose shorn locks now formed the Earth agent's new and lustrous black wig. His soft gentle voice continued: 'Whatever are you thinking of indeed, Mr Wex? Here we are circling this castle in the countryside. You imagine that you are a sailor from overseas. What, I am asking myself, is the chain of associations? Is it that a Pootaran sailor sewed your wig, and you wonder what appearance you will present when we land?

'Oh, but wait. Maybe you're alluding to the architecture down below? In the style, I believe, of the famous mana-temple in Tumio?'

Gurrukal was certainly doing his best to understand Wex-in-league-with-wetwear.

'Not that I've seen Tumio with my own eyes,' Gurrukal added.

Framed in the bulge of the cockpit hood, the keep rose from a balustraded terrace which was cut into by a wide flight of steps. At each corner of the building a stout bastion towered up, sporting an onion dome {*of callipygian dimension and rotundity*} like a buttock presented to the sky {*much more so than like a glans*}. The drum of a dome ascended from the main heap. Upon the dome a squat colonnaded tower supported an upper dome of bulbous rotundity. Undergrowth, and even mature trees, choked much of the area between the salients and the base of the terrace. Patchy efforts had obviously been made in the recent past at clearing the rampant vegetation. Bushes had colonized the terrace itself, taking root in cracks. Lord Beck had hardly kept his abode in prime repair or in readiness for defence. Perhaps down on the ground the effect was charming: a wild garden.

Gurrukal was steering the dovecraft around in a wide slow circle. By now they were over Lake Matijarvi, noted for its luckyfish and sweetfins. Fishing smacks drifted, dozens of lines dangling threadlike in the water which was dappled by shadows of puffball clouds. A couple of keys to the south the houses of the small town were wee loaves crusted with tiles as orange and gingery as the roe from the local catch. Low wooded hills paralleling the Matijarvi were aflush with similar colours. The lake lapped in between two of the castle salients. A jetty led to a gate; the gate, to a path through the tangle. On the landward side they had sighted another gate. Both of those gates were closed. Trees grew so close to the outside of the perimeter that anyone agile could scale a wall.

'Another thing, Mr Wex! You're a bit clumsy.'

Wex's new green gaberdine cloak of many pockets lay over the back of the seat to which he was belted. Loose sleeves of a new purple shirt had ridden up his forearm, revealing a mauve bruise. Gurrukal, never maladroit in his movements, had noted the bruise – and other clues – with those acute brown eyes of his.

'Shall I tell you why that is, Mathavan?'

Should Wex tell him why? Should it remain a secret that Wex experienced no bodily sensation whatsoever, and couldn't possibly be hurt unless his other self relaxed control? (And if so, he would immediately be incapacitated by agony!)

'Please do explain, before we step into an unknown situation.'

Wex should keep this exasperating hateful peculiarity up his sleeve. To be a numb carcass who needed to *think* about each move he made as if steering himself by remote control! To be a rubber capon bereft of touch and smell and taste! {*I am assisting in locomotion. You will not fall down.*}

The need to confide – the need for human compassion – welled in him. {*You confide in me, and I sympathize*}. His wetwear was the cause. {*No, the remedy, the protection, the prophylaxis*}. To tell him thrice seemed excessive.

'Mathavan, my nervous system is switched off. I can see and I can hear but I can't feel a thing! If my other self didn't massage me isometrically I'd succumb to gangrene—'

Wex's woes spilled from him as the olive-clad pilot continued to circle around Castlebeck.

'Oh dear me,' said Gurrukal. 'Poor Mr Wex. Let me think, let me think ... Mr Wex, we masseurs know that touch and pain travel through two separate channels in the spinal column on their way to the brain—'

Could touch be distinct from pain? Had his other self been fooling him?

'If I were to tread your spine with my bare feet—'

{*The pain is in the brain, Roger. Isn't it urgent that we search for Cully?*} Yes, yes, of course.

'My insteps itch to help you, Mr Wex.'

{*Cully, Roger!*}

'It doesn't matter; forget it.'

'Doesn't matter? *Forget it?*' Wex's seeming brusqueness had touched a sensitive nerve. 'Don't you wish the soles of my feet upon your skin? I'd be sure to wear fine silk stockings for you if we had any on board. Such are sadly lacking. Maybe I could set up a profitable business selling such stockings to ladies instead of their woollen socks!'

Why was Wex's mouth hanging open? {*Because your nostrils are blocked*}. He tugged black silk from an inner pocket. He had to look at his fingers to guide them. Noisily he blew his nose.

'Now you put snot upon silk!'

'Please don't be sensitive, Mr Gurrukal. I didn't intend to insult you.'

'I'm the soul of composure. I'm not sensitive. Gracious me, what am I saying when you suffer such a dearth of sensation! It is I who owe you an apology. And admiration for your stoicism. No wonder you wanted to wear my hair. Would somebody who insisted on having my hair tickling their brow and nape—'

'*Your hair doesn't tickle.*'

'No, of course not. What am I saying? Would such a person scorn being trodden on by me? Oh no, I'm telling myself. A follower of the kalaripayit path doesn't take offence, however much he is provoked.'

How garrulous the fellow had become. On the brink of losing his prolonged geographical virginity (as it were), was he nervous? Had a mana-bee entered his bonnet, hairless and hatless though he was?

'Oh, selling decadent silk stockings to ladies might be a smart idea. Yet really I do not think I will choose to settle here when my term of duty is up. What, to go to the stars – to one star at least – and not be able to tell to my fellow peasant villagers about my elite

310

adventures? Few of which have I had before meeting you, Mr Wex! Your condition grieves me. For your information I'm smelling of caraway at the moment. I was chewing seeds earlier.'

Wex sighed. 'We'd better land. Can you set us down on that terrace?'

'It looks broad enough.' The pilot assessed the pompon clouds above, then the foliage below. 'Gentle breeze, estimated force three. There shouldn't be any gusts from round corners, though such buildings are real spindles for flurries . . .'

The retainer who received the two visitors, Pasquil by name, was pleased to hear that they had come from the Earthkeep. He was particularly glad to learn that Mathavan Gurrukal was a medic.

'I'm sure Lord Beck needs help. He seems in distress. He shakes in his sleep. He's suffered an injury I can't explain! And a robbery too!'

'An injury?' asked Wex. 'What kind of robbery? Is Cully here yet?'

'If only Master Cully *was* . . . ! No, I haven't seen him, not in a twelvemonths and more, quite a bit more.'

Pasquil was elderly and gaunt. His grey hair was tied with a black ribbon in a short queue. The muscles of his face and neck stood out as if permanently tensed, perhaps because he held himself straight as a rod. Black leather braces held up black breeches, and his shirt was a starched white. His eyes bulged pronouncedly.

'Could Cully possibly be here without you knowing?'

'Invisibly, do you mean? He'd be eager to help out, not hide himself.'

'I take it you haven't heard any gossip about events at Loxmithlinna!'

Gossip?

The Master was sleeping; not to be disturbed. This was the great project of the dream-meister's life. Castlebeck was under a hush. The staff had stocked the larders and chained the gates prior to their master's aestivation. Why should any cuckoo call at snoozy Castlebeck?

Staff? Why, that consisted of old Pasquil, and Bertha the cook, and handyman Martin and his nephew Young Martin.

'The Master needs help, sirs. I'm sure of it—'

Pasquil led the pair along a gloomy hallway to a grand but dim stairway. Windows were filthy. Difficult to tell whether some

311

panes were cracked or merely cobwebbed. Wex trod carefully. Gurrukal strutted, heels high, one hand on the tammy baton stuck through his belt.

Marble statues of women flanked the base of the stairs. Threadbare smocks draped their nude white limbs. Clothbugs must have enjoyed a nibble for a century or two. Darkly varnished portraits mounted the walls.

Pasquil pointed as they climbed.

'Those two were Lord Beck's daughters by Lady Anna. Dead of old age long before I was born . . . Yon's Lord Beck's father up there. The Sensualist.' Hard to make *him* out.

On the first landing stood another voluptuous nude modestly shrouded in rags.

'So it was Gunther Beck's father who acquired these statues?' asked Gurrukal.

'The Master draped them before I was born, to avoid temptation. Lord Beck is uxorious in the extreme. His devotion to his dead wife knows no bounds.' If Pasquil knew of an exception, he was not about to mention it to strangers.

Carved along the plinth below the nude was a maxim. Wex blew dust away and read aloud:

> Desire wills its own perpetuation, for ever.
>
> S. Sunnuntai

'Could well be your own master's motto too! I wonder if he knows what it says?'

'Lord Beck could read,' said Pasquil, 'but he stopped for the sake of dreams.'

'What's this injury?'

'You will see—'

In a curtained upper chamber a stout flush-faced woman of middle age sat on the edge of a high four-poster bed, her laced bootees dangling. She favoured the bed as perch rather than a more comfy brocaded couch since the bed elevated her enough to peer over the lip of the padded casket wherein lay the naked figure of Lord Beck.

312

Beside the casket was an actual open coffin of tammywood set on low trestles . . .

One did not look immediately at the contraption accommodating the dreamlord, but at that adjacent purple box which housed . . . a human skeleton. Then one quickly looked away – along a cable, one end of which was coupled to the breastbone of that skeleton. The other clamp lay loose upon Gunther Beck's chest.

An oil-lamp burned on a tripod table. Its glow was reflected in an oval mirror lying by the lamp. Light seemed to radiate as much from the mirror as from the lamp, softly pervading the whole shrouded room.

The woman on the bed wore a baggy grey gown. Her dark hair was tied back in a great bun, transfixed by an enormous hairpin of polished yellow hervy horn like a sharp-pronged meat skewer. Keys dangled from her belt. The backs of her hands were tattooed with little blue ladles looking like eternity signs. The upper reaches of her neck were adorned with miniature jugs as if hanging by their handles from her earlobes. On her breast was a horn brooch, of the Queen in silhouette.

'Bertha, it's help,' said Pasquil. 'Just what you prayed for. They're from Landfall, from the Earthkeep.'

Bertha touched the amulet above her heart. 'Saint Lucky be praised.' She kicked her bootees to and fro in exhilaration.

'The Master made us swear not to interrupt,' Pasquil told Wex and Gurrukal. 'But look at him!'

Stretched out naked amidst tubing and dials and a calendar-clock and powercells of alien design lay Beck. Wires were taped to his throat and arms. A springloaded syringe containing yellow juice poised over his thigh. Violet threads marked where skin had expanded then shrunk. The dream savant was so haggard and jaundiced. His cock and nuts were an ugly grey froggy creature such as belonged in a pond. His nipples were torn, the flesh ripped loose. His frame was trembling. Occasionally a spasm intensified the tremor. His eyelids would twitch epileptically.

Pasquil pointed at the split nipples.

'There's the injury, and there's the theft. He wore rings through each nipple. On the chain between was the locket with a piece of Lady Anna's skull in it. That cable was clamped to the locket. As you can see, silver locket and chain and rings have gone! They've been stolen. Not by me. Not by Bertha. Nor, I'll swear, by Martin nor Young Martin. Could a robberbird have hopped in here and pecked the Master's nipples in its greed?'

313

Bertha slid from the bed with a substantial thump. Cautiously she picked up the luminous misty mirror from under the lamp.

'I've been trying to see into his dreams, the way he sometimes used to see into other people's dreams. To see what is so terrible that he twitches so . . .' Uselessly she laid the mirror down again.

'I told you, you need a shaman for that,' insisted Pasquil.

Bertha shook her head. 'Should a stranger pry into the Master's private reveries? And Taiku Setala is dead of premature old age.'

Pasquil indicated the calendar-clock. 'The Master's appointed time is due in just a few more days. Dare we wait? He's dying.'

Dried jade strands of healervine wreathed the lip of the casket and also the canopy of the four-poster bed. Despite the dust of particles released by the split and shrivelled pods, the chamber smelled of sweet fusty mortification mingled with the ammoniacal tang of a latrine – as Gurrukal obligingly whispered to Wex.

Bertha's hand strayed to the brooch of Lucky.

'He made us swear, but our prayers are answered now. Be responsible for waking him, good sirs, and I'll cook you such a fine succulent feast of lamb. The stimulant is in the syringe.'

Gurrukal ejected a droplet on to a fingertip, and sniffed, then wrinkled his nose.

'This fluid has fermented. It would cause a thrombosis to someone so enfeebled!'

Wex and his wetwear examined the dials and wires and powercells and tubes. {*We can easily disconnect him. Though as the guru says*—}

'Forget about feasts for the time being, Mistress Bertha,' said Gurrukal. 'My colleague's no gourmet. What your master needs is some warm weak broth. By which I mean *thin*, and *tepid*. If we free him from all these wires and tubes we can push the casket closer to the bed. I shall hang from the canopy and massage him with my feet to wake him. I shall squeeze his organs gently.'

Bertha reached for the sharp bone pin which pierced her bun. 'Whatever are you saying!'

'I am talking, dear lady, about massage techniques. Open the curtains, and a window too, and snuff the lamp. The air's foetid in here. Fear no robberbird.'

Rubbed back to consciousness, Gunther Beck lay under a blanket upon the faded tapestry coverlet of the bed. Supported by soft satin pillows, he had thirstily sipped broth from a spoon which Bertha held to his lips.

More broth, more.

No, he mustn't. Not yet. He might vomit at the unaccustomed surfeit after months of starvation.

Sweet melancholy air wafted in through the yellow brick embrasure. Sunlight revealed the carvings on the massive headboard and on the columns and on the cornice of ambery harperwood. Birds in flight (soarfowl and harnies and long-necked hikerbirds trailing thin legs behind them) alternated with winged sprites. The faces of the sprites were childlike. Their eyes were shut tight. They were airborne dreaming souls.

Who were these green-clad strangers here in his chamber? One lithe and brown and as bald as a stone, sporting a dapper moustache. The other of prim aspect, though his locks were lustrous.

Why, they were from the Earthkeep! They had saved him with science and sensible advice and foot massage. The jolt-juice would have burst his blood vessels.

Gunther was weak as water, but his need to communicate was urgent, even though his throat was a husk. He rasped about a secret domain of echoes and nakkis where he had found his Anna. *He had found his Anna.* At first she hadn't known him. But later, later she knew him.

She was being seduced by a rogue name of Minkie. *That* was when he first knew him, while the scoundrel was busy knowing her. She had known him, and *yearned*. Yet he was light as a feather. Then a war had begun. Kennan's palace blazed. Snow fell. Eyeno Nurmi – she was the poetess whom van Maanen had sentenced to death – she led monsters against Kennan. Kennan's Snowie soldiers carried off Anna and blonde Paula Sariola on their shoulders while the lecher rode a black bike which jumped. And Gunther had bathed with the Gingerbread Woman in the pool of dreams . . .

'Oh Master,' breathed Bertha. 'Bless Lucky for letting you meet your Lady.'

Pasquil was gripping his leather braces to hold himself the more upright in this heartfelt and soul-searing moment, climax to Lord Beck's devotion.

He and Bertha both stole glances towards a row of oil portraits backed by thready tapestry. One was of a young woman of full oval face, with sultry eyes and inky curls. The next, of the same woman in middle age. The third portrayal was elderly, grey-haired and wrinkled. Yet still the same verve smouldered in her eyes.

'. . . actually *touched* my Anna, *held her*.' Gunther's voice was a creak of rusty hinges. 'That vile wretch Kennan jumped with her out of the dream-domain. Into this world of ours! Somewhere . . .'

A little more broth. Definitely a little more.

'Such vivid dreams,' whispered Gurrukal to Wex. 'Goodness, wars and burning palaces and giant gingerbread women. Monsters too; and the dead brought back to life. After so long he can't distinguish between dreams and what's genuine.'

Gunther struggled to shift himself. 'I must go and find Anna. She must be somewhere. Trying to survive.' He could only wallow feebly under the blanket.

('How appalling that Lady Anna was being seduced . . .')

('Innocently seduced! We shan't speak of this, Pasquil.')

'You must find her,' the dreamlord pleaded. 'Rescue her,' he gasped. 'And tidy the keep for a homecoming.'

'What a gloomy mess this place is,' murmured Gurrukal. 'He can hardly have expected that his wife would truly come back here from the dead. And now he does! What potent dreams.'

Pasquil bent over the prostrate invalid. 'But where *is* Lady Anna, my Lord? And where is this Kennan?'

'I don't know.'

'Your sky-boat can search for Lady Anna,' Pasquil said to the pilot.

'Search where, my dear sir, for the inhabitant of a dream?'

'Lord Beck,' interrupted Wex, 'did you know this Minkie Kennan *before* you went to sleep?' {*A very germane question.*}

Gunther stared hauntedly at Earth's agent.

'I know him now,' he growled.

'Are you aware that Kennan murdered Prince Bertel?'

Gunther tried to raise himself, without success. '*Bertie* . . . ? Bertie's been murdered . . . ?'

{*Kennan fled on a jump-bike to hide himself somewhere. Beck saw the jump-bike in this dream-domain. How could he have encountered a jump-bike before? Gunther Beck must really have dreamed his way into the Ukko-child. Kennan was there; and now he has quit the Ukko-child after losing those battles. Kennan brought some* echo *of Anna Beck out of the Ukko-child along with him too — unless the dreamlord's mistaken! Maybe the monsters are fantasies, but the main gist is true. Kennan knows where the Ukko-child is. So does this* echo *person, Anna. Beck has encountered the* echo *of Paula Sariola. Where's Kennan now? Where's the Anna* echo*? Am I, in a sense, your* echo*?*}

'These aren't just dreams,' Wex assured Gurrukal.

316

The pilot blinked in surprise.

Wex muttered to him: 'My wetwear is convinced, and so am I. If only we can locate Kennan and Anna Beck! She'd probably be a more honest informant than Kennan.'

Gurrukal muttered, 'I thought we were to search for Lord Beck's nephew, not for a dead dream. That was the mission profile, Mr Wex. That was why you were loaned the dovecraft.'

'Cully! Yes. These people need to be warned about that nephew. Maybe you ought to stay here as a bodyguard . . . Which way shall I fly, damn it?'

Gurrukal rested his palm on his tammy fighting stick. 'I don't think we should change our objective in order to chase a ghost, Mr Wex.'

'Kennan, then. Kennan. Kennan. He *knows*. The Ukko-child is Pen Conway's special fascination.'

'She did not tell me anything about Ukko-children.'

'Mathavan, this is what Lucky's looking for! Her own echo. Radio to Pen Conway from the dovecraft. She'll tell you to do as I say.' Wex lurched. {*To do as we say*}, he repeated in a rolling fruity tone.

Warily the pilot backed away. 'I suppose it does no harm to make a radio call . . .'

{*It does do harm! The Isi can intercept the call. I forbid you to call Landfall.*} Wex's hands stiffened.

Gurrukal liberated his shiny baton. 'You may wear my hair, Mr Wex, but the Resident told me to keep an eye on you.'

'Why are you quarrelling?' asked Bertha. 'Don't fight in here. How dare you?' She plucked her long bone pin free and held it out as a deterrent. 'Do what the Master wants! Please!'

'Bertha, take care,' said Pasquil.

'Care of Lord Gunther is what counts.'

'Kennan, Kennan,' cackled a birdy voice. 'Hark to the story, hear the tale!'

A cuckoo had settled itself in the sunny embrasure. Attracted by a window newly open after months of closure and curtaining, and probably by the white dovecraft parked on the terrace, a gossip-bird had come.

Noticing Wex, the bird croaked in alarm.

'Aaaark! Aaaark! Cuckoo-killer!'

Bertha hid her pin back in her bun. The mottled green bird walked around in a circle, ruffling its plumes, flustered. Would it stay? Would it flee?

'Aaark!'

{Duck down out of sight, Roger. Don't let it see you}. Hastily Wex crouched behind the four-poster carved with all those birds.

'Tell your story, sing your tale,' Bertha begged. 'No one means a cuckoo harm.'

'Kennan,' rasped the dreamlord.

The bird seemed addled with shock. 'Ukko-ukkoo!' it cackled. 'Tell the tale about Minkie Kennan. *Aaark. Kaaaark.* Minkie Kennan rode a jump-bike into Kaukainkyla village. *Kaaark.* He left a lady there, with curly hair. *Aaaark.* He left.'

So did the cuckoo. In a flurry it flapped away.

'Coo-coo, come back!' Bertha cried in vain.

Gunther wriggled so feebly on the bed, yet his voice was raucous. 'Anna, my Anna, we're coming to fetch you—'

Wex stood up again. *{Kaukainkyla is a tiny village two hundred keys south-east of Niemi. There is another Kaukainkyla far west of Kip'an'keep. But the Kennan family hold Niemi as their seigniory}.* Therefore Minkie Kennan was heading homeward. *{Not necessarily. Lucky must be thirsting for his blood.}* Why had Kennan abandoned Anna Beck in Kaukainkyla? *{That, we shall discover when we collect her. It's vital that no one else reaches her first. Lord Beck and his retainers must keep her rescue a secret. She knows where the Ukko-child is. Maybe we should take Anna Beck to Landfall for safety?}*

'Listen to me,' said Wex, 'we're going to fly to Kaukainkyla south-east of Niemi immediately, keeping communicator silence—'

'Take me with you,' begged Gunther.

The notion was preposterous.

'I probably don't need any sleep for days.'

Oh, so he would be alert and vigorous, would he? Bright as a new brass button? Even Pasquil and Bertha were shaking their heads.

'You need building up,' said the cook. 'What will Lady Anna think of the way we've looked after you? Or how you've looked after yourself?'

'Can we discuss this privately outside?' the pilot asked Wex softly. Wex nodded.

'Secrecy is essential, Lord Beck. Pasquil. Do you understand? The Isi will be interested in Lady Anna's reappearance, and where she came from.'

'Cuckoos already know about it—'

'That's true, Mr Pasquil. But they don't know about our rescue

318

mission. {*This keep is practically undefended except by weeds.*} Don't you have any more guards you can call on?'

'There's Martin, and Young Martin.'

'How about watchmen from the town? Don't they owe allegiance? I have a warning for you. Beware of Cully if he comes. Don't let him anywhere near Lord Beck. He's been swayed by the Isi against his uncle. He's been trying to resist the sway but he's probably insane. If possible overpower him and lock him up.'

'Cully . . . ?' wheezed Gunther.

'It can't be true,' said Bertha.

'They woke the Master,' said Pasquil. 'They're going to fetch the mistress, whom . . .' He glanced uneasily at the coffin. 'Whom we've never met in the flesh. Why should they invent a slur on Cully?'

'Oh we could have used Cully's helping hands . . .'

'I'll tell you how helpful he is,' said Wex. 'Or rather, how unbalanced he's become. He put out the eye of Lady Loxmith.'

Shocked, Bertha adjusted her hairpin of hervy horn. 'I'll be sitting with the Master. No one will get past me.'

Bones lay in the coffin, a cable clipped to a sternum. Gunther Beck reclined on the bed, enfeebled. The smelly hibernation monitor was like some capsule returned from a unique voyage elsewhere and otherwhere, as though he had sailed in it away over the sky-sickle and back. This chamber cried out to be tidied. So did the whole keep. Would those raggy shrouds be stripped from the sensual statues to celebrate a passionate homecoming?

On the terrace beside the stubby-winged dovecraft, scarcely five minutes later, Wex and his wetwear were both urging Mathavan Gurrukal.

'The Ukko-child is the golden goal—'

'*So you must not use the radio—*'

'We don't want an argument—'

'*Not when we're master of tai-chi, aikido, and karate.*'

'I have the right to commandeer this craft. We mustn't waste time, Mathavan—'

The pilot ran a hand over his shaved skull.

'A golden goal, Mr Wex? And the Resident would approve . . . ?'

'Widen your horizons, Mathavan. You came all the way to the stars.'

'What if Cully comes here in the meantime?'

'He'll be overpowered.' By Bertha. By those Martins. Perhaps
by help from the town. 'He'll be disoriented and muddled.'

'The sky-boat has flown off,' Pasquil told his slumped lord. He
left the embrasure and approached the coffin. 'Shall Martin and
Young Martin take your lady's relics back down to the crypt?'

'Yes . . . Her relics . . . She mustn't see those. How soon will
the Earthfolk be back with Anna? How fast was their dovecraft
flying?'

'Fast as a crossbow quarrel. Faster.'

'Ah,' sighed Gunther. 'When Anna and I had been wedded five
years we went hunting together where the Matijarvi bulges most.
Where did we not go together, she and I . . . ?'

A flurry of plumes. The cuckoo was back on the window ledge.
Warily its yellow eyes scanned the chamber.

Satisfied that the only occupants were Gunther and Pasquil
and the cook, the bird announced, 'Ukko-ukkoo, hark and hear.'

It cackled to itself then continued:

'Minkie Kennan left a lady there with curly hair. For she was
becoming a living corpse . . .'

21 · A Birthday Party for the Maids of Horror

Lucky had moved into the armoured suite in the south wing of
the ravaged aitch-house where Elmer Loxmith had roosted until
he fled by night. She had all the silks stripped from the walls to
expose the cast-iron panelling. Those silks became sheets for
June and Jatta and the others. The Queen would pace the bedchamber and the adjacent reception room, drumming her fingers
over those metal walls. She might almost have been back in the
Katarina again, centuries earlier.

The west wing had been gutted. Explosives and torpedoes had
caused structural damage elsewhere. Every single window in the
aitch-house had lost its glass. Consequently Loxmithlinna town
lost a tithe of glass from its own windows, so as to reglaze the
south wing as quickly as possible. Hardly a palatial refurbish-
ment; however, autumn was here now.

Since the south wing had become the Queen's headquarters, dowager Lokka and paralysed Henzel and Nikki and Lyle Melator and other staff and servants were displaced to a section of an upper floor of the north wing. Elmer's father was now marooned in his wheelchair, bereft of any lift. The new accommodation for the Loxmith family was breezy, whatever drapes one hung up. Soon it would be chilly. They would need to sleep in furs, and wear furs all day long.

Most of the surviving former tenants of the west wing had decamped into town to beg lodgings and charity.

What of the Defence Volunteers who had changed sides? Captain Rolf Haxell (his right arm in a sling) swore an oath of loyalty to Lucky, administered by Serlachius. Haxell forsook his portcullis earrings as an earnest that his priorities had changed. As part of the oath-swearing the Captain was tattooed on one cheek in silver with the spiral cochlea of an inner ear surrounded by few stars, a simplified version of the Order of the Ukko which General Aleksonis wore on his uniform. An honour of sorts, for switching sides! Also, a prominent sign that from now on Haxell would only heed the true Queen.

The *true* Queen? Lucky's status wasn't in any doubt.

Unfortunately, Maananfors was proving more resistant to attack than might have been expected. Perhaps one might have foreseen a stern resistance, in view of the slaughter of the garrison . . .

All those infernal Brindled Isi weapons, besides!

The habitable wings and banqueting hall and land-yard (where a hillock of shovelled glass glittered) were *thronged* these days. Soldiery from Sariolinna, both flesh and wooden. Jaeger-troopers and watchmen from Luolalla. Defence Volunteers. Out-the-House Square, cleared of its leafless curver trees, was the landing ground for sky-boats and flying pods.

One armed pod had already been lost over Maananfors, to a rocket. The small Isi flier had limped back to Loxmithlinna, to smash down clumsily on the waterfront. Maybe Elmer Loxmith could have worked out how to repair it . . . were he in residence!

And Lyle Melator?

Rapping her knuckles around the erstwhile dressing room which was now her office, Lucky was awaiting Elmer's former assistant who had prevailed on Haxell to surrender – lethally, as regards van Maanen's followers.

An act of betrayal? Yet not of treason! Quite the opposite.

After Bekker ushered in Lyle, the wooden Captain remained standing by the door to protect Lucky from any assault. She could rely on Bekker's perfect discretion. His grainy russet face remained expressionless. Not a muscle twitched.

Leaning against an iron panel by the window, head cocked, Lucky scrutinized this new ally, Lyle, who couldn't really be trusted. She had chosen to wear one of Eva's gowns, of mauve satin beaded with amber. Two globules of amber, which were larger than the other golden droplets and sewn in nipple position, contained glitterbugs. This conceit reminded Lucky of the bright insects which had flown towards Jack and June's diminutive daughters, to become part of them. The other beads echoed the amber of her royal chaplet under which her raven hair hung in volatile tumult today. The gown was a bit on the large side, Eva being a sumptuous lass. Or *having* been so.

Should a Queen dress up in her daughter's forsaken costume just because that same Queen now slept in that daughter's marriage bed? Oh it amused her to. The gown mightn't even have been worn till now. Eva had lost her eye for fashion, hadn't she?

From behind his gold-rimmed glasses Lyle was noticing – nonchalantly – Lucky's glitterbug nipples. He wore a faint smile, of appreciative complicity. Lyle cut a fine figure in tight leather breeches and a baggy embroidered cream shirt with capacious sleeves – up which, were what ruses? Lucky felt an impulse to tangle a hand in the auburn halo of his hair, and pull him, pull him where? To his knees? To kiss the amber globules?

'Melator,' she mused. 'A steersman, of sorts. The rudder that really steers the boat, though the skipper imagines he's in charge.'

Lyle inclined his head in discreet acknowledgement. 'Being a few centuries old makes you perceptive, Your Majesty.'

'Or blind, to simple ambitions.'

'What is ambition,' Lyle asked, 'other than a craving which simplifies and streamlines the world so that he who aspires can thrust himself splendidly towards his goal?'

'By devious routes, usually.'

'Those are the twists that the leaperfish perform before hurling itself—'

'—higher up the river.' Lucky nodded. Her fingertips tapped

to and fro on the cast-iron. 'So many things distract me these days.'

'Shall I distract you a little more?' he asked. 'By telling you that Elmer was impotent with Lady Eva?'

Delightedly: *'What . . . ?'*

'Oh it was obvious to me. Elmer really was so gauche. In a vain attempt to work up his passion Elmer whipped Eva every night.'

'Oh, this is *precious.' Thank you, Lyle Melator.*

'That's why silly Minnow chose a crown of whips for herself. Solidarity of Sariola daughters. For once.'

'Whips and pearls! When a cuckoo cackled about that preposterous coronation, I wondered about those!'

'A cuckoo, aha . . .' Lyle's grin was one of connoisseurship. 'Between you and me, I fed the boiled brain of a lamb to a cuckoo and told it to blazon Elmer's problem to the Brazen Isi, in case they might help him.'

'You only had his best interests at heart, of course.'

'The result: the golden Girlem you'll have heard about. Isi motives being what they are, the Girlem then tried to bewitch van Maanen.'

Lucky laughed. 'Pity she failed!' It was some while since she had laughed; and certainly not in the context of *him* at Maananfors.

'In another respect maybe she succeeded, Your Majesty. When I burst in here' – yes, into this antechamber, and into the royal bedroom – 'to evict Elmer and Eva from their home—'

'If Loxmith had still been here, he could have repaired the flier for me, Mr Melator!'

A shrug of apology. 'When I burst in, Your Majesty, it was my strong impression that the couple had finally managed to consummate their marriage – in the heat of the bombardment.'

'How gallantly you phrase it.' One could warm to this Lyle.

Sensing her approval, Lyle asked, 'Could we possibly release Moller from the pillory? He's been in its clutch several days now. He's quite soiled. Those sky-boats taking off and landing around him must be irritating.' Lyle even dared to mention sky-boats. Though hadn't she herself broached the topic? 'He only performed at that sham coronation under protest.'

'Yes, yes. Why do you think I didn't have him whipped and branded? He had to suffer something. I suppose interceding for him demonstrates your worthiness to be the new lord of this battered ruin.'

Lyle demurred. 'Not *lord*, exactly. Populist traditions hold sway here. Maybe Queen's steward, Queen's keeper.'

Lucky drummed. 'That almost sounds like "keeper of the Queen", a remarkable aspiration.'

The man's snubby nose wrinkled humorously. What an insinuating fellow he was. She could have slapped his face, except for a throb of excitement within her.

How could this be, after centuries of strenuous fidelity? Centuries of loyalty to a consort who had arranged his own murder to escape from her! (Dear Bertie never did so. That vile Kennan was entirely to blame.) Maybe she ought to slap Melator's face, even so.

Instead she told Captain Bekker, 'See that the priest is released this evening.' Not immediately. After a decent delay. Her wooden soldier mustn't leave her just yet – not alone with this Lyle, and with temptation.

Why had she chosen the gown with the glitterbug nipples? Was she wishing to celebrate her conquest of the aitch-house in manly fashion by a ravishing?

Yes, Lyle was eyeing her glitterbugs again.

'Don't distract me,' she said. Yet he did. Already the clever fellow did.

How could she contemplate taking a casual lover in the aftermath of Bertie's desertion? What did she know about lovers?

She knew enough about the passions of suitors for her daughters. Jaeger. Fors. Kippan. Mana knows how many. Most recently Elmer Loxmith . . .

Elmer had finally taken his bride's virginity in the heat of battle just next door, in the very room where Lucky herself now dreamed by night of war and vengeance. Dreamed, in a bed where the din of violence had sparked erotic frenzy!

'I suppose,' she said, 'you might more legitimately become a lord if you married the Loxmith daughter.'

Lyle licked his lips, tasting the prospect.

'I don't quite think so, Your Majesty. Though it's good of you to sponsor the idea. Nikki's rather averse to me at the moment. This would take time and persuasion.'

'Her brother's likely to die because he fled to Maananfors!'

'That would distress Nikki, even though she was furious at him because of the way he whipped Eva. What if he doesn't die?

From my point of view he can hardly return to the aitch-house. Not if I'm to be Your Majesty's *keeper*.'

What a clever adviser Lyle would make. Did she want an adviser? Did she want a temporary lover? She'd forsworn any further pregnancies. Was the itch coming upon her again, and Bertie no longer here to appease it?

Lyle wouldn't become longlife by bedding his Queen. No doubt he understood this. He would definitely be temporary in that sense. Much might soon be temporary, when she found her other self! She herself might at last become temporary.

'You're distracting me, Lyle Melator. Thank you for telling me the amusing story of the whips. Well worthy of blazoning abroad.'

Lyle nodded. 'Carnage attracts cuckoos.' If he himself – as someone to be believed – spread this titbit about Elmer and Eva, he would be making a real commitment to the Queen. Worthy of special reward.

'It's the maids' birthday party this afternoon,' she reminded him. 'I hope the banqueting hall will be tidy.'

'Well swept though draughty, my Lady Lucky.' What presumption.

'I'd prefer you to call me Paula, actually. My Lady Paula. In private.' How like the *Katarina* this iron room was. And how unlike. The rap of her knuckles raised an echo – just as a knock sounded at the door.

Ben Prut entered, silver chevrons and shoulder belt over his camouflage leathers. The adjutant peered short-sightedly. His spectacles were clutched in his hand. Lyle wasn't bashful about wearing glasses – ones rimmed with gold.

'Compliments of the General, Your Majesty. Our jump-bikes carrying pillion marksmen skirmished with jump-bikers from Maananfors along the north-western shore of the lake. Those other bikers fought like maniacs, unquote. We lost a marksman from one bike and a rider from another bike, but its marksman was able to bring the vehicle back to base. The flying boat from the fortress has sustained a hole in the hull, and one casualty, but it remains operational. It'll be patched. The General recommends that the royal sky-boat and the fortress-flier don't approach too close to Maananfors for the present.'

So Lucky lacked control of the air, even though the rebels had no sky-boats whatever.

'The General recommends that some of the wooden soldiers practise jump-biking, to form an invulnerable spearhead.'

Hitherto Captain Bekker had stood motionless in his dark blue uniform faced with crimson and gold lace. The high shako with tufted pompon (and silver plate engraved with a tree) made him seem taller than the lofty aide. Now he stirred.

'My men are solid,' he said. 'Unshakably so. Yet jumping from one location to another so swiftly might unbalance them. Wood can march but can it leap? Our mana might be contrary to jumping. I request that I make the first attempt.'

'Jack Pakken might be a good instructor,' suggested Prut.

'I heard from Jatta,' said the Queen, 'how Hubertus Jaeger couldn't walk in a straight line after Jack gave him similar instruction. My Jatta was hoping that I would forbid Jack ever to mount a jump-bike again . . . Do I want to risk the good Captain's equilibrium? Do I? I must think about this.'

Said Prut, 'The General recommends a campaign of attrition rather than a sudden massive assault.'

'It's so exasperating! All because of this damned *resistance*.'

'And Brindled Isi assistance . . .'

'Does Aleksonis suspect that Brindled Juttahats might join the rebels?'

Lyle cleared his throat.

'Yes?'

'An alliance with aliens? Never. Even if van Maanen was losing, he would have to refuse. Otherwise: treason to the human race! Nobody decent would accept the false Queen. Not that many will!'

'He *is* losing,' snapped Lucky. 'He already lost the aitch-house.'

'I volunteer to ride a jump-bike if Your Majesty wishes,' Bekker insisted stolidly.

'No, I must think about this.' Rap-a-tap, rap-a-tap, on the cast-iron wall.

Before she decided anything else, the banqueting hall must be thoroughly purged of the taint of treason.

Just as at the spurious coronation, livers and hearts were hooked within the cagework of wrought-iron foliage screening the now glassless windows. One screen had intercepted a falling bomblet and been blown to pieces. Breeze blew through naked embrasures. Chandeliers hung wrecked.

In a brass frame propped against the tammy-panelled wall at the back of the dais dangled ribbons of canvas. That painting might seem to have been shredded by flying glass. But one knew otherwise. Lucky hadn't wished the vandalized portrait to be hidden away. She would summon Mikal from Pohjola Palace. She would have the painting stitched together and restored perfectly, although not just yet. Keeping it on display in its slashed state implied that van Maanen and Minnow were responsible for all the damage to the house.

On view beyond the cagework was the soot-stained roofless shell of the west wing. Falling debris had sunk two boats in the water-yard. The majority of vessels were intact. If armed, none could match the paddle-steamer which van Maanen had made his flagship, nor could any of them outrun Elmer's *Sea Sledge*. Nevertheless, the portcullis had been raised. The royal army was on the offensive, not the defensive. Van Maanen was unlikely to stage a raid across the turquoise lake. Right now that lake was the dull hue of lead. The sky was turgid with dirty nimbostratus.

Today's feast in honour of June's quadruplets was a sweet feast. Black mustaberry tarts and bubberry pies. Crêpes with blueberry jam topped with cream. Whipped porridge and parfait. Fruit soup and meringues and snowcake – to be washed down with spirits and cordials.

Would the maids rate a similar party each month on the day of their birth? By now those tots could crawl nimbly. They could totter a few steps before sitting down again with a thump. June *could* still cope with a couple in slings, though one at a time was preferable. Fortunately June's daughters had almost stopped suckling, otherwise they might have slimmed her down something drastic. Mince and mash and sweet porridges were acceptable substitutes for her milk.

These days, two of the Loxmiths' maids and a scullery girl generally helped out as nursemaids. This afternoon, however, the four bairns were perched upon little cushions set on high table amidst the bowls and plates. June sat behind one daughter in case she toppled. Jack behind a second. Jatta was another nanny; and Nikki Loxmith a fourth.

Lucky had decreed that her great-granddaughters should wear hooped underskirts shaped like bells and reinforced with wicker. Over these: dresses of pink and silver-grey, the tight bodices tapering to a slender waist before ballooning out. These costumes virtually supported Minx and Minxie and Jinx and Jinxie. As the maids rocked one way then another, their tiny fingers reached into nearby porridge and parfait to scoop and lick. Cream smeared their rosy cheeks. Their eyes, blue as their mother's, were bright. Blonde curls had begun to thatch their craniums. The nymph-whelps cooed happily, appreciative of a large audience.

At one end of the table, elevated on a fat cushion upon her chair, Goody Hilda hunched over, her face bowed almost as low as the tabletop. At the other end lounged Lucky. A family occasion! The only outsider at high table was Nikki, till recently the ranking daughter of the house.

Was the summons to act as nanny a friendly concession? Or did Lucky wish to reach a decision about Elmer's sister? Nikki had come in her best embroidered finery, and she was wearing a bonnet with pink and yellow ribbons.

'I like your bonnet,' Jatta said dubiously to her neighbour. Nobody else had their head covered, though it was cool enough for a hat on this dim day in the draughty hall. Jatta's purple suède tunic (striped with bright felt) and her calfskin trousers were about right for the current temperature.

Nikki's look was doelike yet defiant. 'I last wore this hat when I visited Landfall with my brother. I've never been anywhere else very much, except over the lake to Maananfors. Now everywhere else has come here, with an almighty bang.' Yes, wrecking her home . . . 'Would you like to have my bonnet, Princess? *Haven't you people taken everything else? Today I'm a nursemaid for one of these terrible tots. What will you want me to do tomorrow?*

'Of course I don't want your hat. And I'm hardly a princess any longer, with these queer grandchildren propped on the table. I don't even want to be here,' Jatta confided, 'except to deter my son from risking himself too much. Fat chance, with my mother egging him on. She made me come so that I can flaunt myself in Osmo's keep after she captures it.'

'In Osmo's keep on last Lucky's Day but one, I pitied you, being humiliated in public . . .'

'You were there . . . ?' Jatta reached to steady Jinx or Jinxie.

'I couldn't *do* anything for you then. Damn all the doers of things! Including my blundering brother. What if he'd stayed here? Would he be grinning inanely at the Queen?' Nikki was trembling. 'Now he's lost the lordship . . .'

'Lyle Melator over there looks very sure of himself.'

So many faces, seen between little hooped skirts . . . Paavo Serlachius, ruddy with righteousness. Nils Carlson, whose tattooed lips declared his talent and his defiance of pain. Juke, who met Jatta's gaze momentarily then looked away: a betrayer of his own sister; Osmo's bane. Splendid Aleksonis and Ben Prut and so many more, amid cakes and parfaits and glasses of vodka. Captain Haxell with that silver tattoo on his tripe-like face, lolling next to Melator.

'He's sure of *you*?' Jatta murmured to Nikki.

'I wouldn't have minded that, once . . . Lyle seemed sweet and smart and helpful.'

'There's a blade in every bun, isn't there?'

'Lyle hasn't been paying much attention to me lately. He did speak to me earlier, but he was almost offhand as though I bored him.'

'What more could he want but you? If it's longlife he's after, there aren't any more Sariola daughters available yet, unless my mother intends to give Ester away at fourteen.'

Nikki sounded lost. 'You have so much more *experience* than me, Jatta.'

'I could have done without some of the experiences. But I've never had a brother. You have. Yet he left you here.'

'Because we'd fallen out. He left me to look after Mother and Father. Never asked me. Simply left me. Bombs were falling, the west wing was in flames. He just left me. Left me to his trusted Lyle.'

'To protect you. I once had a protector. Nikki,' whispered Jatta, 'I saw Juke's sister in a vision, wielding a lightrifle.'

'A vision?'

In company with dearest Anni beside a certain pond . . .

That was private.

But Jatta had blurted out to her mother about the vision.

(Long ago: 'Jatta, my chatter, my natter, tell me a tale!' And Jatta had obeyed in panic.)

Perhaps she shouldn't ever confide in anyone else other than Anni.

Yet perhaps she should.

'I saw a vision of glittering flies above a pool, Nikki. Eyeno was asserting herself. I wasn't able to assert myself – not as regards coming here. Or leaving a dear friend behind. My mother was far too frantic. She might have harmed my beloved.'

'You don't have to tell me this—'

'I don't mind. I've had my heart pried into by Juke while he was protecting me. My beloved – *she* – might have been maltreated.'

'Oh,' said Nikki, drawing into herself.

329

Please don't take me under your wing, Princess Sariola. You're too much for me. Maybe all Sariola daughters were wayward. How wilful might Eva have been as Lady of Loxmithlinna if Elmer hadn't bruised her pride, and her bum?

Nikki had flinched away from Jatta. This coincided with Jatta's own wishes to be outside of the brawling world in some private place together with a soul-sister. Though not here, not now. Communion with Nikki, barely begun, already seemed to have faltered. Minx or Minxie was sprawling over to scoop more cream. Nikki concentrated on steadying the dreadful doll upon the table.

A cuckoo was ripping at a raw heart lodged in one of the grilles.

'Coo-coo,' called out Lucky. 'Listen to me: I'm appointing Lyle Melator as lifetime keeper . . . of this keep and this neighbourhood. During his lifetime the Loxmith family are dispossessed.' (Nikki was shuddering.) 'However, old Lord Henzel and Lady Lokka and their daughter shall remain here with an adequate pension.'

Jatta blinked. 'Relax,' she whispered to her neighbour, 'if you can. It's one of Mummy's best pranks.'

Lyle would be fully motivated not to change sides again. Nikki was a hostage. Yet Lyle had little incentive to coerce her to wed him. What could such a marriage add to his status? If Elmer died childless during hostilities, would widowed Eva be the most appropriate *family* heiress? Or Nikki who was of the blood? If Lyle were to wed Nikki and give her a child, wouldn't that child be Lyle's obvious Loxmith successor in the event of his death by poison or by a blade in the night?

During Lyle's lifetime . . .

He would have to hope to win one of the remaining Sariola girls, as each became of age, if he were to prolong that lifetime. He couldn't go a-wooing for a few years yet.

Lyle stood and bowed to Lucky with a droll nonchalance.

The Queen clapped her hands. 'Coo-coo! To my four lively menace lasses I say, *Happy Monthday*.'

The infants all turned to grin creamily at Lucky.

'How far can you conjure flies to fly now? How strongly, my mischiefs? Show us, so that my enemies may hear of the coming of your pests, and fear them more than any bombs and missiles!'

The overdressed miniature maids smacked together their chubby rubbery little paws coated with crumbs and cream. A glittery black insect flew forth from Minx (*was* it Minx?). A simi-

330

lar bug sprang from Jinx (*was* it Jinx?). From all their palms a
stream of flies issued. These rose to circle a wrecked chandelier
in a cloud.

'Coo,' crowed the tiny sisters, gazing upward.

'Coo-coo,' Lucky shouted at the gossip-bird. 'Tell the tale!'

The flies circled busily.

Iron clanked against iron . . .

While everyone's attention was distracted a leanly muscular
figure had entered the hall. Leather scrips and wallets hung from
hooks embedded in his bare honey-pale torso. Heavy weights
hung from an iron belt around his waist, down over a khaki kilt.
A mass of grey hair was piled up and pinned. Such a doggy
face, and such deep-set eyes. The shaman was carrying a wooden
tripod with a bellows-box on top, a round empty hole in the front
of it.

As he advanced between crowded tables his short boots rasped
and plopped. Spikes were on the heels. Suckers were on the soles.
He set down the purple tripod, and called out:

'How about a managraph of the birthday party, Saint Lucky?
Alas, my lens was stolen. I can still play a game of vision. Who
knows what I might see? I still have my sensitive cards. Those
weren't thieved from me. I could put my fingers over the hole
where the lens should be, to cut down the light. Aye, see the
scene in fractions! I remember a previous party in this same hall.
There was meat on the plates, not all these sweets. The hall
wasn't so windy. It's autumn, isn't it, and the downfall of the
year? Oh I could blow away, Your Saintliness. I could blow away
like a leaf!'

Casting around for a familiar face, he spied Lyle.

'Shall I take my boots off, Mr Melator? Ah, but it seems some
damage has already occurred to your fine hall.' He eyed the
circling flies, and sniffed fastidiously.

Juke had risen in astonishment. Voices burbled. Nobody
wanted to subdue a magician in a trance.

On high table the four maids cooed delightedly.

'A fun man—'

      'A joke man—'

            'A trick man—'

                  'A magic man—'

It was that same Hermi who'd been responsible for that legendary lewd ikon of Minnow. Maybe for this intrusion he deserved

a spell in the pillory, except that he wore his own mobile pillory, consisting of weights.

For a week after the bogus coronation of the pipsqueak, Hermi had roamed the aitch-house in a state of confusion, hadn't he? Then he had wandered with his useless tripod into the woods where such an individual belonged . . .

Now he had returned to the place where he'd lost chunks of his memory – where his memory had fractured – to find the aitch-house in a similar broken and topsy-turvy state. He had come back like a seer from a spirit journey.

'Shaman,' Lucky called out to him, 'I understand that the *managraph* of ridiculous Minnow with her tail in the air was burned. You didn't happen to make *two* of them and keep one for yourself?'

Hermi swayed, Hermi clanked.

'Two? Could I have made two? I remember a multitude of managraphs. A myriad alternatives fill my mind to overflowing.'

Opening one of the pouches hanging from his chest, he brought out sepia cards to scrutinize.

'No, no. No Minnows here.'

'Let me see those.'

Plopping and scraping, the shaman advanced to high table.

'Do us a trick,' piped Jinx or Jinxie.

Like some wary animal Hermi sniffed at the menace lass and fanned cards towards Lucky.

'Take one, Your Majesty. I'll guess which it is.'

Lucky seized all of them.

'Do us a better trick!'

'Little girls,' said Hermi sadly, 'I'm not the *maaginen* I was.'

Jack had moved along in a trice to peer over his grandmother's shoulder. Jatta was craning too.

'*What*,' exclaimed Lucky, 'is this?'

Amidst trees there was a cabin made of bones. Hanging above in the sky a-dance with auroras, at no great height, was a big stone potato . . .

Ukko, Ukko, so close to the ground! Hovering over a hut built of bones.

'Is this where my hidden Ukko will reveal itself, shaman? Where is this place?'

'It's just my old home,' admitted Hermi.

Another managraph revealed a blonde woman rising from a flower.

'That's Paula, that's me! No it isn't. It's Eyeno Nurmi. Isn't that so, my Jatta, my chatter? It's your *sister*,' Lucky cried out at Juke in the hall.

Juke hastened towards high table. Mounting the dais, he jostled Jack, and uttered a moan. 'Yes, it's her. She's become a nakki in a flower. Dead, and feeding a daisy.'

'No, that flower's a milkcup,' Hermi corrected him.

'Shaman, was it she who sent me a mana-flower on the night the maids were conceived?'

Hermi clinked.

'I always tell the truth, Your Saintliness. What if there are twelve truths all told, or twenty? I pointed my mana-lens at my home, I pointed it at a flower, I pointed it at Minnow. All I know is that I never sent you a bouquet – not in a cuckoo's beak.' He had understood her glance at the gossip-bird.

'You're addled!' Lucky scattered the cards amongst the plates of berry tarts. Hastily she retrieved the print of the ovoid moonlet looming so low above those trees. With shaky fingers Juke reached past the Queen for the image of his sister. He couldn't pick it up.

'No I mayn't touch—'

A fly fell into a tart, twitching on top of jam, dying.

'Pitter-patter,' remarked Hermi.

Flies were spiralling down from the ruined chandelier. Raising their chubby little fists, the menace lasses wailed. One by one the flies were expiring.

'You aren't quite strong enough yet,' Lucky told the nearest maid. 'Soon you will be. *Soooon*,' she cooed.

Unaccountably Nikki Loxmith burst into tears.

Rain began to fall outside. How dusky it was in the hall.

22 · REQUIEM FOR DEVOTION

'The curly-haired lady was becoming a zombie. *Kaaark*. So Minkie Kennan jumped away from her. Where was this warrior in black leather and gold studs and a high collar hurrying away to? Back to the war between the Queen and the rebel Queen, according to him. He might return to Kaukainkyla in a trice, so he said. Stumpy the Ecstatic didn't believe this. Minkie Kennan had abandoned the lady. Stumpy called for rope and straw and oil and a stake. Otherwise his folk would need to hunt for a hervy and wear shavings of its hooves for a month and a day. *Kaaark.*

'They burned the living corpse with the curly hair and they danced around her, singing loudly so as not to hear screams. She wore little red boots of flame, then big red boots of flame, then a cloak of fire. She blazed faster than a candle. Nothing remained but ashes. Ukko-ukkoo, it is told.'

Cocking its head, the gossip-bird eyed its audience.

Pasquil clung to his braces, shaky as jelly.

Gasping stentorianly, Bertha tore the pin from her bun. She couldn't stab the bird. *Aaaark,* no. Instead she stabbed at the back of her hand, once, and twice, and then again. A howl belched from her. She took pain upon herself to puncture the horror and anguish. Blood welled.

The moan Gunther uttered was as of a tammy tree being uprooted slowly by irresistible force. The tree must either lose all connection with everything it had known, or else crack explosively. Would his spine snap there upon the bed? His moan was of visceral and ultimate despair.

'Ukooooooo—'

The messenger-bird took wing. It went.

Blood dripped from Bertha's hand. She gaped stupidly at the abuse she had done herself on her master's behalf.

'Broth, broth,' she babbled. 'Strong and hot.'

Some people might be able to watch a body being tortured to the point where the crazed victim's eyes knew death before dying. Or worse, where all trace of intelligence vanished from those eyes. Some folks might be able to watch. She couldn't. She blundered to the door. Blindly she tore it open, more by instinct than by thought. She was gone from the torture chamber.

Pasquil had fainted. He had lost hold of himself, and slumped to the floor.

Gunther couldn't flee nor could he faint. He moaned abominably, racked by woe.

'*Uncle*—'

An intruder was at the open window.

It was as if the bird had returned gigantically in the guise of a young man.

A robust young man. Yet so raggy. Cord shirt and breeches were so soiled and torn. His face was filthy. A foul crust disfigured his broad brow. Twigs hung in his dangling mane. He was grinning dementedly.

'I know a tree. I know a creeper. I know a ledge—'

Already he was in the chamber.

What was this body upon the floor? Had he killed someone already? Noticing the open door, Cully dragged the body to the shadowy corridor; dumped it there. Back in the chamber again, he double-bolted the door. From his belt he pulled a knife.

'How many cuts with the knife does it take to end a longlife, eh—?'

Gunther focused incredulously upon the intruder. 'Cully? Cully? Thank mana you've come. Kill me, Cully, kill me,' he begged. 'Put an end to me now. *Kill me.*'

Cully halted, slack-jawed.

'Kill me, Nephew!' croaked the dreamlord.

'What—?'

'Are you deaf, lad? Kill me.'

Cully stared at his knife. No, at *her* knife.

'Kill you? Kill you?' he repeated, stupefied. How could the flesh invite the blade? The plea conspired with the sway imposed on him, catching hold of that sway by the lapels, pulling it forward, unbalancing it utterly. Tripping it, sending it sprawling. The blade fell from Cully's hand. He swept back his unkempt hair. A terrible wonder stunned him. How harrowed and emaciated was the man under the blanket.

'Oh Uncle, I can't kill you . . .'

'You must, lad. I've lost Anna for ever. They made her wear little red boots that burned her to death. She was back in the world again, and now she isn't, for ever.'

A scrabbling at the door. Bolts lurching and rattling. A slapping of palms against the wood.

'Go away,' bellowed Cully. 'Keep away . . . *Pasquil!*' He knew where he was now. He knew whom he had hauled outside.

'Leave us alone, dear man. I'm with my uncle. He's safe. Leave us be!'

To begin with, what Gunther rasped out was all part of the same entreaty to release him from the tragedy. Presently, though, the words became a searching of the ruined foundation of his being, an inquisition into devotion . . .

*

335

How clearly Gunther recalled the intimacies he'd enjoyed with Anna in her youth. And then in her middle years. And finally in her old age too. Yes, *intimacies* even then. Less robust intimacies, but tender ones. A youthful lover was hers in her mid-years, and her late years too; an adorer.

(In the snow, recently, he and she had re-enacted a semblance of shivering intimacy. Kennan had enjoyed *more* of her! Yet a mere once! What price the theft of one grain of wheat from a bushel?)

Gunther had been such a devotee of his Anna. Her gift which granted him longlife might well have imprinted him upon her in the manner of a duckling upon its dam, ardently and for ever, maybe unlike any other man who ever lived. And who continued to live, with her memory.

While Bertha had been in the bedchamber feeding him broth, she had murmured to her Lucky brooch. *His* cult had been of Anna, growing younger in memory, losing the liver-spots from her hands and the lines from her face until at last she corresponded perfectly to the Anna whom he had met once again inside the Ukko-child – in Minkie's bed.

The posthumous role Anna had played in his life – omnipresent as the air he breathed yet invisible except in that sequence of portraits of her (running in which order?) – was perhaps a riddle to himself as much as to his retainers who had never met Anna. Did the portraits stimulate Gunther's memory or confuse it by their constancy, their static permanence? Did Anna's painted eyes truly continue to smoulder? Anna had sanctified – no, elated – his spirit so that little of the monomania or melancholia of a longlife would trouble him.

(*Poor Bertie!*)

She had imbued Gunther with an armature. (*Oh her bones lay in their coffin.*) Her perpetual presence (within absence) finally compelled him to dream his way to her.

Had he ever truly expected to achieve her reincarnation? Or only to arouse a visionary revenant whom he might visit, or who might visit him like a nakki-succubus?

Kennan had abandoned her to a death by fire. Damn him and damn him for ever. What revenge could be complete enough?

Would Cully be willing to find Kennan and kill him, slowly?

'Will you kill him for a whole year? For a month! For a week!' How much could a body endure? 'Will you roast him alive? Will you truss him and douse him with freezing and boiling water till his skin comes off like a sea-eel's? Will you whip him and thrust hot irons into the wounds?'

Ravaged and with his nipples ripped, Gunther already looked as though he had endured torture.

Cully, too. Why did Cully demur? Why did he hang his head?

Could Cully divert the revenge in his soul upon the destroyer of all his uncle's hopes? Revenge had already been diverted. How dangerous to think once again of killing.

'Roasting alive?' said nephew to uncle. 'But you aren't cruel. You aren't cruel at all.'

And Gunther blubbered.

The savant of dreams! Desire was a dream. So was devotion. Was his worship of Anna a product of his dream-skill — or the other way about?

Snakes had implanted the falsest of nightmares in his nephew's heart. His nephew had been a rebellious slave to false dreams, as the young man confessed. Gunther was a master of dreaming, unless his love of Anna was the symptom of a deep servitude.

No wonder the Gingerbread Woman, so gross, had mocked him. No wonder she had compelled him to suckle on her tits. Gunther had delved deep down to the Gingerbread Woman herself. Naturally she was a woman. Wasn't he uxorious? Not a superficial sensualist of the stripe of Kennan!

See what Gunther had made of himself! The sickly ancient lover-swain, pining away. Sick almost to death. Had that been his aim? His last proof of devotion? Driven to this extremity by his brief liaison with Marietta!

How might he express his disordered insights? If only he were a poet.

Why had that poetess Eyeno waged war instead of expressing herself in agonized song? He knew. The cause was called Kennan. Kill him. Slowly. Eyeno might understand Gunther's feelings.

Seen at the gala in such poignant mortification, then glimpsed in dreams . . . Eyeno was remarkable.

Eyeno . . .

Was an impossible new afflatus about to fill Gunther's heart to soothe the devastation he felt? To distract him?

Reaching Anna in his dreams had required him to evade so many distractions. A dream could readily transform itself into a different dream, pivoting upon the axis of one event or another,

337

one encounter or another. The art was to guide the transformations. *He* must remain the fulcrum of decision, nudging the dreaming in one direction rather than another, by sleight rather than force.

The trickiest dreams were those which nested within other mutable dreams. Such had been the devious route to Anna and her habitat – there, where dream became reality, doubling in upon itself. Aye, like a gob of molten glass being inflated within a pliable glass container till somehow the gob became bigger than the bottle which enclosed it; therefore you were within the inner flask. Instead of flexible glass, there were the circumstances and the personae of successive dreams to be negotiated – to be conjured with, en route to that heartland where Anna's echo dwelled, in a place which could alter its complexion swiftly from summer into winter, a place where nakkis populated the bending terrain of desire and wish, yet a place which was also, amazingly, connected to the true world as well as to trapdoors of dream.

If only Gunther had taken Eyeno's route, whatever that had been. Unless Eyeno was, in truth, dead. If only he had taken Minkie Kennan's route instead of following his own dream-itinerary.

He wept. Dryly.

He had no desire to dream again. Although his body was weak as a babe's after the months spent in Elmer's casket, his mind raced, hungry for stimulus. Words must out, however hoarse his throat.

Anna was no more. The horror of it. Cully had refused oblivion to him. His Anna was lost for ever, in agony, in smoke. He prayed she hadn't suffered as much as an ordinary body might!

Back in the bygone days when Blomberg had been prime proclaimer of Kaleva and Paul Vassian was laureate, Gunther had taken Anna to the gala. As they rode towards Yulistalax, how the wind had ruffled her hair, so dark that it was almost a denial of colour yet also such an affirmation of herself, a negative silhouette.

At Yulistalax she had bound her head round with a kerchief so long that the end hung down to her heels. That kerchief blew out behind as a streamer. Anna tucked it through her belt, and it flapped as a tail. Bright ribands, pulled through large silver earrings, fluttered from her shoulders. She was a frolicsome nakki of the air. Her eyes, of roasted-nut hue, had watered in the wind. Was the moisture the result of sheer buoyant happiness?

What of the foibles of a Sariola daughter? Why, to fly a kite. To send up a kitten in a little basket beneath the kite to give the future hunter of birds mastery of the air, if only in its aspirations. To seal the same kitten in a glass carboy and suspend it in the waters of the lake to familiarize it with the native element of fishes. Yet not for long; not till the kitten stifled. Anna wasn't cruel. Her experiments were charming, more symbolic than effective. They were compositions of circumstances. Anna had enclosed her pet songbird in another carboy to hang underwater adjacent to the kitten for a while, fluttering its wings like fins. No harm was done. A magical mood was achieved.

Gunther was included in her compositions. Playfully she purchased Gunther as a slave for a day. Another time she played a Juttahat to his serpent voice. She pretended to be one of his father Frederick's statues come to life. She organized masked balls and pageants at Castlebeck. While she was chatelaine the keep was prosperous. Those areas between the salients and the walls, now choked by weeds and scrub, were parterres of blooms. Guards patrolled the walls.

Behold her in yellow pantaloons and jacket embroidered all over with beads; and ribbons, ribbons through the rings in her ears.

When middle age began to write lines upon her face, those were merely lines of love and laughter, engraved more deeply as the years passed by.

But Gunther's whole inner terrain had shifted, convulsed by a quake which had opened a chasm into which, burning, she had dropped irrevocably out of sight. His grand, impossible project had succeeded. In succeeding it failed vilely.

Zombie. Living corpse. How long might she have endured in that condition? For a decade? For three?

As a zombie, would she have shared this bed of his, carved with birds? Would she have shared his embraces? Would he have committed a kind of necrophilia to offer her physical consolation? Might he have imagined that this intimacy could transfer to her a measure of vitality, a sweet spoonful? Asleep, might he have fled into a fantasy wherein she seemed cured – only to awaken to grey putrid flesh which moved with shallow zombie breath, so unlike the wrinkled perfection of her maturity?

Would Anna the zombie have descended to the crypt, hand in

hand with him – one palm sticky with apprehension, the other with putrefaction – to peer at her bygone bones, she whom nakki-bones sustained?

All this he would have accepted.

Now she was gone, to Surma. Not even to Surma, but to nowhere at all.

He had known a great love, had he not?

Had this actually been a love for *himself*, for herself-within-him? Briefly Gunther felt such rage at her ... *betrayal* of him. How could Anna have forgotten him so utterly as to allow Minkie Kennan to part her legs? To let Kennan fondle and delve her soft nest, which had been Gunther's sanctuary?

For sanity's sake was Gunther beginning to reject the image of her? Never to dream again!

From time to time Cully called out at the bolted door: 'He's safe.' Surely both Martins would be there by now along with Pasquil, silently holding cudgels with which to club Cully. Had Bertha returned with stronger broth into which she had bled?

Gradually the croaky cascade – this wretched rhapsody and requiem – altered course. From rasping whispers Cully discovered so much more than ever before of the driving passion of his uncle's long life: a likeness of Anna Sariola fuller than any portrait, in this hour of his losing her. Was not this anamnesis of Anna – this valedictory recollection of her – becoming a prelude to a kind of amnesia? The reverie was as poignant as the autumn day itself. Gunther lay almost spent yet also compulsively awake. Cully's uncle was like some tree which had cut off its sap and starved its leaves so as to survive a long dark winter of the spirit. A winter to be passed by a fireside, nourished by what possible warmth?

By what indeed?

Hearth and heart, flesh and fireside ... What could Cully propose?

Cully's mother had always felt sure that she had been honoured, and cherished, till guilt supervened. Marietta's resemblance to the middle (and middle-aged) portrait hadn't simply established her as a substitute, a proxy Anna. *She* had been valued in herself.

A mother dishonoured to solace the dreamlord? Installed as his whore for a while? No, no. Far from it.

Her son adopted by way of compensation, or bribery? No, no.

A mirage of rape reared in Cully's memory. Girl in the forest. Pretending to be his sister ... Ach, no. Nor a nakki, neither. A farmer's daughter, deflowered and shamed. That girl had tried to help Cully as Lady Eva Loxmith had.

If Cully's mother entered his uncle's bedchamber once again, if she climbed once more into Gunther's bed of birds, this act of charity – arranged by Cully – might vicariously erase his crime against the girl! The last trace of sway would go away.

'Uncle, you've suffered so much. I'm going to send for my mother. This time, she'll stay here.'

Gunther nodded feebly. Did he understand?

'I'm going to *read*,' rasped the dreamlord. 'I'll drown my talent in a lake of words. The words of others. Captive, captivating. I shan't direct my own dreams again. Find me a *book* from the cellar, Cully.'

High time, indeed, to unbolt the door.

Sizzleflies wafted in through the window. Soon, they would die of frost. What a fine fire of mintywood would burn in Gunther's hearth.

'We had some visitors,' muttered Gunther. 'They went off somewhere, didn't they, nephew? Did you see them?'

'I watched them from a tree.'

'I don't think they'll come back. If they do, send them on their way. I don't wish to be involved in their quests or feuds. She wasn't cruel. Or jealous. She – *wasn't*.'

Absolutely *wasn't*. Her absence was total.

The dovecraft had taken until dusk to reach the vicinity of Kaukainkyla. By that hour it proved impossible to spot any village at all from the air. Gurrukal cruised to and fro for a half-hour of gathering night while he and Wex scanned rolling woodlands for any gleam of lamplight or firelight. Was that outline a cluster of buildings or just a bunch of trees? Was that clearing a pasture or a stretch where trees had burned down to stumps? Switching on their searchlight only brought disappointment. Cloud was patchy, opening windows upon the sky-sickle which cast a spurious lustre across the forest. If Kaukainkyla was hereabouts, the village was blacked out. Maybe everyone had gone to bed early. They might be hoarding their oil for the darkest days of winter when a fellow could go mad with melancholy.

Gurrukal had landed on an island in a river. Long and low,

the island was a leg of bare rock. Spate in spring would regularly scour it clean of any saplings which tried to take root.

There they spent the night, moated by water purling past. Would Lord Beck be lying abed sleeplessly awaiting their immiment return? It seemed unlikely that they *would* return to Castlebeck. Rather, to Landfall with their prize.

Next morning, Gurrukal took the dovecraft up again, and within ten keys they had sighted a modest village lurking in a wooded dale.

From the air, how bucolic. On the ground, how horrific: to find the ashes of a pyre, and then begin to understand the nature of those ashes. The villagers weren't forthcoming. When the dovecraft landed people kept out of sight until Gurrukal fired the wing-guns into the air a couple of times, then dipped the barrels ominously towards the nearest house.

Some women ran out. They waved empty hands placatingly. When it seemed safe, a fat bald man with huge bare feet emerged. Gurrukal opened up the canopy of the cockpit, and Wex interrogated this village spokesman. Though obviously a pugnacious and charismatic bully, the man wrung his hands in a cringing fashion.

A black-clad 'scout' on a metal steed which could disappear to nowhere . . . Name of Minkie Kennan. His prisoner, a zombie, had called him by that name . . .

What zombie?

A she-zombie . . . No name to speak of. A living corpse weren't no real human being no longer.

What happened to her?

The warrior in black dumped the corpse upon the village, didn't he? What do you do with a dead body as might be contagious?

A mound of ashes in the rutted roadway . . .

They had burned her *alive?*

She were definitely dead. Just managing to keep standing up.

What vicious fools.

They had disposed of Anna Beck. They had disposed of her knowledge of the Ukko-child, whatever value it may have had.

Which way had Kennan pointed the jump-bike when he left?

The spokesman shuffled. Oh he knew well enough. Would they swear in Lucky's name to go away?

'Or in Queen Minnow's name?' Wex asked bitterly. How far off course his quest was wandering.

North. The black steed had been pointing north.

Niemi lay to the east. {*Disinformation, Roger. Only a dunce would let people see his true direction. Kennan would be heading anywhere but north.*}

It wasn't Wex's place to take revenge upon these brutes.

Two hundred keys and two and a half hours later, Gurrukal had landed the dovecraft on the promontory within a pebble-throw of the door of the Kennan keep.

Lake Lasinen dozed serenely under a sky of wispy blue. Along the shore tiny bare figures lay on the sand soaking up sunlight. The town over which the dovecraft had just descended was dressed for its own little festival, a week before the gala of voices in Yulistalax. Bunting garnished the mana-kirk and dry fountains, shops and houses. A brass band had been playing in the market square. Kids in fancy dress were running around the streets: little warriors with wooden swords and rifles, sham shamans, blacked-up Pootaran sailors (or were those dusky kids pretending to be Juttahats of the Velvet hue?). The war was far away from here. How many little Luckies were dolled up, and how many wee Minnows?

According to Wex's wetwear this was a local harvest fest.

Certainly it wasn't a homecoming jamboree for Kennan. No pennants flew from the main tower of the keep. No festoons spilled from the windows of the hall. Those were shut tight, as was the ironbound tammy front door. A faint red ghost of a hand marked that door. Saying what? 'Blood on your hands'? 'Don't dare venture out, you inside'? Someone had scrubbed quite hard. Maybe there'd been an eye on the palm: 'We're keeping our eye on you'.

Townfolk were gathering at the landward end of the promontory, to stare at the dovecraft. Cliffs descended steeply to the lake from the broad high causeway where grass had long since grown through gravel. Cliffs descended from the granite walls of the neglected dwelling perched on its spit of land.

Wex tugged an iron handle alongside the door. Within, a bell jangled.

They waited.

Presently the inner hatch of a grille creaked aside. A strawberry face peered out. Stutters spilled forth, as though the rusty bars of the grating were diffracting every word.

Such a family scene it was in that hall with the arch-braced timber roof! Baby in a cradle. Wrinkled old nanny with toothless

343

gums. Two young lads, one handsome, one scraggy and spotty. Snooty young lady in a low-cut gown of lace and muslin, yellow ringlets cascading. Blond acne-blotched layabout. The grand dame in black, adorned with trinkets and spangles.

The two boys had come rushing in evident delight at the interruption to what must have been a bickering monotony. Their frustration at not being able to dash into town to enjoy the fest!

'Can we go inside your sky-boat, sir—?'

'Will you take us up in the sky—?'

Kyli Kennan had swanked into the hall, gratified to receive callers from no less than the Earthkeep.

Dame Inga's smiles of welcome were fulsome, almost seductive; never mind the amount of calculation in her hazel eyes, nor how firmly the jut of her nose suggested tenacity.

'Gentlemen,' she'd enthused. 'Cordials? Wine? Vodka? Lunch? *Beds* for tonight?' Even though it was barely noon.

'An intimate dinner party,' Kyli said wistfully. 'The candelabras lit. Talk of far places. Have you lived on Earth? You must have done.'

'Earth, will you tell us about Earth?' the boys clamoured.

'We'll be needing some alcohol for our fuel tank, madam,' said Gurrukal.

Inga waved a hand. 'In the town.' As though her word was law, irrespective of the handprint on the door.

Fuel for the dovecraft indeed. How long might a jump-bike continue jumping before it stopped? {*I theorize that these bikes recharge themselves by the very act of leaping through mana-space, Roger. They may need periodic servicing, though. By Juttahat engineers. Seemingly the Isi have not tried to build spacecraft or even sky-boats which fly by the same principle. Maybe only something comparatively small can jump.*}

Might Kennan have jumped his way into this keep unseen by night? Ah, but would the Dame be offering overnight accommodation if her son was hiding right now in some upstairs chamber?

Wex had some stern statements to make to Dame Inga. Her son had emerged from his hiding place – which was no use to him any longer. He had kidnapped a woman who was of the uttermost value to Lord Beck of Castlebeck. Then he abandoned her to be burned to death by superstitious yokels. In front of Kyli Kennan and the boys Wex said this bluntly. He needed to speak

344

to Minkie Kennan – not for the sake of justice, but for information.

'What a dreadful thing to happen!' exclaimed Dame Inga. 'I can hardly credit it. Though if you swear it's true . . .' *Please don't go into details.*

Kyli Kennan flushed. 'Who was this lady he kidnapped? Did Minkie ravish her?'

The old housekeeper hissed at the boys and clapped her hands over her ears as if thus the innocent young brothers might be rendered deaf.

'Why,' asked Inga, 'did these louts burn the woman? How terrible to burn a woman, don't you agree, daughter-in-law? Why did they do it?'

'It so happens,' said Wex, 'that she was becoming a zombie.'

'Oh *well* now. So my son took this unfortunate soul under his protection, but her condition terrified him.' Inga beamed reassuringly at Kyli. What fellow-me-lad would want to ravish a living corpse?

Kyli nibbled at a knuckle. 'She was *becoming* a zombie, you say. How about when Minkie kidnapped her?'

'Thuh-thuh-this is all huh-huh-hearsay,' Snowy said loyally.

'It's all very well for you to talk about hearsay,' snapped Kyli, 'with a hundred buzzings in your bonnet.'

'I tu-tu-told you, those have gu-gu-gu-gone.' A grin spread across that strawberry face. 'So mu-mu-much for a shaman's ku-ku-curse. I ku-ku-can think straight now.'

'What was this woman's *name*?' Kyli wanted to know.

'Anna,' said Wex. 'That doesn't matter.' He could hardly explain about Anna having been dead to begin with.

'Doesn't matter? Oh, I'll make it matter. Me, left here pregnant—!'

The baby woke and wailed piercingly.

'Goody, do take the piglet away.'

The squeals intensified.

Gurrukal frowned. 'I believe that child has colic. Cramps in the bowels.'

'Why don't you examine it?' suggested Wex. 'Why don't you and the nurse carry that cradle somewhere else? Massage the infant.'

'Hang on a mu-mu-mu-minute,' warned Snowy. 'Du-du-don't you lay a hand on wee Jo-Jo-Johannes.'

The baby shrieked.

345

'Oh take him away and feed him, Goody,' appealed Kyli.

Gurrukal glanced pointedly at her décolletage. 'Aren't you feeding him yourself?'

'That's none of your business. What was Minkie's relationship with this Anna? Was she really becoming a zombie? Will she have infected him?'

'There's nowt wrong with goat milk,' declared Goody.

'That depends on the breed of goat,' said Gurrukal.

'There's nowt wrong with Dumpling. She eats very nicely in our yard behind the tower. Lactates two years at a stretch, Dumpling does.' *Keep off the subject of zombies and ladies.*

'Ah, but the butterfat content could be too high for the infant's digestion. Too much protein, too little water content. I think you need to water the milk. I would not lay a *hand* on the baby,' Gurrukal assured the acned retainer. 'My method is massage by means of the foot – very gently so in the case of such a little body. Yes, some gentle massage to ease the cramps; and a change of diet.'

Snowy winked at the dame. 'Hey, I'm gu-gu-glad you gents ku-ku-called,' he said. 'Jo-Jo *wu-wu-wu-was* getting on our nu-nu-nerves a bit.'

'*I* suckled my own children,' Dame Inga reminded Kyli, grateful for the diversion.

'If only,' retorted Kyli, 'I'd been able to consult a wisewoman! If people were speaking to us!'

'Ku-ku-come on now,' said Snowy amiably, 'we aren't exactly bu-bu-being bu-bu-boycotted as far as bu-bu-buying stuff goes. Though on the other hu-hand . . .' The other hand being that red one on the front door. Snowy refrained from enlarging on their situation. 'It's really gu-gu-good you gents ku-ku-coming here.'

'This is *not* why we came,' shouted Wex as tiny Johannes continued to yell. 'Gurrukal, please deal with this distraction.'

The pilot had become reluctant to leave. Gurrukal wanted to witness the interrogation. This could hardly proceed while the bawling baby was in the hall. Wex whispered to him, 'This is *exasperating*. Will you please do your duty as a medic!'

Gurrukal and Goody had departed with the cradle. Wailing had receded. The boys lingered. Neither Dame Inga nor Kyli nor Snowy made any effort to scuttle them. And so commenced a prolonged fencing match of minds between Wex and indomitable Dame Inga. Maybe the duel was above the heads of Kyli or

Snowy, though both butted in confusingly. At issue were the whereabouts of Minkie, and more vitally the whereabouts of the hiding place he'd used.

'Nu-nu-nu-never knew wu-wu-where the bu-bu-boss wu-wu-went, honest—'

'Wouldn't tell his own Kiki-liki the secret!'

Inga had glared at Kyli for merely a moment before recovering suavely. 'The secret confided by his father. A men's mystery, Mr Wex! Isn't that so, Kyli? Men's mysteries will ever defeat us.'

'Oh,' said Kyli.

'Yeah,' agreed Snowy. 'Wu-wu-wish I'd bu-bu-been with the bu-bu-boss. Almost fu-fu-feel I was! If only I was wu-wu-with him now. Only Mu-Mu-Minkie knows where he is, or was, eh mu-mu-missus?'

Inga's son had been duped by Prince Bertel. That invitation to a Sariola daughter's wedding had been so disingenuous! Anyway, who cared about such weddings? Longlife, pah. What of it? (Dame Inga was treading thin ice, but Kyli appeared unaware.) A man could be provoked. Given that the Prince's death wasn't wholly Minkie's fault, he deserved protection. Minkie needed sanctuary somewhere secure. Such as in the Earthkeep, for instance. His safety guaranteed, in return for . . . certain information he would supply. As for that zombie woman, whoever she was, Minkie could hardly be held responsible for the actions of louts. Lord Beck might hold Minkie accountable? How unfair. Minkie doubly needed asylum in return for a favour.

'Bring my son back here safely in your sky-boat, Mr Wex. I'll reason with him. He'll listen to his mother. Take him to your Earthkeep, and I know he'll be really helpful.'

'Where do you think he is, Dame Inga? You must have some idea. Or *you*!' to Snowy.

Snowy shuffled. Snowy scratched his blotchy brow. How ought he to decipher Dame Inga's expression? Where would the boss most likely have gone? Think back on Juttie-hunting days . . . Several possibilities.

If Minkie managed to stay out of sight he would be safer that way. If there was a sighting of him, this fellow Wex would race to save the boss.

'Finding Minkie and locating his earlier hiding place are vital to the well-being of this world,' insisted Wex.

'Is that su-su-so?'

The boys were engaged in a whispering squabble.

'What about the drum-map——?'

'Shut up——!'

'Maybe he made another one, and finished it——'

'Boys!' from the Dame. Impatiently, Kosti punched pimply Karl on the nose. Karl howled. 'Mum, Mum, I was just talking about shaman Sven!'

'Oh that shaman won't know anything important,' Dame Inga said hastily. 'My Minkie never liked him much. Nor did Ragnar.'

'But he was making a mana-map, Mum,' whined Karl, 'until Snowy shot a hole in it——'

'Boys, I'm sure that dark man is hurting your little nephew with his feet! Run and see! RUN AND SEE.'

Interpreting their mother's tone accurately, the two boys did indeed scamper for the door.

Wex had stiffened. A fruity voice emerged from his lips. *'A local shaman was making a map . . . showing where Minkie hid? Where do I find this shaman?'*

Startled by the transformation, Snowy burbled, 'Sven du-du-didn't bu-bu-bloody finish it!'

'Where do I find this shaman?'

'In the fu-fu-forest, where do you think?'

Wex's wetwear demanded more precise details.

'Sven Hartzell might have gone wandering,' said Inga. 'And you'll only waste of your time.'

'I do not regard this as a very satisfactory encounter, Dame Inga. What a diplomat you are, in such a worthless cause! How your talents have been wasted by such a family.'

'Hu-hu-hang on. Wu-wu-what do you mean by that?'

Wex ignored Snowy. *'Dame Inga, the ethics of the Harmonious Society prevent me from employing extreme pressure where an alternative course exists. We shall find the shaman or else your damned son.'*

'Whom exactly am I talking to?' the Dame asked staunchly.

'You wouldn't understand. You would allow this world to convulse to protect your disgraceful offspring.'

'I still want to know about this *Anna* person,' insisted Kyli.

'Aren't you staying for lunch?' asked the Dame.

'I don't think so,' Wex replied in his own prim voice.

It was Juke Nurmi who caused the Queen to send an expedition all those hundreds of keys from Loxmithlinna to the realm of Saari, interrupting the war against the rebels . . .

Perched on the hillock of broken glass in the land-yard of the aitch-house, a cuckoo had cackled how Minkie Kennan had shown his face at last. And in which village. And riding a jump-bike. Moreover, Kennan was carrying with him a captive zombie lass, whom he released in the village. Kennan promptly vanished northward, whereupon the villagers burned the living corpse.

When the bird alighted out there in the land-yard, Paavo Serlachius had been discussing the nature of the mysterium with a chastened Moller. Lucky's war-priest was the first to carry the news to the Queen.

Lucky had hurried upstairs with her priest to the long gallery on the top floor to gain a higher viewpoint and perspective. She ejected the guards who were on lookout lakeward. She sent one guard for Juke, and another for Viktor Aleksonis and Ben Prut; and for Jack too, and also for Lyle Melator.

Bedding was strewn along the faded greensward of carpets. Tapestries had been taken down to use as blankets or rolled up into pillows. Most debris had been shovelled out into the lake. Half of the windows had been reglazed, others left gaping to shoot through if need be. Where a stretch of roof had caved in, rain had soaked the woven glade enough for actual fungi to sprout in it. A tubby brass dwarf with red eyes lay upon its side.

Once Lucky's advisers arrived, Serlachius repeated the cuckoo's story. Lucky strode the length of the gallery and back, stepping over bedding and skirting the defunct automaton. Along and back again with her confidants; to and fro.

Where could Kennan have been skulking all this time? Surely not with some ghastly little colony of zombies in a cave. Hardly him! Some misfortune must have overtaken him, to be riding with a zombie.

Where would he be heading to next?

Where had he been hiding?

Where had he jumped away to?

Who had the zombie been, and why?

The key, according to Serlachius, was the zombie. Kennan had been hiding in the place which was the secret of the Kennan men. That place must be the very place which Her Majesty had been seeking all along: home of her twin, and of other echo persons besides. Home of mirror-persons – of reflections in the realm of mana, existing within the offspring of that Ukko which she'd entered long ago. If such persons quit their haven or were snatched away from it they might inevitably become zombie. Serlachius had meditated about this. Surely this was what had happened. Why else would Kennan have kidnapped a zombie unless she had been no zombie to begin with?

Kennan had violated the sanctuary of the Queen's other self. He had abducted an inhabitant of that realm. Why? Out of lust? Or for advantage? The cuckoo in the land-yard hadn't cackled the name of the female zombie. The hen whom Kennan had seized couldn't possibly be . . .

Couldn't possibly be . . .

The Queen's other self? Abandoned by Kennan to be burned to ashes!

Lucky cried out her counterpart's name now.

'Paula! Paula!'

She cried her own name as she paced. In torment she kicked the brass robot. Could Bertie's murderer have destroyed her other self too? No, no, that couldn't be so! She would never find peace and reason.

'Grandmother, Grandmother,' Jack implored her.

Kennan had violated her very being.

'I know where he might have gone to,' said Juke of a sudden.

'*Yes? Yes?*'

'Somewhere where no one would suspect. When my . . . When my . . .'

'When your *sister*,' Lucky prompted him.

'When she and I went to the Velvet Isi nest beyond that bone-hut of Hermi's, Kennan had been hunting Jutties in the forests among the mana-mists. The road's a maze there, and so are the woods. Nobody human goes there if they've any sense. Kennan and his crony Snowy must have known their way around—'

From a pocket Lucky plucked the sepia card picturing the bone-hut with the Ukko hanging low above it.

'That's the meaning of this, isn't it, Paavo? The person who knows about the Ukko-child is hiding in this hut. He *will* be hiding here. That deranged shaman was sent here to show me this as surely as a mana-flower was sent to me at your wedding, Jack.'

Lyle coughed for attention.

'Excuse me, but Hermi wasn't quite so confused when he first turned up here. Either the alien Girlem bemused him after that blasphemous farce of a coronation, or Roger Wex somehow did so.'

Did this matter? Was this important? Oh but that blasphemous coronation! Minnow and van Maanen! *Lucky still had to settle accounts*. Fail to, and what sort of Queen would she be? A failing one. A failed one. Lyle didn't want her to neglect the war against Maananfors where Elmer had taken refuge. Even so . . .

'Supposing the Girlem stole the mana-lens,' continued Lyle, 'on behalf of the *Brazen* Isi.'

Not on behalf of the Velvets who kept a mana-bloom in their nest (but they would never have sent Lucky that flower).

Nor for the Brindleds whose mutant mage Minnow had somehow trounced; the Brindleds who were supplying her and her cocky upstart with weapons . . .

Lucky strode. Which way to turn?

What was Lyle implying by mentioning the Isi? *Think*.

Think of that bloom in the Velvets' nest. Juke had seen it there. The Velvets' nest was quite close to where Kennan had fled.

'Let's not forget,' said Lyle, 'that Hermi made himself out to be something of an intermediary between folks and the Velvet Isi . . .'

What if Kennan bartered his information in exchange for refuge? What if he were able to betray the whereabouts of the Ukko-child to the serpents? Kennan might have butchered a number of their Juttahats in the past, but such knowledge as his must outweigh even deadly grudges . . . if he dared to bargain.

Kennan had to be caught, and *squeezed*. The war must wait a while. The plague flies would be much more resilient *sooon*. In another week, another fortnight. More than a nip of autumn was in the air, but mana-flies should tolerate chills, even wintry cold – not that the war could possibly last so long. Lucky mustn't leave this keep herself, though, must she? That could seem to be a show of weakness or of insufficient interest, as if a war in which people died were merely a whim.

Aleksonis had personally led the expedition to capture the everything machine, but in present circumstances *he* must stay in the neighbourhood of Loxmithlinna.

*

An expedition was concocted: an excursion right across the country. Ben Prut would be in charge of military aspects. In overall command, who better than Jack? He'd been raised in an Isi nest. This expedition must address itself not only to Kennan but to the matter of the Velvet Isi. Jack; but with Juke as a moderating influence.

The royal sky-boat would be crammed with Queen's guards (though Jack shouldn't pilot it); and with some wooden soldiers (though Captain Bekker must stay behind with the bulk of his men); and with a couple of jump-bikes to chase Kennan if or when he tried to make a getaway through the in-between.

Should the fortress-flier also be sent? Aleksonis objected. The Queen mustn't be left without a major flying vehicle. In his opinion the contingent ought to consist mainly of Jaegertroops or Defence Volunteers from the aitch-house, with wooden soldiers providing the backbone of discipline. If a raid were to be made into the Velvet Isi nest, Jaegertroopers were acquainted with subterranean regions, weren't they? As for the Defence Volunteers . . .

Lyle pointed out that his own men – Haxell's men – had recently been *mauled*. It was a long way to send them to the realm of Saari. Personally he volunteered, not so much in the role of a fighter as of a mechanic should the royal sky-boat need an engineer's touch. An overloaded vessel would surely be labouring through the sky.

Debate continued. Were the cream of Lucky's own palace guards to be sent far away from Loxmithlinna, so recently restored to allegiance? On the other hand, were they *not* to spearhead this enterprise? What began as a clear plan developed kinks.

The eventual tally aboard the sky-boat would be equal numbers of royal guards and of wooden soldiers and of Jaegertroopers and of Defence Volunteers. Jack would be in charge of the wooden soldiers and of the guards, two of whom were capable pilots and three of whom were experienced jump-bikers. Juke would be in charge of the troopers and the volunteers, whom he could always bespeak if need be. Ben Prut would be co-ordinator. Lyle Melator would remain at the aitch-house.

Next day, the packed sky-boat did labour somewhat through a dreary sky.

Its first port of call was to be Yulistalax, specifically the meadow below Lord Burgdorf's keep with its tall slim tower of pink granite; there to top up the fuel tanks prior to the long haul onward.

Yulistalax! Where Juke had last seen Eyeno alive. Where he had bartered his own sister to save his skin, betraying her so unforgivably, all because of cocksure Lord Osmo van Maanen. Because of himself too, because of himself . . .

The sky-boat smelled of too much stale breath and sweat and whiffs of fart. The padded leather seats had been removed, except for the pilot's and the gunner's. Packed in like fish in a crate of elegant yellover panelling, they were. Hunkered down around weapons and rations and the two bulky jump-bikes were the green and brown leathers of Lucky's guards, buff leathers of the Jaegertroopers, the umber and bottle-green of the aitch-housemen; and the wooden soldiers too, in blue trimmed with orange, peaked shakos upon their heads topped with white pom-pons. The woodmen's odour was ever so slightly resinous, and freshened the air a little.

Juke agonized as the vessel came in sight of Yulistalax. He was in the Queen's service now. He was part of the thrust to punish van Maanen — on some future day. Van Maanen, and Minnow too. Minnow whom he had never met, though neverthe-less he had shot her down.

Did he wish to treat another woman as damagingly as he had treated his own sister? Maybe he might intercede for Minnow so that her punishment wouldn't be too extreme. Maybe he might be able to offer her some protection — especially if he succeeded in catching Minkie Kennan?

Would that protection be of the same sort as he had lavished on *Jatta*, for his own purposes (though also because she was a victim of van Maanen)?

To protect a woman might atone somewhat for the way he had betrayed Eyeno, and had been betraying her for years in his guilty desires even before the terrible finale . . .

What was Minnow *like*? He had never even set eyes on her. She was van Maanen's accomplice! What fantasy was this, pro-voked by an aerial glimpse of Speakers' Valley?

The terraced three-key-wide bowl was already cleared of sheep. Very likely they'd been driven off into woodland. Nowt better than sheep to keep a forest tidy. Several marquees and booths and a grandstand were up. Carpenters were erecting a second of the slot-together stands which were stored from one year to the next. Don't think about the lass who'd only been hoping to recite some poems while her brother bespoke more powerfully, and riskily . . .

'You're moody,' shouted Jack to Juke over the roar of engines and the shriek of air-intakes. 'I remember this place so very well. Oh how we set the sheep on fire, you and I. *Maaair.*'

Juke remembered Yulistalax all too well. Goal of his ambitions, once, its gala, and now a harrowing needle in his soul. If only. If only.

The town was already dressed in bunting along the maze of lanes. Awnings and corridors of candy-striped canvas linked rows of timber houses, turning them into hostelries for all those visitors who would begin to pour into town very soon. Gala just four days away. By that time the dismal overcast should certainly have cleared. A camp of tents was rising on the foreshore to lodge guests whose purses were too modest to afford a few nights at the Sign of the Goat or the Bellflower. As yet, harbour and shoreline weren't thronged with boats. Nonetheless, Yulistalax was bracing itself for a lucrative flood which would swell the population sixfold. Or would that only be fourfold, in this year of war? Or only threefold?

As the royal sky-boat chugged towards the meadow below the keep, townsfolk looked up and waved, unaware that this big white vessel with vermilion eyes around its portholes was only paying a fleeting visit.

Gala in the offing! How the memory of gala tormented Juke.

If only there was a way to expunge what had happened: the furtive unfulfilled incestuous lust in his heart becoming far too explicit – shouted into his face by van Maanen so that Juke yearned for his horrified sister to lose all knowledge of this by whatever means . . . He'd been drowning in quicksoil. He would have grasped at anything . . .

Could an act of protective gallantry serve to erase so much?

If only. If only.

To make a grand gesture . . . That was van Maanen's forte. Lord Osmo had even made the ostracism of Eyeno an occasion for applause.

To become a hero by capturing Kennan. By invading an Isi stronghold.

Minkie Kennan had lusted for Eyeno casually and trivially. Not dedicatedly like Juke . . .

How easy it had been to bespeak that fellow into impotence. If only Juke could bespeak himself to still his soul and heal the canker festering in it.

How had he, who despised lords for their airs and privileges, come to be the obedient servant of a *monarch*?

354

Why hadn't he followed Eyeno? Why hadn't he trailed after her on her tramp towards death, to save her at the very brink? Why, on account of the look in her eye, in her soft and liquid eye.

Maybe he should put out one of his own eyes, bespeaking the pain aside, or welcoming it. Not till he had served the Queen with the both eyes intent upon his goal! How van Maanen would mock him if he mutilated himself. Not till Lord Osmo was dead could he dream of doing so.

Might Lucky give him Minnow to be *kind* to? (And would he, amazingly, be truly kind – to a person he had never met?) What folly. He had no keep to return to. Only a berth in a cott in a mocky-village. His dad might refuse him even that. He was Lucky's creature now. Her trusted creature.

While Ben Prut arranged for the fuelling most of the soldiers would be stretching their legs and ventilating themselves and peeing and having a guzzle of water. They might be on the ground for an hour. Then onward by midway Keskikyla to Niemi; to Kennan's keep to assure themselves that their quarry hadn't sneaked home. Onward again to Saari city to rest overnight. Unless they were held up at Niemi. In the morning: onward north-east to the bone-house known to Juke.

On Lord Burgdorf's meadow only one sky-boat currently rested amidst long grass: an old derelict belonging to Lord Maxi himself. In another few days would there be half a dozen vessels parked there? Or none at all, if lords were shy of travelling when cuckoos cackled about rival Queens at war?

Now they were landing ponderously, fuselage throbbing.

Maaginen Imbricate being uncomfortable. Leaking droplets of sour musk from anal glands.

Cause being that wild humanbeing riding the jumping-bike. Liberating this mage from Queen Lucky's grotto under her palace. (Tolerable den, though captivity beginning to pall.) In a meadow beyond Great Fjord the wild humanbeing was sloughing this mage and his body-servant like old skin, violently jabbing with elbows and butting with head. Cracking Imbricate's ribs. Tearing anchor-muscles. Ripping sinews attaching ribs to the broad belly-scute wherewith Great Isi can be scooting sinuously over sand or stone or soil if lacking a body-servant to be carrying conveniently with dignity.

Maaginen Imbricate having healing his injuries by mana-mastery within two-three days of distressing incident, while

355

hiding in woods. Body-servant carefully transporting sore Imbricate for three-four weeks of fish-and-fungus-fasting through wilderness towards nearest Isi nest, being Velvet.

Maaginen Muskular of the Velvets receiving Imbricate as esteemed detainee. Remaining in this status. Imbricate being invited into Muskular's den today, soon to be partaking of squirming succulent piglet.

Imbricate being familiar habitué now of the Velvet nest! Sweet chimings. Warm dry fruity breathing. Scampering black Juttahat youngsters assuring Velvets of future servants hearing Isi voices in their heads.

Yet a worldful of humanbeing servants, still wild, awaiting! A homeworld of billions more potential servants, elsewhere. Such a fine game to be gaining mastery of *mankind*, and of the mysterium too. Being two games wrapped up in one another.

Beholding Muskular's den by warm yellow light. *Maaginen* coiling upon her shelf-rock. Indigo glyphs on her purple skin intimating metavision and overvoice. Standing by: her body-servant in sable livery, a Tulki speaker-to-humanbeings. Juttahats sitting at work-desks. Creamy ear-flower from Isi Ukko arising from nutrient flask on pedestal next to great glassy Ukkoscope apparatus. Blue flashes and red sparks twinkling within Ukkoscope, searching the manasphere for concordance with Ukko-in-waiting.

Muskular uncoiling lissomly. Twisting around on her deep rocky shelf as if merely to be flexing herself. Even in that confined space, adopting a glide of the *scrithening* variety – sinister-sinuous. Then in-curling and over-curling again, and rearing high her sleek head. Lustrous eyes appraising Imbricate. Her carmine tongue flicking from under the rostral scale to be tasting Imbricate's harsh anal hint. Muskular emitting a puff of comic caramel, cut with honeyed sympathy.

In coppery livery with black shoulder-glyph, Imbricate's own body-servant upholding weight of coils. Smelling sour in rapport with Imbricate.

Ghost ache from injury *not* being real cause of distress, but sheer pretence! Real cause being *handprint*. Scales being torn off by humanbeing with wig of false hair and two minds in his head squeezing Imbricate out of his moult-skin. Causing *handprint* on Imbricate!

How disfiguring of a somaseer and body-adept. Imbricate being marked indelibly until next moult. Hence Muskular's superior amusement.

Before Imbricate could be marshalling mind and scents and inner words to be projecting at Muskular, Muskular's servant-voice was speaking. Not addressing Imbricate in the speech of precise rattly hissing with which Isi were endowing their servants (and in which Great Narrations are being voiced) but in gobbly quacky humanspeech!

'Conversing in Kalevan,' the black Tulki was insisting. 'Humanbeings coming closer to the Ukko-in-waiting than ourselves with our ear-flower. Ukko being attuned to human deeds, and heeding human tales. Ukkoscope revealing red violence, volatility.'

Imbricate causing his own porter and speaker-to-humans to be replying: 'Ukko's location remaining unknown.'

Imbricate scorning the Velvet strategy, of bloom and skeleton! Conversing in Kalevan? Was rival nest altering its perspective late in the game? Adopting mimicry of humanbeings vocally? Ah maybe this use of alien jabber being allusion to the shameful human handprint branded on Imbricate's hide!

Three rival nests . . .

'Velvets being renowned for your use of sensitive blooms from Ukkos as detectors.' Imbricate stating the obvious. 'Brindled mutant-mage using blooms too. Such a strategy not being unique to Velvets.'

Brazens also forever experimenting with the sensitive flowers found within their own Ukko. Imbricate refraining from volunteering details of the home nest, however. He was continuing: 'Velvets procuring from humanbeings all skeletons they were finding in their original, hitherto only Ukko, for purposes of necromancy.'

Naive of humanbeings to be trading Isi and servant bones. Yet what success was rewarding the Velvets?

Muskular was swaying. Likewise the waxy flower in its flask. Bloom having drunk too much of the *maaginen*'s minor venoms and other juices?

'Velvets collecting and tasting human artefacts quite like this world's robberbirds—'

'Studying products of human behaviour!' Muskular was retorting.

'—while Ukko-cuckoos are gathering story-power.'

'Taming of Ukko-cuckoos being taboo. So: to be studying.' Yes, to be studying, sinuously and circuitously.

Brindled procedure: to be trading, even offering co-operation so as to be enmeshing (not-so-naive) humanbeings. All the while their pariah-paragon meditating and swelling in secure isolation.

Chime of atunement vibrating through the nest.

Imbricate resting his head contemplatively upon the body-servant's mat of ruddy fuzz. Rubbing chin to and fro. Servant coughing softly and huskily. Servant's chin-glands dribbling musk. Puffs of pastel light popping from Imbricate's horns.

Reminding his hostess and detainer: 'Brazen strategy being most varied and vigorous. Exercising humanbeing as body-slave wearing suit of mage-skin. Rearing juvenile human mana-mutant.' This being well enough known from cuckoo-gossip. 'Breeding extraordinary homoform Juttahat possessing free will and loyalty—'

Muskular hissing deprecatingly.

'—who was seducing Sariola longlife giver, becoming pregnant with mutant. Virtually hybrid!'

'Virtually . . .' Erotic vanilla, blended with sour syrup.

'Also breeding homoform sister enchantress. Myself infiltrating Pohjola Palace.'

'Being captured, being the *Maaginen*'s mission?'

Gibe being unworthy.

'Bringing to Kaleva a machine-making-everything.'

'Machine-making-everything being captured.'

'Myself being captured by you, *Maaginen*? No! Coming voluntarily. Seeking hospitality. Brazens being closest to controlling humankind and swaying Ukko-in-waiting.'

Bloom was swaying. Muskular, likewise. The *Maaginen*'s fanged tongue sliding out, beaded with oily dew. Her servant-voice licking maroon tongue out through neat little teeth.

Muskular preening. 'Announcing almost perfect exploit, *handsome Maaginen*! One-eyed human female poet visiting here seeking false eyeball of first-class Isi fabrication. Same female being dream-linked to Ukko-in-waiting! Being potential new Lucky Sariola, we were perceiving. Haaaa.' Hissing satisfaction. 'Being sister of proclaimer Juke Nurmi who was opposing Osmo of Maananfors. Velvets specially creating a *spy-eye* for Eyeno Nurmi to be spying whatever she is seeing, wherever she is being. Artificial eye signalling her location. Haaaa!' Such a coup.

Imbricate lowering his head alongside his servant's.

'Admiring jealously, *Maaginen*. Female poet being where now?'

358

Pausing a while. 'Lord Osmo bespeaking her to be drowning herself last year . . .'

'So she *is* drowning herself?' Imbricate lifting his head up slowly.

Pausing. Smell of wet dog. 'Being unknown.'

'Why not spying through her false eye?'

'Not after she was pulling it out and smashing it.'

'Saaaa . . . Tragic fiasco, then!'

'Effective technique! Being sinuous. Velvets supplying missiles to be eradicating proclaimer Osmo, using proclaimer Juke. Thus Velvets are guiding circumstances.' And becoming effectuators, yes, yes.

He or she who is effectuating, is becoming attuned to the Ukko-in-waiting. Ukko-in-waiting feeding on happenings. Its mana nourishing sways and manias. Effectuating being a kind of swaying. Heroes and heroines becoming the dolls of mana. Eventually all humanbeings becoming puppets of the Isi, just as the excellent Juttahats. Yes, yes.

Chime of attunement.

Muskular seeming intent on provoking Imbricate, however. Repeating gloatingly: '*Hand-some Maaginen . . .*'

Imbricate's side itching furiously where the wiggy man's grip was tearing away scales.

'Hand-some *Maaginen* being handled by humans, being marked by man . . .' Puffs of pastel light popping from Muskular's horns, rosy and violet.

Imbricate being afloat in his servant's arms, anger swaying away, adrift on a resplendent path of illumination. Hearing muted squeaks of piglets behind hatch at the side of her lair. Imagining plump frantic squirms in the belly, spasms of suffocating pink food, satiation. Puff, puff. Vanilla, upon raw pork. Sweet vanilla!

His hostess was swaying him. His servant rocking back and forth. *Her* servant reaching out invitingly, astonishingly.

Muskular declaring alluringly from servant's lips and in Imbricate's head: '¡Kex'qi sukoo qa'zuvi th'raan ¡kexi ¡kikaxi shaaai—'

How could this be happening? He of Brazen clan, she of Velvet clan! Black Juttahat stroking Imbricate's amber-skinned body-servant. Holding him, eyes nictitating, nostrils valving open and shut, liquid pearls leaking from chin-glands. Black male and Brazen male. As paradoxical as Velvet Isi female and Brazen

359

Isi male. As contrary as detainer/detainee. Was she mocking, mimicking, the seduction of humanbeing by a specially bred mana-massaged Juttahat?

Imbricate-male to be achieving dominance and freedom – or submission – in Muskular's coils?

Or being japed?

Mana-light puffing from Imbricate's horns. Black servant pulling Imbricate's servant closer to Muskular's shelf. Squeak of piglets promising feast after rubbing and poking and stroking and twining to be bringing two serpents' cloacas juicily together.

Ukko-flower flexing its petals. No humanbeing words now. Yet still the handprint on his hide.

Muskular being queenly. Displaying whim-lust-cunning. Her game eluding Imbricate. Game needing playing, to be discovering motive for perverse mating of rival *Maaginen*, one of whom being disfigured.

Rubbing, rearing, stroking.

Servants fondling, drooling.

Muskular proving herself unguessable – ripe for becoming Enlightened Precious One.

Ah. Of course! Great Narration impending.

How *Maaginen* Muskular of the Velvets, mistress of ear-flowers, was captivating Imbricate of the Brazens. All preceding and subsequent circumstances being poised upon this pivot.

This being why she is inviting/demanding copulation! Behaviour so unique is embracing Imbricate's personal history within hers. Therefore enfolding Brazen ploys within Velvet manoeuvres. Swallowing like a piglet.

Muskular so precipitate in sexual overture. Necessarily so! Otherwise Imbricate's prolonged presence in Velvet nest might be equating with . . . protracted foreplay. Courtship against her clan's inclinations.

(Narration might be posing this very question!)

Swallowing, as of piglets-in-waiting! Muskular grappling him within her. Pulling the Brazen within the Velvet.

Imbricate ought to be desisting? Refusing at this late moment? His scute is aching again. Two cloacas are rubbing together. Stroking, smearing.

The man called Tomi was certainly Goldi's *saviour*. Despite first appearances he proved not to be her golden one, whom she was swayed to seek.

Her previous saviour, who gave her his pony – the double-minded man with the cuckoo perched upon his shoulder – had glimpsed the goal of Goldi's quest in his mana-lens. He hadn't been able to show her what he saw. Yet he had assured her vehemently that her seeking would not be in vain. When Tomi came into her life he might well have *seemed* to be the person she was searching for . . .

She had dismounted from Goodbrand to bathe in a woodland pool. Blushmoss upholstered the banks with soft pink pillows tasselled by lacy herbage. A chuckling brook fed the pond before seeping onward through a mire of ferns and softsedge. Fat suckerflies were lazing over the ferns, vibrant-winged, a thready tube trailing behind each, their antennae like monstrous eyebrows. Insects didn't bother her if she chose to smell repellent. Spade-leafed larkeries shared the precincts of the pond with frond-dangling leper trees and mounds of mustaberry bushes purple with ripening fruit. Sunshine varnished vegetation and the water. A sailing cloud robbed the world of gloss yet this was swiftly restored.

She had shed her grey fustian cloak. She had kicked off her moccasins which were no longer very pristine.

The place seemed private. Yet peeping eyes had been following that cloaked figure on the shaggy pony. Leper fronds tilted poolwards as if pushed by a breeze. Goodbrand whickered softly. A couple of fellows emerged from concealment.

They whistled appreciatively, as each ogled her brief silver tunic revealing the butter-sculpture of her shanks and thighs, the gilded butter of her shoulders, one with a starflower beauty-spot.

These brothers – or cousins – were squat and brawny. They moved softly enough. Their shirts and knickerbockers were of dull green; their hats of floppy brown felt. Knives were in their belts. Hairs sprouted from their nostrils as though coal-black hammockis lived within.

'What do we have here in our very own woods, eh?'

'Has to pay for safe passage, I'd say.'

'Pay for a bathe too.'

''bout to take a dip, weren't she, Stig?'

'After we dip our wicks, I'm thinking.'

Their words were a mutual mumble of vindication. Erotic frenzy was glazing their gaze.

'Reckon she's a nakki?'

'Never seen the like!' Adjusting his crotch: 'Nor never again, I'm thinking.'

'She'll leave those fancy gloves on, eh, in case she has *nails*.'

Goldi shrilled. Her cry might have been a wild amplified chord on her harp except that the harp was lost at Loxmithlinna. Somewhere a bird shrieked in sympathy or in alarm.

Nostrils wrinkled. Hairy hammockis tested the air.

'She do pong something awful.'

'Like a bucket of pig-shit.'

'Needs a wash first of all.'

'Naw, that's a nakki-sway she's putting out. I think we can put up with it. What a chick, what a hot hen. Do us a dance, darling. Twirl yourself, show us your tail. Fluff your feathers, then we'll play girly sandwich front and rear.'

'Not in the bum-hole, Stig, not with that stench.'

A nudge in the ribs: 'Aw, it's all in the mind, Alf. Ain't we exciting you, nakki-lassy? Dirty talk turns a darling on.'

Hairy hands loosened belt buckles preparatorily. Excitement? Oh horror.

'Tight and hot, hmm?'

'Juicy pussy.'

Goldi shrilled again. Her week and a day of dumbness had elapsed. Yet where was the use of words? Tears started to her eyes. How they would love her to run – to try to leap on to Goodbrand. She would never reach the pony. She would only add spice to their rape.

What beasts humanbeings could become. Isi voices should be controlling them. If she stayed silent and limp, would that frustrate her assaulters and drive them to excess?

Why didn't her stench repel them? Because the vision of her body overcame the effluvium of her glands. Their eyes goggled at her, demented with a need to possess. Were it not for the noxious odour, Stig and Alf might have frothed prematurely in their pants.

'Uuung,' grunted Stig.

The noise meant nothing at all. It also expressed his whole imperative existence, bound up in a sound.

He and his kinsman slouched slowly forward, their awkward gait determined by the swelling of their crotches, as yet unfreed. If Goldi darted in any direction, they would hurl themselves after her willy-nilly. She'd been *designed* to attract alien males. Manipulated to do so. Here was the outcome. Oh the bulging insistent approach of these animals!

But then *he* had arrived at a brisk pace.

Her first thought was that he was a crony of Stig and Alf. Even when he shouted, 'Back off, you boys!' she supposed that he was demanding precedence on account of his superior musculature. Now she must needs endure the attentions of a bull as well as of a couple of bullocks.

Might there be more safety as well as more abuse if a three-some were involved? A pair on their own might egg one another on to get rid of the evidence of their horrid behaviour. A third participant might add a more public dimension.

The newcomer wore tight white leather breeches – with a prominent scrotal bulge along his left thigh. His white leather jacket, unbuttoned, exposed a hairless golden chest of sumptuous proportions. Did he shave that chest of his so that the blue tattoo of a phallic mushroom wreathed in blossom would never fuzz over? His pectorals were so well endowed that those were almost breasts – with bubberry nipples (a gold ring through each) and maroon areolas. His bosoms were of muscle and not fatty tissue. How tanned his skin, how golden. His brawny neck was almost broader than his head. The short oiled brown hair curled back like rippling water. Sideboards were razor-edged. His chin, so clean-shaven, was two tiny buttocks divided by a cleft. His leather-clad buttocks were tight. His waist was almost petite, and his muscled tummy quite tiny. Such gorgeous arched eyebrows and neat wide moustache, and such a slyly impudent expectant smile.

How golden he was. What an awful irony that the *mate* foreseen for her should be a ravisher in the forests, a kingpin of violators.

But no . . .

From his shoulder the newcomer unslung a hooked pole of the kind used to gaff and corral floating timber. From it hung a leather kit-bag.

He let the bag slide to the ground. He slammed the pole, hook downward, into a bulge of pink moss. He flexed his large hands.

'Back off, boys. Leave the lady alone.'

'Uuung?' asked Stig in bewilderment.

'Who the fuck are you?' demanded Alf.

The golden gent's smile widened. 'Ever been tied to a tree by your belts and buggered, boys?' he enquired.

'Hey, that's no way to talk,' cried Alf indignantly. His hand was on the hilt of his knife.

The lumberjack – such he must be – rushed forward. Scooping a hand between Alf's legs, he hoisted Goldi's would-be rapist by the groin and threw him yowling aside. Tossed upon the ground, Alf hunched his knees up almost to his chin, gasping obscenities.

The 'jack turned to Stig, in a scooping stance, hands spread low. 'Who's for a ball-fight, my bold boy?'

Stig raced to the pony. He hurled himself on to Goodbrand's back. He kicked, how he kicked. Snorting, the pony fled with him, away through the woodland.

Single-handed, the 'jack picked up Alf by his unbuckled belt and waistband.

'No don't do it don't please,' blubbered Alf, hanging backward in mid-air, squirming and aching.

'*You* were going to do *it* to the lady.'

'I wasn't, it was a joke, we were wanting a pee.'

'Stiff kind of pee, it seemed! Since I don't fancy you *too much*, I'll give you half a minute to follow your friend.' Unceremoniously the 'jack dumped Alf on his backside.

Alf scrambled up. He gimped away at some speed, nursing himself.

'My pony!' cried Goldi.

'Come back!' the golden fellow bellowed. Goodbrand had gone. Stig had gone. Alf had gone too.

Her saviour's name was Tomi. For a brief while Goldi imagined that he might actually be the lover foretold for her – till gently he disabused her.

Tomi was travelling south to Portti, beyond Tapper Kippan's realm, on the coast. His ambition was to play piano in bars frequented by sailors from Pootara. Tomi was haunted by images of muscular black mariners. Oh to watch them watching him, to admire them while they in turn admired his fingering of the black and white keys: this had become a consuming dream. After the bar closed for the night, what possibilities for a fellow with a cosy room along the street and a taste for lusty lads who'd been

364

long at sea and who didn't care to patronize Momma Rakasta's notorious knocking-shop. If the young lady followed him.

She was most welcome to *accompany* him for a while. She'd had such a shock, poor young lady. Robbed of her pony too. Fellows with big jocks shouldn't inflict themselves on delicate different creatures except in so far as babies were needful. Jocks should sport with other jocks since a jock best understood another jock's cocky nature and needs. If she followed (or at least accompanied) our Tomi.

Such a shock for her. Had she — pardon him — soiled herself? (He wrinkled his nose.) Might she care to clean herself up in the pool while he stood with his back firmly turned?

Already that foul smell had wafted away mysteriously, to be superseded by a scent of fresh soft mushroom gills, and yeast, and sweetness.

Hunkering down, Tomi took a pouch from his bag. Within was tobacco. The weed was pungent with a terebinthinate odour. Her saviour proceeded to roll a long thin cigarette in a leaf of gummed paper as smooth as could be. Inviting her to sit, he presented the tube to her. Puzzled, she took it, she sniffed.

He rolled a second cigarette and stuck this jauntily in his mouth; produced matches.

'Such an upset,' he said. 'Camphor restores calm and modesty, Miss. Cools fever and over-excitement. I use it to soothe myself at times. Though not such times as right now, with *you*, if you follow me.'

Smoke drifted from his lips. He offered her flame, and she copied him.

She coughed a little. 'Camphor,' she repeated doubtfully. 'What is it?'

'Oh it comes from the tarpatty tree down here in the forest lord's region. Many trees down here grow nowhere else, did you know? One kind, the sticky carny tree, can trap and eat flesh of birds and little beasts. That's the opposite of the leper tree. Leans *your* way, it does. Don't fret. A grown person can easily pull free.'

She inhaled some smoke. 'You've been this way before.'

'Never as far as Portti, yet. I'd smoke a cig, and turn back. There's a fable that *somewhere* in Kippan's realm grows a remarkable tree. It's without a name, because no one has found it yet.'

'How can anyone know about it? In what way is it remarkable?'

He grinned. 'I think it looks like other trees. Like a minty or maybe a yellover. It isn't really one of those. It just mimics one

365

of those, to hide how unusual it is. Like you, really, miss. Quite gorgeous to the mundane gaze, I'm sure.' From under those arch eyebrows he assessed her full oval countenance, her dark amber eyes set close, the dimples puckering her chin.

'I'm not a nakki.'

'Of course not. Now the mootapu tree is one to watch out for. Its sap can alter people. Kippan has wooden troopers watching out for him. Just you beware of the fermented sap of the minty. One swig of that nearly takes your head off if you're unused to it. Oh no, you aren't a nakki. But you aren't any ordinary human woman either.'

'I'm a Juttahat,' Goldi confessed. 'I'm a specially bred Brazen imitation of a human woman. I'm an *alien*.'

He winked, and saluted her with his camphorated cigarette. 'Of course you're an alien. To me.'

As Tomi and Goldi journeyed on towards Kip'an'keep, her concept of *saviour* and of *golden mate* underwent revisions. The sway imposed by van Maanen maintained its strength. Yet Tomi's presence engendered in her a definite serenity.

She'd been trained to think in terms of dynamic submission, of herself as both captor and captive, sensually. Could it be that Tomi did represent at one and the same time her destiny and the impossibility of that same destiny? The sway in her was simply unable to perceive this . . . as yet. Maybe Tomi really did embody her hopes and the denial of hope in such a way that, in unfulfilment, she might discover harmony.

Could she accompany him all the way to Portti? Could she live untouched near him, sisterly within his golden aura, pretence of a human woman that she was? If so, she wouldn't be compelled to wander futilely any longer. Would Tomi accept her alien presence close to him as an affirmation of his own desires which were forever directed elsewhere? Might she be an untouched touchstone of his inclinations, authenticating these by the ultimate antithesis, of a mimic woman who was absolutely alien to him?

This might confuse the sailors whom he invited to his room. Ah but she would keep out of his way at such times . . .

Goldi began to hint circuitously.

What would Tomi do during the winter when the harbour was locked in ice, when there were no black-skinned sailors?

A robust fellow could always find work. The log-gaff over his shoulder displayed his mastery of trees.

Could he earn enough money during the summer playing a piano? What if those sailors preferred to play with their puzzles? *What if his dream – for which he had honed and sculpted such a fine body – was a delusion?*

Goldi's thoughts turned to Momma Rakasta's *establishment*, as alluded to by Tomi. Not that Tomi had ever set eyes on those premises personally. (He hadn't visited Portti yet.) Nor would he ever feel the least desire to patronise Momma Rakasta's. Tomi mentioned her whorehouse more by way of reassurance that certain Pootaran sailors felt obliged to fulfil certain cravings other than playing with wooden puzzles. Therefore certain other sailors – the cynosure of his dreams – would harbour equivalent but different appetites.

Goldi herself might find employment at Momma Rakasta's . . .

Merely employment? With her physique and her scents she'd become a queen of courtesans, intoxicating to the sort of sailor-lads whose touch Tomi must always forgo.

'What?' murmured Tomi. 'Me, be a pimp?' He smoothed back his ripply hair. He smiled so drolly. He paused to roll a camphor-ated cigarette for himself, and another for Goldi.

Oh Jarl, Jarl. Jarl was lost. He'd lost his individuality. No longer did Goldi nurse any hope of filching the seed of a longlife to restore Jarl's vitality. What a mirage that notion had been! How much more substantial was her golden escort. Surely he fulfilled Lord Osmo's criteria, even if she failed to experience an overwhelming shock of recognition.

To travel onward with Tomi, absolved of the imperatives of passion . . . To take up residence in Portti under his nonchalant gaze, no more foreign to him than any human woman was . . .

This was not to be.

Settlements in the forest consisted of foursquare tammy cabins caulked with moss: secure identical dens of purple wood. Their casement windows were small. The doorways were low and the thresholds high to resist the chills of winter. As protection against mud at other seasons, several hamlets boasted pave-ments of wood wending between unfelled trees.

Outside one hamlet a lumberyard was stacked with tim-ber already tenoned and mortised and marked for future assembly. A new house for a hen and her hubby could be slotted together in an hour or two. Other lumber could swiftly become a fort, after transport on carts pulled by sturdy draught-mares along forest tracks strewn with bark chippings.

Villagers mostly wore shoes of laced bark and jerkins of bark-cloth mottled brown and green and black. Through an untanned leather girdle there would usually be thrust a large knife, the wooden hilt carved in the shape of a slim hand, its fingers tightly clutching the blade, never to let go of it. Women, flowers of the forest, sported gaudily variegated aprons over their gowns of barkcloth.

What glances of admiration Tomi and Goldi attracted. Such a splendidly well-matched couple. A hero and his hen! The gaff-pole over his shoulder won respect. If any Stigs or Alfs were in the offing, those kept their distance. Tomi had pennies enough (not to mention a handful of silver marks) to buy stew and bread and boiled eggs and grilled chicken. He didn't grudge sharing with Goldi.

Because they seemed so exceptional together, Tomi and Goldi were stopped twice and questioned by wooden soldiers armed with rifles and lightpistols – hard men with a grain to their face who seemed immune to ordinary susceptibilities. Their uniforms and their caps were of brown barkcloth.

Tomi answered easily: that he and Goldi were brother and sister travelling to the coast to find work as entertainers, he as a piano player, she as a chanter. A twin act, he implied. Was he truly contemplating the notion of becoming a pimp in Portti, a piano-playing hustler?

The first patrol extracted an oath of loyalty to Tapper Kippan which would apply for as long as the travellers were in transit. The forest lord, as Tomi told Goldi later, was notoriously protective of his longlife skin.

Of his longlife skin . . .

Dared she dream once more of seducing a longlife to store his seed in her? No, no. She had abandoned any such hope. Chastity, except in golden arms, was part of the sway which Osmo had imposed. *Go until you find a golden mate to bring you joy.*

Might Tomi perform this role at least once, an exceptional once, a charitable once – even an involuntary once, swayed by her odours? If she violated his preferences, and alienated him, how could that bring her joy?

The next patrol cautioned the travellers against straying from the trade road and disturbing colonies of spinneris nibbling fungi in the forest, spinning precious silk for harvesting.

Beware: penalties for serious breach of Kippan's peace include being tied to a carny tree as pillory till a swath of your skin has been consumed – or having your face clamped in a mask of mana-charmed mootapu wood till your features alter for ever to match the grotesque carving of the mask!

Now that they were on the trade road proper – surfaced with bark bedded over stones – they had to step aside from time to time while a cart lumbered past, or a string of heavily laden ponies. Not all merchants opted for this route. Many preferred the south-easterly option of rafting and ferrying and hiring intermediary horses and carts to take them from lake to river to lake. Still, one had to step aside now and then. But not too far aside. Don't disturb the spinneris.

In one of the villages, because rain was sheeting down, Goldi and Tomi spent the night in a hostelry. On finer nights Tomi favoured the open air for kip. He wasn't in a hurry. Was a certain mental barrier, a hurdle of the imagination, confronting him as he approached Kip'an'keep yet again? His spirits might seem buoyant. But was he apprehensive about his erotic, and piano-tinkling, dream becoming a reality? Was he mulling over the matter of this voluptuous alien Girlem with whom he'd become involved?

In the vicinity of Kip'an'keep hot springs abounded, stimulating vegetation to riot around them. The area was an extinct volcanic region – another relic of the chain was the Porttivuono Fjord at the coast itself. (Tomi was something of a plugged volcano, who would erupt pleasurably when he reached the seaport; so he thought.)

One little lake, which the trade road passed by, was a-bubble. Causeways of bulging leaves the size of saddles spanned the hot soup. Chittering blue strider-birds with long toes ran over the saddles, pecking at grubs which seemed to wriggle constantly up from out of the broth. Around the shore swelled yellow fungi as big as boulders of gold, upon which perched other parasitic lilac fungi. Horns of plenty were tall grey vases. Honey-coloured roussel mushrooms as high as stools dripped slime and reeked of fruity oil. Umbrella-size sickeners with broad scarlet caps and green gills smelled deceptively of kastanuts. Braided vines wove steep hummocks.

A few hundred paces beyond such a pond, familiar horzmas and yellovers and larkeries reasserted themselves. Come winter, much of the exuberant growth would have rotted down except where hot soil and steam could still sustain it.

As if such steamy meres were more widespread than was really the case, the weather was sultry now; and the sky a grey blanket over humid air. Electricity crackled. After such a day you rather wished a storm would break.

Finally they arrived at Kip'an'keep, and stood overlooking it, while Tomi discoursed.

The town was laid out geometrically between a long cool lake to the north-west, fed by a river, and a lesser hot lake to the south-east from a rocky isle in which a geysir would spout every two hours.

Each New Year's Day athletic souls would dash through the snowy streets from a hot bath to a cold dunking and back again to hot. Those streets were all paved with planks. Flanking timber a metre high, notched by steps, led up to boardwalks. Before any town had existed here the central area had been a swamp where warm waters mingled with cool. Now both lakes were embanked for a considerable length. Massive sluice-gates were set in both embankments. When summer dust or autumn mud built up, or when spring thaw clogged the streets with slush, one or other of the sluices would be opened to flush the avenues. An army of plodging townfolk would push the water with brooms towards a great gravel pit on the south-west outskirts. On Midsummer's Eve, and again on Lucky's Day, Kip'an'keep remained flooded all night long. Boats and rafts and the boardwalks themselves would host parties until dawn when floodgates at the end of the south-westerly avenues were hoisted to drain the town into the sump of gravel.

The log houses of Kip'an'keep were mostly splendid affairs. Window frames, gables and porches were intricately carved and brightly painted in red and black and gold, and in silver and blue. A tree thrust up its foliage behind almost every building, presiding over a rear garden. Viewed from a rise to the north, an arboreal grid interspersed the bark-shingled roofs, as if the planks of the streets had sprouted and burgeoned. Once you were down in the centre of town, where was a living trunk to be seen? The foliage, yes. But boles and trunks? Trees only rose from behind buildings. In front was the application of the tree in terms of paving-planks and boardwalks.

On the far north-western edge of town, near the cool lake, a building rose amidst a foundation of leaves. The timber mana-kirk with its onion dome was built astride a grove of stout stilt trees.

Eastward of the rise, surrounded by palings with occasional gates, and a little hut by each, was a densely foliaged park: the Kippan arboretum. In the arboretum there supposedly grew two examples – and only two examples – of each and every species and sub-species of tree and bush native to Kaleva.

Between aboretum and hot lake loomed the purple tammywood pile of the Kippans. Barbicans guarded a domed central residence of verandahs stacked above verandahs. These were linked by covered bridges to lesser halls and lodges. Guarding the barbicans were a number of timber forts which could quickly be dismantled, shifted, reconfigured. One or other of those forts was forever undergoing rearrangement to seek the very best vantage and profile. Tapper Kippan had won longlife by wedding Edith Sariola over a quarter of a century previously. Since then he had become obssessed with protecting himself. Continual rearrangement of the defences kept his wooden soldiers and their ordinary counterparts on their toes.

Tomi and Goldi had arrived late of an afternoon of haze and heat, and were loitering by the roadside on a hillock from where one could best view the whole perspective of the town. Carts and walkers passed by. Tomi, though a fount of information, seemed disinclined to tramp on down into the town itself. He mustn't become too involved with Kip'an'keep. Last time, he had let himself be distracted from his goal by sight-seeing, as if that was the reason why he had come to this place. He had worked here for a while. At the paper-mill, look, over there. Beyond the hot lake on the southern edge of town. Can you see an orange roof? Can you just make it out? (But she couldn't.) He had lingered. The year had rolled on, till it was too late to encounter blackskinned mariners two hundred keys further to the south. Tomi had returned northward to his lumber camp, his dream intact but unfulfilled.

Adjacent to that unseen paper-mill was the equally unseen printing works. Tomi used the log-gaff to point, like a harpoon, but he couldn't hook that building into focus. That printery produced *books* for those who could read, as well as for those who couldn't, the mana-priests undergoing their novitiate in seaside Tumio where sailors also berthed.

'Books drain your spirit,' was Tomi's opinion. 'As far as books are concerned, other people's infatuations possess you. That's all very well as regards *the* Book – *Book of Heroes*, you know? Priests need to memorize it and be able to hold it. They're careful not to have words actually put into print anywhere near Tumio . . .' He lowered his voice. 'Some people here in Kip'an'keep actually write little books of their own and have a few copies printed.'

Aye, blame proximity to such books (all be it unread and unreadable) for his earlier failure of nerve. What conflicting fancies might have seeped from their pages? Perhaps blame *the Book* itself, printed so close to the paper-mill? What did *the Book* have to say about the cravings of a man for a fellow man? Yearnings of a fair fellow for another man who must necessarily be black!

Yes, black. How else to affirm the authenticity of the object of his desires except by this blatant antithesis of black and white? Tomi felt sure that no white physique could satisfy him. He would merely be adoring an inadequate duplicate of himself. Whereas a black physique would represent a true counterpart to Tomi, unique and independent of him.

Goldi nodded.

'Can *you* read?' he asked her of a sudden, almost accusingly, as though seeking an excuse to be rid of her.

'No. I'm a chanter.' (And other things besides.) 'I'm hungry. Aren't you?'

Smoked lazed from the crooked chimney of the hut beside a northern gate of the arboretum. Beyond the gate, a bark-strewn pathway wended out of view. Visitors would often buy a picnic from the beldame ensconced in one of the gate-huts. Some lovers would spend a whole warm summer night in the park. Couples came a-courting here where there were only two of each tree. Likewise, each duo's love was special.

'We shan't be out of place in there overnight,' said Tomi. Roguishly he added, 'If a visitor looks for the tree with no name, as I said, it'll be mimicking a different tree. You'd need to discover whether there are *three* of any sort of tree. Which'll be the real one, and which'll be the very image of it? That's why the Kippans only allowed two of each variety.'

Goldi herself was a mimic-person, wasn't she? She drew her cloak tighter to hide her silver tunic and her butter-sculpture skin; and shucked her hood forward to shadow her charming face.

'You're mocking me. Because I'm the only one, of my own variety.'

'And me, of mine?' he asked.

At the door of the shack by the palings Tomi bought fish pasties and a bottle of valleyberry cordial for Goldi to slip into her knapsack. Once the transaction was complete, the presiding crone took exception at Tomi's log-gaff.

'What's that for, then? No carving your tokens in bark!' She leered at his mushroom tattoo. 'Or else your own bark'll be carved.'

'I couldn't easily carve anything, Grandma,' said Tomi, 'not with a hook on the end of a pole.'

She wouldn't be mollified. 'I know you'll be thinking of scratching a couple of hearts high up where you suppose nobody else'll notice! You'd better be leaving that hook here temporary.' Delving down the neck of her black crêpe frock, she produced a whistle on string. 'Or else I'll be calling a woodman.'

Shrugging, Tomi disengaged his bag from the gaff, which he propped against the hut. 'Mind you look after it.'

The crone seized the pole as though it were a long-lost walking stick. 'Collect it when you go home to bed.' She cackled. 'Or else in the morning, whichever's sooner.'

'Silly old bag's jealous of us,' murmured Tomi as they entered the arboretum. 'I've half a mind to tell her my heart's set on lusty sailors . . .'

And the other half of his mind? The other half of his heart? Or if not a half, then at least some tinier fraction? The dimples in Goldi's chin were bedewed but Tomi seemed heedless. He inhaled the fragrance of trees.

'Mightn't be quite so much forest by the coast,' he mused. He pointed. 'Now yon's an albino larix . . . It's odd, don't you think, every tree being different from every other tree? Pairs are never planted together. Being held down by the roots, they can never find each other. Though a tree doesn't care about that!'

Odd, too, was their encounter with a smock-clad fellow of such ugliness that his looks almost transcended the category of beauty and unbeauty. He must have sinned naughtily against the forest lord's peace and been punished. The fellow's nose was a long beak. His chin had recessed nearly to vanishing point. Bumps on his brow suggested budding horns. How his eyes did bulge. Blood was dripping from a cut halfway along his proboscis. Scars webbed his slanted cheeks. His voice was an urgent squeak.

'Whip tree over there – beware! Step too close, and it'll lash out at you. Keep your eyes shut or it'll blind you.'

How could you look out for something if your eyes were shut? However, the fellow – whose head resembled that of an enormous

373

mus – proceeded to shut his goggling eyes. Pressing a scarred hand over his peepers for additional protection, he began to stray in the direction he had warned about, hesitant yet impelling himself.

Did the man suppose that flicks from the whip tree could undo the work of the mootapu mask?

'You have to be really close to a whipper's fronds to come to harm,' Tomi reassured Goldi. 'The mask must have squeezed our friend's brain. Come along.'

He guided her along bark paths deeper into the garden of trees and bushes till they came upon a bench beneath a musktree. Decaying gingery fluff lay all around. There they ate their pasties. Two lovers wandered by, hand in hand. The lad glanced at Tomi in wonder. Tomi winked, and shrugged. From the distance came a faint cry. The ugly man must have encountered pain. Sultry and heady was the air here in the arboretum.

Dew-damp, Tomi and Goldi woke next morning to early sundapple and to a name being barked.

'Tilly!

'Tilly!

'Tilly!'

The caller's voice was gruff and awkward though somehow lacking in adult puff. Were they hearing a child – whose voice, somehow, had broken prematurely? Or the shout of a dwarf?

On to the moss which had been their bed there bounded a chocolate-and-cream spaniel. It glared at Tomi, and growled. Then it stared at the Girlem. The animal was very well groomed. Around its neck hung a collar studded with dark red gems. That wasn't any commonplace collar. It was a necklace – of garnets. A pet wearing jewels!

'You see Tilly?' the spaniel asked Goldi.

'*You can talk?*'

'I'm Out,' said the dog.

Tomi propped himself on his elbow. 'You're *out*? What do you mean?'

'Out! Out!' the dog barked at him. It returned its liquid gaze to Goldi.

'It's a mutie mutt,' whispered Tomi. 'Some fine lady must love it to excess. *Tilly* . . . why, that's Lord Kippan's daughter, his youngest—'

Who was this coming now out for an early morning walk, but

the same young lady herself, trailed on this occasion by a silent escort of two woodmen?

Tilly's features were broad and candid. Her brow was generous. Golden blonde hair hung in loose tresses upon a silk gown embroidered with a hundred different leaves in all the hues of green. She was the very soul of woodlands.

The spaniel bounded and tugged at her hem, then released the silk to yap, 'Tilly, come see.'

Bare-chested, Tomi scrambled up. As Goldi rose, her hood fell open to reveal her bobbed inky hair – did a hint of brazen red show at the roots? The newcomer gazed at the Girlem's mimic-Sariola face, then at those long lace gloves of hers, soiled by travel. The two woodmen stood motionless in the offing, keeping wary watch on that muscular companion.

'Come see!'

'Wait, Out. Wait,' said Tilly. 'Who are you two?'

A strange and lovely woman redolent of floral attar. A magnificent if somehow common fellow with rings through his nipples, raffish moustache, impertinent bulge of tight white leather at his groin, provocative mushroom tattoo.

'I'm just passing through your town, your Ladyship,' Tomi told Tilly. 'I'm on my way to Portti to play a piano in a bar. My friend Goldi here, she's under a sway bespoken by Osmo van Maanen—'

Another sway! Imposed on another young woman! At that Lucky's Day feast in Maananfors Osmo had bespoken the unlucky Jatta Sariola. And now Osmo had swayed someone else of similar countenance . . .

Everyone also knew how Osmo had bespoken that poetess – who had spurned his hectic advances – to go and drown herself far away from him. Not to mention the kidnapping of Princess Minnow which cuckoos had cackled about. *Queen* Minnow, now, would you believe – after a violent battle at Loxmithlinna against his boyhood friend! Tilly's mother Edith had beseeched her daughter to go on her travels to find herself a suitable husband rather than merely amusing herself for ever and a day. Dapper and mannerly though Osmo was, he hadn't quite appealed to the independent spirit in Tilly. Too many people seemed to be swayed domineeringly by him. Perhaps this was in the nature of a proclaimer.

Was Tilly over-indulged by her reclusive father? Perhaps. Yet she wasn't *spoiled* by indulgence . . .

Sariolas were so volatile and headstrong. Maybe Tilly had inherited a streak of this from Edith. Now that Edith was approaching her half-century of life, a bitterness was souring her. Self-pity; grudges and grievances. Daddy remained youthful as ever, though so protective of himself that he could hardly relax except with his favourite Tilly. All the excessive caution of an old man treading on ice. And he, the Lord of the Woods! Mightn't it have been better had he never married a Sariola princess and won longlife? Then Tilly herself would never have been born. Some other daughter of some other mother would be strolling in this arboretum this morning. Or more likely lying abed in Maids' Manor. Yes indeed. Certainly *not* meeting this exceptional pair of travellers.

Of a sudden there crystallized in Tilly an awareness of who this swayed woman in the cloak must be.

Not a woman, precisely! Oh no. A cuckoo had cackled, but Tilly had never dreamed . . . !

'Why, you're the Juttahat Girlem, aren't you? You're the false beauty who tried to daze Osmo at the coronation.'

Goldi stared down at the moss.

Said Tomi, 'Her beauty's real enough.' (Though he sounded ambiguous.)

'You're the Brazen alien lass! The chantress who almost swayed Osmo with her harping—'

'She's alien all right,' agreed Tomi with the most peculiar smile.

'I have no harp any more,' murmured Goldi.

'Tilly, come see!' insisted the spaniel.

'No, wait!'

What could possibly be more worthy of attention than a unique alien female who had almost been able to sway a proclaimer? In this regard the golden lass might almost seem superior to any human woman. (By all accounts Minnow van Maanen could cut the cards when it came to trumping a certain lord's heart – not to mention trouncing an Isi mage . . . What a brat that little rebel Queen might be.)

'Come seeeee—'

'We'll *all* go and see,' commanded Tilly. Her woodmen began to shepherd Tomi and Goldi.

Goldi knew.

She knew at once.

A jolt coursed through her entire being at sight of the extraordinarily *golden* figure sitting on a slumped bough of the moot-apu tree. The insistent sway which had ruled her – irrespective of meeting Tomi – was superseded by an overwhelming certainty of recognition. This ousted all her elaborately wishful notions that Tomi might indeed become her golden partner in a platonic relationship.

What she beheld washed away illusion and any torment of uncertainty.

Of soft beige bark – like vellum – and bowing on all sides, was the mootapu tree. Its portly lower branches rested bloated elbows and knuckles upon the ground. These were vastly larger than the growth higher up and host to sulphurous bracket fungi. Resin oozed from cracks in the vellum, forming orange pendants. Above, short limbs were slim and springy, twigs wreathed in feathery pea-green. The mootapu seemed less a tree than some sagging many-tentacled seabeast colonized by bright yellow coral, with a shrubbery of weed sprouting from its slumped shoulders . . .

The figure seated upon the low bough was of amber, of a cloudy and glossy dark amber. He was of a *supple* amber. That person of jelled waxen honey was swinging a leg to and fro. Such graceful and elegant yet assertive features! Jut of chin and steep planes of the cheeks and firm mouth were definitely male – youthfully so. Of course in this regard mainly one noticed the maleness of musculature and genitals. The thrust of his sinews (junior only by comparison with Tomi's) and that pouch and penis pronounced him masculine – though had he been dressed at all he might have seemed more ambivalent. His scalp was as bald and bare as any other part of him; and his nudity revealed an enigma. His belly was less opaque than the rest of his amber body. Within, as if enwombed, curled a ghostly foetal shape. He seemed almost to be a *pregnant* male . . .

Goldi knew.

A thrill, which almost made the air twang audibly, surely passed between her and him. The air was heady indeed. Tomi gasped. Tilly flushed. The spaniel whined as if in mourning for lost pups. Even the wooden soldiers stirred stiffly. Birds were trilling rhapsodically. All of Goldi's repertoire of scents must have been released at once: attar and yeast and chocolate and more – even the reek of repulsion, such was the totality of her response, informing that golden individual of her fulsome identification of him and with him.

She shucked off her cloak to tally her gilded butter-sculptured anatomy with his lithe amber physique . . .

He was aroused, oh yes. Sliding from the bough, quickly screening that arousal with both hands, he stood dumbstruck. It was Tomi who scooped up the fallen cloak to drape it over the naked golden youth.

Tilly knelt by her spaniel. She didn't seem shocked. Excited, rather. Yet not by the spectacle of the youth as such. By the scents she inhaled. By the event.

'He's Amberman,' she told her dog. 'We call him the son of the forest.'

Ah, but she was informing her two guests, really.

'He hasn't appeared in Kip'an'keep for ages. His mother – oh I'm *sorry*, Out – she felt a miscarriage coming on despite all the spells of her shaman uncle. Do you hear, Out? Her husband had drowned in a boating accident, and her waters were about to betray her too. Her uncle carried her up into the heart of the largest mootapu tree in the woods. There, while he chanted, she miscarried – into a pool of soft resin. He sent her away, but he stayed in the tree himself. He chanted and chewed the bark and spat sap into the resin. Do you hear? Soon the resin took on the shape of a little boy's body – with the living foetus within it able to flex amber limbs and breathe through the amber lips and able, later on, to speak through an amber mouth.

'And able to grow, too, when he needed to grow, by immersing himself again in mootapu resin. That's how it happened, Out, that's how. We don't know if the foetus was going to be a girl or a boy. A boy was what grew. Maybe there's a girl inside the man. So it's said.' Perspiration on her forehead, Tilly glanced from Goldi to Amberman.

Amberman's voice was husky. 'You're a gorgeous goose,' he said to Goldi, marvelling.

'Coo-coo,' called Tilly to the neighbouring trees exuberantly. 'Come, any cuckoo, come. Bear witness, sing the story, tell the tale. Coo-coo,' she sang out.

Hark and hear how the lonesome alien lass met the solitary son of the forest.

What normal maid would willingly have yielded her charms to this Amberman, containing within him that foetus of uncertain sex (miniature yet mature) which operated his amber mocky-flesh? Was Amberman really a *he* (notwithstanding his pouch and his short pole)? Or a *she*?

Or was Amberman of a third sex entirely, of an alien sex astonishing even to a Juttahat Girlem who had been reared to beguile alien males?

When Tomi eventually proceeded on his way towards Portti (log-gaff over his shoulder again, and whistling) he was to wonder whether that old shaman uncle might have swayed Amberman's mother to miscarry – rather than assisting her – in a magical effort to create a new variety of life.

Amberman possessed no special mana-power except insofar as he was in himself an incarnation, an *amberation*, of otherness. In most respects Amberman was a simple child of nature, certainly not a denizen even of a village. He was able to sit in a glade half a day, breathing the world about him. A *nakki* was what the shaman had midwifed, all be it a nakki of human parentage. And this nakki transfixed the Girlem, just as she enthralled him-and-her.

Goldi wasn't a creature of the wild, even if her lover was; but a being of art, more like.

Accordingly Tilly – out of charity and fascination – engaged the Girlem as a maid for herself in Maids' Manor adjacent (by one of those bridges) to the main mass of the family keep. Since two elder sisters were well wedded and away, Tilly had the run of Maids' Manor. Without too much wheedling Tapper's daughter was able to prevail on her cloistered yet indulgent dad to allow the alien housespace – just so long as the Juttahat lass never crossed the bridge to the main building. The Girlem was Tilly's finest toy, to be treated with even more kindness than the talking spaniel whom Tilly had rescued from Lord Osmo.

Of an evening in Goldi's own room in Maids' Manor, her Amberman – allowed past the forts – would visit his mate to clinch, and re-clinch, their alliance; to affirm their mutuality. Then Amberman would be off to the forest again, absent for a day or for several days. Such absences in no way diminished the rapport of these two rare oddities.

What did they prattle about (should a cuckoo be eavesdropping)?

Oh, of Jarl. Though Jarl was as good, or as bad, as dead. Of Tomi; may his dreams of black sailors come true. Of trees and

379

sap and amber. Of snakes and slaves and flesh. Sometimes they merely hummed to one another, a wordless song accompanied by balmy scents. At other times Amberman would trill the songs of birds. Goldi would chime, in crescendo, the notes of an Isi nest. It would seem that an unseen wood was around them (and indeed the floor, of intricate marquetry, implied a totality of forests) – yet that wood was also in smell subterranean and chthonic, a riot of roots, with birds and bugs flying through musty soil which was as etherial as air.

Amberman was Goldi's fittingly brazen – and golden – master; and her mistress too, she sensed (more so, perhaps, than Tilly was her mistress). For whilst in Amberman's arms Goldi felt the sinuous spasms of a foetal girl within his belly. Soulfully and sensually, Goldi was the receptacle for both Amberman's masculinity and his femininity, catalyst (and therefore begetter) of a sexuality as novel and alien to herself as to any human man or woman, or to any Juttahat.

And Goldi at last knew a joy as serene as it was zestful, though elsewhere turmoil seethed.

25 · DEATH BY BESPEAKING

The four mocky-men had stayed at the bone-hut for *weeks*. Lammas's cold cleared up after a few dry days under a roof of jawbone shingles, but Arto's feet continued to protest at the prospect of the final hike by way of Saari and Threelakes and Niemi back to the hovels which were home.

Another reason for staying where they were was that black Juttahats came a-calling several times. The first such occasion was highly alarming, initially, since the mutie combo had never met aliens before. Subsequent visits were disconcerting in a different way.

At the end of the first week of recuperation two identical Unmen named Tulki-nine and Tulki-twenty had presented themselves and begun to pester the mocky-men with questions.

'When Hermi-*maaginen* returning—?'

'Your relation to him being what—?'

'Your relation to each other being what—?'

'Being sent to this truce-house by Lord Helenius—?'

These servants of the snakes seemed highly intrigued by four such disparate fellows, one with brown rope for skin, one with the crust of a pie, one bandy-legged and goaty-eared, and the fourth a werewool.

Was Lord Helenius sending the four to be collected by the Velvets? If so, in exchange for what? ('No! No!' Arto and his friends certainly weren't candidates for an alien collection of human curiosities.) How were ordinary humanbeings esteeming such mutants at these? Mutants being Unmen, in a manner of speaking. Here was an area of potential rapport between Jutta-hats and mocky-men . . .

'So being a *singer*, Sheep-man—?'

A singer, yes, a tango crooner.

'Be singing, be singing.'

Knotty had located his fiddle amidst the jumble of the hut – all those dolls and chronometers and tools and balls of twine and Pootaran puzzles. Pieman found his cymbals. Arto pulled on the new pair of white kid gloves he'd noticed in a drawer. (First he had to snip a hole in the side of each with scissors so that his extra fingers could protrude.)

Lammas had recovered his sweet voice (though early of a morning he would still hawk up some gobs of phlegm). As Knotty sawed the strings, and Pieman whistled and chimed the cymbals, and Arto waved his gloved hands, the werewool had warbled soulfully:

'Within, I'm the same as any other,
'Can't you, won't you, call me brother?
'I lost my love beyond the blue sea,
'Beyond the blue sky, beyond the blue stars.
'She alone ever once kissed me
'On my strange blue skin,
'On my deep blue skin, so pitifully—'

Lammas's skin certainly wasn't blue – no more than the Jutta-hats' was – yet he was singing about the quintessence of aliena-tion. The black aliens in their sable livery listened with utter attention, eyes glazing and unglazing as if tears welled then vanished. Was a whiff of cinnamon a sign of appreciation?

'Do you know what *love* is?' Arto asked Tulki-nine, whose silver shoulder hieroglyph was more complicated than its companion's.

Did *Arto* know? He knew hearth-love for his creaky cott, why yes. And familiarity-love for goat-eyed Ester. He could weep for Eyeno. He could weep. Though he didn't. He let Lammas express all such feelings of loss and emptiness. With gloved hands he directed such expressions of sentiment while himself remaining silent about sorrow.

Grumpily Arto pressed these Unmen: 'Do you people understand about love?' It was a relief to turn the tables and question the visitors. 'Well, do you?'

'Cherishing the voice of a lord in one's head,' recited the Juttahat. 'Being complete.'

'But,' demanded Pieman, 'does a Juttie lad ever love a Juttie lass?'

Ach, had any mutie lass ever loved Pieman, when his body was so hard and horny and rutted that an embrace would scour and scrape her unless she was just as thick-skinned as himself?

'Loving all of ourselves mutually,' came the reply.

'What does that *mean*?'

'Loving, being incompleteness,' suggested Tulki-twenty. 'And incompleteness, being loving. Projecting a vacancy within oneself upon another person so as to be capturing that other person. Only an incomplete Juttahat could be craving in this fashion, exerting emotions compulsively over another.'

So only an Unman without a voice in his head could project his feelings and will and wishes ... Exert his will in the way that a proclaimer did, perhaps? Only such a bereft Unman could conceive the passions or manias or emotional attachments such as constantly haunted the human heart?

In that bone-hut – which was evidently respected as a sanctuary by the Juttahats – Woolly Lammas sang again to them, a song tailored to his notion of the alien heart, and to their way of talking:

> 'Losing your voice from my mind, my Lord,
> 'Your dear tones slipping away,
> 'Leaving me alone without a word
> 'Ever again to be saying
>
> 'Unless to a child, a sister, a lover
> 'Instead of yourself, my Lord gone missing.
> 'How much perfection am I putting aside
> 'In exchange for the hugging and kissing?'

Tulki-twenty asked intently, 'And are you dancing to such songs?'

Lammas told the Tulki, 'I made this song specially for you.'

'So: showing us the steps to be taking.'

Lammas and Knotty demonstrated how to dance. Presently, upon the spiral-patterned rugs of human hair, holding one another and concentrating solemnly, the two liveried Juttahats tangoed slowly: walking together, then taking a sidestep, then promenading sideways ...

The four mocky-men had disposed of almost all the provisions they originally found in the hut: those jars of sea-eel and roe, dried fish and cheeses and rusks. Whoever had once brought fresh milk and tarts to the hut had desisted. Arto and company had been harvesting fungi and berries and nuts from the immediate vicinity, and catching fish in a nearby pool.

When the two Juttahats paid their second visit, they had brought satchels of richly nourishing alien cakes; and again on the third occasion.

Remain, was the message.

Otherwise ... *being collected*, as curiosities?

Lammas warbled. The Unmen harked and tangoed, and went away. The mocky-men played with puzzles from the overflowing cupboards. Outside, the sylvester trees remained blue-bristled as ever but all curver quiffs had become crisply orange and bronze. Days passed by.

Late one afternoon, the hooped door of ribs burst open. Just for a moment the stranded combo imagined that some Juttahat grandee had arrived to learn to dance. Such a blackness of leathers studded with brass! Such huge lapels and cuffs and high collar!

Yet the face was fair. The curly hair was chestnut. The eyes were nutbrown.

No mistaking their former fellow passenger aboard the royal sky-boat when Prince Bertel flew the mocky-men to Princess Eva's wedding! It was Minkie Kennan (who'd scorned their company, though he'd leered at June's bosoms). Kennan the blackguardly murderer.

On that previous occasion he had been dandified in lavender breeches and scarlet kneesocks and a bright stripey waistcoat of green and scarlet. Now he was in ostentatiously tough black leathers.

Kennan pointed a lightpistol around the inside of the hut. Slowly a grin spread across his face.

'Well if it isn't the freaky foursome!' Suspicion darkened his humour. 'What in the name of all that's wonderful are you oddbods doing here? Who brought you?'

'We brought ourselves,' said Pieman. 'We walked.' Pieman's tone might be gruff, but the mocky-men's hearts were thumping.

'You walked, from Sariolinna?'

'All the way.'

'You look as though you did!'

Tucking the weapon away, Kennan stepped back.

'Walked, oh ho. Would you believe it?'

Outside, stood a black three-wheeled riding vehicle with a double saddle. Kennan proceeded to wheel it indoors. A pair of ugly guns jutted from its handlebars. He swung the machine around so that those guns were facing the doorway.

'Don't lay your fingers on this, do you hear? I'm strung-out. What a day. Don't happen to have any vodka with you, do you, fellows?'

Four heads shook.

'So tell me: how did you hear about this place?'

However, they hadn't heard. They had simply happened upon the bone-hut.

Our Minkie hadn't been expecting this. How inconvenient. He was bushed. To judge by the collection of empty jars they had gobbled all available groceries.

Now what's this other grub they offer him appeasingly? Compacted cakes! Concentrated *Juttie* rations, if he ain't mistaken. In the past he'd found similar on Unmen whom he bumped off, before he promised Kiki-liki not to kill aliens.

With bullying bonhomie, Minkie pestered the facts from the mocky-men.

Jutties coming regularly to the truce-hut to be taught how to tango? The werewool improvising songs for the slaves of the snakes? This was so peculiar that it must be bona fide. Come to think of it, mutie freaks and Unmen surely had a lot in common.

Indeed, Pieman became quite forthcoming about how Jutties had lately become dedicated patrons of this tango combo, and *were looking after their interests*. If any harm came to the foursome Juttahats would be very peeved.

Point taken. Word to the wise.

Though Minkie had been aware of the truce aspect of this hut, he hadn't been planning on hanging around in it. Rob it of victuals, flit into the forest; that had been the plan. Rely on the tent packed in his pannier.

'So where's the hermit, anyway?'

At least he wouldn't be obliged to bop that weird fellow on the head. No, he just had four mocky-men to bother about instead.

Hermit? What hermit? The hut had been empty for some while when they arrived. Good. Excellent.

Nevertheless, Minkie could hardly remain for too long in a location known to the locals. Bit of a hero though he might be to them informally, living as they did on the risky frontier between human and alien territory! Sooner or later people would find out about his presence. Tongues could wag. A cuckoo could come a-calling.

Minkie had never exactly thought of Jutties as other than a horde of jabbering (if crafty) alien animals so thoroughly trained by sly and inhuman serpents that they had no minds of their own and deserved exterminating as a noble sport.

What if he could *trade* with this couple of Velvet Unmen who were learning to tango? What if they could do a deal? Whereby he would tell them a certain family secret . . .

That secret was no use to him any more. It ought to be of compelling interest to the Isi; enough so, to impel them to meet his terms.

In exchange . . . No, shudders, he couldn't abide being pent up in a nest of snakes. They must set him up securely in a hut – somewhere in the forest where people wouldn't ever find him. Aye, in one of those little domes of black metal they built, which he had tried to break into once or twice.

As for his previous rampages with Snowy, that would need to be so much water under the bridge. Forgive and forget. Part of the pact. Maybe the aliens could even manage to bring Snowy to him for company. And why not some female company too, seeing as Jutties weren't averse to kidnapping the occasional farmer's daughter? Obviously he and Snowy couldn't carry on hunting Jutties. They would need packs of cards. Cases of vodka. They could tell each other yarns. He certainly had tales to tell to Snowy of his stay in paradise before that bitch Eyeno soured everything. Maids for the asking. Perpetual carnival. A heroic struggle against verrin-men and other monsters.

The bandy-legged mutie with the goaty ears was, of course,

none other than that same damnable Eyeno's *dad*. These freaks were all from her hamlet of oddbodies.

'Now listen to me, you lot,' Minkie said. 'I need shut-eye. It's been a hard day for some folks. You all behave yourselves, and you there Arni—'

'*Arto*.'

'Arto, Arti, whatever it is, if you behave yourselves to my satisfaction – then I'll tell you something interesting about your precious daughter.'

The dwarf exhibited distress. 'About . . . my daughter? What sort of something? She's *dead*, blast you! My Eyeno's dead!'

Minkie laughed. 'Oh no she ain't. Saw her with my very own eyes very recently, I did. Saw her from a distance, admittedly. We had what you might call a difference of opinion.'

'Alive?' Arto wrung his white-gloved hands, superfluous fingers sticking out of the kid skin. '*Where is she? Where is she?*'

Minkie wagged a finger. 'Alive as you and me, but a long way off. My bike jumps a lot of keys in a day. Your reward for good conduct will be what I choose to tell you; and that's the lot for now.'

Spin it out. Keep these muties under control. Until he'd come to an agreement with those tangoing Jutties he could hardly say *where* the bitch was. He would merely trickle titbits out to Arti – no, Arto – and his cronies.

Which special titbits about Eyeno? Her girlfriends? Her gang of monsters? Her brown leather breeches buckled with brass? Her rabid antipathy to a fellow-me-lad who was only trying to have a holiday? Her new-found *power* to be a termagant? He and she hadn't exactly exchanged confidences . . . He would need to be selective in his revelations.

Arto uttered a groan. 'Are you telling me the truth, Minkie Kennan?'

'As surely as you're teaching Jutties to dance. As surely as I'm wedded to Kiki-liki Kennan, née Helenius.'

Very early to doss down, for our Minkie. He was quite worn out what with the bloody drubbing in paradise, that awful disappointment about the hostage lass, and all the jumping he'd done. Bandy-legs would have to remain in torment. *Quietly* in torment, though.

In the wee hours Minkie woke to furtive whispers. Was Arto mumbling sleeplessly to himself or was he conspiring with one of his kin? A brusque '*Shut up*' sufficed to restore peace and quiet.

The following morning, Minkie was cautious in his assurances that the glovemaker's daughter was alive and kicking. Excessively kicking, to be frank. No love lost between herself and Minkie. Tell a lie, hope to die. Actually, his reticence proved more convincing than loquacity would have done – though Arto was still racked by frustration.

'But where *is* she, and how has nobody heard nowt of her?'

'I assure you, old codger, Eyeno's as much the mistress of her circumstances as the Queen herself.' (Damn the bitch.) 'Blabbing right out where she is mightn't help your daughter at all, if you follow me. Mark you, I didn't do her any harm. She just took against me. 'Course, she's prejudiced against men because of the way van Maanen treated her.'

What if snakes and their slaves were to pay a visit to the domain from which she had ousted Minkie? How would Eyeno's band of nakki-monsters cope with an invasion by aliens and mana-mages? Serve her right! Selling the family secret to the Velvets could result in a nifty incidental revenge on the harridan spoilsport.

The day matured towards old age without any Juttie visitors. Our Minkie needed entertaining. Entertainment was at hand in the persons of the combo, though what a shame it was about the absence of any wines or spirits.

In an effort to beguile more information, Lammas pitched some of his songs at the soft marrow of Minkie's soul – assuming that such existed, and mindful that he was a *murderer*, whose attitude to mocky-folk was condescending at best.

To the tune of *Loss Lass*:

> 'Oh where's my lass who lacks an eye?
> 'She turned away, she cannot spy
> 'Me searching desperately.
> 'She thinks I'm playing blind
> 'But it's *me* she left behind.

> 'Oh where's my lass who lacks an ear?
> 'I'm calling but she cannot hear
> 'Me crying crazily.
> 'She thinks I'm playing dumb
> 'Though my heart beats like a drum.

'Oh where's my lass who lacks a mouth?
'Did she go north, or was it south . . . ?'

'Can you possibly sing a song,' asked Minkie, 'about a princess rescued by a fellow who was going to get all sorts of goodies from her? Alas, when he gets her home she becomes a zombie.'

Lammas scratched his woolly head. 'That's a variation on the story of Georgi . . .'

So he sang:

'He saved her from a snake,
'He did it for her sake
'But it was all a mistake;
'She loved the snake, not him.'

'I don't want any snakes in the song!' Minkie began polishing the pillion saddle of his brutal bike with a kerchief. 'You can mention Jutties, though.'

Lammas cocked his head.

'How about:

'He saved her from a Juttie;
'Oh he did it out of duty—
'But he was dying for her beauty . . .'

The singer broke off. 'No, it isn't right, it isn't right at all. I don't like calling them *Jutties*, Mr Kennan, sir. So the song's all awkward. I'm sure they have hearts like you and me. Except, they can't think for themselves. No, it isn't right—'

'Oh feel free to preach at me, Sheep-man.'

Nevertheless, prior to bargaining with the Unmen it could be useful to garner insights into their psychology, to the extent that these muties were any sort of authority on the subject.

'No, go on, I'm listening.'

'I can't say it, I can sing it.'

'Warble away as you please.'

Lammas posed thoughtfully.

'How can I kiss the lips in my mind
'When those same lips swallow me?
'How can I set out, a love to find,
'When there is no hollow in me?'

This wasn't right either. Lammas tried again:

'How can I be kissing lips in my mind
'When those lips are swallowing me—?'

388

'I'm hungry,' said Minkie. The agreement about his refuge must specify that the larder was amply stocked with more than just concentrated cakes.

He made an effort to listen to Lammas – and the idea came into his mind of dancing with a Juttie (no, a *Juttahat*) to seal the deal they would arrive at. While he danced, at which he was a dab hand, the muties would croon and fiddle. Minkie would need to exert all his charm to partner an Unman. Lately his charm had become a bit scuffed. Could do with some spit and polish.

He smiled endearingly. 'Do you know, Lammas, you're really something. I'm impressed. I'm swayed. There's an esteem in my heart that I try to dismiss. But I can't, I simply can't. And you, Arto: you should feel proud of your daughter. She's made something of herself. To tell you the truth, *my* fault's always been admiring a person too much so that it simply offends them. That's why I struggle not to care too much for feelings, as you might have noticed. Or else sentiments would simply overwhelm me.' Why hadn't he always realized this about himself?

'Could we try out a song to appeal on my behalf to Juttahats? Something along the lines of: *He seeks a refuge from the world, with wine and games and a girl, a girl.*' Minkie could turn a phrase if he chose!

Pieman remarked gruffly, 'A refuge far away from any Queens, eh? You'd better be practising *ing*-ing. *Seeking* a refuge. *Wanting* a lass for the winter.'

Minkie simpered.

How long would he need to hide? He didn't fancy dancing solo for months with Miss Bottle. What if even Miss Bottle was missing from his refuge!

Farmer's daughter. Faithful Snowy. Well-stocked shelter. Simple desires, those. The bare necessities.

Lammas, singing about hollows and swallowing, reminded him that Kiki-liki had been cooking up a baby. The hollow in her had been filled up all right. A fellow-me-lad nursed a different sort of emptiness – restless appetites which made him show his teeth and grin and bite the world.

What happened at the Kennans' Keep nauseated Juke.

Due to delay in refuelling and worsening visibility, the royal sky-boat had landed on the bluff by Niemi town later in the afternoon than its pilots anticipated. Veils of mizzle were drifting across Lake Lasinen. The far shore was too murky to make out with any clarity.

Led by Juke and Jack, a mixed band of a dozen guards and Jaegertroopers and aitch-housemen approached the keep in a testy mood.

Should a royal expedition be obliged to jangle a doorbell? Rifle butts beat a tattoo instead, as if preliminary to breaking the door down. That door was of tough tammywood, marked with the ghost of a hand. Butting might have only the faintest effect. A red face thatched with blond locks soon peered from a window above.

'Wu-wu-what is it? Wu-wu-what du-du-do you all wu-wu-want?' The owner of the voice gaped across the causeway at the large sky-boat, around which other armed men were taking some exercise.

Juke breathed deep then bellowed: 'Come down here right away, *Snowy*. This is spoken! Remember me? Open this door.'

'Aa-aa-aa-aa,' spluttered Snowy. He clung to the sill in dismay. If he hadn't already been so red in the face, surely he'd have become florid with the effort to stay put.

'Aa-aa-aa-aa—' he wailed.

'We aren't going to kill anyone, Snowy! Come down! This is bespoken!'

Snowy fairly rebounded.

What should a dozen soldiers do once inside the keep but search it rowdily from bottom to top, while Jack rushed to and fro? What should they do with Dame Inga and Karl and Kosti and Kyli Kennan but herd them into the main hall along with Snowy?

Juke the proclaimer became interrogator. His first subject was Minkie's strawberry-faced crony. Stammering and babbling, Snowy truly knew nothing of where his boss was, or where his boss had been. Was Snowy *aware* that Minkie had reappeared? Oh yu-yu-yes yes yes yes. ('A cuckoo told us,' butted in Dame Inga.) Had Minkie visited home or sent any message? Oh nu-nu-nu-no no no no.

Juke turned next to sturdy-minded Dame Inga. Here he encountered a slippery resistance. Bespeaking Jatta to spill her life's secrets had been like sliding a hand into a pool to tickle a truster fish into his palm and hoist it, docile and gasping, ashore. Bespeaking Minkie's mother was more like trying to grip a wedge of melting ice with oily hands.

Did she know the secret of where her son had been hiding?

Her nose jutted. 'I've no idea where he's hiding, young man.'

Juke hadn't asked where Minkie was skulking *at the present moment*.

'Where was he hiding *before*, Dame Inga? Do you know? Tell me! This is bespoken.'

'Hurry up about it,' added Jack. Sparks and snowflakes danced around him.

'Hurry up, what a hurry we're in. Hiding before, before what? Before what, what do you mean?' the Dame repeated at an accelerating gabble. 'What was he hiding in front of? How can you hide in front of something? What sort of something?' Perspiration beaded her brow. Inga was deliberately working herself into a flummox.

'Poor lad hides in a hut. Water-nakki fell in love with him. She might drag him deep into her lake and drown him, deep in her lake.' How her words slithered away from where they might otherwise lead.

'As raindrops, she came through the roof as raindrops and soaked his bed. She sewed herself a skin of water instead. What a silky beauty she was, so sleek and satiny. He dived into her embrace with his wand so stiff that he burst her—'

'Where was Minkie hiding?'

'In the lake, the nakki-lake. Here comes the wench to get him drenched. Here comes the strumpet blowing her trumpet—'

A reckless resolution was in Inga's hazel eyes. Her greying chestnut hair swung as she gabbled. Her head shook to and fro, *no no no*. The spangles on her black lace bodice sparkled as though Jack had lit a tiny fire in each which brightened with each word-laden pant.

Where was the harm if she told her interrogator where Minkie had been hiding *previously*? She dared not stop to think lest Juke's sway took full hold of her. Did she or didn't she know the present whereabouts of her son? She dared not pause.

Lake lake plunging into a lake . . . Burble about a different lake instead!

'The wet trollop took hold of him in her watery arms. With his wand he filled her with little fishes. Sprats and minnows and elvers. All swimming around in her womb. Why, he'd have food for life, a wife who gave birth to a big fat fish every day, right into his dinner dishy—'

Her boys were goggling at her. Kyli's dainty hand, poised at her lips, suspended a silent scream.

Froth was on Inga's full sensual lips. Threads of blood were in her eyes. Her chest heaved.

What could Juke do? Cry *Hush* and *Hwisht* to silence her — and lose his sway?

A whirlwind was in the hall, whipping up dust and dead flies. Air spun around upon itself. When Juke and Jack and Jatta had been on the back of the wild hervy, the fastboy had gabbled thus. Twitching and sparkling, Jack seemed infected by the memory of that occasion. Was his presence assisting the Dame to wind herself up so hectically?

If only Jack hadn't told her to hurry up. Juke was the proclaimer of the sway. It had swayed away glassily out of his grasp due to Inga's wild determination to go with the flow, all be it to a bogus destination.

The Dame must be suffocating with abuse of air — as Juke himself had been choking when van Maanen made the quicksoil engulf his challenger. She was on the point of bursting! In such circumstances one would shout out at last a terrible disclosure.

Almost, Juke cried quit.

Almost.

'Her womb was a lake. Her chest was a cliff with big boulder breasts upon it and a fish on his dish every day—'

Her froth-flecked lips, her bulging haemorrhaging eyeballs.

Inga gagged.

Blood sprayed from her mouth and from her ruptured eyes in apoplexy.

Briefly she had remained standing then she slumped to the floor, dead as a stone.

Kyli screamed. And one of the two boys fainted.

Juke had left Niemi sick at heart. When he'd been *squeezed* to softness by a superior proclaimer, when he'd been suffocating in quicksoil, what had he shrieked out but a total betrayal of his dearest?

Jack was reticent and edgy. When soldier Ben, Prut's namesake with the fruity breath and mushroom tattoo on his neck, presumed to nudge him and wink and say, 'That'll do nicely as a first instalment on the Kennan account,' Jack lashed out with his fist.

'Just you shut up about it!'

392

Nevertheless this flare of temper didn't diminish the favourable frisson which Ben and the other witnesses of Dame Inga's fate had experienced. This remained quite a whispered topic in the sky-boat until in drizzly darkness they at last reached Saari, to the pilot's manifest relief. Latterly they'd flown perilously low with downward floodlight glaring. Even so, the broad Murame river had been hard to follow. Ben Prut had advised setting down at Threelakes for the night. Juke bespoke him quietly to desist, and encouraged the pilot. Jack chanted about fair wind and good light.

Leave Niemi far behind.

What had they learned from Minkie's mother? Nothing sensible, nothing worth knowing. She had almost certainly known where her son had been. Knowing, she had died. Had he been by a lake? In a lake? Under it? Which one of ten thousand lakes? Were there cliffs in the vicinity of that lake? Why, it could have been Lake Lasinen itself! Only it wasn't.

False clues, false clues. Dame Inga had managed to jumble everything she said.

Death, before divulging.

Comfortable quarters and hot food in the barracks of Lord Helenius vindicated the decision to press on to Saari. Many of the Mint Master's guards were displaced to the stables. Prut and Jack and Juke ate and slept with their soldiery. No bedchambers required in the palace, thank you my Lord; nor seats at high table. These overnight visitors – flying the royal sky-boat even in the midst of the war against the rebels – were on a confidential mission for the Queen. They must keep a low profile.

Of events at Niemi, keep mum. The Mint Master couldn't but loathe Minkie Kennan. But how might he react to news of the death of Dame Inga? His daughter's mother-in-law and protector, after all . . .

How would Kyli fare hereafter in the company of that stuttering crony and those two junior Kennans? No one at the palace in Saari seemed yet to have heard about Kennan's recent reappearance. Cuckoos cackled where and when they wished, unless bespoken to carry a special message.

By the morning the depression had almost passed onward to the west. Jack took an early sprint around Saari to admire the fine canals and fountains and bridges over the busy Murame. Juke didn't. Presently the sky-boat had laboured into the air from the pink-gravelled plaza behind the sprawling thousand-windowed riverside palace.

They flew over forests. Over fields and pastures spreading out around villages. Hereafter each village was a stockaded stronghold. Close-packed and interconnected buildings formed what was virtually one extended house within an encircling timber barricade.

Was the rustic stronghold ahead the last which Juke (and his sister) had reached on their trek to the Velvet nest? Yes, here now, here. This was it.

The bone-cabin would be about twelve keys over that way, deep in woodland. Somewhat further beyond, the horizon was misty, mana-misty.

Juke felt such *qualms*. Jack was grinning with excitement.

26 · UNSADDLED

It was mid-morning when Minkie heard a strenuous throbbing in the sky.

'Stay inside,' he snarled at the muties. He scrambled to a window framed with thigh-bones, its warpy glass puttied with dried clay.

Clouds were fraying into a loose crochet. A pool of blue floated blearily. Cheek to the glass, he spied a sky-boat passing over slowly, commencing a turn.

How well he knew that white fuselage and those portholes outlined in vermilion. That row of eyes: glassy pupils in a blood-shot surround! The royal sky-boat. Lucky Sariola's, come a-searching for who else but him. He harked to the throbbing. The sky-boat was circling, searching for an open space to set down in.

Nobody other than these muties knew he was here. Could one of the muties have happened upon a cuckoo while attending to a call of nature outside? Could those Jutties about whom the combo bragged have sneaked up and eavesdropped? Unmen would hardly alert the Queen by communicator – unless the world was quite topsy-turvy nowadays.

So: why try to land near this hut? Was the sky-boat in distress? Had it suffered damage in the war those wretched villagers babbled about? A war being fought far enough from hereabouts! Why was an important vehicle hundreds of keys from where it ought to be, unless deliberately? How in Surma's name had Lucky found out where Minkie was?

'Shit and shite,' he said.

High time to mount the jump-bike. Already he kept half of the muties' food-cakes stored in its panniers just to be on the safe side. Always best to control the rations. Should he jump in the direction of the Velvet Isi nest in the hope of encountering some Unmen with whom to negotiate? What if they weren't able to parley? What if they couldn't understand Kalevan? And him no longer at the truce hut!

Safer to lie low in the woods for a few days. North-west of here, perhaps ... To the north-east there were those narrow black rubbery roads and mana-mists and the nest itself.

'Listen to me, oddbodies,' he cried, 'that's the Queen's sky-boat that's landing. Same as took us all to Sariolinna. This doesn't bode any good—'

'Not to you,' said Pieman.

'—because I happen to know there's a serious war going on over in the west. When there's a war innocent bystanders such as yourselves get hurt. Whatever the reason for this visit—'

'It's a mystery to us,' said Knotty. Was String-skin being ironic?

'Whatever the reason, for your own sakes it's best to say nothing about me being here. Don't count on a free ride back to those mocky-cotts of yours in exchange for babbling about me.'

Wheel the bike outside. Swing it around. Shoot them all dead to shut them up ... ? (How close were the Queen's men already? Near enough to hear the clatter of gunfire?) Four corpses would be a bit of a give-away. That might only irritate his pursuers, considering the esteem which the mutie combo had enjoyed in Pohjola Palace. Besides, it would be sheer *murder*. Minkie had never murdered anyone apart from figging Prince Bertel who had really been committing suicide. Killing Unmen didn't count. Nor nakkis, neither. Up until now he'd been decent to these muties. They'd given him tips on how to talk to Jutties other than with a crossbow quarrel. Be a shame to spoil a cordial relationship.

He wheeled the bike out through the doorway.

'Our rations!'

'I'm sparing your lives, you know,' he called, and twisted the blue handlebar.

That familiar negative flash of utter darkness. Almost immediately Minkie was amidst some scarlet minty trees.

Swing the bike around. Where's the sun hiding? Where's north, where's west? A robberbird *crukk*ed. Oh look at those bright brass studs.

Twist blue.

This time, the in-between lasted a suffocatingly longer time, similar to when he'd long-jumped with that awful mana-mage. Minkie's lungs were bursting. Dark emptiness pressed upon him. Panic built.

Light and air! A larkery was dangling rusty spade-blades about to drop and moulder. Tarnished copper fronds of a horzma. A green-needled vera. Russet bushes cupping wrinkled berries. A dozen little leppis scattered, gloves of tawny fur scampering in all directions to hide from this sudden giant black predator.

Phew.

Well, whatever had happened, he'd have to twist blue again.

And so he did.

Nothing happened.

The bike was silent. No more soft throb, no pulse. He booted the side of the inert machine, as one might ginger a pony; in vain. Try the guns. Just once, mind, gently. Noisy things.

Briefly he twisted red. No momentary eruption shattered the quiet. No splinters flew from any tree trunks. No dying leaves danced.

He twisted again, violently. Nothing happened at all.

Oh shite.

'Come on, bike,' he urged. He slapped it, kicked it.

In the absence of a more suitable clearing the royal sky-boat had settled across a pond. The ramp-hatch couldn't reach the mossy bank. Disembarking soldiery, led by Prut wearing his glasses, had to wade then empty their boots once ashore.

Their departure left space for Juke to wrestle a jump-bike into position in the hatchway, from which he could point it in the right direction. His pillion escort, armed with a lightrifle, was a sandy-haired aitch-houseman called Karlo whose right cheek had been nicked by shrapnel during the second siege.

Juke jumped into the midst of the woods. Except as a few scraps of winter-white beyond trunks and red-rainbow foliage the sky-boat was barely visible any more.

Jack followed a minute later, bike-borne, accompanied by fruity Ben clutching a lightrifle across his lap.

Ben had begged to ride. His feet were perenially itchy. A few little ulcers on them was the problem. Plodging through a pond could have miserable consequences. ('Sorry I spoke out of turn before. Won't happen again.')

As the soldiery spread out through the trees in the direction of Hermi's hut they yoiked like grannies on a mushroom hunt.

'*Minkie*—!'

    '*Kennan*—!'

        '*Minkie*—!'

            '*Kennan*—!'

These hunting calls co-ordinated the advance, unifying the greens-and-browns, the buffs, the blues, and the bottle-green-and-umbers. Might serve to forewarn, but also to panic their quarry. Silence might have been more discreet. Had the sky-boat been silent as it lumbered towards its landing place? Prut had given no orders for tight lips. His troops needed to know where each person was.

Juke jumped ahead of Jack, Jack following immediately after.

Juke entered the bone-hut, proclaiming, 'Kennan, be still, don't move!' Lightpistol in his hand, fawn hair swept back as if wind-combed, blue eyes intent on a target. Jack in his coppery livery came rushing after him. Karlo and Ben had remained on the bikes.

'*Son?*' exclaimed Arto. '*Son?*'

The goaty-eared little man waved his gloves. 'She's alive! Our Eyeno's alive!' The information arced like lightning from father to son. Couldn't have stayed pent for a moment after Arto set eyes on Juke. Imperatively it proclaimed itself.

'*Eyeno's alive!*'

Juke staggered.

Jack was darting to and fro, peering, sniffing like a hound at the mocky-men and the abundant jumble in the hut.

How Juke's heart thumped with the shock. To find his father here . . . but then to hear that—

'Alive—? But—?'

She couldn't be. Van Maanen had bespoken her to die. Nothing had been heard of her for a year.

'She's alive, me boy, as sure as you and me. She's well.'

Juke supported himself against an open cupboard full of dolls and dismantled clocks.

'Is she . . . at home?'

The astonishing spectacle of his father signified home. But this place wasn't the creaky cott in Outo. It was a shaman's hut built of bones.

Arto wasn't at home.

'How do you know, Dad?'

'Where's Kennan, where's Kennan?' Jack was asking Pieman and Knotty and Lammas all at once.

'*Kennan?* It was that Minkie Kennan who told me, son. He was going to tell us exactly where she is in exchange for us helping him communicate with Juttahats who've been coming here—'

'Kennan was here?' asked Jack.

'He was spinning his yarn out so we'd behave ourselves.'

'How long ago was he here?'

'Five minutes,' said Pieman. 'Or six or seven. With a bike just like them outside—'

'He was lying about Eyeno!' yelled Juke. Her name erupted from him like a quarrel from a crossbow.

'No, he *wasn't*, lad. She's somewhere far off where he'd been skulking. And the proof is this: he'd suffered something gruelling from our Eyeno. I don't know what, but he'd never have confessed anything of the sort unless it had been painfully true and rankling. Not him!'

'Arto's right,' said Knotty.

'Which way did he jump?' Jack whirled around in impatience. 'Five minutes, six, seven! Which direction?'

Said Juke, 'I once swayed him to droop if he ever went near her again—' Ah, jealous covetous brother that he was. Charming Kennan had been trying to ravish his sister!

'Kennan really does know, lad. Then you lot turn up, and off he buggers. Just vanishes away on that contraption.'

As though Juke had caused his sister to be lost a second time!

'Six minutes, seven, eight! Which way?'

Pieman pointed through the doorway. Jack was already lunging towards his bike with Ben upon it, calling, 'Follow me Juke!'

Demon Jack was in the saddle, twisting blue. As the bike

398

disappeared it sucked a stream of leaves into the in-between.

Juke hesitated a while longer.

To catch Kennan, and squeeze Eyeno's whereabouts out of him ... Those Juttahats visiting the hut ... ! Lucky – or was it Melator? – had been right in their suspicion that Kennan might try to barter information about the location of the Ukko-child to the Isi in exchange for protection ... *Eyeno was in the Ukko-child where Minkie had been hiding. She was still there right now. In the Ukko-child!* This realization ravished and ravaged Juke's soul.

To find her, to beg her forgiveness! To expunge what had happened between them. To redeem the memory of furtive incestuous desires ...

How could *she* forget her vile discovery of the squirmings in his heart which had led him to reject her? That, along with the terror of suffocation in quicksoil! Could she possibly comprehend the pressures?

Brought up among mocky-folk in Outo – for whom he could never feel contempt, from whom he could never feel alienation – she had been his true mirror, his female reflection, his focus ... of attention, of comradeship, and ... of passion. *And also of self-love.* Surely he did love himself more than her! Yet she had been his other self too, the self who was not himself. He had adored her in a way that no Minkie could ever comprehend. Cherished her all too deeply.

Could she comprehend – supposing he retrieved her from within the Ukko-child? Supposing he restored her to the world, to a world where van Maanen would be suitably punished?

(Did she want to be rescued? Did she need to be? If not, how would she ever forgive him?)

'For mana's sake, son, are you going to dream there all day? She's alive, I'm telling you!'

Alive. Alive. Kennan knew where.

'This is your chance to make some amends, lad. Otherwise you'll never be welcome back home. Your mum's heart'll stay broken, and mine too.'

Did the old fellow really know all the depths of Juke's passionate deceit? Did *he* comprehend?

'I'll find her for you, Dad, I promise.' Juke was on his way.

'What about us?' bawled Pieman after him.

'Hwisht,' Lammas told his crusty companion, 'hwisht!'

*

Russet boughs and golden branches. Blushmoss unbruised by any recent weight of wheels.

'So where's he gone?'

'Keep quiet, Karlo.'

'I can't hear any—'

'Keep quiet. Breathe in. And hang on.'

Young Jack might go hopping about helter-skelter, hoping to find Kennan by sheer dash. Not Juke. He gathered himself; he breathed deep.

'Bike, your origin is Isi, inspiration of a mana-mage. Your fabric is steel from the forging by their servants. Your path is through mana-space; mana fill my words with force.

'Bike, be my bearer just as a Juttahat bears a mage of the Isi! You can feel Kennan's wake in the in-between, Bike. Swing your wheel where you feel! Follow where Kennan jumped!'

Don't doubt for a moment that you can find him. Finding him's a certainty.

Twist blue.

In the blackness the bike skidded sideways. In the dark a hand clutched at Juke's hip.

Russet bushes. Coppery fronds of a horzma tree. Great rusty leaves of a larkery.

A jump-bike close by.

Its rider wore black leathers studded with brass. Such huge cuffs and lapels and soaring collar. Oh those charming chestnut curls of his! He was shaking the machine and cursing it. No wonder the bike wouldn't shift.

The grappling hand tore free from Juke as Karlo tumbled side-long off the pillion seat. Even before the muted thump, that lone rider was swinging around. Either he'd felt a gust of air or heard the purr of the engine despite all his swear words.

Those endearing nutbrown eyes . . .

The twin guns on Juke's handlebars pointed directly at Minkie. Minkie spread his hands wide apart. *No weapon, no weapon.*

Minkie gawked in wondrous recognition. 'Juke Nurmi! I've news of your sister, Juke! Don't gun me down or you'll never know what I know!' His gaze flicked at Karlo. Karlo was in a crouch, hands pressed upon the ground to reassure himself of solidity. The aitch-houseman had lost his lightrifle. Not here-abouts, oh no. In the in-between.

'Yes, I've news of your Eyeno. She's alive. She's well. There are all sorts of nakki-monsters around her. Terrible things. Verrin-men!'

This, Juke's dad hadn't mentioned.

'Can I get off this bike, Juke? I'm all twisted.'

'Do it slowly. Keep your hands in sight.'

Minkie dismounted in slow motion, hands held wide, the soul of affable compliance.

'What's this about monsters?'

'So you already *know* I've seen your sister? I suppose the oddbodies back at the cabin peached on me. Ah well, they're your kin. And of course Arto's your dad. How can I blame them? Delightful fellows. Actually I'm grateful to them for telling you. Otherwise you might have jumped the gun, as it were.'

'*What's this about monsters?*' Almost in a tone of bespeaking. Almost. Not quite.

Minkie peered at Juke. 'It's a long story, my friend. You'll recall I couldn't help feeling a certain affection for Eyeno, ill-timed and ill-advised though it was. You've no idea how utterly cut up I felt at the way that swinish van Maanen mistreated her at the gala. What could I do to help, though? You'd bespoken me not to go near her. Unfortunately you weren't in much of a position to help her either. Up to your knees in it, eh!'

Did Juke flush with shame?

'Happens to us all sometimes, eh Juke? My heart fairly throbbed to see her so hale and hearty just recently. *Not*, I hasten to add, that I was able to approach a certain chaste hen too closely – for reasons you well know.'

'Where is she, Minkie? What's this about monsters?'

'Oh, those. Her entourage, you might say. I suppose coming from where she does she feels at home with monsters. For the present she's in control of her monsters. Can't guarantee for how long.'

'*Where is she?*'

Ruefully: 'Ah but do you see my dilemma? I need to . . . distance myself . . . from hereabouts. Came here to catch me for the Queen, didn't you? Juke my friend: on the honour of the Kennans – and out of my genuine respect for your sister who *might* be in a spot of bother thanks to her choice of companions – well, if you swear on your sister's name and by mana itself to swap that jump-bike for mine, then I'll tell you.'

401

'Your bike's broken, isn't it?'

Karlo still seemed dazed by his narrow escape from plummeting into nothingness . . .

'I need a chance, Juke. I'm offering you and your sister a chance. Be fair with me. I'll be fair with you.' Minkie gazed around at the glory of the foliage. 'Beautiful world.' An imploring tear was in his eye. 'Shame never to see another autumn – all because the Prince provoked me. That's what happened, you know. Bertel wanted to die. I was merely his stooge. Bertel wanted to escape from Lucky. So do I.'

'You'll take me to her, Minkie Kennan.'

'To her? Oh yes, to Eyeno. What's so hard about saying such a lovely name of a lovely lass, even if she's lacking an eye once again. She really fooled me with that glass bauble that time we first met – not so far from here, really.'

'Do you mean she isn't far from here *now*?' Was Juke shivering, though the day was warming up?

'No, no, it's a longish way.'

To proclaim Minkie to tell, then to ride away on his own bike alone to wherever, with pillion space for his sister. Simply to bespeak Minkie. Juke breathed deeply. The tattoos of lips around his nipples itched.

Minkie's mother gagging, bursting, dying . . . out of loving loyalty to this wheedling scoundrel. A loyalty which had been so lacking in Juke himself . . .

('I killed your mother, Minkie.') He didn't say this. If Juke told Minkie of such self-sacrifice, how would the fellow react? Inga's big little boy might force out some pitiful tears. Would he grieve desolately?

Juke had burst Minkie's mother. He never imagined that the Dame would burst rather than yield. But she had. Wouldn't Eyeno be disgusted at how brutal her brother had been?

He couldn't bring himself to bespeak Minkie.

Minkie peered at Juke harder, puzzled by hope.

'I'll guide you almost all the way to her, then you let me keep the bike. Swear on her name, and by mana too.'

For Juke to swear by mana then to go against the oath would enfeeble him. He would be swaying himself, then defying the sway.

Karlo was still suffering from shock.

'On the way there, Minkie, you'll tell me where it is we're going!' Not in the aitch-houseman's hearing. This was private.

A family matter. To abandon a cranky monarch's cause for the sake of his sister would show Juke's true devotion.

So he swore the oath in Eyeno's name (which he managed to utter steadfastly), and by mana too. Karlo began to protest, but Juke hushed him. The escort had no weapon to back up his words.

Minkie would need to steer the bike. Not Juke. Only he knew where he and his passenger were heading. Though on the way he would tell.

The bike jumped a score of times, emerging in forest, in field, by a lake, by a road. Black void intercut these glimpses.

'Stop next time and tell me!' Juke bellowed during a brief emergence.

'Daren't just yet! In case you cheat me.'

'I swore!'

Twist blue, they jumped.

What happens once can happen more easily a second time.

Our Minkie fired the guns rowdily at a minty tree crowned with scarlet as if already wreathed in flames. An instant later, he was butting his head back. Such a satisfying crunch and howl. His right elbow was stabbing. His left arm was swinging. The mutie proclaimer was toppling, holding his face.

Twist blue; bye to you.

Minkie finally halted the bike in a fenced pasture, causing a minor stampede of ponies. A timbered farm offered the promise of supplementing his rations with some decent meat. Strong spirit too, don't forget. In this life a fellow needed a strong spirit to survive. A soldier type of fellow in black leather, with guns on his impressive bike, could take what he needed without too much trouble.

Would the farmer have a juicy daughter, ripe for adventure? Game for fun, in the shape of a good few months of games in a Juttie cabin away in the wilds?

Oh yes, what about the *plan*? Strayed a bit off course, it had, right at the moment. Queen's troops messing around on the edge of Velvet territory: *could* they have come all that way just for our Minkie? Lucky was cranky enough. Might there be more to their mission? Velvet territory could be a shade too lively for comfort before long. What if this bike suddenly failed, as the other one had? Failed while he was en route to Velvet-ville, and in the midst of royal patrols?

A deal with Jutties might have to wait a while.

Minkie stretched, Minkie yawned. Good to sit astride such a black steed, possibilities still abounding. That skittish bunch of horseflesh cantered to and fro, eyeing the interloper with equine hysterics. A pony might be more reliable than this alien contraption; as well as being less conspicuous.

How did one *dispose* of a jump-bike? Leap off it, just before it jumped into the in-between?

Bit dodgy, that.

Sink it in a lake?

Minkie eyed up the farm. Maybe *charm* was called for rather than bluster. Better still: a judicious blend of both.

Juke staggered to his feet, nose gushing red-hot.

'Pain, wane! Blood, stop your flood!'

He gulped cloying sweet-salty gore, and bespoke again till the flow clotted. The middle of his face was so numb. Minkie might have knocked it into the in-between. Despite the hot bullets the minty tree hadn't exploded. He almost wished it would.

No! It would act as a beacon.

For whom?

By now he was keys and keys away from the bone-hut. *He had better continue putting distance between himself and the hut* – in the wretched hope that Kennan had indeed been heading towards where Eyeno was, however far away.

Faster by sky-boat? Hike back towards the bone-hut? Arrive there in a day or so, only to discover that the expedition had already moved on to its next goal, the Velvet nest?

Return to Prut and Jack? When he'd let Kennan go free! When he'd carried the Queen's quarry away to safety on his own bike! Cheating the Queen. Swindling all the men under his command. And young Jack too.

At this very moment Karlo would be tramping back towards the sky-boat. Soon enough the aitch-houseman would be spilling the beans about Juke's defection and sabotage. Juke wouldn't receive a very trusting welcome. More likely a speedy bullet or a pulse of hot light.

To have whisked away Kennan, who knew where the Ukko-child was . . .

. . . then to have lost him.

Anguish swelled. Most likely Juke's face was swelling too. The woe he felt was of a different brand than could be swayed away by words. How far away was he from Eyeno, travelling on foot? Eating fungi and tickling fish from lakes and filching from farms: how far? When he neared the hiding place of the Ukko-child how would he recognize it, or might he pass it by?

Throw yourself into the deepest lake you can find . . . As though his ears were blocked with muck he heard those words.

How to plumb the depth of a lake? And where?

What were these verrin-men that beset his sister? Amenable at present – but given to bestial behaviour! How would she greet him if he did reach her?

When Kennan threw Juke off, the jump-bike had been pointing directly at the minty tree. Juke hadn't writhed very far while he clutched his face. Here on fallen leaves were imprints of the wheels.

Mark well the lemon of the sun. The bearing must be south-east.

If he tramped for a hundred keys, constantly elbowed aside by forest and water, how far would he veer from true?

Supposing that Kennan hadn't been leading him astray to start with . . .

Juke sank upon the ground in front of the minty, and for a while he wept.

27 · BATTLE OF THE BLOOM

In a den of sand: a two-tiered game-table. Both tiers being rhomb-shaped. Upper board being transparent. Lower board, opaque. Slim transparent central pillar hoisting upper board above lower board. Thin black lines dividing both boards into an array of lozenges.

Thirty lozenges multiplying by thirty: summing up to nine hundred available spaces above (including tower-top position). Below, due to tower, there being eight-hundred and ninety-nine spaces available.

At north apex, and at south, Imbricate and Muskular were coiling rampant. Kneeling alongside Imbricate in sable livery:

Pelki-three, a mover of pieces, memorizer of moves. Attending Muskular: Pelki-two. Behind each mage were standing their voice-servants.

Figures in red glass and green occupying upper board, representing humanbeings including two queens and soldiers, Juttahats and Isi and cuckoos – as well as two blue eggs symbolizing Ukkos.

On lower board pieces being abstract twists of mirror-metal. Nature of pieces and significance of moves being different, below.

Muskular sending thoughts. Pelki-two shifting a serpent-figure sideways several spaces. Then lifting a cuckoo obliquely towards the tower-space.

Mindful of Imbricate, Pelki-three was reaching underneath to turn a mirror-abstract around, then moving another to an adjacent lozenge. Finally, above, Pelki-three was moving a red figure and a green figure and a blue egg towards convergence.

'Too far from tower-square yet!' Muskular's servant was voicing. The purple-skinned serpent with the indigo glyphs swaying ever so slightly yet provocatively.

'Eidolon-queen being reversed, precious hostess,' Imbricate's servant was asserting.

By way of tower-square, when red and green and blue at last triangulating, to be transferring a figure to the underboard where meanings and moving being otherwise!

Muskular yawning, golden droplets oozing from her fangs. 'Eidolon-cuckoo being obscured, handsome *Maaginen*. Being blinded.'

Imbricate's tongue flicking out. 'Being debatable.'

'Precedent being in the Shorter Great Narration Of How The Ancestral Isi Were First Being Carried By Their Juttahats. So: reciting, and counter-reciting?'

Imbricate unwilling for a one-hour pause in playing. Therefore conceding this point.

Sweet being the chiming in the nest of dens . . .

Two days had passed since Karlo's report of how Kennan and Juke had jumped away to wherever.

How could Jack's partner have been such a cheat? Why hadn't he bespoken Kennan to come to heel and yap what they all wished to know? The fugitive's bike had even broken down. Juke had to be the soul of deceit and obsession. Insane, perhaps, so far as his sister was concerned. Demented.

As for the mocky-men at the bone-hut – Juke's own *dad* and cronies – well, they knew nothing worthwhile. Arto's bandy-legged stature, goaty ears, and extra fingers might well prompt the observation that Juke had *always* been masquerading as something he wasn't. And after all the favour which had been bestowed on him; and on the tango combo too!

Short shrift for mutants, then, from the royal soldiery? Jack, mindful that he himself was something of an oddity, interceded to the extent that the four mocky-men wouldn't be harassed nor Arto arrested as an accessory to breach of trust. They would simply be left to their own devices – after a night spent in the vicinity in case Juke returned. (Which he didn't.)

Prut was sceptical about mounting a raid on the Velvet nest – now that the proclaimer had bolted, taking with him one of the two jump-bikes, not to mention his knowledge of the interior of the serpents' stronghold. However, the expedition couldn't simply quit and return to the Queen empty-handed. Prut's career, maybe his skin, would be in serious jeopardy.

Jack, on the other hand, remained full of confidence. Due to his compressed years he might lack experience. (Daddy of four fearsome miniature maids though he was!) Yet he could conjure wild wind and stupefying light and cold. Besides, he'd been raised in an Isi nest. The Brazens' nest and the Velvets' nest shouldn't be too dissimilar.

The morning after Juke's defection, Jack had briefed the assembled Greens-and-Browns, the Greens-and-Umbers, the Buffs, and the wooden soldiers, the Blues.

They would be encountering chambers and curving corridors, fruity air and chimes and pastel light, hibernacula and servant barracks, farrowing places and hydroponic gardens, workshops and a shuttle hangar. Levels of alien town lay under the turf, with several hidden entrances as well as a front door.

A couple of yellover trees had been felled and lopped and dragged to make a bridge to the ramp of the sky-boat. Thus it was with dry boots and breeches that the complement lifted off to fly closer to the nest.

During their stopover no one had spied any Juttahats roaming the woods near the hut, as reported by the mocky-men. Surprise should still be on the side of the royal soldiers. Just as well. To Prut's best knowledge no such force had ever assaulted a serpents' nest before.

'Air buoy us quietly,' Jack chanted as they flew, low as could be over woodland. 'Air be our water. Breeze carry our hubbub high up into the sky out of earshot, eh?'

The vessel did seem to drum less noisily.

Glimpses of narrow black roadway, splitting and joining . . .

Mists drifted up to stroke the pilot's window and the portholes. Mana-mists.

Jack put his mind to these. His hands moved gently, moulding those mists so that vapour thickly wreathed the bulk of the vessel yet only a diaphanous veil lay in their line of travel. As the sky-boat throbbed mutedly onward, wrapped in its own personal cloud, he recited:

'Hide us,

'And guide us

'Through this maze

'Of haze—'

Who needed Juke Nurmi? Not Demon Jack.

Key after key rolled by – till the pilot spied a glossy vacancy within the forest ahead.

Don't set down on *that* exposed expanse by the gateway of the nest. Nor too near it neither!

The pilot veered the vessel. Presently a cloud eased itself into a carbonized misty clearing where a clump of minty trees had burned to the ground.

Prut sent wooden soldiers out to reconnoitre in one direction, and the Jaegertroopers in another. Slowly; take your time – take all day.

Don't snap a twig, especially you lads from the bald uplands. Watch out for disguised hatches or pothole shafts where long tunnels might terminate. Mark them well, but inconspicuously. Beware of booby-traps.

By late afternoon all scouts had returned safely. Reports, reports. No one had stumbled into a trap. No one had found a hatch.

Overnight, the wooden soldiers took turns on picket duty. Most of the Greens-and-Browns bivouacked outside with Jack, where the dense mist grew chilly and clammy.

By mid-morning the soldiers were lurking just within the edge of the woods. Except for Jack, everyone had smeared his hands and face with black lead so as to resemble – at least superficially (uniforms notwithstanding!) – a Velvet Juttahat. Jack, dressed in the coppery livery which he had cherished for so long, was the very image of a Brazen Juttahat. Beyond the forest fringe, mist billowed upon the black sleek tract. In the diffused pearly daylight they watched the two low domes guarding the entrance to the Velvets' lair.

A small team of Juttahats set out at a trot towards the rubbery roadway wending through the woods — far from where Lucky's raiders waited. Four Unmen. Let the patrol head well away.

The substance of the empty expanse seemed vitreous though also flexible. Jack muttered to himself till mist-figures walked upon it within the drifting veils. He coaxed afterimages of the departed patrol, dummies of vapour to confuse watchers in the domes.

He'd brought the jump-bike thus far. But due to Juke's defection he couldn't use the bike in the actual attack. He couldn't allow himself such an advantage over the men whom he'd be leading into danger. Couldn't let them suppose that he too might suddenly jump away to somewhere else if the fancy took him. Jack must proceed on foot into the heart of the nest. Ben, of the tender feet, would remain with the bike. If the alien patrol returned at an awkward moment, Ben must jump to bring the Juttahats within range of the handlebar guns . . .

Presently Jack and Prut and the soldiery began to jog across the open space. Mist was their mask. In the mist they were the phantoms now . . .

. . . almost till they reached the gape of a downward tunnel which those domes flanked. Then hot light seared out from a slit in the leftward dome, and a Jaegertrooper screamed.

As if the sun itself had appeared in the mist exactly where Jack was, he shone. Radiance flared around him. By contrast darkness surged over the domes. Inky mist congealed upon them, forming a crust of sombre ice. The occupants would be blinded, stunned, numbed for an hour.

Jack whooped as the soldiers ran with him into the convoluted lair. They fired hot light and bullets towards Juttahats who appeared along passageways, more to deter than to kill or maim. Those close at hand, Jack stunned and froze.

It must have seemed that a mana-potent Juttahat of the Brazen clan was invading the dwelling leading this swarm of ambiguous figures dressed in a motley of uniforms. Were these humanbeings in disguise? The most ostentatious of the uniforms were worn by impervious persons whom a knife could hardly nick.

No accounting for what was occurring. Responding appropriately was problematic! Youngsters in black elastic were scampering. Clangour rent the air. Not chimes and twangs but urgent jangles.

The intention wasn't to kill gratuitously. If only the soldiers could remember this, once they were empassioned! Wanton killing would provoke a powerful response. Unarmed Juttahats would probably flood to overwhelm the intruders; even to tear people apart barehanded. To be able to withdraw from the nest afterwards called for maximum confusion – and an Isi hostage to be released when they reached the royal sky-boat.

A serpent in a sandy den was swaying; its body-slave was babbling.

Seize this Isi here? (Avoiding its fangs. Woodmen should be immune to venom, at least to the immediate effects.)

It was too soon to encumber themselves. Find the flower first, the flower which Juke had seen.

A Juttahat darted from an archway and levelled a crossbow. A bullet exploded in an aitch-houseman's chest, tearing him open. His corpse collapsed – and the Unman marksman stood limply, doing nothing more. Watching, controlled.

'Don't shoot,' Jack cried at his bustle of soldiers.

Single-shot bow. That Juttahat was making no attempt to reload, nor yet to take cover within the archway. Just gazing, eyes nictitating rapidly, nostrils valving open and shut.

'Not shooting him!'

Weapons wavered.

'Juttie-lover,' exclaimed an aitch-houseman. A lightpistol swung towards Jack.

Jack slapped the gun aside swiftly. 'Not shooting! We were agreeing!'

'Reared an Unman, always an Unman—'

'Excessive violence, you fool,' snapped Prut, 'and we're all dead.' The adjutant's glasses had fallen off earlier and been crushed underfoot. He blinked at the protester, then peered at the Juttahat who still remained. Was the Juttahat terrified yet unable to take a step?

'We shan't take a life for a life, do you hear? If you can't understand this it'll be your own life for insubordination.'

Greens-and-Browns from Sariolinna growled agreement.

410

Sparing the marksman, they headed onward; and no sub-sequent Juttahat ambushed them.

In a long steamy kitchen liveried cooks were sorting and stacking food-cakes, click-hissing to one another ... Of a sudden the slaves were silent and still.

'Rebel and join us!' shouted someone, entirely in vain. Jack shoved an unresisting Unman aside, snatched several cakes and crammed his mouth. Crumbs spilled. He glowed. A Jaegertrooper fired at a demijohn of syrup, shattering glass and releasing a sticky flood. The interlopers passed onward.

Game lacking an obvious outcome, though commencing at an early chime. Consequently mages returning in their servants' arms to the den of the flower.

Rival mages rubbing together. Sweet vanilla, mutual fondling of male servants, mingling of pastel light.

Muskular hoping for Imbricate to be fertilizing an egg within her? Capturing his code and incarnating it. Egg being distantly akin to Ukko by far-fetched metonymy. Muskular being a multi-thinker. Imbricate being ingenious too!

Muscles undulating, mutually massaging, averting the horrid handprint as far as possible, sign of shame. Muskular being exotically stimulated by this mark? As if Imbricate being branded, signalling ownership. Whereas Isi should be control-ling humanbeings! Hand being means of manipulating. Splendid Isi lacking manipulators until obedient servants were heeding Isi minds. Those Of The Hand being ordained as tools of the streamlined shapely perfect ones. Hence the thrill/risk for Braz-ens when breeding those autonomous agents ≪Jarl Pakken≫ and ≪Goldi≫. Those servants proving loyal nonetheless. Lissom Muskular experiencing comparable frisson at emblem of auton-omous alien upon Imbricate's hide?

Discordant jangling!

Jumbly thoughts of many servants:

(Intrusion—!

(Confusion—!

(Humanbeings in many liveries, one in Brazen livery leading—

(Familiarity with Isi habitat—

(Mana-potent Brazen Juttahat looking like humanbeing—

(In Juttahat livery, yes—!

(Blinding onlookers, aah ...)

411

A potent Brazen servant – an autonomous servant – was invading the Velvet nest at the head of an irregular swarm of humanbeings whom he must be swaying!

A servant who was looking like a humanbeing . . .

A servant being able to sway . . .

Jarl Pakken, recovering from his zombie state! But of course. Imbricate's mage-kin were restoring Jarl Pakken's vitality. The autonomous servant wasn't only regaining vigour but attaining great new mana-power. He was leading sway-soldiers to be rescuing Imbricate, whose captivity/hospitality thus being known in the home-nest.

Not leading fighting-servants originating from the home-nest. Naturally not. Provocative of war between nests! Enticing humanbeings instead. Humanbeings serving him. Servant knowing how to achieve this!

Brazen project succeeding.

Not due to mages but to a servant. Him being bred for independence then suffering the living-dying. Receiving the living-dying from the longlife-giving princess. *Yet recovering.* Gaining sway over a crowd of humanbeings. Coming loyally to be liberating the originator of himself: somaseer Imbricate.

Imbricate was swaying against Muskular. Muscles contesting. Mana-light puffing from their horns.

Imbricate was projecting:

Hark, Velvet servants: not harming Brazen servant and escorts! Allowing access to Imbricate-maaginen! Qi'sukoo ¡ku xu'zi zhi'kaxi . . .

Formidable to be emanating in such a fashion to servants of a different hue. Indecision, at least, should be resulting.

Imbricate's body-servant arm-wrestling with Muskular's. Not bumping into the ukkoscope! Not knocking over the bloom!

Imbricate realizing his error. The radiant lad wearing familiar livery being the hatchling of Jatta Sariola! Fastboy Jack, now with hair on his upper lip.

Light swaying Imbricate. Muscles sluggish though mind alert. Body-servant standing paralysed, hands meshed with hands of his counterpart. Still capable of voicing.

Condition of Muskular being similar.

'Both of you being still,' Jack was ordering.

How long could this Jack be maintaining such mana? He was

412

gobbling a cake of servant-food, and clutching another cake in his palm.

Other uniforms in the den, and outside.

Leathers, faces, weapons. Eyes goggling at mages together on the shelf of rock. Gazes darting at inactive servants holding hands. At the vacant ukkoscope monitoring desk. White marble pedestal. Upon it the great glassy ovoid containing tubes and cells wherein blue lights were flickering. At the long-stemmed waxen flower in its nutrient flask, spoonlike petals flexing slowly.

Staring at the flower, at the flower. At the mages. One with shimmery shingle-scales lovely with ochre and ferric glyphs except for the deformity. The other purple, aswirl with indigo.

Reek of human sweat – and resin. Tall peaked hats topped with white pompons worn by grainy-faced persons partaking of the nature of wood. Flesh being rendered wooden. Wood being rendered flexible. Humanbeings metamorphosed by mana.

Jack making the teeth-show of grinning at Imbricate's deformity. Brushing crumbs from his lips, meeting the mage's glossy black gaze with a twinkling regard.

'Why if it isn't Great Mage Imbricate!' Jack's gaze puzzling, and hardening. 'Did Minkie Kennan bring you all the way here from Pohjola Palace? *Was Kennan bringing you, mage?*'

Uncomprehending.

Kennan being the name of the bike-rider carrying Imbricate away from the dungeon before dumping him violently?

Deep implications?

Ambiguously Imbricate's servant was answering. 'Yes, we were escaping.'

The lofty officer with silvery chevrons and shoulder-belt was whispering urgently to Jack, 'Kennan brought the Brazen mage here? *Then* he went to the you-know-what ... The Isi must already know exactly where *it* is!'

'Why haven't they already—?'

'Maybe they can't enter it themselves yet. Maybe it won't allow them to, however hard they try.'

Glancing at the Ukkoscope and the bloom in its flask. 'I tell you, they're all in this together. Kennan was acting for the Isi. Why else did he spring the Brazen snake from the palace dungeon after he'd murdered the Prince?'

'Are you taking my master with you?' Imbricate's servant was asking with feigned alarm. 'Imbricate-*maaginen* was resisting your questions previously.'

413

A clever idea to escape from Velvet hospitality by this ruse? Deserving of as much analysis as a move towards tower-square! Sadly, no time to be deciding. Oh, but being *man*-handled again!

Fleeting whiff of caramel-amusement from Muskular . . .

Muskular's servant was stating, 'A prisoner once may be a prisoner again.'

Muskular wasn't objecting to Imbricate's enforced departure. She wasn't wishing abduction herself. Abduction being necessary to be ensuring safe passage. Oh naturally!

Jack was cramming the remaining cake into his mouth to be freeing his hands. He was lifting the flower flask carefully.

Muskular's voice was warning, 'Our treasure will be wilting without benefit of my venoms.'

Said Jack, 'Oh, I've been knowing such flowers before, and I've been having an influence on them.'

A surprise for her serpentine splendour. *'Being when?'*

'Being in the Brazen nest, Velvet mage.'

Imbricate was deducing that Brille-Estivan must have been superintending Jack Pakken's upbringing . . . Flower still likely to be dying if deprived of accustomed fang-juices.

'Last saw one on my wedding night, in fact.' (He'd been so preoccupied at the time, heedless of bouquets in his eagerness for June.)

Muskular faintly puffing mana-light. Jack glowing. Muskular desisting.

'How many Ukkos in the star-sea?' Muskular's voice was musing. 'Being many. Perhaps.'

'Yes?' the tall bony officer was asking. *'How many?'*

Other voices were clamouring to know. Nervous though these intruders were smelling, to be hearing hints so revealing from an Isi mage's voice! Besides: such a temporary sense of safety in this packed little cavern. Whereas once they were leaving the sanctum . . . Being another matter!

'Precious Isi controlling eight Ukkos,' Muskular was admitting. 'Serving Serpentstar and seven sibling worlds of ours. Shall I be telling a tale?'

A Great Narration impending? Muskular prevaricating with tasty bait, awaiting the waning of Jack Pakken's power?

Green-and-Umber uniform was daring to ask: 'Excuse me, but are there only snakes and Jutties on those other worlds of yours?'

From a buff uniform: 'Are there any other kinds of aliens?' Might these humanbeings be fancying themselves enjoying an

414

audience with a mage, won by their boldness in invading this den?

Muskular reeking of caramel.

Her voice was saying, 'If only one instance of sapient life is occurring – ourselves, including our servants whom we were nurturing – one instance conceivably being the total number. Due to encountering humanbeings, necessarily many sapient species are existing. If two, then many!

'Moreover, be asking yourselves: before the advent of Ukkos at Serpentstar, what were Ukkos engaging in? What narrations were occupying their attention? Be considering nature of the mysterium. These vehicles of mana navigating the star-sea and bestowing powers as well as manias for their gratification so that stories being exuberant. Stories of which other species previously?'

Buff was interrupting: 'Did the Ukkos bring *cuckoos* to your world?'

Tongue flicking out. 'Being bright question. Certain large flying insects native to our world are clicking and stridulating in mimicry of our servants' voices. Such insects being the cuckoos of our worlds.'

Jack was fidgeting, Jack was acting jumpy. The stem of the Ukko-bloom was flexing to and fro. Jack was having no more of this delay.

Which mage to be seizing for safe conduct? Which? The Velvet who was gossiping? Or the Brazen go-between of whom Minkie Kennan was being accomplice? The Brazen who was refusing co-operation, consequently knowing much more?

Seizing for safe conduct only? Or for carrying off all the way back to the aitch-house, into the Queen's custody, restoring to her the prisoner who was previously absconding?

What a jangling cacophony in the air! As of imminent storming of the den.

Three wooden soldiers passing weapons to their comrades. Clumsy clutch of untrained human hands, seizing Imbricate's body. Worse than human clutch, tougher! Restraining this precious one. Three being needed to handle his coils. Hideous and demeaning. Belly-scute aching, fetor leaking from anal glands. Restraining *himself* nonetheless!

No counterattack came during the hasty if tortuous withdrawal from the nest. Jack, aglow, was bearing the flower flask. Three woodmen hustled the stretched-out serpent.

The raiding party emerged between those twin watch-domes into a thinning haze to discover that part of the synthetic expanse between themselves and the forest had swelled elastically into a hill.

That hill was bulging. Its skin was splitting open. Within loomed a hulking black upright slug.

An Isi shuttle-ship had arisen from its subterranean hangar.

'Sweet mana, look at that!'

'Just look at it!'

Oh be hurrying. Soon heat will be pouring and searing. Thunder will be rolling and deafening. Velvets raising that ship as a weapon to be igniting uniforms and wooden soldiers, cooking flesh and captive mage alike, crisping the Ukko-bloom.

Be running, be running.

Imbricate writhing in the effort to propel his handlers. No other way of communicating, intruders having committed the gaffe – so caramel-comical just a chime earlier – of not hustling his voice along with them also.

How, then, to be questioning him after carrying him off? To be kidnapping a Brazen Tulki-talker servant subsequently?

Prut was struggling to see whatever it was which now obstructed their return route. The flanks of the hill were withdrawing. Flowing back upon the plain. Re-forming underneath the shuttle-ship. The ship stood poised for ignition.

'The road!' cried Jack. 'Run for the road!'

Away from the shuttle. Over to where the rubbery black road began. A localized spasmodic blizzard sped along with Jack and the soldiery. The three woodmen carrying the mage were lagging, hindered by the burden linking them together.

If Imbricate being able to coil around chest and shoulders and cling, only one bearer being necessary! Bearer could be jogging along.

Alternatively: lock-step, lock-step as if carrying a sickly Isi!

Imbricate puffing light.

Bearer foot-tangling. Tripping other bearer and self. Imbricate slipping. Wooden soldiers sprawling, mage amidst them. Utter failure to manipulate.

*

416

Astride the bike, Ben peered from the treeline at the upright black ship. Throbs thrummed through the ground. The intensifying vibration set Ben's teeth on edge. The ulcers on his feet began to itch vexatiously.

After the flash and darkness at the domes – half an hour since? – decoy ghosts had disappeared. Since then the mists had become tenuous. Scurrying figures were clearly visible, accompanied by swirls of wind-borne ash. No, of *snow*. The bronze-clad leader must be Demon Jack. Behind him sprinted Greens-and-Browns and Buffs and the others.

These wretched feet of his! He'd soon be no use to man nor beast; nor to himself. Only able to limp and gimp. Couldn't ever put on a burst of speed like those fellows out there in the open. *That* wasn't going to help them much.

Never seen a shuttle-ship take off before. Still, he could imagine. *Whoosh*: a storm of fire, most like. Blast of scorching gases and steam fit to knock you over and take your skin off. Melt any snowflakes, *that* would. Never make it to the woods, they wouldn't.

Oh this damned pulsing in his pins, so aggravated by that ship. Stop the torment somehow. Stop the throbbing. Ben rolled the bike forward into a dip in the synthetic surface and up a rumple. Pointing upward now, he leaned back. The itch, the itch.

Twist red, and fire. Twist everything. Twist blue.

Amidst the rumble from the shuttle Jack heard an irritable rattling as of coins being shaken distantly in a tin cup by an offended beggar. A Jaegertrooper caught up with him.

'Saw a bike over there.' Gesturing, sweeping snowflakes aside. 'It vanished—'

That faint clatter had stopped, but the mightier engine noise was ebbing.

The ship wasn't going to take off after all. It was staying put.

'Head to the right, to the right!' shouted Jack.

Hardly had they altered course than the Juttahat patrol reappeared where the black road emerged from the woods. The Unmen opened fire. A pulse of hot light. A quarrel that fell short. A bullet that sped overhead. Then another bullet, and another pulse.

An aitch-houseman tumbled. A wooden soldier lurched then continued onward, though his shako had fallen off, exposing a

417

polished bald head. The fleeing soldiery returned some fire inaccurately on the run by way of deterrent.

Other Juttahats were spilling from the mouth of the nest. Way back, those three woodmen gave up struggling to reclaim the writhing Brazen mage. They had no choice but to abandon the serpent, and lope in the new direction.

By the time Jack and Prut's force arrived back at the sky-boat the original complement was reduced by a quarter since first setting out. Ben of the fruity breath had obviously jumped heroically into the shuttle. There wasn't even a single jump-bike to stow prior to a hasty departure. Four soldiers had suffered wounds. Only one of the victims, a Jaegertrooper, needed to lie out full-length, sedated numbingly by Jack. The return journey wouldn't be quite as crowded.

The pilot had stayed behind, with four companions, to guard the royal vehicle. As he took the sky-boat aloft, Jack cradled the flower in its flask. Presently the waxen petals began to bunch inward. After a while they flexed apart again. As if gasping for breath, though at a vegetable tempo. Jack murmured coaxingly to the bloom, trophy of the raid.

28 · A WET GALA

Yulistalax may have braced itself for the usual flood of visitors – optimistically, in view of the war! – but a different flood had descended. Gala was going to be a wash-out as never before.

The autumn sun had almost *always* beamed upon the three-day fest of choral chanting and tale-spinning, mana-conjuring and theatricals, poetry and contests of proclaimers. This year rain sheeted down upon Yulistalax, drenching its bunting, turning the maze of lanes into a spate of junior streams.

Downpour soaked the three-key-wide bowl of Speakers' Valley. Water oozed down the turf terraces. The timber grandstands facing Speakers' Stage were awash. That central knoll was becoming an island surrounded by a shallow boggy moat. Bronzed and gilded harper trees around the ridge were too sodden for their strings to thrum. Acoustics were awful. The drumbeat of drops was a burden.

Attendance might have been even scantier if many gala-goers hadn't already committed themselves by travelling considerable distances.

Rain would occasionally desist for ten teasing minutes. Time enough for a recitation on Poets' Terrace. Then the grey grimy cloud mass would resume pissing. Lord Maxi Burgdorf's shaman had bawled himself hoarse and stamped out a sizable wallow in his efforts to dry the sky.

Small joy for the vendors of baked fish and pancakes or for fortune-tellers and hucksters; though hot grog was in demand. Only one bedraggled cuckoo perched on a feeding pole. It seemed as though the gossip-birds had decided that nothing of much note could possibly occur here this year. Scarcely a handful of proclaimers were present. However, Peter Vaara and his drama troupe were about to put on a show in the largest of the marquees, *under shelter*, as a crier was yelling.

It was towards that tent that Bosco was escorting Penelope Conway beneath a large sky-blue umbrella with a fine ivorywood handle. Was there even another such brolly in sight? (When had one been needed at a gala? To bring one from town was to concede defeat.) Possession of the umbrella lent their progress across the squelchy terrace a ceremonial aspect: Pootaran consul and Earth's Resident sharing a mobile canopy.

('Who are those two—?')

('Both black as Velvet Jutties—!')

('Don't you know, lad, she's the Earthkeep chatelaine—')

('Consorting with a Pootaran sailor—')

('Naw, he's the puzzle shop boss in Landfall, take it from me. I once bought a brain-teaser from him for the kids—')

('So why are they arm in arm, then—?')

Arm in arm was the best way to keep reasonably dry. Even so, the lower part of Penelope's olive sari was soaked, and likewise of his pleated robe of gold and saffron.

'Penelope—' Bosco's voice was a rich rumble in their shared shelter. How noble and succulent her name. 'Bear in mind this foul weather ain't any judgement against you for bringing me here. Why, you're the reason I hung around so long in this crazy country.'

'I can't afford to yield to such feelings, Bosco. I asked you along on account of your . . . gravity.'

419

A resonant chuckle. 'Oh both of us have gravity. Portly as can be. That's *good*. I wouldn't want to outweigh you. Miriam don't disapprove of you. She just wants me back home on the island; not nursing buzzings in my bonnet.' He tapped the ivorywood handle lightly against his beaded red fez. 'Such as a buzz for you. One buzz can lead to another.'

Of course he knew that the plump greying woman at his side had surrendered her womb as a promise of emotional neutrality.

'Lately,' she admitted, 'I've been dreaming of the Earthkeep burning like a candle set alight by Wex. I've been dreaming of a glowing moon hanging in the noonday sky just above it, and battles on Harmony Field between Juttahats waving swords and weird beastmen blowing fiery darts from trumpets. *Om*,' she told herself. 'Shelter me from sick consciousness, Bosco.'

'That's why I'm here,' said he, and flourished the umbrella chivalrously.

'There's so much potential for mania here at the gala. Can't you sense it?'

'In spite of the soaking these folks are getting?'

'The weather itself is sick.'

'Oh: a mana-malady. I see.'

'A fever, in this omphalus of mana.'

He scanned the terraced bowl. 'Ain't too many folks in the belly-button today.'

'This isn't actually the omphalus. That's wherever the Ukko-child is. If Lucky does come here, it'll be on the final day. *Tomorrow*. When the proclaimers do their stuff.'

'You still think she'll leave her battling and try to use this gala to summon the Ukko-child? If it exists.'

'Oh but it must exist somewhere within a few hundred keys of here, or else Pootara would be affected by mana too.'

'Gala doesn't seem to be co-operating, Penelope.'

They were staying in adjoining chambers at the Sign of the Lady Lucky. If the Queen arrived and sought rooms over-night, which other inn would she choose for herself and her entourage? Surely Lucky wouldn't dream of expelling Earth's resident from her lodging. Penelope might end up next door to Her Majesty.

Yü was baby-sitting the dovecraft at Maxi Burgdorf's landing field, with a small well-armed team. Penelope wanted Bosco rather than the Chinese aide at her side for any encounter – or confrontation – with the Queen. Yü might be too doctrinaire in her attitude. She might act as if the junior Ukko was Earth's to control by right – supposing Lucky did succeed in summoning it.

Buzz in your bonnet, my daughter. Think om.

Penelope was obliged to be her own daughter since no other daughter was possible.

'*Kaleva's greatest mana-dramaturge will start his performance at any moment—!*'

Bosco let down the sky-blue umbrella, and with Penelope he thrust their way into the marquee. Many wet spectators already were crowded inside, and craning. Bosco used his bulk to clear a passage – but not right to the front where the Burgdorfs were consoling each other noisily about the wash-out. Diminutive Lord Maxi, in burgundy velvet, sported a tall cone-shaped fur hat. Mitzi, taller than her husband, tactfully wore nothing on her soaked coiffure. Penelope didn't wish to become involved in their meteorological grievances. Maxi and Mitzi hushed one another as the spectacle began.

It was dim within the marquee. How large *was* this canvas cavern?

A nocturnal backdrop of purple or black gave the impression of receding indefinitely far away, pulling the black-clad players along with it so that they appeared far in the distance and doll-like. Whole yawning spaces were implied: a stage which was ever so deep, vast enough so to summon a host of protagonists. In the profound depth which the actors inhabited, bodies hidden by inky leotards and hair by skullcaps, faces and hands were afloat.

A moment later – an intake of breath later – Queen Lucky was visibly present on stage . . .

Voices lilted in sing-song style. Despite the distancing and the beating of rain on canvas the voices of the homunculi were audible almost within one's head.

Penelope knew that wilful figure not so much from recollections of portraits as from imperative certainty, and exclaimed to Bosco, 'Why, she's already here!'

'What—?'

'Lucky's actually here, taking part in—' Penelope bit softly on her lip, and Bosco squeezed her arm sustainingly.

'Illusion, illusion . . .'

Illusion, yes. Yet also a revelation of recent happenings, conjured so vividly that one saw not disembodied hands and faces but bodies, gowns, uniforms. Peter Vaara had met the Queen just a little while ago . . .

Vaara – that *must* be the dramaturge himself – was a seductively villainous van Maanen.

Whom had he seduced but that petite princess at his side? How Minnow strutted. How Minnow swanked. A Juttahat approached her. Humbled and subservient, the alien staggered under the burden of a half-glimpsed Isi of daunting size whose vast wraith-coils reared aloft. This monster waited on Minnow's whims – resentfully so, but she had extracted an oath from it. Otherwise it would happily bite her head off.

Lucky seemed so far away from Minnow and Osmo. Nearby in reality, she was distant in the illusion. Her war-priest was praying. Moments later the priest was a stiff wooden soldier, holding a bundle of babes in his arms . . .

> 'And the Maids of Horror
> 'Spread plagues tomorrow—'

What were those squalling nymphs which the actor conjured?

Vaara and his troupe were excelling themselves, not merely swaying their audience to witness what was known already, but to experience a version of what the players themselves had lately beheld – and the consequences of those events. It seemed that a divination was occurring here in this marquee in which tracts of space were reduced to pocket size, and where afterimages of the actors multiplied, evoking royal guards fighting, townsfolk dying, sickly soldiery, the march of wooden men.

Twisting and trembling, a sphere of light hung ghostly under the canvas vault. A chandelier high in a hall. A distorted moon. The Queen was summoning it. She was beckoning with all her will. The other Queen – Minnow – was trying to repel the light while the bloated serpent loomed over her.

The glow swooped down; and though there was only herbage underfoot a crash resounded as of a great glassy weight impacting upon a stone floor.

Gleams of light flew amongst the audience. Spectators batted with their hands as if assailed by a swarm of phosphorbugs, bright *zizzing* insects everywhere.

Who was this *bright* new player who appeared from out of the backdrop itself? His youthful face and Brazen livery were aglow!

Tilted in one hand he held a vase containing a wilted saggy bloom the hue of mildew.

Even Osmo/Vaara and his troupe paused in amazement.

And who was this cloaked soaked fellow with the curly black hair thrusting his way through the audience accompanied by a bald brown man in a sodden olive uniform?

'*Wex!*' exclaimed Penelope. '*Gurrukal!*'

The Indian pilot peered, then veered towards Penelope and Bosco.

'Ah, madam, so here you are.'

'Mr Gurrukal? But how—?'

'Oh, we landed our dovecraft alongside yours. Hardly the weather for flying!' Urgently and confidentially: 'We failed to find Cully, you see, madam, but we did help the dreamlord awake and after we learned how Minkie Kennan had reappeared—'

'Are you in training to be a cuckoo?' enquired Bosco.

'Later, tell us later,' Penelope told the pilot.

Wex had reached the players.

'Jack Pakken,' he called out. 'Jack, it's *you*.'

There was commotion in the audience.

'*It's Lucky's demon grandson!*'

A couple of Lord Burgdorf's guards, in serge with crimson-cockaded caps, shoved their way to the fore. One was brandishing a cudgel. The other, a crossbow.

'Your Lordship,' the former announced loudly, 'the royal sky-boat has landed nearby—'

'What? What?' cried Maxi Burgdorf.

'*Wooden soldiers* have carried a wounded man into a booth, calling for a physician—'

'Find one. Find two.'

'The Queen *is* here,' Penelope breathed to Bosco.

The dramaturge had hoisted both black-hidden arms exultantly, white hands suspended like hoverbirds above him. What a day of days, despite the rain. His mana-drama was attracting protagonists, originals of its masquerade. So it seemed.

'You,' Jack said to Vaara, 'take this.' He thrust the flower flask in Vaara's direction. Jack's lustre was ebbing away.

Lowering his arms, Vaara accepted the offering as though this were a bizarre floral tribute – limp and languishing though the bloom was, on the very verge of expiry.

'Make the flower seem strong again, Peter Vaara.' A tremble in the fastboy's voice. 'Make it seem healthy, will you?' Notwithstanding his 'tache he was very youthful of a sudden, a weary lad appealing to an illusionist.

Nonplussed, Vaara scrutinized the sick petals, the feeble stem.

Wex – or his wetwear – was reaching out to grasp a prize.

'Did you pluck that from inside the Ukko-child, Jack? No, you couldn't have done ... That's where it's from, isn't it? *Does it point the way – like a dowsing rod?*' As soon as Wex's hand brushed the bloom a petal fell off. Then another. Swiftly the flower fell apart. The stem hung like wet string.

Jack Pakken rushed away through the audience, which parted to avoid a brush with his strangeness. In the rain, at a stall, he was seen to grab a couple of breadboxes stuffed with pork and baked fish. Very soon he was back aboard the big sky-boat decorated with those vermilion eyes. Many members of the audience had followed outside, to gawp and debate, despite the drenching.

'Appeared out of thin air, didn't he—?'

'Idiot, there's a flap at the back of the marquee—'

'Is Lucky herself in the sky-boat—?'

Wex hadn't tried to pursue Jack. Instead, he was questioning Peter Vaara. How anonymous the dramaturge looked now that his show had paused. Mathavan Gurrukal was hovering beside Penelope, impatient to tell his tale. Should she hear him out first? Should she buttonhole Wex? The Queen, the Queen was in her sky-boat just outside.

Om, she told herself.

'I must meet the Queen,' she told Bosco.

'Penelope, why don't I go and ask if she's actually here?' Such a *reliable* voice, his. So sonorous and sensible.

'You're right. I shouldn't leave Wex to his own devices.'

Preceded by their two guards, Lord Maxi and Lady Mitzi were impatient to cut through the spectators. Bosco, who was ahead of them, unfurled his brolly – like a great blue bird with a single white leg and a twisted foot launching itself skyward.

Maxi was delighted. 'Why thank you, my man! Hmm, an *ivorywood* handle if I'm not mistaken, and you black as boot polish.'

Wee Maxi peered at the big man's splendid garment, then up at his fez. 'What are you, the Prince of Pootara, gracing my gala? My apologies for the rain, but you came well prepared. A Pootaran doubter! Thank you, thank you.'

'We don't actually have any aristocrats, sir.'

'Well, you're certainly one of nature's gentlemen!'

'Actually, sir, I'm the consul in Landfall.'

'Are you! You deserve to be.' Lord Burgdorf stuck out his hand – for the umbrella.

'Do let me hold it, Maxi,' said his wife. All be it dumpy, Mitzi was still half a head taller.

'Why not allow *me*?' offered Bosco. 'I take it that you're planning to visit the royal sky-boat.'

So the Pootaran consul held the brolly sidelong and at arm's length over the lord and his lady. Water bounced into Bosco's face and dripped from his fez. Halfway to their goal, they were intercepted. A bespectacled man of advancing years with a trowel-blade of a chin stepped in front of the party. Silver threads ornamented his green brocade robe. A four-peaked cap of black velvet perched on a grizzled head. Dripping, he blinked through blotched glasses.

'Your Lordship, I'm compelled to postpone the poetry contest.'

'Compelled? Compelled by whom?'

'By this deluge!' A sneeze gathered itself, and erupted.

Maxi dithered.

'Come with us, Lutainen,' said Lady Mitzi. 'If we're about to meet the Queen, let us have our laureate with us. Maybe you can recite an ode.'

When they arrived at the boarding ramp a lofty officer, decorated in silver, was descending. He peered short-sightedly.

'Lord Burgdorf? My compliments, and may we request refuelling?'

Not the Queen's compliments. No, not hers.

The sky-boat, which had dropped in briefly at Lord Maxi's landing field almost a week earlier, no more conveyed the Queen than it had upon that previous secretive occasion.

Secrecy was of less consequence now. Ben Prut was happy to reveal that this expedition was returning from an assault upon the Velvet Isi nest. With surprise on their side and with the help of Jack Pakken, the Queen's united forces had invaded the serpents' dens and emerged successfully, bar some casualties. Unprecedented foray. Exceptional. A feat of heroes. Van Maanen and his rebel chit would be well advised to pay heed.

425

The why and wherefore of this attack upon the Isi, far away from Loxmithlinna and Maananfors, remained opaque. Likewise whatever *else* the expedition might have been busy at. Could the main aim have been to demonstrate Lucky's invincibility to van Maanen?

Jack Pakken was remaining aboard the boat. He couldn't present himself to His Lordship. Too fatigued! The royal force must return to Loxmithlinna as soon as the rain let up, after refuelling.

Quite a feat of navigation and piloting to have reached Yulistalax during the present foul weather.

Why had the sky-boat come down in Speakers' Valley rather than at the much more convenient landing field beside the Burgdorf's keep? Alcohol for the engines would need to be fetched all the way from town. Had the pilot been afraid of crashing into the tall slim granite tower of the keep, which in more favourable visibility he might have used as a great guidepost?

Ah, no . . . Jack Pakken had insisted on here as the landing site. He'd sensed such an affinity. A vortex of mana was spinning around a certain marquee. He'd seemed to hear burning sheep bleating.

So said General Aleksonis's adjutant.

Wee Lord Maxi must swallow another disappointment.

Penelope broke in upon Wex's quizzing of Peter Vaara and his black-clad troupe.

'That flower's done with,' she said. 'It's almost rotting.'

'Oh hullo, Pen,' said Wex. 'We tried to find a shaman near Niemi who makes mana-maps—'

'I do hope you've regained your senses, Mr Wex.'

'*My senses?*'

'I meant—'

Wex jerked. '*I am still protecting my partner from pain, Miz Conway.*'

Vaara eyed Wex with considerable interest.

'What a curious case of ventriloquism. Though the lips move, the speaker is someone else.'

'What exactly are the Maids of Horror?' Penelope demanded of Vaara.

Why, those were the quadruple offspring of a mutant lass and of Demon Jack. Precocious wasn't the word. Born speaking, near enough. The four miniature maids of malice could conjure plague-bearing flies to launch against Lucky's enemies. Peter

426

Vaara had performed by royal command after their mana-baptism. The maids would be more mature now, almost ready to spread their diseases – maybe by being carried swiftly into enemy territory on those jump-bikes, Vaara surmised . . .

Plague, to be launched at *Minnow*. Hideous disfiguring torments. Bound to be ugly and ghastly. Swiftly or slowly lethal? *Plague*.

{*The agony of bursting buboes. Gaping lockjaw rictus. Arching of the spine till it snaps. Those are symptoms of plague.*}

Minnow must be warned of the threat – by communicator message to Maananfors.

{*To be overheard by any eavesdropper? Earth's agent intervenes in the conflict of rival Queens!*}

Something must be done. Minnow, beware of flies. Pin up sticky paper. Hang out pomanders. Sleep in mosquito netting.

{*Maybe this will not be such serious plague. Bubo plague was spread by fleas not flies.*}

'Mathavan, what do you know about plague?'

'Why should I know anything?' retorted the Indian. 'Plague is a disease from the Dark Ages; and when I say Dark Ages I'm referring to your own cultural heritage.'

'Do we know a cure? A prophylaxis?'

'Perhaps you hope I might trample on the bodies of the victims, healing them with the sweat of my feet?' Gurrukal rubbed his scalp briskly. Hair had begun to grow back, sprinkles of black pepper all over his pate.

'Do *we* know a way of halting plague?' *Us. Within.* Wex twitched with a minor paroxysm.

'*I have no more information on such an archaic disease, Roger,*' his wetwear chose to say aloud.

'At least I wouldn't feel anything if I caught a plague!' Wex retorted in his own prim voice.

'Excuse me, sir,' said Vaara, 'I believe I could expand my troupe to include an extra player such as yourself. Two for the price of one, so to speak!'

Ignoring him, Wex turned to Penelope. 'I need to go back to Maananfors to observe the course of this war—'

Bosco had returned, soaked and minus umbrella.

'I'm sorry, Penelope, but the Queen isn't here at all. And what's more . . .' He spread his well manicured and empty hands. 'No umbrella. Little Lord Burgdorf needed a consolation prize. We're

427

going to be drenched unless we stay in here till this deluge eases . . .'

When the rain did ease, the royal sky-boat would be heading back to Lucky's base in Loxmithlinna.

Should Roger Wex be allowed to take the dovecraft – by a different route – to the van Maanens' keep? Penelope found herself unable to decide. In Bosco's company she felt that her position was compromised.

An Earth observer ought indeed to be witnessing the conflict from one side or another. Wex had no clout with Lucky. With Minnow: why, that was another matter.

'What I think,' murmured the Pootaran consul, 'is it's better if this Ukko-child stays hidden away—'

Oh but the Ukko-child had been found already, by Minkie Kennan, currently missing. And in a dream Lord Beck had found his dead wife, or a semblance of her, preserved within it, according to Gurrukal. And a certain Paula Sariola was ensconced in the Ukko-child too – that other self whom Lucky sought. Would Gunther Beck broadcast what he knew? Was Kennan even now selling his own information to the Isi, and perhaps selling the human race into the bargain?

Lucky had sent her demon grandson to attack the Velvets, those being the nearest Isi to Niemi . . . where Wex had failed to find Kennan. Wex had arrived too late at Kaukainkyla to see more than the embers of Anna Beck's pyre. Penelope didn't wish to think for too long or too graphically about this event. (Might Lord Beck go mad when he learned of this, if he hadn't already?)

As regards Roger Wex, maybe a pattern was emerging. By following his impulses – and the promptings of his wetwear – Wex was *almost* arriving at the right places at the right times. If he persisted would he finally converge upon a crucial pivot, an axis of events?

If not, then a plague upon him.

Om. Om. Drum of raindrops. Bosco's steady hand upon her arm.

The injured soldier in the tent had been a participant in the attack on the Velvets. He could be questioned while he mended. In return for Bosco's gift of the brolly Lord Burgdorf would surely allow an interview.

'Mr Gurrukal,' said Penelope, 'would you be willing to fly our

428

dovecraft to Maananfors along with Mr Wex despite war and threats of pestilence?'

Wex was nodding his head reassuringly.

The Indian massaged his scalp and scrutinized Penelope.

'I shall be seeing more of Kaleva than ever I expected . . .'

She took him to be accepting the commission. Indeed, this was a commission from Earth's Resident.

'Meanwhile,' she asked, 'would you use your medical skills on behalf of that casualty in the tent? Till the rain eases.'

'Till the royal sky-boat leaves,' said Wex. 'Thanks, Pen.'

PART THREE

MOONRISE

Minnow was sitting cross-legged in her ivorywood throne late that morning, doing her best to wax a ski, when Roger Wex and the Indian medic paid their regular call to enquire about Osmo's ailment . . .

What a dazzle of snow there was outside the casement windows, beyond the immediate strip of shade cast by the mansion. Minnow's Manor: that's how this guest house was fast becoming known. To its rear stood Maids' Manor where Tilly Kippan lived, numbering among her domestics that Brazen Girlem! Queen Minnow, Osmo, and entourage weren't the only exiles hereabouts.

Minnow's ground-floor throne room was modest but it commanded a partial panorama of white-swathed Kip'an'keep and the so-called Cool Lake, now glazed with ice. The view was partly occluded by a tammywood fort undergoing hasty reconstruction. If you stood at a window you could see to the leftward the jut of a barbican. In the other direction, further away beyond another purple fort, was the celebrated arboretum.

Bundled in her protective brown quilted coat, and with stockinged feet tucked under her, Minnow may have looked shivery, though a stove warmed the air. As often, her crown of leather and pearls was askew. The ski, its yellover sole upright, rested across the arms of the throne. With her wax-daubed buffing leather she seemed intent on coaxing notes from wood which was silent except for occasional squeaks. A pile of other skis lay on the parquet floor, and variously coloured pots of wax.

The genuine instrument, the Isi harp, lay in the half-open drawer below her throne. Its music soothed Osmo's bouts of fever considerably, though banish the cause it couldn't. Not as yet.

The room reeked of mustoreum. So did most buildings and garments in Kip'an'keep these days. Pomander balls were strewn about on floors and furniture. Balls were stuffed into pockets. Balls were worn in pouches. Blended of healervine pods and the anal glands of the musti (or alternatively sickener fungi), goat urine, and turpenoids from the tarpatty tree – then blessed by a

433

shaman or by a priest in the Kirk in the Trees – these pomanders were a definite deterrent to Lucky's plague flies. (Or rather, her devilish *great-granddaughters'* flies.)

Could those mana-pests survive the freeze which had now suddenly descended on Tapper Kippan's realm? The flies had been largely responsible for the fall of Maananfors . . .

Here too, a similar disaster? Here too, in spite of the stink of mustoreum? The pervasive protective stench made Kip'an'keep seem rotten, as if inviting surgery by Lucky's forces.

'How is he this morning?' asked Wex.

Wex wore a linen pouch around his neck, approved by his wetwear. His tone was one of circumspect concern and a wry self-denying gallantry. Hadn't he flown to Maananfors specially to warn Minnow about the impending plagues (though a cuckoo had already cackled)?

When the fly-borne diseases arrived at Maananfors, and when Osmo was infected, hadn't Wex offered to evacuate Osmo and Minnow in his dovecraft? Whatever the merits of this offer Osmo was obliged to refuse. He couldn't seem to advantage himself; couldn't skedaddle in advance of his supporters. An orderly withdrawal – overland and all together – was the only, if grievous, option.

Now that Wex was robbed of all physical sensation, did this incapacity of his add a tragic dimension to his continuing crush upon Minnow (incontestable in her presence), or an element of utter farce? Maybe his other self colluded in the absurd infatuation as a lifeline of sanity for poor Roger, to whom the reek of mustoreum was as unnoticeable as the smell of a roasting lamb would have been – or the aroma of a woman's hair.

Wex had been quick to confide his inadequacy to Osmo and Minnow so as to avert any pique on Osmo's part. Wex was as harmless as a capon. He could safely consort with anyone's wife. A kiss would be no more palatable to him than a spoonful of porridge.

Such a confession coaxed sympathy – even fascination. Such, at least, was Osmo's reaction. The Earthman had a personal proclaimer within him which could numb his senses as surely as Osmo had numbed and dumbed the Girlem.

Aside from offering his assistance, Wex was undoubtedly spying on Osmo and Minnow. Since Wex certainly wasn't doing so on behalf of Lucky, who cared if he was snooping?

Well, Osmo cared, in a positive way. If it seemed that Landfall (and even Earth) supported him and Minnow, however tenuously, some advantage might accrue. Right now, any asset was a blessing.

'He sweated a lot,' Minnow informed Wex, 'and he had to go to the toilet a lot. The last two times he peed brown blood. He drank a lot of water sweetened with cordial. This morning he peed pink, then his waters ran clear again. He's resting, but feeling bloated. The colostrum pudding didn't do much good.'

The first flush from the udders of a cow whose calf was stillborn, rich with immunojuice, stored since summer in a bottle in one of the ice-rooms, had been used as the main ingredient in that pudding; but Osmo seemed hardly to have benefited.

He couldn't bespeak himself better. True, he wasn't worsening – but nor was he remotely well. If only he'd been longlife! Then he would have thrown off the blight. Perhaps his efforts at proclaiming – allied with Minnow's harping – were having a salutary effect to the extent that dying didn't seem to be an issue. Only wretched malady! Bloody pee and bloat. Still, his power to proclaim was severely impaired; and so, by default, his leadership. He had to pretend as best and bravely as he could.

No need to feign with Minnow. Nor with Wex or Gurrukal.

But with Sam Peller: ah, that was another matter. Fortunately Sam was mostly away with the troops, fighting in the forests, resisting the advance of Lucky's men and woodmen.

With Tapper Kippan it might be another matter too, except that the forest lord kept to his inner sanctum for days on end. Daughter Tilly knew the truth about Osmo, but she seemed not to be telling her dad. Tilly had offered the colostrum.

As for Elmer and Eva, why, Elmer was genuinely longlife – and he had forts and rockets to play with. If Elmer perceived an advantage over Osmo, it wasn't one which Eva wished him to press to Osmo's detriment. Where could such an advantage lead? Only to her mother's mocking supremacy. Cuckoos often cackled how the Loxmith family were dispossessed from lordship of the aitch-house for as long as Lyle Melator lived. To undermine Osmo would bring no benefit beyond a certain bitter satisfaction. Even this was unappealing now that Eva had recovered her poise and had reached a droll accommodation with her kid sister.

With the reluctant acquiescence of Tapper Kippan, ailing Osmo still remained in nominal charge of the ill-fated war against Lucky.

For some while now events had possessed their own momentum. Probably it was as well that they did. Otherwise would Kippan have co-operated in the first place?

It wouldn't be true to say that the glittery insects had descended upon Maananfors in swarms. There were never huge numbers of the flies. Half a dozen here. A dozen there. A couple of dozen elsewhere. In addition to loners – which were sneakier. At any one time there could have been no more than a few hundred or maybe a thousand of the plague pests besetting Maananfors – a trivial number compared with the normal suckerflies and sizzlers and pollenflies and sweatsippers of summer. Certainly no clouds of mana-flies darkened the sky. But when a plaguefly stung a person the consequences were usually grim.

Some victims' heads ached, fit to burst. Eyes were bloodshot from the pressure. Viscous humour exuded into the tubes of the hair. These dilated to admit globules of blood so that the engorged locks hung heavy and clotted. If a sufferer took a knife to their hair in despair, the ends oozed unceasingly.

Stung limbs of other victims would swell agonizingly. People mutilated themselves to gain relief. Self-inflicted wounds became septic and gangrenous.

Other victims bled internally. Bowels and kidneys ached. Constipation, diarrhoea, nausea . . .

Not every sting, nor even repeated stings, proved fatal. People were affected to different degrees. Nevertheless scores of townfolk young and old died in utter distress. Others went insane. Many more were incapacitated. Swat a fly, and another would soon be buzzing nearby.

Bailiff Septimus leaked blood through skin become porous and hypersensitive. The plump fellow screamed till he died on a saturated bed. Venny the cook's hair was a bloated mat. Deafened and dizzied, the sauna steward drowned himself.

Inevitably the defence of Maananfors faltered. Raids by immune troops and wooden soldiers intensified.

Per Villanen, brother-in-law of Osmo's former mistress (whose dad had likewise died in Osmo's service), began to agitate publicly about all the deaths and misery which the rebellion was causing. He would appear on the waterfront or in the sculpture park to harangue scared citizens, then he would make himself scarce.

Hans Werner also took up rabble-rousing. During the water-borne assault on Loxmithlinna Werner may well have beaten the

drum for the van Maanens but only because Lord Osmo had
bespoken this fisherman's hand to stone. Now he brandished his
useless fist and railed against the keep. People harked to him,
though the black blem on his cheek, so floridly framed by a tattoo,
seemed malignant, and everyone recalled how he had slashed
Anna Vainio and her cousin. Weighed down by his stone fist,
Werner was caught by men of the Blue Watch and chained in
the pillory in the sculpture park, gagged so that he couldn't
speak, food for plague flies (which, however, seemed to shun
him).

And Osmo himself was stung . . .

At first Sam Peller tried to deny the evidence of the effect of this
bite on his lord, though at the same time insisting that there
was no option but to evacuate and retreat southward into Tapper
Kippan's domain. They must retreat in strength, while strength
remained. The forest lord would be forced to fight them or allow
them free access to his territory to carry on the struggle against a
demented tyrant who might sacrifice everyone's freedom of mind.
Armed with Brindled weapons, jump-bikes, rockets, the Blue
Guards and Blue Watch wouldn't be so easy to repel. If blocked,
they would fight like verrins. Whereas together Kippan's woodmen
and the men of Maananfors would have a fair chance to resist
Lucky. Plague flies wouldn't find victims as easily in the forests
as in a single exposed town.

Besides, a cuckoo blazoned that during the weeks of the slow
war before the advent of the flies, a certain armoured battle-wagon
had been brought south laboriously from Sariolinna by ferries
and overland to assist in an assault on Maananfors.

Retreat – and lure Lucky onward. Communicate with
Kip'an'keep to this effect? What, and risk refusal? No. Retreat en
masse. Enmesh the forest lord. Once he conceded passage to
Osmo's men Kippan would automatically become Lucky's enemy.
Of this Sam assured Osmo, without quite meeting his sickly eye.

Weapons and supplies were loaded on carts. Some would travel
by lake and river. The ivorywood throne must accompany Queen
Minnow, of course. Crustily, old Alvar elected to remain in the
keep along with his reams of notes and his Chronicles forever in
progress. How preposterous to cart those away into the wilds where
any unlettered soldier might set light to them to heat some soup
while Alvar's back was turned.

Doubtless Lucky would dispossess the van Maanens of the lordship once she occupied Maananfors – just as she'd dispossessed

437

Elmer. By all accounts she hadn't revenged herself much on the elder Loxmiths or on Elmer's sister. Osmo's sin was greater, but would she be vicious to Alvar – when he was a historian almost without bias? She must respect his chronicles of her world. And he must safeguard them. All his work had been composed in that study of his in the keep at Maananfors. A superstition haunted Alvar that anywhere else he mightn't be able to put pen effectively to paper – not even at Kip'an'keep, source of that paper and those pens.

Before Osmo abandoned Alvar and his keep, father and son (who was panged by spasms in the guts and by a sick headache) had embraced tenderly.

'You need an heir,' Alvar had advised quietly.

Oh yes. And an heir in the womb would inflame Lucky even more! Minnow showed no signs of pregnancy as yet. When would Osmo be able to perform again in that department? Even if his rod could become stiff a sick man shouldn't attempt to impregnate. A lame-brained oddity might be the result.

Before final departure, rites for soldiers who must leave their homes were carried out by Pappi Hakulinen. Inept though Osmo's mana-priest sometimes was, on this occasion he excelled himself in the appropriate melancholy vein – perhaps since he himself wouldn't be leaving, and if the troops left, so would the plague flies. Yes, the priest must stay behind owing to a bout of gout, an odd affliction in such a fellow as him and a sad reflection on the efficacy of the hervy-horn amulet he wore round his neck.

> *'The swan flies,'* Hakulinen had chanted.
> *'Who will gather the feathers it drops?*
> *'Who will gather your bones from a distant forest?*
> *'Still left on the shelf is your harmonica;*
> *'Still here on the wall is your fishing net.*
> *'Like white sylvester trees or ivorywood*
> *'The grieving girls are left . . .' (But some would be left with gory hair!)*
> *'In spring when cuckoos cackle of lust*
> *'Where will you be then, my boy,*
> *'Apple of our eye? And on sauna night*
> *'What hens will hope for delight?*
> *'For the last time mother beats you*
> *'And the beasts are in sister's care.*
> *'Mother, oh mother, why cry . . . ?' (Why, for fear of dying of plague! Or of being raped by an occupying army!)*

438

> *'Your son's toys stay behind!*
> *'I lay you in a coffin;*
> *'I bury you in a grave.*
> *'Don't cut off your toe to lame yourself*
> *'Or your lord will shave your head.'*

It was as when Eva had wedded Elmer: the banes, the rejection, the slights – in order to finesse protection and, in the case of the soldiers, an eventual safe return . . .

'Shall I examine him, Your Majesty?' asked Gurrukal.

Minnow shook her head. She buffed the ski, and for a moment the wood sang faintly. 'I have another idea—'

'Is it connected with skis?' asked Wex. 'Why are you polishing those?'

'To keep my hands busy while I'm thinking! And to seem useful while others are fighting,' she added frankly. 'Waxing isn't a simple matter, you know. I've had instructions from an expert. Tilly Kippan sent him to me. Actually, my informant dictated a little book called *The Art of Wax*. He told it to a scribe and he had some copies printed at his own expense. He recited aloud to me from his *Art of Wax*, full of wit and beauty and slippery insights memorized during years of waxing! I'd call him a philosopher. When I'm Queen in Sariolinna I'll invite him to court. It's really important,' she confided, 'to have a court philosopher so that one doesn't become cranky like Mother. *Isn't it?*' she asked herself.

'Would you be Queen in Sariolinna, Your Majesty?' asked Gurrukal. 'Not in Maananfors?'

'Where the palace is, of course. Isn't that the idea? Should I abandon the Northland? Who should I abandon it to?' She buffed busily. 'I'm the true Queen. Queens reign in palaces. When they're victorious.'

At the moment none of this seemed quite feasible. Of course she had to act as though it was. Cloth in hand, she adjusted her crown. Wex almost moved to assist her. She had tipped the crown askew in the opposite direction.

Her hair would have no scent. His fingers had no feeling. Her husband and lover lay sick next door. Such a slippery situation. He must retain his equilibrium. His other self was always helpful as regards balance.

'Doesn't wax make skis skid dangerously?' he asked.

He recalled the statue of Lucky which Minnow had inveigled him into taking apart. Thanks to Minnow's enthusiastic misdirected efforts he imagined soldiers sliding confusedly about like harnies landing on ice. Who was this expert whom the forest lord's daughter had directed in Minnow's way?

'But,' Minnow cried in puzzlement, 'you *must* wax skis. Firstly, to waterproof them. More importantly, so that they'll stick to the snow – temporarily, without holding you back once you move. Stick and glide, stick and glide – that's the whole virtue of wax. Snow crystals embed their points lightly in the wax under your weight whenever you pause. Then you glide onward smoothly. That's really essential.'

Wex had to admit, 'I didn't realize.'

'Did *neither* of you realize?'

Petulantly Wex told himself, 'So we know everything about wigs, do we, but nothing about ski wax!'

Briefly Minnow favoured him with a sympathetic smile.

'But Your Majesty,' enquired Gurrukal, 'in what way will waxing Prince Osmo help him?' Lately, the Tamil pilot had developed a taste for titles. 'Gracious, he's altogether too sore for a massage.'

'Wax *Osmo*? That isn't my idea! I was thinking of enlisting the help of . . . the Girlem,' Minnow concluded in a whisper. 'I'd very much like you to be on hand, Roger. She mustn't abscond with the harp, you see.'

Though loath to sound a reluctant note Wex asked, 'Wouldn't a few guards be more effective? Why me?'

Exasperatedly: 'Do we want the whole world gossiping about Osmo's illness, and about desperate remedies? Do we want people tattling how I appealed to a rogue Juttahat hussy to help him? The very same lass who tried to enchant him at my coronation! Goldi might daze any guards with her scents – whereas you, Roger, you can't smell anything. You're dead to odour. Anyway, you're trained in pacification, aren't you?'

What an intimate invitation this was for an agent at the court of the rebel Queen. What a show of bosom confidence in him.

'Will you act as my go-between, Roger? Will you ask the Girlem? In my position how can I appeal to her directly? She might refuse. Osmo bespoke her harshly. Though things turned out well for her, didn't they?' Minnow wrinkled her nose. 'How will she cope with the stench in here? I must sweep this mustoreum out before our meeting. Every last smelly ball! If only there'd been as much mustoreum in Maananfors!'

'Would it have made a difference?'

'Oz being a prime target, do you mean? Why wasn't I a victim too?'

'I think your brush with the Viper made you immune to the stings of mana.'

'I do believe you're right. But I can't heal Osmo on my own, just stabilize him.'

In all innocence Gurrukal spoke up. 'He's endowed with long-life, Your Majesty—'

'Will you shut up!' Minnow shouted at the masseur. 'Just go away. I'm trying to think. Buzz off!'

Was this outburst a sign of Sariola instability? With a bow and a sour grimace the pilot-medic began an exaggerated retreat from her presence.

'Get out of here faster!' To Wex, who was nonplussed: 'Not you, Roger, not you, I'm sorry, I'm still thinking how to reward the Girlem if she helps—'

Gurrukal had departed, upset by royal rudeness.

'Goldi already has her Amberman, doesn't she? Just as Osmo proclaimed! Maybe you can put it to her that his words blessed her – even if he was vexed because of the trick she tried. Actually, he's her benefactor. Somehow Oz sensed her potential for happiness. Don't let her suppose that meeting Amberman was just a fortunate coincidence. It was ordained, wasn't it? Osmo helped her on her way, even though he was irritated.' Furiously Minnow polished the ski across her lap. 'Oh to fall in love with such an oddity! She's alien, of course. No accounting for tastes. Don't let her doubt, Roger.'

'Basically she has *already* been rewarded, courtesy of Osmo.'

'I don't know how else I can appeal to her short of giving her the harp back.' Disentangling a stockinged foot, Minnow kicked shut the drawer under her throne. 'She could use it to amplify her talents. I can't return it to her.'

'You may need to return it temporarily as a gesture of trust.'

'Oh dear. Stress how she owes her happiness to Osmo even though she tried to cheat him.'

Wex jerked and blinked.

{*Your husband never became longlife at all, did he, Minnow? Something went wrong . . .*}

441

Minnow burst into tears. She almost hid her face in the waxing cloth but thought better of this.

'Damn it and damn you, *yes*,' she snivelled. 'Yes yes yes. I shan't tell what went wrong, if that's what you're hoping! You mustn't tell Gurrukal – nor anyone.'

Wex was himself once again. 'Of course not,' he promised.

'I didn't make Oz into a *zombie*! His illness isn't that. A fly stung him. That's why he's sick.'

How best to comfort Minnow? With an arm around the shoulder? That ski was such a barrier. How unsuitable to hug a Queen on her throne. How invidious to exploit this moment of vulnerability.

Minnow's eyes glistened, wide and wet. 'You mustn't tell the Earthkeep!'

From an inner pocket of his cloak Wex offered her a length of black silk, with which she mopped her face.

'You mustn't, Roger.'

'I promise.'

'Does your other self promise too? Tell me, wetwear!'

'Such a revelation might seriously jeopardise your position. Does any one else know about this but you and Osmo? Does he know?'

'Oh Oz understands. He's so much more understanding than I ever thought possible.' Spoken with a passionate fondness which Wex could only envy.

'I, too, understand Roger similarly, Minnow. That's why I guard him from pain, except as regards emotional pain. Without emotions he would be robotic, and I would be only a programme.'

'Poor you, unable to feel.'

'We do feel. I feel more keenly since his senses of touch and taste are disconnected.'

Fleetingly horror showed on Minnow's face. Was the wetwear tricking Wex so as to replace him? Swiftly the silk veiled her features. When she let the kerchief drop, she was composed again.

'That's why I'm asking your help, because you shan't be able to smell Goldi's scents. That's really important,' she assured herself. 'Who else knows? That's what you asked, isn't it? Actually, Eva and Elmer both know. They won't take advantage. She'll keep her gob bunged, and his. Sam *knows*. Sam Peller. At the same time he doesn't. He couldn't take it in. Couldn't admit it. You'll persuade the Girlem, won't you, without mentioning any of this?'

Wex nodded. In his own prim voice he assured her, 'Osmo *must* get well.'

How alone Minnow seemed at this moment, even though Osmo lay abed in a neighbouring room. Alone, as if she wasn't truly in Roger's company at all. She was adopting a mask with him. Had he failed to hear something vital? Was his hearing becoming faulty? Or his memory?

{*Om*}, said his other self. {*As Minnow is to Osmo, so am I to you. Inseparable. Naturally she feels alone when he is absent. Our feelings for her can never be fulfilled even if he dies. We must console one another, Roger. Do you understand?*}

If only he could experience agony just for an instant, briefly to restore physical sensation. Just for a moment: one single gush of pain, too short-lived to provoke a scream, too sudden to tell apart from rapture. To grasp a hot coal and feel the heat yet not experience the hurt of it momentarily – till numbness returned in a trice. Let his nerves blaze in Minnow's presence for a fraction of a second!

{*Beware: the Girlem might sense this as a weak point in our armour. We might fail Minnow.*} This mustn't happen.

'For you,' said Wex to Minnow, 'I sacrifice sensation.'

She ducked to scoop more wax on to her cloth, and he could only see the bowed black frizz of her hair, from which her crown almost fell off.

'Please keep the kerchief,' he told her, 'with your tears upon it.' He mustn't crave for any fetishistic keepsakes.

Still she didn't meet his gaze. Bent over, she buffed the sole of the ski more than any ski could possibly have needed.

Keep control, Sam Peller thought, as he glided along a snowy road towards a fort which blocked the route southward, a fireproof barrier iced like a cake. Beneath his skis and clinging to every tree was cold wool. Cold clutched at his heart. The woolliness softened his judgement so that the world seemed silently cushioned, not crisp with threat. The dingy murk of amorphous cloud was so low that a crossbow quarrel might disappear into it. So much dirty wool above denied the possibility of genuine daylight. Would there only be this depressing half-light for months? Ach, sun might be shining somewhere, a low sun lighting the land yet remaining oddly elusive.

Control of troops, and self-control . . .

How could one control oneself when one's very own self was in doubt? Since the onset of winter, so abrupt and premature, Sam had been wearing a white quilted coat over his blue

443

leathers, red chevrons stitched to the shoulders of the coat. A fur hat, bleached white, augmented his silver hair. His hair seemed to have bunched out into a dense hugging fog. With his whey face and white beard he might appear to melt into the scene save for those hovering chevrons: lips of fire, of blood.

He halted to survey the defences – and to marshal himself. Plumes of his breath puffed out like unvoiced words made visible, blankly, empty of any sense.

He hadn't heard anything in the hall at Maananfors that day when Lady Eva railed at Osmo.

Oh but he had.

'Dead: that's what happens to men who aren't longlife.' 'You aren't longlife, Prince Osmo!'

This was amply proven when Osmo succumbed to the sting of a plague fly.

Sam had been so sure that Osmo had become longlife thanks to Minnow's gift. Longliving and resilient. It shouldn't have mattered so intensely that Osmo had somehow failed to achieve this boon, and was still an ordinary mortal man. Ach, it wouldn't have mattered as much until the advent of the mana-flies!

It did matter. The shock of learning of Osmo's failure had plucked at the fabric of Sam's certainties about his own self. Thread after thread had unravelled. Away slipped a sway which had sustained Sam's soul for the best part of two decades.

Somehow, Osmo had blundered in bed. Or maybe Minnow hadn't been a virgin bride. Maybe the mutant Isi mage had interfered with her; filched her gift. For some incredible reason Minnow had confided in her elder sister – perhaps to make amends for the seizure of the aitch-house? The circumstances didn't matter. The upshot did.

The upshot was that Osmo would grow old and die.

So therefore, likewise, would Sam.

Be old for ever, Osmo had bespoken Sam after Sam had held him roughly under the water of that pool so long ago. And Sam had duly aged on the journey back to the keep so that the strapping lad who set out returned as a grizzled man who appeared to be sixty years old if he was a day.

Old for ever. Always that age. Never more, never less.

Longlife, at the price of losing his youth and his subsequent ripe years, leaping all of those at once to a venerable state from which he would never decline. Old, of a sudden; but *never any older than that*.

So Sam had always assumed. He'd had to assume this, otherwise he would have gone insane. Maybe his vigilant devotion to Osmo's interests had been a kind of lifelong insanity.

Be old for ever.

A lie, a fraud. Those words had actually possessed a totally different significance. Be old for as long as you live. Live the life of an old man. Lose your youth, lose your ripeness; be old before your time. Quite simply that. The angry malice of a boy. Words of spite spoken in haste.

Sam had merely been passing time until he should reach the age to which his physical appearance corresponded. Actually, he still had quite a few more years to serve of this dire obsessive indenture. But once he finally reached his target age, of sixty years or so, he would commence a physical decline . . . towards infirmity and the grave.

Assuming that he didn't die in this war! Assuming that Lucky didn't put an end to him. And to Osmo and Minnow and how many others, by gun or plague fly or bombshell, due to inattentiveness on Sam's part, failure to be a careful general.

Due to wool-gathering when he should be watchful.

The rump of Osmo's forces and Tapper Kippan's men and woodmen in their native forests, and in alliance, ought to be able to carry on resisting Lucky and stop her from advancing on Kip'an'keep. Brindled munitions still came by Isi sky-boat to the resistance army. Mustoreum from Kip'an'keep kept most flies at bay. After a while you got used to the smell unless you were finicky.

Sam couldn't afford to be finicky or else he would never complete his indenture. Perhaps the absurd bond *protected* him. How could he die before he arrived at an appropriate age?

Ach, such logic was a way of sneaking Osmo's original proclamation into spurious legitimacy once more, by a back door!

A lie. A fraud.

Yet a fellow must persist staunchly in the course he'd chosen. Otherwise he'd be nothing, and ridiculous. Even if the course was absurd. Yes, even so. Be staunch, be constant. Years had slipped away. There was no reliving those years now in some different style. Efficient loyalty to *Prince* Osmo and to his young Queen was the only path of integrity and self-control, the only governing pattern. Loosen that, and Sam's identity would disintegrate. He would have lost everything, including himself, the shell of self he had painstakingly secreted.

Earlier this morning, one of the jump-bikers had shot a dog while out on patrol. A Spitz had dashed out of hiding and leapt at the biker's throat. Fending the hound off with an arm would have been the instinctive reaction, resulting in bites. Instead the rider had twisted blue and jumped a little way, then swung his bike round and calmly shot the animal. He'd brought the blood-stained carcass back with him quickly before the cold even had time to chill it. Sam had peered into the Spitz's glazed dead eyes and had seen faintly, far away, a face which wasn't his own in reflection. Momentarily he'd imagined that it was his *other* face: the face of the fellow he might have been if Osmo had never bespoken him. But of course the Spitz was one of Lucky's seeing-eye dogs. The fading face was that of its trainer, gazing into a mana-mirror somewhere else ten or twenty keys away. The trainer had lost his snoop-hound and years of attunement all for nothing. The biker hadn't even been nipped.

Don't forfeit all those years of self-attunement, Sam, for the sake of an impulsive bite.

30 · MOTHER OF THE WORLD

Even though the bulk of Lucky's forces had pressed on into the forest lord's domain Lucky herself stayed in Maananfors. She remained there with Jatta and Serlachius and an adequate number of guards and some wooden soldiers so as not to seem like a vagrant camping out in the woods. By all accounts Osmo and his chit had a roof over their heads in Kip'an'keep. The genuine Queen shouldn't resort to a tent or bivouac.

The matter of Juke's betrayal preyed on her mind. With whom could she best express her chagrin and frustration but with Jatta?

The stoves were hot in that hall which had until recently been Osmo's pride. And Minnow's pride too? Maybe this keep had been a touch humble for Minnow compared with her mother's palace! People of small stature sometimes got above themselves. Minnow seemed to have taken this trait to excess.

The tapestries of trees suggested a summery day. However, the cascade of light coming through the windows wasn't honeyed. Yesterday had hardly been a day at all, only a twilit shroud. Today was bright but harshly so; snow-light. Premature winter had even iced the turquoise lake already.

The hall felt unfriendly and vacant. Vacant, too, was a certain notorious niche in the wall. That recess in the pink granite was where Cammon the tyrant had once stood petrified. Prior to the hasty evacuation, someone – Minnow herself? – had torn down the brass rod and arras. Lucky was lounging in Osmo's abandoned chair, staring at the niche. Beside her yawned a gap where the ivorywood throne had been. Oh that couldn't be left behind for her to inherit.

'Do you think she meant that as a message to me?' Lucky asked Jatta. '"The nook awaits you, Mummy. If only my hubby can bespeak you!"' The Queen laughed. 'I'm not afraid to try it for size. Are you, my Jatta? You suffered humiliation in this hall. You should own every single part of it.'

Jatta, in her tunic trimmed with variegated felt – of vermilion and pea-green and orange – was dressed just as when two summers before she'd burst into Osmo's hall to beg in vain for sanctuary. On that earlier occasion her tunic had been soiled and slashed, her calfskin trousers caked in mud, and her coaly hair awfully hacked. Now her short hair showed some style, though Anni wasn't here to trim and tend it lovingly.

In a swirl of purple gown Lucky descended to where Jatta was leaning against a woven larkery tree, distancing herself. She seized her daughter by the arm, and propelled her towards the empty alcove.

'Climb up, my Jatta, and chatter to me!'

Reluctantly, Jatta complied. Feeling foolish and vulnerable, she posed while her mother scrutinized her. The high-roofed hall seemed even more vacant now.

'My finest of daughters! Grandmother of my wonderful menace lasses, who gave me this town! We should be friends and confidantes, you and I, just as we were when you were a little girl.'

Aye, a little girl shivering in her room, and scared, anxious to appease this mother of so many superfluous daughters . . .

Was it flattery to be addressed as the granddam of miniature minxes and jinxes who wafted pest flies from their mischievous little paws?

'Can I please step down?'

447

'No! Not till—' Seeming to hear a noise, Lucky stooped and from the back of her scarlet suède boot pulled a knife.

'Nobody's coming,' protested Jatta. 'There's nobody else here. You're safe in Maananfors.'

'Who says I'm not?' The captured keep was adequately guarded. The surviving servants wouldn't dare harm Lucky. Nor would those able-bodied townsfolk who hadn't fled with Osmo. Too cowed by the plagues, they were. Victims – *surviving* victims – still bled from the hair, from the bowels, from the bladder. The agents of the Queen's retribution (and their mum, June) were with the mass of the army; but they'd made their mark.

Osmo's sway over the town was gelded. Two discontents, Per Villanen and Stone-hand Hans, were serving as 'administrators'. Old Alvar, locked upstairs in his study, hardly posed any threat. The blade remained in Lucky's hand, blocking Jatta's descent.

'Not till you tell me what happened when the stone man came to life.'

'I hardly saw him, Mother! I was hustled out.' Jatta squirmed. Did some trace of the tyrant remain, he who had imposed his will on women so much more horridly than Jarl exerted his sway over her? 'Then I fled.'

'Ah yes, with *Juke*.'

'No, Juke waylaid me.'

'The deceiver . . .'

Did Lucky imagine that Jatta was holding back some vital clue to Juke's conduct? Jack, on his return – empty-handed – from the intrusion into the Velvet Isi nest, had told how Juke had jumped Minkie Kennan to safety because Eyeno was supposedly alive, and inside of the Ukko-child, which might or might not be hidden under a lake, which might or might not be near cliffs. Might Jack have told his mother something extra – something seemingly trivial yet all-essential – which Jatta needed to be pressed to bring to mind, with the point of a knife? On the night of Jack's wedding he hadn't told his grandma that he knew a bit about Ukko-flowers, and she had cremated the bloom!

'My Ukko-child's hidden in the east,' mused Lucky. Certainly it was nowhere to the south of Maananfors. She mustn't stray further in pursuit of van Maanen and his Minnow; mustn't let herself be out of touch in Kippan's forests. Let her army, and Jack, and the Maids, and Captain Bekker's wooden soldiers attend to the rebels.

In the inner bailey stood the royal sky-boat, and the fortress-flier and two flying pods. *Don't send those where rockets might shoot them down.* Lucky might need rapid transport herself. She couldn't fly away to the east with her guards and Serlachius without any clear destination. She had to stay somewhere near her army. That place was here, where she had promised to flaunt herself and flaunt Jatta. She imagined that Osmo might be dying by now. And Minnow? She hadn't ever killed a daughter before . . . Her knife wavered.

Were Kennan and Juke inside her Ukko-child at this moment? Were the Velvet Isi scanning that Ukkoscope of theirs, awaiting their opportunity? Why hadn't the expedition destroyed the device! Surely Juke had understood about the Ukkoscope. Juke was a traitor.

How hollow her victory here at Maananfors. How lonely.

'We should hold another feast,' she told Jatta.

Oh yes: just as after the occupation of Maananfors! Three-meat stew and fish stuffed with chanterelles, roast goose and blood soup – while in the town people's hair bled. Whom might she invite to a new feast? The best of her previous guests had gone onward to war. Prut and Aleksonis, Nils and Bekker, Jack.

Summon Lyle Melator from Loxmithlinna? *Around*, not across, the crusted lake. Not Lyle, no. She might find herself in bed with him. He would call her Paula in private. Thanks to him cuckoos cackled in Maananfors how Elmer had whipped Eva. But they also squawked how Elmer Loxmith was longlife now, and Osmo's ally again. Away in Kip'an'keep the birds would be gossiping about Elmer and his whip, and about the revenge of the Northland, and how Jack had brought about the freeze so that the ground would be firm for the war-wagon.

Had Jack truly caused the bitter weather, the plummeting of temperature? If so, he was becoming a prodigy.

Just three mornings earlier, as snow was scudding, the communicator in the keep had chimed. Aleksonis must speak to the Queen immediately.

The General told her how Jack had conjured up cold; and how cold had come overnight – of which she was well aware. The Maids needed swaddling. The troops urgently needed skis and sledges. While these were being commandeered and transported, the royal advance was delayed. Aleksonis implied a setback, without broadcasting blatantly about one. Kippan's forces, by contrast, only needed to open up their winter stores to equip themselves and Osmo's rebels.

Jack was certainly no saboteur, even if he'd failed to bring back the Ukko-flower. What had possessed him? He'd chattered to the General about the war-hervy which was even now trundling towards the zone of conflict. Frozen ground and a soft cushion for its broad high wheels to roll over! Now he wasn't saying anything, as though the cold had nipped his tongue.

That armoured vehicle would more likely bog down in a drift, its wheels coated with wool crushed into ice. What had possessed Jack?

Lucky had spoken to Jack over the radio, sternly though patiently. Gradually he'd found his voice.

'A war needs winter,' he'd rhapsodized. 'Slaughter in the snow. Bloodflowers blooming. It's how a war for final victory should be fought. I saw this last night! So I shouted and I sang and I spun around and beckoned frost and snow. Snowflakes didn't just swirl around me. They poured from the sky all over. War's beautiful in winter, Grandma.'

'Listen to me, my best boy,' she'd begged him, 'what prompted you?'

'Snowscapes,' he'd whispered, 'and bloodflowers; and a feeling, such a powerful feeling – that there's been a war before, just like this, so this is how it must be again.'

'When was this other war? Where was it?' she'd persisted.

'It was a mana-war, Grandma, an invisible war that no one else saw. So I sang and I spun around. What did I do?' he'd asked in sudden shocked realization, voice crackling with static or with emotion. 'How could I have done so much? All this wool, and the cold . . . My daughters can still conjure flies from their mitts!'

She had soothed him, from afar. She had calmed him.

After so much effort in transporting the war-wagon from Sariolinna, would it ever now arrive at the area of hostilities?

How fitting that the vengeance of the Northland upon the rebels should feature ice and cold.

So Lucky had praised Jack.

Something prodigious had happened: an eruption of mana into the world. Jack had been a pivot for this, a hinge upon which a greater door turned, a closed door which was now beginning to open. There was such a sense of imminence.

Lucky had reassured Aleksonis.

'Jack will be able to freeze van Maanen solid, and Minnow too. Once you fight your way through he'll shatter them. He's the Mana Kid, Viktor, that's what he is.'

She must reassure herself too.

'I once asked you to call me Paula,' she reminded her daughter. 'Do you remember?'

'Yes!' Yes indeed: that chilly room high up a tower, the anxiety, being forced to tell a tale which a little girl could hardly understand.

'I want to call *you* Paula for a while.' Still that knife was in Lucky's hand. 'Even though your hair isn't blonde. It ought to be.'

Should Jatta's hair turn white with fright? Keen to every cue, she inhaled her mother's aroma of spicy yeasty buns and shrimpy piquancy.

'How will you greet me, Paula, when you meet me?' Lucky asked her huskily. 'How shall I greet you?'

What reply could Jatta make, which would satisfy? Her mother wasn't seeing a daughter before her, elevated upon the pink granite nook. Had she ever truly seen any daughter of hers, as their own person? The portrait gallery in Pohjola Palace was full of herself, and only herself. Daughters were warped portraits which went their own way, discarded, sold to suitors, false faces which peeled off and blew away.

Paula: Lucky's twin, the sane immaculate double in whom Lucky believed so frenziedly . . .

'I've missed you, dearest,' suggested Jatta.

'*Dearest?* What's this then, Paula?' Lucky's voice was a knife-edge itself. 'Are you confusing me with someone else? With someone called Anni, perhaps! A peasant slut who sleeps with aliens and anyone else!'

Jatta could have struck her mother across her prominent peachy cheek, so like her own. She dug her fingernails into her palms.

'I feel for Anni,' she whispered, 'as you feel for your twin.'

'Ohhh!' The exclamation escaped like some vast billow, uplifting. 'To compare something so momentary with . . . a yearning of centuries! Besides, pretty Paula, you *are* my twin. Don't forget it!' Or else the knife might lurch . . .

Would Lucky, in a burst of madness, really injure the mother of *prodigious* Jack, grandmother of the menace lasses? Would she really harm this very special daughter? Permitted, for now, to be Lucky's mock-equal, her counterpart!

'We've missed one another so,' attempted Jatta.

'Have you really missed me?' asked Lucky sombrely. 'Were you thinking of me all these years, envying my power and palace and daughters galore? My fine Prince too. No need to envy him now! What did you know of me in dreams and mirrors? *Did you envy me? Did you yearn?*'

'We meet afresh, sister. It's all sweet, all clean, all new.'

'Ah but did you miss me . . . at Kaukainkyla, Paula? (I'll scorch that place). Was that you, there, dragged out of your dream by Kennan, and decaying, and burned to ashes? Was that you?' The knife dipped. It dropped upon a waxed yellover floorboard. Lucky was trembling violently. 'Oughtn't I to feel a terrible pang if my other self was destroyed?'

Jatta spoke diffidently. 'Mother, you've been fretting about this privately for weeks and weeks. You need to talk about it now. Daddy's dead. There's no Bertel to confide in. Do you want me to love you, instead? Is that why I'm standing up here like a statue brought to life? Do you want to bring a friend to life but you don't know how, after our differences?'

Lucky stared at Jatta through moisture in her eyes. 'When daughters continually grow old and die, how can I cherish any?'

Hesitantly Jatta stepped down on to the floorboards glossy with reflected snow-light. She kicked the knife and it skittered away.

'Stop the war,' she pleaded. 'Forgive Minnow and her husband.'

'What, when she calls herself the true Queen? How can you say so, Paula?' Although so close, Jatta's mother was still far away from her. Lucky tugged the chaplet from her hair – which tumbled into disorder – and rummaged the circuit of amber beads through her hands. She needed to clutch something.

'I'm defending our legacy. To gain it I exchanged you for myself, this incomplete self of mine.'

'If you find me, you can . . . relax, at last.'

'Were you at Kaukainkyla, Paula? Was it you?'

'Juke must know who Kennan kidnapped,' said Jatta. 'He'd have found out.'

'And cheated me . . .' Fists tightened on the beads. 'What a lot you know about Juke, my chatter.' Lucky drew away. 'You won't be Paula. You can't even pretend.'

This had been a childish game of fright and feigning, as in the palace in the past. How Jatta's heart went out to Minnow, whom her miracle demon son was going to freeze, if he could. Jatta might once have refused to wed, to spite her mother. Minnow had crowned herself with whips and pearls. In her mother's dark narrow eyes Jatta saw lunacy like a thin red worm writhing in each.

Anni, Anni, be safe in Sariolinna.

'The rapids might turn to ice,' said Jatta on sheer impulse. Anything, to distract.

Lucky considered this observation as though it held a cryptic meaning.

'The rapids,' she repeated.

Soon after the fall of Maananfors, while the plague-pestered and demoralized town was host to so many royal guards and wooden soldiers and buff Jaegertroopers and aitch-housemen resentful of how their home had been exposed to such jeopardy and damage, a royal picnic had been held at the cataract a couple of keys from the keep, out of sight of corpses in streets and wretches with bloody hair – a picnic for the Maids.

The cascade had delighted the little lasses. Jack and June had folded paper boats and pinned a bright ribbon to each to race down between the spume-sprayed boulders. The paper came from Alvar van Maanen's study. However, the pages in question had no writing on them as yet. Who knew what bias a spate of unknown words might give to the course of the toy vessels?

'Frozen *rapids* is a contradiction,' said Lucky. 'Why are you always determined to contradict me?'

At this point Paavo Serlachius came into the hall. Fresh from the courtyard, the ruddy-cheeked priest blew on his hands. He stamped snow from his shoes, and announced that a cuckoo was cackling some curious news from the roof of the storm hut outside the outer gate.

News from Castlebeck: longlife Lord Beck, widower for a century and a half, was to wed a certain Marietta, a woman in her middle years who happened to be the mother of Cully, the same who had put out Eva Loxmith-Sariola's eye.

Good for Cully, was Lucky's immediate reaction. News of this marriage seemed irrelevant.

Not to Serlachius. After Moller's release from the pillory in Loxmithlinna for the offence of presiding at Minnow's coronation, Elmer's mana-priest had confided in Serlachius how Elmer Loxmith had built a special cradle for Gunther Beck.

453

Forever besotted by the memory of his Sariola bride who had died ages ago, Gunther the dreamlord hoped to hibernate and dream his way to his dead wife, Anna.

Anna?

Lucky could barely remember who Anna might have been to have aroused such adoration and fidelity.

Beck had evidently awoken from his protracted slumber. What was *peculiar* about the news was that the dreamlord's devotion must have encountered an almighty rebuff or defeat. A quite devastating reversal.

Serlachius was much exercised by the mysterium, not least by the abrupt advent of winter for which Jack had so recently been a conduit, or so the demon lad had claimed. Serlachius wanted leave to go to Jack's side to monitor him and guide him. Maybe a pilot could fly the corpulent priest crammed into a pod on a one-way trip to the war front. A priest militant *ought* to be with the army, not here a hundred keys away from the action. Alas, the Queen wouldn't quit Maananfors, and insisted on his staying with her. Was Serlachius only using this gossip about Gunther Beck as a pretext to pester Lucky again?

Not at all. If the dreamlord were to find his dead wife anywhere, it must be as an echo-person in the Ukko-child where Lucky's own twin abided. What could have constituted such a total defeat for the dreamlord that he would wish to obliterate, even desecrate, all memory of his quest? Surely he would have continued to pursue that quest if he had simply failed, as yet, to find his Anna.

Therefore Beck had succeeded. But then all hope had been wrecked.

Beck's Anna must have been the zombie, the decaying echo, whom Kennan kidnapped and whom those rustic ruffians at Kaukainkyla burned. Not Lucky's other self, but Anna Beck-Sariola. Lucky's blonde twin still survived in the secret place.

Lucky's joy was inordinate. She roared with laughter. She skipped. Snatching portly Serlachius by the hands, she swung him around. Seizing Jatta, she pranced about the hall, bumping herself and her daughter into tables and benches bruisingly. This maternal embrace was almost a punishment. Lucky halted, bosom heaving; and Serlachius proceeded to hint that maybe the bearer – or rather, the interpreter – of such news might fly south to join Jack . . .

Ah, but Lucky's gratitude *did* know bounds. Chortling, she shook her unkempt head. How could she do without her precious Paavo? She must inform herself much further about Gunther Beck. If he had found (and lost) his Anna, could he possibly have encountered Lucky's other self too?

Beck of Castlebeck, several hundred keys from here . . . An old crony of dead deceitful Bertie's! Bertie had run into Beck at the gala where he'd paraded daughter Eva as a lure for Loxmith. And for vile van Maanen too.

They must radio to Castlebeck. No, they mustn't do any such thing! Let any eavesdropping Isi overhear about Lucky's inner-most hopes? Oh, no.

She must fly to Castlebeck herself in the royal sky-boat.

Just as Jack and damnable Juke had flown far off, to worse than no avail – aside from the distinction of Jack and Prut having invaded an Isi nest?

She mustn't leave Maananfors yet. In a snow-veiled camp in the midst of nowhere, would a cuckoo have gabbed such news? How wise to stay here.

Her Paavo could fly to Castlebeck . . . Not in a pod, to be sure! Aboard the royal boat, or in the fortress-flier. No, those might be needed. Against Kip'an'keep, when her forces broke through. (When. Or if. Drat the untimely winter. Though cold and dark-ness appealed.) If the whereabouts of the Ukko-child became apparent the sky-boats would be needed right here, and immedi-ately, to transport her and guards.

She must inform herself about Beck.

'*Moller* knows about Beck,' she mused. 'Lyle Melator must know *all* about the cradle project!'

Why hadn't Lyle told her? However canny Lyle was, he mustn't have realized the special significance. Paavo could hurry by sledge to the aitch-house, skirting the lake of course, not cutting across it and tumbling through inchoate ice . . .

'So that's why Beck was so gutsy!' exclaimed Jatta. 'He was cramming blubber on to himself so that he could sleep for ages.'

Lucky whirled. 'You've *met* him?'

No, not met. When Jatta sought sanctuary here she had hailed the gross blond baby-faced dream savant first of all – 'Right there, on high table, Mother!' – mistaking him for Lord Osmo. Juke had identified Beck for her later on, when they were travel-ling, though Juke hadn't known a great deal about him.

Who had Beck been sitting next to? Who was he closest to? Lucky must know everything!

Why, Beck had been next to a dandified older figure in a black and gold jacket, black stains on his fingers. *Alvar van Maanen.*

Him upstairs: Osmo's dad, held prisoner along with his *Chronicles*. An intimate of Gunther Beck's.

On a wall by the foot of a grand staircase – as in the hall itself – there now hung a portrait of Lucky. The tammywood frame was carved with leaves not unlike so many tongues of purple fire, though naturally a tammy tree was fireproof. During a thorough search of the premises prior to her taking occupation, these paintings had both been found in a subterranean ice-room cut into the granite upon which the keep stood, and of which it was built. They were concealed amongst cold carcasses – put there to chill the everlasting Queen by association? By proximity to lamb cadavers to imply her fate? Or her imprisonment in a stone cell!

A maid in starched white apron and linen bonnet was jostling the painting askew. This wasn't the first, or even the fifth, time that this portrait and the other one in the hall had been found hanging lopsidedly.

'You!' shrilled Lucky.

The slim lass swung round. Flaxen tresses, little dolly features, piercing blue eyes with a pronounced squint. Spying the subject of the portrait, the maid crouched rather than curtseying.

'Saint Lucky,' she whimpered. The mother of Kaleva herself, with her red-faced mana-priest and her daughter who had mated with an alien!

'What do you think you're doing? What's your name?'

'It's Amelie. I were just adjusting your ikon.'

'You were slanting it cock-eyed.' Cock-eyed as herself. 'So you're the one who's responsible!'

Wailed the maid, 'It's so as *nakkis* don't sit on the frame.'

'Oh indeed? The wooden leaves would prick their bums. Now your bum will be thrashed, Amelie. Paavo, call a wooden soldier. Tell him to put this chit over his hard knees and paddle her with his hard hand.'

The maid grovelled. Wide, her eyes stared quite out of focus. 'Saint Lucky, beat me yourself, I beg. Touch me so I shan't catch the bloody pangs.'

'Nobody else will suffer now, silly,' said Jatta. 'Not hereabouts. Not any more.'

456

'Please thrash me yourself, Saint Lucky,' begged Amelie.

'Why should I?'

'Cos, cos . . . it was me as put yer ikons in the ice-room to protect 'em. I knew otherwise they'd be daubed on or worse.'

'Is this true?'

The maid squinted extravagantly. 'True as me name's Amelie. I did it ages ago, straight after Sam Peller first turned them to face the wall in case you could see through them what was going on. Oh they was noticed to be missing but nobody knew who took them or where they went.'

'My loyal child!'

'Some people blamed Seppy Hakulinen cos then he wouldn't go with the fleet to the aitch-house—'

Serlachius snorted. Osmo's mediocre mana-priest had been relegated to the kirk in town.

'Some people even blamed Osmo's dad, cos yer portraits were a sort of *chronicle* in paint. But I hid 'em, cos you're my saint. Why, you're the mother of the world. My saint coming here is magic. Please beat me with yer own hands, if,' and her voice trailed off, 'I'm to be beaten.'

Of course she wasn't to be beaten. Lucky raised her by tugging her tresses, and planted a kiss on her squinty blue eye – which made Amelie gasp out, 'Oh thank you, thank you.' Lucky winked at Jatta suggestively. *Is it thus with you and Anni?*

Mother of the world! What the maid babbled was true. For centuries, Lucky's daughters had been bearing children who bore or sired children. By now her blood must be in many Kalevans who had been born here. Tens of thousands of people must be related to her, distantly and dilutedly. Men and women in Saari and Tumio, in Portti and Yulistalax, in Verinitty and Luolalla. People who knew nothing of the connection, no more than she herself knew. Normal people, mana-talents, mutants even. Her harvest was vaster than just a hundred-some daughters. Harvest, likewise, of the Ukko which had transformed her.

'You might be my granddaughter a dozen times removed,' she told Amelie.

Jatta's lips moved: *Pity yourself.* She kept her counsel.

A tabby cat slunk towards them, then paused to stare – not at maid or Queen or priest but at a shadowy patch of wall where nothing obvious was visible. The animal's tail switched to and fro a couple of times in umbrage or apprehension, its mind irrelevantly obsessed with some phantom of its imagination.

Abruptly it scuttled away for a reason which perhaps equally eluded it, panicked or chagrined because it had no idea what it had stared at, or why.

'Shall I still call a soldier?' asked Serlachius, just to be sure.

Of course not. Alvar awaited.

A fug of smoke heady with rum and nutmeg filled the stove-hot study. Noon sunlight exaggerated the flux of fumes. Lucky's first action was to march past a couch heaped with blankets, and a commode hung with sachets of pot-pourri, to the window to thrust it wide open. Some flakes fluttered in on an icy draught. Outside was a cuckoo perch, with no entrails hanging on it, only a few icicles. The window commanded a snowy panorama of town and lake, boats frozen at their moorings, most prominently Osmo's futile flagship. *Sotko's Daughter* had been too large to pilot southward. Stripped of its armaments, the paddle-steamer was abandoned.

Serlachius wafted the door to and fro before shutting it. Jatta coughed, as if suffering a recurrence of the awful chestiness which had been bothering her when first she came to this keep.

Osmo's dad, in mulberry dressing-gown and slippers, had risen to his feet from out of a rocking-chair by a heaped desk. His droop-bowl tammy pipe puffed like some steamer funnel. His bare shanks were corded with several varicosities, though otherwise he was trim with almost lady-like skin, delicately crinkled rather than wrinkled. He'd been scribbling on a sheet of paper upon a tray – which he now clutched protectively across his midriff.

A spindly dumb-waiter held a used porridge bowl, eggcup with emptied shell, a broken roll amidst crumbs of others, and a milk-stained glass, the historian's breakfast still awaiting clearing. Lucky promptly occupied a high-backed leather armchair beside this.

Books crowded two cases on either side of a painting of a windswept hero leaning into the wind. Globe of the world. Heaps of black notebooks. Bundles of papers tied with ribbons. Numbered ledgers. Thick candles in holders, wax-knotted. Recently there'd been no oil for Alvar's lamp.

'It smells like a *bonfire* in here,' said the Queen.

After the initial shock of her arrival, Alvar did his best not to seem perturbed by such a remark. Setting the worktray, then his pipe, aside he said, 'I'm sure my tobacco saved me from your flies! If only my son had taken up smoking. Smoking prevents dementia too, do you know? That's how I can cope with all the tangled nests of stories.'

'Sit down. I want to hear about your crony Gunther Beck's quest for his dead Anna. I hear that he's going to remarry – a Marietta.'

'Remarry?' exclaimed Alvar. Sinking back into the rocking-chair, he groped for a black notebook. 'I've been so cut off, relying on a scullery lad twice a day, and no offal allowed me to attract a cuckoo! What can have happened to Gunther?'

Lucky leaned forward angrily. 'Are you asking me? Do you imagine you're about to *interview* me?'

Avarice and appeal gleamed in Alvar's eyes.

'Oh how I need to, Paula Sariola!' (And Lucky twitched uncontrollably.) 'May I? Can I? There's so much to find out.' Alvar glanced fleetingly at Jatta, who had evaded his questions on an earlier occasion. Jatta was merely one daughter. Here in his room right now was the source, the wellspring.

'You're forgetting your position,' Serlachius reproved him.

Alvar persisted, pen poised in inky fingers. 'It's all that gives meaning to me – mapping the weave of events.'

Lucky knitted her fingers together, knuckles cracking. 'How many people in the world,' she asked Alvar, 'do you calculate I'm related to by my blood?'

Since her daughters wrought a physical change in their husbands by giving them longlife, maybe – by some kind of infection – she herself had combined intimately with Osmo, with Elmer, with many men, in addition to her relationship by descent to so many living souls.

A sudden perspective opened: of similarity to herself, as if she had fractured into ten thousand shards all reflecting herself in askew and partial guise – and about, somehow, to be reunited, just as she would be reunited to her original self: the much-experienced suffering self reconciled with the pristine self, preserved for her salvation . . .

Alvar shivered at the cold draught from the window.

'How many?' he repeated. 'That's a hard question. I'd need to draw up such long lists, and there'll be gaps . . .'

'Here's an easier one!' she cried. 'How did Beck find my other

459

self? How did he find Paula? If you can't answer this your *Chronicles* are worth nothing.'

Alvar licked his lips.

'Gunther used Isi hibernation hormone given him by a shaman called Taiku Setala, who received it from the mutant Isi mage known as Viper, whom your younger daughter—' *Don't mention Minnow.* 'Taiku Setala died dreaming other people's dreams instead of his own—'

'Do you mean that Beck dreamt *my* dream? Because he'd lived long enough? Not as long as me, but long enough! Oh if we live long enough we dream of the beginning. The dream will become real to us – but Beck has been getting in my way!' Leaping up, Lucky rushed to the window and gripped the snowy side of the sill, her fingers sinking in as though the underlying fabric itself was soft. 'I'm so lonely!' she screamed into the frigid air.

'Mother,' appealed Jatta.

'Mother of the world,' Serlachius said awkwardly, aping Amelie's words.

Lucky bit at her lip. 'It's the strain of waiting so long!' (And Alvar scribbed so swiftly.) 'Time had to pass, didn't it? Enough time for stories to feed the child. I couldn't find myself till now. Beck couldn't conceive how to find his Anna. They're cruel, cruel, the Ukko and its child. Giver of mana, sucker of life-juice.'

'But,' protested Serlachius, 'the Ukko provided a world. The mysterium blesses us. How else could our lives be lived?'

'I curse the Ukko and its child,' shrieked Lucky.

'Don't, Majesty—'

'Why shall I not if I wish?'

'Mana heeds you.'

'And frustrates me!'

'Consider the freeze. This isn't a normal onset of winter.'

She agreed, she agreed. 'It's the end of warmth, and life. A terrible change. An abolition. Jack should have danced warmth instead! A sweltering fire . . . to burn Kip'an'keep.' Swinging round, she glared at Alvar, scribing away. 'Setting light to its paper factory!' Snow gloved her fingers. 'I suppose it's the wrong time of year for a heatwave. My Jack caused this freeze, old man, so much younger than me! Do you hope for a spurious kind of longlife for yourself – even now, Alvar van Maanen – by accumulating all those stories of other people's lives? Jack'll freeze your son solid. Then I'll melt him into soup, and pigs will slurp it up.

460

His'll be the shortest longlife ever! Frost and fire, frost and fire,' she chanted.

'I've been looking at my portraits downstairs,' she added ominously.

'They've turned up?' asked Alvar, eager for facts.

'The carving on the frames is like tongues of flames wreathing me.'

Alvar recollected. 'Those are *meant* to be leaves.'

'Tongues of flame, you futile old man.' *The idea of a bonfire had taken root and sprouted.* 'You can't tell me where Beck found Paula, can you?'

Alvar could try, oh yes he could try – in the awful extremity which he sensed to be impending. He could tell her so much about the dreamlord and his dead wife and ramifications. Starting when? Starting where? Witness the mounds of ledgers and notebooks and piles of beribboned paper inked with *Chronicles*.

'He doesn't know,' interrupted Jatta. Alvar had seemed to intervene for her at that Lucky's Day feast in the hall. A night's shelter. Change of clothes. Most likely Alvar had only wanted a chance to interrogate her. She should protect him from Lucky's lunacy. 'How can he possibly know, Mother?'

'In that case he's useless; and so is all this paper. Fit for paper boats, fit for paper sky-boats . . .' Sweeping bundles of manuscript aside, Lucky tugged a ribbon loose. She flattened out a sheet inked with constipated yet scuttley writing. She began to fold it. 'I last saw those rapids two hundred years ago,' she reminisced. 'Is my visit properly recorded?' Matches, intended for Alvar's pipe, spilled loose on to the desk. She struck a match, aimed the dart, lit its wing. Immediately she threw it through the open window. Burning, it sped out.

Alvar uttered such a moan of loss.

'Oh this is too slow.' Lucky snatched up a whole ribboned sheaf, lit the edge, tossed the bundle out.

'Don't,' begged Alvar. 'It's the history of your reign.'

An appeal of no consequence.

'Can't I remember whatever I need to?'

'Don't,' croaked Alvar. 'Osmo isn't longlife. He isn't.'

'*What?*'

Her vandalism ceased.

*

461

Lucky yelled for the cuckoo which had brought word of Gunther's marriage. *Coo-coo*, wherever it was! *Coo-cooooo*. She slashed her hand on a spur of the perch, blooding the snow.

When it arrived, the scaly green bird eyed the study and occupants with its big yellow eyes, ears cocked. What a cornucopia of silent inked cackle the room contained – and would continue to contain; now would continue to. However, the bird only knew the spoken word.

'Say in Kip'an'keep,' Lucky told the gossip-bird, 'that Osmo van Maanen isn't longlife at all. His Minnow was too small for him!'

'No she wasn't,' muttered Alvar miserably.

Lucky rounded on him in his rocking-chair.

'How do you know? Were you peeping through a keyhole to record it all?' The Queen laughed zanily. 'Her keyhole was too tiny, so he used her bum instead. Because he's a *shit*. And she's a shithole. Bird: tell how he isn't longlife because he bodged the job.'

She stared at her hand, beginning to heal already. The hand moved towards a sheaf of script. 'You really don't know exactly *how* he bodged?'

'I swear I don't,' vowed Alvar.

'Let's see now,' said Lucky to Jatta. 'Together we ought to be able to work it out. Don't you think? Mother and daughter putting our heads together in private? I shan't feel so alone then.'

Years ago, to relieve such pressure as this, the young Jatta might have insisted, 'I love you, Mummy, I love you.' Now she whispered, 'Paula.'

Where was the other self, the sweet sane self?

'Go, bird, go!' ordered Lucky. She flapped some paper at the cuckoo then set the paper down safely again once the bird took wing.

Outside, how glittering was the scene – as if the sky-sickle had descended and swathed itself across the whole landscape. The midday seemed more silver than gold. A bank of dirty cloud was looming low in the distance, though. By dusk not very many hours hence there'd be no sickle to see, nor stars, only flakes of darkness falling, snow which might seem more like soot.

31 · NAKKIS ON THE RUG

At first Goldi was reluctant to yield to Wex's persuasions, even though the man with two minds had told her where to find Amberman and had even given her his pony.

Was her brief idyll so soon to be curtailed by involvement in human affairs – in the fortunes of the van Maanens from whose presence she'd been expelled with a binding sway? Now Lord Osmo and his little lady had pursued her here. Themselves, they'd been forced to take an unexpected trip. The details of the war were vague to Goldi. She did not wish for a sharper perspective.

To have Lord Osmo in her sway, reliant upon her! Such had once been a goal. Though not her personal goal. It had been a goal of her illustrious masters. No voice had ever whispered in her mind to enforce the attempted seduction of Osmo. With reasonable justification her masters had presumed on her loyalty. She'd been bred and moulded and made ready. Jarl, too, had been loyal – loyal enough! Loyal to the status of Juttahat, which was his, which was hers. Neither he nor she could ever imagine identifying wholeheartedly with these wild human-beings. Yet she hadn't been bindingly compelled to carry out her mission, no more than Jarl had been. She had chosen to do so (and failed). The hope which secretly impelled her had been futile. She had ceased to cherish it after Lord Osmo bespoke her so tormentingly.

Nevertheless, it was true what Wex said. Osmo had set her on a course towards fulfilment, to an amazing consummation, with Amberman. Osmo had set her *fortuitously* on her course, not out of foreknowledge. He hadn't intended future delight for her but endless frustration.

Osmo had been too powerful for Goldi to trip-trap, once his spouse had raised the alarm! Now that he was diminished by illness she could assail him with her scents and her chanting. She was actually being invited to do so in order to heal him! She could *succeed* now that success would be a pointless distraction, subversive of the joy which she had found for herself.

Nevertheless, when Osmo would have treated this Girlem even more harshly the young rebel Queen had interceded . . .

Wex suggested that debts should be repaid, including the debt to himself. He finally begged her, 'Do it for love.' For the love she had found in an amber embrace, a love as unique as *she herself* had formerly been unique (and lonely), notwithstanding her delusions about Tomi.

Do it for love.

For the sake of another love too, so she'd guessed.

A vain love which that double-minded man nursed for Minnow.

Wex was the closest approximation she knew of to a fellow Juttahat, though truly no Juttahat other than Jarl could be – or could have been – a fellow to her. Why did Wex's other mind not control him more wisely?

In another respect it was his utter master, as she'd discovered.

Their encounter had taken place in a reception room in Maids' Manor. When Wex intruded, she'd been dusting glassware, dressed in black frock and starched white lace-trimmed apron and mobcap. A log fire smouldered in an open grate on a plinth of granite, doing little to relieve the chill. The cold didn't bother the Girlem at all. She was still hot from Amberman's embraces of the early morning, before her lover had absented himself to wander among the snowy trees of the arboretum, as goldenly naked as ever. Should her Amberman heed cold when his body was built of no ordinary flesh but of resin? As Wex was about to depart after pressing his appeal, he took a chunk of wood from the pile of fuel and placed it upon the fire.

Perhaps he did this so as to emphasize *ardour*. Perhaps to show that he knew what was best to do in the circumstances, because males often feel proprietorial about fires. That chunk had proved to be mintywood. Mintywood shouldn't have been in the pile. Instantly it blazed up under his hand, flames flaring. A sweet green reek pervaded the air, almost ousting the stink of mustoreum.

Wex had leapt back but without uttering any cry of anguish. 'Damn,' he'd murmured. That was all. He didn't feel the pain, though his palm looked seared! He mustn't leave till she knew why – or how could she make up her mind about his request?

A confession emerged from him.

After Wex had given Goldi his mount and parted from her, he had killed the cuckoo which rode him, and had been engulfed in mana-fire. A blaze tortured his nerves without quit. His other self had cut him off from bodily feeling and smell and taste. He was a creature who could only hear and see, reduced to ears and eyes.

No wonder he must love – impotently, and in vain! Such control as his inner voice exercised over him must admit some degree of licence, or else his incarceration in a numb carcass would be unendurable. Imagine if *she* could not feel the caress of her Amberman, the rhythms of his limbs, the foetal girl in his womb turning and flexing, seeming to flex him so that when he entered Goldi his discharge was like that elf's tears . . . of joy; a gush of liquid amber, beads of aromatic resin retained in a secret place within the Girlem without any other consequence than a shining clarity.

Not to be able to smell, nor feel! Oh to liberate Wex from his cruel restraint, which must be the worst of sways. She, who had been struck dumb for a week and a day, could appreciate the misery which he kept bravely concealed.

Yet if she were to involve herself . . .

First she must consult her mistress.

She had gone to Tilly in a chamber which had once been a nursery. These days the room was bare of furniture apart from a tall stove tiled in pink. Most of the floor was occupied by a rug upon which were set out little wooden carvings of forest-nakkis.

Tilly played a game with these figures which had lasted for years. The rug was patterned with silhouettes of trees branching and rebranching, a maze of curving and crooked pathways. Along these paths Tilly would move her little wooden dolls to the accompaniment of a tale grown so complicated in the telling that perhaps only nakkis understood it any more, a tale of love and treachery and ambition and quarrels and reconciliations. Tilly would often pause in her quiet narration to question one or other of her nakkis, and would impersonate a squeaky or gruff or silky reply. Also on the rug were arranged several small pieces of polished agate and onyx and lapis, make-believe holystones supposedly giving the power to cast various sways or be freed from a sway.

The rug was a forbidden zone. Only Tilly could venture upon it. Green-gowned, Tilly was kneeling on a fat moss-green velvet cushion. On an identical cushion sat the cream and chocolate spaniel, tongue lolling out. The spaniel would listen to Tilly's story unfold. Out couldn't hope to understand much of what she

465

heard but she was grateful to be the audience and occasionally would growl a word to herself gruffly.

Today was different.

Near the middle of the rug, in a wooden eggcup, stood a lighted candle. Beside the candle several figures lay on their sides. Tilly seemed perplexed.

'Lippa and Larkery and Vine are *dead*,' she appealed to Goldi in distress.

'Is that why the candle is lit?' asked the Girlem.

'I never wanted them to die . . . It was Musky who insisted on the candle. Then all three of them died one after another.'

Tilly leaned forward towards a knobbly figure, golden tresses dangling like fleecy foliage. 'Didn't you insist, Musky?' In a quiet croak she answered herself, 'Ach, this wretched war.'

'War,' growled Out.

'Maybe they'll come to life again—' The Girlem knelt alongside her mistress, upon hard parquet.

'Come to life . . .' Tilly frowned, her generous brow creasing. 'They weren't really alive to begin with, except in my imagination.'

What an imagination was hers. So debonair and even flirtatious to outward eyes, Tilly led this secret life, telling a convoluted tale to herself within her erstwhile nursery – a nursery, still, so it seemed. Yet she had always played her story-game without delusion. Perhaps she should have begun to dictate her meandering narrative to someone who could write it down? Perhaps she should have had it printed in a book? Where better than in Kip'an'keep! That book might have been as big or bigger than the *Book of the Land of Heroes* . . .

By the time she could have decided to do so, her story had been in full flood for years. No turning back to the beginning again. Who else but she would have known the preliminaries? Lacking those preliminaries, the subsequent ramifications would surely elude any audience other than herself.

Suppose that Tilly's Tale could have been memorized by storytellers for recital during dark winter days and nights, that nakki-narrative might have begun to influence the folk of Kaleva in their lives in minor rivalry to the *Book of Heroes* itself.

This wasn't her intention. Tilly's tale was a personal sanctuary, granting her a delicious sense of autonomy.

'Has a part of my imagination died?' she asked the alien Girlem. 'I never had any mana in me, Goldi. This is all my mana, here upon the rug. Do I throw those three into the stove now? Musky insisted on the candle – as a new sort of sway-stone! Actually, I dreamt of that candle last night. I dreamt that our tammy keep became afloat in liquid soil and liquid rock like melted wax. Now I've let Lippa and Larkery and Vine die. Not that I ever liked Vine much, but . . . something's coming to an end,' she whispered. 'My story, I think!'

'If I knew the story well enough,' said Goldi, 'I could help you continue it endlessly. Did no one ever die before in your tale?'

'I didn't want to lose my friends, my nakki-voices! Even if I didn't like them equally. I don't care for deaths, Goldi. Even if it's the death of a dog! Sometimes my nakkis *altered*, they changed. But now three are dead. I can't call them back. What *is* that candle, really? It's the light at the end of my story.'

Surely Tilly wished van Maanen well again. If Goldi tried to cure Osmo by her scents and chants – and by playing the Isi harp again! – would Tilly's father view such an intervention as a piece of alien meddling which might menace him? A possible prelude to the Girlem crossing the covered bridge into the main body of the keep with mischievous intent upon Lord Kippan? Goldi couldn't bear to be chased away from here. Despite her mistress's distress at the death of characters in her story, Goldi broached her dilemma.

'Osmo bad to Out!' yapped the spaniel. The bitch shook herself, exposing her neckwear of garnets. 'Osmo be sick and sick.'

The Girlem released an aroma of golden serenity, and the spaniel sighed, as did Tilly.

'Are you trying to sway me,' enquired Tilly with a sad smile, 'or are you asking my advice?'

'Your advice, mistress. Being your trusty maid.'

'Being your own person too. Like me.' Tilly contemplated the fallen nakki-figures and the candle flame. 'Selfishness,' she announced, 'is what occurs when your own self isn't enough. When it isn't ample, isn't bounteous. You jealously corset your pygmy self, and it shrinks a little bit more, though it seems denser and stronger. My dad, alas, is like that, youthful and hearty though he looks. This keep is his corset. Though I love him, I say so.'

Her father couldn't stop Osmo and Minnow from coming here because he was *inside* this corset of his own contrivance like an oster tight in its shell, cosseting himself while waves broke across his realm. Forts were forever rebuilt and woodmen were patrol-

467

ling dutifully, but the centre was ever more vulnerable and scared.

'For Osmo also to be weak is . . . a shabby thing. I think my father must realize this. Listen, Goldi: if necessary I'll tell Daddy that *I* asked you to help Osmo. Otherwise our shell might crack! I'll tell Daddy you'd sworn not to use your wiles, and,' smiling wistfully, 'your scents, but I persuaded you, my alien housemaid, I persuaded you. What do I do about Vine and Lippa and Larkery, though? Do I let the candle burn down into a pool of hot wax?'

'*Tilly!*'

The door had opened. Clad in deep purple, darker than the fabric of the keep, Tilly's mother glided forward. When had she ever trespassed in this room before? Her lean angularity made her seem even taller than she was. Edith Sariola had been the skinniest princess for a generation, a svelte and graceful sapling once.

Edith had been desiccated by the knowledge that she had bestowed life itself upon a once exuberant hubby – only for him to harbour her gift like some miser instead of profiting. Tapper Kippan would outlive the youngest sapling in his forests (and herself, of course, herself) but his life would be vegetative. By now he wouldn't even travel with wooden guards as far as the arboretum, which represented his domains in miniature. In his shuttered suite Tapper indulged in euphoric drugs from a fungus of the hot springs. Aside from the pleasure, the effect was to speed the passage of time for him. A day seemed to be an hour long, though brimful of delight. It was as if he was outrunning the rest of the world yet at the same time was compressing exquisitely what ordinary mortals must eke out. Through trusted, privileged bailiffs (not *one*, but a balance of bailiffs) Tapper kept a rein over his realm so that his peace would be protected. Really, recent events had happened too quickly for him to decide on a policy.

With Tilly – who was as young as his wife had once been – Tapper was indulgent and even ebullient. As for Edith . . . why, in other circumstances she might have kept her looks perfectly intact through middle age. Now she seemed to wear a new line on her face for each week which elapsed, and regarded herself bitterly as a sacrifice to Tapper's cloistered felicity.

Tapper's hair was as golden as Tilly's, and that of the two elder daughters whom Edith was privately delighted to have married off so that they departed. Edith's own dark hair was greying.

Tapper had long since ceased to heed her melancholy except perfunctorily. He'd offered her the drug to speed her own days. She refused, determined to endure every morose dry moment and not hasten headlong for his convenience.

'Playing with your alien maid, are you then?' asked Edith, in the dull lowered voice of self-pity which might so easily erupt into recrimination. 'I declare she's as privileged as . . . a talking dog. You do bestow your blessings, don't you, daughter? If you'd won Lord Osmo's heart there would never have been all this violence in our forests and plague flies and stink. You must marry soon. Marry, and leave me to my own miseries. Even an alien oddity can marry an amber nakki. Isn't she an example to you?'

Edith wrinkled her nose. Goldi kept her gaze downcast.

Edith continued more sharply: 'That's why I advised your father to let you admit this alien lass to service and let her lover visit her here in Maids' Manor. Didn't you realize?'

Tilly doubted that this was true. However, once her mother asserted something to be the case then she fully believed it to be true – at least until she asserted something contradictory. Tapper paid little heed to Edith. Edith must pretend otherwise.

'That's why I don't mind all those *brawlers* straying into our territory. Where there's war, there's a sense of emergency. Sudden passions occur. It's high time you stopped playing with dolls, Tilly. Still a virgin, indeed.'

Tilly looked up.

'Oh, perhaps I am not *that*, Mother.'

'What do you mean? Does your Girlem pleasure you – *with a candle in her hand*?'

Tilly flushed with a fury hitherto unknown to her. Her mother had gone too far this time in expressing her bile. Altogether too far. It was high time she was enlightened.

'Let me tell you, Mother,' cried Tilly, 'I've lain with soldiers who were going to take the oath of wood and drink the sap! Oh yes, I've done that several times. Soldiers loyal to us Kippans. They appreciated what I did – and afterwards they would have no hold over me. Because they were entering a different kind of existence. Right? Yes, Mother, I've done *that* – to explore the sensation.'

Distraught, Edith tottered. She lurched on to the rug of branching pathways.

'No!' cried Tilly. 'I'm sorry—'

Her mother kicked over wooden figurines.

'Stop it, you're scrambling the story – I'm sorry!'

'Whore,' cried Edith. She crunched a nakki beneath her shoe, trying to grind the wood into the weave.

'No!' yapped Out. The spaniel launched herself at Edith's ankles. The candle was knocked from the eggcup.

White smoke flowed across the whole rug. Or was it white fire? Tilly and Goldi both scrambled to their feet. Edith shrieked and danced clear. The spillage was more like bubbling steaming milk. Out retreated, barking. For a moment the rug seemed to be the top of a great incandescent candle, a molten lake: of seething wax, colourless burning gas. Next moment, only a halo was hovering upon the weave. No fallen candle to be seen in the glow, only an empty eggcup.

The Girlem chanted alien words, sibilant and clicking.

'*Mana*,' moaned Edith. '*Mana*. I never knew that's what your game was all about. My daughter's a secret shamaness. With a Juttie apprentice. Is it the other way about? Has your Girlem shown you how?'

'No!' cried Tilly.

Within the halo light tiny nakkis were stirring. Wooden figures began to move. Those figures which had fallen stood up.

'Larkery! Lippa! Vine—!'

Small voices chittered at Tilly, and she covered her ears. The participants in her long-standing story had come to life, mischievous wee nakkis.

Miniature flowers sprang up from the weave: with hearts of sunny yolk and coronas of white petals – a forest of daisies – as if long-dormant seeds had lain in the furrows in a loam of dust awaiting germination not by moisture but by waxen light.

Wee worms writhed, as though insect eggs had also hatched. No, those were *Isi*, ever so tiny. The rug seemed to bulge, becoming a hillock as the air distorted, lens-like. Nakkis raced along the routes of the rug through the flower forest, up-slope, down-slope, along contour lines, personae pursuing one another this way and that, her story run riot, quite out of her control.

'No, stop!' she squealed. Stop, before any nakki darted from the rug into the rest of the room.

The spaniel Out launched herself upon the bulging fabric, and rampaged. She seized a nakki in her jaws. She shook it furiously, cracking it, tossing it aside. She seized another, and another. Out was a monster in their midst, necklaced with jewels. Their

470

squeaks were an unintelligible chorus, raucous but minor.

Of a sudden the halo evaporated. It was as if a wave broke and dissipated, hissing. Out fled from the rug as it subsided. Daisies were grey cobwebs collapsing into dust. Worms withered into threads. Figurines lay scattered, many lacking legs or arms or heads.

With each extinction in the dog's jaws, a spark had seemed to enter Goldi, and a puff of afflatus. She sensed that she had been terribly blessed. She must bless in turn, to rid herself of this endowment both marvellous and awful. She didn't need it. She already had her Amberman. Amberman was all she needed. Oh to pass this bestowal onward. To Osmo. To Wex as well. To bestow. But not to control, not to try to dominate. She must grant a blessing with perfect benevolence. Benevolence had been of the essence of the tales which Tilly had woven, and which had become so uncannily animated.

Tilly panted, the breath gone out of her along with the tangled lives of her figurines. The spaniel was panting too. Stooping, she hugged Out to her. She squinted at Edith through her tresses. Her mother was casting around for somewhere to settle, or else she would surely fall. Edith reeled towards the tiled stove and slumped in its lee, her back to the wall panels.

What Tilly had told her mother about soldiers was true. She had hardly conveyed the fullness of the experience.

A couple of years before her acquisition of Out she had been roaming the arboretum, alone on that occasion, for who would harm her? A fresh-faced young fellow had been dallying near one of the two mootapu trees, weeping softly. He was going to become a woodman the very next day. He had begged to become one because of some cruel ostracism by fellow villagers, youths and maids alike. The youth was mourning the certainty that now he would never know the embrace of any woman of flesh and blood; and soon he wouldn't care about this. Meanwhile his care spilled out of him in a wistful adieu. He'd also heard that woodmen while dormant dreamt deliciously. By losing his tormented flesh maybe he would find hallucinatory happiness.

Spontaneously Tilly offered herself to him. The youth didn't know that she was Kippan's daughter. He imagined that she was a nakki of the woods, a precursor of the transformation he would undergo.

471

Willingly she gave herself to him. And that was the first sexual encounter for Tilly too.

That youth had regarded the trickle of hymenal blood on her thighs, and blood's anointal of his rod with wonder, realizing then that she was no nakki and amazed at her generosity, a charity which made even more poignant his own self-sacrifice. He had nestled his head upon her bare loins while she stroked his hair, inhaling her intimate odour with exquisite tenderness, he who would harden irrevocably.

Twice thereafter she had sought out fellows who were on the eve of change to help them bid farewell.

But to accept a regular *husband*? That wouldn't be to give herself, but to be taken.

What had been given here in this room? And what had been taken from her? Was this moment a closure – or a preliminary? A candle, prompted by a dream of calamity, had overflowed. Her story was no more. Its elements had erupted from her rug, and now lay fractured. The story had ended so abruptly that its absence would take days to register. Her alien maid seemed quickened with purpose. Should Tilly herself weep like the fresh-faced youth on the brink of miraculous consummation?

Minnow reached between her legs into the drawer beneath the ivorywood throne to produce the silver harp. She riffled the strings. Chords rippled. Osmo sighed.

'I suppose you'll be needing this,' Minnow said to the Girlem. Goldi hadn't resumed her seductive short tunic but remained dressed in domestic's clothing, perhaps as an earnest of good intent. 'I'm grateful to you,' Minnow added. ('Well, I *shall* be grateful,' she qualified under her breath, 'depending on the outcome.')

No particular craving to seize the instrument showed in the Girlem's stance or expression. No greedy anxiety in that regard. Nevertheless there was tension in her bearing as she contemplated Osmo, lounging wearily in a leather armchair, wrapped in a thick woollen dressing gown, depleted and reduced – and Wex too, the middleman of this venture. Wex clutched his green gaberdine cloak around himself even though he couldn't feel cold, nor heat. In fact it was warm in the throne-room. Enacting this pretence of normality, Wex was watching Minnow with such a giving gaze.

Two oil-lamps burned. The windows were curtained against

472

night and swirling snow. Doors were bolted. There'd be no inter-
ruptions, no intrusions.

Osmo stirred. 'I treated you a little intemperately,' he said to
the Girlem, wincing as he spoke.

She beamed. 'Oh that is forgotten. You set me on my course
to happiness. You could have bespoken me to choke – not to be
able to breathe. Now I must lull you again, to stupefy the sickness
in you. If I can! To pluck the sickness out paralysed. To rekindle
you with sparks of mana.'

'I'll . . . relax,' Osmo promised uneasily. The Girlem had
glanced towards Wex as though some double agenda was on her
mind.

'*Trust*,' whispered Wex. 'I do.'

'Well, *you* have a supervisor in you!' Osmo muttered. Minnow
was smiling encouragement and utmost fondness.

'Once I begin,' said Goldi, 'please don't try to stop me. Try not
to join in my urgings, Prince Osmo. Nor you, Queen Minnow.'

'You'll need to explore the origins of my illness—'

'I know, I know.'

'—thoroughly . . . Do you know enough about it?'

'Roger Wex has told me the details, Prince, including what
cuckoos have blazoned.' Every one of the details? Including his
failure to seize longlife? Wex didn't know about that. Or did he?
'I'm an accomplished chanter.'

Osmo gestured, limply: *proceed*. He breathed shallowly. For a
few moments human woman and alien mimic shared custody of
the silver harp. Only gently and gradually did Goldi accept the
instrument from Minnow's hands. She busied herself adjusting
pegs and tuning pins.

> '. . . Maids of Horror, Menace Lasses,
> 'Sent the fly that bit his earlobe,
> 'Putting poison in his bloodstream,
> 'Baneful toxin, blighting venom,
> 'Gnawing at the Prince's kidneys,
> 'Causing lesions and pink urine,
> 'Robbing him of mana-power,
> 'Gagging all his proclamations;
> 'Jinx and Jinxie, Minx and Minxie
> 'Are the names of those four pixies,
> 'Daughters of a fatal wedding
> 'Of a mutant and the fastboy,

473

> 'Son of Jatta who sought safety
> 'In the hall of Lord van Maanen . . .'

Was Osmo's rejection of Jatta an ultimate source of his sickness?

On and on, and around and around, Goldi's tale had been tracing and chasing itself for an hour and more to the accompaniment of ravishing arpeggios and rippling chords as more and more circumstances shuttled into the fabric – even Wex's affliction by agnosia to free him from agony. The lingering hint of mustoreum had long since been overwhelmed by intoxicating fragrance. The audience of three was as lulled as could be.

The assault by scent and sound became a storm as the Girlem at last declaimed sinuously and lustily:

> 'The name of the fly was—'

For an instant she paused before choosing, before seizing the name from the necessities of her narrative . . .

> '—Minxie,
> 'Begetter of his malady,
> 'Milady of his misfortune,
> 'Be purged from his healing waters,
> 'That words from his heart speak strongly,
> 'And a man with two minds may know
> 'Fragrance of flowers, zest of food,
> 'For *love* is the name of release!'

Sparks and scintillae flashed from the Girlem's hands – or from the reverberating strings of the harp. Borne upon a bombardment of honeyed scents, these sparks settled upon Osmo who jerked as if stung, and upon Wex who lurched and who inhaled as avidly and sorely as a new-born first breathing air, and began to sneeze into his senseless hand.

Disappointment darkened Wex's face. He beat his brow with a fist, but softly.

'I smelled for a moment. Such sweetness. It's gone. I sneezed it out of me. Wetwear, you took the smell away—'

His other self informed him aloud: *'The smell brain is ancient, fundamental. So is pain. I protect you from distractions.'*

Fatigued, the Girlem glowered at Wex, or rather at the wetwear within him.

Shivering, Osmo rose. 'I felt I was drowning,' he slurred. 'As when Sam held me under that pool without a breath to breathe

. . . Drowning in words and musk and music. I submitted, I did submit – to an alien spirit.'

'Now you surface unharmed,' said the Girlem. Giddily she made her way to Minnow and restored the harp to her.

In the dark morning Osmo woke refreshed. He had slept all night long. His kidneys no longer ached as if they were bruised and rotten. He did not fear the pressure in his bladder, an urgency as familiar as his piss-erection. Nor was his head banded with tightly screwed brass. Lighting a candle, by which time his cock softened, he peed into a chamber pot: a stream of liquid straw.

'How is it?' asked Minnow, leaning from the bed.

'Pure.'

He rejoined her under the blankets. 'Flame die down,' he called; 'this is spoken.' The candle guttered, strangled. Tapestry upon the wall receded into oblivion. His own flame was roused. His candle was stiff, his wick of nerves pulsing. 'I feel . . . bountiful,' he whispered. 'Shall we try to make a baby? Is this the right time, my duckling? I've lost count.'

The right time, with an army of wooden soldiers and royal guards and Jaegertroopers and aitch-housemen trying to reach them?

'Our child will be born in high summer – ebulliently. I want a little Minnow.'

'You already *have* one, silly!'

'How about a little Oz?'

'I don't know if I want to be a *mother*, considering how mothers behave . . .'

'Think of the sprat as a sister – no, better, a friend, just as you're my best of friends.'

'Well now, it *is* the middle of the month for me . . . No bungs in the offing; only yours.' Raising herself, she caught hold of him, to squeeze softly, so that he moaned. 'If I ride you, the seed might spill out . . .'

Throwing back blankets, he tumbled her. He knelt between her knees. In the darkness he lifted her lean legs shoulder-high. 'We'll do *this* the right way round—'

Minnow giggled, as did he.

'Untie the knot from the egg,' she purred; 'make a hole in the shell and slip inside . . .'

Tongues met. Words were flesh and muscle and nerves a-throb.

*

475

Light asserted itself at last upon snow-cloaked Kip'an'keep, and a cuckoo came to perch on a post outside Minnow's Manor, attracting a small crowd of Keepers from their work. It was Sam Peller who came indoors to tell Osmo and his wife. Sam had been riding for most of a day and a night on a succession of mounts from the war zone. In defiance of his earlier resolution he'd made the long journey to reassure himself about Osmo.

He arrived just in time to witness the cuckoos squawking at Osmo's very door. The secret was being blabbed. Osmo was ephemeral, not longlife like the forest lord – all due to ineptitude, sheer incompetence. What sort of leader was *he*?

Bleakly Sam trudged to join his lord – only to find Osmo flushed with vitality. He and Minnow were in their bedroom, dressed and breakfasting on caraway crispbread and slices of Emmenthal cheese. They were chuckling together. Cheerful wasn't the word. The only tears were those in the eyes of the cheese which was weeping ripely.

It wasn't merely that Osmo's sickness had remitted. He might never have been sick to begin with.

Sam himself was hoary, snow-flecked, blue with cold, dog-tired. If amazed relief hadn't been his overpowering emotion he might have felt defrauded, cheated of tragedy. Sam was the first to tell them about the bird.

Not even bothering to pull on their heavy quilted coats, Osmo and Minnow hastened outdoors to confront crowd and cuckoo. Elmer and Eva had joined the gathering in the snow. The gangly engineer stood diffidently, conscious of inquisitive challenging glances. How would he react to this public humiliation of Osmo? Eva, eye-patch in place to protect her hollow from the chill, seemed furious with the bird. As soon as she spied Minnow, Eva shook her head several times, tight-lipped, abjuring any role in what was happening. This was their mother's doing. Only then did Eva register Osmo. She actually raised her patch to see him more clearly before realizing the futility of this move.

Osmo planted hands on hips and shouted, 'Shut up, cuckoo! Don't listen to slanders, fellows. I'm well; very well indeed. I'm going to be visiting the forts today, and our rocket batteries that protect this fine city from molestation.' He tugged at his chestnut locks. 'Nothing wrong with my hair, you see! Nothing wrong with any bit of me. I've thrown off the plague. If this isn't like longlife, I don't know what is.'

Like longlife, perhaps . . . Nor had his hair ever been bloated

476

with blood. Now was the time for hyperbole. From the lips of a proclaimer would a little hyperbole be queried too closely?

'Actually I feel pissing good.' So saying, despite the cold, he opened his pants. 'I piss on that cuckoo and I piss on Lucky.' Into the snow he urinated exuberantly, cratering the white wool with a bowl of yellow slush. 'What's more,' he announced, 'my Queen and I are going to have a baby heir; and this is *spoken*.'

'You wouldn't likely have a full-grown one!' shouted someone cheerfully. Supportive laughter rang out.

'No fastboys for us, nor menace lasses! Those mutie monsters appeal to the mad old sort of Queen who'd ruin this world with her quirks and make people's hair weep blood till they're as mad as she is. I'm,' and he grinned, 'for decency.' Only then did Osmo tuck his pisser away, provoking hilarious approval.

Seeming to rise above mere snow in her platform boots, Minnow grinned genially, her hastily donned crown cock-eyed – adored by Osmo, and only less so just then by most of the onlookers.

Sam sagged. He needed a hot drink, sweet buns, a warm bed. 'By the way,' he mumbled, 'a biker scout spotted her war-wagon—'

'Should I ride to our troops, do you think, Sam, since I'm feeling so lively?'

'The war-wagon was making slow progress. I didn't think the matter merited a communicator message . . .'

But rather a journey by day and by night (night being much longer than day)? Leaving the front to its own devices? Oh the real reason was so obvious: the conflict in Sam's mind.

'Shall I go there by pony sledge, Sam?'

Ten years since, Tapper Kippan had sold his family's sky-boat to the richest merchant in Portti whose son then crashed it in the sea. Kippan hadn't even needed the money. He would be living a long time, and never intended flying anywhere again. The news of the crash had confirmed Kippan in his seclusion.

'But of course, there's Wex's dovecraft—!'

Could the dovecraft be involved directly in the war? Not so long as Lucky refrained from committing her sky-boats. An offer of evacuation was humanitarian. To transport Osmo in the role of a war leader would be very provocative.

Sam gathered his wits. 'In my opinion you're better off at a keep in this town than dossing in the cold.'

'Ah but now I can proclaim again.'

477

Sam was too tired to advise. When he wobbled, Osmo gripped an arm to steady him. 'Be strong, Sam; this is spoken.'

Sam shook his head. 'Don't. I feel the flow . . . You'd be burning both ends of my candle. It's food and sleep my body needs.' A fanatic gleam entered his eye. 'My powerful Prince,' he whispered. His journey had not been wasted.

Minkie pissed upon a hoar-frosted tussock, wondering whether the herbage might feel grateful for this hot donation – or as shockingly assaulted as a fellow-me-lad tossed from a bath of ice into boiling water.

A foreboding of punishment, perhaps? Who could punish Minkie for anything? He had found his farmer's daughter: gauche nubile Sal of the long crinkly ginger hair and freckles all over. He had wooed her away with his charm and with the magic and power of his bike – well away from her homestead.

The notion of exchanging the bike for a bareback pony had failed due to lack of bridle or reins. He and Sal had found a deserted cott in fair repair by a woodland mere. He'd made forays by jump-bike to a decent distance in various directions to stock up on rations by theft or by bluster or by playing the part of a royal soldier requisitioning what he needed in the Queen's name. No booze, alas. He was obliged to limit his ferrying to victuals, twice as much as would be needed for a man alone – but he couldn't have done without Sal to keep him warm and gratified.

The cott had yielded some fishing lines and hooks and a rusty ice saw and axe, stored under a hatch in the floor. A hearth awaited logs. Minkie's campaign tent, stuffed with dry herbage, served as a mattress over which to pull Sal's fur-trimmed cloak.

Quite a come-down for a fellow-me-lad. Not exactly what he'd envisaged (aside from Sal). But needs must. He mustn't risk using the jump-bike again (and who could say when it might quit?). So he sank it in the mere, a little way offshore. Steel pony, steel pony? What steel pony? Never heard of such a thing. I'm just a lover with his lass. We like to be by ourselves.

Sal was quite mesmerized by Minkie. She would have purred like a cat when he stroked her, if she'd possessed a purr, and she almost did. Never had he charmed any girl to such a degree. Sal was oblivious to the contrast between the farm from which she'd decamped, and this meagre cott. She absolutely *knew* that Minkie was on a royal mission which required him to hide himself, and wait. Why, Minkie knew Saint Lucky well. He'd stayed in

Pohjola Palace! He'd been a friend to the Prince, before the Prince met with an accident.

Minkie was less enchanted by his situation. However, he resolved to charm himself for a change – using Sal as his mirror. Otherwise he might become abominably bored and she might seem tiresome in her naivety rather than charming.

How *did* he habitually exercise his charm? Why, by wishing as abundantly as he could to sway a person in his favour.

By gazing closely into Sal's eyes for ages as if doting on her as much as she doted on him, by seeing the reflection of himself there, he began to experience a euphoria akin to hers, a sense of ample and caressing rightness as regards his circumstances.

Like a shaman's soul on a spirit journey surely his soul was ripening towards a revelation of its own sufficiency to itself. He would emerge from this restricted experience as an admirably serene person.

He began to worry mildly whether he might not be becoming addicted to this drugging doll. He had never felt so close to a woman before (not even Kyli, during his intoxication with her) though actually he was close to himself. Oh he wasn't in love. He was forever investing in Sal's eyes his essence, almost hiding himself away in her, caching himself. What a perfect hiding place, if a fellow had to hide. It came to him fancifully that he might one day change places with her so that he might look out of her eyes at himself, and inhabit her woman's body whilst she occupied his place instead. She'd feel a mite bewildered by the transformation, yet surely ecstatic, for this must be her perfect reward: to become the object she adored.

Of course our Minkie couldn't enter a woman in such a way. Not as yet . . .

As time wended by, might he achieve this feat by sheer concentration – by an application of the will more prolonged than any he had ever undertaken?

Why, then he could walk freely away to wherever he chose, unrecognized and unrecognizable in woman's flesh. As a lass might he be vulnerable to ravishment? Ah, but he would still exert his charm . . . Indeed, perhaps the true reward of a seducer was to become the *subject* of his erstwhile desires so that desirer and desired were one. If his enemies should capture this farmer's daughter wearing his body, who would believe her protestations?

This project of Minkie's became all-involving. Sal exulted at the attention paid to her.

Almost all-involving. Certainly it passed the days.

Meanwhile, the mere froze over, quite suddenly and severely. Time to saw a circle in the ice, and sit Sal beside it with a line and hook. Shouldn't take long to make a decent catch. Fish would dart to the hole for oxygen.

Finally Juke had come upon the bones of a horse. Its ribcage could almost be hoops for a tent, if he tore down evergreen boughs to pile on top. Snow had begun to scud from the west, and afternoon-night was falling fast. His belly was as empty as that of the horse, which had evidently caught its reins on the tortuous limb of a fallen tree. Some withered leather still remained. Riderless, snared by the muzzle, the animal had starved years since.

So would Juke.

Where better for a traveller to curl up tightly than inside a creature which had been fleet of foot, with keen nostrils, an emblem of speedy journeys to destinations? Except that this pony had blundered and panicked and died, held by the mouth it could no longer feed.

Death was what Juke must meet, rag tied round his forehead, hiding his left eye.

Quite a while since in his fruitless hunt it had come to him that just as he had virtually sent his sister to her death, so must he send himself to his death so as to rediscover her. No ordinary hiking and searching was yielding her hiding place. Maybe the place was further on. Maybe he had passed it already. How could he be sure?

Therefore, at noon one day, he bespoke his reflection in a mirror of water trapped in a shallow bowl in the top of a boulder. Scavvy-birds had been using this bowl as their bath. Bright spray, as they fluttered their wings, had attracted him. Juke had let the remaining water settle then he peered at himself, at his sweptback hair, at his farseeing eyes. Seeing too far, perhaps, and seeing too much, for one who searched for a half-blind sister. Therefore missing her, missing her so.

He mustn't look for life – namely hers, preserved – but for the death she had somehow evaded, and which must now, being denied, beckon him instead. Need he travel as far as her physical hiding place? Could he court death precisely where he was? Could he bespeak himself to strangle himself, strong hands inflexibly squeezing the well-sheathed cordy muscles of his neck? Could he bespeak himself not to breathe?

In his asphyxiation, eyes popping, vision distorted, might he perceive luminous ghosts of her footsteps tracking across the land? And learn the true direction she had taken?

Breathing deep, he began to chant in one long slow discharge of air:

'Breath, die,
'Sigh away,
'Away sigh,
'Breath die . . .'

Quieter now, stooping forward, his bellows emptying out. Soon their inner skins might stick together.

'Away sigh,
'Sigh away,
'Breath die . . .'

The words of proclaiming weakened as he willed himself towards a collapsed, locked silence. No longer could any words leave his lips. With an agonized determination he withheld his breath—

—till dizzily he slumped upon the boulder, stunning himself. Willy-nilly his nostrils sucked in water: sharp gravel into his chest. Air, air like blades with which to cut the gravel free then explode it from out of himself in racking raw-edged coughs.

The world spun around him giddily, land aglow with light, a black sun swallowing up that light.

When he recovered his aching wind and the balance of the world, he tore off a shirt sleeve for a slanting blindfold to cover his left eye. This was how his sister had seen her way: flatly. How could he have spied the route to her in depth, in full – but false – perspective?

She possessed an inner eye, too, which saw *elsewhere*. Nonetheless, he now felt more fully identified with her than at any stage hitherto. Surely she had died to herself while trudging through a flatness akin to the collapse of her dreams.

Maybe he backtracked for a score of keys or more to try a new approach. Maybe he circled like a duck blinded in one eye and in a bit of its brain, unable to reconcile itself to a one-sided pond. Trekking in a state of somnambulism, Juke traversed a dream-world. This was the real world of lake and forest and mists and rocks but deprived of significance. It funnelled him towards an alternative realm of dream, or of nightmare.

481

Sometimes, clear-skied, the sickle shone upon him, bridge of death or cascade of mana, Eyeno's especial shattered moon, her precious gewgaw-words scattered low across the sky. Cold and hungry, feeding scantily on berries and fungi and raw fish bespoken from pools, suffering as Eyeno must have suffered, Juke was resonant with her at last. No luminous footprints showed. Yet he felt himself to have become Eyeno. Surely he banished his demon, for how should he lust furtively for his very own self?

Juke kicked at the long-dead pony. Ribs cracked and crumbled. Fat flakes were settling like daisies. Perhaps he was going to die tonight. But not crammed inside a barrel-bellied skeleton! A path of snow-daisies led upward into gathering darkness. Were those her ghostly footprints at last? He should climb. To reach a more exposed place where the cold was even more bitter?

Punishing himself, blades in his lungs, he mounted tilting slippery rock, sometimes on all fours by feel. *She* had suffered like this. He was her, almost completely at last, approaching death.

Presently the ground levelled. And a frisson of mana invaded him.

Snowflakes were phosphorescent with brittle inner light. Faintly, fitfully, his surroundings became illuminated in patterns of glinting dots. He must be seeing with Eyeno's inner eye, experiencing a hint of her other mode of vision! The scene flickered as if that inward eye were blinking, an eyelid fluttering inside the brain. Hints of distance showed – otherwise he might have walked over a brink. He spied, just in time: the lurking chasm, the gulf. More hints emerged. Down below he glimpsed patches of a frozen snow-dusted lake. He was up on a high escarpment, overhanging an icy crust deep down.

Despite the murk, sprays of snow-sparks scintillated, revealing outlines. Such glints must be within his own head. He fully believed that they corresponded to fragments of the actual vista. Was this his vindication and deliverance: to begin to see in Eyeno's style?

Giants lurked nearby. No, those were *boulders* high as a house. The great rocks stood poised where some glacier had abandoned them an aeon ago. Juke could curl up in the bleak shelter of those stone abodes without any rooms in them; and freeze . . .

Then, just then, what had merely glinted became general. Murk withdrew. The whole extent of the lake became luminously visible. Its crust of ice was crazing, cracking. Water bubbled up, steaming and frothing. As he stared from the clifftop a gust of warmth enveloped him – a rush of warmth, an embrace!

He could see for a key, two keys, along the cliffs or down across the seething water. Astonished, he tugged the blindfold from his brow. True depth assaulted him. All scuds and swirls of snow had evaporated from the vicinity.

That lake below was surging, boiling.

Tremors ran through the rock. One of those boulders teetered and toppled. Juke sank to his knees. His eardrums throbbed at a pervasive low-pitched groan.

The lake was swelling, arching. Waves poured towards the shores as a vastness thrust itself upward. A massive bulge of rock broke the surface, steaming liquids cascading from its sides. *Ukko was rising*: the Ukko sought by Lucky, Eyeno's refuge. *Ukko was rising*: a stone moon born from the lake which now was no lake at all any longer but a downward deluge, a hundred cataracts tumbling into a billowing steam-wreathed gulf of a depth he could not guess. The escarpment to which he clung seemed twice as high yet dwarfed by that great progress upwards.

The top of the ovoid moon was level with him, lambently flickering as if tongues of white flame roved over its surface.

The summit rose above him. He was gaping at flanks from which fell soil and mud like drool.

The base of the Ukko-child cleared the cliff line. Pallid lightning forked from its base down into the hot vaporous abyss. Cliffs might crack at their roots and tumble into the steaming vacancy.

His sister was inside that moon. He'd found where she was. She was departing. Up into space, home of all other Ukkos? He stood and semaphored his arms and screamed, 'Eyeno, Eyeno!'

Juke might as well have tried to bespeak a mountain to obey him. The moonlet continued ascending. Cloud roiled and wreathed around the Ukko-child, fading it from view. On the edge of a steaming lustrous emptiness he gawked upward, dumbstruck.

32 · FLOWERCHANT AND CANDLEFIRE

In the heart of the rebuilt village of white wooden houses was
a sward where silver-spangled hens pecked. A mass of daisies
bloomed upon the turf. Ducks cruised an oval pond. Near the
water towered a communal swing. Six lasses sat side by side,
gauzily clad and beribboned. Holding hands as they rocked to
and fro, they sung blithely:

> 'Oh our home is here,
>> 'So what do we care
> 'If our home was elsewhere
>> 'Once?'

> 'Well here we are now,
>> 'Clasp hands and chant,
> 'And banish the memory of
>> 'Once!'

> 'Put Once in a pail
>> 'With a handful of hail
> 'And throw it in yon
>> 'Pond—'

'Will you stop it!' cried Eyeno. She clapped a hand across her
empty socket. At the back of that little hollow, of a sudden, such
a gruelling pang! Stick a finger in, hook it out. No, she mustn't.
The pain, already fading (be calm) was just a memory of her injury.
Oh but surely this sharp pressure from within was something
else. The pang had come so unexpectedly, taking her unawares.
She imagined that something small and hard was trying to be
born from her head – something which had been quickened in
that pool where the ginger beast-woman wallowed, in the tiny
navel of everything far from here. Tiny, though in its own com-
plexity quite as large as hereabouts . . .

Inga was immediately solicitous. Freckled hands hovering
a-flutter: 'Is it that pain again? Let's sit. Lay your head in my
lap.' Lay it in the haven of a taffeta gown of azure and perse,
silky and lustrous. 'I'll stroke your brow. I'll make you a daisy
chain. A chain to bind your pain softly.'

'No . . .'

484

'You might make me a daisy *crown*!' suggested Paula. Her gown was of purple and gold these days. Just recently she had unwoven her pigtails. Her blonde hair had flooded upon her shoulders in rivalry to Eyeno's mane, if less yellowy. But then Paula had plaited her pigtails together again. Couldn't quite make up her mind what appearance to present.

'How about a crown, Inga?'

'I wasn't offering *you* daisies!'

Eyeno could see Inga's soul: a slender azure chimneyflower spotted with golden beetles, her wealth of freckles. Paula was the soulflower itself, alabastine and copious. Irregardless of her peachy skin, her chubby cheeks, her scent of spiced buns, she was the soulflower supreme.

Except in the neighbourhood of the candle-palace, within its warm aura, the landscape remained devastated and chilled. The echo-lasses were still so many flowers of the meadows. Flowers! You knew just when a flower would bloom each year, smiling, fragrant, and young. Flowers were for memory. Flowers remembered themselves perfectly, and so in a sense they remembered nothing else, never changing.

Yet poor lost Anna had recovered her memory of life. Paula likewise. Paula remembered her girlhood and adolescence in the cold dark void, the deadly enemy which had to seem like a familiar friend. Paula knew now that she'd become a Queen of a world, in a different existence close by. This puzzling knowledge was making her volatile. She was halfway vain and assertive and fickle yet still winsome too. She was a girl imagining herself to be a monarch but not comprehending the consequences, oblivious to centuries of vehemence, agitations and obsessions, fevers of the soul.

Fevers of a flower . . . ! Eyeno had once been the daisy. That daisy had been crushed into a smear of shit. Was she now the bloodflower?

'Thank you Inga, but I don't need any daisy chain.' Eyeno hitched up her breeches of brown leather buckled with brass. Such had she worn, with a similar ruffled white blouse, when she had tramped into this village before it was burnt . . .

Nakkis had restored the village to something resembling its previous state. Previously there hadn't been quite such a pond, so suggestive of the pool of lost words where the monstrous mannekin roosted.

Since the war nakkis had restored themselves to villagers.

Now they worked in vegetable plots and storehouses where flour and fruits and nuts appeared and in a bakery and in a dairy. Lasses might join the nakkis to hoe a few rows or churn some butter or twist some pastry before tiring of the activity. An echo of the war sometimes betrayed itself in a nakki's sudden feral grin, a manic stare, an outburst of cackling laughter. How much better if no nakkis were here at all! But needs must. So many refugees to care for – blithe and carefree once again.

Paula helped. She practised giving orders without seeming quite au fait with authority, and achieved puzzled compliance from lasses (for a while), or provoked droll protests or giggles. Inga tried to help too to please Eyeno.

Most lasses were intent on forgetting the recent past. They didn't look up at the smutty cloud cloaking the upcurving landscape, or away beyond the environs of their village where all was still a frozen waste as though no longer required as an abode. Beasts howled beyond the perimeter of life. The lasses didn't wrinkle their noses at the odour of greasy gas nor stray too near to what Minkie's palace had become: those spectral walls, translucent, incandescent, source of the area's warmth and vitality. Through a permanent funnel in the clouds the sun-eye looked down preferentially upon the village, an oasis amidst waste and winter. Eyeno had heard tell of such places in the south-west, near that town where books were printed. She could no longer read any words. When the sun-eye faded to a wan disc overnight, to a moon unlike any which shone on Kaleva itself, the wraith of the candle-palace was an albino aurora, blinding bright, rising compactly from the ground.

She knew she must finally brave that palace of hot light . . .

Meanwhile – *'Why shouldn't I have a crown?'* – what of Paula, naively bumptious, would-be Queen of a village? Must there be silly competition between herself and Paula?

'Look, Paula,' said Eyeno, 'I've sold gloves and gold dust to merchants—' She meant that she was so much more experienced. The allusion was far too elusive, more like a line of verse. Could it be that lost words were returning to her? The war had made her something of a proclaimer. Could she become both poet and proclaimer at once? Could a poem proclaim as evocatively as a power-chant? (Though quite dissimilarly!) Could a poem cause analogies of its images to come to pass?

One day, she recalled, *Moon will plunge*
Into warm world . . .

Eyeno could remember the mood of poetry. The uprising within
from the source, the afflatus, the nativity of jouissance – that
revelatory rapture, the joy of emergent meaning, all senses
stirred, sense being heard; being neither the slave of meaning nor
the master; words of such transparency that they nevertheless
seemed to become objects in themselves, actualities, more visible
than what they named or implied.

Gaseous fire was nearby.

No, she didn't wish for a daisy chain. Nevertheless the idea
had lodged: of a chain of flowers, a chain of words.

The ground was trembling. Or was she herself shaking?

The lasses on the great swing had resumed their refrain.

> 'Oh what do we care?
>   'We'll wash our hair,
> 'Drape sable silk before our
>   'Eyes—'

'Shut up all of you!' yelled Paula. 'You're giving me a headache.'

'Oh we're sorry!' called one lass, and laughed.

The pang stabbed Eyeno again. Poetry was emerging in her.
That was it! She must release it in a flood. The daisy-strewn turf
pulsed under her feet.

A nakki-fellow came scampering. He clutched a handsaw.
Curly blond locks framed the face of the carpenter. What a pretty
face his was. One cheek was adorned with a heartbell tattoo.

Urgently: 'Eyeno, Eyeno, there are thingth to thee in the
palace! Dark thingth in the wallth of fire!' The lisp accented the
fellow's femininity. 'Come, come!' he clamoured.

Eyeno accompanied him, and Paula and Inga too. En route, other
nakkis formed an escort. A score and more lasses joined the
procession, sufficiently piqued by curiosity that they would brave
an approach to the spectral palace. Egging one another on, quite
a throng advanced towards the walls of lambent gas – all trace
of bridge and moat had long since disappeared.

On close approach, the heat was not intense. Rather, warmth
spread evenly throughout the whole neighbourhood of the village.
Yet one sensed that to step through the shimmering boundary
might be to set oneself ablaze, to become a candle oneself!

True to report, within the palace was a rippling scene wrought in darkness. A vista of high cliffs, a frozen lake, appeared and disappeared. Accelerated clouds and snow billowed into the long bowl of that lake and out again, veiling and unveiling. How suggestive of the rest of the terrain beyond the village, how reflective, though more dramatic with its heights and depths. How inimical to life that view seemed. Lasses shuddered and shivered, and almost fled. But there was a mesmeric sway to the apparition.

'What is that awful place?'

'That's the lake I dived into, Paula—'

To think that Eyeno had once contemplated re-entering the lake underwater and swimming upward to the base of those cliffs to chase after Minkie and Anna. Impossible.

Ragnar Kennan must have left by that route . . .

'It's the world outside we're seeing—'

'*That's* my realm? There are giant snakes in it too? No wonder they stay underground! What kind of realm is that? You *dived* into that lake?'

'From a clifftop. See where those boulders are—' Swirls of snow hid those stones, perched like pebbles. A person would be a tiny insect.

'Don't look at it,' begged Inga. 'It's horrible. Let's go back.'

Paula was chastened by the spectacle. 'I don't think I really want to be a Queen at all . . .'

Such a pang assaulted Eyeno inside her head below her brow. Momentarily she was robbed of vision. She cried out:

'Aiieee, *darkness*—'

And this was the first word of poetry to emerge for a long long while, in response to that negative scene within the gassy brightness.

'Near the dense centre of a sun,' *she declaimed*,
'Where light crashes into light
'Is it utterly dark
'Or is it blinding bright?'

The pang had gone. Pressure persisted. Words poured forth.

'Within the heart of a moon
'Where dark to darkness clings
'Is there a light unseen?
'Can any gleam take flight?'

488

And this was only the beginning.

> 'I bathed in a spring, imagining
> 'A bird with tripe on its beak,
> 'Squawking: "The snake and its servant
> 'Are two, and are one besides."
> 'Oh black men of Pootara,
> 'Why can't you hark to cuckoos?

> 'Two cuckoos sat in a curver tree
> 'And cackled, *Ukoo*, at the sky
> 'Where the silver sickle unpeeled
> 'A potato moon on high.
> 'Oh black men of Pootara,
> 'Why can't you hark to cuckoos?

> 'A gossip sat in a harper tree,
> 'With a wax bloom in its beak.
> 'Oh where is the Queen's bed of love?
> 'That's the very place I seek.
> 'Oh black men of Pootara,
> 'Why can't you hark to cuckoos?

> 'Cuckoo's mate perched in a minty tree
> 'Soon to explode into flames.
> 'Blossom forth, undeflowered,
> 'Unlock the volcano of names!
> 'Oh black men of Pootara,
> 'Why can't you hark to cuckoos?'

Eyeno rocked to and fro. Images assaulted her, unseen until they bespoke themselves. A Queen's bed strewn with white blooms . . . A bloom had been sent to the Queen to provoke an attack on a snakes' nest so that there would be strife involving *her own brother*. Black sailors tussling with wooden puzzles. A minty tree incinerating a cuckoo . . . Stories, stories from the moon-child's hoard.

Paula and Inga had linked arms with her, not to pull her away, nor yet to support her, but to sway in rhythm with her. Other lasses, likewise. Nakkis too. Linking and swaying. The ground seemed to be rocking as if to dislodge itself, seesawing, from its roots.

That sequence of curver tree, harper tree, minty, wasn't right. Naming all the trees of Kaleva could serve to embrace the world in a *wooden* frame. Never forget the chain of flowers. Flowers

489

were for fertility, enlisting beauty to its cause. Flowers were creative organs, painted and scented sensually. Flowers were the heralds of thought and word, for their food-packed pollen had once permitted beasts and then people to evolve, to arise. She must be a flower not a tree (even though trees could blossom too).

Before that dark vista of cliff and lake within the luminous walls Eyeno rocked in rhythm with the lasses, and sang out a riddle:

> 'What is my name but a bloom's?
> 'What is my name but a flower's—?'

An image of the gross gingery sow in the pool of words intruded. The sylph of stars fleeted by. Sylph or sow: which was the true incarnation of the moon-child?

Eyeno continued:

> 'For chimneyflowers are my lady's fingers,
> Long and azure and far-reaching;
> 'Bellflowers are my lady's ears,
> 'Ringing with stories, far-hearing;
> 'Pink heartbells are her toenails,
> 'And her fingernails: yellow narciss;
> 'What is her navel but a milkcup?
> 'What starflowers spark in her eyes?
> 'What am I then but a bright daisy?
> 'Alas we guessed wrong; three tries!'

As Eyeno and the lasses rocked, the world rocked with them. As they swung back and forth, the world tilted in accompaniment, away from equilibrium and back again. In her pool was the gingerwoman rolling her arse to and fro? A motion suggestive of childbirth, or maybe of constipation! No regular childbirth, this. An egg of rock must rock itself out of the cup in which it had long rested.

Eyeno's head ached. Words were composing themselves insistently of their own volition, just as when she had once told fortunes.

> 'What I am then but the bloom
> 'Unfurling its bloody petals
> 'Through a bed of virgin snow,
> 'Piercing the soft frigid wool
> 'In violation of its whiteness,

> 'Deflowering by its flowering,
> 'Fragrance of rape and murder . . .'

The ground lurched. The gassy walls wavered. In the black panorama the lake was cracking. A thousand decapitated daisies flew hither and thither, aglow, snow-bright. Water was bulging upward, boiling. On a cliff-top Eyeno spied the little insect of her fears clinging – just as a stone dome breached the surface of the lake, a moon arising, breaking the waters which tumbled off its sides.

She cried in alarm:

> 'But no, I'm not the bloodflower,
> 'So guess again, guess thrice!
> 'What flower seems of candlewax,
> 'Creamy petals curly as ears?
> 'I bloom in moon-child meadows
> 'I can outlive the years.
> 'My name is—'

No name came to her, no name at all.

Bloodflower, bloodflower, muttered her pulse. *Bloodflower*, beat her heart.

She recognized that insect on the cliff-top. Amazingly it was her brother. Juke who betrayed her. He was rising haggard from his crouch. He was waving his arms. Eyeno strained forward, pulling free from Paula and Inga. She jerked to a halt – so that *he* should not lure her into the flame of the candle to be consumed. Juke had shrunk to a mote. The moon was rising swiftly into clouds.

Eyeno swung round, her mouth agape in a stupid way which she despised in others. In her astonishment she had almost cried out Juke's name. Oh no she hadn't. She wouldn't have done so. The name she had wished to call out – the name of the bloom – was an empty space, a vacancy in her. Into her parted lips trickled a taste of blood.

Inga exclaimed: 'Your eye's bleeding!'

A moment later: 'But you have two eyes, *two*!'

Awareness came of a pressure in the socket – of a swelling, a ball pushing her lids apart – as when she had worn Ruokokoski's false eye and the Isi eye. Eyeno's fingers fluttered. She felt how a globe filled her orbit. The touch blurred her vision. She snatched her hand away. Suddenly the world was full. She could see depths, distances.

Tears bleared those distances till she wiped away sobs and a smear of blood. She could see twice as much as ever before; see in full. Her inner eye had emerged: born on its chord, breaking through a membrane of bone softened by the pangs.

'A new eye, a new eye,' clamoured Inga.

Eyeno gasped: 'What does it look like? Is it like an eye at all? Is it like my other eye?'

To be able to see, yet not to see this above all!

Hesitantly: 'It's blue—'

A blue less intense than that of her brother's piercing eyes?

'A sort of pearly blue—'

'Yes, yes?' Straining her eyelids wide.

Paula intervened. 'What Inga's trying to say is that it doesn't have anything else in it. That's all there is: pearly blue.'

'But I can see with it . . . Surely there's—?'

'There isn't.'

'That's all?'

'That's all.'

'Do I look—?'

Grotesque? More of a mutant than before?

Paula considered, and judged: 'Why, it's pretty . . . It's lovely. A smooth blue opal.'

'That's true,' said Inga. 'Honestly, Eyeno, it's true.'

A moon had been born. At the same time an eye had been born.

'Did I choose an eye,' Eyeno asked herself, 'instead of the name of the bloom? Did I, Gingerwoman?' she called. The voice of the moon-child, sow or sylph, eluded her.

Seen in the candle-walls, the moon was rushing low through clouds, through clear sky, images flickering. The moon had ascended only so far then had commenced a sidelong journey.

'Cuckooth are watching uth from the ground,' announced the carpenter. He gestured affectedly with his saw.

Below the course of the moon cuckoos must be turning their yellow gaze upward to register its passage. What cuckoos saw was reflected in the candle-palace. Time without and time within were following a different pace. Paula peered at her dark frosted realm then rounded on the nakki. 'Where are we going to?' she asked.

'Yes, where are we going?' echoed Eyeno.

This effete carpenter seemed to have become the voice of the moon-child now. He cocked his pretty head on one side. He simpered at Eyeno then eyed his first questioner coyly.

'Why, to end a thtory, and begin it. To put Paula and Paula together again. What will we thee, when yourthelf meetth your other thelf? Who will be the lucky one?'

Eyeno had thought she was mistress of circumstances, empowered by the ginger sow. The awareness came to her of how very *recently* she had entered the moon-child – compared with Paula, heedless centuries old. Eyeno's prize was merely the resurgence of poems, and an opal eye – not a capacity to guide and foster something as complex and childish, as old and as young as this entity.

'The lucky one?' cried Paula, petulance edging panic. 'I entered your creator. I caused you!'

'Thith in turn cauthed you.' The lisp was sinister now, not winsome at all. Oh the ventriloquism of a puppet operated by a ginger sow who embodied the moon-child! The carpenter smirked. 'I can conjure a copy of any perthon. I gathered dead daughterth to decorate me, a garland for the thtoryth I'm hearing, a friezth.'

A decoration . . . Inga and Gretel and Gerda and Maria. Not Paula, no. Paula was more essential. She was one end of a string, the other end being Queen Lucky.

'What would you have done,' demanded Eyeno of the carpenter-nakki, 'if Minkie Kennan had succeeded in taking Paula away on his bike?'

'Why, I would have conjured another copy from my memory.'

Paula shuddered. Through clenched teeth she muttered, 'I'm *me*.'

Cold tiptoed down Eyeno's spine. 'Did *I* die when I came here?' she breathed. 'Am *I* a copy too?'

The carpenter seemed sympathetic. 'No, no, you entered me, ath Paula entered my creator.'

'If I leave, will there still be a copy of me here for ever?' *Poor other me! How would she know which me she was?*

'You entered me,' repeated the puppet. 'Only two rogueth and a dreamlord have done tho, otherwithe. Until now, until thoon . . .'

Whoever knew how to seize the initiative would steer this moon. Would that be the Queen of the Northland? When Paula

493

met Paula – if this occurred – what would happen between the reflection and the demented original? A furious struggle, which the reflection must surely lose?

Eyeno faced the candle-fire. Her new depth of vision brought vertigo. If she rushed forward she might fall right out of the moon into the scene below. The moon was hanging over the edge of a town, a huge potato hovering. Either time had paused, or the moon had. A space-flier stood poised on a broad disc of snowy ground lapped by a narrow bendy iced lake. Little lights glowed in a hulking brick ziggurat dusted with snow. A dome was visible – and a block of a building with what seemed to be an inverted umbrella fixed upon its roof. The sky-sickle arched across clear sky in the south. Indeed, almost all the sky was clear . . . here over Landfall. Sickle's glow and the fainter though closer luminosity of the moon limned the view eerily. The globular wrapped-around perspective was akin to the upswooping internal terrain of the moon-child. Yes, she might fall forward into that spectral sphere and plummet all the way to the unforgiving ground to become a smear of shit upon the wool.

A tiny star moved high across the sky . . .

In Landfall someone had panicked. In Landfall someone thought that the Isi had discovered how to manoeuvre one of their Ukkos close to the ground as a war-ship. The cartographic satellite happened to be passing over. In Landfall, someone clawed at a console.

A thread of hot light lanced between the top of the moon and that rushing star. An instant later: another. Which was the source: moon or star? Did the star initiate hot light? Did the stung moon trace the direction with mana-light?

Eyeno knew that tiny hurrying star well enough. When stargazing in Outo she had marked the passage of the Earthkeep's artificial moonlet. It would move out of sight so soon. It wouldn't reappear promptly. What use was its lance of light unless it could melt a stony moon thousands of times its own size?

Lightning licked from the moon's underbelly. The umbrella on the roof of that brick block filled with silver fire. Fire haloed the whole building. Then the building erupted. Bricks flew outward like a mob of scavvy-birds from a cat. The tiny star had already gone, bending away beyond the horizon.

In a spasm of shifting scenes the moon moved onward. Curved

494

dark woolly land warped giddily into semi-visibility, into sight, out of sight.

33 · CONVERGENCES

The platform extension of Minnow's left boot had broken loose as she and Osmo fled from the manor house towards the arboretum, chivvied by Sam. She'd nearly ricked her ankle. Sam had wrestled the boot from her foot. Right boot likewise. Else she'd have been lurching along hipety-hop.

She stood in woollen socks. Those socks were sodden and muddy. Not chilly, though. Scarcely! Air was sultry as could be, and soil was warm underfoot.

'Sweet mana,' breathed Sam, 'will you look at it—?'

Through parting billows of vapour, regard the hell-pit which most of Kip'an'keep had become. If the stink of mustoreum had been unpleasant, that of the earth's open bowels – and of town consumed – was a scorching reek fit to take the breath away. The meagre daylight would have been dismal grey were it not for the glow of lava and fires staining the blanket of dense cloud and drifting steam a hideous orange hue.

Small in her socks, Minnow tore open her quilted coat to ventilate herself, exposing a gown of ambery satin which now seemed too long for her, as if she had dressed in thoughtless haste. Oh on the contrary she'd had ample time to perch her crown of leather and pearls upon her frizz and count most of the observable log-houses in Kip'an'keep besides by ghastly moonlight (if she'd cared to) before the convulsions began. Now she seemed waif-like. All refugees from the cataclysm were strays right now.

Osmo, too, feeling the need to cool himself, flapped his reinforced quilt open.

'Be careful,' Sam fussed. 'Those coats give good protection.'

'It hasn't rained rocks for a while,' Minnow retorted. Earlier hot gravel had fallen, blasted from the sump at the south-west of town.

Figures were moving about in the fitful haze amid the leafless trees and bushes and the evergreens. Escapees from keep and forts had fled to the arboretum because trees have roots. The

495

fenced garden was a great trembling raft. Hitherto it had held together save for a few narrow fissures. It hadn't slid downhill into the pit, as the keep had slid.

'Osmo, is that you—?'

Tilly Kippan was with the Girlem. Goldi was pulling Tilly along, steadying her. Both were disarrayed and dirty. Blood had dried on Tilly's broad brow. A tress had crusted to her skin. The spaniel barked at Tilly's heels, speechless, a terrified animal. Maybe the dog would sink its teeth into Tilly to be fully assured of her companionship.

'Daddy stayed in the keep! Too druggy to know the danger. Thought the moon coming down was a dream. Bailiff Boris wouldn't drag him out. And my mother, well, my mother—'

'What about Lady Edith?' asked Sam.

Tilly choked.

Goldi volunteered: 'Lady Edith wishing to watch Lord Kippan die. Yes, that's what she wanted most.'

'To be with him, to be reconciled . . .'

'No, Mistress Tilly, to witness his longlife ending suddenly, more suddenly than he could ever have expected. But maybe he is still surviving.'

The hulking keep had slithered sidelong into the gulf, shedding verandahs, and twisting askew. Its wreck had lodged against one side of the sunken moon. The tammywood structure resisted fire but smoke twisted up from within, from ruptured stoves and burning furnishings. Disintegrating forts had tumbled further, into bubbling lava – ruddy and orange – in which the moon was submerged to the midriff. Did mana-fire flicker in that narrow moat or only plumes of burning gas?

'Unless he's dead of asphyxiation or heatstroke,' said Sam. 'Who's in charge now, Miss Kippan, if the forest lord's dead? The rival bailiffs? Or yourself?'

Tilly tugged her tress free of her brow, reopening a wound. 'No one's in charge . . . *That* thing's in charge. That terrible Ukko! Like a huge stone verrin! The town's destroyed. It's in charge of nothing. Nothing at all.'

The spaniel barked senselessly, the same noise over and over. Goldi called into the steam-drift: '*Amber, where are you? Where are you, my Amberman?*'

'Obviously you're in charge, my Prince and Proclaimer,' Sam said to Osmo.

Osmo gestured emptily at the moon in the hell-pit. 'Proclaim, at that? It's like a great stone eyeball in a bloodshot socket . . .'

'I did trounce a mutant mage,' Minnow mumbled diffidently. She slammed her small fist into her palm. 'Did my mother send that thing here to crush us? Is she in charge of it now? Has she succeeded? When? *How? Where?*' This was a question which she and Osmo had already asked one another fruitlessly.

Osmo half-enclosed his wife in his coat and murmured: 'Remember our baby.'

Minnow evaded the additional protective insulation. She slipped from his squeeze. 'Oh I'm sure that's really important right now,' she muttered to herself. 'Half a gram of baby. Not even that. A minim. Maybe we should take to our heels before these trees stroll down into the pit? I can gestate in a hut like Jatta – but hunted by Mummy's troops.' She clenched her teeth. 'I did trounce a mage! Oh shit. I left the harp in the throne . . . *Damn it, my throne!*'

Minnow's Manor had crumpled into the pit, as had Maids' Manor, and much more besides. Altogether too much more . . .

When the mad moon had loomed into view, like a cloud of phosphorbugs it brought with it a lambent radiance which the snow and ice mirrored. Sentries in forts and watchmen in town blew screech-whistles soon enough, a piercing chorus to greet this false winter dawn. Hardly anyone in Kip'an'keep could have been asleep or indoors by the time the moon poised itself over the town: a luminous hill in the sky, lightning flickering across its base.

'Ukko, Ukko!' rose the cry from here, from there.

No Ukko had ever descended and hung above the ground. No Ukko had ever shone with its own intrinsic brightness. Ukkos swung through space, tiny in the upper distance, their lustre borrowed mainly from the sun, and a little from the sky-sickle. Here was certainly Ukko, *hanging ponderously if airily overhead; and not very far overhead, either.*

What could this prodigy be but the Ukko-child *which Lord Osmo had warned that Queen Lucky was searching for? Blessedly it still hung out of reach – unless you had one of those jump-bikes which were all at the war front . . .*

News of the moon's advent would be a beacon to Lucky as a lantern to a bug, crazing her to come here to Kip'an'keep by any means as soon as could be, uniting her hatred of van Maanen with the object of her desire.

Overhead it hung, aglow.

Waiting . . . for what?

For the forest lord's men to rear a rickety tower of tree trunks and planks high enough up to reach it, tearing up boardwalks and the timber paving of the streets? For woodmen to dismantle the forts and re-erect them vertically?

Mana-priests at the kirk upon the stilt-trees petitioned the Ukko-child to bless the town by its presence, to work some wonder, to impart a revelation of the nature of the mysterium. They might all become mana-bishop in Tumio, a collective episcopacy akin to the administration of Tapper Kippan's domain by a trio of bailiffs. Right now Kip'an'keep was the centre of mana-study in the whole of Kaleva.

Citizens who couldn't endure the sight of a hill hanging over them fled with bundles of belongings through snowy streets to the frozen forest. These were the lucky ones. Many others stayed to goggle and gawp.

Presently the temperature began to climb – out of chill into mild, into warm. Snow and ice melted to slush; to running water. Ice retreated across the cold lake, thinning and vanishing. In the hot lake, always balmy and unfrozen, the geysir spouted – then a few minutes later it squirted once more. Again and again it discharged scalding water.

In the streets planks steamed as the soil and stone under them heated. Tremors shook the town, and Kippan's keep. Trees in gardens nodded their crowns. Window glass cracked.

Before long houses and plank-streets were riding upon warm agitated sludge as the ground emulsified beneath them. The kirk in the trees danced to and fro.

And then the embankment of the hot lake and its sluice gates had subsided. Heated water poured out to submerge the buckling streets. People were wading with disorderly useless urgency, tumbling, staggering, screaming. The bank and the gates of the cold lake also collapsed, releasing a vaster flood.

Spray billowed. Gravel exploded from the sump.

The principal roar was of a subterranean paroxysm as if the earth's bowels were emptying out – preparatory to an engulfing.

This occurred in stages.

A swathe of swamped quaking town below the moon slumped downward by several metres. The muddy floor of the hot lake subsided too. Ten minutes later the surface sank abruptly again. The roar became a rending shriek. Not long afterwards, town and flood and lake-bed collapsed into a steep basin of wreckage and spate. Vapour exploded upward hiding even the moon.

When the main gush of steam finally drifted to join the clouds, a bowl was ruddily a-churn with lava. Forts had tumbled down·ill. Kippan's keep had slid steeply. The moon itself was setting down into the crater.

The survivors would need to organize shelter for themselves. Right now the arboretum was balmy, almost sweltery; but even so. The survivors would need to organize food – in one of the snow-bound forest villages nearby? Nothing was left of Kip'an'keep apart from a few outlying huts such as those at the arboretum gates. No rockets defended the area now. Nothing remained to defend. *Oh on the contrary: the Ukko-child there in the hell-pit!* Defend that lethal treasure from Lucky at all costs.

Defenders were few; weapons likewise.

Elmer and Eva joined the group. Then a score of wooden soldiers. Some were scorched, their barkcloth uniforms charred. A few Blue Guards came, one moaning about a burnt hand. Wex stood outside the palings, staring intently at the moon lodged in the hot crater, his hand still bandaged from the minty burn. One of the forest lord's bailiffs arrived, the same stocky Boris – sweaty in furs and strawberry-nosed – who had refused to drag his lord out of his sanctum. One of his co-bailiffs had been absent from town, arranging for supplies to be sent to the war. The other co-bailiff must have died.

It was natural to gravitate to the arboretum. The tree garden was close to danger yet here was the last relic of Tapper Kippan's lordship in the vicinity apart from that twisted smoking wreck of the keep lodged in the torrid pit. Wex continued to gaze covetously at that. Kippan couldn't still be alive. He'd be roasted and stifled. Edith Kippan, too. The same for anyone who might be mad enough to try to climb down the steep slope to the debris abutting on the Ukko-child. Wex moved forward; Wex moved back.

'Come here, Roger!' cried Minnow. *'Come here now!* I order you to!'

Dragging his feet, Wex complied. Skirting the palings to the gap where sods had slid, he entered the steamy garden. His prim face was smutty with ash. Cinders dusted his wig.

'What are you thinking of, Roger?'

It was his wetwear which replied:

499

'*The Ukko itself doesn't appear too hot to walk on. We could reach its surface via the remains of the keep. Those form a bridge, do you see? For a suitable person there should be a way inside the Ukko. Else, why is it here?*'

'Obviously to squash Kip'an'keep!' cried Eva. She asked her younger sister: 'Isn't Mummy already inside of that horror, telling it what to do?'

'Oh well, if she *is*, then that's that, I suppose!'

'Don't you think she is?'

A raucous voice chirped in answer:

> 'The old Queen's in Maananfors Keep,
> 'Where she woke from a troubled sleep!'

A rustle of rusty foliage high in otherwise bare branches: a cuckoo was looking on.

'Gossip-bird,' cried Osmo, 'hark and hear me: are you the Ukko's voice?'

The cuckoo harked, cocking its cupped feline ears; and mutely it continued harking.

'If she's really in Maananfors,' said Sam, 'she isn't in charge of that thing *yet*.' His tone insisted that his Prince of Proclaimers should *do* something.

Bailiff Boris eyed Osmo then Tilly. Shakily he said, 'I appear to be the administrator in charge of this region's forces, most of whom are quite a way from here—'

Sam cleared his throat. 'Might I remind you that you're speaking in front of the true new Queen, and her general, namely myself?'

'You aren't *with* those forces at the moment, Mr Peller . . .' The bailiff waved his hand mordantly. 'How can this disaster be recouped?'

'*Quite*,' said Sam to Osmo.

If Boris had abandoned Tapper Kippan in the hope of some personal advantage, the sight of the moon resting in the crater which had been a town was profoundly sobering. 'I grieve for your parents, Miss Tilly,' he said.

'Do you indeed?' said she. Her spaniel growled at the bailiff.

He was backing away, his eye on Osmo rather than on the dog. Abruptly Boris turned and fled.

'Wait!' shouted Minnow. 'Bespeak him, Oz!'

Osmo was too late. A swirl of mist had swallowed Boris up. Wooden soldiers stirred uneasily and seemed about to sneak away but Osmo bid them, '*Stay, woodmen; it's spoken.*'

'He'll have a long way to go,' said Sam, 'to try to arrange a surrender to ingratiate himself with Lucky. Keys and keys, by day and night, once he finds a mount. She'll fly here as soon as she hears.' He nodded towards the eavesdropping cuckoo. 'She won't be able to stop herself. I suppose she'll stop by her army to take on some troops. Then she'll sail right over the fighting. Only a few of us are left here now. No forts, no rockets, no nothing, just a few guns.' He rubbed his palms together. 'Viewed one way, here's our chance to ambush her. She won't be the only one hurrying here, if you want my opinion!'

Minnow muttered to herself, 'So it would be cleverer to enter that lump of rock . . .'

'Quite!'

Elmer was making juggling motions with his long bony hands. 'So many *tonnes*. And it could float. Defied gravity . . .'

'The Brindleds have been helping us so far,' suggested Eva. 'I don't suppose that'll continue . . .'

'Oh, Brindleds and Brazens and Velvets will be racing here,' Sam assured her. 'Along with all the Jutties they can bring.'

'It really *is* rather like an eyeball,' Minnow mused. 'If you think of it as an eyeball, Oz, that reduces the scale a bit! Doesn't it?' she quizzed herself.

Wex shaded his eyes. 'Too much steam to see an entrance clearly. Too blurred! How hot is it really down there, on the Ukko itself?' Warm enough, certainly, in the arboretum on a winter's day.

How else than accompanied by generation of heat could the moon-child have quarried a resting place for itself? Should it have balanced itself upon the ground? Wex shuddered.

'This body can encounter heat without experiencing pain. Still, entering the crater without protection might damage us so that our body fails to function.'

'Wetwear!' yelled Minnow. 'You aren't going to march Roger down into that all on your own!'

'If my host fails, how should I survive? Still, the security of Earth may require this.' How fruitily, how unctuously phrased.

'Wetwear, try to consider Roger's feelings.'

'Feelings?'

'Think about your *own* survival, is what I meant.'

'Ah yes, I am quite an individual, aren't I? I have a face you cannot see.'

'Roger mightn't have any face if you force him to climb down there.'

501

'He would lose his face? And maybe mine would supersede it . . . Maybe a mootapu mask would protect us.'

'And change his face to yours? What are you thinking of? I don't see any mootapu masks lying around!'

'Maybe,' said Tilly acidly, 'he fancies carving one from a tree in here.'

A lithe figure hoved in view. Creased olive uniform; natty tache; such bright white pupils in a brown countenance.

'Ah, Mr Wex,' exclaimed the Tamil pilot, 'you're alive—' Mathavan Gurrukal eyed Wex's wig as an earnest of this. Gurrukal's left arm was stiff, wrapped tightly in torn cloth securing his tammy baton as a splint.

'Where is the dovecraft?' demanded Wex's wetwear.

Gurrukal regarded the spectacle beyond the garden. 'I have seen sights, oh gracious—'

'Where is the dovecraft?'

With a grimace of discomfort Gurrukal raised his splinted arm then lowered it back against his side. Must be snapped or fractured at the elbow. Or the radius or the ulna.

'I took our dovecraft aloft but suffered a slight calamity. It's broken.'

His arm, or the dovecraft?

Both!

'The Ukko-child pulled me off course, do you see?'

'Damn damn,' cursed Roger. His wetwear had relaxed hold in chagrin. 'We could have landed on the moon.'

'In exactly the way that Lucky will,' said Sam. 'And Isi and Jutties.'

'The accident was not my fault,' protested Gurrukal.

'Did you radio Pen in Landfall to tell her what's happening here?'

Gurrukal was offended. 'Oh and inform those Isi of the circumstances? After I'd repaired my arm, single-handed and with the aid of my teeth?'

Assertively: 'You were right not to use the radio. I have not used the communicator in our cloak till now. Mr Peller, how sure are you that the Isi might already know?'

Sam nodded impatiently at the scaly glaucous cuckoo.

'Several hours for other dovecraft and oliveclads to arrive here from Landfall . . . About the same for sky-boats from the Brindled and Brazen nests – if they know, if they know! A good while longer from the Velvet nest . . . Queen Lucky will arrive first, if she knows.'

'Ex-Queen Lucky,' Minnow corrected the wetwear half-heartedly.

'Shall we take the risk of radioing?' Roger asked himself, struggling back into possession of himself. Presumably he hoped to avoid an unprotected descent into the pit. 'I believe we should.' He delved in an inside pocket of his cloak, to produce a squat communicator, from which he untelescoped a slim aerial. He paced aside for privacy. Gurrukal quickly joined him.

('*By the way, Mr Gurrukal, what do you mean by saying it pulled you off course—?*')

('It felt so. All right, I was distracted! I was flappy—')

('*So other dovecraft and sky-boats could land safely on the Ukko—*')

('If they could cope with the contour—')

Attar and yeast and essence of chocolate drenched the air.

'Amber! My Amberman!'

The Girlem darted to greet the naked golden youth with that foetal form in his belly. Seeing that figure for the very first time, Osmo gaped, and Minnow too. Amberman's visits to Maids' Manor had always been discreet. Osmo inhaled. He shook himself to banish a dizzying lewdness. He had sprayed golden piss to impress a crowd. This was no time to repeat his exhibition.

'Oh my,' squeaked Minnow.

Elmer slid an arm grandly if clumsily around his wife, and Eva rested her locks against his shoulder, sighing.

Amberman embraced Goldi. Her lover was already staring beyond her at the hell-pit.

'Resin of the rocks,' he sang out. His tone was of enchanted simplicity. 'Resin of the earth. So much amber.' A veritable moat. Plainly Amber felt a powerful affinity for lava. The foetus inside him was moving. Goldi clung to her lover, wafting sweet amorous scents which were sedative too, a superfluity of joy tranquillizing the rapt recipient so that Amberman trembled feebly.

The cuckoo was also affected. Up in its tree the bird croaked sonorously like some cracked bell:

> 'She who would steer me seeks
> 'The name of the bloom
> 'A gingerbread woman wears
> 'In her ginger hairs.
> 'Her words shall melt like candlewax;
> 'Reform to shape that name.
> 'Oh black men of Pootara,
> 'Why can't you hark to cuckoos
> 'When a town is melted by candle-fire?'

503

The gossip-bird rocked from side to side. Suddenly it fell off its branch. Down it fell, flapping to retard its descent. The bird almost bounced as it landed. Yapping, Tilly's spaniel scampered towards it. Squawking indignantly, the cuckoo beat its way back into the air, and off – over the palings, then out over the pit. For a while the bird glided on thermals, around and around. Then it dived upon the great stone bulge, diminishing, disappearing amidst vapours.

'Poetry,' said Osmo caustically. 'Shall I be a poet too? *When a cuckoo lands on a moon, Oh it crows a crazy tune.*'

'Flying might be the best way to get down there' – Wex was rejoining the group – 'but communication with Landfall seems to be stone dead!'

Amberman tugged in vain towards the gap in the palings, while Goldi chanted softly in his ear.

'*A phalanx of wooden soldiers could shelter us as we descend,*' Wex's other self told Osmo. '*Cannot a prime proclaimer protect us from heat and harm if he's with us?*' 'Fastboy Jack could certainly chill the atmosphere,' said Wex. He and his wetwear seemed to be taking turns with increasing ease. Minnow eyed him with concern.

'Well, I trounced a mana-mage,' she muttered.

Elmer was busy with his juggling act again. 'I got the every-thing machine to work—'

'Did you indeed?' retorted Osmo. 'This moon-creature isn't a machine. It's an entity as unbalanced as Lucky herself. Obliterat-ing Kip'an'keep, killing thousands of people! Thousands! Not scores or hundreds, but probably a few thousand. Each with their own lives, which Goldi here could tell, if she knew them, till the cows came home, and stop us from doing anything. What a ter-rible waste of life.'

'*You* waged war,' protested Eva. 'You attacked our aitch-house.'

'Beware what you say! Your aitch-housers butchered my garrison.'

'If death's what this thing's been suckling on, no wonder it squashed a town!'

'Stories hinge on conflict,' said Wex, '*apart from in the Harmonious Society*', and end in disaster or in re-integration, *or both, fluctuating until the very last moment*, depending on chance and choices, {*though really chance is a misnomer for spontaneous choices occurring without conscious decision.*'

'Oh really?' Queen Minnow puffed herself up. She adjusted her

504

crown of whips and pearls. 'Well, let's not bicker. We'll just have to try to control that thing down there.'

Osmo toyed with his moustache, then he inhaled tentatively. 'If I'm to proclaim us a safe route down into that, first of all I'd better eat a big breakfast.'

He eyed Sam as the likeliest provider, but it was Goldi who spoke up.

'There ought to be food in the grannies' huts by the gates—'

'Unless other survivors are already filling their bellies.' Tilly's voice shook. 'I think they might still be too shocked to think of eating.'

'Eat!' yapped the spaniel. 'Me hungry!' At the sound of a well-loved word Out had regained her vocabulary.

Precious *Maaginen* Viper rearing her great head against the roof of her sky-blue den, being coated with her moulted skins transforming surroundings into a shingly luminous envelope. Due to recently swallowing body-servant who was shedding his beige livery and squirming perforce down her throat, Viper being gorged.

Body swelling and deflating upon that bulge of stifled body-servant, three full days to be digesting. Yet Viper thrusting the tented scales of her head towards the ceiling. Raising upward the sharp tooth projecting out of her upper lip, she was tearing the coating of skins.

Juttahat with pad for polishing her splendid scales being knocked aside by that armour of iridescent streaky ochre decorated with sepia glyphs. Juttahat with Ukko-flower in chalice of Viper's fang juices backing against curving azure wall, taking refuge in passageway.

Viper slicing blue membrane of roof, tooth grinding against rock. As if due to this friction, pastel light puffing from *Maaginen*'s horns. Oily vanilla drenching the air.

Time to be hatching from this egg-cave! Ukko-cub having arisen, revealing the stone pod of its rainbow self, a rainbow gaudy with blood of its birthing, blood of humanbeings, flaming lava. Precious *maaginen* soon arising from womb-cave to be asserting affinity, gentling and controlling. Tooth grooving rock, seeking fracture to be splitting eggshell den apart.

Sending powerfully: *Brindled-kin, Brindled-kin, be coming. Be bringing biggest of sky-boats down into Precious One's mana-*

maze. Be emptying nest for escort. Be hoisting Precious One in cradle beneath sky-boat. Be transporting Precious One to be taking occupancy of Ukko-cub where candle-flame is burning warmly amidst winter. Be sending all jump-bikes there too. Such potent images after monstrous gestation. *Maaginen* only ever once being flawed — by sprat-princess once tying her tongue, long and thick and rosy as skinned sea-eel. *Rejecting image of sprat-princess!*

Pastel light puffing. Rock splitting open. Soil trickling, soil deluging. Be coming, be coming. Great Narration impending: Exalted *Maaginen* taming the starfaring Rainbow-Within-Rock on behalf of Brindleds, paragons of Isi, then achieving guidance of wild humanbeings' minds.

Be coming. Be coming.

Be waiting a moment! Why was precious *Maaginen* ingesting weighty body-servant prior to bursting from den?

Why was *Maaginen* burdening her impeccable self when sensing important events impending? Succumbing to such sudden hunger not making sense!

Unless . . .

Maaginen appraising herself. Certain recent sensations and scents being disregarded as distraction from mana-currents alerting herself to those impending events! Be recalling those sensory hints which recent meal was muffling. Be examining herself!

Amazing truth becoming evident. *Precious* Maaginen *being pregnant!* Onset of pregnancy provoking feeding frenzy.

How being pregnant?

How how how how how how?

Being no Isi male visitors to Viper's den for many years. Sperms being storable for years in a serpent's body. Yet *Maaginen* long since outgrowing any serpent-suitor. Long since! No suitor whatsoever visiting this den. No Isi would be contemplating wooing this *monstrous mutant mana-mage*.

Female Juttahats likewise could be storing male Juttahat sperms . . . Could Juttahat female also be storing Isi sperms? Was Viper previously eating servant being vessel for serpent sperms? Being sent into Viper's den as act of mischief?

Preposterous! Impossible!

Whence, then, this mysterious fertilization of Viper? By *herself*, parthenogenetically? Virgin-conception? During some passionate personal frenzy?

506

Viper not being prone to personal erotic frenzies! Juttahat servant with polishing cloth never trespassing within Viper's cloaca, nor stroking a certain part of neck! Viper pursuing momentous mana-mission.

Yet erotic frenzy *was* occurring. Occurring a year since: during deplorable visit of sprat-princess! Viper was swaying princess and proclaimer lord to be copulating. Sway was miscarrying. Princess was bunging up *Maaginen*'s mouth and mind.

That being moment of mana-parthenogenesis! Consequences being delayed; now becoming overt!

Be visualizing a snaking line of embryos becoming a chain of foetuses, conceivably fifty foetuses for a serpent of such size as eminent Viper, maybe a hundred foetuses each strung upon a placenta. Such feeding frenzy to be satisfying. Most foetuses certain to be stillborn due to oxygen deprivation when placentas all pulling each other loose in labour. Otherwise, too many Isi!

Maaginen being pregnant!

Because of sprat-princess!

How galling yet how gratifying. Gratifying and galling at once. Pregnancy being intrinsically pleasing.

Brazens attempting hybridization of wild humanbeings and loyal Juttahats ... Was magnificent *Maaginen* achieving strange fusion of humanbeing aura and serpent-species within her own fertile womb, so that her offspring (those surviving, considering the likely myriad of the pregnancy) could be manipulating humanbeings easily as willing servants?

Maaginen being mother-to-be after decades in den! Due to sprat-princess!

Both vexed and euphoric, Viper thrusting upward. Cold lumps and wedges of soil avalanching. Mighty *Maaginen* shoving, body flexing, tented head-scales digging. Pressure of body-servant in belly pushing ribs outward. Armour of scales being tougher than any other Isi's. One head-scale snapping alas. Frozen soil being hard. Mana-puffs softening the resistance. Calling servants with digging tools? Oh no. Vigorous pregnant Viper giving birth to herself from her cave.

Citric odour of puzzlement lacing pepper of purpose and unctuous oil of imminent accomplishment aboard Velvet Isi sky-boat. Sky-boat having landing by searchlight and sickle-light on frozen pasture to be solving conundrum of captured ≪Minkie-Kennan≫. This, at tactician Pekular's insistence. Pekular's esteem being

507

previously wounded due to invasion of nest by uniforms including wooden persons led by Demonjack. Ergo, Pekular especially insistent: hasty oversight shall not be flawing so crucial a mission.

Esteemed *Maaginen* Muskular being capricious in bringing honoured Brazen hostage Imbricate along with herself as witness on this mother of all ventures. Admittedly, Muskular lauding her Velvet self and nest over ambitious rival Brazens. Even so! Imbricate swaying Velvet Juttahat defenders during deplorable assault, after which Brazen mage being retrieved.

Faint odour of peculiar equivocal erotic complicity between Muskular and Imbricate. Pekular being sensitive to oddities. Too many oddities aboard this sky-boat. Imbricate being one. Gaunt exhausted captive Juke-Nurmi being two – though highly acceptable as witness of the rising of the Ukko-cub and being brother of the half-blind human female poet therein, she being sensitive to the Ukko-cub long since.

Human male ≪Minkie-Kennan≫ being three. Being dazed and bewildered during capture, confused and terrified thereafter, this ≪Minkie-Kennan≫ now appealing to haggard Juke-Nurmi that *he* really being a *she*, Sal by name; and somaseer Imbricate agreeing . . .

Recalling: back in Velvet nest Ukkoscope flashing indications, urgent and at-last-coherent, of imminent *emergence* – even though ear-flower being lost to raiders. Imperative chiming. Nest galvanizing. Sky-boats departing southwards, throbbing and thrumming, airtubes moaning in labour. Sky-boats arriving over chasm, recently being lake below cliffs. Cliffs being twice as high now, lake having drained away into depths. Lingering luminosity, steam arising. Searchlights probing, finding human witness on heights, stupefied by awe and hunger. Landing. Juttahats collecting witness, unresisting. Witness proving to be brother of poetess!

Apprehending witness without much protest. Feeding some foodbars and water to him; reassuring, questioning. Proclaimer witness regaining some weary vigour and sombre stroppiness. Despite food-aid, chanting (if memory serving correctly):

'Not missing my supper,
'No, missing my sister,
'Missing her yellow silk hair,
'Missing Eyeno reciting,

'Her blue eye inviting
'Not a kiss but a prayer
'From her brother: *forgiving*
'For the thorn in the heart
'The prick in the loins
'Virgin yet violating.
'Moon lying under a lake
'Being no reflection, ah no,
'Being no moon in our sky.
'In a moon departing,
'In a moon, a stone moon!
'Ukko, Ukko: *why?*'

Juke-Nurmi bespeaking himself in anguish. Proclaimer becoming poet?

'Gelding me, sickle in the sky,
'Trimming my words to make amends,
'Shaving me, shriving me—'

Proclaimer forsaking power?

After capture of Juke-Nurmi, Ukkoscope revealing mana-wake westwardly. Not up into orbit, but traversing wintry woodlands and ice-lakes. Such a mass to be sustaining in mid-air! Juke-Nurmi effervescing somewhat when being told. Chance of following Ukko-cub. Chance of storming citadel of sister.

Sky-boat with escorts tracking the mana-wake. Presently instruments detecting faint anomalous muffled *ping* of jump-bike in resting mode. Puzzling Pekular. Why being so far from anywhere? Having emerged from within the Ukko-cub as it was passing by? Pekular ordering minor detour and landing in spite of protest by Muskular.

Juttahats abducting ≪Minkie-Kennan≫ from lakeside hut whilst ginger-haired female lurching away into forest, flailing and reeling. Juttahat claiming to be recognizing ≪Minkie-Kennan≫ from past brawls. Imbricate endorsing; no mistaking smells! Any Isi remembering two thousand scents perfectly; a somaseer mage maybe remembering four thousand. Juke-Nurmi ranting at captive ≪Minkie-Kennan≫ – revealing that ≪Minkie-Kennan≫ was previously *entering* the Ukko-cub under the now-drained lake! ≪Minkie-Kennan≫ being acquainted with interior of Ukko-cub! Such an important prisoner. Pekular's detour being fully justified.

Journey continuing. Mingling odours of Juttahats cradling lightweapons and crossbow-rifles crowding on saddles projecting from walls or else holding straphangers. Sandpits where mages coiling. Piquancy, cloy, ambiguous fragrance of seers, *reek* of unwashed bearded Juke-Nurmi arising from armpits and crotch in warmth of cabin. Pastel lights softly showing roof décor of dunes and moons: sinuous waves and discs. Thrumming duty-thoughts of Juttahats, Great Narrations inspiring servants.

Then: distraught ≪Minkie-Kennan≫ starting to protest that *he* being female named Sal. Despite ≪Minkie-Kennan's≫ body smells, somaseer Imbricate beginning to agree: this body harbouring the mind of another. Momentous discovery if true. Requiring landing for full assessment. Ukko-cub responsible for exchange of minds?

Returning to the vicinity of that hut so as to hunt escapee through the forest? No, this being quite intolerable.

Nevertheless: debating, delaying.

'I ain't Minkie, I ain't! You got to make these monsters believe me, mister—!'

Lucky had been sleeping in the bedchamber which once housed Osmo's mother Johanna. A faint fruity smell impregnated the room. This had nothing to do with that woman's death; everything with Johanna's erstwhile passion for the reek of fruit in decay. Despite cleaning of all cut-glass bowls and bedding after Johanna's demise that odour still lingered in the very fabric of the chamber, in floorboards, in wainscot, in furnishings. Lucky found the odour tantalizing; so here she slept at nights.

Jatta was obliged to doss here too, upon the couch by the window. Mother and daughter, together.

Thus it was Jatta who was roused first by the screeching of a cuckoo on the frozen feeding post outside. Her mother, snuggled in the spacious bed, a moment later. Oh, it was a bed broad enough for mother and daughter both. To sleep side by side was unthinkable.

'Light a lamp! Let it in, my Jatta!'

Let it in quickly so that Lucky could hear what the gossip-bird had to say at this early hour – or in the hope that other people mightn't hear? Not so long ago a cuckoo had cackled about a robust Osmo pissing in the snow outside Minnow's Manor at Kip'an'keep contrary to expectations, and about the wretched sprat even starting a family for him.

510

Jatta almost knocked over one of the brass lamps before finding matches and lighting the wick. An odour of burning fish oil mingled with the faint sickly-sweet mustiness of fruits long since decomposed. Floral garlands on the plastered uppers of the walls made of the bedchamber a sad bower. Revealed at the snowy window: a green fluster of scaly plumes, cupped feline ears, big yellow eyes, a beak clacking open and shut.

'You slow bitch, let it in!' Lucky was sitting bolt upright, jet hair a-tumble, silk counterpane clutched around her.

Hugging her rug around herself, Jatta admitted arctic chill from the dark courtyard.

The bird peered into the chamber. 'Hark and hear,' it croaked. 'Kip'an'keep is destroyed. The forest lord's city is drowned and burned and crushed—'

'*What?*' Scrambling from bed, Lucky wrenched silk around herself.

'Ukko-ukkoo, it is sunken, buried, obliterated.'

Lucky shook with excitement. 'Oh *Jack*, oh *Viktor*, oh *Bekker*—!'

'Mother, your army can't possibly have done that!'

'How dare you try to spoil . . . !' Lucky sagged. 'No, they can't have . . . not so suddenly, not so quickly. *Lies! Vile lies! Vile stupid lies!* As if I'd believe it. As if my army would quit. Or be lured so naively. Resistance melting away then my army rushing onward into a trap . . .'

'Mother, the army know perfectly well they haven't even reached Kippan's town, let alone—'

'You're right. So the message is aimed to sway *me*. To delude me, as if I wouldn't pay attention to reality! The mad Queen cries, "I've won, let's all go home. Kip'an'keep doesn't exist any more."'

'Kip'an'keep doesn't exist any more,' cackled the bird.

'This is van Maanen's doing. Isn't it, Jatta, isn't it?' How could Jatta possibly know? 'Thank mana you're here with me, daughter. My daughters are all alike, aren't they? They hate their mother even if they pretend to love her.'

When had Jatta ever pretended any such thing? Oh when she was a little girl. Out of fear. Fear which she had purged from her heart . . . except in so far as dear Anni might be harmed.

'Cuckoo,' Jatta said to the bird close by her. She had never looked so closely into a cuckoo's eyes before. Within one eye the lamplight reflected like an inner candle-flame. Despite the rug

511

around her she shivered convulsively. 'Sing the whole story, tell the whole tale.'

The bird cocked its head. It shat on the icy windowsill. 'Ukko,' it said. 'Ukkoo. The moon-child has risen. From a lake far away—' (Lucky crushed silk into her mouth to prevent herself from interrupting the cuckoo.) 'The moon-child has flown across Kaleva. She has settled down upon Kip'an'keep, melting and crushing—'

Silk tore. Lucky was dancing disconnectedly, moaning into her gag as if in torment. For a moment wild suspicion haunted her smoky narrow eyes. Then exultation drowned any doubt. She was jerking, quaking. She had to sit upon the bed. She held her heaving chest. The silken bung popped free.

'A fire to burn Kip'an'keep,' she gasped. 'Cruel Ukko: it's what I commanded. *My* Ukko-child, at last. At last! With myself await-ing me . . .'

'Awaiting,' echoed the cuckoo.

'And it destroyed a whole town,' whispered Jatta.

The bird eyed Jatta. 'To claim thomething great, there muth be great travail,' it lisped. Whose voice was it mimicking? A voice blurred by distance, heard through a blanket.

'A whole town . . .'

'An enemy town, my Jatta! But still, a town of mine. All towns are really mine.' Lucky rocked to and fro as if in labour. 'Why did the Ukko-child go there? It's what I wished. Van Maanen and his sprat are dead.' She panicked. 'If cuckoos are cackling then the Isi will be heading for my Ukko-child! We're closest, aren't we, Jatta? Of course we are. That's why it went there too. Obviously. Now the missiles are destroyed. And the printing press. My Ukko-child's a lusty bawling pugnacious one, a brat kicking over the toys. Me and myself will tame it. We'll tell it new stories. Stories of alien serpents and their slaves and daugh-ters whom aliens fucked. We'll take it to the worlds of the Isi. We'll be the greatest mana-mage. We'll be the serene Queen of Snakes, myself and me.' How hectic her voice was. 'We'll live another four hundred years, long after you're dead, my chatter.'

'Dear mana,' whispered Jatta.

'Shall I take you with me? Your Jack, of course; and the Maids . . . Your whole family, my Jatta! *Jack* – he has to be with me at Kip'an'keep to freeze any snakes' snouts!' Lucky was rushing to the door.

She shrieked along the pitchy corridor: '*Guards, guards, rouse! Paavo, where are you? Are the sky-boats ready? Lights, lights! We're leaving!*'

34 · LANDING ON THE MOON

Horrified and heartsick, Eyeno mourned for the dead of Kip'an'keep.

She and those with her had seen the moonlit, snowlit town in spherical perspective. Very soon, tiny refugees had been scurrying away from under the looming moon almost too fast for the eye to follow. Time enough for most people to evacuate their homes. Whole crowds failed to seize this only, early chance. And then had come the melting and the quaking and the breaking of the waters, before steam gushed up to hide the agony of annihilation.

As witnessed from within the moon-child the momentum of destruction had been so swift.

'Stop it, stop it,' she had begged the carpenter-nakki. She was already almost too late. Almost! That was the horror. If only she could have conquered her vertigo! If only the name of the flower could have come to her! If only she had thrown herself into the candle-palace crying out that name, maybe the extermination would have paused.

Why had the moon-child granted her a new perspective if this also made her dizzy? Surely the havoc wreaked upon Kip'an'keep was partly her own havoc. *Moon plunging into warm world.* Bloodflower legacy of the war against the Snowies. Volcano of names. Her wounded eye socket: a throbbing crater. Yes, yes. And idle thoughts about *hotspots* associated with Kip'an'keep, the place where books were printed which she could no longer read!

Now that the moon-child had descended into that crater of its own creation the view within the candle-palace was of an abstract angry madness: tongues of fire, curlicues of bubbling lava, a scalloped wheel of chaos.

'Who'll claim me?' asked the carpenter, swaying. 'And who thall *I* claim ath mine?'

*

When Osmo and Minnow emerged into that grey icy world within the moon-child, were they glad of their quilted coats! How bitter the air; how nostril-cutting. Snow blanketed tracts of grim woodland and open wastes. So pale the scene, so leached of light – except in one direction where radiance beaconed in the gloom. Quite far away wan shafts of some sort of sunlight competed with the eerie luminosity of a ghostly edifice seemingly made of combusting gas.

They could see across hoary treetops to that distant place because the land curved upward. Indeed all directions were upward, gently so, then perhaps more steeply. From their vantage point they only saw as far as they did because rolls and coils of ashen cloud curved upward in tandem with the terrain. Those clouds resembled some antique wig worn upside-down or the convolutions of a brain turned inside-out. The interior of the moon-child was so huge, a different type of space . . .

Minnow was glad to be wearing boots. They'd been commandeered from the shortest of the Blue Guards. Even with the fellow's socks pulled over her own those boots were still a size too big.

Goldi clutched to herself a cloak obtained from another guard. Those guards had been only too glad to abandon their chance of accompanying this particular expedition. Indeed the escort had finally resolved into four wooden soldiers – one of whom had fallen into the lava from the perilous if hefty bridge of the wrecked keep. Amberman held Goldi close to him as if his golden body must communicate heat.

During the descent into the pit *she* had been hugging *him* so that his affinity would not lead to a fatal plunge. Amberman had been at his most malleable then – softened, as it were. Manoeuvrable. Too long in traversing tammywood wreckage, and her lover might have begun to adhere to it. Now the bone-racking chill stiffened his amber anatomy without apparently discomforting him.

Sam Peller scanned the austere landscape from side to side. As if in response to his misgivings a hidden creature howled forlornly, hungrily. Then another. Then a third.

Wex waved his bandaged hand. 'That tower of light! It's like the mana-light I stepped into which took me to Landfall and tortured me—'

Aye, till his wetwear had divorced him from sensation.

514

'There isn't this much volume inside the ferry-Ukko, Lucky's Ukko. Or could there be—?'

The arctic air smelled greasy. After the dazing fumes within the pit this frigid odour was cleansing. Earlier, *reek* had almost stifled them; heat had almost overcome them . . .

Elmer had stayed behind with his wife, because Eva couldn't see well enough with one eye to accompany her younger sister. Such was the excuse. Elmer's empty-handed juggling had failed to offer the instinctive engineer an inkling of how he could try to manipulate something as huge and powerful as the Ukko-child. It eluded his grasp.

And as for Mathavan Gurrukal, why, his arm was broken.

Tilly had also stayed behind at the granny's hut where they had eaten rusks and cheese and sausage. Those nakkis racing pell-mell upon that surging rug in her playroom – a rug which at one moment had seemed like a molten lake! – must have been a warning of imminent catastrophe. She had failed to heed it because she failed to understand it. How could she possibly have interpreted such an omen? Whatever her poor mother may have thought, Tilly was no secret shamaness. At least she still had her talking spaniel to keep her company.

The party had scrambled and slithered down scree and dirt to the ruin of Kippan's keep. How the wreckage creaked and groaned. Spars of verandah fell off to tumble deeper and float and start to smoulder lazily, even if the wood was tammy. The venturers had to totter and crouch and haul their way along ruptured tilted corridors and through pancaked rooms as fast as could be. Fast was far from easy. The collapsed fabric offered some shelter from the heat radiating upward, if not from hot gases. How strenuously Osmo had proclaimed protection for them all. Across a rift in the floors they had spied the bodies of Edith and Tapper Kippan tangled together unmoving under a fallen beam. Couldn't detour to investigate. The couple would have been lying a long while pinned amid scorching fumes; Tapper Kippan's longlife had surely expired.

Finally they had scrambled on to the rugged hillside of naked rock quite near to a vent which led within . . .

To Wex, frosted trees in the distance seemed like eruptions of magnetized iron filings pulled upward by a force rather than growing organically.

'The Ukko makes the scale smaller inside itself,' he mused. 'The scale, yes that's it, the scale . . .'

'And a tree in the distance is truly smaller than a tree close by. When you arrive in the distance you too have become smaller. Maybe a kind of relativity applies. Looking back, you'll see the tree you left behind as tiny in proportion to your own location—'

'Does that mean,' asked Minnow, 'we'll need to travel further to that mana-lighthouse than seems to be so?'

'We ought to have brought *rations* with us,' Sam said gloomily. 'Granny's hut wasn't exactly bursting at the seams! *Does* it mean that, wetwear?'

'This is precisely how the Ukkos travel the vast distance between the stars, by shifting scale in mana-space, upward, then downward again – but downward elsewhere. I have an announcement. You must tell this to Landfall if Roger meets with a fatal accident. The whole universe must in a sense be an Ukko of space-time – of which we're all reflections on a minuscule scale, yet equally intricate. The whole universe is within an Ukko, yet the outer limit – which is nowhere definable – is also the very core. We are within the universe but the universe is within us. Adjust our perception of scale, and we can shift a moon across a galaxy—'

'Does this mean we have further to *walk*?'

'An Ukko can shift itself thus by means of mana-energy. There is such vast potential power in everything that exists. Energy is locked up in mass. Yet there is vastly more power inherent in what we term "nothing" – in the potent void vacuum, the sea of mana from which a whole universe can explode into being. Our universe is but a bubble in mana-space. Very likely there are many universes: clusters of bubbles from which new bubbles bud—'

'Wetwear, how *far* do we have to hike?'

'Hidden within the potent – the omni-potent – primary nothingness are curlicues of virtual spacetime which the Ukkos navigate. Mere tiny twists yet in essence titanic! The travelling is a question of scale – of navigating the tiny, which is so self-similar to the very large, and therefore equivalent to that vastness!'

'Obviously the wetwear has become a shaman,' observed Osmo. 'Must be all the mana hereabouts.'

'Roger, snap out of it and answer me!'

But the wetwear persisted in its rhapsody.

'From tiny to vast the transition is betold. Tales and word are the agent of transition – for tales are all metaphors by which one thing becomes another, significantly. Creatively, transformationally. Words are all frozen metaphors, reflections of real things which have become arbitrary yet obey structure. We are story incarnate, my Roger,' insisted Wex's other self. *'What appears arbitrary about events is really a dynamic structure in operation. A universe emerges arbitrarily. Because of this arbitrariness, not otherwise, it evolves speedily into*

structure. *If conditions weren't arbitrary in the moment of emergence, this telling of itself could not occur. One element compels another which fits, and is self-fitting. This is what the Ukko absorbs by its feasting upon the stories of events: the dynamic of being, the transformation of events whereby desire becomes actual, and dream becomes a deed. The degrees of freedom allowed by mana enforce patterns of happenings and the interplay of people. Oh it was capricious yet essential that we should use a satellite to shoot a bird from our shoulder. I have such a feeling of unfolding cosmic magnitude, reflected in the twists of events—'*

Wex struggled. 'It's you who has flipped, wetwear, not me.'

'—and thus I become . . . a self. This Ukko compresses space inside itself. It can compress within itself the space it travels through from star to star. Often "Gods" appear to beings, and are capricious in their conduct – reflecting the manias of beings without which there could be no tales or transformations. The tale of the universe is one of vast creation and destruction occurring constantly, though over times and distances too great for the sky to seem other than peaceful. Ah yes, I am becoming a self. Shall I be bodiless or embodied? Shall I cleave to the mind of this Ukko to steer it on behalf of the Harmonious Society – or shall it furnish me with flesh and a face?'

Wex slapped himself brisky even though he wouldn't personally register the blow. His head rocked.

'Is this Ukko creature in touch with your protoplasmic circuits now, wetwear? Can you steer it?'

'I feel, I feel—'

'Well, I certainly don't!' Wex shuddered, and whispered. 'If you leave me . . . will I be in torment? Can you gain a body here?'

'Something wants our bodies!' squealed Minnow, pointing.

From clumps of glacial trees three verrins had emerged. The brindled brown carnivores reared upright, the better to see, long bald whip-tails balancing them. The beasts were as tall as Osmo would have been with Minnow riding on his shoulders.

Each dropped back upon four feet. Each came loping through the snow, snouty and savage and ravenous.

Two-handed, Sam sighted his lightpistol. The wooden soldiers aimed lightrifles and a crossbow. Hot light pulsed. An explosive bullet flew. Three verrins tumbled headlong . . . They vanished amidst the woolly blanket.

Just adjacent to where the beasts had disappeared, three fierce verrins were racing towards the group, teeth bared.

Hot light pulsed again. Two verrins toppled and vanished. Two verrins replaced them, rushing onward. Two more verrins surged from out of the snow as if they had lain hidden till now. Five beasts were racing for the kill. Goldi moaned.

'Remember Viper's maze, Oz!' cried Minnow. 'Shrink them! Scale them down, like Wex says! Don't fire at them, Sam. Don't fire, soldiers—'

Osmo heaved his breath.

Plumes billowing in the chill – as though his words were more substantial than ever before – he bellowed:

> 'Shrink and shrivel,
> 'Shorten and dwindle, verrins!
> *'This is spoken.'*

More than spoken: trumpeted.

> 'Shrivel and shorten,
> 'Shrink and dwindle!
> *'This is bespoken.'*

As the beasts rushed closer they became smaller. Then smaller still. They still came onward. Now they were having to leap to make progress through the snow. Killing frenzy and feeding frenzy propelled the diminishing bodies forward in a series of bouncy jumps.

By some mutual agreement the beasts converged upon Minnow. By now they were reduced to frantic furry finger-lengths. These launched themselves at her boots. She pranced. She crushed one then two. Finally all five lay broken-backed and gut-burst.

The clouds of Osmo's words wandered compactly through the air. He blew on his hands. He brushed his moustache to clear away some crystals. How would he replenish his power without rations? On the other hand, would he need to here where mana saturated the locale?

'Heed no hunger or fatigue,' he announced. 'Heed no cold,' he told Goldi especially, and her skin glowed. Fragrances wafted from her, sweetening the greasy air.

Amberman was holding his belly, that translucent womb, sanctuary of his anima.

'I need a piss,' said Osmo.

'And so do I,' agreed Minnow. She had no wish to retreat into the cave from which they had come. The wooden soldiers crouched around her, backs turned to the young Queen as she bobbed down to pull up coat and satin gown and stain the snow yellow with a welcome gush.

*

518

More than one portal having opened in the upper shell of the Ukko-cub according to twinklings in the Ukkoscope. Vapours veiling precise observation.

Low sky glowing lava-orange. Smoke particles of combusted town adrift in atmosphere. Wheezing air-tubes sucking in heavy pollution while sky-boat circling with escort vessels. Wholesale obliteration of a city, scooping out hot pit for the Ukko-cub to be nestling in, evoking horrid images of an Isi nest suffering similar fate.

Such devastation implying rejection by Ukko-cub of association with obstreperous humanbeings? Alternatively: *great injury; great gift?*

Balance and counterbalance being central tenet. Juttahats – Those-Of-The-Hand – bearing burden of service to Isi to balance boons of speech, of technology envisioned by Isi of yore, of voices in the head guiding wise-conduct in place of primeval savagery. Humanbeings-Of-The-Hand likewise benefiting in future by radiant guidance of splendid illuminated Isi! Isi of manipulative minds requiring hands to serve. How else were minds becoming manipulative except by lack of hands? Hands must be serving minds.

Even so: *great injury to humanbeings; thus great gift?* Devastation being excessive otherwise?

Aerial survey and instruments detecting (subject to error) no sky-boats upon Ukko-cub itself. Despite delay (in no way solving enigma of ≪Minkie-Kennan≫) yet due to very early warning by Ukkoscope, Velvets apparently first at the scene.

Ah but trace-echo of sky-boat pinging from land beyond large tree garden. Juttahat lookout acutely identifying *dovecraft*, white hull upon snow amidst trees, seeming badly damaged.

Earthkeep dovecraft!

Agents of humanbeing homeworld here already? Dying in crash or surviving? Ruin of forest lord's keep of rooms and corridors and verandahs jamming between crater-wall and side of Ukko near lava-line amid hot fumes: incombustible tammywood forming hazardous bridge. Negotiable by humanbeings? Wearing wet cloaks and holding breath? Bringing spacesuits in dovecraft? Using mana-umbrella?

Be bombing that bridge to remove it!

Pekular demurring. Explosions shocking to Ukko-cub. Triggering robust response. Only resulting in incombustible wreckage lodging lower down in smaller pieces.

Ruin therefore remaining unbombed.

So: sky-boat and escorts descending perilously upon bulging Ukko-cub. With aid of mages, black tyres softening into strong quick-setting glue analogue. (Be clinging tight, be staying upright!) Noses of vessels pointing upslope so the sky-boats should not be rolling over, tumbling towards lava. Hatches opening, admitting foul stink.

More than one entrance to an Ukko being a perplexing novelty . . . as novel as any Ukko being upon a planet's surface! Imbricate mooting whether Ukko inviting more than one boarding party. Should body-servant be carrying Imbricate to an entrance of his own for balance as delegate of the Brazens?

Not being likely! Game being almost won. Convergence of blue eggs and Juttahat-figures. Serpent-figure descending from tower-square to the underboard. Figuratively so.

Pekular insisting on one quarter of armed Juttahats guarding portal and sky-boat housing Ukkoscope as well as escort vessels. Two quarters deploying across surface of Ukko-cub to be finding and interdicting other openings.

Two other Velvet mages to be accompanying Muskular on her quest within. Muskular insisting on Imbricate being included in the penetration as Brazen eyewitness of Velvet triumph. Velvet Juttahats to be escorting captive Juke-Nurmi in event of problems with poetess. Also escorting ≪Minkie-Kennan≫ as witness of interior of Ukko-cub and meddler therein – though ≪Minkie-Kennan≫ still protesting persuasively, pathetically, non-identity with Minkie-Kennan, identity as Sal, some doting farmer's daughter with long gingery hair (now abbreviated to chestnut curls).

Juttahat sentries likely becoming dazed by fumes and gases arising? Two mages remaining in sky-boats to be bolstering those sentries' alertness.

Sky-boats adhering tightly to stone. Juttahats lifting mages. Juttahats propelling Juke-Nurmi and ≪Minkie-Kennan≫. Other Juttahats bearing numerous weapons. Muskular leading, coiling above body-porter. Great Narration culminating imminently, victoriously.

Jack whistled. 'Look, there it is and they're fighting over it!'

A steaming potato-moon lay embedded in a crater. Here and there upon its surface tiny Juttahats were in combat. Black liveries of the Velvets, beige liveries of the Brindleds. On one flank of the moon three sky-boats were parked alongside one another at an acute angle near what looked to be a hole. Higher up on the opposite flank a larger vessel lay tilted precariously on its side, attached to a peculiar ... drogue-anchor? Surely not an anchor, but rather a sling, a sleeve which must have been suspended beneath the vessel in flight so as to convey some large long cargo which wouldn't fit aboard. Several smaller grounded sky-boats formed a protective cordon sheltering this empty sleeve and a vent in the surface ...

Jack rubbed his hands briskly over his knees clad in coppery-coloured fabric. 'At least the Brazens aren't here yet!'

'We're late,' snapped Lucky. 'Late late late!'

Extricating Jack and Captain Bekker and Prut from the war front had proved time-consuming. Maybe the rebels had been planning to launch an early-morning ski-borne raid, irrespective, to try to wreck or capture the battle-wagon; for the armoured vehicle had finally reached Lucky's forces. When the royal sky-boat and the fortress-flier landed beside the tented camp – after conspicuously criss-crossing the forest in search of its current location – an attack perhaps became inevitable ...

In her urgency Lucky had dragged Jatta out into the snow with her.

Such a pack of royal guards and Jaegertroopers and aitch-housemen – hardly distinguishable from one another in their goggles and mitts and woollen knickerbockers and coats of double cloth, an outfit perhaps less effective at keeping out cold than at permitting vigorous exertion without overheating. Hence the number of bonfires. Those were being used to heat rye porridge.

So many ponies, carts, and sledges. Stooks of skis stacked on their points to preserve the curvature of the tips.

Oh, and the armoured vehicle, but that was of no consequence now.

General Aleksonis had forsaken his splendid uniform. He was wearing knickerbockers instead of those excellent form-fitting breeches which Lucky had so admired. Her Majesty must forgive this adjustment to wintry circumstances. To pull on wetted breeches would lead to pneumonia. The General couldn't carry off Demon Jack's trick. What trick? Why, Jack's Juttie livery had finally lost its dirt-repellent quality, and begun to smell. June had boiled the Brazen fabric for her young hubby in melted snow and soap, leaving it to simmer overnight.

*Right now Jack was sitting in a chilly tent drying the livery
upon himself by a summoning of intensified body heat, acting as
his own personal sauna-brazier. The four Maids – wrapped up
in thick little coats and fur-lined leather bootees – played outside
that tent, lobbing snowballs instead of plague flies. On Lucky's
approach, escorted by the General, the Maids bombarded her and
Jatta, chorusing:*

   'Have you—
      'Brought us—
         'Any sweeties—
            'Sweeties?'

*Lucky hadn't brought any. (And Jatta thought of mignon
eggs . . .)*

*'Grandmother—! Mother—!' Still busy drying his livery by will
power, Jack was also much preoccupied by a name confided to
him, in exchange for not looting her house, by a wisewoman in a
village which the royal forces had overrun. He promptly overwhelmed Lucky with a spate of telling.*

The name: progeria.

Progeria *was the name of a very rare disease characterized by
extremely precocious development, premature ageing, and early
death. Dire details of Jack and his daughters had preceded
the army, cackled by cuckoos. The wisewoman had been
acquainted with a case akin to his and to theirs thirty years
previously . . .*

*A boy had been born to new immigrants whom the mana-priests
of Landfall had assigned, by tin divination, to this part of the
forest lord's domain. Those immigrants had been medics on
the far-off Earth. During their transit through mana-space in the
Ukko-ferry, in their dreams their minds had been ransacked by
the Ukko and left in some disarray though dominated by the
notion of this strange time disease which they happened to have
encountered on Earth. By mischievous whim of the Ukko their
first son born on Kaleva was fated to recapitulate their experience
of* progeria. *Their son gained his second set of teeth when he was
three months old. By the time he was six months old his teeth
were yellowing and rotting. His hair was white by the time he
was two.*

Progeria: *misbehaviour of the pituitary gland. Affecting the
hypothalamus in the brain, which was part of the time-keeping
system. Consequently their son had lived at a different rate to
ordinary people, dying of old age when he was ten, though without*

attaining adult stature – unlike Jack, though not unlike his four daughters . . .

Jack had already evaded the curse of progeria by passing it to the Maids. Now that the proper word was known – by way of the wisewoman of the woods, by way of the medic couple who had been meddled with – Nils the young proclaimer had begun using that word to stabilize the Maids so that they might grow more normally. Those temperamental lasses were a challenge to Nils. A point of pride to prevail!

'Isn't it wonderful, Grandma? Isn't it wonderful, Jatta?' As a consequence of these ministrations, it seemed that the Maids might make no more plague flies . . .

It was several gabbling minutes before Lucky could prevail over Jack.

Ukko-child arisen! Kip'an'keep obliterated! Plague flies irrelevant. Likewise the hostilities themselves . . .

Ben Prut had arrived by then. Bekker too. The Captain of the wooden soldiers retained his fine uniform since he felt no cold whatever. Numerous other soldiers were crowding outside the flap of Jack's tent. Soon there was a crowd behind a crowd.

('Our Queen's going to lead us—')

('No she ain't, she just shouted that the war's over—')

('How can it be over—?')

('Hwisht, she's shouting that Kip'an'keep's destroyed—')

('The war's a waste of time—')

('The steel hervy! We brought yon all the way from Sariolinna—!')

('Tapper Kippan has to be dead, and that vile van Maanen and his chit—')

('Our real enemies are the Isi now, she's saying. They're her rivals for the Ukko that's appeared—')

('The Ukko that squashed Kip'an'keep—')

('She's in a frantic rush to leave us, not lead us, you deaf fool—')

('Taking Demon Jack with her—')

('And Bekker's Timberlads and the young proclaimer too—')

Distant commotions, cries and horn-calls from the picket lines, the beginning of turmoil . . . What a scramble, what a scattering. Porridge spilling on bonfires. The battle-wagon roaring to life to interpose itself beyond the grounded sky-boats, spitting fireshots into the forest. Flick of hot light, zip of bullets. Wooden soldiers forming a cordon around Lucky. No, it wouldn't be a wise idea to run for the royal sky-boat.

What if it and the fortress-flier were crippled? What a wicked waste of time when the war no longer had any purpose!

Lucky had seethed with frustration even as her troops sustained the perimeter. How could she strip officers and soldiers away while such skirmishes were going on? Someone must proclaim a truce, a peace.

Where were Aleksonis and Prut and the young proclaimer and Jack? Busy, busy.

How should the rebels believe such a huge claim, of the elimination of Kip'an'keep? This might seem a lie too large.

At last calm returned. The last sniper had either skied away or been shot. Injuries were tended. Corpses were counted. A wooden soldier was prising a bullet out of his arm.

And then came the dispute with Jatta, which quickly involved Jack too, back now from the action. Nils Carlsson must stay with June and her menace lasses to continue controlling their progeria. Lucky mustn't try to take him with her. Or else Jack wouldn't go with his grandmother! And whom did she value more?

Oh all the damned delay.

Now as a result of the delay Velvet and Brindled Juttahats were brawling sluggishly all across the pocked surface of the Ukko-child. Blacks and Beiges fought ineptly as if drugged. An alien would stumble, another would stagger. One rolled all the way down the hillside of the Ukko into the moat of lava. As the royal sky-boat circled, into view came the remains of a substantial keep lodged deep down the side of the crater. Much higher up the rocky flank of the moon-child, contested by Juttahats, a vent was visible.

'Late, late, late!'

'Hush, Grandma, hush—'

Lucky stuffed a wad of gown into her mouth. Rocking to and fro, Jack glowed as he conjured cool quietude and frozen moments. Serlachius chanted softly: words of mysterium. The pilots communed by radio. Sloth seemed to paralyse Juttahats in the area below. In suspended stillness, both boats descended to bracket that aperture, the royal boat groaning and shuddering. Lucky shook with the intensity of her anticipation, and anxiety.

35 · INTEGRATIONS

'Hark and hear,' lisped the nakki-carpenter, 'they're coming thoon.'

Inside the spectral palace the whorl of fire had burned itself to blackness, to a bloated inky bum-shape a-flicker with gingery lightning. Upon that bifurcated inky bum perched a blank black head sporting a topknot. The silhouette of the Gingerwoman! A stream of sparks gushed upward, their shimmer suggestive of the star-sylph, an image forever forming and dissolving.

'Who are coming?' asked Paula who was a soulflower.

'Who?' asked Inga, slender chimneyflower.

'Who?' asked Eyeno of the opal eye.

Why, a monstrous mutant mage was sliding across the snowscape never minding the bulk of servant slow to be dissolving in her belly. Amber-skinned Juttahats jogging alongside. Lacking jump-bike outriders, jump-bikes having failed shortly after entry into Ukko-cub.

Viper being too bulky for even a dozen servants to be carrying upon their shoulders with any ease in either lockstep or freestep. Pastel mana-light lubricating her journey, leaving a rosy snaking trail as though thin blood leaking from her underside due to straining herself.

Why, three regular purple mages were being carried like wraparound tubas by black-skinned Juttahats in sable livery, and one brassy mage by a coppery-clad servant. Being hustled along was a humanbeing fellow with chestnut curls, nutbrown eyes, generous brow and mouth and impishly snubby nose and stubble on his chin astonishing to him ('How can I recognize anything here? I'm just a girl! My name's Sal!'). Also being propelled: a haggard bearded figure with fierce blue eyes and greasy fawn hair jutting back: 'I tell you my sister will be *surrounded* by monsters! *Minkie* told me so.'

'No I didn't. Not me! Ain't me, I swear. Minkie took my body and gave me his! It's a nightmare. I loved him so. When I goes to sleep, will I wake up as me again? His *thing's* between my legs all the time, bulging and aching—'

One monster having already rushed out from a snowy thicket, half-humanbeing, half-verrin, howling *food, food*, heading for Juke-Nurmi and his Juttahat warder with hungry intent, a nightmare being embodied. Lightweapons failing to fire, though being tested earlier just after entering the Ukko-cub. Cartridge in rifle failing to detonate. Bullet flying from crossbow failing to explode on impact, although verrin-man being punched and spinning around before resuming frenzied rush. Ordinary crossbow quarrel (being urged by mage-words) penetrating the beastman's forehead, attacker collapsing.

Most weapons being only useful as *clubs* now? Arms mainly useful for wrestling?

Why, Captain Bekker had made the same discovery. Yet he and his wooden soldiers – in their deep blue uniforms and peaked shakos – were staunch as cudgels. Short-sighted Ben Prut and his detachment of royal guards – in knickerbockers and double-cloth coats – were more disadvantaged. Demon Jack was dashing to and fro, solicitous of Lucky as she tramped resolutely through the chilly gloom towards the zone of light, that sunny village with its glowing ghastly keep. Jack was also attentive to Jatta. He gobbled cabbage and mincemeat in soft pastry parcels from a big greasy paper bag to sustain his gusto.

'Have a pig-in-a-blanket, Jatta Mum,' he urged. 'They're lovely.'

Shaking her head: 'You'll burst, my fastboy.'

'It's like our hike away from Maananfors when I was just little, isn't it, Jatta Mum? All hurry, hurry.' Long ago in his lifetime, though not so very long either . . . 'You and me and Juke, eh?'

'Damn that Juke!' swore Lucky. 'Could have been helping me. I pardoned him, I patronized him.' Her teeth chattered with chill and rage and tension.

'I'm helping you, Grandmother. I'm more than Juke. I'm the master of wind and light and cold. The light that stuns, the cold that chills.'

'And you brought dear Anni to me,' murmured Jatta ruefully, though not so as her mother would hear.

'Warm up, Grandmother. Have a pig-in-a-blanket—'

'No! It was glacial in space when I found my Ukko. That's why it's so frigid now. The cold, the dark . . . It's so big in here! So much bigger. Where are all the labyrinths and cochleae and chambers? Maybe we're only in one of them. Maybe this is the wrong one. Ah, that bright place is the meadow with the waxy blooms! Why isn't the air sweet? It's gassy. Greasy as that grub in your gob, Jack! Where are the skeletons of serpents and Unmen? Oh but those wouldn't be here. Where's Paula? *Where am I?* Don't call me Grandmother. I'm young. I'm old, so old, from so many bitchy silly daughters. I don't mean you, Jatta-chatter. You're here with me at the end, and the new *start*.'

'I'm sure I wish to be.' Not so as her mother might hear.

Why, Sam Peller likewise discovered the treason of guns. He had fired at a pillar of snow which suddenly lurched forward from against a tree trunk. The pillar shed handfuls of its woolly covering, revealing patches of red leathers and a leering blotchy scarlet face. Without being lanced by any hot light the figure fell rigidly and lay still. Sam shook his pistol and fired again without effect. His gun had quit.

Wex stooped by the frozen corpse. He brushed cold wool from the features. The hair was as bleached as Sam's own.

'He's Snowy—'

'Of course he's snowy!' said Minnow. 'Isn't that plain as potato pie?'

'No, I mean he's *Snowy*, Minkie Kennan's crony. From Niemi Keep.' Wex's hands brushed again. 'There's a long dart sticking through his chest. It was pinning him to the tree . . .'

'Woodmen,' Sam instructed the escorts, 'test your lightrifles.'

Which they did. None fired.

Mana could certainly have this effect on weapons, though never yet so comprehensively. Here was the cauldron of mana, all be it a cold one.

'We'll use our knives if need be,' Sam said gloomily. 'It wasn't our guns that stopped the beastmen, was it? Really our guns were never any use.' He gazed at Osmo. 'My Prince and Proclaimer: you'll see us through.'

'Of course he will,' said Minnow. 'Or my name isn't Minnow van Maanen.'

Wex hunched over the corpse. 'This must be a false body created by the Ukko-child out of Kennan's mind while he was here . . . A mana-festation.

'*A psych-clone.*'

His hands strayed over the stiff body, almost longingly, though what could he feel?

527

'My Amberman being a mana-festation too,' Goldi said proudly. 'He – or she – and I: each being unique.'

'If we run into Juttahats,' Sam asked her warily, 'will you still feel so unique?'

The Girlem wafted reassurance. 'Aren't I the only Juttahat who can sway with my scents and my chants? Do you fear I'd succumb to an old allegiance?'

Her Amberman was rocking, holding his or her midriff. 'Goldi, I'm—' He or she whistled birdsong as if to regain his or her wind. 'I can't say—'

'What's wrong?' Goldi knelt in the snow before him and laid her hands over those protective hands. 'You miscarried into a pool of resin in a mootapu tree,' she told him. 'Your uncle chanted and chewed and spat. Amber formed your wonderful limbs, firm and flexible and free from any frailty.'

Gently though firmly she prised his palms free; and exhaled – or did she gasp ever so slowly?

Double vision in a cloudy mana-mirror of honey-amber! The blurred womb within, habitation of the foggy foetus, contained another shape occupying the same space: a ginger silhouette of rotund torso, blank orange head and bun, aflicker as if a hundred tiny fingers were flexing. The foetus turned within this phantom.

'Thall I be born of mythelf?' lisped Amberman. 'Thall I give birth to mythelf? Thall I lie my amber cocoon down in labour, legs wide?'

'You can't!' Goldi stared at the golden genital pouch and cock so close to her, so sculptural. 'You being male, having no birth canal!'

'Thall my belly thplit open, then?' Amberman's midriff heaved. As Amberman staggered, Girlem clutched both his hips to steady her lover. Anxious fragrance flooded from her.

'Thall I dithcard mythelf to give you a whelp, a fastbrat, to hang at your tit?'

'No, no, it's *you* I love! You!'

'But thith ith me, and all the retht ith my wrapping.'

'My harp, my harp—'

'—is lost,' wailed Minnow. 'And I'm so sorry it is. Help her, Oz,' she urged. 'Help Goldi. Proclaim! Control this! Tie an egg into a knot: that kind of sway. Stop the baby being born. Keep it where it is.'

'No, don't say so! Or our own baby might—'

528

'Control', declared the wetwear. '*A test of control: that's what this is.*'

Osmo dithered.

Wex advanced upon Amberman. He thrust Goldi aside. He sent her sprawling. Such lust and yearning were in his fruity voice:

'*After the baby departs, do I take this amber body for my own? Wearing my hidden face. Conforming to my conception of me. Becoming natural bronzed flesh, natural muscles and bone. My mind within. Give birth, Amberman, give up your golden envelope. Accept the baby, Girlem, the wise loving talking baby, sister of your soul—*'

Minnow slapped Wex fiercely across the face.

And he screamed. Oh such a scream, as if he were dipped into fire. The force of his scream flung him upon the snow, writhing and howling.

'Don't leave me!' Wex shrieked. His words were raw tortured sinew, a flayed cat being pulled to snapping point between two hounds.

Minnow disregarded him. 'If my Oz can't proclaim,' she vowed, 'then I will. Amberman, hark and hear. Child of resin, man of amber with a girl's essence: remain yourself. Shadow, submit to me!'

She had to yell to compete with Wex's shrieks. Tugging her crown from her frizz, she tore it asunder, scattering pearls like hailstones upon the snow. She freed a handful of black leather snakes, little whips which she flailed furiously.

'Leave Amberman alone, I say. This is spoken, bespoken, respoken. Shadow going, no more showing. Baby unborn, belly untorn.'

Amberman relaxed – and slowly pressed palms across that blurred window upon the womb.

'I am ... all right,' said Amberman in an everyday voice – husky though with a trill in it as of a soft whistle through golden teeth a little too widely spaced.

Goldi rose to clasp her released exotic lover to her, and to sigh an exhalation of sweetness.

'My Amberman!'

'My luscious goose!'

Minnow rounded on Wex. He still writhed, squealing the breath out of himself. Stooping, Minnow belaboured him with her fistful of thongs.

'Shut up, shut up!'

This lesser tickle appeared to penetrate his agonized seizure.

Subsiding, he clawed feebly at snow. Minnow grinned at Osmo. She let the thongs fall.

'No high boots, and now I've ruined my crown.'

Wonderingly: 'You don't need it, do you?'

'Hoping,' called Goldi, 'hoping you haven't harmed your child.'

'Now don't you go *ing-ing* at me,' teased Minnow, 'even if you are in a fluster, or Sam'll suspect you're still a Juttie at heart.'

'My Queen,' said Sam, abashed.

Wex had rolled over. Sitting up, he hugged himself.

Sheepishly: 'You hit me, Minnow . . .'

'The temptation. Desire edging out duty so that I wasn't paying enough attention. You took us by surprise . . .'

'And then I hit you again. Both of you, Roger.'

'Both . . .' Wex hugged himself tighter as if shivering with shock.

'The chance has gone . . . We must share each other . . . for ever. Share each other. Only in Roger's dreams will I wear my inward face.'

'Let's face it, Wetwear,' said Minnow, 'if you'd entered Amberman's body you'd have looked like . . . like some brass robot made by Elmer. Yes, like a robot, not like a lusty suntanned chap at all. Amberman is wonderful.' ('Oh yes,' sighed the Girlem.) 'But *you'd* have been a bit ridiculous.'

'A mutie freak,' agreed Osmo. Right away he shook his head, reproving himself. 'I'm sorry, Amberman. Sorry, Goldi. And I'm sorry I didn't proclaim quickly enough. No, I'm not really sorry – because that gave Minnow the opportunity. She trounced that shadow, she tamed it.'

Throughout his passion Wex's wig had remained in place. He checked that his skull-discs still were hidden before staggering erect again.

'Why,' he asked, 'did the shadow's voice lisp like that?'

Osmo thought for a moment. 'The words aren't right yet. They need clarifying. Focusing.'

And now they are coming into the warm bright village of white wooden houses and daisies and spangled hens and bakery. They're coming from the four winds, or at least from three and a half winds (one group skirting the palace of gaseous fire).

The scene is almost gala at Yulistalax drug-dreamed by a shaman. Nakkis dash to and fro. Refugee lasses marvel: at a gargantuan Isi mage, its armour of scales a streaky iridescent ochre adorned with sepia ciphers. Pastel light puffs like rosy steam from horns on a head the size of a bull. She heaves herself forward, leaving a wide smear, glistening, fading. She's attended by amber-skinned Juttahats in beige livery.

Other lasses gape at three mages coiled upward around ebon-skinned body-servants with matching liveries, and another brassy mage with his brazen servant. Chins resting upon these Juttahats' fuzz-skulls: alien duos with serpentine head upon humanoid. A curly-haired human prisoner bucks and begs in the grip of black hands. A gaunt bearded fellow strains forward dementedly.

And see: here's a hectically hobbling Queen wearing an amber chaplet upon disorderly jet-black hair. She shares the lineaments of those onlooking lasses as if she were once the model for them all. A brooding daughter accompanies her, and a burly priest, and a meagrely moustached young man, aglow and coppery-clad. Around his head snowflakes swirl like phosphorbugs (at dusk, though this is daylight). An escort of apprehensive flesh-and-blood guards and of resolute showy soldiers with wooden faces.

And look: at a naked young man whose anatomy is of flexible amber on the arm of a gorgeous golden lass (in a maid's linen and lace – she has shucked off a cloak in the warmth). These two tramp along in company with a moustached lord and his ragamuffin princess and a vigilant white-haired bondsman and a fellow in a cloak whose hairstyle seems unnaturally tidy, and a trio of woodmen.

These four groups still have to converge on the sward with the pond and the great swing. From various houses here and there nakkis in bandsmen's uniform come out to greet them. They're bearing trombones and trumpets, horns and bugles and tubas. The nakkis strike up a jaunty carnival march, *tum-ti-tum, tootle-too, tum-ti-tum-ti-tum*. To rouse spirits? To quell hostility? The bandsmen aren't all close to each other, yet all still play in concert.

As four crowds sweep on to that sward, a woman with silky yellow hair aflutter comes sprinting; a woman with one blue eye and one eye which is an opal. She's wearing breeches and a brass belt and a ruffled white blouse. A willowy lass follows less speedily. A lass with blonde pigtails lingers in her approach.

'Stop your playing!' Eyeno bawls at a bandsman here, a bandsman there. 'Stop it, I tell you!'

Oh no, Minkie's carnival must not resume – or fire-darts might soon be flying from the mouths of trumpets.

531

That monstrous serpent writhing its way on to the sward ... Other Isi being carried like tubas. So many Juttahats – and soldiers made of wood. A naked person, all of amber. And Osmo van Maanen, bespeaker of her exile and death by drowning!

And a bearded yet so familiar figure in the clutch of those black Juttahats who had once fashioned an eye for her ...

Juke, glimpsed on the headland above that lake far away, and now so suddenly here!

And with *Juke*, none other than *Minkie Kennan* ...

How electric the air is with mana, with tensions of a tempest about to break, of the four winds about to fight. Mages puffing pastel light, Juttahats flexing muscles, touching hilts of knives, Demon Jack poising himself. Crossbows cocking.

Eyeno's chances have slipped away, away, for want of the name for a bloom.

Viper scenting a sprat, and surging.

'She's monstrous, she's mutant, and she's *here*—!' Minnow doesn't retreat. She stands her ground. Viper halts. Rears a huge head. Opens a mouth vast enough to accommodate a Minnow easily, venoms dripping.

Minnow being in this Precious One's mind! ('So you hatched yourself at last. Eaten any good servants lately? This wild Juttie says: you shan't be making a meal of us.') *Wild Juttahat? Oh the sprat meaning herself. Yet nearby being an altered Juttahat female, fruit of the foolish Brazen experiment, heeding no voices, wafting her own autonomous swaying scents, seemingly friend to this sprat. This Precious One scenting without even troubling to be seeing: rival lesser servant-borne mages including a Brazen, the Brazen quite failing to be controlling that Girlem. Girlem's strange mutant male companion shockingly having a foetus within him. This Precious One being pregnant too, all because of—!* ('I fertilized you? Through your gob? I caused you to conceive? Oh that's precious!') *Pregnancy being precious, swaying even an Enlightened One.* ('I think I deserve a little gratitude. How about a bargain between us not to try to dominate each other? We'll work out something about this Ukko. I'm the new Queen of Kaleva, after all. I can make bargains. How about some help with these *lesser* mages? Maybe with certain people too. How about it, Enlightened Precious Pregnant One—?')

Sprat being impertinent and glib. However: sprat nesting in

Viper's mind, not Viper in hers. So be casting a sway of limited harmony, or at least of non-havoc.

Certain people!

Minnow's mother is advancing upon her skimpy daughter, almost clawing the air out of the way. The sheer bulk of Viper is a deterrent. Amongst the onlookers are so many echoes of dead dreamy daughters that Lucky is dizzy. Might the peering ghosts suddenly swarm upon their mother like scavvies upon some meat? Where, where is her true self? Does Minnow matter, or vile van Maanen, except that they're here to distract her, to spoil the moment if she lets them? Difficult to ignore those two.

'Bitch!' she shouts. 'Bastard!'

'Calm yourself, Mother,' Jatta begs.

Yes, calm, calm. Or how shall she find her other self?

'Mysterium of mysteria,' exclaims Serlachius as he scans so many similar faces, and goggles at the giant mage, at the nakkis, at the woman with an opal eye.

'Eyeno Nurmi!' Osmo cups his hands to call across the duck-pond. 'I treated you disgracefully—'

Osmo can hardly succumb to remorse at such a moment. His apology abbreviates itself to a gesture embracing Amberman: *See how I've become friendly with freaks.* Nudged in the ribs by Minnow: 'You too, Jatta Sariola: I treated you shamefully—!' Her fastboy, full grown, is dancing attendance on Jatta. He's eyeing Osmo up. Osmo's gestures includes the Girlem: *Look, I respect all sorts of women, even alien ones.* Diplomatic gestures, these, even if they're sincere. Osmo can't afford to beg pardon any more fulsomely. Lucky is ripping the air again. To claw Osmo and Minnow aside. To unmask her heart's desire. To acquire the power of the Ukko-child. Her attention veers to Minkie Kennan in the grip of a Juttahat. She bares her teeth. 'You killed my Bertie!'

Oh no he didn't. He isn't he. He's she. She's Sal. Sal has nothing to do with murder or a madwoman or – how he or she shrinks from the accusing gaze of the poetess! – or with these nakki-bandsmen, either.

≪Minkie-Kennan's≫ protestations arousing suspicions of a mage whose Voice is clamouring: how can ≪Minkie-Kennan≫ possibly be recognizing Eyeno-Nurmi or Queen Lucky or *nakki-bandsmen* (such being obviously so, due to shock of proximity to the poetess) unless being genuinely Minkie-Kennan? Having hallucinated and charmed himself successfully into believing

533

himself to be someone else of another sex, to be hiding himself, protecting himself! Such a charm, such a charm!

Lucky's attention is on Juke, who still strains towards his sister though less vigorously.

'You *betrayed* me!' cries that Queen.

Eyeno is watching her brother with a clear blue gaze and an opaque opal blankness as Juke mouths . . . nothing powerful at all, but plaintive strangled phrases.

'Not missing my supper! No, missing my sister! Missing Eyeno reciting . . . !'

What do such pretty sentiments mean to Eyeno now? Has Juke's ambivalent yearning for her proceeded to the stage of mimicry – by which he might conceive an image of her soul within him, possess her spirit, usurp her?

'Geld me, sickle in the sky . . . !'

Aye, by abjuring his masculinity and his male rage. That rage is no longer directed at Osmo who injured his sister so.

Osmo can only remain extremely wary of a mutie who caused his former mistress to die horribly and who shot down his skyboat – even if the result was joy with his Minnow.

Mage Imbricate being bitterly aware of the wiggy man who disfigured a fine new hide with the mark of his hand . . .

Such a reciprocity of recriminations! Only Viper's sway of limited harmony is keeping this mêlée from tumbling into havoc, unbalancing.

It's a sway which Minnow supports; and Goldi, with her fragrance.

Surely chaos must come, pitching Velvets against Brindleds, woodmen and fleshmen against Juttahats and against one another – whereupon nakkis will become bestial once again.

She who steps uncertainly through the mob wears blonde pigtails. Her peachy skin, her chubby cheeks, her full oval face and her close-set smoky eyes are the perfect reflection of Lucky (save for the hue and style of hair). Or perhaps not the *perfect* reflection. Several centuries of passions have exercised Lucky's physiognomy in modes and moods which Paula has not known and only recently has begun to imitate. Near perfect enough, their twin resemblance. Near enough. Except for the hair, the blonde hair which was Lucky's once.

Both women hesitate.

Like a duck coming in to land upon its ascending reflection in a pool – becoming in the final moment one fused creature – will

Lucky rush toward Paula, and Paula toward Lucky, to become melded together, the hand entering the kidskin glove, the glove engulfing the hand? Will the resulting solitary woman's hair be blonde or black – or grey with instant antiquity?

Where's the benefit to Paula in embracing this stranger, herself?

To gain many more memories, to inherit a realm from which she had been kept apart in exile, surrounded innocently by echoes of all her daughters?

Shuddering, Paula glances for a moment at *snakes* which have invaded. One of them's colossal. At aliens. Compulsively she must meet Lucky's trembling fervent scrutiny again, that demanding yet terrified desire. Terrified, yes, to confront herself lost for so many centuries, but preserved.

The Queen who wears a crown of amber paces towards her twin, and her pigtailed twin towards her. Paula, possessed by a curiosity so intense. Should Osmo proclaim to prevent this? Jack is gesturing up a gust which sucks the two women close, and closer. There's an inevitability. Even though approaching one another slowly, the two women seem to fly with arms outstretched, wings in this wind of self-attraction.

They meet.

They bump.

And the world jerks – as if the Ukko has rocked in its cradle-crater. Vision lurches; swims out of focus. Much of the village is shrinking out of sight, fleeing away. The inner world is changing scale and perspective. Are all the witnesses of this becoming giants? Far forests and frozen lakes are dwindling to sheer texture on walls. Rolling banks of cloud are merely clinging vapours.

As focus returns shrunkenly, here is a meadow and some cotts and a pond inside of a great cave luminously aglow. The crowd has shrunk too. During that blurring rift of vision nakkis have disappeared—

—and echo-lasses too!

All those blithe refugees – where are they?

Gone, gone, into the memory of the Ukko-child.

All those daughters of Lucky have disappeared, compressed out of this region by the collision of the fair twin and the dark twin – who between them bracketed the existence of those daughters.

Where are Gretel and Gerda and Maria? Gone away, gone away.

Where is tender willowy Inga, Eyeno's temptation? Inga alone still lingers on the fringe of the living. There's appeal and alarm in her eyes as she beckons to Eyeno from beyond guards and Juttahats: *Be with me. Me with you.* Already Inga seems vague. A song seems to fade: *Oh what do we care? We'll wash our hair. And hide our faces in silk—*

Juttahats jostle momentarily, hiding Inga from view, and that moment is for ever. She can no longer be seen.

'Be with me,' Lucky says to Paula. 'Me with you. My conscience, my consort. I loved a man. He left me. Preferred death to me. He must have known there'd be no space between you and me. What can be finer than to find oneself again, fresh and young and without all torments of memory?'

'With no memory?' replies Paula. 'Oh I remember the *Katerina* perfectly well! The cold and the dark of space, and the fear we had to love. There's been a war here, you know . . . sister. I'm not naive.'

'I never had a sister, a sister-self, before.' Lucky leans her head on Paula's shoulder. 'Help me to forget . . . No, not to forget! Think with me, breathe with me, thrill with me, weep with me.'

'You could have had a hundred sisters,' butts in Jatta. By now everyone is so much closer to one another.

'All of my daughters, yes. The pressure . . . Ukko's maddening influence . . . the sway to conceive, and see my harvest reaped and reaped again . . . Cruel! Cruellest to taunt me with their ghosts.'

'Those were my friends.' Paula's plump cheeks are moist.

Lucky kisses her tears. 'I'm sure the Ukko continues to remember them. Doesn't it remember almost everything?'

Creamy waxen blooms grow in the meadow – and starflowers and heartbells and a slender azure chimneyflower. Eyeno is hurrying to pluck one of those waxen blooms. Juttahats are stirring. Mages are staring, tongues licking out to taste. Ripples pass along Viper's massive frame.

'How do we tell the Ukko what we want?' asks Paula. 'What is it we want? You're a woman of a boisterous world. I'm a woman of *here*, and of hope. There's been a war . . . Is it peace we want?

Peace as in the void of space? Peace as in the emptiness, in the caressing *killing* dark? Peace as in a pasture?'

From the pond arises such a glow.

Much abbreviated, the candle-palace spans the water. No lambent silhouette is within it now. From the water rises an obese hairy body of orange-brown. Moon-buttocked, gorbellied, bulgingly bosomed, a legless vat of flesh, with a globe of a head.

A snub-snout, a split of a mouth, red sunken eyes, jug-ears. Henna hair spills from a topknot. Hairs prickle erect all around her anatomy. Armless hands waggle. On one sloping shoulder perches a petite sylph of stars.

Mages puff pastel light. Jack glows, and daisies adorn his livery then fall from it like snow. Minkie dribbles at the sight of the mana-festation's ginger hair. A guard swoons. Ben Prut peers myopically, mystified. Sam Peller shakes his snowy head repeatedly as if he alone is a dupe of hallucination. Agog, Serlachius wrings his hands and sinks to his knees.

A voice rumbles, like a mouthful of dumpling in broth:

'WHAT ITH MY NAME? WHO WILL PRONOUNTHE IT? WHO WILL BETHPEAK ME THUITABLY?'

Eyeno brandishes the waxy flower she has plucked.

'It's this, it's this—' She inhales the odour. She recites:

> 'I bloom in moon-child meadows,
> 'I can outlive the years.
> 'My name is—'

She falters.

Juke cries out to her, 'Ear-flower – that's it! Or: Eye-flower!'

Eye or ear, eye or ear?

'What's its name in here?' Lucky clamours at Paula. 'What do you know it by?' Paula knows no special name.

A Juttahat Voice is calling out a clickety hiss of alien syllables. Wex's wetwear is warbling permutations of possibilities: '*Korvakukkavahakukkavoidekukkasilmakukkakorvavaha—*'

'Shut up!' Minnow tells Wex.

Resplendent Viper being well aware of at least fifty synonyms for the Ukko-flower being used in a spectrum of situations. ('Oh are you? Well, spill them out one by one! And don't you use your Voice.')

How close does a sprat need to be to a mage to stay attuned if she chooses? Viper once extracted the name for unlocking Minnow's girdle, the secret name which her girdle knew. Now

Minnow will snatch those shifty synonyms from an Enlightened Precious One while tying Viper's tongue. Part of the bargain, part of the bargain. Right? Tugging Osmo by the hand, she's hurrying towards Eyeno.

(*But all of those synonyms being evasions, verbal ruses. After long meditation, being evident that no single name being inherent at all, all names being arbitrary though metaphorical, meaning being conveyed by will, determined by desire. So maybe the name being* White Rainbow *or* Chalice of Tales!)

Why, the name can be whatever Minnow chooses! Just so long as she chooses effectively. Why doesn't Eyeno realize this?

Ah, Eyeno's too troubled by the responsibility, by the violence there's been in here, by the wreckage of Kip'an'keep, by Minkie's presence and Juke's, by the disappearance of Lucky's dead daughters.

As mages' Voices call out alien names and as Wex resumes his clattering babble, Minnow hauls reluctant Osmo to confront Eyeno face to face.

Her silky yellow hair; lovely little moles on her cheek and neck, more endearing than any starflower tattoo, a little like the constellation of the nakki perched on a chanterelle . . .

'Won't you introduce us, Oz? Don't I have a right to meet your one-time flame of passion politely?'

Rising on tiptoe, Minnow cocks her frizzy head on one side to squint up quizzically at the opal eye, the blue eye.

How embarrassed Osmo is. Juke is shouting out in anguish, 'Leave her be, leave her be!' Osmo manages to mumble, 'Eyeno Nurmi, this is my Queen, Minnow.'

'Queen,' the poetess repeats. '*Queen* . . .'

Since Minnow has raised a hand, Eyeno reaches to touch it, if only with the tips of her fingers, the Ukko-bloom held slack in her other hand.

'Hullo there, Eyeno! I do hope we can be friends, despite you-know-what—'

Eyeno licks her upper lip. She ignores Osmo so close to her.

'This must be the most absurd proposal of friendship anyone has ever made.'

Minnow beams. 'Oh I don't know. Osmo kidnapped me. Look at us now. I do love your eye, by the way.'

Despite herself, Eyeno almost smiles. 'You'd hardly have enjoyed the business of obtaining it. Ever since I was a girl I seem to have been searching for an eye . . .'

538

'That one really suits you, believe me! Take it from someone who trounced a monstrous mage and can read her mind, which is why I wanted this chat.'

'*Now?* You want some chit-chat?'

'This can hardly wait.' In a whisper: 'You can simply choose the name, you see.'

'I'm *trying* . . . It has to occur. Maybe the name is Queenflower, for all I know — and maybe that's why you're bothering me. I only have one more guess, you see, Minnow.'

'Ah, but *listen*, Eyeno. This is really important . . . Your flower can have whatever name we choose, whatever name we tell it to have. Has to be a suitable choice, though, not a selfish one, I think. *Queenflower* would be confusing — being as how there are two Queens here right now: me and Mummy. A name like Eyeno's Eye would be wrong, if you choose it yourself. I think! Well, it seems to me you have the power to bespeak the name! Oz here will back you up, won't you Oz?'

'Is it two Queens — or three?' asks Eyeno. 'There's also Paula!'

Lucky, her arm round the waist of her twin, is heading their way determinedly.

'Don't meddle, you witch!' Is it Minnow or Eyeno who is the witch? 'This Ukko's ours!'

Oh yes, by virtue of her and her twin meeting up at last. Hadn't Paula been waiting inside the moon-child through four centuries for Lucky to make her claim?

Lucky can't rake the air any longer. Having found her original self, how should she let go of her? Jatta is interfering, and trying to calm her miracle son who is in a dither.

Is the real threat from the poetess? From rebel proclaimer and junior Queen? Or from the vast alien serpent who seems so strangely passive and indecisive? Or from the Brazen mage, now being borne forward by her porter, accompanied by Velvet mage?

Odour of caramel and woodsmoke and caraway. Click-hissing of Juttahat words shouted toward the Girlem, and then in Kalevan too: 'You being our creature, our creation. Assisting me!'

Goldi releasing blithe fragrances. 'Being *myself*! Alone! Not alone now.' She has her Amberman, as unique as herself.

Puffing pastel clouds, Viper asserting Resplendent Self over lesser mages. Being pregnant thanks to the sprat-princess.

Still, in the pool, in the glow, the monstrosity waits for an answer.

539

'Minnow, how dare you meddle so much! I want . . . I want *this*.' The whole Ukko, everything.

'Mummy, don't you think maybe you already have your prize?'

'I'm not a prize!' protests Paula.

Lucky is almost shedding tears of frustration. 'I have to have this. Don't you see? If Paula and I can't stay here . . . Why, outside, she could become – like Anna Beck!'

'*Anna!*' Oh Eyeno has to know. '*What happened to Anna?*'

'She became zombie. Yokels burned her to death.'

The author of Anna's fate is wriggling in the grip of a Juttahat, shaking like a leaf, eyeing the ginger hair of the presence in the pool, trying not to stare at that compelling reminder of Sal's mane, but glancing again and again . . .

'Poor dear Anna . . .' Eyeno almost crumples the Ukko-flower. Almost. 'And the name of the bloom is—'

'No!' Minnow butts in. 'Don't say that, whoever Anna was! Or the snakes will seize their chance.'

'I must stay here.' Lucky is actually appealing to her elfin daughter. 'Don't you see? Otherwise . . . Minnow: I'll give you my realm if it's what you want. You can be the Queen. Someone has to be. It's no great joy. Is Osmo really longlife now?'

Osmo laughs. 'Shall I piss on the grass?'

'If you're really longlife my land will have an immortal *King*, marrying again and again—'

'Don't be wicked, Mummy. Maybe you do need a part in all this. Maybe the snakes even need a part.'

Osmo is quite taken aback. 'What are you saying, Minnow?'

'Just that the Isi maybe deserve some share—'

'Of our minds? Of our free will?'

'Viper is pregnant on account of me. And I'm pregnant too! We have a few interests in common, her and me.' She claps her hands. 'I know a name for the bloom.'

At which, Wex breaks off from his exhaustive chanting.

'Don't work mischief, I beg you! Take statues apart, but don't lose us this entity! Please, dear girl! It's ready for flight. It's trimmed for its virgin voyage to the stars.'

'To the Isi stars.' Minnow winks at him.

'Oh yes,' says Lucky. 'Yes. That's where. Of course that's where.'

*

540

And Minnow whispers in Eyeno's ear (though Eyeno has to bend
to hear). And Eyeno thinks for a while, then she recites to the
gingerwoman in the pond:

> 'I bloom in moon-child meadows,
> 'I can outlive the years,
> 'My name is *Lucky's Harvest*,
> 'I'm Ukko's eyes and ears.'

'Say it louder,' demands the being, who is no longer afflicted
by a lisp. Prodded by Minnow, Osmo bespeaks the verse in chorus
with Eyeno. This is the name of the harvested bloom. Not a
selfish name. Not a partial name.

And oh, that flower will bloom in glades here and there across
the land from time to time, where it never grew before of its own
accord. Will a few specimens maybe even appear in Pootara, to
be rooted out by the rationalists?

Some people may call it the Queenflower, or the Moonflower.
Named after the only moon which most Kalevans had ever spied,
which from its hiding place had brought frenzies and manias to
nourish itself, and once out of hiding brought destruction to a
town where the *Book of Heroes* was printed. Or named after a
Queen who was also frenzied and manic until she met her stolen
self again (and who may still – should one venture to say? – be
peculiar).

The heady scent of Lucky's Harvest will empower those who
find it. Or it will make them mad. In other respects mana will
not manifest itself so readily once the moon-child quits Kaleva,
leaving behind those rare buds of itself. Cuckoos will only cackle
infrequently. Rationalists will rejoice. Mana-priests and shamans will indulge in nostalgia.

The only moon they ever spied . . . ! Some of the people, anyway, during the moon-child's transit from Loom Lake to
Kip'an'keep!

Yet the Ukko-child is to offer Eyeno a true moon for the Kalevan sky. Eyeno's Moon.

This is the promise: other Ukkos will come in cavalcade. They
will suck all the debris of the sky-sickle into a solid sphere out
in orbit beyond the region where tidal forces can tear a moon
apart.

Such a molten sphere it will be at first. Later it will cool and harden and grace the sky with its waxing and waning, and with its fullness just like her opal eye.

Will Eyeno's Moon be as bright as the sky-sickle was? Ah no. And tides . . . Won't people get their toes wet? Won't the sea slop over the low quays of Tumio and Portti and spill through the streets every day? To lose one town – Kip'an'keep – is bad enough!

Bad, bad. Evil. There will be no new moon.

Yet in the moon-child's mind the evil is part of life itself. Once upon a time consciousness dawned. Thereafter: such a dynamic of desire, lust as well as love, vanity and also true love of self, perfect and imperfect pride, loyalty yet likewise revenge – a spiral at once leading up to the stars yet also to an abyss, to bigotry as well as to knowledge supreme, to sublime will but obsession too. Without this flow life would have no story at all, nor the cosmos a revelation of itself through the ears of its Ukkos. Consciousness: a cage – its bars defining the openness beyond, even while captives fight over crusts and lusts . . . generating tales, the chattering expression of existence.

How much more complex to ally with this moon-child than when Lucky first entered hers! This Ukko wants a new epos for a new epoch: a tale of snakes-and-people, people amongst serpents; and at last its clients have discovered this for themselves, or else the decision would be worth nothing. Because they arrive at such a decision, so also does the Ukko.

Yes, yes, Queen of serpents, you and me, Paula . . .

Yet Lucky has abdicated, hasn't she?

Or being a tale of serpents amongst people on the human home-world . . . ?

At Goldi's roguish hint, Viper rears her head; and Wex panics. The Harmonious Society must remain unshaken, telling itself its tales of mutuality. Wex must return to Landfall to report a failure, a wildness let loose. In a voice at once prim and fruity he protests.

In amazement Wex touches his own lips, his face. He can *feel*. 'Who am I?' he asks himself. 'Who am I?' he asks Minnow.

'Roger Wethead,' she tells him.

And in that naming, is his awakening to a fuller self. Who had that fussy fellow with bees in his bonnet been? And who had that overseer been? Yet he feels no estrangement from the past.

542

He chortles. He guffaws in delight – prompting Jack to grin and caper, and Amberman, child of nature, to hum rhapsodically. Huge and tiny, near and far: almost, Roger Wethead understands the scales of existence as an Ukko might understand those.

And then he understands much more.

'Those skeletons!' he exclaims, and hurries towards the Velvet mage in the arms of her body-servant.

Over the years Landfall has traded almost all the skeletons of Isi and Juttahats found aboard Lucky's original Ukko in Earth's asteroid belt. The Ukko destroyed its alien passengers so that there shouldn't be a premature encounter between the species. It erased the tale of how to arrive at Earth. The Velvets have been trying to recover a lost narration, to put flesh on the bones.

Yet a long game indeed was needed before Earth and the Isi stars could meet directly. Now at last the real encounters can begin, in Isi space. The Isi are a more widespread race, a more powerful race, really. Better materials, better tech-toys – dependent upon a symbiosis with slaves who possess hands, which impels the serpents to think in terms of body-slavery. And in terms of balance, balance. Slave cultures are always ultimately vulnerable to some other less static culture. Oh all those Great Narrations of the Isi, dictating patterns, as indeed the *Book of Heroes* imposed patterns upon Kaleva – patterns of wildness, however! Of mana-magic.

The Isi are mesmerized by their patterns. Old Earth is static, too . . . By now Earth almost has acquired its own voices-in-the-head, of sweet reason. Earth might soon possess these in a wetwear actuality, of which Wex was a prototype.

People and Isi: prisoners of themselves, their very own Juttahats! So vulnerable to more dynamic alien beings, wherever those might be.

For Osmo and Jack and Wex, and Lucky with her twin, and Eyeno and Minnow and Goldi the free Juttahat, to journey to an Isi world will be to inject a wild mind-virus which will save a society from ultimate inertia – and thereafter Earth too – not in a ruthlessly invasive and domineering way but impishly, mercurially, the trickster's way.

Inspired, Roger Wethead babbles of this to the Velvet mage – and to the Brazen mage, and the Viper.

Resplendent Viper rears her head, fangs dripping, odours of musk and camphor venting from her gape. Only on Kaleva, under the sway of a moon-child, could Viper have been mutating so. Not on an Isi home-world where mages are more like most humanbeing mana-priests, intent on the mysterium though not often experiencing mighty surges.

Prevailing upon the lesser mages (particularly upon clever Imbricate) to be perceiving surprising validity in the wiggy humanbeing's words. Brindled Isi will be gifting shuttle-ship to rendezvous in orbit with the rising moon.

Sprat being in Viper's mind. Sprat peeping through Viper's great eyes, Minnow's own eyes being closed, a trick of vision communicable to Imbricate.

Imbricate's body-servant stepping forward to be surrendering its burden, at least temporarily, to a sprat. Imbricate baulking. Not being held by human hands! Being disfigured once already!

'Oh but I see exactly how to hold you best, little mage—!'

'*Little!*' complaining his Voice.

Pumping herself up: 'I mean little compared with my monstrous mutant mage. There's a hand-hold, just here! Just so!'

Girlem's fragrance inundating the air, rapturing sighs from many. Imbricate yielding. Osmo bespeaking strength and lightness of load.

Staggering, Minnow accepts the Brazen mana-mage. Imbricate coils up around her chest and shoulders, forming a twisted tuba, and rests his head upon her frizz. She shuts her eyes again. Imbricate raises his head almost in affront.

'Oh my,' exclaims Minnow, 'this is a much better height to see from! Who needs platform boots? All of a sudden I feel as tall as Eyeno.'

And Eyeno laughs at last. And Eyeno winks her opal eye.

Hark and hear.

Epilogue · A Letter to Pen

I hope you can decipher my economical writing! I don't believe I've ever sent a letter to anyone before, for the obvious reason that most recipients would be quite unable to read it. I've tried to speak with you in Landfall three times already by communicator. Always the voice which answers is that of your aide. I think she is your aide – the Chinese woman called You. She prevaricates about fetching you, Miss Conway. I do not trust the tone of her voice. Three times is quite enough. Hence this epistle which I shall be sending by ski-courier.

It's as well that I arranged with you to print my history, now that Kip'an'keep has been wiped from the map! Assuming that I ever polish my history into shape. There's a definite sense of closure now that the Ukko-child has gone, and cuckoos have mostly stopped gossiping.

Will that Ukko ever return from the Isi stars, from its mission of constructive mischief? Oh that final flood of cackle before the birds shut up! I was hard put to note down all that I heard myself, not to mention collecting other people's testimony.

At least now I don't need to worry about resuming the lordship of Maananfors, blessedly plague-free, though still suffering the consequences of the war. Not now that Elmer and Eva have taken responsibility, supported by troops still returning, and by the other survivors who never admired Hans Werner or Per Villanen.

Lyle Melator is a problem, of course, on the other side of the lake! Holding the Loxmiths hostage, Nikki not least. Maybe Queen Jatta will be able to put that house in order after she has established herself in Sariolinna, with that Anni by her side. High and low together.

If only the new Queen had stopped here en route instead of rushing back to Pohjola Palace in the royal sky-boat as if she was under a sway. Probably this keep holds bad memories for her. In the event, peace was decreed by communicator (as I presume you know). Rumour is, that she'll wear that snakeskin suit under her tunic and entertain serpents in her palace.

I very nearly lost my Chronicles, Miss Conway. They could so easily have been burnt. Lucky was on the verge of doing so out of spite. I can imagine half a dozen other ways in which the war might have destroyed all my work. That's why I'm asking you to send a dovecraft here with some kind of data-copier such as you described when I visited you – what is it now, five years ago? Maybe six. That's the purpose of this letter, written with chilly fingers on a gloomy frozen midday. Please send a dovecraft to Maananfors, to Alvar van Maanen.

Now that I've begun scribbling, my fingers itch to note down what I've gathered about *Juke Nurmi* and *Minkie Kennan* travelling away <u>together</u> from *Kip'an'keep* towards *Niemi* – if they ever arrive there on their wintry trek. What a wretched bond of penance arose between those two! *Ben Prut* has been here – he's responsible for the logistics of returning Northerners to their home and Jaegertroopers to *Luolalla* and such (though aitch-housemen go their own way). He was in the *Ukko*, and he confided to me how Juke shrieked, 'Take me with you!', but *Eyeno* refused, though her eye leaked so. On her return (if ever) enough water will have flowed under bridges. Kennan, still pretending spasmodically to be a woman whom he'd cheated, stuck close to Juke. Will Juke and Minkie need to pass by way of *Castlebeck* on their wintry route east? How can *Lord Beck* and *Cully* possibly tolerate that! Minkie will need to pass himself off as a lass trapped in the wrong body. *Lucky* grew blasé about revenge in the euphoria of her reunion and the elation of new purpose. *Eyeno* could hardly fail to tolerate *Osmo*, especially as my son is so gracious – as well as being *Minnow's* beloved. Ah Minnow, the serpent-bearer!

Of course Queen *Jatta* and *Anni* can hardly have any children themselves. But there are certainly grandchildren: the four Maids, which in my opinion is an awkward situation . . .

Not to mention *Princess Ester* and the other younger daughters who are now in Queen Jatta's care! Will Jatta continue, I wonder, the tradition of wooing to win longlife? Until these six maids are all in turn wed? She, a woman-lover!

Has your brown-skinned pilot who broke his arm somehow reached *Landfall* yet after seeing more of *Kaleva* under snow than anyone might wish to?

But I ramble. *Miss Conway*: *Peter Vaara* the dramaturge is now wintering with his troupe in our poor town where there are numerous empty homes, inspiring himself for some spectacular theatrics in the spring. Vaara declares that you were associating on very friendly terms with the black consul of *Pootara*. I hope and trust that you aren't intent on quitting Landfall for the rationalist island; or at least not yet. Do please send a dovecraft to safeguard my <u>Chronicles</u>.

Vaara and his troupe came here quite perilously by a series of mishaps – but I ramble! Please assist me. Pen to pen, as it were.

And now: closure,

> from *Alvar van Maanen*,
> ex-Lord of *Maananfors*,
> Chronicler of *Kaleva*.